KATHLEEN E. WOODIWISS

"A LEGEND!"
tlanta Journal and Constitution

"A PUBLISHING PHENOMENON!"
The New York Times

"THE FIRST LADY OF THE GENRE!"
Publishers Weekly

THE WOLF AND
THE DOVE

"A FLAMBOYANT, FAST-PACED
PAGE TURNER!"
Fort Worth Star-Telegram

"SENSUOUS, ROMANTIC...
A TENDER LOVE STORY!"
Hartford Courant

"OUTSTANDING!"
Port Chester Globe

KATHLEEN E. WOODIWISS

The Wolf and The Dove

AVON BOOKS ◆ NEW YORK

THE WOLF AND THE DOVE is an original publication of Avon Books.
This work has never before appeared in book form.

AVON BOOKS
A division of
The Hearst Corporation
1350 Avenue of the Americas
New York, New York 10019

Copyright © 1974 by Kathleen E. Woodiwiss
Published by arrangement with the author
Visit our website at http://AvonBooks.com
ISBN: 0-380-00778-9

First Avon Books Printing: March 1974

AVON TRADEMARK REG. U.S. PAT. OFF. AND IN OTHER COUNTRIES, MARCA
REGISTRADA, HECHO EN CANADA.

Printed in the U. S. A.

UNV 70 69 68 67 66 65 64 63

The Wolf and The Dove

A Myth

In times of yore when druids roamed the northern forests of England and held their sabbaths in the dark of the moon, a young man grew enamored with battle and violence and studied the arts of war until none could best him. The young man called himself "The Wolf" and preyed upon the people for his wants. In time his feats came to the ears of the gods on the high mountain between earth and Valhalla. Woden, King of the gods, sent a messenger to destroy the upstart who took tribute from the people and challenged the fates. The two met and drew blades and their battle raged for a fortnight of new moons from the white cliffs of the south to the bleak rocky shores of the north. The warrior was truly great, for even the messenger of Woden could not destroy him, and returned to the mountain to admit his failure. Woden pondered long and deep, for it was written that who could best a messenger of the gods would gain eternal life on earth. Woden laughed, and the heavens above The Wolf trembled. Then the air was rent with bolts of lightning and peals of thunder, and the youth stood bold with blade drawn.

"So you've won eternal life," Woden roared in mirth. "And you stand before me with your sword ready for battle, but foolishness was never part of valor and I cannot let you ravage here unchecked. You will have your imortality, but you shall wait on Woden's will to ply your trade."

And with a mighty gust of laughter he rose and lightning struck the insolent blade. A cloud of smoke rose slowly upward. Where the youth had stood, now glowing red and slowly cooling crouched a great iron wolf, a snarl frozen on his lips.

It is rumored that in a deep valley near the border with Scotland there is a dark glade wherein stands the statue of an iron wolf, brown with rust and twined with creeping vines, moss greening its legs. It is said that only when war rages in the land does the mighty wolf stir and become a warrior—bold, strong, invincible and savage.

And now William's hordes crossed the channel and Harold rode from the north and war drew near—

October 28, 1066

The clash of battle rang no more. The screams and the moans of the wounded were silenced one by one. The night lay quiet and time seemed suspended. The autumn moon, bloody hued and weary, shone upon the indistinct horizon, and the distant howl of a hunting wolf shivered down the night, locking the eerie silence tighter upon the land. Shreds of fog drifted through the marsh over the split and hewn bodies of the dead. The low wall of earth, weakly buttressed by stones, was covered with the heroic shroud of the town's butchered manhood. A young boy of no more than twelve summers lay beside his father. The great black bulk of Darkenwald's hall rose beyond this, the shaft of its single watchtower piercing the sky.

Within the hall Aislinn sat upon the rush-covered floor before the chair from which her father, the late lord of Darkenwald, had ruled his fief. A rough rope was knotted about her slender neck. It bound her by its length to the left wrist of a tall, dark Norman who rested his mail-clad frame upon the rough-hewn symbol of Lord Erland's status. Ragnor de Marte watched as his men tore the hall apart in a rampaging search for the smallest item of value, climbing the stairs to the bedchambers, slamming heavy doors open in their search, rummaging through coffers, then casting on a cloth spread before him the more worthy trophies. Aislinn recognized her jeweled dagger

9

and gold filigree girdle, torn from her hips only a short time ago, thrown into the pile among the other treasures that had graced her home.

Arguments broke out among the men over some coveted piece, but were quickly silenced when her captor issued a sharp command. Usually the object of the squabble was grudgingly added to the growing heap before him. Ale flowed freely, liberally swilled by the invaders; and meats, breads and whatever else was at hand were devoured upon discovery. This iron-thewed knight of William's horde who held her tipped his own hollowed bull's horn and freely sampled the wine that filled it, unconcerned that her father's blood still darkened the mail on his chest and arms. When nothing else occupied him, the Norman worked the rope, causing the rough strands to brutally test the soft white skin of Aislinn's throat. Each time the harsh chafing brought a grimace of pain to her features, he chuckled cruelly at having wrung some reaction from her, and his victory seemed to ease his morose mood. Still, to see her cringe and beg for mercy would have far better suited him. Her manner remained alert and watchful and when she faced him it was with a calm defiance that rankled him. Others would have grovelled at his feet and pleaded for his pity. But this maid—there was something about her which seemed to take a slight advantage from him each time he jerked the tether. He could not fathom the depths of her reserve but determined he would test it well before the night was out.

He had found her with her mother, the Lady Maida, poised in the hall when he and his men crashed through the heavy door, as if the two of them would stand against the whole invading Norman army. His bloody sword ready in his hand, he had paused just inside the door while his men hurried past him to search for others willing to fight for their own, but finding nothing more than these two and the barking, snarling hounds to greet them they lowered their weapons. With a few well placed kicks and blows they subdued the dogs and chained them in a corner then turned to the women who fared no better.

His cousin, Vachel de Comte, stepped toward the girl, intent upon seizing her for his own. But instead he encountered Maida who threw herself into his path seeking to stay him from her daughter. He tried to push the older woman aside but her clawing fingers found his short knife

10

and she would have snatched it from its sheath but he felt the grasp, and swinging his heavy-gauntleted fist, laid her flat. With a cry, Aislinn had fallen to her mother's side and before Vachel could claim her, Ragnor moved between and yanked away her snood, spilling free a shining mass of coppery hair. The Norman knight twisted his hand in it and drew her struggling to her feet. He dragged her behind him to a chair and threw her into it, tying her wrists and ankles to the heavy wooden structure so that she could interfere no more. Maida was dragged, still stunned, and lashed securely at her daughter's feet. Then the two knights joined their men in the sacking of the town.

Now the girl sat at his feet, defeated and near the gray hinterlands of death. Still, she mouthed no pleas or words for clemency. Ragnor knew a moment of uncertainty as he recognized that she possessed a strength of will few men had.

But Ragnor had no inkling of the battle that raged within Aislinn in her effort to quell her trembling and present a proud mien as she watched her mother. Maida served the invaders with feet hobbled together to prevent her from taking a full step. A length of rope trailed from the bindings and the men seemed wont to step upon the tail. Their guffaws rose loudly when Maida fell upon the floor, and with each fall Aislinn blanched, better able to take the punishment herself than watch her mother suffer. If Maida bore a tray of food and drink and fell crashing with her burden, the merriment was doubled and before she could scramble up, she fetched a kick or two for her clumsiness.

Then Aislinn's fears pricked her anew and she was held breathless as Maida stumbled against a thick-faced soldier, wetting him with a pitcher of ale. The man seized Maida by the arm, his large, hamlike hand easily encircling its thinness, and forced the woman to her knees, where with a thrust of his foot he booted her away. A small bag tumbled from her sash as she fell, but Maida quickly rose beneath the Norman's curses and snatched it up again. She would have returned it to its place, but with a shout the drunken soldier caught her hand and tore the bag from her grasp. When Maida reached out to grab it back, her insolence aroused the man's ire. He clubbed his fist against her head, sending her spinning, and Aislinn started for-

11

ward, a snarl upon her fair lips and feral gleam in her eye. But the blow only seemed to amuse the man. The treasure forgotten for the moment, he followed and swung again at the staggering woman, then catching her shoulder, began to beat her in earnest.

With a wrathful shriek, Aislinn came to her feet but Ragnor pulled hard on the rope, sending her sprawling into the reeds and dust. When she could draw a breath again from her bruised throat, her mother lay senseless and unmoving while her assailant stood above her, waving the small sack in triumph and howling his glee. Impatiently the man tore it open to see what prize it might hold, then finding it contained nothing more than a few dried leaves, scattered the contents with a vicious curse. He flung away the empty pouch and delivered a hearty kick to the limp form at his feet. With a dry agonizing sob, Aislinn threw her hands over her ears and closed her eyes tightly, unable to bear the sight of her mother so abused.

"Enough!" Ragnor roared, relenting at last as he saw Aislinn cringe. "If the hag lives, she will yet serve us."

Aislinn braced her hands on the floor and glared at her captive through dark violet eyes smoldering with hatred. Her long coppery hair fell in wild disarray about her shoulders and heaving bosom, and the sight of her was like an untamed she-wolf meeting her foe. Yet she remembered the dripping red sword that Ragnor had held as he came into the hall and saw in her mind the fresh blood of her father spattered on his shining mail hauberk. She fought the panic that threatened to rob her of her last strength as well as the grief and self-pity that would have brought her to submission. She swallowed back a rush of tears at the emotions experienced for the first time in her life and for the deep, tormenting knowledge that her father lay dead upon the cold earth, unblessed and unshriven, and that she was helpless to remedy it. Was mercy so lacking in these men of Normandy that even now, when their battle was won, they could not fetch a priest and see to the proper burial of the defeated?

Ragnor gazed down at the girl where she sat, her eyes closed and her lips parted and trembling. He could not see the battle that shredded her resistance. Had he stood then, he might have won his desire to see her crushed in fear

12

before him, but his mind wandered to the base-born knight who would claim all of this surrounding him.

Before dusk they had come, galloping boldly up to the hall in the manner befitting conquerors, to demand the surrender of the town. Darkenwald found itself unprepared for this foe. After William's bloody victory over King Harold at Senlac a fortnight before, word spread that the Norman Duke marched toward Canterbury with his army, having lost patience with the English, as they, although defeated, refused him the crown. Relief had swelled the spirits of Darkenwald, for his direction was away from them. But they had not accounted for the small forces that had been thrown out to seize or harass the settlements along William's flanks. Thus it was that the lookout's shout of Normans approaching had deadened the hearts of many. Erland, even though greatly loyal to the late king, had known the vulnerability of his holdings and had meant to yield the day had not his wrath been provoked beyond endurance.

Among the Normans it was only Ragnor de Marte who felt unease with his surroundings as they rode across the field, past the peasant's huts, toward the gray stone manor where the lord dwelled. As they drew up before the hall he gazed about him. There were no stirrings in or about the outbuildings and to all appearances the place seemed forsaken. The main entrance, an iron-bound door of hard oak, was drawn closed against them. No light from within illuminated the oiled and thinly scraped skins that were stretched tight over the lower windows of the hall, and the torches mounted in iron sheathes on either side of the door had not been lit to ward off the darkness of the approaching night. All was still within, yet as the young herald called out, the heavy door was slowly drawn open. An old man, white of hair and beard, tall and robust of frame, emerged, holding an unsheathed battle sword in his hand. He closed the door behind him and Ragnor caught the sound of a bolt dropping into place behind it, then the Saxon turned to consider the intruders. He stood quietly, guardedly, as the herald approached unrolling a parchment. Confident in his mission, the young man halted before the elder and began to read.

"Hear ye, Erland, Lord of Darkenwald. William, Duke of Normandy, claims England his by sovereign right—"

The herald read in English the words Ragnor had

prepared in French. The dark knight had thrown aside the parchment given him by Sir Wulfgar, a bastard of Norman blood, for to Ragnor's mind it was more a demeaning plea than a rightful demand for surrender. What were these Saxons but ignominous heathens, whose arrogant resistance warranted crushing without mercy? Yet Wulfgar would deal with them as honorable men. They had been beaten, Ragnor thought, now let them be shown their masters.

But Ragnor grew uneasy as he watched the reddening face of the old man while the words continued to descend, calling for every man, woman and child to be brought out into the square and be branded with the mark of slave upon their brow and for the lord to give himself and his family over as hostages against the good behavior of the people.

Ragnor shifted in his saddle, glancing nervously around. There was the cackle of a hen which should have been roosting and the cooing of a dove in the cote. A slight movement drew his attention toward an upper wing of the manor where the outer shutter of a window had been pushed open the barest degree. He could not see into the darkness behind those rough wooden planks yet he sensed someone there, watching him. Growing cautious, he flung his red wool mantle back over his shoulder, freeing his sword arm and the hilt of his weapon.

He gazed again at the proud old man and somehow glimpsed his own father in his manner—tough, arrogant, not willing to give a rod unless a furlong had been won. A sense of hatred swelled anew within Ragnor's breast and his dark eyes narrowed as he viewed the man with a loathing stirred by the comparison. The old Saxon's face darkened even more as the herald read on with the outrageous demands.

Suddenly a chill breeze stirred against Ragnor's cheek and set the gonfalon above their heads flapping as if it were sounding a death warning. His cousin Vachel muttered low behind him, now beginning to feel the tenseness that made Ragnor's sweat start beneath the leather tunic he wore under his glistening mail. His palms were moist in his gauntlets as he moved his hand to rest upon the hilt of his sword.

Suddenly the old lord let out an enraged bellow and swung his sword with demonic fury. The herald's head top-

14

pled to the ground before his body slowly crumpled across it. Confusion delayed reprisal for a split moment of time as serfs armed with haying forks, scythes, and crude weapons swarmed from hiding. Sir Ragnor shouted an order to his men and cursed himself for allowing them to be taken by surprise. He spurred his destry forward as the peasants leapt at him, their hands reaching upward to claw him from his saddle. He hacked right and left with his sword, splitting skulls, severing hands from outstretched arms. He saw Lord Erland fighting before him, taking three Norman soldiers at once, and the impression passed him that Harold might still be king if he had had this old man by his side. Ragnor urged his mount through the mass of men, his target the lord of Darkenwald, for he saw him now in a reddish haze that would only ebb when he felt that ancient body sinking beneath his sword. The peasants tried to drag him down, sensing his intent and only bloodied the turf with their efforts. They fought gallantly to save their lord, only to lose life themselves. They were no match for men trained to war. The mighty destry plodded over fallen bodies until at last he was urged on no more. Lord Erland looked at the uplifted sword and his death came swiftly as de Marte buried it deep within his skull. Seeing that their lord had fallen, the serfs broke and ran, and the din of battle yielded to the wails of women, the cries of children, and the heavy thudding of a tree trunk ramming against the door of Darkenwald in an effort to break the barrier behind.

From where she sat at Ragnor's feet, Aislinn watched her mother's form anxiously for any sign of stirring and felt some relief when Maida finally moved. A soft groan was heard, and the woman managed to raise herself to an elbow. She stared dumbly around her, still befuddled by her beating. The one who had levied the blows came to her again.

"Fetch me ale, slave!" he roared and raised her by the scruff of her garments and hurled her toward the keg of brew, but her hobbled feet could not catch her and she sprawled again.

"Ale!" the man shouted and threw his horn at her.

Maida stared blankly at him, not understanding until he cuffed her and pushed her toward the barrel once more. She struggled to her feet but the soldier stepped on the

15

rope, tripping her and sending her down hard upon her hands and knees. This seemed to better meet his pleasure.

"Crawl, bitch! Crawl like a dog," he laughed and she was forced to serve him on her knees. As she gave him the full horn other men called for her service, and soon she was again hobbling about bringing ale and wine to them with the aid of the two serfs, Hlynn and Ham, who had been caught fleeing the hall.

Maida served the Normans, but her bruised lips began to move and she crooned in a sing-song voice. The Saxon words penetrated Aislinn's consciousness and with a horror she labored to hide, she realized her mother heaped vile threats upon the uncomprehending men and pledged the curse of every slimy demon of the swamp upon the enemy's ears. If but one had seized upon Maida's meaning she would without much hesitation have been spitted like a roasting pig. Aislinn knew that their survival hinged on their captor's slightest whim. Even her betrothed was in unsafe hands. She had heard these Normans speaking of yet another bastard who, under William's rule, had gone to Cregan to obtain that town's surrender. Was Kerwick dead too, after fighting so gallantly beside King Harold at Hastings?

Ragnor gazed at Maida and thought of the regal poise and vintage beauty she had shown until his man struck her and marred her face. He could find no hint of the former woman in the painfully shuffling, dirty creature who stumbled about her labors with a twisted face and gray-streaked auburn hair matted with blood and dirt. Perhaps the maid at his feet saw herself as she stared so intently at her mother.

A scream tore Aislinn's attention from her mother, and she glanced around to see the serving girl, Hlynn, being pulled back and forth between two of the soldiers who were arguing loudly over her. The timid maid, just entering her fifteenth year, had never known a man and now faced the nightmare of rape at the hands of these ruffians.

Feeling the girl's terror, Aislinn bit into her own knuckles to keep from echoing Hlynn's frightened cries. She knew only too well that soon she would be prey to a man's passion. There was a rending of cloth as Hlynn's gunna was torn from her breasts, and a restraining hand clamped down roughly on Aislinn's shoulder. Cruel, calloused hands snatched and pawed at the young girl's body,

16

bruising the tender flesh. Aislinn shuddered in revulsion, unable to drag her eyes away. Finally one of the men stunned his rival with a blow to the head and rose, lifting the thrashing, screaming Hlynn in his arms and strode out the door with her. In despair, Aislinn wondered if the girl would survive the night, and she felt the odds seemed high against it.

The dreadful weight upon Aislinn's shoulder became suddenly unbearable. Her violet eyes flashed their loathing as she turned once more to glare at her captor. The Norman's eyes returned the challenge and a slow sneering smile crept across full and generous lips, mocking her defiance. Yet as her stare grew more contemptuous and unwavering, his grin faded. Aislinn felt his fingers tighten upon her, bruising her shoulder. Unable to further contain herself, Aislinn shrieked in rage and lifted her hand to strike a blow to his cheek, only to have him catch her arm and force it behind her back until she was crushed against his hauberk. Her face was nearly pressed to his, and his hot breath touched her cheek as he chuckled at her helplessness. She struggled to wrench herself from him as his free hand moved with deliberate slowness over her body, sampling with crude lust the soft ripe curves beneath her garments. Aislinn trembled at his touch, loathing him with every ounce of her being.

"Filthy swine!" she hissed in his face, deriving small pleasure from the startled expression on his face that her French words had brought.

"Eh!" Vachel de Comte sat up sharply, his ears pricked by a feminine voice speaking words he could understand. He had not heard such since they had sailed from Saint-Valery. "By damned, cousin, the wench is not only beautiful but learned as well." He kicked in feigned disgust at the late lord's saddle. "Bah! 'Tis your luck to get the only wench in this heathen country capable of understanding you when you give her directions in bed." He grinned as he relaxed back into his seat. "Of course, I must take in account that rape does have its drawbacks. But since the maid can understand you, mayhaps you can coax her into a more congenial mood. What does it matter that you killed her father?"

Ragnor threw Vachel an ugly scowl, and let Aislinn fall to his feet again. His superiority over her once more had slipped a notch, for the wench knew French when he had no inkling of her language.

"Be silent, cub," he snapped at the younger man. "Your prattling annoys me."

Vachel pondered Ragnor's mood and smiled. "Dear cousin, you do worry overmuch, I perceive, or else you would see the jest with me. What can Wulfgar say when you tell him that we were attacked by these wretched heathens? The old man was a wily fox. Duke William will not blame you. But which bastard do you fear most? The Duke, or Wulfgar?"

Aislinn sat more alert now as Ragnor's features darkened with ill-concealed anger. His brows drew together like a gathering storm cloud.

"I fear no man," he growled.

"Oh-ho!" Vachel hooted. "You say that bravely enough, but do you mean it? What man here tonight does not hold some uneasiness within him for the deed done here? Wulfgar gave his command not to draw the villagers into battle, yet we have killed many of those who were to be his serfs."

Aislinn listened carefully to the words the men spoke. Some were strange to her ears but she managed to understand most. Was this man, Wulfgar, whom they spoke of with such apprehension, to be feared above these terrible invaders? And was he to be Darkenwald's new lord?

"The Duke has promised Wulfgar these towns," Vachel mused. "But they are of little value without peasants to work the fields and herd the swine. Yes, Wulfgar will have words to speak and in his usual manner not one will be uttered in trivial tones."

"Nameless cur!" Ragnor spat. "What right does he have to possess these lands?"

"Yea, cousin. You are justified to feel resentment. It does test even me. The Duke has promised to make Wulfgar lord here while we, of noble house, have been given nothing. Your father will be greatly disappointed."

Ragnor's upper lip drew back in a sneer. "A bastard's loyalty to another of his kind is not always just to those more deserving." He lifted a glossy tress of red gold hair from Aislinn's shoulder to idly rub it between his fingers, enjoying the silky texture. "I'd swear William would make Wulfgar pope if he could."

Vachel stroked his chin thoughtfully and frowned. "We

cannot with truth say Wulfgar is altogether undeserving, cousin." What man has ever beaten him in a joust or bested him in a fight? At Hastings he fought with the fury of ten with that Viking ever near to guard his back. He stood his ground when we all thought William dead. Yet to make Wulfgar a lord—aaah!" He threw up his hands in genuine disgust. "That will no doubt give him the thought that he is our equal."

"And when has he ever thought otherwise?" Ragnor quipped.

Vachel's gaze shifted to Aislinn as she gave his cousin a contemptuous look. Youthful she was. Vachel surmised her less than a full score years, mayhap eight and ten. Already he had seen her fiery temper. It would not bend easily to obedience. But a man with an eye for beauty might find cause to overlook this flaw, for he was confident it was the only one she possessed. Her new lord, Wulfgar, would no doubt be pleased. Her copper hair seemed aflame around her and caught the light of the flickering firelight within each thick curl. An uncommon shade for a Saxon. Yet her eyes were what took him completely off guard. Now in her rancor they burned dark and purple, glowering as she felt his perusal. But when her manner was calm her eyes were a soft violet, clear and bright as the heather that grew on the hillsides. The long, sooty black lashes that rimmed them now lowered and fluttered against ivory skin. Her cheekbones were fine and high, and the same gentle pink that shone upon them graced the softly curving mouth. The thought of her laughing or smiling titillated his imagination, for she possessed good white teeth, unmarred by the blackish rot that many other fine beauties were plagued with. The small, slightly tilted nose was lifted proudly, defiantly so, and the stubborn set of her jaw could not disguise the daintiness of its line. Yea, she would be a hard one to tame, but the prospect appeared thoroughly enjoyable, for though she was taller than most and slender, she was not lacking the full curves of a woman.

"Aah, cousin," Vachel concluded. "You'd best make merry with this damsel tonight, for the morrow may see Wulfgar with her."

"That lout?" Ragnor scoffed. "When does he ever bother himself with a woman? He hates them, I swear. Mayhap if we find a fair squire for him——"

19

Vachel smiled wryly. "If that were but true, cousin, we could have him beneath our thumbs, yet I fear he is not so inclined. Yea, he shuns women like the plague in public, yet I believe he has as much of them in private as we. I have seen him giving one or two damsels his perusal as if pondering what merits they possessed. No man looks at a woman in that fashion when some lackey tempts him more. That he manages to keep his affairs private is only one more thing about him that seems to fascinate his women. But 'tis baffling to me why the fair damsels at William's court dangle their kerchiefs and posture so inanely before him. They must be tempted sorely by his cursed aloofness."

"I have not seen so many wenches fawning over him," Ragnor retorted.

Vachel chortled in glee. "Nay, cousin, and you wouldn't, for you are usually more than properly entertained yourself. You are far too busy leading fair damsels astray to be troubled with those who fancy Wulfgar."

"You are indeed more observant that I, Vachel, for I still find it hard to believe that any maid should covet him, cursed and scarred as he is."

Vachel shrugged. "What is a little mark here and there? It but proves a man is daring and brave. Thank goodness Wulfgar does not boast of those small attributes of battle like so many of our noble friends. I can almost bear his wretched dryness more than those boring tales of doing and dare that are told and retold."

Vachel beckoned for his drinking horn to be refilled and Maida came trembling to accommodate him. She exchanged a hurried glance with her daughter before slipping away to return to her mutterings and ravings.

"Never fear, cousin," Vachel grinned. "We have not lost this game yet. What care we that William favors Wulfgar for a time? Our families are of some importance. They will not long tolerate this usurpery when we make this outrage known."

Ragnor grunted. "My father will not be overjoyed when he learns I have gained no lands for the family here."

"Do not be bitter, Ragnor. Guy is an old man and has old thoughts. Since he won his fortune he naturally assumes it is easy for you to do the same."

Ragnor's hand gripped his drinking horn until his fist

whitened about it. "There are times, Vachel, when I think I loathe him."

His cousin shrugged. "I am impatient with my father also. Can you imagine him threatening me that with the next bastard I make on some wench he will throw me out and cut off my inheritance?"

For the first time since breaking open the doors of Darkenwald Ragnor de Marte threw back his head and laughed. "You must admit, Vachel, you do your share."

Vachel chuckled with him. "And you cousin, are not one to call the kettle black."

"True, but a man must have his pleasure," Ragnor smiled and his dark eyes fell to the red-haired wench who sat at his feet. He caressed her cheek, and his mind became intoxicated with the vision of her slender body pressed tightly to his. Beginning to feel impatient for her, Ragnor caught his fingers in the fabric of her gunna, tearing it from her shoulders as she tried to wrench free. The hot, greedy eyes of the invaders turned quickly to feast on the half-revealed bosom swelling above the torn garment. As earlier with Hlynn they shouted encouragements and obscene jests, but Aislinn did not relent to hysteria. She held the separated garment together, and only her eyes spoke of her hatred and contempt to each. One by one the men were silenced by her gaze, and they drew away to swallow their discomfort with a large gulps of ale, mumbling among themselves that this wench was surely a sorceress.

Lady Maida clutched a wineskin frantically to her bosom, her fingers white with the pressure of her grip. In pain she watched Ragnor fondle her daughter. His hands moved slowly over the silken flesh and beneath her garments, trespassing where no other man had dared before. Aislinn trembled in revulsion, and Maida choked on the fear and hatred that seemed to congeal in her chest, making it impossible for her to draw an easy breath.

Maida's eyes raised to the darkened stairway leading to the bedchambers. In her imagination she saw her daughter already struggling with Ragnor upon the lord's bed, the one she had shared with her husband and where she had given birth to Aislinn. Now Maida could almost hear the cries of pain drawn from her daughter by that fearsome knight. The Norman would have no mercy nor would Aislinn plead for it. Her daughter had the stubbornness and pride of Lord Erland. She would never beg for herself. For another, perhaps, but not herself.

Maida moved into the deep shadows of the hall. Justice would not be served until her husband's murderer had felt her revenge.

Rising to his feet, Ragnor drew Aislinn with him and wrapped his arms close about her supple body. He chuckled as she squirmed against him trying to get free, taking brutish delight in the painful grimace that crossed her face as his fingers tightened on her arms.

"How be it that you speak the tongue of France?" he demanded.

Aislinn tossed her head up to meet his gaze yet remained silent, her eyes cold with loathing. Ragnor considered her haughty demeanor and released her from his savage grip. He thought no amount of torture could wring the answer from her lips if she refused to tell him. She had kept mute before when he had commanded her name. It was only her mother who had rushed to tell him when he threatened the girl with violence. Yet he had ways to humble the most arrogant of damsels.

"I pray you speak, Aislinn, or I shall strip your garments from you and let each man here take his turn on you. You would not be so royal then I vow."

Reluctantly Aislinn replied, standing soberly against him. "A traveling troubadour spent much time in this hall during my years of childhood. Before he came upon us he wandered from country to country. He had knowledge of four tongues. He taught your own to me because it amused him."

"A traveling troubadour who amuses himself? Where was the jest? I see none," he returned.

" 'Tis said your duke from his childhood fancied England upon his platter. My merry troubadour knew of this tale for oft would he play for the high born of your country. Twice or thrice in his youth he even pleasured your duke until he cut off his small finger for singing the tale of a baseborn knight in his presence. It pleasured my troubadour to have me learned in your language, that if one day the Duke's ambitions were realized I could call you the scum that you are and have you understand me."

Ragnor's features darkened but Vachel chuckled in his cup.

"Where be your gallant troubadour now, damoiselle?"

22

the young Norman inquired. "The Duke is no more fond of being called a bastard today than when he was a youth. Mayhaps your man will find his head missing instead of a finger."

Sarcasm dripped from Aislinn's words. "He is where no mortal man can reach him, quite safe from your duke."

Ragnor's brows lowered. "You remind me of unpleasantries."

Vachel smiled. "Your pardon, cousin."

The sight of Aislinn's meagerly clad shoulders gleaming smoothly above her tattered gown turned Ragnor's thoughts in another direction. He bent and swept her into his arms amid a shower of angry protests and a surprising variety of titles. He chuckled at her efforts to escape until she nearly lunged out of his grasp, then he crushed her against him, smothering her efforts in an iron grip. He grinned as he lowered his head to hers and his mouth was upon her lips, wet and searing. Suddenly he drew back in pain. A small trickle of blood ran from his bottom lip.

"You vicious little viper!" he choked.

With a low growl, Ragnor tossed Aislinn over his shoulder, jolting the breath from her as his hard mail slammed into her belly, and stunned, she hung half senseless. Snatching up a candle to light his way up the darkened stairs, he crossed the hall and mounted them, leaving the noise of the rowdy invaders behind as he entered the lord's chamber. He kicked the door closed and setting the candle aside, strode to the bed and he spilled Aislinn unceremoniously onto it. There was a glimpse of long, slender legs before she scrambled up and tried to leap from the bed. The rough rope around her throat frustrated her effort and brought her up short. With a cruel smile, Ragnor began to wrap the thong about his wrist again and again until she knelt close before him, facing him as a wary dog faces its tormentor. He laughed at her undaunted stare and loosened the rope from his wrist, tying it to one of the massive posts at the foot of the bed. With a casual slowness he began to undress, dropping his sword, hauberk, and leather tunic carelessly upon the floor. He crossed to the hearth, donned now only in a linen chainse and the chausses, a garment combining tight-fitting hose and underpants. Her apprehension mounting, Aislinn tore frantically at the rope around her throat, but her fingers could make no dent in the hard knot. He stirred the fire

23

up and added more kindling, and by its warmth he drew off the linen shirt and the woolen chausses. Aislinn swallowed convulsively as his body emerged lean and muscular, giving her little encouragement that she could hold him off by strength. He smiled almost pleasantly as he came to her and reached up to rub his knuckles gently against her cheek.

"The bloom from the thorn bush," he murmured. "Yea, 'tis true, and you are mine. Wulfgar gave me leave to take a suitable reward upon completion of his orders." Ragnor chuckled as if amused. "I cannot think of a more appropriate recompense than to have the most valuable possession in these towns. What is left is hardly worth my notice."

"Do you expect reward for slaughter?" Aislinn hissed.

He shrugged. "The fools should have known better than to attack armed knights, and slaying the messenger of the duke drew the old man's lot to a certainty. We've done a good day's work for William. I deserve reward."

Aislinn shuddered at his callous disregard for the lives he had spilled. She lunged away from him off the bed to the limits of the tether.

Ragnor threw back his head in a roar of laughter. "Would my little pigeon fly from me?" He twisted his hand in the rope and began to draw her to him. "Come, dove," he cooed softly. "Come, dove, and share my nest. Ragnor will be gentle with you."

Sobs struggled from between her clenched teeth as Aislinn wildly fought the pull of the rope. Finally she was held on her knees before him. His hand held the knot tight beneath her chin, forcing her head back so she stared up at him with rolling eyes and gasped for breath. He reached behind him and snatched up a wine skin lying atop a chest.

"Have a taste of wine, my dove," he coaxed, his face close above. hers as he forced the brew between her lips. Aislinn choked and gasped then swallowed the burning fluid. He held the skin to her mouth till she fought again for breath. Releasing her, he sat back on the bed, tipping the skin above his own mouth, half drinking, half bathing in the dark red brew. He lowered the skin and his eyes gleamed as he wiped the stain from his face and rubbed his chest where it had spilled. Laying the skin aside, he reached out to draw on the rope. Aislinn had less strength

24

to fight this time, and he pulled her close until their faces were but a hands' breadth apart. His breath, sour with ale and wine, almost made her retch, but suddenly his hand was in the neck of her gown and with a swift downward thrust he tore her garments from her and threw them aside. He released his hold abruptly and she stumbled back in surprise. With a smile, he lay back on the bed and took a long pull of wine without taking his eyes from her as she tried in sudden fear and shame to cover herself.

"Now come to me, little dove. Do not fight so," he cajoled. "After all, I'm not without influence in William's court, and you could do far worse." He leered at her in drunken grace, his eyes sweeping every tempting curve of her body. "You could be thrust beneath the churning butts of those cloddish oafs below."

Aislinn's eyes grew wide and she strained again at the stubborn knot.

"Nay, nay, my dove." He grinned and reached out, giving the rope a tug, pulling her sprawling to her hands and knees. She stayed there, gasping with pain and frustration but raised her head to glare her hatred. With a half snarl upon her face and her long hair tumbled, glowing with reddish gold lights, she seemed again as some feral beast crouched wild to do him battle. There was a quickening in his loins and a yearning for her grew with every moment. His eyes darkened.

"Aah, no dove at all," he murmured huskily. "But a vixen, all in truth. If you will not come to me, then I must come to you."

He rose from the bed, and Aislinn gasped, for he stood there before her bold as a man can be. He strode forward, desire burning in his eyes and a half smile playing on his lips. Aislinn straightened and backed away cautiously. An icy riverlet of fear ran along her spine and cold trickles spread through her body until her breath came fast and ragged, almost in a sob. She wanted to scream, to cry out her terror much as Hlynn had done. She felt the burgeoning wail congeal in her throat, and she fought the suffocating dread of utter hopelessness. Still he stalked her, the same evil leer twisting his lips, the same bold, unblinking hawk-like stare eating of her every move until the tight rope brought her in a circle against the foot of the bed and she could retreat no further. Her limbs hung like leaden weights and refused to obey her will. The shadows blurred behind him, and the handsome, cruel face filled her vision. In the flickering firelight his long, lean body seemed lightly furred. The panic rose and choked her until she could barely breathe. He reached out a hand and laid it against her breast, and with a cry Aislinn twisted away, but he held her and pressed forward until they tumbled onto the furs spread upon the bed. She was caught, pinned beneath him. The room swam before her, and his voice was oddly muffled in her ear.

"You are mine, damoiselle." His words sounded slurred and indistinct. He brushed his face against the slim column of her throat and his breath, hot and heavy against her flesh, seemed to sear her to the bone. His mouth caressed her breast as he muttered again. "You are mine. I am your master."

Aislinn could not move. She was in his power and she ceased to care. His face swam close before hers, her vision blurred. The weight of his naked body pressed her down deeper into the furs. It would soon be over—

Maida gazed down at the entwined couple now silent and still. She threw her head back and let her laughter override the waves of merriment from the hall. The peal of a hungry wolf rent the night and the two sounds were mingled. Below in the great hall, the rowdy invaders were silenced as a chill spread its cold fingers up their sturdy backs. Some crossed themselves, never hearing the like before, and others, thinking of Wulfgar's rage, thought he had already come.

26

Aislinn woke slowly, hearing her name called from what seemed a long distance away. She struggled to awareness and pushed at the heavy weight across her bosom. The Norman stirred beside her and rolled away, freeing her from the dreadful burden of his arm. In slumber Ragnor's face seemed innocent, the violence and hatred hidden behind the mask of sleep. But as she gazed down at him, Aislinn sneered her contempt, loathing him for what he had done to her, remembering too well his hands upon her body, his hardened frame pressing her down into the furs. She shook her head in distraction, knowing now she must worry that she would bear him a child. Oh, God forbid!

"Aislinn," came the voice again, and she turned to see her mother standing beside the bed, wringing her thin hands in a fearful worry.

"We must hurry. We've not much time." Maida pushed a woolen gunna at her daughter. "We must leave now while the sentry still sleeps. Make haste, daughter, I pray."

Aislinn heard the whimper of terror in her mother's voice, yet no emotion stirred within her own bosom. She was numb to all feeling.

"If we are to escape, we must hasten," Maida urged pleadingly. "Come, before they all wake. For once think of our safety."

Aislinn struggled from the bed, tired and bruised, and

27

pulled the gunna over her head, unmindful of the prickly texture of the woolen material without the familiar kirtle beneath. Afraid she would rouse the Norman, she cast an uneasy glance over her shoulder. But he slept on undisturbed. Oh, she thought, how pleasant his dreams must be for him to rest so serenely. No doubt his victory on her had sweetened them considerably.

Aislinn whirled and went to stand at the window, flinging the shutters open with an impatient movement. In the sharp white light of the dawning sun, she appeared pale and wan, seeming as fragile and delicate as the morning mist rising from the swamps beyond. She began gathering her hair, raking knots from it with her fingers. But the memory of Ragnor's long, brown fingers thrust through it, hurting her, forcing her to bend to his will, made her stop abruptly. She whipped the heavy swirling mass forward over her shoulder, letting it tumble loosely down over her bosom to her thighs and strode across the room.

"Nay, Mother," she said in firm decision. "We will not flee today. Not while the honored dead lay prey to the ravens and wolves."

With purposeful strides, Aislinn left the room, leaving the old woman to trail behind in helpless frustration. Scrambling in her wake to the hall below, Maida stepped gingerly over the snoring Normans sprawled carelessly in drunken slumber upon the floor.

Like a silent flowing wraith, Aislinn moved before her. With a heave of her slender form she swung wide the scarred door of Darkenwald, then staggered to a halt, half choking at the reeking stench of death. Her gorge rose in her throat and with an effort of sheer will she fought the retching down. She stumbled past the grotesque forms until she came to that of her father. He lay rigid now, his shoulders pressed to the faithful sod, his arms flung wide with his sword grasped in his knotted fist and a snarl of defiance still curling his lips.

A single tear slid over Aislinn's cheek as she stood silently mourning him. He had died as he lived, with honor and with his own life's blood quenching the thirst of the soil he loved. She would miss even his rages. What misery, despair! What loneliness, death!

The dame drew up beside her and leaned hard against her, panting heavily in the thickened air. Maida stared down at her slain husband and drew a long rasping breath.

28

Her voice started in a low moan and ended in a raking screech.

"Ah, Erland, 'tis not fair you should leave us thus with thieves ranging the hall and our own daughter a good night's toss for yon shaven ass!"

The woman fell to her knees and grasped her dead lord's hauberk as if to draw him up. Her strength failed and she knelt pleading in despair.

"What will I do? What will I do?"

Aislinn stepped across his frame and pried the sword from his hand. Grasping the once-loving arm, she sought to drag the corpse away to a softer place of rest. Her mother seized the other hand but only to work the great signet ring from the gnarled finger. At Aislinn's gaze she looked up and whined:

" 'Tis mine! Part of my dowry! See, my father's crest." She waggled the ring in Aislinn's face. "It goes with me," her mother pleaded.

A voice rang out, startling them. The old woman jumped, fear twisting her face. She dropped the hand and sped with amazing agility across the littered battlefield to disappear in the brush at the edge of the swamp. Aislinn let her father's arm sag back to the ground and turned with calm deliberation that surprised even herself to face this unknown threat. Her eyes widened at the sight of the tall warrior astride a great stallion, the likes of which she had never seen before and which bore the man as easily as if he were but a lad. The mighty stallion seemed to pick his way almost daintily among the fallen toward her. Aislinn stood her ground yet felt the strings of terror tug at her as this giant apparition approached, making her markedly aware of her own woman's frame and her vulnerability. The man's brow was shadowed by his helm yet from behind the nose guard steel gray eyes seemed to pierce her through. Aislinn's courage melted before his glare and she swallowed convulsively as the cold hand of fear gripped her.

His shield, portraying a black wolf rampant on red and gold with a bend sinister, hung from his saddle. Aislinn knew by it that he was a bastard. Had it not been for awe and fear inspired by his height and the sheer size of his huge mount, she would have hurled the taunt in his face. As it was she raised her chin in a gesture of helpless defiance and met his eyes, her violet eyes speaking her hatred.

29

His lips curled in contempt. The French words rang clear and a rankling sneer could be heard in the tone.

"Saxon swine! Is nothing safe from your thievery?"

The notes of Aislinn's voice rang higher but with the same sneer as she replied in kind. "What sayeth thou, sir knight? Cannot our brave Norman invaders see us bury our dead in peace?"

She gestured in mockery to the field of slain.

He snorted distainfully. "By the stench you have dallied too long."

"I dare say, not long enough one of your companions will say when he wakes and finds me gone," she spat in return. Despite her will to still them tears brightened her eyes as she returned his glare.

Without moving the man seemed to relax back into his saddle as he studied her more closely. She felt his gaze glide leisurely over her. A sudden breeze molded her woolen gunna to the curves of her body and presented great detail to the observing eye. As his glance traveled upward it paused brazenly upon the full rounded bosom heaving with her anger. Aislinn's cheeks grew hot and flushed under his slow, careful appraisal. It maddened her that he could make her feel like some nervous milkmaid being considered by her lord.

"Be thankful you had more to offer Sir Ragnor than these," he growled as he too gestured at the dead.

Aislinn stuttered in rage, but he swung down from his steed and came to stand before her. She fell silent as his hard gaze penetrated her. He removed his helm and held it casually in the crook of his arm while he released the upper catches of his coif and pushed it back from his head until it lay across his shoulders. He smiled leisurely, measuring her again, and his hand went out to lift a soft curl from her breast.

"Yea, be glad you had more to offer, damoiselle."

"They gave the best they had. Would that I could have taken a blade and given as much."

He snorted and half turned away, surveying the carnage in apparent disgust. In spite of her words, Aislinn studied him with detached interest. He stood tall, at least two hands higher than herself though she was not of short stature. His tawny hair was tousled and streaked by the sun, and though the long coat of mail was heavy, he moved with an easy strength and confidence. She surmised that in courtly garb he would draw many a sigh from a maiden's breast. His eyes were wide set and the brows well arched above them though, when as now he was angered, they drew down and blunted his long, thin nose and lent to his face the intense look of a hunting beast. His mouth was wide, the lips thin yet finely curved. A long scar that ran from his cheekbone to the line of his jaw grew pale and the muscles beneath it worked as he ground his teeth in anger. In a quick movement he turned to face her and Aislinn's breath fled from shock as she found herself staring into cold gray eyes. His lips drew back from strong, white teeth and a low growl rumbled in his throat. Aislinn was stunned by the wild look of him; it was as if he were a hound on a scent. Nay, more than that. A wolf set to wreak vengeance on an ageless enemy. He whirled from her and with long strides almost ran to the main portal of Darkenwald and disappeared within.

Once he stepped inside it was as if thunder shook the hall. Aislinn heard him bellow loudly and the heavy walls echoed with the noise of the scrambling invaders. Her anger forgotten, she listened and waited. Her mother crept to the corner of the building and gestured imperiously for her to come. Reluctantly Aislinn turned her attention to the task that lay before her and reached to take her father's arm to drag him away. But she started when a great yelp rent the air and glanced up in alarm to see Ragnor being thrown naked from the door. His clothes and sword followed and came to rest beside him in the dust.

"Imbecile!" his evictor raged, coming to stand on the steps above him. "Dead men are useless to me!"

Her eyes gleaming with obvious satisfaction, Aislinn watched and relished the sight of Ragnor scrambling awkwardly to his feet suffering greatly from this indignation. His lips drew back in a snarl as he grabbed for his battle sword, and the gray eyes above him flashed a warning.

"Take heed, Ragnor. Your stench can rise with your victims."

"Wulfgar, you son of Satan!" Ragnor choked in rage. Recklessly he beckoned the other near. "Come hither that I may skewer you properly."

"I do not care to joust with a naked, braying jackal at the moment." Noticing Aislinn's interest, he lifted a hand toward her. "Though the lady wishes you dead, sorrowfully I have use for you."

31

Ragnor jerked about in surprise to see Aislinn watching him with amusement. His face darkened with his wrath and humiliation, and the angry twitch of his lips were stilled as he bit them. With a muttered curse he snatched up his chausses and donned them before crossing to her.

"What business finds you here?" he demanded. "Why have you left the hall?"

Aislinn laughed low and her eyes were full of loathing. "Because it suited me to do so."

Ragnor stared at her, considering how to effectively quell her rebellious nature without marring her beauty or the soft, lovely body he could remember all too well against him. It would be difficult to put aside that delicious memory. He had never before seen a wench with the courage to match a man's.

Reaching out, he took hold of her slender wrist. "Get into the hall and wait me. You will soon learn that you are mine and must obey me."

Aislinn snatched her arm away. "Do you think that because you have bedded me once you own me?" she hissed. "Oh, sir knight, you have much to learn, for never will I be yours. My hatred of you will set me against you all the years of my life. The blood of my father cries out from the earth, reminding me of your deed. Now his body begs burying and whether you will it or not, I am bound to do it. You can only stop me by spilling my blood also."

Ragnor caught her again roughly by the arms, his grip biting painfully into her tender flesh. He was aware that Wulfgar watched them with great interest, and Ragnor's frustration grew that he could not frighten this stubborn wench into doing his bidding.

"There are others more capable of burying him," Ragnor growled low through clenched teeth. "Do as I command."

The lines of Aislinn's jaw grew rigid as she looked up into his flashing black eyes. "Nay," she breathed. "I prefer it be done by loving hands."

A silent battle raged between them. Ragnor's hand tightened as if he would strike her, then without warning he flung her from him, making her reel and stumble to the dirt. He came to stand above her, his eyes raking her slender form. Aislinn hurriedly pushed down the gunna over her thighs and returned his stare coldly.

"I yield this once, damoiselle. But do not test me again," he warned.

"Truly a kind knight," she taunted, rising to her feet. She rubbed her bruised wrist. Her look of contempt held him for a moment and then moved passed him to the tall warrior standing at ease near the steps of the hall. That Norman met her look and smiled, a touch of mockery twisting his handsome lips.

Aislinn turned abruptly, missing the thoroughly appreciative gaze he swept over her. She bent, taking up her father's arm once more, and began to tug at him. Both men stood watching and finally Ragnor moved to help her, but she thrust his hand away.

"Be gone with you!" she cried. "Can you not leave us in peace for this brief moment of time? He was my father! Let me bury him."

Ragnor dropped his hands to his sides and did not try again to help but went to put on his clothes, feeling the bite of a chill wind against his scantily clad body.

With great determination, Aislinn dragged her father away from the courtyard to a spot beneath a tree a small distance from the hall. A bird darted between the branches above her head, and she observed his flight, envying his freedom. She continued to gaze after the bird, unaware of the approach of Wulfgar behind her. But as a heavy object was thrown down at her feet, she started and whirled to face him. He indicated the shovel.

"Even loving hands need some tool, damoiselle."

"You are as kind as your brother Norman, sir knight," she flung shortly, then she lifted a lovely brow. "Or is it 'my lord' now?"

He made a stiff bow. "Whatever you wish, damoiselle."

Aislinn's chin raised. "My father was lord here. It does not sit well with me to call you Lord of Darkenwald," she answered boldly.

The Norman knight shrugged his shoulders, unperturbed. "I am known as Wulfgar."

Having hoped to vex him, Aislinn now felt only discontent. The name, however, was not unknown to her, for she remembered clearly Sir Ragnor and his cousin speaking of him the previous evening with hatred. Perhaps she was taking her life into her hands by seeking to stir this man's anger.

"Perhaps your duke will give these lands to some other

after you've won them for him," she returned flippantly. "You are not lord of them yet and may never be."

Wulfgar smiled slowly. "You will learn William is a man of his word. The lands are as good as mine now, for England will soon be his. Do not place your hopes upon false desires, damoiselle, for they will lead you nowhere."

"What have you left me to hope for?" Aislinn asked bitterly. "What have you left England to hope for?"

His brow lifted mockingly. "Do you give up so easily, cherie? I thought I had detected a small bit of hell-fire and determination in the swing of your skirts. Was I wrong?"

Aislinn's temper flared at this taunt. "You laugh at me heedlessly, Norman."

He chuckled at her anger. "I can see no daring swain has ever ruffled your pretty feathers before. No doubt they were all too besotted with you to put you in your place."

"Do you think you are more capable of doing so?" she jeered. She tossed her head toward Ragnor who watched them from afar. "How will you go about it? He has used pain and violated my body. Will you do the same?"

She glared at him through rising tears, but Wulfgar shook his head. Reaching out, he lifted her chin.

"Nay, I have more thorough methods to tame a wench such as yourself. When pain brings nothing, pleasure can be the weapon."

Aislinn thrust his hand away. "You are over confident, Sir Wulfgar, if you think to master me by kindness."

"I have never been kind to women," he returned casually, making a shiver of fright pass through her body.

Aislinn searched his eyes for a moment but found nothing to indicate his meaning. Without a further word she picked up the shovel and began to dig. Wulfgar watched her awkward movements and smiled.

"You should have obeyed Ragnor. I doubt that being in his bed should cause you this bother."

Aislinn's eyes were cold with hatred as they turned on him. "Do you think we are all whores to find the easiest way out?" she demanded. "Would it surprise you to know that I find this infinitely more pleasurable than having to submit to vermin." She looked meaningfully into his gray eyes. "Normans—vermin. There is no difference I think."

Wulfgar spoke slowly, as if to let his words fall with effect. "Until I have bedded you, damoiselle, reserve your

34

judgment of Normans. You may prefer to be ridden by a man, instead of a braying braggart."

Aislinn stared at him aghast, unable to make a reply. He seemed to state a fact rather than issue a threat, and she knew with certainty it would be just a matter of time before she would share a bed with this Norman. She considered his tall, broad-shouldered frame and wondered frantically if she would be crushed beneath his weight when he decided to take her. Despite his words he would probably bruise her like Ragnor and take delight in the pain he caused.

She thought of the many men whose offers of marriage she had rejected and scorned until her father, losing patience, had chosen Kerwick for her. No regal wench now, she mused, but a lowly maid to be used and then thrown to the next one down the line who favored her. She shuddered inwardly at the thought.

"You may have conquered England, Norman, but I warn you, you will not master me so easily," she hissed.

"I warrant it will be a contest more enjoyable to me, wench. I will take great enjoyment in the fruits of my victory."

Aislinn sneered at him. "You conceited lout! You think me one of your weak-willed Norman whores to spread myself at your beck and call. You will soon learn better."

He laughed. "A lesson will be taught, but to which of us remains to be seen. I am inclined however to favor myself the winner."

With that he turned and strode away, leaving her staring after him with her temper sorely raging. But for the first time Aislinn noticed that he limped. Was it some wound gotten in battle or an affliction of birth? Vehemently she hoped that whatever it was it caused him much pain.

Becoming aware of Ragnor's eyes upon her, Aislinn spun about and struck at the earth with the shovel, damning both men. Furiously she stabbed at the ground as if it were one of them she beat at. As she continued, she noticed the two men had begun to speak heatedly. Wulfgar's tone was low but anger rumbled in his words. Trying to salvage some of his pride Ragnor spoke with constrained ire.

"I was told to secure this place for you. The Duke's English advisors said that naught but ancient and unskilled

35

hands could raise sword against us here. How were we to know that the old lord would attack us and that his serfs would seek to slay us? What would you have had us do, Wulfgar? Stand and die and not lift up our weapons in defense?"

"Did you not read the offers of peace I sent with you?" Wulfgar demanded. "The old man was proud and had to be approached tactfully if blood was not to be let. Why didn't you take more care instead of riding in here like conquerors to demand his home? My God, are you so inept that I must be with you every step of the way showing you how to deal with men of such stature? What did you say to him?"

Ragnor sneered. "Why are you so sure 'twas not your words that angered him? The old man attacked us despite the cleverness of your plea. I did naught save let the herald read the parchment you gave me."

"You lie," Wulfgar growled. "I offered him and his household terms of treaty and safety for the laying down of his arms. He was not a complete fool. He would have accepted surrender to save his family."

"Obviously you were wrong, Wulfgar," Rangor smirked. "But who is there to prove otherwise? My men know nothing of this heathen tongue, and the herald was most prolific in it. Only I and the herald saw the document. How are you to prove your charges against me?"

"There is no need for proof," Wulfgar snarled. "I know that you murdered those men."

Ragnor laughed contemptuously. "What is the price for putting a few Saxons out of their misery? You killed more at Hastings than these few churlish clods here."

Wulfgar's face was stoney. " 'Twas because Cregan's strength was rumored as greater that I went to take it, thinking you had the good sense to persuade an old man to give up a futile fight. In that I see I erred and I regret my decision in sending you here. The old man's death means nothing. But the peasants will be difficult to replace."

These words cut Aislinn deeply and she missed the ground she hacked at and fell over the shovel. She hit the turf hard, almost knocking the breath from her. Gasping in pain, she lay quietly in her misery, wanting to cry out her anger and torment. To these men a single life was unimportant, but to a girl who had loved and respected her father, his had been a most dear life.

The heated conversation ceased and the men's attention turned to her once more. Wulfgar bellowed for one of the serfs from the hall. It was Ham, a sturdy youth of three and ten, who stumbled out with the help of a Norman boot.

"Bury your lord," Wulfgar commanded but found little understanding in the lad's eyes. The Norman gestured for Aislinn to tell him his meaning, and in resignation she handed the shovel to the boy. She watched solemnly as he dug the grave, aware of the Norman bastard rousing the invaders from the hall to drag away the dead.

Together Aislinn and Ham tied her father in a wolf pelt and dragged him into the grave, placing his mighty sword upon his breast. When the last shovelful fell atop him, Maida came forward timorously to lay across the mound of dirt and sob out her sorrows.

"A priest!" she wept. "The grave must be blessed."

"Yea, mother," Aislinn murmured. "One will be fetched."

This small bit of reassurance Aislinn would dare offer Maida, though she had no clue as to how she might send for a priest. Darkenwald's chapel, deserted after the death of its priest several months back, had been reduced to rubble by a fire shortly after. The friar at Cregan had served the people of Darkenwald in the absence of another clergyman. But to go for him would be taking her life in her hands even if she could manage to leave without being seen, which was highly unlikely. Her horse was tied in the barn where some of the Normans made their pallets. She knew the full weight of her helplessness and was strongly aware of her inability to give Maida much comfort. Yet her mother was treading dangerously close to madness and Aislinn feared that disappointment would push her over the brink.

Aislinn lifted her gaze to where Wulfgar stood. He was taking the armor from his horse, and by this action she knew he intended staying at Darkenwald rather than at Cregan. Darkenwald was the likely choice, for though the town had fewer people, the hall was larger and more suitable to the needs of an army. Erland had planned it so with forethought for the future. Built mostly of stone, it was less susceptible to fires and attacks than the hall at Cregan which was built entirely of wood. Yea, Wulfgar would be staying and by his word Aislinn knew she would be serving his pleasures. With her own fear of being claimed anew by this fearsome invader, she found it difficult to offer encouragement to anyone.

"Lady?" Ham began.

She turned to see that the lad was looking at her. He, too, had become aware of her mother's state and now looked to Aislinn for authority. His eyes questioned. Guidance was what he sought in dealing with these men whose very language confused him. Wearily Aislinn shrugged, unable to give him an answer, and turning from him, she slowly walked toward Wulfgar. The Norman glanced around as she approached and ceased his labors. With great hesitancy Aislinn moved closer to man and beast, surveying the huge horse in some awe. She felt more than a little apprehensive coming near him.

Wulfgar stroked the silky mane, holding the bit in his hand as he looked at her. Aislinn took a deep breath.

"My lord," she said stiffly. The title came hard, but for the sake of her mother's sanity and that these men of Darkenwald might have a Christian burial, she would swallow her pride for a time. Her voice grew stronger with her determination. "A small request I might ask—"

He nodded, saying nothing, but she was aware of his eyes, keen, yet dispassionate upon her. She sensed his distrust and she wanted to curse him for a foreigner, an intruder in their lives. She had never found it easy to appear docile. Even the times her father raged at her over some disputed point, such as her reluctance to choose a suitor, she would stand stubborn and willful, unafraid of his thundering anger while other people would cower before him in what seemed mortal fear for their lives. Yet Aislinn knew when she wanted her way that gentleness and pliancy would soften his ageing heart and turn it toward her will. Now she would turn that same guile upon this Norman, and she spoke in measured tone.

"My lord, a priest I pray. A small thing to ask—but for these men who died—"

Wulfgar nodded his consent. "It shall be attended to."

Aislinn sank to her knees before him, humbling herself for this brief moment. It was the least she could do to insure a proper burial.

With a growl Wulfgar reached down and yanked her to her feet. Aislinn stared up at him in surprise, her eyes wide and searching his.

"Stand upright, wench. I respect your hatred more," he said and turning, strode into the hall without another word.

Serfs from Cregan, well guarded by a handful of Wulfgar's men, came to bury the men of Darkenwald. To her amazement Aislinn recognized Kerwick among them as they trudged closer, following behind a huge, mounted Viking. Overcome with her relief at seeing him alive, Aislinn would have run to him, but Maida caught her gunna and clung to it.

"They will slay him—those two who fight over you."

Aislinn saw the wisdom of this and was thankful to her mother for this small bit of sense. She relaxed and watched him furtively as he neared. There was some difficulty with language as the guards tried to show the serfs what they were to do. Equally confused, Aislinn wondered at Kerwick's game for she had taught him the French tongue herself and he had been an apt student. Finally the peasants understood and began to sort and prepare the bodies for burial, all except Kerwick who stood as if dazed, gaping with horror at the terrible sight of the slaughtered men. Suddenly he turned away and was sick. There was laughter from Wulfgar's men, and Aislinn silently cursed them. Her heart went out to Kerwick; he had seen so much war of late. Yet she wanted him to rise and show these Normans dignity and strength. Instead he was letting himself be the object of their ridicule. The mirth gnawed at her and she whirled away and fled into the hall. She felt shame for him and for those who abased themselves so before the enemy. With her head lowered, oblivious to the men who leered at her, she walked straight into the arms of Wulfgar. He had removed his hauberk, leaving the leather tunic in place and now stood with Ragnor, Vachel and the Norseman who had arrived with Kerwick. Wulfgar's hands swept her back as he lightly held her.

"Fair damsel, do I dare hope that you are impatient for my bed?" he mocked, lifting a tawny brow.

It was only the Viking who guffawed his delight, for Ragnor's face darkened, and he glared at Wulfgar with jealousy and loathing. But it was enough to spur Aislinn's temper, already seething beyond caution. Her humiliation was past bearing. Her pride burned like a flame, engulfing her, goading her to unreasonable action. With a flare of white rage burning within her, she drew back her arm and struck a stinging blow across Wulfgar's scarred cheek.

The men in the room held their breaths in stunned surprise. They full expected Wulfgar to lay this saucy wench on her back with his fist. They all knew his manner with women. Generally he had little use for them and at times showed his complete contempt by turning and striding away when one had attempted to draw him into conversation. No woman had ever dared strike him before. Damsels feared his dark moods. When he bent his cold, ruthless gaze upon them, they fled out of his way to safety. Yet this damsel, with so much to lose, had braved far more than any other.

In the brief moment Wulfgar stared at her, Aislinn regained her senses and knew a sudden prickling of fear. Violet eyes met gray. She was as horrified by her action as he was astonished. Ragnor appeared pleased, not knowing his man. Without word or warning Wulfgar's hands were upon her like slaves' armlets, jerking her to him and crushing her against him in a powerful embrace. Ragnor had been lean and hard, well muscled, but this was like being thrust against an iron statue. Aislinn's lips half parted in surprise and her startled gasp was abruptly silenced when his mouth swooped down upon hers. The men hooted and howled encouragement, and Ragnor was the only one who found cause for dissatisfaction. With reddened face contorted by violent rage, he watched and his hands clenched at his sides to keep from tearing them apart.

The Viking crowed. "Ho! The wench has met her match!"

Wulfgar's hand moved behind Aislinn's head, forcing her face to slant against his, and his lips twisted across her mouth, hurting, searching, demanding. Aislinn felt the heavy hammerlike thud of his heart against her breast, and she was aware of his body, hard and threatening, pressed tightly to her slender form. His arm was clasped around her waist in a merciless grip and behind her head she felt his hand, large and capable of crushing her skull without effort. But somewhere in the deepest, darkest, unknown recesses of her being, a small spark was ignited and flared upward, awaking mind and body from their coldly held reserve, and singeing, scalding, fusing them in one whirling mass of sensation. Her whole consciousness was stimulated by the feel, the taste, the smell of him, all pleasurable and acutely arousing. Her nerves flooded with a warm excitement and she stopped struggling. As if with a will of their own her arms crept upward around his back and the ice melted to a fiery heat that matched his own. It mattered little that he was enemy nor that his men watched and crowed their approval. It seemed there were only the two of them. Kerwick had never possessed the power to draw her from herself. His kisses had aroused no passion within her breast, no desire, no impatience to be his. Now, clasped in the arms of this Norman, she was yielding helplessly to a greater will than her own, returning his kiss with a passion she had never known she possessed.

Wulfgar released her abruptly and to Aislinn's utter bewilderment he did not seem at all disturbed by what to her had been a shattering experience. No amount of force could have brought her down so low. She felt shame and realized her own weakness to this Norman's rule, weakness based not on fear but on desire. Aghast at her own response to his kiss, she struck out at him with the only weapon left her, her tongue.

"Nameless cur of Normandy! In what gutter did your sire seek your mother?"

There were sharp intakes of breath in the hall but reaction to her insults flickered only momentarily across Wulfgar's brow. Was it anger she saw? Perhaps even pain? Oh, that was doubtful. She could not hope to wound him, this iron-hearted knight.

Wulfgar raised an eyebrow at her. "Strange is your display of gratitude, damoiselle," he said. "Do you forget your request for a priest?"

Violence drained from her, and Aislinn was appalled at her own stupidity. She had sworn the graves would be blessed, yet by her own idiocy the dead men of Darkenwald would lay dishonored. She gaped at him, unable to utter a plea or apology.

Wulfgar laughed shortly. "Fear not, damoiselle. My word is my oath. You shall have your valued priest as surely as you will share my bed."

Laughter swept the hall at his words, but Aislinn's heart gave a sickening lurch.

"Nay, Wulfgar!" Ragnor cried in a burst of rage. "By all that's holy, you shall not trespass here. Have you for-

41

gotten your oath to me, that I should choose as my reward anything that pleasures me? Give heed, for I choose this maid as payment for capture of this hall."

Wulfgar turned slowly and deliberately to face the furious knight. He spoke with wrath rumbling low in his voice. "Seek your reward in the fields yonder where it is being buried, for that is what your payment shall be. Had I known what price I was to pay, I would have sent a knight less foolhardy."

Ragnor made to lunge at Wulfgar's throat but Vachel leapt forward to grab him by the arms and held him back. Ragnor struggled to free himself yet his cousin would not loosen his grip.

"Nay, 'tis folly, cousin," he hissed in Ragnor's ear. "To fight the wolf when we are in his den and his kind wait to taste our blood. Think, man. Have you not already left your mark upon the wench? Now bastard will wonder whose bastard she will whelp."

Ragnor relaxed, considering this. Wulfgar's expression did not change, yet the scar across his cheek whitened against the bronze of his skin. The Norseman sneered his contempt at the well-born cousins and his voice rumbled low.

"I perceive no contest. The seed of a weakling falls shallow of its mark yet the strong always knows fertile ground."

Aislinn smiled with a secret contentment, gloating over their argument. They fought among themselves, these conquering foes. It would be simple to aggravate their anger and watch them kill each other. She lifted her head proudly again, her spirits thriving on their heated words, and found Wulfgar's gaze upon her. His gray eyes seemed to look within her inner soul and search out the secrets hidden there. A corner of his mouth lifted into a smile as if what he saw amused him.

"The maid has not had her say," he remarked, turning to Ragnor. "Let the girl choose between us. If it be you, De Marte, then I will give no dispute. You have my leave to take her."

Aislinn's hopes were crushed, leaving her in confusion. No battle here, for Wulfgar would give her over without quarrel. Her intended ploy had failed.

She saw that Ragnor looked at her with open desire and his dark eyes held a promise of tender reward. Wulfgar,

42

on the other hand, seemed to mock her. He would not fight for her. Her bruised pride screamed to take Ragnor, demanded she scorn the bastard. She would delight in wounding his ego. But she knew she could not yield anything to Ragnor. She loathed him as any crawling, vile thing from the swamps. And if this was vengeance on him, small though it be, she would not cast it aside.

Her answer came doubly hard when the Norman guards led Kerwick into the hall. Standing in the midst of these towering men who commanded attention just by their mere presence, Aislinn could not hope to go unnoticed. Her bethrothed saw her immediately. Feeling his tortured gaze upon her, she raised her eyes slowly to his troubled face and found misery and despair. He seemed to make a silent appeal but for what she was unsure and even more doubtful of her ability to grant it. He bore no visible wounds, yet his tunic and braccos were dirt-stained and his golden curls were snarled and unkempt. He had always been a scholar, favoring books and learning to war. He seemed out of place now, a gentle man among fierce invaders. Aislinn could only pity him, yet there was nothing she could do, not when the enemy waited for her answer.

"Damoiselle," Wulfgar pressed. "We await your pleasure." The last word was stressed as he smiled tauntingly. "Which of us will you choose as your lover?"

She saw Kerwick's eyes widen and in the pit of her stomach there was a coldness that would not ease. She felt sick, suffocated by the lustful stares of the men who stood about the room watching with great attention. But she cared naught of them. Let the idiots pant. And the pain in Kerwick's face he must bear himself. If she but spoke any word, she would only lay his pride open to the Norman's scorn.

She gave a sigh of resignation. She would have the matter behind her.

"So I must choose the wolf or the hawk, and I know the hawk and his cries are more of the raven caught in a snare." She placed a small hand upon Wulfgar's chest. "Thus I choose you. So, lover, 'tis your lot to tame the vixen." She laughed ruefully. "Now what have you gained by this play of straws?"

"A fair damsel to warm my bed," Wulfgar replied and added with a hint of mockery, "Have I gained more?"

"Never," Aislinn hissed and glared at him.

Ragnor silently raged, his tightened fists the only evidence of his irritation. Over Aislinn's bright head, Wulfgar stared into his face and spoke slowly.

"It was made clear in my orders that each man should get his fair share of the booty. Before you go about your duties, Ragnor, you and your men leave what you have gathered for yourselves there." He gestured to the pile of loot taken the previous evening. "Duke William will want his share first, then and only then will come payment for your work."

Ragnor appeared on the verge of violence. His jaw tightened while his hand opened and closed about the hilt of his sword. Finally he withdrew a small pouch from his jerkin and going over to the gathered loot, tossed the contents onto it. Aislinn recognized her mother's great ring and several gold pieces belonging to her father. One by one as Ragnor looked on his men passed him, dropping their treasures onto the heap until it had grown half again its size. When all had done, Ragnor turned on his heels and strode angrily from them, shoving Kerwick out of his path as he left the hall with Vachel following close at his heels. With the huge door closed behind them, Ragnor struck his fist into his hand.

"I'll kill him," he swore. "With my bare hands I'll tear him limb from limb. What does the maid see in him? Am I not a handsomer man?"

"Ease your anger," Vachel soothed. "Time will see his end. The wench seeks only to spread strife among us. I saw it in her eyes as we quarreled. She does bloodthirst after all Normandy. Beware of her as you would a viper, but know that she can be of asset, for she has no more love for Wulfgar than we."

Ragnor straightened and sneered. "Yea, and how could she? Bastard and scarred that he is, no woman could cherish him."

Vachel's eyes gleamed. "We will give her time to infect the wolf with her winsome beauty, and then when he is weakened, we'll set the trap."

"Yea," Ragnor nodded slowly. "And the wench is the one to do it. I vow she has cast her spell upon me, Vachel. Still do I have a yearning in my loins for the vixen. With every inch of my being I remember her against me as nature bore her, and I would throw her down and have her again if afforded some privacy."

"Soon, cousin, soon you'll bed her again and the wolf will be no more."

" 'Tis a promise I'll hold you to, Vachel," Ragnor flung. "For I am bound to have her, one way or the other."

The few men of Darkenwald who had been taken captive were freed after spending the night tied in the cold October air. They stood about, still numb and stunned by the defeat of the day before. The women came to the square with food and water and those who found their men fed them and led them home. Other wives named the slain and then stood dumbly while their husbands and sons were laid in the holes. Still others who searched the faces of the living and dead but to no avail, went away wondering if they would ever see their kinsmen again.

Aislinn mournfully watched it all from the door of the hall. The slain were buried by the serfs from Cregan who labored under the direction of two of Wulfgar's trusted knights. Aislinn had overheard them speaking of yet another who had stayed at Cregan with a few men-at-arms to see the peace was kept there. Her mother, with split and swollen face, went to the grave beneath the oak and lay a small spray of late flowers upon it. She crouched and, as if speaking to Erland, gestured and wept in her hands.

Aislinn's father had been some three score and five years when he was slain and his wife was only two and ten. Though he was gray when she was still in the full bloom of womanhood, there had been a love between them that made the days seem bright and gay. Aislinn had known an older brother in her youth but a plague had come to the villages and he succumbed. Thus she had known the full dotage of her parents since, and the hall had been a place of love and kindness, away from the run of conquerors who flooded England like the tides. Erland had been wise and brought them through a multitude of kings. Now, though, it seemed the destruction of war had descended here to rest with a vengeance for its long absence.

Maida rose wearily, seeming lost and forlorn as she wrung her hands and gazed about her in misery and despair. She began to make her way back to the hall, her feet lagging with each step as if she were reluctant to meet the strange faces that now seemed to fill every corner of the place. Several of the women approached her with their woes as they had for years and pleaded her assistance, unmindful of the trauma that held her mind. She listened for a while, gaping at them from behind swollen lids as if in a stupor. Aislinn shivered and a sob rose in her chest as she watched her mother, her once-beautiful mother, who now seemed more of a mindless idiot than a stately dame.

Maida threw up her hands as if she could stand no more of the women's complaints and gave a shriek. "Begone from me!" she railed. "I have troubles of my own. My Erland died for you and now you welcome his slayers with little more than a frown or two. Yea! You let them enter my hall, rape my daughter, steal my treasures from me—argh!"

She tore at her hair and the townswomen drew back at her ranting, wide eyed and fearful. With a slow, painful gait she walked toward the door then paused on seeing Aislinn.

"Let them find their own herbs and bind their own hurts," she mumbled through her swollen lips. "I have had enough of their aches, lumps and sores."

Aislinn watched her go, knowing a deep grief and anguish. This was not the mother she had known, so full of love and compassion for the townfolk. Maida had spent a life going into the swamp and forests to seek out roots and leaves then drying them, mixing potions, salves and tisanes to heal the hurts and ills of all who came to her door. She had carefully tutored Aislinn in the art of healing and saw that she too knew the herbs and where to find them. Now Maida cast the people from her and would not bend to their pleas, so Aislinn must take up the responsibility. She accepted it as a blessing, thankful for the labors to ease her mind.

Thoughtfully Aislinn rubbed her hands down the woolen gunna she wore. First she must clothe herself against the Norman's prying eyes, then to work.

She mounted the stairs and entered her own chamber where she scrubbed herself and combed her hair, then donned a soft kirtle, slipping a fresh gunna of light mauve wool over it. She smiled ruefully as she smoothed the latter. No girdle or even a necklace to grace the garment. The Normans could not be outdone in their greed.

Aislinn gave the skirt a last pat, determined not to think of it again and left her chamber to fetch the potions from her mother's room, the same one she had shared with Ragnor only the night before. She pushed the heavy door open and stopped short in surprise. Wulfgar, apparently naked, was seated before the hearth in her father's chair. At his feet knelt the Viking who was bending at some task over his thigh. They both started at her entrance. Wulfgar, half rising from his chair, reached for his sword, and Aislinn saw that he was not naked after all but wore the brief loin cloth common to his profession. She noted also that a dirty, blackened rag clung to his thigh and Sweyn's huge, blunt fingers were still resting on it. He relaxed back into the chair and set his sword to rest, seeing no great threat from this slim maid.

"I beg your pardon, lord," Aislinn said coolly. "I came for my mother's tray of herbs and had no thought that you were here."

"Then fetch what you came for," Wulfgar directed, his eyes skimming her, noting her change of attire.

Aislinn went to the small table where the herbs were kept, then turned with the tray in her hands. The men were again preoccupied with the bandage, and drawing closer, Aislinn could see the dried blood that stained the cloth and the angry red swelling that had begun to creep from beneath the bandage.

"Take your clumsy hands away, Viking," she commanded. "Unless 'tis your wont to play wet nurse to a one-legged beggar. Move aside."

The Norseman lifted questioning eyes to her, but he rose and stepped away just the same. Setting her tray aside, Aislinn knelt between Wulfgar's spread knees and

48

carefully lifted the edges of the cloth, peering under and testing it gently. It was stuck to a long gash on his leg and the whole oozed with a yellow fluid.

"It festers," she mused aloud. "You would have torn it anew."

Aislinn rose and went to the fireplace where she dipped a linen cloth into the steaming kettle of water that hung over the glowing coals, then drew it out with a stick. With a crooked smile she dropped the hot wet cloth over the bandage, causing Wulfgar to rise halfway out of his chair. He tightened his jaw and forced himself to relax. He'd be damned if he'd let this Saxon wench see his pain. He stared up at her as she stood with arms akimbo and some doubt of her skill showed in his eyes, but she gestured to his leg.

" 'Twill loosen the crust and draw the wound." She gave a short, satirical laugh. "You treat your horses better than yourself."

Whirling, Aislinn went to where his belt and sword lay and drew the short knife from its sheath. At her movement Sweyn eyed her closely and moved nearer his huge war ax, but she only went to lay the blade in the coals of the fireplace. On rising from the task she found both men watching her with something less than complete trust.

"Do the gallant Norman knight and the fierce Viking fear a simple Saxon maid?" she inquired.

" 'Tis not fear I feel," Wulfgar replied. "But your tender arts are ill laid on Normans. Why do you minister to me?"

Aislinn turned away from him and bringing her mother's tray of potions, began to crumble a dried leaf into goose grease. As she stirred the mixture into a yellow salve, she answered.

"My Mother and I have long been the healers of this burh. So do not fear that I will maim you with lack of skill. If I would betray you, Ragnor would place himself in your stead and there are those who would suffer beneath his rule, not least of all myself. Thus for a time I will wait on my vengeance."

"A good thing." Wulfgar nodded slowly as he met her gaze. "If your vengeance was out, I fear Sweyn would not take kindly to it. He has wasted much of his life trying to teach me the ways of women."

"That great hulk!" she scoffed. "What can he do that has not been done to me, other than end my slavery?"

Wulfgar leaned forward and spoke evenly. "His people have long studied ways of slaying and what they do not know they are very wise at guessing."

"Do you threaten me, my lord?" Aislinn asked, raising her eyes to him and pausing in her stirring.

"Nay. I would never threaten you. Betimes I promise but never threaten." He gave her a long look then leaned back in his chair. "If you lay me low, I would have a name to place to you."

"Aislinn, my lord. Aislinn, late of Darkenwald."

"Well, do your worst, Aislinn, while you have me at your mercy." He smiled. "My time will come soon enough."

Aislinn straightened, sorely nettled that he should remind her of what was to come. Sitting the bowl of salve on the hearth beside his chair, she knelt and braced her side against his knee to hold it steady, feeling the iron-thewed hardness of his leg against her breast. Lifting the dampened cloth, she neatly peeled away the bandage, baring a long, red, oozing gash that ran from just above his knee almost to his groin.

"An English blade?" she inquired.

"A token of Senlac," he shrugged.

"The man's aim was poor," she retorted harshly as she examined the wound. "He could have spared me much a hand's breadth over."

Wulfgar gave a snort. "Get on with it. I have much that needs my attention."

Nodding she fetched a bowl of hot water and seating herself again as she was, began to wash the open flesh. When all the blackened tissue and gouts of blood were removed, she brought the knife from the fire then noted that Sweyn picked up his ax and came to stand nearer. She met the Norseman's calm, deliberate stare.

Wulfgar grinned sardonically. "So that you will not be tempted to remedy the Saxon's aim and spare yourself my company in bed." He shrugged. "Sweyn's own manhood is so often and mightily tested he would see mine preserved as well."

Aislinn turned cold, violet eyes to him. "And you, my lord?" she sneered. "Do you not wish for sons?"

Wulfgar waved her question away wearily. " 'Twould goad me less if there were no chance of that. Too many bastards are about these nights."

She smiled wryly. " 'Twould do me no ill either, my lord."

She laid the glowing blade against the wound and drew it quickly down the length of it, sealing the flesh and burning away much of the poisoned part. Wulfgar made no sound as the sickening stench of scorched flesh choked the air, though his body jerked taut and his jaw tightened with his effort. This done, Aislinn rubbed the salve in and about the slash. She took from a plate on the hearth handfuls of moldy bread and, wetting it until it made a thick paste, packed it upon the wound then bound the whole tightly with clean strips of linen.

Aislinn stood back and surveyed her work. "This should stay for three days untouched, then I will remove it. I would suggest a good night's rest till then."

"It eases already," Wulfgar murmured, a bit pale. "But I must be about or it will set and leave me lame."

Shrugging, Aislinn gathered her potions on the tray and would have left him but as she moved behind him to fetch other linens, she noticed a chaffed spot behind his shoulder that showed signs of the reddish color that bespoke of poisoning. She reached out to touch the place and Wulfgar twitched and turned to stare at her with just enough of a start showing on his face to make her laugh.

" 'Twill not need the searing, my lord. Just a small knife prick and a balm to sooth it," she said and began to tend it.

"My ears betray me." He frowned. "I swear you vowed your vengeance would wait."

A knock on the door interrupted and Sweyn opened it to admit Kerwick with a load of Wulfgar's belongings. Aislinn glanced up as her betrothed entered, but quickly bent her eyes to her labors and carefully kept them there lest she give a hint to Wulfgar, who watched the young man place the clothes and chest near the bed. Kerwick paused, and seeing Aislinn's averted gaze, left without a word.

"My bridle!" Wulfgar snorted. "Sweyn, take it back and see they do not bring the Hun to my chambers."

When the Norseman had closed the door behind him, Aislinn again took up her tray to leave.

"One moment, damoiselle," Wulfgar bade her.

Aislinn turned to wait his leisure and watched with detached interest as he pulled himself from the seat and

51

gingerly tested the leg. When he was assured of its strength, he pulled a shirt over his head and went to throw open the shutters. He turned then and gazed about the room in the new light.

"This will be my chamber." His tone of voice was distant. "See your mother's things are moved and the room well cleaned."

"Pray tell, my lord," Aislinn sneered at him. "Where shall I put them? In the sty with the other English swine?"

"Where do you sleep?" he asked, giving no heed to her temper.

"In my own chamber, unless I find it taken."

"Then place them there, Aislinn." He looked directly into her flaring eyes. "You will have little need of it henceforth."

Aislinn blushed hotly and swung away, loathing him for his bold reminder. She waited for him to dismiss her and the room grew silent. She could hear him moving about, poking at the fire and slamming the lid of a chest. Suddenly his voice rang loud and harsh.

"What is that man to you?"

Aislinn whirled and stared at him confused for a moment.

"Kerwick. What is he to you?" he repeated.

"Nothing." She managed to gasp.

"But you know him and he knows you!"

Aislinn regained some of her poise. "Of course. He is the Lord of Cregan and we bartered much with his family."

"He has nothing left to barter. He is lord no more." Wulfgar watched her closely. "He came late, after the village surrendered. When I bade him yield he cast down his sword and made himself my slave." He almost sneered the words as if demeaning Kerwick.

Aislinn replied in a softer tone, more sure of herself now. "Kerwick is more of a scholar than a warrior. His father trained him as a knight, and he fought bravely with Harold."

"He left his spleen on the sod over a few slain. No Norman respects him."

Aislinn lowered her eyes and hid her own pity for Kerwick. "He is a gentle person and those out yonder were his friends. He talked with them and set down verses of

52

their toils. He has seen too much of death since the Normans came to our land."

Wulfgar clasped his hands behind his back and stood huge and imposing before her. His face was shadowed by the light from the window, and Aislinn could see only those gray eyes calmly gazing at her.

"And what of those who did not die?" he questioned. "How many have fled and hid in the forest?"

"I know of none," she replied and it was only half a lie. She had seen some reach the edge of the swamp when her father fell but could not name them or say whether they were still free.

Wulfgar reached out and lifted a tress of her hair and felt its rich, silken texture. Those eyes would not free her from their intensity. Aislinn could feel her will weaken, and the slow smile that spread across his face told her she had played no deep game with him. He nodded.

"You know of none?" His voice was heavy with satire. "No matter. They will soon come to serve their master as will you."

Wulfgar's hand fell to her shoulder and he pulled her near him. The tray rattled in her hands.

"Please—," Aislinn whispered hoarsely, afraid of the lips that stirred her so. "Please." The word came in a half sob.

His hand slid down her arm in a gentle caress then dropped from her.

"See to the rooms," he commanded softly, still holding her with his gaze. "And if the people come to you, treat them as well as you have me. They are mine, too, and precious few."

Outside the chamber Aislinn nearly collided with Kerwick in her haste to leave. He bore in his arms more baggage for the lord, but she hurried by him, knowing her flushed face would betray her. She flew to her own room and as she gathered her belongings fought to control the trembling that beset her fingers. She was in a rage that the Norman could so upset her. What strange power burned in those cold gray eyes that sneered at her.

Aislinn came from the hall to watch with dismay as some dozen serfs were led into the yard. With their ankles tethered they could only hobble along together beside the mounted horsemen. On his great war horse Wulfgar

53

looked all the more fearsome to these simple folk who trembled for their lives. Aislinn bit her lip as one lad, seeking to escape, broke from the rest and hopped away as fast as his bonds would allow, but he was no great test for Wulfgar's stallion. Riding up behind the boy, Wulfgar caught him by the scruff of his shirt and hauled him across the front of the saddle. The youth, yelping for all he was worth, received a silencing blow across his buttocks and rode back grimacing in pain but silent. Wulfgar discarded his load in the midst of the peasants who scrambled frantically to get out of the way of his mount.

They were herded into the square like trussed swine, and Aislinn released a sigh of relief when she saw that none were wounded. She stepped back as Wulfgar rode up before her and dismounted.

"You did not kill any in the forest?" she questioned anxiously.

"Nay, they fled like any good-blooded Saxon would," he threw at her.

Aislinn glared at him as he raised a mocking gaze to her and turning on her heels, stalked into the hall.

A semblance of order fell on Darkenwald and compared to the previous night they supped in what was almost a tranquil atmosphere. The Normans were established and there was no bickering, for each man knew Wulfgar was lord here. Those that envied him dared not challenge him. Those that respected him thought him worthy.

Aislinn found herself occupying her mothers' rightful place as lady of the hall and was conscious of Wulfgar's dominating presence beside her. He conversed with Sweyn who sat on the opposite side of him and generally seemed to ignore her which she found most bewildering since he had insisted that she feast with him, indicating that particular place beside him. She had been reluctant to do so. Her mother had been reduced to scrambling for scraps with the other serfs, and Aislinn thought it only proper that she share the same fate of Maida.

"A serf's place to dine is not beside the lord," she reminded him caustically when he bade her take the chair.

Wulfgar's cold, penetrating gaze bore into her. "It is, when the lord commands."

During the feast Kerwick remained close by Wulfgar's table, offering them food and wine as a common servant.

Aislinn found herself wishing him someplace else. She hated the miserable guise of defeated resignation he wore. Ragnor, too, did not relent in his careful perusal of them but with his dark eyes, watched their every move. Aislinn felt his hatred of Wulfgar as if it were a solid substance and grew somewhat amused that he should be so annoyed by the bastard's possession of her.

The possessor of a blackened eye and a swollen jaw, Hlynn timorously brought ale to the Normans, flinching when they barked at her or reached to fondle a breast or buttock. Her clothing had been repaired by a piece of twine, and the men's regalement became enlivened by a wager among them over which would be the first to break it. The fearful girl, not understanding their language or wager, walked into many a trap set by the conniving Normans.

Maida appeared unconcerned by the girl's distress but seemed more interested in the scraps of food flung to the hounds laying underfoot. At times Aislinn would see her cramming a stolen morsel into her mouth, and her own waning appetite was little improved by the knowledge her mother was going hungry.

Hlynn's repairs held until the meal was nearly complete, but in his frustration, Ragnor vented his anger upon the unfortunate girl. Catching her into his brutal grasp, he cut the cords with his dagger, pricking the tender breasts and pressed his cruel mouth to the youthful flesh, ignoring her tearful and terrified struggles.

Aislinn's stomach heaved and she looked away, remembering those same burning lips against her own breasts. She did not glance up when he strode out the door carrying the girl, but shuddered uncontrollably. After some moments she lifted her head, having regained some small bit of her composure, and found Wulfgar's eyes upon her. Weakly she reached for her wine and drank it down numbly.

"Time has swift wings, Aislinn," he commented, watching her. "It is your foe?"

She would not meet his gaze. She knew his meaning. Like Ragnor he had become bored with the feasting and was thinking of other entertainment.

"I repeat, damoiselle, is time your foe?"

She turned to him and was surprised to find that he was leaning toward her, so close that his warm breath touched

55

her cheek. His eyes, almost blue now as he gazed at her, delved deeply into her own.

"Nay," she breathed. "I think not."

"You are not afraid of me?" Wulfgar inquired.

Aislinn shook her head bravely, setting the brilliant tresses astir. "I fear no man, only God."

"Is He your foe?" the Norman pressed.

She swallowed and glanced away. What manner God would let these men of Normandy invade their homes? But it was not for her to question a reasoning so great as His.

"I pray not," Aislinn replied. "For He is my only hope. All others fail me." She raised her chin haughtily. " 'Tis said your duke is a devout man. Having the same God as we, why has he killed so many of us to achieve the throne?"

"Edward and Harold both gave their vows 'twould belong to him. 'Twas only when Harold closeted himself with the dying king that he saw a chance for his own and proclaimed Edward's last word was that he should have the crown. There was no proof he lied, but—" Wulfgar shrugged. "By right of birth, 'tis William's crown."

Aislinn turned sharply to stare at him. "The grandson of a common tanner? A—"

She stopped aghast, realizing what she had almost said.

"Bastard, damoiselle?" Wulfgar finished for her, peering at her questioningly. He smiled wryly. "A misfortune that befalls many of us, I am sorry to say."

Her cheeks flushed with color, Aislinn wisely lowered her gaze from his all too perceiving eyes. He straightened back in his chair.

"Even bastards are human, Aislinn. Their needs and desires are like those of other men. A throne is as appealing to an illegimate son as one that's proper born, perhaps more so."

He rose from his seat and taking her arm, drew her up to him. He raised a taunting brow and there was an odd gleam of amusement in his eyes as his hands slipped about her narrow waist, pulling her supple body against his much harder, much larger one.

"We even yearn for our comforts to be eased some small whit. Come, lover, I've a need to tame a shrew. I am weary of men and fighting. I seek gentler sport this night."

Her glaring eyes gave venomous retort to his jibe and before her lips could follow up the assault, an enraged, bellowing cry rent the hall. Aislinn started around to see Kerwick charging toward them with a dagger in his hand. Her heart leaped and she could only stand frozen, waiting for his attack. Whether it was herself Kerwick sought to slay or Wulfgar she could not say. She cried out as Wulfgar thrust her behind him, and prepared to meet Kerwick's attack barehanded. But Sweyn, never trusting anyone too fully, had been watching the young Saxon closely and thought his regard of the maid more than a bit harrowed, and now acted swiftly. With a backward motion he flung a mighty arm against Kerwick that sent him sprawling to the floor. With a heavy foot the Viking ground the younger man's face into the rushes as he easily wrested the dagger from him and threw it clattering against the wall. The Norseman raised his battle axe to sever his head, and Aislinn screamed in horror.

"No! God's mercy, no!"

Sweyn looked at her and every eye in the hall was turned to them. Aislinn struggled up, sobbing in hysteria as she clung to Wulfgar. She clutched his leather jerkin.

"No! No! You must not do him harm! Spare him, I beg you!"

Maida crept forward and stroked her daughter's back, whining her fear. " 'Tis sire first slain, then betrothed. They leave you no one."

Wulfgar whirled on the woman and Maida screeched, falling back under his fierce gaze.

"What say you, hag? Is he her betrothed?" he demanded.

Maida nodded, terrified. "Yea. Soon they were to wed."

Wulfgar glanced from Aislinn to the young Saxon and settled an accusing glare upon the girl. Finally he turned to Sweyn who waited.

"Take him to the dogs and chain him there," he barked. "I will deal with him on the morrow."

The Viking nodded and jerked Kerwick to his feet by the back of his tunic, lifting him for a moment completely off the floor.

"Be assured, little Saxon," the Norseman chuckled. "This night you have been saved by a wench. You have a good star protecting you."

Aislinn still shook uncontrollably from terrible fright,

57

but she watched solemnly as Kerwick was dragged to the end of the hall where the hounds lay. There he was thrown among them, sending the pack yelping and snapping at each other. In the confusion no one saw Maida hurriedly conceal Kerwick's dagger within her garments.

Aislinn turned to Wulfgar. "I am indebted to you," she murmured softly, her voice quavering but growing stronger with her relief.

He grunted. "Are you? Well, we shall see in a moment how grateful you really are. You turned on me in rage when I granted your request for a priest. You lie to me and declare that milksop of a boy is of no importance to you." He laughed with scorn. "Better you had told me yourself he was your betrothed than let the old hag spill the news."

Aislinn's anger flared anew. "I lied lest you should kill him," she replied heatedly. "'Tis your way, is it not?"

Wulfgar's gray eyes appeared dark and stormy. "Think me the fool, damoiselle, to slaughter valuable slaves so easily. But he would surely have met his death just now had not the crone told me he was your betrothed. At least knowing that, I can see the reason for his foolish act."

"You spared him now, but what of the morrow?" she asked intently.

He shrugged. "What of the morrow? My fancy then will see my will out. A dance from a gibbit mayhap or some other entertainment."

Aislinn's heart sank. Had she saved Kerwick from a quick death now to see him hung or tortured to amuse the Normans?

"What are you willing to trade for his life? Yourself? But this is not fair. I do not know what I bargain for." Wulfgar took her wrist. "Come, we shall see."

Aislinn tried to pull away from him but his fingers tightened upon her arm, and though she felt no pain under his touch she could not get free.

"Do you fear you're not worth enough to save a life?" He mocked. Aislinn resisted only lightly as he drew her with him up the stone stairs. He dismissed the guard who stood at the chamber door and flinging it wide, pushed her inside. He closed and barred the door behind him then turned, folding his arms across his broad chest as he leaned against the wall. A smile crept across his lips.

"I await, damoiselle." His gaze measured each rounded curve of her body. "Anxiously so."

Aislinn held herself with dignity. "You have a long wait, messire," she said distainfully. "I do not play the harlot."

Wulfgar smiled slowly. "Not even for poor Kerwick? Pity. On the morrow he will surely wish you had."

Aislinn glared at him, hating him with all her being. "What do you want of me?"

He shrugged his great shoulders leisurely. " 'Twould be a fit beginning to see the worth of what I bargain for." He smiled. "We are quite alone. Do not be timid."

Aislinn's eyes flashed. "You are loathsome!"

His grin deepened. "Few women have said as much, but you are not the first."

Aislinn glanced around in desperation for some object to hurl at him.

"Come now, Aislinn," he cajoled. "I grow impatient. Let us see your worth."

She stamped a slender foot. "No! No! No! I will not play the whore!!"

"Poor Kerwick," he sighed.

"I hate you," she screamed.

He did not appear concerned. "I have no great love for you either. I detest lying women."

"Then if you detest me, why this?!" she demanded.

Wulfgar chuckled. "I don't have to love you to bed you. I desire you. That is enough."

"Not for me!" she cried, shaking her head furiously.

Wulfgar's shoulders shook with his laughter. "You are no virgin. What difference is one more man?"

Aislinn stuttered in rage. "I have been taken once against my will," she stormed. "That does not mean I'm a slut."

He looked at her from under his brows. "Not even for Kerwick?" he taunted.

Aislinn choked back a sob and whirled in helpless frustration. She stood quivering in anger and loathing fear, unable to bear his mockery. Slowly she unfastened her gunna and let it fall to the floor. A tear slid down her cheek. The kirtle followed the gown and lay in a heap around her slender ankles.

She heard Wulfgar approach and he came to stand before her. His eyes burned and seemed to brand her where they touched as his gaze traveled slowly down her body and then slowly upward again, measuring every soft, splendid curve with a thoroughness that seemed to draw her very breath from her. Aislinn stood proud and tall, hating him, yet knowing a strange excitement stirring in her youthful body as this man stared at her.

"Yea, you are lovely," Wulfgar breathed, reaching out to fondle a well-rounded breast. Aislinn steeled her body, yet to her shamed surprise felt a sweeping pleasure beneath the warmth and gentleness of his hand. He traced a finger between her breasts downward to her narrow waist. Indeed, she was beautiful, long of limb, slender bodied, yet with swelling breasts, ripe and delicately hued. They loomed eager for a man's caress.

"Do you find me worth a man's life?" she bit out icily.

"Most certainly," he replied. "But that was never the case."

Aislinn stared at him in bewilderment, and he smiled slowly into her eyes.

"Kerwick's debt is not yours. His life is his own. I give him that. Yea, there will be punishment for him because he had dared much and must be properly rewarded. But nothing you can do will change what I have set aside for him."

Aislinn went livid with rage and she struck out at him in her fury, but Wulfgar caught her wrist and pulled her hard against him. He chuckled unmercifully at her as she struggled to free herself. Aislinn felt his hands in contact with her body, momentarily touching here and there in his attempt to subdue her, and he seemed to enjoy her efforts thoroughly. He smiled into her flashing eyes.

"My fiery vixen, you are well worth any man's life, even if all the kingdoms in the world were at stake."

"You knave!" she cried. "You beggardly oaf! You—you bastard!"

His grip tightened to iron intensity and his smile faded. He held her so closely their bodies seemed to merge into one. Aislinn gasped in pain and bit her lips against crying out. Her thighs were caught tightly to his and she knew his raging desires. Her head swam and she could only whimper in agony in his cruel embrace.

"Remember one thing, damoiselle," Wulfgar said coldly. "I have little use for women and a lying one even less. The next time you lie to me you will suffer greater shame than you just have."

With that he thrust her from him, and she fell in a heap upon the floor at the foot of the bed and lay quivering, her body aching, her shame intense. Aislinn heard him move and glanced up to see him lift a length of chain her father had used to leash the dogs. As he approached her with it, she cringed in terror. Had her words provoked him so that now he must beat her to have revenge? What hell had she sought, trying to flee from Ragnor's grasp? He would kill her, she was certain. Her heart drummed in her ears, and as he bent to her, she gave a gasp and leapt away, kicking at him as she tried to flee his outstretched hands. He dropped the chain and bounded after her.

"Nay!" she shrieked and eluded him by running under his arm. She darted past him in a spurt of strength and flew to the door. Her fingers tried to lift the bar, but even lame, Wulfgar was fast, and he was close, a menacing step behind her. Aislinn could almost feel his breath upon her neck. With a cry, she flung herself from the door toward the hearth, her mind churning, trying to outwit him. But to her horror, her foot caught in the edge of the wolf pelt spread before the fire and she stumbled. Before she could regain her balance, he dove at her, throwing his arms about her middle. As they went crashing down, he twisted his body so that he bore much of her weight against him and took the full impact of the fall upon himself though it caused him no slight discomfort as his leg was jolted. Aislinn had no time to wonder if he meant it thus, for she was too busy trying to escape him. Her limbs flailed about as she sought to free herself, then she turned in his restraining arms to press a frontal attack. She saw the error of her ways when he laughed and pinned her to the floor beneath him.

"Let me go!" she gasped, thrashing her head from side to side. She was shaking uncontrollably until her teeth chattered, yet she was not cold for the heat of the fire near scorched her skin. Though she felt his stare upon her face she would not look at him but kept her eyes closed. "Let me go! Please!"

To her amazement he rose and drew her to her feet. He peered down into her tearful face with a twisted smile, reaching up to brush some of her wildly cascading hair from her cheek. Aislinn wrapped her arms before her to hide her nakedness from him and returned his gaze sullenly, feeling bruised and battered.

61

Wulfgar laughed and taking her slim hand into his, led her back to the end of the bed. He picked up the chain again and with a dry sob, Aislinn strained away, but he pushed her down to the floor. There to her utter amazement he fastened one end of the shackle to the bed and the other around her ankle. Now she gazed at him in complete bafflement. Glancing into her face he read her confoundment and apprehension. He smiled.

"I have no wish to lose you as Ragnor did," he mocked. "There are no longer any brave and foolish Saxons for you to bury, therefore I doubt that you would tarry so close to Darkenwald's door if you were left free to roam while I seek my rest. The chain is long and gives you some freedom."

"You are overkind, milord," she retorted, anger riding again over her fears. "I had no inkling your strength was so lacking that you must chain me while you do your worst to me."

"It saves energy," he laughed. "And I can see I'll need all the assist I can get to tame the shrew."

He rose and strode from her back to the hearth where he began to disrobe, setting his garments neatly aside. Aislinn contemplated him broodingly as she huddled naked upon the cold floor. Garbed only in chausses, he stared pensively into the flames, absentmindedly rubbing his thigh as if to ease the ache. She noticed that once inside the chamber he gave almost imperceptible favor to the wounded limb.

Aislinn sighed as she tucked her knees beneath her chin and idly wondered at the battles he must have fought. A long scar marred the bronze chest as if someone had laid a broadsword across it. Several smaller scars marked his body and the muscles beneath the sun-darkened skin gave evidence of a hard, rigorous life and of much time spent wielding a sword and riding a horse. It was easy to see he was not a man of leisure and even less difficult to guess the reason why she had not evaded him. His waist was trim and his belly hard and flat, the hips narrow and his legs long and well-shaped beneath the stockinged garment.

Now in the flickering light he suddenly seemed drawn and haggard and Aislinn could almost feel the exhaustion that sapped his strength and drooped his frame. She experienced a quick pang of pity for this Norman foe, realizing that he must be driving himself by will power alone.

Wulfgar sighed and stretched his weary muscles. Then sitting down, he removed the chausses and laid them aside with his other clothes. As he turned toward Aislinn her breath caught in her throat, for the sight of his male nudity brought her fear to the fore once more. She shrank away, trying to cover her own nakedness. At her movement Wulfgar stopped as if remembering her presence and read the fear written in the violet eyes she raised to him. A tawny brow lifted and mockery curved his lips as he reached to the bed where he seized several wolf pelts. He threw them to her.

"Good night, lover," he said simply.

There was stunned bewilderment as well as relief in her expression as she stared at him for a moment. Then she hurriedly wrapped herself against the chill and settled herself gratefully upon the hard stone floor. Blowing out the candles, Wulfgar pulled himself to the middle of her parents' bed, and soon his heavy breathing filled the room. Aislinn snuggled deeper into the furs and smiled, content.

Aislinn was rudely awakened the next morning by a lusty whack upon her buttocks that brought a screech of pain from her. She started up in agony and came face to face with an amused Wulfgar who sat on the edge of the bed grinning at her. Handing her garments to her, he watched appreciatively as she quickly donned them, feasting his eyes on the impudent breasts and the soft, ivory thighs before she snatched her kirtle over her head.

"You're a lazy wench," he chided. "Come, get me water to wash by and help me dress. My life is not so leisurely as yours."

Aislinn glared at him, rubbing her abused posterior.

"You also sleep soundly," he said.

"I trust you slept well, my lord," she said, tossing her head to look at him. "You seem rested at least."

Wulfgar gave her a slow appraisal that seemed to penetrate her simple garments and smiled, his eyes warm and glowing. "Well enough, damoiselle."

Aislinn's color deepened and she hurried to the door.

"I'll fetch water," she said and fled from the chamber.

Maida sidled up to her as she filled a pail with hot water from the kettle hanging above the fire in the hall.

"He bars the doors or sets a guard to it," the old woman whined. "What must be done to save you from him? He's not an easy man for you, the beasty. I heard your screams last night."

"He didn't touch me." Aislinn said in some wonder. "All night I slept at the foot of the bed and he didn't touch me."

"What manner man would do that?" Maida demanded. " 'Tis naught from mercy, I vow. Wait 'til eventide and he'll take you. This time, do not linger. Flee. Flee."

"I cannot," Aislinn answered. "He chains me to the bed."

Maida screeched in dismay. "He treats you like an animal."

Aislinn shrugged. "At least he does not beat me." Remembering otherwise, she rubbed her buttocks. "Only a bit."

"Huh, he would kill you if you crossed him."

Aislinn shook her head, recalling the moment he held her tightly pressed against him. Even in his anger he did not abuse her. "Nay, his manner is different."

"How do you know? His own men fear him."

"I am not afraid of him," Aislinn returned proudly.

"You are foolhardy!" Maida whined. " 'Twill gain you naught to be stubborn and proud like your sire."

"I must go now," Aislinn murmured. "He is waiting to wash."

"I'll find a way to help you."

"Mother, leave be! I'm afraid for you. That one called Sweyn guards his master's back like a hawk. He'll kill you if you dare anything. And I find Wulfgar more acceptable than these other jackals."

"But what of Kerwick?" Maida hissed, glancing toward where he lay huddled asleep among the dogs.

Aislinn shrugged. "Ragnor ended that."

"Kerwick does not think so. He still wants you."

"Then he must realize it is a different world than a week ago. We are not free. I belong to Wulfgar now as he does. We're no better than slaves. We have no rights other than what we're given."

Maida sneered. "Strange, daughter, I should hear you say that, you were always the haughty one."

"What have we to be arrogant about now, Mother?" Aislinn questioned wearily. "We have nothing. We must think of staying alive and helping each other."

"Your blood is among the best of Saxony. Your sire, a great lord. I will not have you whelp a bastard's brat."

Aislinn looked hard at Maida and her eyes flashed their

anger. "Would you rather have me produce a bantling for Ragnor, my father's murderer?"

Maida wrung her hands in consternation. "Do not scold at me, Aislinn. I think only of you."

"I know, mother," Aislinn sighed, softening. "Please, at least wait a time and let us see what kind of man Wulfgar proves to be. He was angry over the killings. Mayhaps he will be a fair man."

"A Norman?!" Maida shrieked.

"Yea, Mother, a Norman. Now I must go."

When Aislinn opened the chamber door, Wulfgar scowled at her. He was half dressed.

"It took you long enough, wench," he growled.

"Forgive me, my lord," she murmured. She put her burden down and raised her eyes to his. "My mother feared for my safety last night, and I only paused to reassure her that I suffered no harm."

"Your mother? Which one is she? I saw no lady of the hall, yet Ragnor said she still is about."

"The one you refer to as hag," Aislinn said softly. "She is my mother."

"That one," he grunted. "She was ill-used by some heavy fist, I vow."

Aislinn nodded. "I am the only one she has left. She worries about me." She swallowed hard. "She speaks of vengeance."

Wulfgar peered at her, now fully alert. "Do you seek to warn me? Will she try to kill me?"

Aislinn's gaze fell nervously. "Mayhap. I am not certain, my lord."

"You tell me this because you do not wish to see her slain?"

"Oh, God forbid!" Aislinn gasped, beginning to tremble. "I would never forgive myself if I let that happen. She has taken enough from the Normans. Besides, your duke would slay us all if you were killed."

Wulfgar smiled. "Your warning is taken and I will look after her and will tell Sweyn to take care."

Releasing a grateful sigh, Aislinn lifted her gaze to meet his. "I thank you, messire."

"Now, girl," he sighed heavily. "Help me finish dressing. You've tarried too long for me to put that water to good use. However, I shall want a bath tonight and my anger will be sorely aroused if you delay too long then."

The hall was empty but for Kerwick when Aislinn followed Wulfgar down. Her betrothed was still chained with the dogs but now he was awake. He watched her as she crossed the room behind Wulfgar, never wavering a moment in that intense regard of her.

Maida came to serve them herself and scurried to place warm bread, meat, and softened honeycombs before them as Wulfgar seated himself before the table and gestured Aislinn to a place by his side. Kerwick's gaze had remained steadfastly on his former betrothed until Maida brought the food. Now his hunger for that stuff was even more important. Maida waited until Wulfgar served himself and Aislinn then took the rejected heel of bread and gave most of it to Kerwick, keeping only a small piece for herself to gnaw on. As she squatted near him and exchanged whispered comments with him, it was apparent the two had found some common ground and now shared confidences in their grief. Wulfgar studied them over his meal, and then suddenly his belt knife rang on the table, drawing the attention of all. Aislinn saw a quick flash of anger pass his features, leaving them taut but thoughtful. She puzzled at what had disturbed him, but his voice broke her train of thought as he spoke tersely.

"Old hag, come here."

Maida seemed to crouch even lower as she sidled in front of the table as if she expected more blows to descend upon her.

"Stand up, woman," Wulfgar commanded. "Straighten your back, for I know you can."

Slowly Maida drew herself to her full height, slight though it was. When she stood straight backed before him, Wulfgar leaned forward in his chair.

"Is it you who was known as Lady Maida before your master was slain?"

"Yea, lord," Maida bobbed her head in a birdlike manner. She glanced nervously at her daughter who sat tense and waiting.

"And is it you," Wulfgar questioned further, "who was lady of this hall?"

Maida swallowed convulsively and nodded once more. "Yea, lord."

"Then, dame, you do me ill service when you play the fool. You dress in rags and fight the dogs for food and bemoan your lowly station, when if you displayed the courage of your husband and had decried your status, you might now reside as is thy wont. You play me false before your people. So I bid you now, seek your garments and clothe your frame, and in the course of such, wash the filth from your body and do not carry this game beyond my endurance. Your daughter's chambers will be thine. Now get thee hence."

As she withdrew Wulfgar returned again to his meal. When he glanced up he found Aislinn watching him with an almost tender expression upon her face.

"Do I perceive a softening in your heart for me, damoiselle?" He laughed at her scowl. "Beware, maid. I will tell you true. After you will come another and then another. There are no strings that can tether me to any woman. So guard your heart."

"My lord, you greatly exaggerate your appeal," she replied indignantly. "If I feel anything for you, 'tis hatred. You are the enemy and you are to be despised as such."

"Indeed?" He smiled slowly into her eyes. "Then tell me, damoiselle, do you always kiss the enemy so warmly?"

Aislinn's cheek flushed scarlet. "You are mistaken, lord. It was not warmth, merely passive resistance."

Wulfgar's grin deepened. "Shall I kiss you again, damoiselle, to prove that I am right?"

Aislinn returned his gaze with distain. "Far be it for a serf to argue with a lord. If you imagined response, then who am I to say you nay?"

"You disappoint me, Aislinn," He chided. "You give up the game too easily."

" 'Tis that, milord, or suffer through another kiss or worse yet another mauling such as I had last eventide. I fear my bones will not take another crushing as you seemed wont to give them. I would much rather concede."

"Another time, damoiselle."

Kerwick withdrew to the shadows as the great door was flung wide and Ragnor swept into the hall, his breath curling around his head like streamers of fog. He paused before Aislinn, and bowed shortly.

"Good morningtide, my dove. It seems that the night has well agreed with you."

Aislinn's mouth curved upward into a winsome smile. If he could play this game of polite nonsense, so could she.

"Yes, sir knight. It pleased me well."

She sensed his surprise and was aware of Wulfgar's

amused gaze upon her. At the moment she thought she hated both men equally.

" 'Twas a chilled night to be warmed by a wench," Ragnor remarked casually and turned to eye Wulfgar. "You might taste that maid, Hlynn, if you tire of thorns and nettles in your bed." He grinned, rubbing his thumb against his torn lip. "She'll do whatever you command without a struggle and her teeth I'll wager aren't nearly so sharp."

Wulfgar grunted. "I prefer a livelier game."

Ragnor shrugged and seizing a horn, poured himself a hearty draught of ale from the flagon while Wulfgar sat quietly, waiting the man's good time.

"Aaargh." Ragnor cleared his throat and banged the empty horn down. "The peasants are up and about their labors as you ordered, Wulfgar, and the men set to guard against thieves and roving bands of looters and in the twain to watch the villeins."

Wulfgar nodded his approval. "Set patrols to ride the perimeters of the lands." Thoughtfully counting with the point of his knife upon the rough-hewn planks of the table, he continued. "Make each group consist of five men to return three days hence and send a new group every morn except for the Sabbath. Let each group take a different way, one east, one west, one north, one south. The warning should be a trumpet sounded at the mile mark or a fire burned at the five. Thus we know that each patrol completes its ride and should they not, we are warned."

Ragnor grunted. "You plan well, Wulfgar, as if you always deemed it your due to be made lord of lands."

Wulfgar arched a brow at him but said nothing and the conversation stiffly turned to other things. Aislinn noted the two men as they talked, wondering at the difference in them, for where Ragnor was arrogant and superior and demanded the allegiance of his men, Wulfgar was calm and reserved. He led by example rather than by orders and simply assumed that his men would follow. He did not question their loyalty but seemed to know that each would lay down his life rather than disappoint him.

Aislinn was still considering these points when she raised her eyes and with a gasp half rose in reflex, for there at the head of the stairs stood her mother as Aislinn had known her for many years, small of stature, yet proud beyond her size. Maida stood now poised in her own

69

clothes, clean and with a head rail covering her hair and draped to hide much of the swollen face. She strode down toward them with the grace and bearing that seemed natural to her and Aislinn's heart swelled with gladness and relief. Here was her mother indeed.

By his silence Wulfgar gave his approval, but Ragnor came to his feet with a roar and before any could stop him, leapt forward and snatched at Maida's hair. The veil came loose in his hands and with a screech Maida fell to the floor, the idiot's grin again twisting her face. It was doubly cruel for Aislinn to watch her beloved mother fade and the hag return, for now with her shoulders hunched and whimpering for mercy at Ragnor's feet she seemed no more than some wretched crone in stolen finery. Aislinn caught her breath in a sob and fell back into her chair again as her mother whined louder.

Ragnor raised his fist in rage at the old woman. "You dare dress yourself in rich clothes and strut before your lords like some regal wench at court. You Saxon sow. 'Twill bring you naught, for I will have wolves chewing at your stringy bones!"

He bent to seize her, but Wulfgar's fist came down hard on the table.

"Hold!" he commanded. "Do the old one no harm, for she is here and thusly gowned at my request."

Ragnor drew himself back and faced the other. "Wulfgar, now you reach beyond yourself! You set this hag above us! 'Tis William's way to set aside the lords who resisted and all their kin and place instead our own, our heroes who took the field and won the day. You take from me my reward, yet you set this one before the Saxon oafs and—"

"Do not let rage cloud your vision, Ragnor," Wulfgar retorted. "For surely even you can see that these poor wretches could not long bear to see their former mistress abused and reduced to feed among the dogs. On her behalf they'd seize up arms and come again to take us. There would be naught to do but slay them until there were but aged men and swaddled babes to serve us. Now would you have it so that we, soldiers of the Duke, should tend the fields and milk the goats? Or leave these Saxons some small touch of pride to assuage their fears and have them meet our bidding until we own the land in truth and 'tis too late for them to blow the horn and rise up against

70

us? I yield them nothing, but they will say 'tis much more. In the end they will pay my taxes, and I will be the one who gains. No martyr ever suffered in comfort. No saint ever died in gold and silk. 'Tis no more than a gesture from me to them. She is their lady still. They will not know that she but serves my will."

Ragnor shook his head. "Wulfgar, I have no doubt that should William ever fall, you might prove his long lost brother and might weedle your way to the very crown. But mark me well." He smiled with a touch of venom. "Should you ever err, in truth I pray, that I should be the one to see it and be the one to swing the axe that separates your bastard heart from those winsome lips that sing songs of righteousness and bait the worthy to a cruel end."

With a bow of mockery he left the hall, and as the door banged shut behind the dark knight, Aislinn flew to her mother's side. She sought to calm her, for the old woman still groveled on the floor and whimpered in confusion, not knowing her tormentor had left. Aislinn placed an arm about her shoulders and holding Maida's head to her breast, rocked to and fro and whispered softly against her hair.

With a start Aislinn realized that Wulfgar had come to stand beside them. She raised her eyes to his and saw him regard Maida with something akin to pity.

"Take her to her chamber and tend her."

Aislinn bridled at this uncalled-for command, but his broad back had swung and he was already striding to the door. She stared after him a moment, enraged that he could so easily use their pride for his own end, but she turned her attention to her mother again and helping her to her feet, she guided Maida slowly up the stairs and into her own former room with tenderness born of love. There she calmed her mother's fears as best she could, putting her to bed and smoothing the gray-streaked hair as the woman's mewlings turned to sobs and the sobs to the uneven breaths of troubled sleep. The room was silent as Maida rested her weary mind, and Aislinn quietly put the place to some order, for the search after booty had left it in sore disarray.

Aislinn went to the shutters and set them ajar to catch the warming morning breeze. As she did so, she heard a voice droning on and recognized the words calling for twenty lashes. Leaning out the window, she gasped at the panorama before her. Kerwick, stripped to the waist, was lashed to the frame of timbers set in the town square, and Wulfgar stood beside him, helm, gauntlets and mail removed and hanging from his sword which was thrust into the ground to support them. So weaponless, but as a lord he stood ready to mete out punishment. He held an arm's length of heavy rope which had been unbraided for two thirds its length and small knots tied in the end of each strand. As the words ended, the very breeze died, and the scene froze for a moment, then Wulfgar's arm rose and fell with an eager swishing sound, and Kerwick jumped against his bonds. A low moan rose briefly from the gathered townspeople, and again Wulfgar's arm rose and fell. This time the moan came from Kerwick's lips. On the third stroke he was again silent, but on the fourth a short scream was torn from his lips as his back turned to fire beneath the lash. By the tenth the screams turned to gurgles and the fifteenth he only jerked against the straps as the lash fell. As the twentieth stroke was laid the townspeople sighed in one breath, and Aislinn broke from the window, sobbing and breathless, flushed and dizzy as if she had held her breath throughout his punishment. Her sobs turned to choked curses as she ran from the chamber with tears streaming down her face and struggled with the weight of the great door. Feeling herself a part of his torment, she came to Kerwick's side, but he hung senseless against the timbers, and she whirled to face Wulfgar with the fury born of frustration.

"So, you must seize this poor man from the hounds to vent your whimsy upon his helpless back!" she raged. "Was it not enough that you stole his lands and made him a slave?"

Wulfgar had dropped the cat with the last stroke and had turned and was wiping Kerwick's blood from his hand. Now he spoke from rigid self-control.

"Woman, this fool sought to slay me in the midst of my own men. I told you then his fate was sealed and not yours to dally with."

"Are you so high, my lord," she sneered, "that you take to your own hands vengeance upon this man whose own betrothed he saw mauled before his very eyes?!"

Wulfgar was not pleased and his frown darkened. He stepped closer and spoke with a harder tone. " 'Twas my heart he sought to pierce. Thus my arm should strip his back bare and lay thereon the strokes of justice."

Aislinn lifted her chin and opened her mouth to speak, but Wulfgar continued.

"See you them!" He swung his arm to the townspeople. "They now know that any foolery will be met by that same justice and that the lash may well shred their hides as his. So taunt me not with your tongue of innocence, Aislinn of Darkenwald, for 'twas your game, too. And you who hid the truth should endure some of his pain." His gray eyes pierced her. "Be grateful your tender back will bear no share. But you may learn from this my hand is not forever stayed."

With this Wulfgar turned to his men.

"Now shear this fool," he bade them. "Then let his fellows salt his wounds and give him ease. Yea, shear them all! Let them wear the Norman mode this season."

Aislinn stared at him with some confusion and knew what his words meant only when Kerwick's hair was clipped and his beard shaved from his face with a well-honed blade. A new murmur rose from the townspeople, and men turned to flee only to find their way blocked by the Normans, and they were seized one by one and dragged back to the square where they met a part of Kerwick's fate. Some rose embarrassed and fingering their nude and pinkish chins and shortened locks, fled the public eye in mortal shame, for now they bore the Norman brand and had lost their Saxon glory.

Aislinn's fury regained its throne, and she left the courtyard to return with purposeful gait to the lord's chamber where she sought out her mother's scissors. She had unbound her hair and with unreasoning anger raised the blades to her tresses when the door flung wide. A blow stunned her wrist, and the tool fell from her numbed fingers. She gave a startled gasp as a great hand gripped her shoulder and spun her about. Steel-cold eyes quenched her anger.

"You test me sorely, maid," Wulfgar growled. "And I warn you now. For each bright lock you shear the lash will fall once upon your back!"

Aislinn's knees trembled and she shook with fear, for she had not known the towering black heights his rage could reach. It dwarfed her own, and within his iron grasp

73

she felt the idiocy of her notion and could only whisper hoarsely:

"Yea, lord. I yield. Please, you hurt me."

There was a softening in Wulfgar's gaze, and his arms slipped around her, crushing her to him. His voice was hoarse as he whispered:

"Then yield me all, damoiselle. Yield me all."

For a long moment her lips were smothered beneath his passionate kiss, but even in his rough embrace she could feel herself softening and a warm glow beginning deep inside as his mouth moved upon hers, brutally snatching her will from her.

His lips withdrew and he looked at her strangely, his eyes clouded and unreadable. Then she was flung backwards across the bed. In long strides he went to the door then turned and stared at her, this time in disapproval.

"Women!" he snorted and slammed the door closed behind him.

Aislinn stared at the door and knew more confusion than she had seen in his face. She was aghast at her own reaction. Her mind tumbled over itself in bewilderment. What manner of man was he that she could hate him so intensely yet at the same time find pleasure in his embrace? Her lips responded to his against her will, and her body yielded almost gladly to his greater strength.

Wulfgar strode out of the hall and barked an order to his men as Sweyn came to him, carrying his hauberk and helm.

"The maid is spirited," the Viking remarked.

"Yea, but she will learn," Wulfgar said curtly.

"The men wager upon which will be tamed," Sweyn returned slowly. "Some say 'twill be the wolf who finds his fangs drawn."

Wulfgar looked at him sharply. "Do they now?"

Sweyn nodded, helping him fasten the hauberk. "They do not understand your hatred of women as I do."

Wulfgar laughed as he stretched out a hand to place it upon his friend's sturdy shoulder. "Let them wager if it so amuses them. You and I know a mere maid is oft swallowed for a morsel before she can thrust her hand into the wolf's mouth."

Lifting his head, Wulfgar surveyed the horizon beyond the town. "Let us be off. I have a desire to view this promised land of mine."

The hall was quieter with only a token of Wulfgar's men set to guard it. Aislinn felt almost at ease with fewer stares directed her way. Quietly she went about treating wounds. Wulfgar had directed his men to seek her out that she might tend their injuries, and she had spent most of the day at this task. Toward evening she had purged and cauterized the last of these, much to her relief, for the sickening smell of burnt flesh and the sight of gaping wounds had set her stomach aquiver. Yet for all of this she was thinking of another who needed her attention and wondering where they had taken him. It was a short time later when that question was settled in her mind. Two serfs carried Kerwick into the hall and gently laid him among the hounds. The dogs swarmed around him, yelping and straining at their leashes, and Aislinn frantically drove them away.

"Why do you leave him here?" she demanded of the peasants, whirling to face them. With their shortened locks and naked faces, she hardly recognized the two men who had been born in the town and were of an age a full score older than herself.

" 'Twas the Lord Wulfgar's directions, my lady. As soon as his wounds were salted and he came around we were to bring him here to the dogs."

"Your eyes deceive you mayhap," she said with a bit of ire as she swept her hand toward Kerwick who still lay unconscious.

"My lady, he fainted on the way here."

Dismissing them with an impatient gesture, Aislinn knelt beside her betrothed and tears sprang anew.

"Oh, Kerwick, what must you suffer because of me?"

Remembering with frightening clarity Wulfgar's warning of the whip's ability to tear her own flesh, Aislinn surveyed the Norman's handiwork, feeling a new dread rise up to shake her senses.

Ham came with herbs and water, tears still streaming down his face. With short-cropped hair his youth was all the more apparent. He dropped to his knees beside her and handed her the stuff, gazing sadly upon Kerwick's raw back. As Aislinn stirred a mixture into a smelly unguent, she paused to brush aside a stray curl with the back of her hand and caught Ham's doleful countenance. The lad felt her attention and hung his head.

"Lord Kerwick was always kind to me, my lady," he

murmured. "And they made me watch this. I could do nothing to help him."

Leaning forward, Aislinn began to spread the thick salve over Kerwick's mutilated flesh. "There was naught that any man of English blood could do. This was their warning to all of us. Their justice will come swift and hard. They will surely slay the next person who assaults them."

The young man's face was twisted in a moment of hatred. "Then two will pay with their lives. The one who murdered your father and this Wulfgar who has dishonored you and done this deed upon Lord Kerwick."

"Do not yield to madness," Aislinn advised.

"Revenge will taste sweet, my lady."

"Nay! You must not seek to do such a thing!" Aislinn cried, distraught. "My father died a hero's death, in battle and with his sword in his hand. He took no few of them with him. Yea, his songs will be sung long after this invader leaves our land. And as for this lashing, 'twas the gentler thing, for Kerwick's head was surely forfeit with his foolish act. Wulfgar did not take my honor but the other, Ragnor. Now there's a cause for vengeance if ever there was. But hear me well, Ham. 'Tis mine to seek, and by all that's holy my honor shall prove worth that Norman's blood." Then she shrugged and once more spoke with logic. "But we were beaten fairly and for a time must yield the day. You should not dwell upon yesterday's loss, but rather seek the morrow's gain. Now go, Ham, and do not bring upon your back this striped pelt of foolishness."

The lad made as if to speak, then bowed to her wisdom and retreated from the room. Aislinn turned again to her labors and found Kerwick's blue eyes upon her.

"Foolishness?! Stripes of foolishness?! 'Twas your honor I sought to save." He made as if to move but winced in pain and ceased the effort.

Aislinn was shocked by his bitterness and could venture no defense.

"You seek your vengeance in an odd manner. You enter almost gladly to his chamber and no doubt pursue his death by spreading yourself beneath him. Damn! Damn!" he groaned. "Does your oath mean nothing? You are mine! My own betrothed!" He tried again to move but cried aloud and sank back to the floor.

"Oh, Kerwick," Aislinn started gently. "Hear me out.

Be still, I say." She pressed him down against his efforts. "The potion will soon draw the pain and soften the hurt, yet I fear no like remedy will sooth the injury I feel from your tongue. I was taken much against my will. Listen to my words and do not rage so. These are knights well mailed, and you are naught but servant now, without a blade to do your will. Lest your head roll loose upon the village sod, I beseech you do not seek what must now be done by a coward's tool. You know their judgment will be harsh, and I would not have you spread upon the block for the sake of what little honor I have left. Our people need a voice that will effect some justice, and I would not leave them without an intercessor so they must find their judgment from the Norman lash. Heed me now. Do not make me hew another grave beside my father's. I cannot honor vows broken against my will nor would I hold you now to take a soiled bride. I execute my duty where I see it. 'Tis owed to those poor fellows who held my father lord and did his bidding to the end. If I can but ease their hardship some small whit, I will do well. So do not judge me too harshly, Kerwick, I pray."

Kerwick sobbed miserably. "I loved you! How can you let another man hold you? You know I wanted you as any man desires to have the woman he loves, yet I was only permitted to dream of you in my arms. You begged me not to dishonor you before our marriage and like a fool I complied. Now you have chosen that one as your lover as easily as if he were some long-known swain. How I wish I would have taken you as was my desire. Perhaps, then, having had you, I could drive you from my mind. But now, I can only wonder at what pleasure you give my enemy."

"I pray forgiveness," Aislinn murmured softly. "I did not know how I would hurt you."

He could not bear her kindness and buried his face in the straw and sobbed hoarsely. Miserably Aislinn rose and stepped away, realizing she could soften the pain no more, neither of his back nor of his mind. In God's will, time perhaps could do what she could not.

A small sound came from the door, and Aislinn glanced up to see Wulfgar standing inside the portal with legs spread, hands holding his gauntlets and gray eyes regarding her. Her coloring deepened under his perusal, and in distress she wondered what he might have overheard, but she calmed as she remembered the Norman did not understand their language.

She whirled and fled up the stairs, feeling his eyes following her and only knew relief when she was safe behind the chamber door. With a sob she threw herself upon the bed to weep out her torment there, feeling as if all the heartache in the world was her own. Kerwick could not understand her choice, why she had taken the Norman lord. He thought her a slut who groveled at the bastard' feet and placed herself in his hands to escape a few hardships. She wailed the louder when she thought of that Norman and his scoffing and pummeled her hands into the pelts in sore aggravation, hating him with all her being.

He thinks me here to serve his whimsy, she raged silently. But the wolf has much to learn, for he has not had me yet nor will he ever, not as long as I can outwit his simple Norman logic. Ere that, he will find himself tamed.

So intent was she upon her thoughts, that Aislinn did not hear the chamber door open and close but started violently when Wulfgar spoke.

"You seem intent on flooding the channel with your tears."

She turned and in one movement threw herself from the bed, glaring at him. She sniffed her woes to silence then turned to him, smoothing her disarranged hair. Her eyes were still red with tears but an angry blush at being so surprised partly concealed this.

"My troubles are many, Lord Wulfgar, but in main they seem to descend from you," she sneered. "My father slain, my mother abused as a slave, my home looted and my honor brutally stolen. Have I then no cause for tears?"

Wulfgar's eyes had followed her and now a smile broke his manner. He turned a chair to face her and seated himself, casually slapping his gauntlets against his thighs for a moment while he watched her.

"I concede the tears and cause, so shed them if you must and fear no ill from me. Indeed, I find your fortitude to this moment beyond most women's. You bear your burdens well." He laughed lightly. "In fact, misfortune seems to agree with you." He rose and stepped toward her until she had to raise her chin to meet his gaze. "For in truth, my vixen, you grow more beautiful with each moment." Then his face hardened. "But even a handsome wench must know her master." He raised his gauntlets in his hand and dropped them to her feet. "Pick them up and know that as you do so you are mine. Like these gloves you are my possession and no other's."

Aislinn's violet eyes flashed with revolt. "I am not a slave," she stated haughtily, "nor a glove that I can be worn and then be cast aside without a mere thought."

His tawny brow raised and his lips curved into a slow, sardonic smile. Still his eyes were like cold steel, smashing down the fortress of her will.

"Can't you be, damoiselle? I could do it. Yea, I could. I could mount you this moment and ride between your thighs and hence be off about my duties with no thought of you in mind. You rank yourself too highly, for you are indeed a slave."

"Nay, lord," Aislinn said quietly but with a soft determination that shook his own resolve. "A slave has passed the choice of death and sees no other road but miserable obedience. If it comes to that and my worth is done to all, I shall not hesitate to seek that haven."

Wulfgar reached out a wide hand and cupped it beneath her chin, drawing her near and holding her motionless before him. His eyes softened to a stormy gray and his brow knitted for a moment as he could feel her passive resistance.

"Yea," he murmured softly. "You are no man's slave I think." Then he withdrew his hand and turned away in a manner suddenly brusque. "But do not press the point, damoiselle." He looked at her over his shoulder. "Lest I reconsider and choose to prove the issue."

Her cheeks reddened under his stare. "And in that moment, lord, what then?" she returned. "Will I be just another wench to pleasure you for a time and then forgotten like your gloves? Has no damsel led you fair and dwelt upon your mind?"

Wulfgar laughed softly. "Oh, they've played and spread their skirts. But I've taken my ease of them and none has yet stuck in my memory to dwell for any time."

Aislinn saw victory near and raised her gently curving brows to ape his offhand manner.

"Not even your mother?" she mocked and thought the argument won.

The next moment she quailed in fear. His face darkened; his eyes flashed. And as he trembled in rage she thought a blow would momentarily descend upon her.

"Nay," he snarled through gritted teeth. "Least of all that noble dame!"

He spun about and with angry strides left the room. Aislinn stood confused. His transformation had been so abrupt that she knew beyond a doubt that his mother would find no love in her bastard son.

5

Wulfgar stormed out of the hall and strode across the courtyard, setting his face toward the lowering sun and letting the anger drain from him. Suddenly there was a shout from the yard and an arm pointed. Wulfgar looked to the direction indicated and saw a cloud of black smoke billowing upward from beyond the brow of a hill. He roared a command and several men jumped to their mounts as Sweyn and Wulfgar swung up into their saddles. Great hooves tore up the brown autumn turf as they charged away from the hall.

Several moments later they had topped the crest of the hill and were thundering down toward the outlying cottage where a great stack of straw and a small shed smoldered furiously, sending out the dense cloud they had seen. The scene spread before Wulfgar made his hackles raise in anger. Seven or eight bodies lay strewn about the place, among them the two yeomen he had sent as guards. The rest were a ragged bunch and bore the long Norman shafts from the yeoman's bows. As they neared the hut a crumpled splotch of color became a young girl, brutally abused and now sprawled dead in the shreds of her dress. An old woman, bruised and blacked, crawled from a ditch and fell sobbing at the young girl's side. Perhaps a dozen men fled on foot across the fields, but what caught Wulfgar's eye were six mounted riders disappearing into a far copse. He shouted to his men to ride down the ones in

81

the field then with a nod to Sweyn, those two took up the
chase of the mounted ones. The great destriers knew their
work and their muscles bunched and stretched as they settled into a mile-eating gallop that bore them down rapidly
upon their tiring quarry. As they gained ground, Wulfgar
drew his sword and raised his voice in a wrathful, wordless war cry. Sweyn's rumbling bellow sounded in chorus
beside him. Two of the riders slowed and turned to face
their pursuers. Wulfgar swung beyond their reach to pass
them, but Sweyn took them full on his great charger,
crashing one to the ground while his ax thudded deep in the
chest of the other. A glance behind told Wulfgar that
Sweyn was in no danger as he stood and battled the sur-
vivor. Wulfgar turned his attention to the four ahead of
him. These raiders, thinking the odds with them, also
slowed and set themselves to do battle. Again Wulfgar's
spine chilling cry rang in the woods and his great steed
never paused in stride but flung itself full weight into the
lesser horses. Wulfgar's sword and shield rang with their
blows, then the long blade whined and split one from
crown to shoulders leaving him dead in the saddle as his
horse stumbled away. The fury of the charge took man
and beast through the others. Under the guidance of
Wulfgar's knee the Hun skidded to a halt and spun to the
left so that as the great blade swung wide it was given added impetus and crashed through the shield of another to
bite deeply into his neck. The man gave a gurgling
scream, and Wulfgar raised his foot and kicked the body
clear of his blade. The third man lifted his arm to strike a
blow, then stared in numb horror at his armless shoulder.
The blade returned to end his pain in a short thrust and he
fell beneath the thrashing hooves. The last, seeing the fall
of his comrades under the flashing steel, turned to flee and
caught the raging blade full across his back. The force of
the blow sent him head first into the roiling dust.

Sweyn came to join the fight but found Wulfgar surveying the bloody scene and carefully wiping the blood from
the long sword. The Norseman scratched his head at the
ragged, unkempt men who littered the ground but who
bore the weapons and shields of knights.

"Thieves?" he questioned.

Wulfgar nodded and set his sword again to its sheath.
"Aye, and by the looks of them they raked the bloody
field at Hastings for their treasures." With his toe he

turned a shield that lay at his feet, presenting its face, which bore an English coat-of-arms. "The scavengers did not even hold their own kind sacred."

The two warriors gathered the horses and lashed the bodies to them. They led their meager caravan back to the cottage as the sun's last edge sank below the western horizon. There in the deepening darkness they buried the dead, marking the graves of three with crosses. Eleven of the men in the open field had surrendered without fight. Two had raised their swords and won a very small piece of ground with them.

Wulfgar gave the old woman a horse, small payment for the loss of her daughter, but with a sense of surprise at his generosity she accepted it, wondering at this new lord of Darkenwald.

The thieves were lashed together in a single line with a rope about their necks and their hands tied behind their backs. As the small party wound its way back to Darkenwald the moon rose high above.

Dismounting before the manor, Wulfgar gave commands for his men to secure the thieves and post a guard over them. Dismissing the rest, he made his way into the hall. He paused inside the door, gazing to where Kerwick lay asleep amid the hounds and his brow puckered thoughtfully. With the afterthirst of battle, he crossed the room and poured himself a hearty draught of October ale. As he sampled it, he went to stand above the defeated Saxon. The strong brew warmed his belly and began to ease his tensed muscles, and as his eyes swept the young man he smiled ruefully.

"Methinks you cherish the virtues of the wench overmuch, my English friend," he murmured. "What has it gotten you but a frayed back?"

His words fell unheeded and he turned away, flexing his sword arm. He drew another large horn of ale to help him on the way to the bedchamber and strode lightly on the stairs. He eased open the door to the room. The light was dim within the chamber, for there was only the low flicker of the fire and one lone candle burning. Wulfgar smiled to himself as he noted the large wooden tub half full of warm water and more steaming in a great caldron on a hook in the fireplace. A trencher of meat, cheese and bread lay warming on the hearth. At least this wench, Aislinn, would serve him a few comforts and as his slave could be taught obedience. His eyes lingered upon her slender form curled in the large chair in front of the hearth and the sleeping face that seemed without flaw. Her hair in the firelight seemed like molten copper and her fair complexion was no less than perfect. Wulfgar stood for some time partaking of the slumbering beauty before him. Her soft lips were parted as she breathed in repose, her cheeks slightly flushed with the warmth of the fire. Her breasts rose and fell against the cloth of her garments, and for a moment all thought of other women was clouded in Wulfgar's mind. He bent low and with his finger carefully lifted a loose curl from her cheek and brushing it against his lips, inhaled the fresh clean scent of it. He straightened abruptly, for he had mistaken the rousing effect the fragrance would have on him. As he did so, his scabbard clanked against the chair. Aislinn woke with a start of fear but as her eyes fell on him she smiled dreamily and stretched and sighed.

"My lord."

At the sight of her lithe form unfolding, Wulfgar felt the blood begin to pound in his temples. He retreated to a safe distance and raising the horn of ale, took a long pull in an effort to steady his hand. He began to remove the accoutrements of his profession and set them aside. Sweyn would send a young lad in the morn to clean the filth and grime of battle from them and oil and polish the leather and metal until it shown.

Wearing a light linen chainse and chausses, Wulfgar searched out the horn of ale and turned to Aislinn. She had curled again in the chair, watching the movements of his long, rugged body with something akin to admiration. As his gaze fell to her again, she rose and went to place a new log upon the fire.

"What delays your rest, damoiselle?" he asked curtly. "The hour is late. Was there something you wished of me?"

"My lord demanded a bath to wait him upon his return and I've kept the water and his supper warm. 'Twould not be of much matter which comes first. They both await you."

He peered at her. "You were not anxious about your own safety with me gone? Do you trust the Normans so much?"

Aislinn faced him, folding her hands behind her back.

"I heard that you sent Ragnor on some errand from here, and since I am yours your men stay their distance. They must have a great fear of you."

Wulfgar grunted, ignoring her jibe. "My hunger would make naught of a full roast boar. Give me food that my bath should be leisured."

As she turned to obey his words, his gaze was drawn to her slender back. He observed the graceful swing of her hips, remembering too well the sight of her without her garments. She passed close to him in placing his food on the table, and he again noticed her delicate scent, like lavender in May. The victory of the day had sent his spirits soaring, the strong ale warmed him, now the nearness of her and that tantalizing scent sent his blood coursing through his body as never before. She turned and found his intense though somewhat brooding gaze upon her. Even by the flickering light of the fire and the candle, he could discern her heightened color. She seemed to hesitate and as he approached her, she retreated a step. He paused beside her, gazing down into her violet eyes. Reaching out a hand, he placed it upon her breast and felt her heart jump against his palm.

"I can be as gentle as Ragnor," he murmured huskily.

"My lord, he was not gentle," she whispered, standing awkwardly beneath his touch, not knowing whether to flee or to fight. His hand did not caress yet rather rested upon her as if he were weary and any slight movement might drain him of strength. His thumb brushed against the peak of her breast.

"What have you there, maid?" he teased. "It interests me."

Aislinn's chin lifted a notch. "You have sported with this game before, my lord, and wouldst play me for the fool. I could relate nothing which is not already known, for you have seen me at my barest and know full well what lies beneath my gown."

"Aaah, you speak coldly, wench. The fire needs warm your blood."

"I would prefer, my lord, that you cool yours."

With that Wulfgar threw back his head and his laughter rang in the room. "Oh, I think I will find pleasure here, in and out of bed."

Aislinn pushed his hand away. "Come sup, my lord. Your food grows cold if you do not."

"You talk as a wife and I've yet to make you my mistress," he chided.

"I was tutored carefully upon wifely deeds," Aislinn retorted. "Not those of a paramour. It comes more naturally to me."

Wulfgar shrugged. "Then think of yourself as my wife if it pleases you, my little Aislinn."

"I cannot without benefit of a priest," she returned coldly.

Wulfgar regarded her with amusement still. "And could you then after those few words were spoken?"

"I could, my lord," she said serenely. "Maids are not oft allowed to select their husbands. You are as any other man except that you are Norman."

"But you have said you hated me," he pointed out with mockery.

Aislinn shrugged. "I have known many girls who hated the men they married."

Wulfgar pressed closer to her side and cocked his head to better gaze down upon her fine profile. His warm breath touched her cheek, yet Aislinn stared straight ahead of her, seeming oblivious to him.

"Ancient men to be propped upon their brides with helping hands?" he perceived. "Tell me true. Was it not old and decrepit men these maids hated?"

"I cannot remember, my lord," she replied flippantly.

Wulfgar chuckled low as he reached to lift a curling tress from her breast, his fingers brushing boldly against that soft place. "I perceive that you do remember, damoiselle. A wench would not whine at having a strong and virile groom to keep her company in bed and pass the winter nights with," he murmured. "Nor would you find such boredom in my bed."

Aislinn turned mocking eyes to him. "My lord, do you beg for my hand?"

Wulfgar straightened and peered down at her with raised brows. "What? And have that chain about my neck? Never!"

He stepped away, but she faced him squarely.

"And what of your bastard sons?" she queried. "How do you deal with them?"

He grunted. "So far there have been none." He regarded her leisurely as a taunting smile lifted a corner of his mouth. "But with you it might be different."

Aislinn's cheeks flushed with hot anger. "My gratitude for your warning," she quipped with sarcasm, no longer cool and composed but aggravated. She hated him because he seemed to enjoy her rage and could raise her wrath at will.

He shrugged. "Mayhap you are barren."

"Oh!" Aislinn choked in unrestrained fury. "'Twould please you well, no doubt. No bastards then would you have to claim. But 'twould be no less wrong to take me without vows spoken between us."

He laughed and sat at the table. "And you, wifely maid, have the determination of an ox. If I made you my wife, you probably have thoughts that you could soften my hand and save your people. To sacrifice yourself for peasants and family, a great gesture." His brows drew together sharply. "But I do not value your noble-mindedness."

"The priest did not come today," she said, abruptly changing the subject as he turned his attention to his meal. "Did you forget your promise to have him bless the graves?"

"Nay," Wulfgar replied, chewing his food. "He's journeyed elsewhere, but upon his return to Cregan my men will hasten him here. In a few days perhaps. Have patience."

"Some of the townfolk spotted Hilda's farm burning. Thieves probably. Did you catch them?"

"Yea." He peered at her. "Did you doubt it?"

She returned his stare without wavering. "Nay, lord. I have already found that you are a man who gets what he sets out for." She turned aside. "What will you do with them?"

"They slew the woman's daughter, and I killed four of them," he said. "My men a like number. The remaining thieves swear they had no part in the murder though most of them had their turn upon the girl, no doubt. On the morrow they will feel the lash for being there and work out the wergeld to repay the old crone for her daughter. After that they will belong to me as my slaves."

Aislinn's heart trembled, not for the men but at the memory of the whip in this Norman's hand. "Your work will turn tiresome," she murmured.

"I will not do it. The men from your town will deal out the punishments in the old woman's stead."

"You have strange ways," she said, puzzled at him.

He chewed a mouthful of meat and only held his gray eyes on her. Finding his stare unnerving, Aislinn sought some simple chore for her fingers.

"Did the thieves turn and fight?" she inquired softly. "Usually they're a cowardly bunch. They've been here before to plague my father."

"Nay, but for those Sweyn and I followed."

She gave his long frame a quick glance. "And you were not wounded?"

Wulfgar leaned back and met her gaze. "Nay. Except for these." He turned his palms upward to show her his hands, and Aislinn gasped, seeing the large blisters across them. "The gauntlets are of use, damoiselle. I was foolish to leave them behind."

"You must have used the sword fiercely."

"I did. My life depended upon it."

When he stood up and began to disrobe for his bath, Aislinn turned delicately away to some other task. Though it had always been the custom for the women of the hall to help visitors wash, her father had refused to let her give assistance, and she knew his distrust of men and their appetites to have been the reason.

"A pretty lass you are," Erland once told her. "And you'd whet the passions of a saint. There is no reason to brew trouble when it can be avoided."

So, she had remained ignorant of a man's body until Ragnor.

Wulfgar stripped to the brief loin cloth and then called her. Aislinn glanced over her shoulder and saw that he gestured toward his leg and the bandage there. Fetching the scissors he had earlier struck from her hands, she came to him and kneeling, snipped the binding and peeled the poltice away. The wound was beginning to heal remarkably well, and she bade him to be careful not to break it open. She picked up the rags and kept her eyes averted until she heard him splash in the tub.

"Will you join me, damoiselle?"

Aislinn whirled with a start, eyes wide, and stared at him increduously. "My lord?!"

Then he laughed and she knew he was only teasing her again, but his eyes swept her from toe to top and glowed with a warm and determined light.

"Another time, Aislinn—perhaps when we know each other better," he smiled.

Aislinn blushed hotly and withdrew to the shadows. From there she could watch him without being observed in return, though several times he glanced in her direction, trying to see into the darkness that shrouded her.

Finally he rose, finished with his bath, and stepped from the tub. In her corner she sat quite still, not daring to go near lest his passions should rise again and without his clothes between them her fate would be quick and sure. It was wiser to stay out of his grasp.

When he spoke to her, she started.

"Come here, Aislinn."

Apprehension traced its icy fingers along her spine. She hesitated, wondering what he would do if she fled from him as she had done the night before. She saw that he had forgotten to bolt the door. Perhaps she could reach it in time. But the idea quickly ebbed. She rose on trembling limbs and walked to him delaying each step as if she were going to meet her executioner. Standing before him, she felt small and helpless; her head barely reached to his chin, yet for all of her fear she met his gaze with bravado. She found he was grinning at her in his mocking way.

"Did you think I had forgotten the chain, my lady? I dare not trust you that much."

Relief flooded her features, and she stood quite docile as he bent down before her and secured the piece around her ankle. Then without another word he bolted the door, blew out the candle and climbed into bed, leaving her standing in thankful confusion. Finally she turned and moved to the end of the bed where the wolf pelts still lay on the floor. Feeling his eyes upon her she slid out of her gunna, leaving on the kirtle for modesty, and began to loosen her hair. It was free and she was combing the bright tresses with thoughtful strokes in the glow of the warm fire, wondering at this man who had her within his reach and yet did nothing, when she glanced his way and found that he had raised up on an elbow and was staring at her intensely. She stood rooted, unable to move.

"Unless you are prepared to be my companion in this bed tonight, wench," he said hoarsely. "I suggest you delay your grooming until the morrow. My mind is not so weary that it cannot remember what charms lay beneath that linen, and it would be of little concern to me that you are not willing."

89

Aislinn nodded mutely and quickly sought her furry bed, pulling the pelt high under her chin.

Several days passed with no more disastrous events, still Aislinn did not forget Wulfgar's warning, though she found herself being treated more as a serf than any mistress. She mended his clothes and brought his meals and helped him dress. During the days he seemed oblivious to her. He was occupied with his men and with setting up defenses in the event they were attacked by raiding thieves or loyal Saxons. Word came from William that the army was detained because of illness and that Wulfgar was to hold there until they were able to march again. Wulfgar accepted the message without verbal utterance, yet eyeing him Aislinn thought he seemed almost to welcome the respite. Sometimes she watched him from afar. He seemed completely in command of every situation that arose. A brave but foolish serf, barring the doorway of his simple dwelling against their search for weapons, received a choice of whether he wanted his home burned down around him or if he'd rather let them enter. The poor fellow was quick to understand the ultimatum when Wulfgar ordered a torch lighted. He was even more prompt to submit his cottage to the search, which turned up a few various and crude weapons. At their insistent questioning he finally got across the fact that the weapons were there before the Normans came and he knew of no conspiracy among the serfs to overthrow the new lord.

When the chamber door was bolted against intruders and they were alone together, Wulfgar's gaze would settle upon her, and Aislinn again would realize that she treaded upon thin ice. His gray, brooding eyes followed her about, watching her with an intensity that set her fingers to trembling. In her separate bed, she was conscious of the fact that he lay awake for long periods of time.

One night she woke cold and shivering upon the floor and rising, tried to reach the hearth to stoke up the fire, but the chain around her ankle was forbidding and would not allow her to move the distance toward it. She stood in indecision, trembling with the cold, her arms clutched around her, wondering how she would get warm. A movement behind her made her turn as Wulfgar swung his long legs over the edge of the bed and sat up. Just a shadow of his naked body was visible in the darkness.

"You are cold?" he questioned.

A chattering of teeth answered him as she nodded. Drawing another pelt from the bed, he came to her and pulled it around her slender shoulders, wrapping it closely about her, then he went to the hearth to throw splinters and logs upon the glowing embers. He squatted before it until flames curled around the wood then came to her. He bent and freed her ankle, flinging the chain away, then rose to stare down into her eyes. The firelight etched his profile.

"I will take your word that you will not leave. Will you give it?"

Aislinn nodded. "Where else would I go?"

"Then you are free."

She smiled her gratitude. "I did not like being chained."

"Neither would I," he replied brusquely and returned to his bed.

After that, Aislinn was allowed more freedom to roam where she would. She could walk through the town without having someone following close behind. It seemed in the past no one was guarded as well as she. However, the day Ragnor returned and approached her in the courtyard, Aislinn found she did not go unobserved even now. Two of Wulfgar's men made themselves plainly seen.

"He guards you well and gives me duties elsewhere," Ragnor muttered, glancing around. "He must fear losing you."

Her mouth curved upward. "Or else, Sir Ragnor, your ways are well known to him."

He scowled at her. "You seem pleased with yourself. Is your master such a grand lover then? I would not think it. It seems he would prefer pretty fellows to beautiful women."

Aislinn's eyes widened innocently as a sparkle of devilment brightened them. "But, sir, you do jest of course! Such a great and strong man I've never before met." She saw his mouth tighten and grew fond of her game. Her voice softened. "Dare I admit he makes me swoon?"

Ragnor's face was stony. "He is not handsome."

"Oh?" she seemed to question. "Methinks him so. But then, that has little to do with it, don't you agree?"

"You are toying with me," Ragnor surmised.

She affected a mien of sympathy. "Oh, sir! I pledge thee true, this is not so. Do you say I falsify my yearnings? Do you speak that I cannot love one who is naught but kind

91

and gentle to my heart and sets my every limb afire with his most tender words?"

"Then what is it that you see in him?" Ragnor demanded. "I would know."

Aislinn shrugged her shoulders. "Good, sir, I know your time is precious and I would not bend your ear for the many hours it would take to explain why a woman finds one man her own true lord and the many deep and most private matters shared by both that would seal the bonds between them. Why, I cannot begin to explain—"

A thunder of hooves rent the peace of the town, and they turned to see Wulfgar and his men approaching on horseback. Wulfgar scowled, drawing his mount to a halt beside them. He dismounted and handed the reins to his knight, Gowain, and turned as his men rode on to the stables.

"You return early."

"Yea," Ragnor replied sourly. "I scouted north as you bade me, but 'twas no use. The English have taken to their homes and closed their doors against spying. 'Tis beyond me what they do beyond their walls. Mayhaps they sport and ease themselves upon their wenches as freely as you seem to do on this maid."

Wulfgar glanced at Aislinn to see her heightened coloring and watched as she squirmed uncomfortably.

"The maid says you play the game well," Ragnor said, raising a brow as he regarded the bastard.

A slow smile spread across Wulfgar's lips. "Does she now?" He dropped his hand casually upon Aislinn's shoulder and caressed the nape of her neck though he felt her stiffen under his touch. His grin deepened. "She pleasures me well also."

"I say she lies," Ragnor flung.

Wulfgar chuckled. "Because she fought you? As any damoiselle, she responds more readily to a gentler touch."

Ragnor sneered his contempt. "She doesn't look much like a lad, Wulfgar. I'm wondering how you have mistaken her for one."

Aislinn sensed Wulfgar's rising anger in the tightening of his fingers upon her shoulder, but he spoke easily, his temper carefully masked.

"You speak heedlessly, my friend. I did not know you desired the damsel at the cost of your life. But I forgive you, seeing that the maid is one to make any man reckless. I might be also, if placed in your position." His hand slid to Aislinn's waist and he squeezed it lightly as he pulled her against his side. "You would do well to seek Hlynn out. On the morrow you will leave to join the Duke by his command. You will have precious little time for wenching then."

He turned from Ragnor, sweeping Aislinn along with him, and mounted the steps to the hall. As they entered Kerwick glared at them from where he sat chained with the dogs, and his face darkened with rage and jealousy as he watched the Norman pass a light caress across Aislinn's buttocks before releasing her. So intent was he upon following Wulfgar's hand that Kerwick missed the angry glare Aislinn threw at the Norman and in return, his taunting smile. Aislinn whirled and fled up the stairs, calling for Hlynn to fetch her water. Wulfgar leisurely watched her flight until she banged the chamber door behind her then slowly turned to Kerwick.

"Little Saxon, if you could speak my tongue I would congratulate you on your fine taste. But you and de Marte are unwise, wanting the maid as you do. She has sliced your hearts upon her platter and tossed them carelessly away. You will soon learn as I have not to trust women." He drew a horn of ale and lifted it as if in toast to the chained man. "Women. Use them. Caress them. Leave them. But never love them, my friend. I have been taught this lesson well from childhood."

Wulfgar went to stand by the hearth and stared pensively into the fire as he finished his ale. Finally he turned and mounted the stairs. He entered the bedchamber but to his surprise found the room empty. With anger pressing down upon his mood he whirled, wondering what game the vixen was now playing upon him. He could allow that she might have need to seek revenge on Ragnor, but he'd be damned if he would let himself be the object of her vindictiveness. Irately he strode to the door of the chamber he had given her mother and without pausing threw open the door. Aislinn started as the portal banged open, clasping her arms across her naked breasts, and Hlynn jumped, almost dropping the pail of water she was pouring into her lady's bath. The girl backed away fearfully as Wulfgar approached and came to stand beside the tub to gaze down on Aislinn who glared at him and choked red with her anger.

93

"Do you mind, my lord?" she gritted indignantly.

He smiled and her skin burned as her cheeks grew darker under his slow, deliberate stare. "Nay, damoiselle, I do not mind."

Aislinn sat back in a huff, splashing water over the side of the tub and onto him. She eyed him distastefully, loathing his casual manner that, she was sure, marked them in the girl's eyes as lovers.

Wulfgar gestured toward Hlynn. "I believe Ragnor is looking for her."

"I have need of her," Aislinn answered shortly. She swept her hand indicating her bath. "As you can plainly see."

"Strange," Wulfgar mocked as he feasted his eyes upon her swelling breasts. "I thought you bathed at morningtide, when I am gone."

"Usually I do," Aislinn retorted. "But with so much mauling, I felt in need of extra cleansing."

Wulfgar chuckled and rubbed the nape of his neck. "Tell me, damoiselle, is it because you cannot stand the thought of De Marte riding another wench that you keep the girl with you?"

Aislinn threw him a murderous glare. "De Marte may enjoy any Norman slut of his choosing, but Hlynn is unused to the crude ways in which you foreigners take a wench. He hurts the girl, and if you had any compassion in your soul, you would not give her so freely to him."

"I have no part in the arguments of women," Wulfgar shrugged, reaching out to tease a stray lock of coppery hair which tumbled from the heavy mass of curls tied upon her head.

"I know," Aislinn snapped. "You seek to discredit me in the sight of my betrothed with your fondling of me. If he were free, you would not handle me so casually."

He laughed lightly as he perched upon the rim of the wooden tub. "Shall I free him, damoiselle? But I think the little Saxon is far more fond of you than you of him."

He glanced toward Hlynn who all but cowered in a corner away from him. His tone was impatient as he questioned Aislinn.

"Does she have to look so frightened? Tell her it's her mistress I fancy in my bed, not her."

Aislinn considered the trembling girl. "My lord wouldst do you no harm, Hlynn," she said in English. "Mayhap if he can be persuaded, he'll even give you his protection. Calm your fears."

The pale-haired girl settled herself to sit upon the floor, still wary of the tall Norman, yet filled now with a certain confidence that her lady could save her if anyone could.

"What did you tell her?" Wulfgar questioned.

Aislinn rose from the tub, reaching for a linen to wrap about her and felt Wulfgar's devouring gaze upon her. She quickly covered herself and stepped out to stand beside him.

"I said you wouldn't hurt her," Aislinn answered. " 'Tis what you told me to say."

"If I knew your tongue, I could be sure you do not play me for a fool."

"A man makes himself a fool. 'Tis hard for another to do so unless the first allows it."

"You are wise as well as beautiful," Wulfgar murmured. He ran a finger down her arm in a slow, unhurried caress, and Aislinn turned to look pleadingly at him. She stood so close that the side of her leg brushed against the inside of the thigh he had perched upon the tub. It was as if a charge of a storm's bright fire arched between them with the contact jolting each with an abrupt shock of passion. Aislinn felt weak and unsure with his nearness. Wulfgar's reaction was more physical and his breath drew harshly between his teeth as if he had been struck a blow. He clenched his fists in the effort to endure her nearness without snatching her into his embrace and stilling the throbbing in his loins then and there. He knew Hlynn watched them and he was amazed that he could respond so quickly to a wench when others looked on. He was grateful for his mail hauberk, but his self-control was sorely shaken by the dampened cloth Aislinn had wrapped around her. Though it had proven a most strenuous feat, he had steeled his body against his raging desires as he watched her bathe. But with the proximity of her supple form with only the wet linen draping her, he found it more of a task to think logically than he had before. His passions rode him hard and goaded him almost beyond the limits of his own iron will.

"My lord," Aislinn murmured softly. "You have said we are no more than slaves. It is surely your right to give Hlynn to anyone of your choosing, but I pray you will be merciful with her. She has always served well and is willing to do so again but not in the manner of harlot for your men. Her feelings are tender. Do not tread upon them and make her loathe you as well as the men who take her. Please be compassionate. She has done nothing to warrant such cruelty."

Wulfgar's brow lowered. "Are you bargaining for another life, Aislinn? Are you set to share my bed that this girl may not have to yield to Ragnor?"

Aislinn took a deep breath. "Nay, Wulfgar. I am pleading, only that."

Wulfgar stared at her. "You ask much but are willing to give nothing in return. You have come to me for yon Kerwick, now this girl. When will you come for yourself?"

"Is my life at stake, my lord?" she questioned, her eyes searching his.

"And if it were?" he pressed.

"I think I could not find the way to play the whore for even that," she answered slowly.

"Would you come freely if you loved me?" he asked. His gaze penetrated into the depths of her soft eyes.

"If I loved you?" she repeated. "My love is all I have left that I can give of my own free will. The man I loved would not have to beg me to be a bride or to give him all the rights that brings. Ragnor took what I held for my betrothed, yet my love is still my own to gift a man or withhold as my heart would bid me."

"Did you love Kerwick?"

She shook her head slowly and answered truthfully. "Nay, I have loved no man."

"And I no woman," he returned. "Yet I have desired them."

"I desire no man," she said quietly.

His hand caressed her cheek and moved downward to the slim column of her throat. He felt her tremble beneath his touch, and smiled with a hint of mockery.

"I think you lightly ply a maiden's dream, damoiselle."

Her eyes flew to his face and she saw that he was laughing at her. She lifted her chin proudly and would have retorted angrily to his quip, but he shushed her by placing a finger upon her lips.

"The girl, Hlynn is bidden to attend you 'til Ragnor leaves on the morrow. He will not seek long for her ere he finds another. And unless you wish to act in her stead,

I bid you stay close upon my hand for your own welfare. It is common truth 'tis you Ragnor wants and he is no different in that respect than any man of his camp or mine. While my men will keep their distance, his may not. I think you would soon discover the safety of our nest in yonder chamber if left to your own defenses."

Aislinn smiled and a dimple flirted at the corner of her mouth. "I am quite aware of the benefits of sleeping near you, my lord, if not with you."

Wulfgar grinned like a devil, and he rose and walked to the door. "You will soon learn those benefits also, my lady. Rest assured."

At the evening's feast, Aislinn sat at her usual place beside Wulfgar but found Ragnor had taken a chair next to hers. He feasted his eyes upon the brilliant hair coiled in a glorious mass upon her head. Her creamy skin glowed with a luster of youth and a healthy blush of pink flushed her cheeks, setting her eyes a-sparkle. As she turned to answer a question Wulfgar presented her, Ragnor's eyes raked her slender form adorned in forest green velvet and lingered a moment where her hair was lifted from her neck, baring a soft, tempting nape. He knew a deep, fermenting hunger that he could not ease, and he felt cheated, robbed of this sumptuous prize by the bastard's own greed and lust. He bent to her.

"He sends me to William," he muttered. "But he will not always be able to keep me from you." He brushed his knuckles gently along her sleeve. "I can give you more than he. My family is important. They can be counted on when I want to further my position. Come with me and you will not regret it."

Aislinn pushed his hand away in distaste. "My home is Darkenwald. I seek no greater treasure."

Ragnor studied her. "Then you will go with the man who possesses this hall?"

" 'Tis Wulfgar's and I am his," she replied coldly, thinking to settle the matter, and turned her attention to Wulfgar while Ragnor leaned back thoughtfully in his chair and mused on her answer.

After the meal Wulfgar left the hall for a short time, and Aislinn sought the safety of his bedchamber as he directed her to. But she did not count upon the fact Ragnor waited for her in the shadows of the narrow hall outside the room. He stepped from the darkness, and she halted abruptly in her stride, taken by surprise. A confident smile twisted his handsome lips as he came to her and took her by the arms.

"Wulfgar is careless with you, Aislinn," he murmured huskily.

"He didn't consider you had lost your senses," she returned icily, trying to pull away.

Ragnor's hand slowly moved over a rounded breast and came to rest upon her hip.

"I never thought the memory of a wench could haunt me as yours has these past days," he said hoarsely.

"You only seek me because Wulfgar has claimed me," she retorted disagreeably, pushing at his hard chest. "Let me go! Find some other wench to fondle and leave me be."

"None pleases me as well as you," he murmured against her hair, the hot blood surging like a swift river of passion through his veins. He reached behind him and pushed open the chamber door. "Wulfgar will tarry with his horses and his men, the fool, and Vachel has promised to sit at this door to watch upon his return. He'll warn us with a rap on the wood when the bastard approaches. So come, my dove, we've no time to lose."

Aislinn struggled now in earnest and sought to claw his face, but Ragnor caught her wrists before she could sink her nails in to do him damage and drew her arms behind her, crushing her against his chest. He held her in a savage grip as he grinned down into her piercing glare.

"Upon my word, vixen, you're a livelier tart than that simple girl Wulfgar would give me." He chuckled as he thought of the other man. "He'll see I am not one to settle for meager fare when a feast of delicacies tempts me more."

Ragnor swept her into his arms and strode into the chamber with her, kicking the door closed behind them.

"You crawling vermin! You viper from Hades!" Aislinn railed, straining against his overpowering strength. "I'll die before submitting to you again!"

"Doubtful, my dove, unless you can command yourself to die in the next few moments. Now relax and I will be gentle with you."

"Never!" Aislinn screeched.

"Then have it your own way," he replied.

He threw her onto the bed and fell upon her before she

could roll away. Aislinn fought him as any wild thing afraid of capture and a fierce battle raged between them. She lunged beneath him in an effort to escape and her hands quickly followed his to replace the clothing he pulled away from her limbs. If her strength would last until Wulfgar came back— But she had no way of knowing when he would return, and she was swiftly losing ground in her struggles to preserve what dignity she had left. Ragnor was tearing at her garments, ripping the gunna from her bosom. She felt his warm, wet mouth upon her breasts, and she shuddered in loathing.

"If you can bed that boar, Wulfgar, with ease," he murmured hoarsely against her throat, "then you might find real pleasure with a more experienced lover."

"You stumbling clod," she choked, straining away from his insistent ardor, "you're a weedling youth compared to him."

Suddenly they both started as a loud crash resounded in the room. It seemed to vibrate the very walls of the chamber. With a jerk Ragnor rolled from her and stared agape at the source of that noise. Aislinn struggled up to see the door flung wide and Wulfgar standing inside its frame. At his feet lay the now subdued, limp and moaning Vachel. With a casualness that did not lend to Ragnor's comfort, Wulfgar leaned against the doorway and placed his foot upon Vachel's chest. His gaze first swept Aislinn, assessing the damage done to her as she hastily clutched her clothing over her bosom and covered the gleaming, pale thighs from his regard, then settled upon her tormentor whose pallor was well justified.

" 'Tis not my wont to kill a man over a woman," Wulfgar said slowly. "But you, Sir de Marte, draw my patience perilously thin. What is mine I hold and I can allow no one to doubt my possession. It is good that Sweyn came to tell me of some mischief he perceived brewing here with Vachel lurking in the shadows outside my chamber door. If you had proceeded further on the maid, you might have missed the dawning of the sun."

Wulfgar turned and gestured outside the chamber and Sweyn came into view. Aislinn sat up and a delicious grin spread across her features as she watched the huge Viking come and drag the well-born Norman from her side. Ragnor struggled and cursed the Norseman and his lord as Wulfgar leisurely smiled.

"Throw his carcass in the nearest sty," he bade Sweyn and then gestured toward Vachel. "Then come fetch this one here and do him the same. They should find sweet companionship there and reminisce upon the hazards of trespassing upon my property."

When the room was emptied of their presence, Wulfgar closed the door and turned to Aislinn. She wore a bright, happy smile of gratitude but as he came forward, she quickly vacated his bed.

"Sir Ragnor will surely have reason to want your hide after this injury to his pride," she grinned, her face beaming with her delight over his humiliation. "Without running Ragnor through you have served his pride a hearty blow. I could not have thought to settle my revenge upon his frame with such thoroughness."

Wulfgar continued to view her lithe form as she strode jauntily past him like some regal wench, carefully holding the shreds of her bodice together.

"And that must certainly please you well, Aislinn, to have us quarreling over you. Which one of us, I pray, will you be most pleased to be rid of? I am more a threat to your peace of mind than he."

Aislinn faced him and smiled slowly into his gray eyes. "My lord, you think me a fool? I do not dare walk the simplest path without being assured your claim upon me is my protection. That I have not yet paid for that defense I well know and am grateful for, but I continue to hope you will be of a gallant nature and not demand such unworthy payment from a lady unwed to you."

He snorted. "My nature is never gallant, Aislinn, least of all towards women. You may rest assured that you will pay and pay well."

Her lips remained curved in a beguiling smile and her eyes were aglow with a sparkle that would have bedazzled a man less fierce. "I think, my lord, that your growl is worse than your bite."

His tawny brow arched. "Think you so, damoiselle? Then one day you will wish you had given me more credence."

With that he blew out the candles and undressed by the glow of the fire, then flung himself upon the bed to take his rest. In the shadows of the room, his voice came stern and harsh.

"On the morrow you will wear a dagger for your pro-

100

tection. Mayhap it will discourage other attacks upon your person."

With a shrug and a smile Aislinn nestled down upon her bed of furs and sought the benefit of slumber, thinking dreamily of how the firelight played upon his bronze skin and the way the muscles of his back rippled with every movement.

There were only a few descriptive words that floated to Aislinn's ears of Ragnor's departure the next morning. Rumors were that the manner of his going was hurried, angry, and darkly silent. Aislinn grinned to herself as she heard, gloating over her good fortune to have seen his put down and went merrily about her duties with a lighthearted mood and step. The familiar and welcome weight of her girdle about her hips and the accustomed dagger in its sheath added to her confidence. She did not feel quite as naked wearing the belt. Wulfgar, himself, had brought it to her as she dressed that morning, and in his usual manner, brushed away her thanks with a satirical quip that spurred her anger.

It was late in the afternoon when Aislinn, sitting beside Erland's grave with her mother, glanced up to see a man wearily trudging his way through the woods toward the hall. She watched him for some moments sensing there was something odd about his appearance, when suddenly she realized his hair was shaggy and long and his chin was wreathed by a beard. She gasped in surprise but abruptly hid her astonishment from her mother who looked up at the sound. She smiled reassuringly and shook her head and Maida bent her head again to gaze sadly upon the mound of dirt, rocking back and forth as she continued with her low, whining song.

Aislinn cast anxious glances about to see if some Norman had also sighted the man, but no one stirred. She rose with an air of calm that she struggled to attain and strolled leisurely toward the back of the manor. When she was reassured no one watched or followed her, she turned and darted across the clearing into the thickest edge of the swamp then made her way back toward higher ground and the place where she had seen the man, playing little heed to the sharp branches and small shrubs that tore at her mantle as she ran through the woods. She caught sight of the fellow still plodding along through the trees and recognized Thomas, the knight and vassal of her father. With a cry she hailed him, overcome with joy and relief, having thought him dead. He stopped and on seeing her, began to hurry toward her, meeting her half way.

"My lady, I despaired I would ever see Darkenwald again," he said, tears coming to his eyes. "How is your father? Well, I hope. I was wounded at Stamford Bridge and could not travel with the army when it moved south to meet William." His face saddened. "These are bad times for England. It is lost."

"They are here, Thomas," she murmured. "Erland is dead."

His face twisted in his grief. "Oh, my lady, 'tis sad news you bear."

"We must hide you."

He glanced up in alarm toward the hall, his hands upon his sword, only now realizing the import of her words. He saw the enemy about the courtyard and where some had approached nearer to where Maida sat.

Aislinn dropped a hand upon his arm in an urgent manner. "Get to Hilda's and hide there. Her husband was killed with Erland and her daughter slain by thieves. She will welcome your company. Go now. I will follow when I am sure no one watches and bring food."

He nodded and hastened to escape through the trees. Aislinn stood watching after him until he was well out of sight, then made her own way back to the hall. With Hlynn's help she quickly gathered bread, cheese and meats and hid them beneath the folds of her mantle. In her haste she passed Kerwick, forgetful of his presence, but he reached out and grabbed her skirts, almost making her drop the food.

"Where is it you go in such a flutter?" he demanded. "Is your lover waiting?"

103

"Oh, Kerwick," she cried impatiently. "Not now! Thomas is back. I go to see him."

"Tell me when your lover will loose me." He held up his chains. "These chains are burdensome and my mind grows weary and dulled. I would have some task to occupy me besides keeping the hounds from my neck. They loose them before me." He indicated the dogs roaming the empty hall, and asked in desperation, "What must I do to get free?"

"I will speak with Wulfgar this eventide," she replied.

"What sweet thing will you promise that you have not already given him?" he questioned bitterly.

She sighed. "Your jealousy eats at you."

Angrily Kerwick yanked her down to him, causing her to drop her bundle, and pulled her roughly across his lap. His mouth crushed upon hers, bruising her lips as he forced them apart. His hand ripped at the fabric over her bosom.

"Oh, Kerwick, no!" Aislinn gasped, tearing her mouth free. She pushed against his chest. "Not you, too!"

"Why the bastard and not me?" he demanded, moving his hand over her bare breasts. His face appeared pinched and hard, contorted by desire, and his caress was rough and brutal. "I have the right, not him!"

"Nay! Nay!" she choked in rage, pushing at his hands. "No words were spoken by a priest to seal our bonds! I belong to no one. Not you! Not Ragnor! Not even Wulfgar! Only myself!"

"Then why do you crawl into the Norman's bed like some docile bitch?!" he hissed. "You sit with him and dine and your eyes are only for him. He gives you the slightest glance and your tongue stumbles over words."

" 'Tis not true!" she cried.

"You think I don't notice, when there's naught else to entertain me?" he railed. "My Lord, you crave him as any starving man craves food! Why?! Why?! He is the enemy and I, your betrothed! Why do you not show me the same kindness? I have need for your body, too. All these months I have remained chaste to honor you. My patience is at an end!"

"Do you take me here with the hounds then?!" she questioned furiously. "Do you care so little for me that you must satisfy yourself as your lowly bedmates do—

those hounds?! With no regard for their bitches?! At least Wulfgar does not treat me so!"

He gave her a violent shake. "Then you admit you prefer his embraces to mine?"

"Yea!" she blurted out, tears of pain and anger springing forth. "His touch is gentle! Now loose me before he comes."

Abruptly he did so, flinging her away with an oath. In the past days as he sat chained with no other distractions for his mind to rest upon, he had watched her with Wulfgar and sensed her affections slipping from his grasp. Always proud and distant with other men, the winsome woman came to surface when she was in the presence of that devil Norman. She was like an unlit candle, slim, cool, remote until that one called Wulfgar entered and set her aflame, and then she became a light that enchanted and beguiled. It was doubly hard for him, her betrothed, to watch, knowing he had never been capable of the feat which seemed so easy for the Norman. And that knight did not treasure his wealth but vowed his contempt for women in a language he thought not understood. That man had stolen his love from him without the simplest effort. Yet if there was a chance of winning her back, Kerwick promised himself, he would take it and snatch her from the wolf's power.

Regretfully he reached out for her hand, making her recoil and look at him with suspicion.

"You are right, Aislinn. This jealousy gnaws at me. Forgive me, my dearest love."

"I will see if Wulfgar will set you free," she said quietly and left him, clutching her mantle closed over the shreds of clothing and her small bundle of food. She had not time to change her garments now when she feared Wulfgar would return to the hall.

Hilda was waiting at the door of the cottage and quickly let her in.

"Is he well?" Aislinn asked softly, glancing toward Thomas who sat before the hearth in a dismal mood, hanging his head.

"Yea, only his heart needs healing, lady, as mine does," Hilda returned. "I will care for him here."

Aislinn gave her the food, taking care the mantle did not slip away from her torn bodice. "If anyone should see these meats, tell them 'twas I who stole. I would not have you chastened for my deeds."

"It does not matter if they should kill me," the old woman returned. "My life is nearly over and yours is just beginning."

"Wulfgar will not kill me," Aislinn said with a small measure of confidence. "Now, is there place for Thomas to hide if they come searching? They must not find him here."

"Never fear, my lady. We will find a secret place."

"Then I must go." Aislinn turned toward the door. "I will bring more food when I can."

She had opened the door and was about to step through when she heard Hilda cry out in alarm.

"The Normans!"

Aislinn glanced up, fear chilling every nerve. Wulfgar stood before the door, flanked by two of his men. Aislinn froze as his steely gray eyes pierced her. He stepped forward to enter the cottage, but she blocked his path, seeking to make a barrier of her slender form. With a grunt of contempt for her effort, he stretched out a hand and moved her easily aside.

"Nay! He has done nothing!" she cried, clinging to Wulfgar's arm in desperation. "Leave him be!"

Wulfgar glanced down at the slim hands clutching his sleeve, and his voice held a warning note when he spoke. "You go beyond yourself, Aislinn of Darkenwald. This matter does not concern you."

Aislinn glanced fearfully toward Thomas who stood braced for battle. Need yet another Saxon fall beneath a Norman sword? The thought brought a coldness to her belly and she knew she must do what she could to forestall further violence.

Her eyes held a plea for mercy as she lifted them to Wulfgar. "My lord, Thomas is a valiant warrior. Must his blood be spilled now after the battle is done because he fought honestly for the king to whom he and my father owed their loyalty? Oh, seigneur, show wisdom and mercy here. I will pick up the gauntlets and be your slave."

Wulfgar's face was stony. "You bargain with what is already mine. Do you try again to influence me? Loose me and set your mind on other matters."

"Please, my lord," she whispered, tears welling forth.

Without word, Wulfgar disengaged her fingers and set

her from him then turned and approached Thomas as his men brushed past Aislinn and took their places behind him.

"You are called Thomas?" Wulfgar questioned.

Thomas looked toward Aislinn in bewilderment.

"My lord, he does not speak your language," she explained.

"Tell him to lay down his sword and come with us," Wulfgar directed.

As she repeated the words for Thomas, the vassal eyed the three men warily.

"My lady, are they bound to kill me?"

She glanced uncertainly at Wulfgar's back, the broad shoulders covered with mail, the hand casually resting upon his sword. If he could kill four armed thieves who set upon him, one weary and hungry Saxon would offer him little difficulty if he chose to slay him. She could only rely upon Wulfgar's mercy.

"Nay," she replied, with some assurance mounting. "I think not. The new lord of Darkenwald deals fairly with men."

Thomas, with some hesitation, reversed his sword and laying it across his palms, presented it to Wulfgar. Accepting it, the Norman lord turned and walked toward the door, catching Aislinn's arm and steering her out ahead of him as his men fell in behind Thomas and followed them out. In the sunlight Aislinn glanced up at Wulfgar in confusion as he continued to draw her with him. His face held no emotion and he gave her no heed. She dared not question his intent. His strides were long and swift. She had to step quickly to keep pace and many times stumbled over ruts. She felt his hand tighten upon her arm lending her support. Then she tripped in front of him, letting go the mantle in an effort to check her fall. He drew her up by the arm he held, and his gaze dropped to the torn garments baring her bosom. His eyes widened in surprise as her white breasts boldly thrust through the rent cloth, then they narrowed as they dropped to her sheathed dagger and finally lifted to her face. There the cold steel held her gaze and seemed to burn into her brain and seize upon her very thoughts until she was certain he knew the full truth. She stood breathless until he gathered the mantle about her shoulders so she might hold it better and took her elbow again.

The silence continued between them until they reached the hall and he freed her, then as he seemed to turn his attention to Thomas, she ascended the first stone steps to the sleeping chambers in hopes of changing her gunna. With a voice that boomed within the hall, he halted her.

"Nay!" he bellowed and thrust his finger toward her.

Aislinn's heart quailed in her bosom, and she glanced toward Kerwick in dismay. His startled face etched her own apprehension of Wulfgar's penetrating gaze. Near her, Maida whined fearfully, wringing her hands. Slowly and with a quiet dignity, Aislinn turned and descended the stairs and went to him.

"My lord?" she questioned softly. "What is thy will?"

His voice was gruff, cold. "My will is that you honor me with your presence until I bid you go. Now find a perch to rest thyself."

She nodded and sat on a bench by the table. Swinging round, Wulfgar pointed to Kerwick.

"Loose him and bring him here!"

Kerwick's color waned and he struggled back against the Normans who sought to take hold of him. He was outnumbered and soon faced Wulfgar. As he appeared to shrink beneath Wulfgar's hard gaze, Sweyn chuckled.

"The little Saxon quakes in fright. What has he done now to make him tremble thus?"

"Nothing!" Kerwick cried. "Unhand me!"

He bit his lips as Sweyn laughed.

"Ah, so you do speak our tongue. Wulfgar was right."

"What do you want of me?!" Kerwick demanded, glancing toward Aislinn.

Wulfgar smiled slowly. "Thomas here does not know our language. You will give me assist."

Aislinn almost breathed a sigh of relief, yet with Wulfgar there was nothing done without purpose. Why was she not asked to translate since they knew her learned in this way? Her brow grew troubled and she puzzled as she studied Wulfgar closely. He spoke easily, watching Kerwick rather than Thomas, not even glancing toward the disconcerted vassal.

"Speak with this man and tell him thusly: He may be a slave and chained with the thieves or he can retain much of his former place but for three things. He must lay down his arms and not raise them again unless so bid by me. He must crop his hair and shave his face as is our

108

manner and he must swear fealty to the Duke William on this very day."

While these things were repeated to Thomas, Wulfgar came to Aislinn's side and placed his thigh upon the table leaning forward and half sitting. Aislinn gave him little notice, for her attention was centered upon Kerwick and Thomas and their discussion. Thomas's main concern seemed to be the loss of the larger part of his glorious blond hair, but he acquiesced and nodded his agreement vigorously when Kerwick bared his own back and showed him the stripes thereon.

With a start Aislinn became aware that her mantle had fallen open and glancing downward, confirmed that her breasts lay open to Wulfgar's chance gaze. Looking to him, she saw her fears realized, for his gaze was not chance but rested hungrily upon the display. She blushed profusely and clutched the front of the cloak to her as his hand moved to rest upon her bare shoulder. She felt warm and flushed as his long fingers slowly traced her collarbone, the line of her chin and down the curve of her neck, returning to lay upon the first gentle swell of her breast. Shaken and addled, Aislinn became conscious of the fact that the conversation had ceased and glanced up to find Kerwick glaring at them with reddened face and clenched fists, obviously fighting for what little self-control he could muster. Suddenly she knew Wulfgar's game and started to speak, but the hand tightened upon her shoulder, and when she looked around those gray eyes caught hers and though his lips smiled and were silent she was warned not to interfere.

"Methinks you dally, Kerwick." He spoke without raising his attention from her. "Get the business done."

Kerwick choked and struggled with words. His voice started haltingly then as he continued deminished in volume.

"Speak up, Saxon. Your speech grows slurred. I would hear the sound of my words in your English tongue."

"I cannot," Kerwick suddenly cried, shaking his head.

"And why not?" Wulfgar demanded almost pleasantly. "I am your lord. Is it not meet that you should obey me?"

Kerwick jerked his arm toward Aislinn. "Then leave her be! You have no right to caress her thus! She is mine!"

Abruptly Wulfgar's manner changed. His great sword sang from its sheath and with a long stride he reached the

109

fireplace. There, with both hands on the hilt, he brought the blade whining downward to split in twain a large log lying there. Then reversing his grip, he thrust the point through the heavy seat of a wooden bench nearby. He strode to Kerwick who though still angry was pale and struggled to present a defiant mien. Wulfgar stood before the younger man, legs spraddled and arms akimbo. When he spoke, his voice fair trembled the heavy timbers that arched the hall.

"By God's own word, Saxon," he thundered. "You try my temper sorely! You are no longer lord or landed but a simple serf! Now you maul with outraged passion what is mine!" His voice lowered to a mere growl and gesturing to where Aislinn sat in dire fear, he continued. "You both speak the French tongue well, but she gives me pleasure too, and you most certainly do not! Though I would not pursue my business with a woman hanging to my tails, your life is by far the cheaper. Do not quest this issue again if you would live another day." Almost quietly, he added, "Do you see the truth of my words?"

Kerwick lowered his gaze and bowed his head. "Yea, lord." Then he raised himself to full height and squarely faced Wulfgar, though a tear slowly traced its way down his face. "But 'twill be difficult, for you see, I loved her."

Wulfgar felt a first inkling of respect rise up within him for this lean Saxon and some stir of compassion for him. He could feel sorry for any man tormented and bedeviled by a woman, though he could not see their foolishness in letting themselves be drawn to such ends by a simple wench.

"Then I count the matter done," Wulfgar stated flatly. "You will not be chained again unless you bring it on yourself. Now take this man and see that he is sheared then bring him to make his vow before a cross."

As his men followed Thomas and Kerwick from the hall, Wulfgar turned and crossed to the stairs. He had mounted the first few steps when he glanced toward Aislinn, who sat quietly in dumb confusion, and paused to wait for her. She turned and raised her eyes to him.

"You seem at a loss, damoiselle," he mocked and then grew serious. "The men of this town are welcome to return to their homes. Winter draws hither and 'twill be the labor of every sound body to keep hunger from the door.

110

So if you find more, do not hide them but bring them to me in no fear of their lives. Now I bid you come and seek some replacement for those poorly used garments that we may dine and ease our hunger. I do hope your gowns have not been reduced to the point you have no change for that rag. It is simple to see that if you are put upon again by some lusty male that I will have to draw from my purse a sum to clothe you. You may in a short time, damoiselle, come to cost me more than you're worth. I hope I shall not have to share my coins with some lowly dressmaker since my monies are hard earned and I have better use for them."

With a haughty air, Aislinn rose. With all the dignity she could muster she mounted the stairs, passing him and leading the way to the chamber, all under his amused stare. He closed the door behind them and moved about the room, shedding the heavy mail and setting it to its place. Aislinn stood watching him in indecision, well aware of her lack of privacy and of his offhand manner with her. When he turned to the hearth to warm himself, she knew it was the most she could expect and that she would have to make the best of it. Turning her back to the room, she hastily dropped the mantle to the floor and stripped the ruined garments from her. Perhaps it was some small sound from Wulfgar that made her clutch the kirtle to her breast. She looked his way and her breath caught in her throat for he stood now staring at her with eyes hot and burning with the passion he made no effort to disguise. His gaze slowly traveled the length of her flawless back, touching the long, slender legs and the rounded hips with eyes that seemed to scorch her with their searing heat. Aislinn felt no embarrassment. Indeed, a slow pleasant warmth tingled through her. With an effort she lifted her chin and questioned him coolly.

"Does my lord pleasure himself or does he wish me to pleasure him? Please allow me an answer before I clothe this simple frame that you may not have to part with a precious coin for my garments."

His eyes rose to her face, and she saw the passion die. His brow darkened and without a word he stumbled from the room.

Dark clouds of wintery gray smothered the dawn as a first splattering of rain turned into a roaring downpour

111

that soaked the earth and sent sheets of water cascading from the roof. Aislinn stretched contentedly upon her furry bed and turning, snuggled deeper into the warmth of the pelts, half opening an eye and seeking the source of light that roused her, wondering if Wulfgar had risen in the early morning hours to open the shutters. She gazed out for a moment at the falling rain, enjoying the restful sound, then a shadow moved across the window, and she came to her feet realizing Wulfgar was already up and dressed. He wore a tunic and leather braccos and did not seem to mind the chill which prompted her to seize a fur and wrap it close about her.

"My lord, forgive me. I did not know you wished to rise early. I'll get food."

"Nay." He shook his head. "I have no business pressing. The rain woke me."

She walked to the window to stand beside him, brushing a glossy tress from her face. Her hair fell about her in loose curls that many times defied a sober braid. He reached out and lifted a heavy lock from her breast as she peered up at him.

"You came quite late to bed, my lord. Was there some trouble?"

He looked into her eyes. "I crawled between no wenches' thighs if that is what you mean."

With a flush of color she leaned forward out from the window to catch the rain within her cupped hands. She scooped it to her mouth, giggling gayly as some dribbled down her chin and plummeted to her bosom, wetting her light kirtle. She held the dampened cloth from her breast, shivering at the crisp chill of the water. As she reached out for more she felt Wulfgar's eyes upon her as she played.

For a moment she stared out the window at the country-side, very much aware of his manly presence beside her. His nearness stirred some strange, pleasurable spark that flickered along the ends of her nerves.

"My lord," she began slowly without glancing his way. "You have said you do not wish my gratitude, yet I feel dearly thankful for your mercy to Kerwick. He is not so shallow-witted as he has seemed. I cannot think why he has acted so foolishly. In truth, my lord, he is clever with his mind."

"Until it is dulled by a wench's treachery," he murmured thoughtfully.

Aislinn turned to him sharply, taken aback by his harsh words. An angry flush rose to her cheeks as she stared up into those gray eyes. "I had always been true to Kerwick. Until that choice was taken from me by your man."

"I wonder, damoiselle, if your loyalty would have stayed fast if Ragnor had not bedded you."

She drew herself up, looking at him squarely. "Kerwick was the choice of my father, and I would have honored that choice to my dying day. I am not a fickle maid who falls in any bed to be wooed thereon by every passing stag."

He considered her quietly and she raised a questioning gaze.

"But tell me, sir, why do you fear women and their infidelity so?" She saw his scowl blacken. "What makes you hate women and loathe the one who gave you birth? What did she do?"

The scar across Wulfgar's cheek went livid, and he struggled with himself to keep from striking her, but in her eyes he saw no fear, only a calm, deliberate look that quietly questioned. He whirled and in irate strides crossed to the bed, grinding his fist in his hand. He stood silent for a long time as violent rage gripped him in its power. Finally he spoke over his shoulder with a voice sharp and brittle.

"Yea, she gave me birth but little else. First she loathed me, not I her. For a small boy who begged for love she had none and when that lad turned to a father who would be one, she destroyed that too. They cast me away like something begotten in the gutter!"

Aislinn's heart wrenched at the thought of a small lad having to plead for affection. She did not know why she suddenly wanted to go to Wulfgar and hold his head close to her breast and smooth the troubled frown from his brow. Never in her life had she felt such tenderness for a man, and she was at a loss as to how to cope with her emotions now. This man was enemy and she wanted to soothe his hurts. What madness was this?

She went to Wulfgar and gently laid her hand upon his arm, gazing up into his eyes in humble apology. "My tongue is sharp and quick to wound. 'Tis a fault I'm oft reminded of. I beg your pardon. Memories so sad should be left buried."

Wulfgar reached up a hand and caressed her cheek. "I do not trust women, fair to say." He smiled stiffly. " 'Tis a fault I'm oft reminded of."

Aislinn's eyes held him softly. "There can always be a first time, my lord. We shall see."

The firelight danced along the blade of the sword as Wulfgar held it up and with his thumb tested its edge, then he bent again to honing out the nicks. He had discarded his tunic with the warmth of the fire and the long, sinewy muscles of his back and arms rippled and played in magnificent rhythm with his movements. At her place by the foot of the bed, Aislinn sat mending his chainse. She had laid aside her gunna and wore only a white kirtle. Seated crosslegged on the pile of furs and with her hair loose and flowing over her shoulders, she looked like some wild Viking bride of old. Perhaps some of the blood from those seafarers coursed in her veins, for the warmth of the fire and the sight of this man half naked and closeted with her for the night made her pulse beat faster. She bit through the last thread and the thought crossed her mind that were she that savage Viking maid she might rise now and go to him and caress that sleek and shining back, run her hands down those mighty arms—

A chuckle burst from her as she considered what might be his reaction. At the sound of her laughter Wulfgar's gray eyes rose and regarded her quizzically, and Aislinn turned her attention quickly away from him to folding the garment and putting aside her needle and shears. Wulfgar jerked and cursed lightly and raised his thumb to show her a tiny gash where a drop of blood welled brightly.

"Your humor wounds me," he quipped. "Does the sight of me amuse you so?"

"Nay, lord." Then she blushed deeply for her own haste in denying his accusation betrayed to a small degree her interest. She was amazed at herself, for it seemed now she almost enjoyed his company and would even seek him out on any plausible excuse. What truth lay in Kerwick's words? Was she more the smitten maid than the vengeful vixen?

Wulfgar returned to his labor as she took up another of his garments and began to mend it with careful attention. A light tapping at the door disturbed the domestic tranquility of the scene and upon Wulfgar's answer Maida entered and bobbing to the lord seated herself close by Aislinn.

"How fared your day, child?" the mother inquired in a chatty voice. "I saw you not, for ills and troubles kept me busy in the town."

Wulfgar gave a derisive snort at this woman talk and bent close to his blade as he whetted it carefully. Aislinn, however, arched her brows in question, for she knew her mother now cared little for the people and even less of their sicknesses but spent most of her day in seclusion wherever she could find it, plotting vengeance upon the Normans.

As she saw Wulfgar's attention elsewhere, Maida lowered her voice and spoke in the Saxon tongue. "Does he not leave you unguarded a moment? Since the morning's fare I've sought to speak with you but I always find some Norman perched by your side."

Aislinn made a motion for Maida to cease, glancing quickly toward Wulfgar in apprehension, but the old woman shook her head and almost spit out:

"That bumbling ass does not know our gentle tongue and probably could not follow our thoughts if he did."

Aislinn gave her the point, shrugging her shoulders, and the old woman continued anxiously.

"Aislinn, heed the Norman not but listen carefully to my words. Kerwick and I have set a way to escape and I bid you join us in the hour when the moon sets." She ignored her daugher's startled stare and took her hand. "We would leave these southern sties and fly to the north country where they are yet free and we have some kin. We can

116

wait there until a new force is raised and then return and free our home from these vandals."

"Mother, do not do this thing, I pray you," Aislinn pleaded, trying to keep her voice level and calm. "These Normans are too many and they patrol the countryside. They would ride us down in the fields like thieves. And Kerwick, what will they do to him if they take him this time? They will surely choose harsher measures for him if he is caught."

"I must," Maida hissed and then again more calmly. "I cannot bear to see these lands once mine now trod by Norman heel and to give this one"—she jerked her head over her shoulder towards Wulfgar—"the pleasure of hearing 'my lord, my lord' from my lips."

"Nay, Mother, 'tis foolery," Aislinn argued. "If you are so bent then go, but I cannot, for our people still bear the yoke of the Norman Duke and at least this lord"—she cast her eyes toward Wulfgar—"bears us some compassion and yields us small concessions however sorely won."

Maida saw her daughter's gaze shift and soften and she sneered. "Aaiieey, that my own flesh, my own tender child should set her heart upon a Norman bastard and desert her own kind for his lowly company!!"

"Aye, Mother, bastard perhaps and Norman true, but a man and a kind of man I've never set my eyes upon before."

Her mother snorted. "He rides you well I see."

Aislinn shook her head and raised her chin a notch. "Nay, Mother, never that. This is my bed where we sit and I've gone no further, though sometimes my mind betrays me and I wonder what adventure there would be seeking that fate."

She motioned to her mother and they again spoke in French of woman's things and doings. As they continued Wulfgar rose and returned his sword to its sheath and left the room without so much as a glance toward them though both watched quietly until they could hear his footsteps going down the stairs. Aislinn now pleaded in earnest with her mother to cease her useless planning and see more to the people of the town that she might ease their plight somewhat and not lead them to paths of revenge where they would find only the lash or the headman's block.

Some moments had passed before Wulfgar returned,

hitching up his chausses as if he had but yielded nature's call. With a surly grunt in their direction he seated himself and taking up his shield began to rub it with an oiled cloth.

Maida came to her feet, giving Aislinn a gentle caress across her cheek, and bidding them both adieu slipped out of the room. Aislinn sat deep in thought, her contentment gone and worry beginning to take deep hold, until she raised her eyes and found that Wulfgar had paused and was looking at her with an almost gentle smile on his lips. She puzzled at his manner, for he nodded silently and returned to his work, but in some subtle way he seemed to be waiting for something.

Long moments dragged past. Wulfgar labored on and Aislinn's nerves stretched taut with tension. The break came abruptly. Maida's shriek rang from the hall and there was a loud crash and a scuffling and then silence. Aislinn's eyes flew wide in horror and garments and sewing were flung in every direction as she ran to the door, threw it open and fled to the stairs overlooking the hall. There she halted in puzzled perplexity. Her eyes fell first on Kerwick, bound and gagged and chained with the dogs. His eyes blazed in fury but he wasted no more effort in struggling. Maida choked out curses as she hung helpless in Sweyn's great arms, her feet high off the floor. She was dressed again in rags and a large bundle lay on the rushes where it had fallen. A slow anger began to build in Aislinn and her eyes darkened as it grew. She whirled in a high rage as Wulfgar's voice came from the stairway behind her.

"What makes you seek to leave my room and board? Do you hate your home so much? Do you not find justice and reward here for labors well performed or is it perhaps that you find the northern moors more attractive?"

Three pairs of eyes turned to him and two jaws fell open as the three of them realized he had spoken in flawless English. Aislinn's face burned as she knew then just how much he had heard from her very own lips. Her thoughts raced back to all the times she had spoken in his presence when she had felt assured he could not understand her, and her shame mounted.

Wulfgar descended the stairs, passing her, and strode to where he could look Maida in the eye. He gestured to her frayed and tattered garments.

"You old hag, I've seen you here before and did I not say if I found you here again that I would treat you as you deserve. Sweyn, tie this crone with the dogs and free that fellow's arms before they eat him."

"Nay!" Aislinn shrieked, flying down the stairs to stand before Wulfgar. "You will not do her thus!"

Wulfgar ignored her and gestured to Sweyn, and the Norseman did as bade. When it was done, Wulfgar stood before the leashed pair and spoke almost as a stern father to his errant children.

"You will no doubt find warmth in each other tonight. I bid you think well and converse on this evening's game while you rest. Seek the wisdom of it all and remember this: Where I play the game you are but innocents of the world, for I know the way of courts and kings and men of politics and have played their games in earnest upon a battlefield. Have a good night—if you can."

He bent to scratch one great hound behind its ears and thump its ribs in good comradery, then turned to Aislinn and without a word took her arm and led her to the stairs where he paused for a moment as if in thought.

"Oh Sweyn." He turned. "Loose the dogs for a run in the morning and see if those two then can act like loyal slaves. They may even have their freedom if they promise to give up this foolishness."

For his thoughtfulness Wulfgar received a murderous glare from Kerwick and a strangled curse from Maida. He shrugged and smiled almost pleasantly.

"You will feel differently on the morrow."

Without further ado he proceeded to the chamber, his fingers firm and unrelenting upon Aislinn's arm. A dog yelped as Maida's foot found his ribs.

Wulfgar had closed the door of the chamber behind them and was just turning when he caught the full force of her open hand across his cheek.

"You chain my mother with the dogs!" she cried. "Then you will chain me beside her!"

Aislinn pulled her other arm back to strike again but found it seized in an iron grip. It did little to dampen her rage and she swung her foot against his shin, winning her freedom as he grimaced and grabbed his leg in pain.

"Cease, you vixen!" he bellowed. "Take care!"

"You played us for fools!" she screeched, stepping lightly away to seek something heavy to throw at him. A

119

drinking horn shattered against the door behind him as he ducked out of its path.

"Aislinn!" he warned, but she was already grabbing for another piece.

"Aaaah, I hate you!" she shrieked, hurling it at his head. She did not wait to see that he dodged out of its way also, for her eyes were already searching for other weapons. With two long strides Wulfgar was upon her, wrapping his arms about her, pinning her own to her sides. Aislinn gasped as they closed tightly about her and felt his rock-hard chest against her back.

"Your anger is not because of your mother!" His voice thundered in her ear. "You know the merits of the whip had I laid that to her. You cannot but agree this is the gentler way."

Paying no heed, Aislinn squirmed and struggled to get away. "You've no right to degrade her."

" 'Tis *your* pride you think has been damaged and you seek revenge because of that."

"You played false with me!" She sought his foot with her heel.

Wulfgar's arm slipped around her thighs to still the movements of her legs and he lifted her clear from the floor.

"Had I played falsely with you, wench, you'd have shared my bed by now."

There was no answer for that and she could only shriek and squirm. He sat her down roughly in a chair.

"Now sit until your temper cools, my pretty vixen. I have no intention of letting those hounds nibble on your flesh."

"I will not stay here in this chamber with you!" she cried, bouncing to her feet as he stepped away.

"You needn't worry," he mocked, smiling roguishly as his eyes swept down her body. "I do not intend taking advantage of your willingness."

She flew at him and sought to lay another blow, but he grabbed her arms and pinned them behind her, crushing her against him. Her fury muffled against his chest, she lifted her foot to stamp upon his and immediately gained her release as her knee struck between his loins. Wulfgar groaned and stumbled back upon the bed as Aislinn looked at him in surprise, wondering what she had done to cause his pain, but she was without mercy and leapt upon

120

him to press the attack. With an arm outflung Wulfgar tried to hold her off, but her fingernails raked across his chest, clawing deep furrows.

"You bloodthirsty vixen," he choked. " 'Tis time I taught you a lesson."

He caught her wrist, dragging her face down across his knees, but before his hand could descend upon her, Aislinn wiggled from his lap and slid to the floor. Determined to mete out this punishment he deemed well deserved, Wulfgar reached down to draw her back, and Aislinn started violently as his hand met the bare flesh of her hip. The loose kirtle had slipped up and was twisted about her waist, leaving her lower body naked. Her eyes widened and her purpose changed abruptly. Now she fought to escape him as her raging anger dissolved in rapid waves and was replaced by a flooding fear.

She tried to pull away but his hand held her wrist in an iron grip and Aislinn felt herself relentlessly drawn to his lap. Her long hair twined about them hampering her battle, but her sharp teeth found his hand. Wulfgar grunted in pain and released her arm, then as she snatched away, reached for her again catching his fingers in the neck of her kirtle. There was a rending tear and the garment split from top to bottom as she straightened.

Aislinn stared down in mute horror at her own nakedness while Wulfgar's eyes feasted greedily upon this glowing bounty. Her skin gleamed like pale gold in the warm light of the fire and her breasts, full and ripe, rose tauntingly between the remnants of her garment. His outraged hunger, long stemmed, flamed to its most fervent height.

His arms closed about her and in the next moment she found herself wrapped in her hair and torn kirtle and sprawled on her back upon the pelts of the bed. Wulfgar's eyes met hers and Aislinn read in them that his time of waiting had come to an end.

"Nay!" she cried, flinging up an arm to ward him off, but he caught her hands and dragged them beneath her as his knee thrust between her thighs. Her weight lay on their arms and she gasped in pain at his brutal grasp. She began to curse him but her words were smothered as his mouth crushed down upon hers. Her head was forced back, arching her spine until her breasts were pressed full against his chest. His lips burned and beneath his deep, penetrating kiss she felt suffocated. He kissed her eyelids, her

121

cheek, her ear passionately, murmuring soft, unintelligible words, and Aislinn dimly realized the raging ardor she awoke in him. Her panic rising, she lunged against him and met the hardness of his thigh between her loins. It only served to impassion him further. He pressed forward as she shrank away and released her wrists. Still she could not move in the tangle woven by her hair, kirtle and bedclothes. He cast his garments away and Aislinn gasped as he pressed boldly against her. He lowered her shoulders to the bed, freeing her hands from beneath her, yet holding them against her sides. It seemed that every inch of their bodies touched. Aislinn writhed and fought beneath him but the movement of her body only sharpened his desire. His mouth traced downward to her breasts and the blistering heat of his lips seared her flesh until she felt as if she were on fire. A strange warmth began to grow in the depths of her body and her pulse quickened. His mouth returned to take hers and she found herself clasping him to her and yielding to his flaming kisses, allowing herself to be swept away by his consuming passion. She gasped, half in surprise, half in pain as a burning ache spread between her thighs. She struggled furiously and sought to push him away, crying out. But he paid no heed to her protests as his lips moved against her throat. His hands easily caught hers as she tried to scratch him and he held them secure in an iron grasp, leaving her no defense as he had his way with her. Finally the towering passion was spent and Aislinn could only sob in anguish until he withdrew from her and moved away. Angrily she flung herself into a corner of the bed, tearing off the irreparable kirtle and snatched covers over herself. Between her sobs of rage she laid every curse she could think of upon his head.

Wulfgar chuckled at her fury. "I would not have guessed it, but I must allow you're one of the liveliest bits I've had in a long time."

Smothered shrieks bore testimony to the rankling of his words.

Wulfgar laughed again, running his fingers along the four furrows across his chest. "Four strips of flesh for a romp with a vixen! Hah, but 'twas worth it and I'll gladly pay the price again."

"You crawling vermin!" Aislinn choked. "Try it and I'll take yon blade and extend your navel to your chin!!"

He threw his tawny head back and his guffaws filled the

room. Aislinn's eyes narrowed and she fumed silently in rage. He crawled beneath the furs with her and smiled as he looked her way.

"Mayhaps there is one consolation for you, Aislinn. This bed yields more comfort than the floor."

He chuckled and turning from her, presently went to sleep. Aislinn lay awake by his side, listening to the sound of his deep breathing until it seemed to vibrate within her own head and his words wore heavily upon her mind.

Forgotten already? Yea, he said he could do it, but could she him? Could she forget the only man who even now in her anger tortured her thoughts? She could hate him, loathe him, but forget him? There was great doubt in her mind that she would ever be able to. He was in her blood and she would not stop until he too was plagued by thoughts of her night and day. Play the witch or play the angel, she would have her way! After all, was she not proud Erland's daughter?

Aislinn slept then with the ease of a child and woke drowsily in the middle of the night to feel Wulfgar's warm body molded against her back and his hand lightly caressing her. Feigning sleep she submitted to his questing hand, but where his fingers touched her flesh seemed to burn and waves of delight tingled through her every nerve. He brushed his lips against the nape of her neck and his warm breath touched her skin. Aislinn quivered, closing her eyes with a sense of ecstasy. His hand slid down over her belly and with a gasp Aislinn rolled over on her stomach but found her hair caught beneath him, forbidding escape. She rose on an elbow and looked at him. His eyes glittered in the low light of the fire.

"I lay between you and the sword, cherie. You'll have to cross me to get it."

Reaching out, he took her by the arms and drew her against his chest, forcing her head down until her mouth met his. Her lips trembled beneath his flaming kiss and she sought to turn away but he rolled over with her, pressing her down into the pillows.

Aislinn's eyes came slowly open to view the bright ray from the waning autumn sun which had found its way between the shutters to trace a long path upon the stone floor. Tiny motes of dust glittered as they drifted across the beam of light. Lazily Aislinn remembered when as a

123

child she had sought to trap those motes in her hand while her parents laughed from the bed. Suddenly she came full awake remembering the hours passed and who now shared her parents' bed with her. Though they lay untouching she felt Wulfgar's warmth beside her and by his heavy breathing she knew him to be asleep. Carefully she sat up and tried to ease herself from the bed, only to find escape impeded by his hand resting in the curling tresses of her hair. Biting her lip Aislinn gingerly pulled the coppery lengths from beneath him. Her heart gave a sudden lurch when he stirred, thrusting out a knee toward her, but relief flooded through her when she saw that he did not wake.

Aislinn gazed down at him, letting her eyes measure him slowly. His face in repose possessed a boyish charm that disarmed her. She wondered at the mother who had turned him out without feeling remorse and knew such a woman had no heart to soften. Aislinn smiled wryly to herself. How bravely she had once decided to use this Norman to turn enemy against enemy. Yet he had made her waver from her purpose. Instead she was the one caught in a trap between her people and this man. This Wulfgar had played her game better than she. Had he not used her to rouse Kerwick's anger on more than one occasion, baiting the Saxon by fondling her in his presence?

Oh Lord, that she should fall victim to a man who at every turn of the hand could outwit her. She, Aislinn, who could ride a horse as well as a man and think as fast. Her father had claimed her better than any boy her age. She was bright witted, stubborn to a fault, Erland had bragged with a fond gleam in his eye, and more cunning than any young whelp who sought knighthood from any king. She was half boy, he had laughingly declared. She possessed the face and body of a beautiful temptress while her thoughts were sound and logical.

Aislinn almost laughed aloud and the impulse was strong, for she did not think herself especially clever at the moment. She had wanted to hate Wulfgar and show him that he was just another lowly Norman to her, to be loathed and despised. But the days had passed and his company had become more tolerable and her manner more congenial. Now to her further degradation, she had become his mistress.

The word stung her with its irony. Proud, aloof Aislinn at the beck and call of a Norman.

It took an effort to keep from flinging herself from Wulfgar's side, for an overwhelming desire to flee from him welled up within her. Instead she eased her body from the bed, shivering as a draft caressed her with icy fingers, and she clenched her teeth tightly to keep them from chattering. The kirtle she had worn lay on the floor in shreds and she dared not risk opening the coffer for a fresh one. The woolen gunna lay draped over the chair by the hearth and going to stand close to the burnt-out fire she yanked the garment on, shuddering slightly as the rough cloth rubbed against her skin.

She donned a pair of soft hide boots and grabbed a wolf skin to wrap about her shoulders then made her way silently from the room. As she crossed the hall Aislinn saw that the dogs were astir but Maida and Kerwick were still huddled on the straw in the corner. If they were awake they gave no sign.

With a low creak of hinges Aislinn pulled open the door and slid outside. There was a chill in the air but the low sun had begun to warm the land. The morning was clear and seemed to have a brittle quality about it as if a sharp sound might shatter the very air. As she crossed the yard Aislinn saw Sweyn with a small group of men on a distant hill riding horses about, working the cold from the great destriers. She desired no companionship and turned in the opposite direction toward the swamp, for she knew of a private place.

In the warm bed Wulfgar stirred, half awake, half feeling the thrusts of Aislinn's soft hips against his loins as she fought with him. In search of that warmth and softness he reached out a hand but found only the empty pillow. With a curse on his lips he shot up from the bed and surveyed the room.

"By damned, she's gone! That vixen has flown!" His thoughts flew. "Kerwick! Maida! Blast those two and their plans! I'll wring their skinny necks!"

He leapt from the bed and ran to the stairs stark naked. Looking down toward the corner of the hall, he found them still chained. But where could the wench have gone?

Maida stirred and he retreated hastily to the bedchamber. He hugged himself against the chill of the place and hastened to toss small splinters on the glowing coals and blow up a flame. Upon these he threw sticks and a small log, then stamped around looking for his clothes. In his search he tossed her torn kirtle on the bed without regard for the damage he had done.

A sudden thought rushed across his brain. My lord, she's gone alone. That little wench has set out by herself.

He hurried now to dress, pulling on woolen chausses, chainse, boots, and a soft leather jerkin. Worry began to gnaw at his mind, for she was slight and helpless enough and if she should come across the path of some maurauding band— The memory of Hilda's daughter lying dead in the shreds of her clothing flashed to mind, and the thought would not finish itself. He now snatched up his sword and mantle and ran through the hall and out to the stables. He slipped a bridle over the head of that huge roan who had bore him through many battles and throwing the reins over his neck, seized a handful of mane and vaulted to his broad back. He spun the animal out into the brisk air and encountered Sweyn and some of the men returning from working their steeds. A short question determined that none of them had seen the maid that morning. With a touch of his heels, Wulfgar sent the destrier on a wide sweep around the hall seeking some trace of Aislinn's direction.

"Aaah, there it is," he sighed with satisfaction. A faint path where her feet had swept the dew from the grass. "But where does it lead?" He glanced up. "Mon Dieu! Directly into the marshes!" The only way he could not follow swiftly on horseback.

The steed daintily picked its way as he guided it along the trail on the ground. Other thoughts crossed his mind as apprehension and doubt began to nibble again around the edges of his consciousness. She might have mistaken her step and even now might be struggling in some bubbling black bog. And then, in a distraught temper she might not be above seeking some deep hole and throwing herself into it. A nagging sense of urgency made him touch his heels to his mount's flanks and press it into a faster pace.

Aislinn had walked some distance along the winding path which she and the local folk knew well, for she had often trod these ways in search of herbs and roots for her mother to make her potions. With sure memory she found the clear stream with sloping banks and sparkling water. Light shades of mist still hung in the shadows where the sun could not reach. She felt a need to cleanse herself. Wulfgar's sweat still clung to her and she could smell his scent upon her which brought too many memories to bear of the night gone by.

She threw her garments over a bush and waded shivering into the cold depths of the pool. She caught her breath and gasped but splashed and swam about until the first hard chill had passed. The icy currents cleansed her and sent the blood rushing through her veins. Above her the sky shimmered in the brilliance of after-dawn and the last trailings of fog began to lift from the forest. Water rippled over rocks near the shore, the sound soothing to her troubled spirit, and she reveled in these calming moments. The nightmare of her father's death, her mother's beating, and Darkenwald's fall into Norman hands seemed far away, belonging to another time, another place. Everything here seemed untouched, unspoiled by the wars of man. She could almost imagine herself an innocent again but for Wulfgar. Wulfgar! She could remember well the smallest details about him, his handsome profile, the long, lean fingers which had strength to kill, yet could be gentle and pleasure giving. She quivered at the memory of his encircling arms and her peace was gone. With a sigh she waded out. The water swirled around her slender hips before she glanced up to see Wulfgar astride his stallion, calmly watching her from the bank. But in his eyes some strange emotion dwelt. Was it relief? Or more likely passion at her nudity? A chill breeze swept her wet body and she could not suppress a shudder nor the urge to cross her arms over her breasts.

"Mon seigneur," she implored. "The air is cold and I left my clothes there on the bank. If you would—"

He seemed not to hear her. His eyes lowered from her gaze and she felt their bold caress against her body like a physical fondling. He urged his destry forward into the water until he stood beside her. For a moment he stared at her and then he reached an arm down to lift her dripping wet to a place in front of him. He doffed the heavy mantle and swung it about her shoulders, carefully covering her and tucking the edges beneath his knees. Shivering Aislinn snuggled close against his warmth. She felt the heat of the beast beneath her and the chill began to leave.

"Did you think I had left you?" she ventured softly.

His only reply was a noncommittal grunt as he turned his mount and touched his heels to its sides.

"But you did come after me." She leaned her head back

127

against his shoulder that she might look into his face and smiled. "Perhaps I should feel honored you even remembered me after so many others."

Her remark passed him for a moment until the point of it stung him and he gave her a quick angry glance.

"The others were little more than brief passing affairs, but you are my slave," he growled. "And you must know by now I always take good care of my property."

He knew that his words had struck home for her body stiffened against him, and when her voice came again it carried the sharp edge of anger.

"And what price do you place upon me?" she asked. "I cannot break the sod nor tend the swine. At chopping wood, alas, I could not heat the meanest hut, and until last eventide the best you could find of me was mending clothes or tending some minor wound."

He chuckled lightly at her tone and sighed deeply. "Aaah, but last night! Your softness bodes of much I've overlooked and your warmth holds great promise of joyful nights to be. Rest assured, cherie, that I have in mind a task quite worthy of your meager frame, one well suited for your talents."

"As your paramour?" she snapped and raised her head again to stare at him. "A bastard's whore? That is what they call me now." She gave a short, bitter laugh. "How better then that I should serve the part?"

She choked off a sob and he could find no comment worthy of speaking, and they rode in brooding silence to the hall. The huge hooves churned the turf and skidded to a halt before Darkenwald. Aislinn wasted no time in hurling herself from the back of the beast, or trying to, for she hung frustrated in the folds of the mantle as it was still tucked firmly beneath Wulfgar's knees. As her rage mounted Wulfgar laughed and let go with one knee, sending her sprawling naked to the ground between the hooves of the destrier. The well-trained horse stood motionless, for even the slightest brush with those great hooves would have marred her irrepairably. Aislinn scrambled awkwardly to safety and rose to stand with fists clenched in rage. Wulfgar threw back his head and laughed aloud. Finally he gathered up the cloak and tossed it to her.

"Here, clothe yourself, cherie, for surely you'll catch a chill in this fresh air."

There was nothing for Aislinn to do but snatch the

mantle around her but in the act she surreptitiously cast her gaze about to see what other eyes might have beheld her nakedness. Her fury ebbed somewhat as she saw that no one witnessed her shame.

Now cloaked she tossed her head with arrogance and without waiting for Wulfgar to dismount turned and strode to the postern, catching the garment to her, for within its enormous folds the slightest movement drew drafts of cold air over her already chilled body. She pushed the heavy door open far enough to gain entrance, stepped within and there she stopped, for Wulfgar's men crowded the hall and with them were some she knew as Ragnor's mercenaries. She could hear his voice across the room, giving the Normans news of Duke William.

"Soon he will be able to ride again, and he will not let this insult subside. They chose another over him, but these English will soon learn William is not to be denied. He will crush them without mercy and He *shall* be king."

His words stirred the men. Their voices grew louder as they discussed the matter among themselves. Aislinn could no longer hear what Ragnor was saying, and wide shoulders and helmets blocked her view, preventing even a glimpse of the knight.

Suddenly the door swung wide and Wulfgar stood behind her. He glanced around in surprise to see his men gathered here, and as the oaken panel came closed, men turned and stepped aside, making a path for them to the stairs. Wulfgar moved his hand almost comfortingly to the small of Aislinn's back and urged her forward. She saw many eyes take in her damp hair and bare feet and knew that those who observed her must think that she and Wulfgar had only just returned from some cozy woodland tryst.

Aislinn could now see Ragnor standing on the first step of the stairway. Sweyn stood farther up the stairs, watching calmly while Maida crouched beside him, her arms clutched before her holding a tattered garment clasped to her breast. As Wulfgar and Aislinn moved forward, Ragnor turned to meet them. His dark eyes traveled the length of Aislinn's slender frame, taking in the bare feet and the wet hair. As their gaze met and clashed, his lips parted as if he would have spoken. Instead he turned abruptly away, ignoring her, for any slight he might have given her would only have been too well understood by

129

these men who had witnessed her selection of Wulfgar over him. He continued his tirade and though he spoke to the men his eyes insolently engaged Wulfgar.

"And 'tis well met I trow, that a strong hand rules best and a conquered heathen works best when oft reminded that he is conquered." He paused and waited for Wulfgar's reaction. He found nothing but a tolerant smile as Wulfgar waited for him to finish. "These simple churls must be taught that we are schooled beyond their pagan ken. The soft hand will drop the reins while the iron hand will push the steed where it wills."

Ragnor folded his arms across his chest almost as if challenging Wulfgar to reply. The men waited for the clash but in the silent room Wulfgar spoke softly.

"Sir de Marte, must I advise you again that my men are soldiers. Would you have me waste them tilling the fields while peasants hang all around on gibbets?"

A commotion stirred in the hall and a red-faced friar pushed his way free of the press of bodies and came forward.

" 'Tis good," the wheezing man panted. "Show mercy to your neighbors of Brittany. Blood enough has been spilt to Satan's Hell. Good Lord," he cried, clasping his hands together as if in prayer. "Preserve them all. Yea, 'tis good, my son, to set aside the devil's work."

Ragnor turned in sour temper upon the long-robed man of God. "Saxon monk, you shall shortly behold your own end if you prattle further."

The poor priest paled and withdrew a step, and Ragnor turned again to Wulfgar.

"So, the brave bastard is now the English champion," he sneered. "You protect these Saxon swine and coddle this English bitch as if she were the Duke's own sister."

Wulfgar stood almost relaxed. He shrugged. "These are all my serfs and in serving me, they serve the Duke William. Would you slay even one and serve in their stead to feed the dogs and swine and set the geese about at night?" He raised a questioning brow. "Or would you mayhap serve in the place of any of those others you've already slain? Now I would not treat a Norman so, but I am set to wring a tythe for William from this weary land."

Ragnor's eyes rested upon Aislinn for a moment and grew warm in ill-concealed desire. He turned to Wulfgar, smiling almost pleasantly, and spoke low so that only those nearest heard.

"My family serves me well, Wulfgar. What of yours?"

Ragnor's smile faded as he heard Wulfgar's reply.

"My blade, my mail, my horse and yon Viking are my family and they've done me more faithful service than you could dream."

For a moment Ragnor was at a loss, then he looked to Aislinn again. "And what of her, Wulfgar? Will you claim the bastard she spills whether it be yours or mine? And how may you tell whose brat it is?"

The darkening scowl on Wulfgar's face assured Ragnor that his words had struck home, and his lips curved with mockery.

"What of your family then—your blade, your mail, and the wench's brat?" He laughed with amusement and reached out to cup Aislinn's chin in his hand. "We should have a handsome son, my sweet, full of courage and fire. Too bad the bastard will not marry you. He hates women, you know."

Angrily Aislinn slapped his caressing hand away and stepped to face Wulfgar.

"You are no better than he," she spat in low tone. "Had I my wits about me I would have fought you to the end of my very strength and torn your flesh asunder rather than yield! You amuse yourself lightly at my expense."

Wulfgar rubbed his chest and with unseemly humor bade her cease her ranting. "It seems, Aislinn, that your titled duties as to last of strength and my torn flesh have been most sternly dispensed. None but I could witness this, cherie, that it was only greater force of arms that made you yield to me."

Wulfgar caught her wrist before the hand could strike his face, then twisting slowly drew her close until their lips were all but met. His eyes smiled into hers.

"Should I shout it loud for you?" he whispered. "That you have yielded in this moment but still hope to carry the day?"

"My lord! My lord!" Aislinn sought frantically to turn his attention, for she was most aware that another besides Ragnor watched them closely. "The friar!"

Amid shouts of encouragement from his men there rose a troubled voice.

"Ahem! My lord—Sir Wulfgar. We have not met before

but I am Friar Dunley. And you have asked me here." As Wulfgar turned to him he continued in a rush of words. "I have come to bless the graves, but 'tis obvious to me that other needs are sorely wanting. The affairs of God in this good town are not well met. 'Twould seem that many of the maids were sorely set upon and even some were married. So 'tis wholly grievous, my lord, the church can not afford to view these matters lightly, nor yield without atonement made to those unfairly taken. I deem it wise to offer coins in goodly sum to the husbands and betrothed to those where wedlock vows were promised or accomplished."

Wulfgar cocked an eyebrow and half smiled at the man as he pressed the issue further.

"And then, my lord, to those yet unbetrothed I bid those men who did the deed should carry the maid to wedlock—"

"Hold, father," Wulfgar admonished, holding up his hand to stem the flow of words. "It seems to me that a tidy sum of money offered to the swains of those whose unwilling favors were roughly taken would reduce the fair and tender ones to the level of whore, and what man would sell the virtue of his lady fair? A tidy sum, indeed, when all of England lies with aching thighs. 'Twould beggar the richest crown to pay the due. And I am none of those but only a poor knight and cannot meet the tally were I to deem it a worthy notion. As to the course of wedlock for the rest, I see them soldiers one and all." He gestured to his men. "They are a goodly sort to fight a war but not the kind a maid would seek to share a hearth. All would go with the next call to arms and some would stay upon the field of battle to leave the wench with brats aplenty hanging to her skirts with no way to feed them but to ply her wares upon the street and thusly set aside a good intent to end no better than before. Nay, good priest, I say let them ply their plight as it falls today. What good, will in time surely come. What evil, most has been already done, and from my hand can hardly be undone."

"But, my lord." The friar would not be gainsaid. "What of yourself? You are landed now and privy to the Duke. Surely you will not leave this poor wretched girl to suffer for unkindly acts which were no fault of hers. You are bound by your very oath of knighthood to protect the fairer gender. Do I stand assured that you will take her at the least to wife?"

Wulfgar scowled as Ragnor threw back his head and guffawed his delight.

"Nay, father, neither that," he said. "My knighthood binds me not to that extent. And then of course I am a bastard and I cannot ask tender ears to share the brunt of slurs and oafish jests from those of brutish wit." He looked pointedly to Ragnor. "It has been my lot in life to see the cruelest stabs and deepest wounds are given by the shrewish tongues of that same sex that prides itself on tender hearts and gentle manners and mother's love. I bare no special spot for women's weepings nor do I seek to yield them more than they deserve. Nay, chide me not, for I am hard in this concern."

With that he turned his back but the friar halted him with further speech.

"Lord Wulfgar, if you will not wed her, then at least set her free. Her betrothed will yet accept her as she is."

He turned to indicate Kerwick who stood quietly nearby and found the younger man's eyes resting dolefully upon the girl.

"Nay! I will have none of that!" Wulfgar roared and whirled again upon the friar. Openly struggling, he regained his composure. He spoke with a lower voice but with a hardness that could not be denied.

"I am lord and master here. Everything you see is mine. Do not trespass needlessly upon my good will. Go tend your graves as I have bid you come but leave the other matters to me."

The good friar knew when to stop. With a sigh he mumbled a prayer, made a sign and left, with the men following. Aislinn did not dare aggravate Wulfgar and even Ragnor was strangely subdued. Sweyn stood as always, silent.

The graves were blessed and Aislinn returned to the bedchamber to seek some privacy. Instead she found Wulfgar staring moodily out the window upon the far horizons. In his hand he held the contents of the packet Ragnor had given him as the priest spoke his prayers over the graves. Sweyn stood before the hearth with an arm braced above it and with the toe of his shoe idly nudged loose embers back into the fire. They glanced around as she entered and mumbling an awkward apology, Aislinn made to withdraw again, but Wulfgar shook his head.

"Nay, there is no need. Come in. We are finished."

Hesitantly Aislinn entered and closed the door behind her, feeling the weight of both men's eyes upon her. She blushed lightly as they continued to stare and turned her back to them when Wulfgar spoke to Sweyn.

"I will leave it in your hands."

"Yea, sire," came the reply. "I will watch and guard."

"Then I can rest assured, knowing so."

"It will seem strange, Wulfgar, after these many years— We have always fought well together."

"Aye, but there is duty and I must be certain the matter is in safe hands. Hopefully it will not be for long."

"They are stubborn people, these English."

Wulfgar sighed. "Yea, but the Duke is more so."

Sweyn nodded in agreement and then took his leave. Aislinn continued picking up the pieces of the drinking horn she had shattered against the door the night before and set them aside, avoiding Wulfgar's gaze. She glanced around for her torn kirtle, in hopes she could with some skill mend it to a useful state, for she did not have many gowns left. But her efforts proved fruitless, for it could not be found.

"My lord," she said, her lovely brow knitted in her confusion. "Have you set eyes upon my kirtle this morn? I know it was here."

"I laid it on the bed," he replied.

Aislinn turned, knowing it was futile to look again. She shrugged, throwing aside the pillows.

"It is nowhere, seigneur."

"Perhaps Hlynn removed it," he offered without much interest in the matter.

"Nay, she would not enter here without your permission. She is frightened of you."

"The garment will turn up somewhere," he said, rather irritably. "Put it from your mind."

"I have not many," Aislinn complained. "And no money to buy more linen. The wool is rough against the skin without the softness of a kirtle. And you have already said you will spare no coins for my clothing."

"Cease your prattle, wench. You sound as the other nags who beg for a fat purse to tide them over."

For a brief moment Aislinn's chin trembled, and she turned her back to him to hide this weakness that was utterly strange and foreign to her. Crying for a torn kirtle when all England was laid waste. But was it for her kirtle she wept or for herself? She, strong, willful and determined, now weakened and brought low by a man who loathed women and just this very moment compared her to the unsavory trollops who trudged the camps of the armies.

Aislinn swallowed back the tears and lifted her chin. "My lord, I beg naught from you. I only seek to keep what is mine as you are wont to do."

She busied herself tidying the room without further speech, willing herself to shrug away the low humor she had fallen into. When finally she glanced at Wulfgar, she was halted by the brooding gray eyes that held her. She looked questioningly at him.

"Monseigneur?" she murmured. "Am I to stand unjustly condemned of some monstrous deed that I have no recog-

135

nition of doing? Truly, I did not ask you to purchase me clothing. Yet you stare at me as if you wished to see me flogged. Do you hate me so much, my lord?"

"Hate you?" Wulfgar snorted. "And why should I hate you, damoiselle, when you are the very measure of any man's desire?"

Her mind flew, skimming over the details of their conversation spoken a few moments before and could find no cause for his dark and grim countenance. Then the memory of Ragnor's words hit her with an impact that nearly knocked the breath from her.

"Do you fear that I may carry another man's child, m'lord?" she asked boldly and watched his eyes grow stormy gray. "You must find it difficult to bear the thought that I might be carrying your child already and that you will never be certain it is yours."

In annoyance he growled. "Be silent."

"Nay, sire." She stubbornly shook her head and the tousled, unkempt curls danced about her shoulders. "I would know the truth now. What if I am with child? Will you speak the vows with me to save an innocent from the fate you have suffered?"

"Nay. You heard my answer to the priest," Wulfgar replied.

She swallowed hard. "I would know one thing more, if you will be generous," she managed. "What assurance have you that you have not already gotten some wee bastard from your loins? Were your women barren as you perhaps hoped I would be?" She saw his scowl deepen and knew her answer. She wanted to laugh and at the same time cry. "You would enjoy me better if I were like your other women, wouldn't you?" She came to stand close in front of him and gazed up into his stony face. The lines of her jaw were tense with the effort she made to appear calm. "I desperately hope that I am barren, for I do not think your child would please me."

He winced at her words and stood obstinately silent until a thought stung him. He pulled her roughly before him and his scowl grew ominous as he searched her face.

"Whether it pleases you or no, Aislinn, do not think that honor is righted by sacrificing yourself. I've heard tales of women ending their lives because they could not bear their shame. But 'tis foolishness to me."

136

"Foolishness?" Aislinn smiled softly and knew that she taunted him. "I think it a worthy notion."

Wulfgar shook her hard until her teeth rattled and her head threatened to snap from the slim throat that supported it.

"So help me, wench, I will have you chained to my side to be assured you do nothing foolish."

Aislinn jerked from him and her stare was piercing though tears blurred her vision. "Never fear, noble lord. I hold life very precious. If I am with child, then I will surely bear the babe some months hence, whether you claim it or no."

Relief flooded his features. " 'Tis well, I would not have your death on my conscience."

"Pray, who would then be your whore?" she retorted bitterly.

"Aislinn," he said in warning tone. "Soften your words. I grow tired of being pricked by them."

"Indeed, my lord? I would not think such a fearsome knight could be afraid of a mere girl's tongue."

"You let blood with yours," he flung.

"I pray forgiveness, sire." She feigned a humble appearance. "Does my lord suffer much from it?"

"M'lord! M'lord!" he mimicked, ignoring her gibe. "I have told you my name. Are you set against using it?"

Aislinn lifted her chin proudly. "I am your slave. Would you have a slave speak so familiarly with you?"

"I command it of you, Aislinn." He bowed gallantly as if she were some regal queen.

She nodded briefly. "Then as you command—Wulfgar."

He came to her and taking her by the shoulders, held her still. His hard gaze bore into her.

"You choose to be a slave at your convenience, but I will it otherwise. As long as I have spilled my seed I will make the most of it."

His mouth crushed down upon hers, smothering angry words, and forced her lips apart in a fierce, hungry kiss. Aislinn's mind tumbled in its own confusion as she struggled briefly to pull away, but his arms folded tightly about her in a merciless grip that would not permit her to move. His lips left hers and pressed hotly against her throat. Aislinn could feel the heavy pressure of his loins against her own and saw herself surrendering to his masterful embrace. Desperately she fought for control.

137

"My lor—Wulfgar! You hurt me!" she gasped breathlessly. His mouth covered her face and throat with raging kisses. As his lips met hers again she moaned and tore her mouth free. "Loose me," she demanded, now more furious with herself than with him because she could not still the wakening desires in her own body. "Loose me now, I say."

"Nay," he murmured thickly, bending her arm backwards over his arm. Her breath caught in her throat as his mouth touched her breast and his searing breath seemed to burn through her garment. His hand slipped under her knees and he lifted her up within his arms. Amid her heated protests he carried her to the bed and there, laying her down, began to undress her. He spread her hair upon the wolf pelts until it flowed like silk across them and as he stood back and removed his own garments, his devouring gaze ranged the length of her splendid beauty.

"'Tis not decent!" Aislinn gasped in outraged modesty. The color of her cheeks deepened, for in the revealing light of day their bodies seemed to brand their nakedness upon the very image of her mind. She saw him as she had never seen him before, a bronze-skinned warrior that could have stepped from a tale of pagan lore, a beautiful, marvelous being, to be captured and tamed if possible that one might keep it by one's side. She exclaimed, "The sun is high up!"

Wulfgar chuckled and fell on the bed beside her. "That has little to do with it." He met her gaze and smiled into her eyes. "At least there shall be no more secrets between us."

Aislinn's coloring mounted high to ride her cheeks and set them aflame. There was admiration in Wulfgar's stare as he swept his hand over her body, making her tremble under his light caress, and he marveled at the velvety texture of her soft skin.

There was no stopping him, for Aislinn felt his determination in the pressure of his hands upon her, insistent, eager. But she was just as resolved to lay completely passive under him. In his own good time he took his pleasure, and it was only after he withdrew that he showed any sign of displeasure with her. He lay on his side for a moment with a frown creasing his brow. Aislinn dared not smile her triumph but returned his gaze with a coldness that mirrored her lack of response.

"It occurs to me, cherie," he murmured softly, tracing a

finger between her breasts. "That you resist not me but yourself, and I would wager the time will come when I will but touch you and you will beg my favors."

Aislinn gave no sign that she heard but continued to stare at him. He sighed somewhat pensively and rose and picked up his garments. As he turned to gaze at her, letting his eyes move admiringly along the path of her slender legs, Aislinn sat up, snatching a pelt over her nakedness. She threw him a sullen look and he shrugged and laughed and under her watchful eye began to dress. When he stood clothed, he bent and swept her garments from the floor and handed them to her. As she took them she glanced toward the door as if in invitation for him to leave, but he shook his head and a corner of his mouth slowly lifted into a smile.

"Nay, I'm not going—yet. You'll have to get used to me, my lovely Aislinn, for I will not be denied my pleasures by your modesty."

Aislinn glared at him and rising defiantly, dropped the pelt to the floor. With natural grace she moved past him to stand before the hearth and was unaware of the glint of passion that returned rapidly to his gray eyes as she walked before him in the glory of her unadorned beauty. Before the fire she faced him and met his stare and for a second glimpsed some of the bewilderment at his own emotions in his face.

Suddenly from without there came a shout that strangers approached Darkenwald, and Wulfgar turned as if relieved by the interruption. Belting on his sword, he hurried from the room. Thinking that perhaps more of Erland's men were returning from battle, Aislinn now hastened to dress. Slipping into her kirtle and gunna, she left the chamber, throwing her hair absently over her shoulder. She fled down the stairs and met Ragnor as he was crossing the hall. He blocked her path and as she tried to step around him, he moved again to halt her flight. She gave him a withering look.

"Shall I call for aid or will you let me pass?" she demanded in brittle tones. She could see Wulfgar standing just outside the hall waiting for the strangers' approach. "Did not Wulfgar warn you before to leave me be and did you not suffer some embarrassment for your last handling of me?"

"Some day I will kill him for that," he murmured, but

139

he shrugged and smiled, reaching out to pull a coppery tress from over her shoulder. "I brave death and shame to be near you, my little Saxon wench, as you can see."

Aislinn tugged at her hair, but he would not release it.

"And if you had your way, no doubt you'd string me up on a gibbet when you tired of me," she retorted sarcastically.

He chuckled at her anger. "Never you, dove, Never would I treat you so harshly."

"I am a Saxon," she pointed out. "Why not?"

"Because you happen to be a very beautiful one." He laid the bright curl against her breast, his fingers lingering as they brushed against her. "I see he entertains himself well. Your cheeks are still flushed."

Her coloring deepening, Aislinn tried again to brush past him but he caught her arm.

"Do not hurry," he murmured.

"Let me go!" Aislinn demanded in low, raging tones.

"Will you not send me away with a kind word?"

Aislinn raised her brows in question. "Do you go again? How soon?"

"Do not appear so anxious, my little dove. You injure me sorely."

"In your absence the chance of ravishment is greatly reduced," she replied tartly. "But tell me, why do you bother with me? Are there no women where you go?"

He bent closer and whispered as if he told a secret. "Thorns, all. I wager for the rose."

He placed a quick, warm kiss upon her lips before she could draw away then laughed at her flaring temper. Stepping out of her way, he swept his hand before his breast.

"I shall treasure that kiss always, my sweet."

Haughtily Aislinn swept past him and went to the door, turning her attention upon the covered cart and accompanying knight which approached the hall. The cart paused beside one of Wulfgar's men standing beyond the hall and at a word from the occupant, the man's arm lifted toward Wulfgar. The odd train continued and as it drew near Aislinn could see that a rather thin young woman with flaxen hair drove the cart. The horse before her was old and limped, and though he bore the scars of many battles he would have been a noble beast with better care. The knight's mail was well worn and of an outmoded cast. The man himself was robust of frame and long of limb, almost equaling Wulfgar. His destrier also had seen better days and the dust of the road covered his dapple coat thickly. The woman drew the cart to a stop before Wulfgar and surveyed the hall.

"You've fared well enough, Wulfgar." She rose and not waiting for his assistance, climbed to the ground and came to him. She waved a hand encompassing the cart and knight. "At least, much better than we have."

At the woman's familiarity Aislinn felt an instant hostility and a sinking feeling of dread. The face lifted and she saw the cool and frail beauty of its fine, aristocratic features and the pale, ivory skin that seemed without flaw. The woman was older than she, perhaps nearing thirty, and bore herself proudly. Aislinn's own heart trembled within her bosom, for she could only wonder at what prior claim this woman had upon Wulfgar.

The old knight drew up and gave Wulfgar a salute as one lord to another. Wulfgar returned the gesture and the two measured each other for a long moment. The mounted one grounded his lance and doffed his helm and Aislinn noted the fall of white hair, long in the Saxon manner, yet the face showed pale on the cheeks where a beard had been recently shaved.

Her brow knitted in puzzlement to see this armed Saxon knight at Darkenwald. Then there was something familiar about the man also, though his face was strange and he bore no crest on his shield.

Wulfgar spoke and an odd note rang in his voice. Aislinn thought it was as if he fought some inner battle.

"The lodging is poor and lean, my liege, but you are welcome here."

The old man stayed in his seat as if rejecting the welcome. "Nay, Wulfgar, 'tis no fortnight's lodging we seek." The elder's eyes stared straight ahead over his steed's head and when he continued his voice was husky as if the words came hard. "I am cast from my land by your Normans. The Saxons half believe me a traitor, for I could not go to battle at Harold's side. My household has grown small yet I cannot support them fairly for my possessions are few. Thus it is, I come to you to beg for shelter."

Wulfgar shifted a foot and gazed at the lowering afternoon sun and then back to the other man who still sat rigid and proud. Wulfgar spoke and his voice was strong and sure again.

"It is as before, my lord, you are welcome here."

The old man nodded and relaxed and closed his eyes for a moment as if gathering his strength for some further ordeal. He braced his lance across the rear of his saddle to the ground on his left and hung his shield upon its upper end. He placed his hand beneath his right knee, grimacing with pain as he raised that member, and sought to bring it across the wide pommel. Wulfgar stepped forward to assist him but was waved back. With greater effort the old knight succeeded but gasped as his leg swung against the flank of his horse. It was Sweyn now who came forward, brushed aside the wave of dismissal, lifted him clear of his mount and set him erect, taking the weight of his body against his own. They stood thus as the old man smiled at the Viking and then laid a clenched fist against his chest where it was seized in a huge hand and roughly shaken.

"Sweyn. Good Sweyn." The man nodded. "You have not changed."

"A little older, my lord," the Viking returned.

"Yea," the stranger sighed pensively. "And so am I."

The woman turned to Wulfgar. "We thirst greatly. The dust was dry upon the road. May we have drink?"

Wulfgar nodded. "In the hall."

For a second time that day Aislinn was made aware of her ruffled appearance as she felt first the woman's and then the man's gazes fall upon her. The tousled red hair and the small, slender bare feet showing beneath her hastily donned garments were all too obvious to both strangers. With a touch of color rising to her cheeks, Aislinn self-consciously smoothed her gown under the woman's quizzical stare. Sweyn glanced away with indulgence toward his lord, for there was no mistaking the change in her appearance. The fair-haired woman came forward to the foot of the steps and stared upward at Aislinn with curiosity. Ragnor approached to stand at the door beside Aislinn and the woman's brow lifted sharply at his lazy smile, for he seemed almost to flaunt the girl before them. She glanced back to Aislinn in contemplation of her proud bearing then turned toward Wulfgar for some explanation of this scene but found him striding toward the maid. She watched in considerable bewilderment as he mounted the steps and took the girl's hand, drawing her to his side. For a brief moment Wulfgar met

142

the woman's bemused stare and a bit of mockery crept into his gaze.

"This is Damoiselle Aislinn, daughter of the old lord of this hall. Aislinn, my half-sister, Gwyneth," he said, lifting his hand toward the woman. He felt more than saw Aislinn's surprise and turned his hand toward the old man. "Lord Bolsgar of Callenham, her father."

"Lord?" Bolsgar repeated. "Nay, Wulfgar. The times have changed. You are now lord, but I only a knight without arms."

"These many years have I thought of you as Lord of Callenham and 'tis hard to change," Wulfgar replied. "I fear you must humor me."

Aislinn smiled at the old man who glanced from Wulfgar to her with a troubled frown. "The old Darkenwald was always honored when guests paused to pass the time in its hall. You would have been welcomed then as Lord Wulfgar makes you welcome now."

Ragnor stepped forward to press an introduction and bent low over Gwyneth's hand. At the touch of his warm lips, the coldness she felt at first encounter with him melted into a bubbling spring of pleasure. She smiled into his eyes as he straightened and Ragnor immediately sensed a new conquest near at hand. He turned to Wulfgar and grinned.

"You did not tell us you had kin here, my lord. William will be interested in knowing of this."

"No need to hasten your tale to him, Sir de Marte. The story is no news to him," Wulfgar assured the knight.

Dismissing further questions, Wulfgar turned and pushed the door wider then strode down the steps again to Bolsgar's side. He took the old man's arm and brought it across his own shoulders to help Sweyn get him into the hall. Aislinn ran to drag a large, heavy chair close before the hearth and ordered food and wine brought to the weary travelers. She set a stool before the chair and the two men eased the older one into the place she had provided. The Saxon grimaced in pain as Wulfgar gently lifted his leg upon the stool, but the old man sighed deeply in relief as he settled back in the chair. Kerwick drew near to watch as Aislinn knelt beside Bolsgar and began struggling with the leather trappings binding his leg. This she found difficult for the leg was swollen. Using her small blade in a sawing motion she sought to cut them off until she realized as Bolsgar stirred in his chair this only brought new pain. Wulfgar knelt beside her, unsheathing his own knife and easily slipped his blade beneath the coverings and with a single pass slit them open. The old man gestured Aislinn away as she reached to pull them apart.

"Wulfgar, take this girl from here. 'Tis no pretty sight for young eyes."

Aislinn shook her head. "Nay, I will not be sent away, Sir Bolsgar. I have a strong stomach and"— She looked into Wulfgar's eyes as he regarded her—"I have been called stubborn; you must allow."

Amusement crept into the steel gray eyes. "Indeed she is."

Aislinn frowned at him. Gwyneth had drawn near and stared down at the two as Maida scurried to serve her and her father food and drink.

"How is it to be among the conquerors, Wulfgar?" Gwyneth inquired.

Bolsgar looked at her sharply. "Curb thy tongue, daughter."

Lazily Wulfgar shrugged his great shoulders and bent with Aislinn over the elder's leg. "Better I would say than being among the defeated."

Any reply to this remark was completely silenced as the leggings were drawn away, revealing the bloated, red, festering wound. Gwyneth choked and abruptly turned her back and allowed Ragnor to assist her in moving her plate and goblet to the lord's table where he entertained her liberally with the courtly ways of a Norman knight.

A stench rose from the dirty coverings about the old man's leg and even Aislinn swallowed heavily. Wulfgar steadied her with a hand upon her shoulder, but she shook her head and peeled the legging back further.

"Tell me what must be done," Wulfgar urged, noticing her pallor.

"Nay," she replied softly. "I will do it."

She took up a wooden pail and turned to Kerwick. "The bog—do you know the place?" At his nod, she handed the bucket to him. "Fetch me this full of the blackest of the mud."

Without further word he hastened from the hall and for a change no one questioned his intent.

Wulfgar frowned up at his stepfather. "How came you by this, lord?" he inquired. "Was it by Norman hand?"

"Nay," the other sighed. "Proud I would be if it were so, but 'twas no enemy who brought this thing upon me—only myself. My horse stumbled in a rut and fell upon my leg before I could jump free. A sharp stone cut my leggings and tore the flesh and now the thing worsens despite what I do for it."

"Did you not ask to have it tended?" Aislinn inquired in surprise. "It should have been cared for at once."

"There was no one to ask."

Aislinn glanced toward Gwyneth but did not voice the question. Yet her thoughts strayed to the times she had tended her own father's wounds and wondered at this sister of Wulfgar.

Aislinn took quick command. "Wulfgar, bring the kettle of water from the fireplace. Mother, fetch clean linens from the chests, and Sweyn, prepare pallets before the fire."

Bolsgar's brow lifted and his lips broke into a smile as he noted that even the knight warrior did not question her but made haste to do her bidding. The girl herself went about the hall gathering handfuls of dusty cobwebs from the darkest corners with complete disregard for possible occupants. Now Wulfgar and Sweyn helped strip the mail from him and placed him upon the bed. Aislinn returned to his side where he now lay on the pallets with his back comfortably settled upon a mound of pelts. She slipped her hand beneath his heel and lifted his leg, removing the remains of his legging and in its place put a soft goatskin, tucking the edges underneath until it cradled the wounded member and held it steady. She turned the leg carefully until the wound was uppermost and the stench that rose from the gaping wound almost made her retch. She took a piece of linen and with a quick motion tore it in half but then paused, raising her gaze to meet that of the older man, her concern showing in her troubled brow.

" 'Twill hurt, my lord," she warned. "But it must be done."

He allayed her fears with a smile and gestured for her to continue. "I have felt your gentle touch, Lady Aislinn," he admonished her. "And I doubt that you can pain me beyond my endurance."

She dipped water from the steaming kettle into a smaller wooden bowl and wetting the cloth, began to wash the ichor from the torn flesh. Aislinn looked up again as his

145

foot trembled. He still smiled at her but sweat beaded his brow and his hands tightly clutched the mattress.

Carefully she washed and cleansed until Kerwick threw open the door and gasping for breath, placed a dripping bucket of black slimy muck beside her. She seized a shallow dish and threw into it a handful of the odorous mud, there adding the cobwebs and with her fingers mixed the two into a thick paste. This she pressed into the wound where the skin was torn and spread it liberally over all the bruised and discolored flesh. When this was done, she dipped more cloths in the hot water and folding them gingerly packed them close about the leg on all sides, pulling the goatskin tightly over the whole and tucking it under until it held them firmly in place. She sat back pausing for a moment as she wiped her hands dry and looked at Bolsgar.

"You must not move this, lord," she told him firmly. "Not one small bit." Then she smiled and rose. "Unless 'tis your desire to wear a wooden peg and make a funny track." She lifted her gaze to Wulfgar. "Mayhaps Sir Bolsgar would find a draught of cold beer to his liking."

The old man smiled his thanks and when the proffered horn was drained, slowly closed his eyes and it was not long before sleep overcame him.

Ragnor left the hall with Wulfgar and Sweyn and after showing Gwyneth to a chamber where she could rest, Aislinn sought her own privacy. In the room she shared with Wulfgar she stood beside the bed, gazing at its rumpled pelts, almost feeling again the warmth of Wulfgar's body pressing upon hers. With a small cry, she whirled and went to stare out the window, remembering Gwyneth's appraisal of her and knowing well what the woman's thoughts must be. Gwyneth had watched them in the hall, hardly taking her eyes from them except when they were drawn by Ragnor. What would Gwyneth think this eventide when she must sit beside Wulfgar at the table and then later come with him to this same bedchamber? Oh, surely he would not flaunt his mistress before them. And yet, at the door, he had claimed her by the casual taking of her hand and seemed not to mind Gwyneth's stare. Other men would have felt discomfort in presenting a mistress to their kin and in such obvious disarray. Aislinn's cheeks burned at the thought of how she must have looked to them. She shook her head in dismay and spread her hands over her ears as if to blot out some accusing voice that screamed:

Harlot! Harlot!

She calmed herself and, turning her attention to the window, saw the Normans on a distant hill rehearsing the maneuvers of battle, but she whirled away from the sight, not content to watch them in that display of their trade, knowing many countrymen had found death at their hands.

She bent her attention to arranging the chamber and improving her own appearance. She braided her hair with yellow ribbons and donned a kirtle of soft yellow and a gunna of tawny gold with embroidered trimmings around the long, trailing sleeves. About her hips she placed her girdle of fine wrought metal links and in its sheath her small jeweled dagger, the symbol that she was something more than a slave. A thin-textured snood of silk she placed upon her head. She had never taken such minute care with her dress since Wulfgar's coming and wondered at his reaction, if he would even notice. Kerwick might muse at her attire and certainly Maida, for this was her best gown, the one she had been saving for her marriage to him. What good would it do her if she could not win that stubborn knight of Normandy?

Darkness had descended when she went down to the hall. The trestle tables had been set up to feed the men but as yet they had not returned. Gwyneth paced the hall and Aislinn noted that she had freshened her hair but still wore the travel stained garment she had arrived in. It seemed an unwise choice to have donned her own finest gown and she wished her mind had not been so set upon Wulfgar that she allowed herself to blunder so badly. But it was too late for afterthoughts.

Gwyneth turned as Aislinn came down the stairs and her eyes swept her from small slippers to the silk snood covering her bright head.

"Well, I see the Normans at least left you a change of garments," she said with a touch of venom. "But then, I gave naught of my favors to them."

Aislinn halted in her step, her cheeks flushed with hot anger. She bit back a sharp question as to how Gwyneth had been fortunate to be among the few women of English blood to escape rape by the Normans. No doubt they had honored her as Wulfgar's sister, but what gave her the right, Aislinn wondered, to ridicule those who had been dishonored? With rigid control she crossed to the hearth where the old man still slept. For a time she stood gazing down at him, letting compassion for this aged Saxon knight wash away the bite of Gwyneth's words. As Ham came into the hall and approached her she turned.

"Mistress, the food is waiting to be served. What must we do?"

Aislinn smiled. "Poor Ham, you are not used to these hours the Normans keep. The promptness of my father spoiled you."

Gwyneth spoke firmly as she joined them. "These Normans should be taught something of promptness. Let them have a taste of cold food but I prefer mine hot. Serve me a platter now."

Aislinn moved her gaze until it rested upon Gwyneth, and she spoke with a calmness she did not necessarily feel. " 'Tis the custom of this hall, Lady Gwyneth, to wait upon the lord when he has not told us otherwise. I would not discredit my lord with my haste."

Gwyneth made as if to reply but Ham turned and left them, not questioning Aislinn's authority. Gwyneth frowned and lifted a brow at the younger girl.

"These serfs should be taught respect."

"They have always served well," Aislinn replied in Ham's defense.

The sound of horses approaching broke the stillness of the evening and Aislinn went to draw open the door. She waited as Wulfgar pulled his stallion to a halt before the steps and swung down. He came to her as his men led the horses away, and for a moment he paused beside her, letting his gaze range the length of her slender frame. With a soft glow in his eyes he murmured:

"You do me honor, cherie. I had not thought your beauty could be enhanced, but I see that perfection can indeed be improved upon."

Aislinn blushed lightly at his compliment, knowing that Gwyneth listened and observed them carefully. Wulfgar bent to kiss her mouth, his lips parted and eager, but in some confusion Aislinn withdrew and held out a hand toward the other woman.

"Your sister is famished, my lord," she said quickly. "Will your men be long?"

148

He lifted a brow sharply. "My lord?! What is this that you've forgotten so soon, Aislinn?"

She threw him a pleading look, her cheeks growing warmer now. "You were so long," she replied, trying to distract him. "We were wondering if we must dine alone."

Wulfgar grunted, giving her a scowl, and went to warm himself before the hearth, stepping carefully when he saw that the old man slept on. He stood with his back to the heat, his legs spread, his arms folded behind him and his somber stare followed Aislinn as she crossed to the door of the small cooking chamber just off the hall and gave instructions for the meal to be served. She returned, no less observed, and felt tacit disapproval in his gaze.

As Bolsgar stirred Aislinn went to kneel beside him and pressed her hand against his furrowed brow. He was warm to the touch, yet not overly much she decided. She gave him water and then with a satisfied sigh, he lay back upon the pelts again. He glanced around him, first seeing his daughter who had come forward and then Wulfgar who stood silently watching them all. The younger man presented his back to them and touched the toe of his shoe to a slow burning log in the hearth. He drew in a slow breath and looked up to some distant spot.

"You have not told me of my mother, sire. What of her? Is she well?"

The old man seemed to take his time in answering. "A year ago this December she died."

"I had not heard," Wulfgar murmured. He remembered her as she appeared when last he saw her, looking much like Gwyneth. He had no trouble recognizing his sister for that memory was etched upon his mind as if he had just seen her hours before staring silently after him as he rode away with Sweyn.

"We sent word of her death to Robert in Normandy," Bolsgar said.

"I have not seen her brother these past ten years," Wulfgar returned quietly, thrusting those haunting memories of his mother aside. "Robert always considered me an unwanted burden."

"He was paid well to care for you. He should have welcomed that."

Wulfgar snorted derisively. "Yea, it bought him plenty of ale so he could spread the news wide that his sister had cockolded a Saxon and that his nephew was in truth noth-

149

ing more than a bastard. It seemed to amuse him that no man claimed me as son."

"You were brought up as a proper-born son. You gained your knighthood," the old man pointed out.

Wulfgar sighed. "Yea, Robert made me his page and saw me schooled, but only after Sweyn reminded him of his obligations with no less than a threat."

The old man nodded slowly. "Robert was a frivolous man. I could not have hoped for more, I suppose. 'Tis good I sent Sweyn with you."

Wulfgar's features were strained and drawn. "Did you so hate me that you could not bear the sight of me?"

Aislinn lifted her gaze and her heart went out to Wulfgar, for she had never seen him look so miserable. As she glanced at Bolsgar she saw his eyes were brightened with tears but none came and the noble face was unreadable as he stared into the fire.

"For a time I hated you after learning the truth," Bolsgar sought to explain. "It was a great soreness not to have sired a son like you. I thought you my first born and I had a father's pride in you. For you I neglected my other son. You rode swifter and raced harder than anyone ever and seemed to have the very secret of life in your veins. I could not take much comfort in the weak, frail boy who came after you. You were my very life's blood and I loved you more than myself."

"Until my mother told you I belonged not to you but some Norman she refused to name," Wulfgar murmured bitterly.

"She thought to set right a wrong. I took more delight in some man's bastard son than my own children and she could not bear to see them slighted. She was willing to take the shame upon herself to set things aright for them. I could not condemn her for that. Nay, 'twas my own gall that rose and made me set you from me. You who were the wind at my side, my shadow, my joy—but no son of my loins. I turned my heart to my own son and he grew strong and quick, then in his prime died. Would that I could have died in his place. But I am left to care for a railing maid whose tongue rivals her mother's." The old Saxon grew silent and pensive once more, and returned his stare to the flickering flames that warmed them.

Aislinn saw the injustice of it all and felt sympathy for the boy who had been rejected first by the mother and

150

then by the father he had known too well. She wanted to reach out and touch the man now and soothe his hurt. He seemed the more vulnerable, for she had known him only otherwise, always strong, like the unscalable fortress, and she wondered if his heart could ever be reached.

Thoughtfully she rose and went to sit in the great chair before the fire to better consider him.

"We sent you away to your mother's country, little knowing you would return in this manner." Bolsgar's voice was husky as if he struggled for control. "Did you know your brother died upon the hill of Senlac?"

Wulfgar's head snapped up and he looked hard into the old face. Gwyneth whirled and stepped to them, her eyes flashing.

"Yea, the Norman thieves killed him. They killed my brother!"

Wulfgar turned his attention to her, raising a brow. "Norman thieves? You mean me, of course."

She lifted her chin. "The thought does seem to fit you, Wulfgar."

He smiled almost gently. "Be careful, sister. The manners of the defeated must always please the victor. You would do well, woman, to take some hints from my Aislinn." He came to stand beside the latter's chair and gazed down at her as she in turn watched him passively. "She plays the vanquished one so well"—his fingers toyed with a heavy coppery braid—"that I sometimes wonder if I've really won at all."

With his words, laughter tugged at the corner of Aislinn's lips and played around the edges of her eyes, but she gave no other sign and only Wulfgar took note. Idly he brushed a finger across her cheek.

"Yea, sister, you would do well to let the maid give you tutoring."

Gwyneth trembled with rage as she took a step toward him. Wulfgar turned to face her, lifting a tawny brow in mockery as he watched her lips tighten and her eyes narrow.

"You wish to say something more, Gwyneth?" he inquired.

Her bosom heaved with the wrath she felt. "Yea," she hissed. "And I say, brother, I wish it had been you who died instead of Falsworth." She spat the words at him, ignoring Bolsgar's plea for silence. "How I loathe you and

151

despise the fact we must seek your charity to survive these wretched times." Gwyneth turned upon Aislinn who sat amazed by the hatred she saw in the woman's face. "You see fit to hold this wench before us as an example. But look how grand she clothes herself. Not exactly what the tragic women of England are wearing, is it?"

"Be thankful that I still live, sister," Wulfgar said tersely. "For indeed you would be cast out to make your bed upon the cold earth without me here to give you these few comforts."

"What is this?" a voice interrupted, and Ragnor approached from the door as men drifted in behind him to settle themselves at the tables. "A family quarrel so soon? Tsk. Tsk." Ragnor feasted his eyes momentarily upon Aislinn, admiring the sleekness of her figure in the yellow gold of her gown, before he quickly took Gwyneth's hands in his and drew them to his breast. "Aaah, sweet Gwyneth, has the fierce Wulfgar shown his fangs? Pray pardon his manners, my lady. Or give me leave and I will take him to task for you, for I cannot bear any insult to your grace and beauty."

Gwyneth smiled stiffly. " 'Tis natural that a brother finds quicker fault with his sister than would a stranger scarce known."

"Even if I were a lover full known," Ragnor murmured huskily with warmth, bending over her hand. "I could never find fault with you."

Gwyneth pulled away with heightened color. "You take too much upon yourself, sir knight, to imagine that we could ever be lovers."

Straightening, Ragnor smiled slowly. "Dare I to hope, damoiselle?"

Nervously Gwyneth looked to Wulfgar, who watched them quietly. Taking Aislinn's hand and pulling her to her feet, he indicated the head table to his sister.

"Let us sup on friendlier terms, Gwyneth. We might as well, since we will be seeing much of one another henceforward."

Gwyneth whirled abruptly away and allowed Ragnor to take her hand once more and lead her to her chair. As she settled into it he bent toward her, his eyes lightly caressed her.

"You stir my heart and set me aflame. What must I do to gain your kindness? I will be forever your slave."

152

"Sir de Marte, you speak boldly," Gwyneth stammered, her cheeks taking on a rosy hue. "You forget that my true brother was killed by Normans and I have little love for them myself."

Ragnor slid into the chair beside hers. "But, damoiselle, surely you do not blame all Normans for your brother's death. We were bound by oath to do as William commanded. If you must hate anyone, then hate the Duke but not me, damoiselle, I pray."

"My mother was Norman," Gwyneth murmured softly. "I did not hate her."

"And you must not hate me," Ragnor pleaded.

"I do not," she breathed.

A grin spread across Ragnor's face, showing flashing white teeth, as he caught her hand. "My lady, you have made me very happy."

In her confusion Gwyneth turned her attention away and watched Wulfgar assist Aislinn into the chair beside his own. Her eyes grew cold once more and she stared hard at the younger woman, feeling the web of hate twine about her. A bland smile curved her lips.

"You did not tell us you married, brother."

Wulfgar shook his head. "Married? Nay. Why so?"

Gwyneth's attention shifted to Aislinn, and her pale eyes glittered.

"Then this Aislinn is no actual kin. I had thought her some prized and valued bride the way you honor her."

Ragnor snickered and appeared thoroughly amused. He toasted Aislinn casually when she bent a frigid glance upon him, then he leaned close to whisper some amusing anecdote to Gwyneth which prompted her to burst gaily into laughter.

Aislinn folded her hands tightly in her lap, bristling at the sound of their amusement. She lost all appetite and longed to be any place but where she was. The meat Wulfgar placed upon her plate went untouched and her wine remained untasted.

Wulfgar considered her for some time, then casually remarked, "The roast boar tastes pleasantly well, Aislinn. Will you not even try it?"

"I do not yearn for food," she murmured.

"You will grow thin if you do not eat," he scolded lightly, sampling his own meat. "And I find bony women lack much of the comfort of rounded ones. You are pleasantly soft though you are not as sturdy as you need be. Eat, it will do you good."

"I am strong enough," Aislinn replied, not making any effort to obey him.

A tawny brow arched. "Indeed? I would not have guessed it by that weak play you gave me some hours ago." He rubbed his chest and grinned roguishly. "By damned, I think I would have the vixen back rather than that limp-kneed twit I had beneath me then. Tell me, cherie, is there not another woman that resides in your comely frame who would come betwixt the two, with not so much the shrew but certainly more lively than the other?"

Aislinn's cheeks flamed. "My lord, your sister! She will hear, and already she wonders at us. Would it not be best to treat me with less familiarity?"

"What, and have you slip into my chambers when darkness is dense and no one can see?" He laughed and his look consumed her. "I could not be that patient for you to come."

"You jest when I am serious," she rebuked him sternly. "Your kin suspect we are lovers. Would you have them know I am your mistress?"

He grinned slowly. "Shall I announce it now or mayhap later?"

"Oh! You are impossible!" Aislinn said in a huff and in a somewhat louder tone that drew Gwyneth's attention from Ragnor. When the woman turned back again to speak with the knight, Aislinn leaned closer to Wulfgar.

"Do you not care what they think?" she questioned. "They are your family."

Wulfgar grunted. "Family? In truth I have none. You have heard my sister speak of her hatred for me. I did not expect more, nor do I owe her an explanation for the way I live my life. I will not be bound by her frowns or thoughts. You are mine and I will not put you aside because kin have arrived."

"And neither will you marry me," Aislinn added softly.

Wulfgar shrugged. " 'Tis my way. I own you. That is enough."

He glanced away, but half braced himself for her reaction. After a long moment of silence when none came, he turned again to face her and found himself staring into wide violet pools which hid the thoughts behind them. The hint of a smile rested lightly upon her lips then deepened. Her beauty held his attention like strong cords upon his mind until she laughed lightly, breaking the leashes with the musical sound.

"Yea, Wulfgar, I am your slave," she half whispered. "And if that is enough for you, then it is enough for me."

Wulfgar sat back puzzling at her reply but Gwyneth interrupted his thoughts.

"Wulfgar, surely you do not intend feeding all these Normans through the winter." She swept her hand to indicate the hall. "We will certainly end that season by starving if you try."

Wulfgar glanced around at the twenty odd men who feasted hungrily upon Darkenwald's precious store of food before considering his sister.

"There are more, but they ride guard. They keep the hall safe from raiders and thieves. They protect my people—and you. Do not question their food again."

Gwyneth drew up in a huff, eyeing him distastefully. Another stubborn man to deal with like her father. Was there not one with wits enough to look after their own?

A short time later Aislinn rose, begging pardon from Wulfgar, and went to see to the comfort of Bolsgar. She dampened down the cloths upon his leg once more then instructed Kerwick to keep the fire stirred up during the cold hours that the old man would not suffer a chill and to watch him during the night. If he turned for the worse, she was to be called without delay.

Kerwick studied her. "Shall I awaken Maida to fetch you?"

Aislinn returned his gaze and sighed. "It seems that I am without secrets. Even the crudest harlot can have some hidden sin. But I?" She laughed low. "I must have my deeds announced from the highest hill. What does it matter if you come yourself?"

"Did you expect privacy when your lover rules men?" he asked sharply. His eyes dropped to the floor and the muscles in his cheeks flexed with the tension he felt. "Must I honor this thing between you two as a marriage? What is expected of me?"

Aislinn shook her head and spread her hands wide. "Kerwick, you and I can never go back to where we were before the Normans came. The door has closed between us. Forget that I was once your betrothed."

"There is no door that stands between us, Aislinn," he said bitterly. "Only a man."

She shrugged. "Then a man, but still he will not let me go."

" 'Tis your charm that holds him," Kerwick charged. He lifted a hand to indicate her gown. "And now you dress to entice him. If you do not wash your face or rub sweet scents upon your body, then he will turn some other's way. But you are too vain to let it happen."

Despite her efforts not to, Aislinn burst into amused laughter. Kerwick's lean face reddened as she continued unceasingly. He glanced nervously toward Wulfgar and found the Norman scowling blackly at them over his horn of ale.

"Aislinn," Kerwick gritted between his teeth. "Cease this madness! Would you have me flogged again?"

She tried to choke back her laughter but fell to giggling. "I am sorry, Kerwick," she gasped. "I am bedeviled."

"You laugh at me," he growled, folding his arms across his chest. " 'Tis my wretched garments you abhor and ridicule. You would have me like him, your Norman lover. So proud of his frame he must strut about like a cock at dawn. My clothes have been stripped from me. What would you have me wear in their stead?"

Aislinn sobered and laid her hand upon his arm. " 'Tis not these simple clothes that do you ill, dear Kerwick, but lack of washing."

Kerwick set her hand from him with some regret. "Your lover watches and I have no desire to feel the sharp teeth of the hounds upon me this night nor the sting of the whip. You'd best join him to ease his mind."

She nodded and went to kneel beside Bolsgar, drawing a fur rug over him. The old man closely watched her as she bent over him and when she drew back, he gave her a tired smile.

"You are overkind to me in my ageing years, Lady Aislinn. Your fairness and gentle touch have brightened my day."

"Your fever weakens your mind, I fear, sir knight." Still, she smiled at his words.

He lightly brushed the back of her hand with his lips and lay back with a sigh, closing his eyes. Aislinn rose and without another glance to Kerwick, crossed the hall to where Wulfgar sat. The Norman's gaze followed her as

156

she approached, never wavering until she moved behind him to stand at his chair. There Aislinn could consider him without being observed in return. He was relaxed now after the meal and paid his half sister the barest courtesy as she plied him with questions about his holdings and his status with William. She complained that his manner of dealing with his serfs was much too lenient, for they were a crude lot and needed a firm hand to keep them in check. As she offered this last advice Wulfgar slowly shifted his glance to Ragnor who lounged back in his chair, seemingly content with himself and Gwyneth's conversation.

"I'm glad you have the ability to make judgments so swiftly, Gwyneth," Wulfgar returned and his sarcasm passed her by.

"You will soon learn that I am very perceptive, brother," she said, a knowing smile curving her lips as she raised her eyes to Aislinn.

Wulfgar shrugged, reaching behind him to take the girl's hand and draw her closer. "I have nothing to hide. 'Tis common knowledge the way I live and manage my holdings."

To Gwyneth's irritation he began to toy absently with Aislinn's slender fingers and caress her arm. At his continued fondling Aislinn grew uncomfortably warm and flushed. The smile of contentment stiffened upon Ragnor's face and he turned to fill his drinking horn to the brim. Gwyneth's own words slowed to a halting, stumbling speech as anger weighted down her tongue, and Aislinn could not help wonder if this was another game he played with them all. Wulfgar rose with a half smile, and dropping an arm over Aislinn's shoulder, spoke in jest to the young knight, Gowain, who had boasted quite heavily of his own swordplay that afternoon.

" 'Tis not your talent that keeps you astride, lad," Wulfgar grinned. "But your winsome face. At its sight every man thinks he has found himself some sweet wench and dares do no harm to the fair damsel."

Laughter shook the hall as Gowain reddened but smiled in good humor. Wulfgar rubbed his knuckles softly against Aislinn's arm as he continued to banter jovially with his men, and in her confusion she failed to see Gwyneth glaring at her. Had her look been of steel it would have severed Aislinn's heart in twain.

The look became even more piercing a few moments

later when Wulfgar retired up the stairs with the girl, his hand riding upon her narrow waist.

"What does he see in that slut?" Gwyneth demanded, flinging herself back in her chair to pout like some spoiled child who had been ignored.

Ragnor averted his gaze from the slender figure mounting the stairs and finished his ale with an angry gulp. When he bent near Gwyneth's cheek, he quite artfully managed a charming smile.

"I would not know, my lady, for my eyes hold only you within their sight. Aaah, would that I could feel you beside me, your body hungrily pressed to mine, I would know the joys of paradise."

Gwyneth laughed low. "Sir de Marte, you give me cause to fear for my virtue. I have never been courted so boldly."

"I've not much time," Ragnor admitted roguishly. "I must leave on the morrow to join William." At her obvious disappointment, he grinned. "But never fear, sweet damsel, I shall return, even if it is on my deathbed."

"Your deathbed!" Gwyneth cried in dismay. "But where do you go? Must I fear for your safety?"

"Indeed, there is danger. We Normans are not popular with the English. They would throw aside William's claim and choose another. We must persuade them that he is the best choice."

"You boldly fight for your duke while my brother amuses himself with that trollop. He is truly without honor."

Ragnor shrugged. "She only sends him away happily."

"Wulfgar goes with you?" Gwyneth questioned in surprise.

"Nay, but soon. Alas, my fate may come more swiftly and no one cares."

"I care," Gwyneth confessed.

Ragnor caught her hand against his breast. "Oh, love, those words are sweet to my ears. Feel my heart pound against these confines of my chest and know how I yearn for you. Come into the meadow with me and let me spread my mantle upon the ground for us. I swear I will not touch you, only let me hold you for a time before I go."

Gwyneth blushed hotly. "You are very persuasive, sir knight."

His hand tightened upon hers. "Damoiselle, you are too beautiful for me to resist. Say you'll come. Send me away with a small token of your kindness."

"I shouldn't," Gwyneth argued weakly.

"No one will ever know. Your father sleeps. Your brother amuses himself. Say you'll come, love."

She made a small consenting nod.

"You will not regret your generosity," Ragnor murmured huskily. "I will go first and prepare a place then come to meet you. Do not delay, I beg."

He pressed his lips passionately against her hand, sending wild waves of excitement flooding through her body, then rose and hurried from her.

Wulfgar leaned in fatigue upon the door as he closed it behind him, noting with gratitude the steaming bath that awaited him.

"You manage this household as if you were born with the talents of seeing to the comforts of many," he commented, watching Aislinn cross the room as he began to disrobe.

She smiled over her shoulder at him and there was a hint of mischief in her eyes. "My mother early taught that responsibility."

Wulfgar grunted. " 'Tis well, you will make a good slave."

Aislinn's laughter rang with a note of wry mirth. "Will I, m'lord? My father once said I had a most untamed nature."

"And in that matter I believe he was right," Wulfgar replied, lowering himself into the wooden tub. He leaned back with a sigh. "Still, I like the matter as it stands."

"Aaah," she returned. "Then you are content to produce bastard sons?"

"You have not proved capable of bearing any man a bastard as yet, cherie."

"The test of time has not yet ripened, my lord." She chuckled low as she removed her gunna, standing with her back to him. "Do not pin your hopes on fantasies. Most women are known to be quite fertile. You have just been fortunate in your adventures, that is all."

"Not fortunate—careful," he corrected. "I have made it a habit of inquiring upon the lady's status before indulging."

"You did not ask me," she pointed out.

He shrugged his broad shoulders. "I assumed you did not know, which you don't. 'Tis the disadvantage of young virgins."

Aislinn blushed hotly. "Then you have never had a virtuous maid, monseigneur?"

" 'Twas by choice."

"Do you boast that should you have desired one, you could have had such a maid?" Aislinn questioned with care.

"Women are not very discriminating. I could have had many."

"Oh," Aislinn choked. "How confident you are! And I am only one among many of your harlots!"

He peered at her obliquely as he idly rubbed a sponge across his chest. "Let us say, cherie, that you have proved the most interesting thus far."

"Perhaps it is because I am not so old as your other women," she snapped. Whirling she angrily strode to the tub where she postured saucily for him, touching her breasts, her waist and hips as she pointed out her assets. "Perhaps my bosom does not hang so low or my legs bow so wide. I have a slim waist yet and my chin does not disappear into folds. Surely something must have tempted you to take me without first your usual precautions."

Gray eyes bright with amusement, Wulfgar reached out an arm and with a quick movement pulled her into his bath. Aislinn shrieked and fought to remove herself from his lap.

"My kirtle!" she sobbed, tears coming quickly as she held the dampened cloth from her skin. " 'Twas my finest and you've ruined it."

Wulfgar only laughed the more. He pressed his face near to hers and smiled into her flashing eyes.

"Your head would be swollen with conceit if I yielded that you are by far the fairest or that you would bedevil any man into forgetting his convictions. Indeed, you would grow cocky and vain if I hinted that you are more beautiful than any woman I've ever seen." He tightened his grip as she strangled with unreasoning fury and struggled against him. "You might even become overconfident and think that I would never turn to another woman because I thought you more desirable than any other. Therefore, I do none of this, and I do you a kindness. Your heart might soften toward me and you would cry and cling to me when I choose another to replace you. I want no strings that are difficult to break." And he added as if giving her warning. "Do not fall in love with me, Aislinn, or you will be hurt."

Aislinn's eyes brightened with turbulent tears as she glared at him. "Do not distress yourself. You are the last person in all of Christendom that I would fall in love with."

Wulfgar smiled. " 'Tis well."

"If you despise women as you claim, why do you warn me? Do you caution all the women you have affairs with?"

Wulfgar loosed his grip and settled back against the tub. "Nay, you are the first, but you are younger than the rest and more tender."

Aislinn smiled thoughtfully as she propped her arms upon his chest, laying her chin on her hands, and gazed into his eyes.

"But still, I am a woman, monseigneur. Why are you kind to me when you have not been with others? You must feel something more for me than you did for them." Her grin deepened wickedly as she traced a slim finger along the scar marking his cheek. "Beware, m'lord, do not fall in love with me."

He caught her under the knees and behind the shoulders and set her dripping wet from the tub. "I love no woman nor shall I ever," he stated flatly. "For the moment I find you entertaining. That is all."

"And after me, m'lord, who then?"

Wulfgar shrugged. "Whoever meets my fancy."

Aislinn fled across the room to a darkened corner behind him where she crushed her hands over her ears. She trembled with frustrated anger and was sure he would never intentionally allow her to gain advantage. It was a game he played with her because of his contempt for women, never allowing her the smallest measure of confidence in her relationship with him, never allowing her to draw close to the man inside the shell. He ridiculed and taunted womankind while he watched their reactions in calm amusement, teasing with deliberate patience until the time when they would break or flee from his abuse. But he had not fully found her depth, Aislinn thought, nor drawn the bounds of her mettle. It was truly a battle that raged between them. While he casually cautioned her not

161

to fall in love with him, she sought out every softness in his professed armor of hatred.

Shivering in the wet kirtle, she doffed it and quickly slid into his bed, drawing the pelts up high under her chin. When he joined her there a few moments later she feigned sleep, resting on her side with her back to him. Though she could not see him, she felt his attention on her, and smiled secretly to herself, wondering his next move. It was not long before she learned. His hand upon her shoulder pressed her down upon her back and she found herself staring into warm gray eyes as he bent over her.

"Damoiselle, you are not asleep," he mocked her.

"Would it matter?" she inquired with a hint of sarcasm.

He shook his head as he lowered his mouth to hers. "Nay."

Gwyneth stepped into the moonlit clearing and caught her breath sharply as a hand closed upon her shoulder. She swung round with a start, remembering the large, rugged men who had crammed the hall at the feasting hour, and knew an instant prickle of fear. At sight of Ragnor's smiling face, however, she laughed softly in relief.

"You came," he grinned.

"Indeed, sir knight. I am here."

Ragnor bent, sweeping her into his arms, and quickly carried her a short distance into the woods. Gwyneth's heart beat fiercely at the swiftness of his actions. She giggled nervously, looping her arms about his neck, feeling herself small and helpless in his strong embrace.

"You make me forget my sanity," she whispered against his ear. "It is hard to realize we met only this morn."

Ragnor halted in his stride and pulled his hand from under her knees, letting her limbs slide against his until her toes reached the ground.

"Was it only today we met?" he asked hoarsely, tightening his arms about her until he could feel every curve of her thin body pressed to his. "I thought centuries had passed since I left you in the hall."

Gwyneth's head reeled giddily. "Oh, it was only years, my darling."

His mouth crushed down upon hers feverishly as they strained against each other in their passion. With great skill Ragnor loosened her gunna and kirtle, letting them fall to her feet and pushed her gently down upon his mantle spread out upon the ground. His eyes for a moment traveled the length of her body glowing silvery in the moonlight. He caressed her small breasts while his thoughts played idly upon a rounder, fuller bosom, remembering the soft creamy skin and curling coppery tresses twining wantonly about a beautiful body. In his imagination he saw Wulfgar's hands taking possession of its perfection. Ragnor jerked sharply with his irritation, making Gwyneth cry out in fright.

"What is it? Does someone come?" she asked, frantically grabbing for his mantle to cover herself.

His hands stayed her movement. "Nay. There is nothing. The moon plays tricks with me, that is all. I thought there was something moving there, but I was mistaken."

Relaxing back into his arms, Gwyneth slipped her hand beneath his tunic and slid it over the hard muscles of his chest.

"You have me sorely at a disadvantage, sir knight," she breathed. "I am very inquisitive."

Ragnor smiled and began to remove his garments.

"That is better," Gwyneth murmured in approval when they lay discarded. "How handsome you are, my dearest. You are dark like the warm earth and strong like yon oaks. I had not thought men could be beautiful, but I was mistaken."

Her hands moved over him boldly, stirring the hot flames of passion.

"Be gentle with me," she whispered against his throat and lay back upon his mantle. Her pale eyes were like stars in the night, glittering and distant until Ragnor bent over her, covering her narrow frame with his, and then they slowly closed.

A wolf howled in the distance when Ragnor finally sat up, wrapping his arms about his knees as he gazed through the darkness toward the dim light coming from the lord's chamber window. As he watched a figure of a man shadowed the square and then moved out of sight to reappear again shortly. The dark silhouette flexed its arm, and Ragnor grinned, hoping the practice of arms that day had affected Wulfgar's pleasure, and knew otherwise as he thought of it, for his own tired limbs had little hampered his. The black shape turned in profile toward what Ragnor knew was the bed. He could almost see the bright hair

163

spread across the pillows and the small, oval face soft and perfect in sleep, as if he were the man at the window.

How intensely he desired revenge. At times he could almost feel it within his grasp, yet it was allusive and much like that damsel who slept in the lord's bed, irresistible and untouchable, ever taunting. His body stirred quickly at the memory of the wench in his arms. The thought gave him no rest, plaguing him day and night until he knew that he would not be satisfied until she belonged to him. He smiled, knowing that he would have revenge upon Wulfgar by taking her. Even if Wulfgar harbored no affection for the girl there would still be his pride to suffer.

"What are you thinking of?" Gwyneth murmured softly, reaching out to caress his lean and muscular ribs.

Ragnor turned and took her in his arms again. "I was just thinking how happy you have made me. Now I may go to William with your sweet memory riding atop the highest peak of my imagination." He pulled her chilled body closer against his. "Do you shiver with the cold, ma cherie, or the fierceness of our love?"

Gwyneth wrapped her thin arms about his neck, pressing her body to his. "Both, my dear love's heart. Both."

The first rays of the sun struck the frosted trees, making them sparkle as if spread with rare jewels, and the doves stirred in the cote. Ragnor gave a quick thump upon the door of the lord's chamber and pushed it open on the sleeping couple. With a warrior's instinct for danger, Wulfgar rolled from Aislinn's side and snatched up his sword lying on the stone floor. Before the door ceased its swing he stood ready to meet a foe. For a man who but a moment before slumbered peacefully at the side of a maid, he now seemed fully alert and quite capable of meeting any attack directed toward the occupants of that room.

"Oh, 'tis you," Wulfgar grunted, sitting back upon the bed.

Aislinn roused much more slowly, raising up to stare at Wulfgar in sleepy confusion and failed to notice Ragnor standing near the door in the dimness of the room. The small pelt she clutched more revealed than covered her breasts and it was toward this view that Ragnor stared. Following his gaze, Wulfgar saw the reason for his great attention and lifted his sword toward the intruding knight.

"We have an early morning visitor, cherie," he said and watched calmly as she started in surprise and hurriedly covered herself.

"Why came you here to my chamber at this hour, Ragnor?" he inquired as he rose to sheathe his sword.

Ragnor swept his hand before him and bowed in mockery before the spectacular form of the naked man.

"Your pardon, my lord, I did but want to take my leave of Darkenwald and desired to know if you wished anything further of me before I turn my horse upon the road. Mayhap you desire me to carry a message to the Duke."

"Nay, there is nothing," Wulfgar replied.

Ragnor nodded and turned to go, then paused, facing them again. A slow smile grew upon his lips.

"You should be careful of the woods at night. Wolves range the groves wide. I heard them close in the late hours."

Wulfgar raised a questioning brow, wondering who might have entertained the roving knight this time. "The way you make your rounds, Ragnor, 'tis certain you'll shortly replenish the populace of Darkenwald."

Ragnor chuckled. "And who should give birth first but my fair lady Aislinn."

Before he sensed the wrath his words had wrought, a small vessel glazed his ear and crashed against the door behind him. Ragnor looked at Aislinn kneeling in the middle of the bed with clenched fists holding a pelt close about her. He rubbed his ear and grinned, admiring the beauty her rage stirred forth.

"My dove, I'm overwhelmed by your passionate nature. Are you so tormented because of my love of last night? I assure you I did not think of your jealousy."

"Aaah!" Aislinn shrieked, glancing around for some other object to throw. Finding nothing in reach she flung herself from the bed. She crossed to where Wulfgar watched in silent amusement and snatched at his sword, only to find it too heavy for her to lift.

"Why do you stand and laugh at his jibes?!" she demanded of Wulfgar. She stamped her foot in rage. "Make him show respect to your authority."

Wulfgar shrugged and returned a smile for her glare. "He plays at games like a child. When he plays in earnest I will kill him."

The grin faded from Ragnor's face. "I am at your call, Wulfgar." He smiled stiffly. "At any hour."

He left the chamber without further ado, and for a long moment Aislinn stared in deep thought at the closed door before finally commenting.

"Monseigneur, I believe he sees you a threat."

166

"Do not let your fancies lead you astray, cherie," Wulfgar bade her shortly. "He is from one of the richest families in Normandy. He hates me, true, but it is because he thinks only blooded men should bear titles." He laughed. "And of course, he wants you."

Aislinn whirled to face him. "Ragnor wants me only because I belong to you."

Wulfgar chuckled as he drew her to him. He raised her chin until he could gaze into her eyes. "Somehow I cannot imagine his wrath if I had taken Hlynn from him."

His arms swept under her, lifting her up against his chest.

"M'lord," Aislinn protested, struggling in his embrace. " 'Tis morn. You must be about your duties."

"Later," he said huskily and silenced further argument by a fiery kiss that left Aislinn weak and tingling and unable to find any logic in resistance. He was stronger and she would only prolong the misery by fighting him.

Gwyneth swept down the stone stairs, feeling gay and thoroughly in love with the world this early morning hour. She had watched Ragnor ride off only a moment before and knew that her heart went with him. In the hall the men sat at the trestle tables, taking bread and meats. They paid her little heed, for they bantered among themselves and their laughter rose heartily at their own quips. Before the hearth Bolsgar still slept and glancing about for a familiar face, Gwyneth found only Ham and the young man Aislinn had spoken and laughed with the night before. They served Wulfgar's men and did not seem to take notice of her yet when she strode to the lord's table and took her place Ham shortly approached with food.

"Where is my brother?" she demanded. "These men here seem to be at their leisure. Does he not give them tasks to perform?"

"Aye, m'lady. They only wait for him. He has not come from his chambers yet."

"His laziness spreads like a plague," she said in derisive tones.

" 'Tis his usual custom to rise early. I would not know what keeps him."

Gwyneth leaned back in her chair. "The Saxon wench, no doubt."

Ham's face reddened with anger and he opened his

167

mouth to make a reply then snapped it shut again before uttering one. Spinning on his heels, he strode to the cooking chamber without a backward glance.

Gwyneth picked at her food absently, half listening to the men, half musing on the night before. When Sir Gowain entered with the knight, Beaufonte, the Normans called a greeting and beckoned them over.

"Were you not to ride to Cregan this morn?" Gowain inquired, turning to Milbourne, the eldest knight.

"Yea, lad, but Wulfgar seems wont to stay in his chamber instead," Milbourne replied with a chortle. He rolled his eyes and smacked his fingers in a gesture that was not lost upon his comrades who guffawed their delight at his silent wit.

Gowain grinned. "Mayhaps we should see to his welfare to be sure he does not lie abed with his throat slit. The way Ragnor slammed about and cursed him before he took to road, 'tis most likely they had another row."

The elder knight shrugged. " 'Tis over that girl again no doubt. Ragnor has had his blood up ever since he bedded her."

Gwyneth started in surprise, all senses stunned and reeling in confusion. Her breath came hard as if someone had struck a blow against her chest, and she thought she could not bear the pain.

"Aye," Gowain smiled. "And 'tis no small matter taking the wench from Wulfgar either, if he is bound to keep her. But she is a prize I'd gladly fight for, were I Ragnor."

"Aah, lad, she's a hot blooded one," the elder laughed. " 'Tis best you leave her for a man with experience."

Their conversation ceased abruptly as a door banged closed on the upper level. Wulfgar came into view and strode down the stairs, buckling on his sword. He saluted his sister, who eyed him coldly.

"I trust you rested well, Gwyneth."

He turned without waiting for a reply and went to his men.

"So, you think you can dally because I do. Well, we shall see what better men you are for it." He broke off a piece of bread, picked up a piece of meat and went to the door, where he turned again and considered them. He smiled leisurely.

"Why do you delay? I am for Cregan. What of you?"

They scrambled after him as he strode out, knowing

they were bound for a rigorous day, and they stumbled over themselves as they hastened to catch up. Wulfgar was already in his saddle, chewing on the bread and meat, as they scrambled to mount. When they regained some order about them, he swung his large steed about, tossing the remaining bread to Sweyn who stood watching with amusement, and set the spurs to the Hun's flanks to send him thundering off in the direction of Cregan.

Gwyneth slowly rose from the table, feeling sick inside, and walked carefully to the stairs and mounted them. In front of the lord's chamber door she paused, her hand trembling violently as she reached out for the latch, then she drew back sharply clutching the clenched fist to her breast as if she had just touched fire. Her ashen face looked sharp and hardened in the shadows and her pale eyes seemed to pierce the very wood that separated her from the peacefully sleeping form on the other side. She knew a hatred now that exceeded the contempt she felt for Wulfgar, and she vowed quietly in her misery that the Saxon wench would feel her wrath.

With measured care, as if she were afraid some slight noise would awaken the other to the malice she felt, Gwyneth backed away from the door then slowly moved on down the hall to her own small chamber.

When Aislinn woke a short time later, she dressed and went down to the hall to learn that Wulfgar had gone to Cregan. Sweyn had been left in command of the hall and was at the moment trying to mediate a petty squabble between two young women over an ivory comb given to one of them by a Norman soldier. Aislinn strolled outside to stand on the steps and listen in amusement at Sweyn's attempts to placate the two. One swore she had found it, the other claimed her companion stole it. Very capable of dealing with men, the Viking found himself completely at a loss to settle this argument.

Aislinn smiled, raising a brow in mockery. "Why, Sweyn, you can always cut their hair in the Norman fashion and they would have little use for the comb."

The women turned to her with a start, their eyes wide, their mouths hanging open. The sudden grin upon Sweyn's face quickly decided one to give up the comb and remove herself forthwith to some place distant from him while the other quickly retreated in the opposite direction.

Aislinn could not keep the tide of merriment from sweeping her away into mirthful laughter.

"Ah, Sweyn, you are human after all," she smiled brightly. "I would not have believed it. To be confounded by mere women, Tsk. Tsk."

"Blasted wenches," he grumbled and shaking his head, stalked into the hall.

Bolsgar's health was improved from the day before when his color had held to a waxen gray tone. Now his complexion once more glowed a leathery bronze, and at midday he did away with a hearty meal. Aislinn changed the poultice on his leg, gently cracking away the dried mud and drawing with it long gouts of the poisoned matter. She saw that the wound was already beginning to knit and that the flesh around it had taken on a healthier ruddy hue.

It was toward late afternoon that Gwyneth came downstairs and approached Aislinn.

"Do you have a mount? I wish to see this land Wulfgar has gained."

Aislinn nodded. "A swift and mighty Barbary mare, but she is uncommonly spirited. I would not advise—"

"If you can ride her, I suspect I will have little trouble," Gwyneth replied coldly.

Aislinn struggled with words. "I am sure you are well acquainted with a saddle, Gwyneth, yet I fear Cleome—"

She was silenced abruptly by the woman's murderous look. Aislinn folded her hands and quietly stepped aside before the hatred she saw. Gwyneth turned and ordered the horse to be saddled and escorts provided for the ride. When the mare was brought forward, Aislinn tried once more to caution the woman and instruct her to hold the reins firmly but again she met that glowering look that chilled any words to silence. Aislinn winced as Gwyneth laid her whip heavily against Cleome's flanks and sent the mare leaping ahead of her mounted escort. In dismay Aislinn watched them ride away and did not feel comforted with the direction they took, which would lead them to Cregan. It was not the destination that worried Aislinn but the countryside along the way. The paths were clearly laid but if one wandered from them there were many vales and gullies to snare the careless rider.

With apprehension sitting heavily upon her shoulders, Aislinn sought to occupy her time with matters dealing

170

with the hall. But as it turned out she spent most of the afternoon hearing complaints from Maida about Gwyneth's manners and lack of courtesy. Aislinn listened as long as she could then retired in frustration to the bed-chamber. She could not approach Wulfgar about his kins-woman, for he hated women enough without added as-surance that they were worthy of his contempt. He might consider her too critical of Gwyneth and be unwilling to lend a fair ear. Still, in a morning's time his sister had made herself felt. She had spent the morning pawing through Maida's coffer seeking gowns for herself, then grew petulant and sharp, for all of Maida's garments were too small. Though she was thin Gwyneth was as tall as Aislinn and not of the tiny frame of the older woman. Shortly after she had commanded her meal to be brought to her chamber, Gwyneth had slapped Hlynn and caused the girl to cry over no matter worthwhile. She excused her action by saying Hlynn was too slow to obey her orders. And now Gwyneth roamed the countryside on Aislinn's fa-vored steed.

Roamed the countryside indeed, for Gwyneth knew not where she went. It was simply a race. Her temper was high and her spirits were low. The very sight of that young Saxon wench enjoying the hospitality of her brother was enough to set her nerves on edge. But the crude reve-lation that her lover first had the woman ended any small chance of friendship they might have had between them. And if that was not enough, Wulfgar openly flaunted the slut as if she were some worthy maiden when in fact she was Wulfgar's whore, at his beck and call, a captured slave. The bitch had the nerve to claim this mare as hers. What right did a serf have to own a horse, least of all a slave? She had nothing herself, not even a suitable gown to wear upon Ragnor's return; all her possessions had been taken by the Normans. But Aislinn had fine clothes which Wulfgar allowed her to keep. That jeweled dagger she wore was worth a goodly sum.

Gwyneth laid the whip again across Cleome's side and whipped her into a frenzied gallop. The two escorts fol-lowed at a distance, sparing their animals the headlong pace. Accustomed to the firm and knowledgeable grip of her mistress, the mare could find no authority in the loose reins. She chose her own way over the solid path and gave her rider's commands only the briefest attention. The ef-

171

fect was simply to send Gwyneth's rage to a higher level and in absolute fury she jerked the reins and the horse fled from the path into the dense woods. Now Gwyneth whipped the steed soundly until finally it threw out its head and began to run with long, swift strides, crashing through the brush. Some fear rose as Gwyneth realized what she had begun, for branches whipped and vines tore at her, yet the mare plunged heedlessly onward, up the hills and through the dales. Gwyneth could hear voices calling from behind bidding her halt, but the mare had the bit in her teeth and gave no mind when the reins were tugged. The maddened beast pressed onward, harder, faster. Gwyneth felt panic bite deep now. A narrow gorge lay ahead yet the horse thrashed on in agony as if some raging monster tagged close behind her heels. She gave no pause but leaped into the gorge. Gwyneth screamed and threw herself from the saddle as the mare hurled downward through branches and brush to fall with a sickening crash to the rocky bed of the ravine. The two escorts came crashing through the woods and drew their horses to a stop. Gwyneth rose, her rage far from satisfied; she forgot her fear and her own foolishness and spit words out with venom.

"You brainless beast!" she railed. "You low-born nag! On open path you prance along but take to the woods and you flee like the hunted stag!"

She brushed leaves and the matted forest turf from her gunna and sought to rake some from her tangled hair. She glared at the horse wheezing in pain at the bottom of the gulley and made no effort to ease its agony. One of the escorts dismounted and went to stand close to the edge. He turned with a sickly smile upon his face.

"My lady, I fear your mount is broken badly."

But Gwyneth flung her head and spun about. "Aaah, that stupid nag, couldn't see a hole as big as that! Good riddance that she should be broken!"

A new sound came and heavy thundering and a crashing in the brush drew near. From the dark shadows of the wood, Wulfgar rode into view followed by his men. He pulled his great red warhorse to a halt beside Gwyneth and her escorts and his scowl raked them.

"What goes here?" he demanded. "Why are you here? We heard a scream."

The mounted escort gestured to the gorge and Wulfgar approached closer. He scowled heavily as he recognized

172

Aislinn's mare lying at the bottom. Many times he had stopped to stroke the fine beast and feed her a handful of oats. He whirled to face Gwyneth.

"You, dear sister, riding a horse and one I gave you no word for?"

Gwyneth flicked a dried leaf from her skirt and shrugged. "A slave's horse, what would it matter? Aislinn will have little use for it now; her duties lie in your chamber."

Wulfgar's face grew rigid and it was with a great effort of will that he spoke below a shout. " 'Twas a good nag you slaughtered by your wretched carelessness! Your utter disregard for another's property, Gwyneth, has wasted a valuable steed."

"The mare was ill tempered," Gwyneth replied evenly. "I could have been killed."

Wulfgar bit off a sharp reply. "Who gave you permission to take the horse?"

"I need not have permission from a slave," she retorted haughtily. " 'Twas Aislinn's horse, thereby it was available for my use at my discretion."

Wulfgar's hands clenched into tight fists. "If Aislinn is a slave, then what she owns is mine," he rumbled low. "For I am lord of all this and everything here is mine. You will not abuse my horses nor my slaves."

" 'Twas I who was abused!" Gwyneth flung back in high rage. "Look at me! I could have been killed riding that beast and no one warned me that I would be taking my life in my hands. Aislinn could have stopped me, yet I think she would have me dead. Not a word of warning did she utter."

Wulfgar's frown became ominous.

"Really, Wulfgar, what do you see in that driveling wench," Gwyneth inquired. "I would think you spoiled for lesser creatures after being accustomed to the ladies of William's court. She's a scheming, conniving little bitch and she will have your head as well as mine in the end."

Wulfgar whirled abruptly, jerking the great steed about to face his men. Lifting an arm, he gestured for them to set off.

"Wulfgar!" Gwyneth cried, stamping her foot. "The least you can do is dismount one of your knights and give me a horse for the return."

He turned his head to stare at her stonily for a long

173

moment, then glancing about him spoke to her mounted escort.

"Take her up behind you, Gard. Let her ride the rump of your horse back to Darkenwald. Perhaps she will learn the value of a worthy steed on the return."

He moved his gaze back to Gwyneth who eyed him coldly.

"Nay, dear sister, the least I can do is to finish the work that was so carelessly begun."

He bit the words off as if they were distasteful to him and swung down from the Hun. He tied the reins to a nearby bush and made his way down the steep side of the gully until he stood near Cleome's head. Reaching down he took the mare in a firm grip by the lower jaw, stretched her head upward until he looked into her great soft eyes. Cleome struggled gallantly to rise but with two quick thrusts of his dagger Wulfgar cut the pulsing veins in each side of her throat and then gently lowered the head again. In great vexation he returned to his own mount. Slowly the sounds from the gulley quieted until only silence hung heavily in the forest.

Wulfgar whirled the Hun about with a jerk at the reins and urged the huge steed forward until he had rejoined the party. It was in a sharp tone of voice that he bade Gwyneth's other escort to return and collect the trappings from Cleome. The group continued on in silence against the darkening day until they reached Darkenwald where a shout from the lookout heralded their approach.

Wulfgar saw the blue of Aislinn's gunna as she left the door to wait upon them, and Gwyneth's words fell heavily upon his thoughts. What web of contentment had the Saxon wench woven about him that he could feel at ease with his back turned to her? Was he someday to have that small dagger he had let her keep thrust between his ribs? She had stated herself that she was safer with him alive and this was true, but what of later? Would circumstances in the future warrant his death and would she be the one to carry out the execution? Lord, he could not trust any woman! His jaw tightened as he considered how greatly he enjoyed her company. She would be difficult to replace, for she pleasured him well. He'd be a fool if he let his sister's accusation goad him into putting her aside. A more winsome bedmate a man could not find. As long as he held his trust from her, he could gratify himself with her

174

and suffer no consequences. He almost smiled again, yet he remembered the mare and knew he would have to be the one to tell Aislinn of her loss. Sourly his thoughts turned back to Gwyneth. Another woman whose idiocy he must contend with, but this one gave him no pleasure.

Aislinn stood silent as they neared. Sweyn had come from the hall and waited beside her. She blushed lightly as Wulfgar met her gaze, unable to forget his passionate caresses of that morning, but he scowled and glanced away, barking an order over his shoulder at his men. In mean temper he drew the Hun to a halt and dismounted, throwing the reins to Gowain. Ignoring Aislinn, he brushed past her into the hall, flinging the door wide with a bang.

Aislinn knew only confusion and she looked from one to another of the men as they led their horses away, but each avoided her gaze and no one spoke. Aislinn turned, wondering at their manner and spied Gwyneth mounted on behind one of her former escorts. Aislinn glanced around in further bewilderment, seeking some sight of the small mare among the huge Norman steeds, but try as she might she could not see Cleome. She faced Gwyneth again and watched her dismount and brush at her skirts. In sudden apprehension Aislinn stared at the streaks of dirt marring the other's gown. Gwyneth raised cold eyes to hers, seeming to dare her to ask. Swallowing a cry of dismay Aislinn whirled and followed Wulfgar with a rush. She found him seated at a table, staring at its top with a horn of ale in his hand. He lifted his gaze to hers as she came to stand before him.

"You left Cleome at Cregan?" she asked softly, almost knowing better.

He sighed heavily. "Nay. The mare broke her forelegs and I had to ease her pain. She is dead, Aislinn."

"Cleome?!" Aislinn half laughed, half sobbed. "But how? She knew the paths well."

A sharp cutting voice came from behind her. "Hah! That stupid nag could not find her way through the simplest of paths, yet she did find her way into a hole and threw me in the course of it. Why, she could have killed me! You did not warn me of her meanness, Aislinn."

"Meanness?" Aislinn repeated in confusion. "Cleome was not mean. She was a fine beast. There was no horse swifter than she."

"Hah! You can ask my escorts of her temper. They saw her themselves and can vow to my truth. What would you gain with my death?"

Aislinn shook her head, completely baffled. She felt Wulfgar's steadfast gaze upon her. It was as if he, by his silence, questioned her, too. She attempted to laugh.

"You jest with cruelty, Gwyneth. It was my horse you killed."

"*Your* horse!" Gwyneth scoffed. "You claim a horse? A mere slave?" She smiled into Aislinn's wide-eyed gaze. "You mean my brother's horse, don't you?"

"Nay!" Aislinn cried. "Cleome was mine! My father gave her to me!" She glared at sister and brother and choked. "She was all I—"

The rest was torn in sobs. Wulfgar rose and laid a hand upon her arm as if he would comfort her, but she jerked angrily away and fled from them to seek what little comfort privacy could afford her. She had mounted the stairs when Gwyneth's voice rang out.

"Hold! You do not leave before you're bidden!"

Even Wulfgar was taken aback and he peered questioningly at his sister. She turned to him.

"I am your sister while that simpering bitch is but a slave! A captured slave!" she stormed. "I thump about in bare feet and rags while you take this English whore to bed and dress her in the finest gowns! Does it seem fair that kin should suffer so while slaves enjoy the privileges of your hospitality? You hold her up before my father and myself as if she were some badge of courage that you've won, and we must eat the scraps from your table while you place the bitch by your side where you can fondle her at your leisure!"

Gwyneth missed the lowering of Wulfgar's brows. Aislinn had frozen at her command and had turned and even with the rage burning inside of her noticed the gathering storm on his face.

Bolsgar struggled up on an elbow. "Gwyneth! Gwyneth, listen to me!" he commanded. "You will not speak to Wulfgar in this manner. He is a knight of William and they have conquered this land. Though I have not been defeated in battle, I am stripped of my lands. We did come here begging and are here on his mercy. If I am your father, you will not abuse his kindness."

"My father indeed!" Gwyneth poised herself before him

176

and gestured to his blank shield with her whip. "Were you my father when you sent my brother to his death? Were you my father when my mother died? Were you my father when you took me from my home and led me across half of England to this filthy hovel because we heard the Normans speak of this bastard, Wulfgar, here? 'Twas I who was injured today, my life almost forfeited. Do you take a slave's side against that of your daughter or will you for once be *my* father?"

She opened her mouth to continue her attack, but Wulfgar's voice preceded hers and in thundering tones silenced her.

"Cease your prattle, woman!"

Gwyneth whirled to face him and met his hard, piercing eyes.

"Mind your manners here!" he commanded in a low angry tone, taking a step forward. "Mind them well, my sister. You have called me bastard. So I am. But 'twas not of my choosing. And you complain that your fair mother died. 'Tis true, but of what? 'Tis my thought she died much of her own will. My brother, gallant knight for Harold, died upon a battlefield. No man sent him. 'Twas his oath, his honor, that took him there. He died a man for the cause he chose. But what of my cause, sister? Where was my choice? You! Your brother! My mother! Your father! You all cast me to these ends. You sent me far across the seas so that I would not blemish your good name and bring embarrassment to you. I was young and knew no fault of blood, a mere lad and knew no other father but one."

He turned to Bolsgar.

"And you say, my lord, that my mother sought to set a wrong aright?" He laughed coldly. "I say she sought the vengeance of a shrewish wife, for who was harmed by her words? She? But little. My sister?" He bowed, gesturing to that one. "None at all, for she was the fairest in my mother's sight. My brother? Never, for he became the favored one. You? Deeply, I wouldst think, for you and I were truly father and son. But you in honor to her cast me out, sent me far away to that foppish sot who took the coins you sent and gave me for my care but the meanest share.

The steel gray eyes settled coldly upon Gwyneth again.

"Do not lecture me on what I owe my family again.

177

You take what is willingly given without complaints, for I feel no deep obligation here. You criticize my pleasures freely." He swept his arm toward Aislinn. "That, too, is my affair and none of yours, for I will have her whether you say yea or nay. Be careful when you speak of whore and bastard, for I am not opposed to striking a woman. Many times have I been tempted and may one day yield that urge. So be warned.

"Now the mare you took without my word is dead and I am one to feel a fondness for a good steed and she was a fine piece of horse. As to your claim that she was ill tempered, I say she was but a trifle shy since Aislinn has not been allowed to ride her these weeks since my coming. I would rather think it was this reason that caused her loss and nearly yours. We will leave it at that, and I will hear no more accusations without proof. Further I would suggest you try to console yourself with a lesser wardrobe than you may have been accustomed to. I have neither the patience nor the inclination to hear your naggings about such things. If you feel yourself abused, speak with the women of England and learn of their losses and what they've suffered."

He ignored Gwyneth's furious expression and strode away to the center of the hall where he faced her again.

"I must leave to do the Duke's bidding on the morrow," he said, drawing Aislinn's startled gaze upon him. "The journey is of a length I cannot know but when I return I hope you have been reconciled to the fact that I am master here and will run this manor and my life as I see fit. Sweyn will be here in my absence and you will give him due respect. I will leave coins to see to your needs, not because you demand them, but by reason that it was my intention. Now I tire easily of women's prattle and I bid you to test my patience no further. You are dismissed, dear sister, and if you question that, it means you are free to retire to your chamber."

He waited until she whirled in silence and fled up the stairs, passing Aislinn without meeting her gaze and slammed the door of her chamber behind her. Aislinn lifted tearful eyes to his and in their violet depths Wulfgar recognized the anguish there. For a long moment their eyes held and then he watched her turn, observing the square set of her shoulders and the gentle swing of her hips.

While holding herself proudly erect, she slowly mounted the stairs.

Wulfgar became aware of his stepfather's gaze and turned to face the older knight, half expecting some reproof. Instead there was the slightest trace of a smile on Bolsgar's lips. He nodded his head ever so slightly and then leaned back, rolling his head upon the pelts to stare into the fire. Wulfgar's gaze swept on to Sweyn who stood just inside the door. The Norseman's face was void of expression, yet the two old friends knew each other's thoughts. After a moment Sweyn turned and left the hall.

Picking up his helmet and shield, Wulfgar mounted the stairs. His tread was heavy as if he almost forced his feet to take the steps. He knew Aislinn sorely felt the loss of her horse. He thought himself capable of dealing with her rages, but what of her sorrows? Superior strength and force would not alleviate the pain of this needless waste of the Barb. He blamed himself mostly for what had happened. He could have prevented it all by a simple word, yet his mind had been on other matters, his duties and these estates that would need guarding in his absence.

He entered his chamber and closed the door softly behind him. Aislinn stood near the window with her head resting against the inside shutter. Tears made wet paths down her cheeks and fell unheeded to her bosom. He watched for a time and then with his usual care removed and put away the trappings of his profession, his hauberk, his helm, his sword, his shield, each to its place.

In his own mind he was unattached and needed no woman to clutter his thoughts. He had lived his life hard and vigorously. There was no place in it for a spouse, nor had any wench ever made him yearn for a mate. Now, he felt hampered by the lack of gentleness in his life. He didn't know in what manner to approach a grieving maid and express his regret. There had never been an occasion when he had to or even wanted to. His affairs with women had been brief and without depth, rarely going beyond a night or two with the same one. He took women to appease a basic desire. When he became bored with them, he simply left them without explanation. Their affections or feelings mattered naught. Yet he sympathized with Aislinn's loss and felt compassion, for he had experienced some sadness himself at losing a favored steed.

As if some inner knowledge guided him, he went to her

and took her in his arms, hushing her tearful sobs against his strong and hardened chest. Tenderly he brushed dampened hair from her cheek and kissed each tear from her face until she lifted her mouth to his. Her response surprised him pleasantly yet a fleeting moment of confusion at her moods swept him. Since first taking her she had tolerated his advances as any slave would her master, seeming anxious to place the moment behind her. But his kisses she fought, turning her face away when she could, straining against him as if she were afraid of yielding some victory to him. Now in her woe, she met his kiss almost eagerly, her soft lips parting warm and moist beneath his mounting ardor. Hot blood surged through his veins, beating fierce and turbulent like a storm at sea. He dismissed the wonder of her reaction as he raised her in his arms and bore her now soft and willing to his bed.

A thin silvery beam of moonlight crept effortlessly between the closed shutters, invading the chamber where Aislinn lay asleep curled warm and secure, protected in the arms of her knight. Yet in wakeful repose, Wulfgar stared at the shaft of light, reflecting upon the moments passed, unable to pick any logic from his own confused mind.

Aislinn woke as the first gray hues of dawn were seeking their way through the shutters and lighting the room. She lay savoring the warmth of Wulfgar's body and the feel of his muscled shoulder beneath her head.

Ah, my fine lord, she thought, running the tip of her finger along his lean ribs. You are mine and 'tis only a matter of time, I think, before you know it also.

She smiled, half dreaming of the night passed yet basking in the soft, still moments of the present. She rose up on an elbow to further study her lord, marveling at the handsomeness of his features, and found suddenly his arms locked around her pulling her to him. Surprised by his feigned slumber, she gave a gasp and struggled in his embrace. His eyes came open and smiled into hers.

"Ma cherie, are you so eager for me that you must wake me from a sound sleep?"

Her face flaming, Aislinn sought to pull away but his grip was firm and unbreakable.

"You are conceited," she accused.

"Am I, Aislinn?" he questioned, the corner of his mouth lifting as his gray eyes sparkled. "Or is it your greed for

180

me? I think you must carry some warmth in your heart for me, my little vixen."

His mockery burned her. " 'Tis a lie," she returned sharply. "Would a Saxon seek out a Norman?"

"Aaah," he sighed, ignoring her protests. "I will be hard pressed to find a wench so entertaining upon the road, and one that bears some affection for me, never."

"Oh, you swollen-headed buffoon," she cried, straining against him. His arms tightened about her, crushing her naked breasts to his chest, and his smile deepened at that pleasure.

"Would that I could take you with me, Aislinn, I would not find boredom. But alas, I fear so soft a one could not bear the battle march and I would not risk so fine a treasure in a foolish game."

His hand moved behind her head, forcing her lips down to meet his. He kissed her long and passionately, his mouth searing and bruising with its insistence. Again Aislinn felt her will to resist weaken. Wulfgar rolled over with her until his weight held her down, but there was now no need for force. Her hand slipping behind his neck attested to her frailty. The building fires that ran like molten lead through her veins and throbbed with pulsating agony in the depth of her belly only made her seek more heartily his appeasement. That same intense yearning began to sweep her as it had only a few hours ago when her young body had responded eagerly to his almost with a will of its own, meeting his with each deep thrust. Yet when he had moved away she had still ached for his caresses and known a strange hungering frustration she could not explain.

Shame at her earlier behavior and the thought of his mockery now cooled her passion. He used her, then taunted her for feeling some warmth for him. Was there no softness within him? How could she feel cold and distant with him when even his kisses drove her beyond the brink of sanity? Could it be that she was indeed falling in love with him?

The thought sobered her like a pail of icy water. She jumped, making him lose his grip on her and she twisted away, half dragging him with her as she scrambled to the edge of the bed.

"What the devil?" he cried and reached out to draw her back. Another moment there would have been no need for

181

battles. Now he was eager and ready and perturbed with her. "Come here, wench."

"Nay!" Aislinn shrieked and threw herself from the bed. She stood braced for action, her bosom heaving, her coppery hair cascading wildly around her naked body. "You laugh at me and then seek your pleasure! Well, find it on some whoremonger's crone."

"Aislinn!" he barked and flung himself after her. She screeched and leapt out of his way, putting the bed between them.

"You go to fight my people and you expect me to send you off with my good tidings! Heaven help me!"

She made a very fetching sight standing in the shaft of light, her slim body glowing golden in the early rays. He paused in rounding the end of the bed and leaned against a massive post regarding her with amusement. She glared back at him defiantly, aware of his nakedness, his passion, his strength, yet determined to salvage this small bit of pride.

He smiled slowly. "Ah, cherie, you make it hard to think of leaving, but I must. I am a knight of William." He approached her with measured tread and she eyed him with suspicion, ready to fling herself across the bed again if he made a move to take her. "Would you have me neglect my duty?"

"Your duty has taken too many English lives. When will it end?"

He shrugged and replied easily. "When England has bowed before William."

With a quick movement he reached out and grabbed her arm, taking her off guard, and snatched her against him. She struggled furiously but to no avail, for his arms were clamped securely about her. He chuckled at her efforts, thoroughly enjoying them and with a frustrated groan Aislinn halted her movements and stood stock still against him, aware that doing otherwise only aroused his passions further.

"You see, Aislinn, it is what the lord of the manor dictates, not what his slave wishes."

Aislinn made a strangling, enraged sound beneath his kiss and would not relent to the beckoning excitement of his searing lips. Instead she held herself cold and rigid against him. After a long moment he drew away and met the mockery in her gaze.

"For once, Wulfgar, my Norman knight," she breathed, her violet eyes glowing with the warmth he did not find in her lips. " 'Tis what the slave wills—"

She danced away as his hands fell from her and curtseyed prettily for him. Her eyes swept him from toe to head and knew his desires had not cooled.

"Mind you dress, lord. These days would chill even the stoutest of men."

Grabbing up a pelt she pulled it close about her and gave him a impishly wicked look as she grinned. Turning on her heels with a low laugh, she went to the hearth, there to lay small logs upon the still warm coals. She blew upon them but drew back in haste as the ashes flew up and sat back upon her heels rubbing her reddened eyes while Wulfgar's amused chuckles filled the room. She made a face at his mirth and swung the kettle of water on its hook over the building heat as he crossed to the warmth of the fire beside her and began to dress.

The water steamed and she went to where his sword and belt hung and there found his scabbard knife and returning with it, began to whet it on the stone of the fireplace. He raised his brow in wonder at her actions.

"My flesh is much more tender than yours, Wulfgar," she explained. "And if you would go about barefaced you should keep it so. The burr upon your chin does sorely chasten me and since I've seen this shaving done so well upon my people, I would think it not unseemly that you would allow me the single honor to return the favor."

Wulfgar glanced at her small dagger lying atop her gunna, remembering his thoughts of the day before. Was his death warranted now when he must go and fight her people? Should he tell her he was not one to waste lives needlessly? By Heavens, he would know the truth now. He nodded.

"Perhaps your hand is gentler than most, Aislinn," he replied. He took up a linen and dipped it into the kettle. Wringing it out, he shook the piece free to cool the steam and leaning back in a chair, laid it several folds across his face.

"Ah, Wulfgar, what a tempting pose you make," Aislinn quipped, considering him. "Would that it had been a moon ago that a Norman throat be laid bare before me—"

She rose and stood over him fingering the blade. Wulfgar removed the towel and their eyes met as he lifted a brow. Her mouth curved and she grinned devilishly, tossing her long hair with a shake of her head. Her tone became quite casual.

"Ah, but were I not so afraid of my next master the temptation might be far greater."

The benefit of her humor was the solid whack of his large hand upon her buttock, bringing from her a small shriek and a more eager manner. She slowly plied the well honed blade along his cheeks until the same had lost their bristles and were again smooth. When she was done he rubbed a hand across his face, marveling at the fact she had not cut him once.

"A better manservant a knight could never have." He reached beneath the pelt and pulled her down onto his lap. His gaze burned deeply into hers as he murmured hoarsely, "Remember that you are mine, Aislinn, and I will not share you."

"Do you treasure me after all, m'lord?" she murmured softly, tracing her finger lightly over the scar on his cheek.

He did not answer her inquiry but said, "Remember."

It was with a definite hunger he pulled her against him and kissed her, this time tasting the warmth and passion he knew her capable of.

The morning was cold and wet with a brisk wind sweeping the rain across the hills and in through every crack that plagued the manor. Small wisps of the chill breeze crept beneath the outer doors, bringing with them trickles of water and stirring the frosty air within the hall. Aislinn huddled deeper into the woolen shawl and with cold-numbed fingers picked a small crust of bread to nibble as she crossed to the hearth where Sweyn and Bolsgar sat. The newly kindled fire was just beginning to drive the chill from the hall, and she took a seat on a small stool beside Bolsgar's chair. In the days following Wulfgar's departure, her fondness for the old knight had grown, for he reminded her much of her own father. He was a cushion that softened Gwyneth's harsh railery and made life bearable when that woman was about. He was kind and understanding when his daughter was not.

Aislinn often sought his counsel over matters concerning the hall or serfs and knew the wisdom of his advice had come by his own experience through the years. Sweyn often came seeking his opinion as well and more than not stayed to enjoy a horn of ale and reminisce upon the days when Wulfgar was still looked upon as a true son. When these moods struck the men, Aislinn sat quietly and listened in rapt attention as they spoke of the young lad with fondness and praised his feats. Their manner was proud, enough to make a person wonder if each had not had a part in siring the boy.

There were times when Sweyn would spin tales of his adventures with Wulfgar and their life as mercenaries. Bolsgar listened with an eagerness easily discernible. At an early age Wulfgar left the house of de Sward, and he and Sweyn found their sustenance by hiring out as soldiers of war. Their reputation grew until their services commanded the highest prices and the demand for them was constant. It was in this time the Duke heard of Wulfgar's prowess with a sword and lance and called the pair out of France to join him. The friendship between knight and nobleman began at the first moment of their meeting, when Wulfgar declared without ado that he was bastard and that only coin brought his allegiance. Taken with the other's frankness, William pressed him to join forces and swear fealty to him. It was a matter quickly done, for the Duke was a persuasive man and Wulfgar found in William a man he could respect. At his present age of three and thirty, Wulfgar had been with the Duke for several years and was well set in his loyalty.

Aislinn now looked at the Norseman and the old knight where they sat and knew that if Gwyneth had been present, she would have berated them severely for wasting time. As she chewed her crust, Aislinn mused on Wulfgar's sister. How different she was from either her brother or her father. Wulfgar had no more than ridden over the hill when Gwyneth began to reign as mistress of the hall. She treated the serfs as low, contemptuous beings there to serve only her. She gave no pause to interrupting their labors and setting them about on some petty errand. It seemed to completely infuriate the woman for the peasants to go to Aislinn or Sweyn for approval before doing much of what she bade them do. The woman had taken charge of the larder as well and doled out food as if it were she who had paid dearly for each grain of wheat. She measured the meat in portions and scolded loudly if some was left on the bone. She made no accounting of the poor serfs who came and waited hungrily for scraps to be cast from the table. It became a game for Bolsgar and Sweyn to cheat her meager ration and fling large meaty joints to the watchful peasants. When she noted this, Gwyneth seemed to take their treachery to heart and ranted long on their wasteful ways.

The serenity of the morning was suddenly shattered as a piercing shriek rent the quiet of the hall. Aislinn rose to her feet with a start as her mother came flying down the stairs waving her arms in outraged passion, calling for all the demons of hell to come forth and plague this daughter of Satan. Aislinn stared at Maida in astonishment, half convinced that she had passed the border of reason and fled into the depths of madness. Gwyneth strode to the head of the stairs and with a smug smile on her lips gazed down upon them as Maida scuttled behind her daughter's skirts. Aislinn faced Gwyneth as she leisurely descended and came to them.

"I caught your mother stealing from me," Gwyneth charged. "Not only must we abide in the same hall with serfs, but with thieves as well. Wulfgar will hear of this. Mark my words well."

"Lies! 'Tis lies!" Maida shrilled. She held up her hands in appeal to Aislinn. "My spider eggs! My leeches! They were mine! I bought them from the Jews. Now they are all gone." She cast an evil look at Gwyneth. "I but ventured into her chamber to find them."

"Lies?" Gwyneth gasped indignantly. "I find her rummaging in my room and I am named the thief? She is mad!"

"My mother suffered greatly at the hands of Ragnor and his men," Aislinn explained. "The things were of use in ministering to the hurts of all. She valued them highly."

"I threw them out." Gwyneth drew herself up in righteous pride. "Yea, I threw them out. Let her keep her playthings from this hall. I will have none of them crawling about my chamber."

"Gwyneth!" Bolsgar snapped, sorely vexed. "You have no right to act thus. You are a guest here and must abide in Wulfgar's way."

"*No right!*" Gwyneth railed in a fit of temper. "I am the only one here of kin to the lord of this hall. Who denies my rights?" Her pale blue eyes flashed and dared them all to answer. "I will see to the welfare of Wulfgar's possessions while he is gone."

Bolsgar gave a derisive snort. "As you see to mine? You lay out food as if it were yours to give. Wulfgar leaves us monies and you toss out a few coppers and horde the rest. You have never seen to anyone else's welfare that I know of."

"I only keep it safe from your free hand," his daughter retorted sharply. "You would squander it as you threw away our gold. Arms! Men! Horses! What good did it do you? Had you held a few coins back, we would not have had to beg for a crust and lodgings."

The old man grumbled into the fire. "Had I not been bestowed with two nagging females who demanded the best of everything, I might have been able to send more men with your brother and we would not be here now."

"Aye, blame poor mother and myself. We had to beg you for even a few coppers to buy a gown. Look at my gunna and see how well you kept us," Gwyneth berated him harshly. "But I am here now and the only kinsman of Wulfgar. I claim the rights of blood, and I shall see these Saxons do not abuse his generous nature."

"There are no rights of blood." Sweyn was so bold as to enter the fray. "When he was cast out, your mother did not claim him as her son either. Then she denied his kinship also."

"Keep your tongue still, you lickspittle lackey!" Gwyneth snarled at the Viking. "You polish Wulfgar's armor and guard his door when he sleeps. You have no say here. My words will stand. That woman will keep her vermin from this hall!"

"Aaaiee!" Maida wailed. "I can not have my chamber safe from thieves even here in my own hall."

"Your hall!" Gwyneth scoffed. She laughed jeeringly. "By William's hand you are set away from these walls."

Aislinn's temper flared. "By Wulfgar's command we are held here and given these abodes."

Gwyneth's wrath would not be stayed. "You are serfs here! The lowest kind! You can hold no possessions!" She thrust a finger toward Maida. "You, you sniveling old crone, prance about this hall as if you were still the lady of it, when in truth you are no more than slave. I will not have it."

"Nay! She is here at Wulfgar's will." Aislinn cried, her ire raised at this senseless attack upon her mother. "Your brother even stayed Ragnor's hand when that knave would have set her out."

The other woman's lips curled in contempt. "Do not call a true-blooded Norman knight by your Saxon names!" She whirled on Maida again. "By what right do you claim a place in this hall? Because your daughter beds the lord?"

She chuckled scornfully. "You think that gives you Norman rights, old hag? What say you when the lord returns with wife and throws your precious kin to his men? What rights then will you sport? A mother of a whore?! 'Twould do you ill to even stay upon these lands. Yea! Begone from here, out of my sight. Find some hovel where you can take your bony frame, but get thee gone. Clear your chamber of those vile pests and get out of this hall! Get out!"

"Nay!" Aislinn cried. " 'Twill not be so! Wulfgar, himself set her in that room. Do you challenge his command?"

"I challenge naught." Gwyneth spat. "I see only to his good."

"Aislinn?" The whisper came softly and the girl looked down as her mother tugged at her gunna. "I will go. I will get my things. They are few enough now."

There were tears in Maida's eyes as she spoke and a chaotic flow of emotions flickered across her face. As Aislinn opened her mouth to speak, the old woman shook her head negatively and crossed to the stairs and slowly mounted them, her thin shoulders sagging with defeat. Aislinn glared her voiceless rage at Gwyneth, standing with clenched fist as the other smiled tauntingly.

"There are times, Gwyneth,'" Bolsgar slowly ground out, "when you sicken my gut."

His daughter glowed in her triumph. "I cannot see why you bemoan her leaving, father. The crone has marred this hall long enough with her rags and twisted face."

He turned his great shoulders away to stare stonily into the roaring blaze on the hearth. Sweyn did likewise for a space then heaved his bulk up and left the hall. Aislinn glowered on until Gwyneth strode away and seating herself in Wulfgar's chair, began to daintily pick at a trencher of mutton Hlynn had placed there.

Maida descended the stairs with a ragged pelt covering her back and a small bundle in her arms. She paused in the doorway, turning a pleading glance to her daughter. Aislinn gathered the shawl tightly against the cold and wet outside and followed her mother. They shivered together as the north wind caressed their meagerly clad bodies and a frosty mist dampened their hair.

"Where am I to go now, Aislinn?" Maida wept, wringing her hands as they crossed the courtyard. "Should we not go before Wulfgar returns and seek a place far from here?"

"Nay." Aislinn shook her head. It was difficult to speak calmly when she wanted to tear at Gwyneth's hair and vent her rage upon the other. "Nay, mother mine. If we leave the people will suffer and would have no one to ease their hurts. I cannot betray them to Gwyneth's shallow mercy. In any cause, there is war upon the land. 'Tis no time for two women to wander about."

"Wulfgar will cast us out if he returns with a bride," Maida insisted. "And we will be no better off than if we were to go now."

Aislinn lifted her gaze to the distant horizon as she thought of the last night spent in Wulfgar's arms. She could almost feel his hands upon her again, caressing, touching, arousing until it seemed each single nerve cried out for him. Her eyes grew soft and dreamy. The mere memory of their play now set her breasts and thighs aflame and a hunger grew within her. But what of him? Had he truly been hers then or was she to find herself put aside for another woman upon his return? A brief vision of Wulfgar holding some wench within his passionate embrace loomed upward before her and the delicious excitement that had swept her youthful body was crushed in a wave of anger. Of all the men who had desired her hand and begged her father to consider them worthy of her, she must now be the paramour of one who loathed women and did not trust them. She almost laughed aloud. What irony to have been so proud to those who pined for her and to find herself a slave to that strange Norman who declared that he could forget her as easily as some glove. Yet there had been a proven need for the gauntlet. Aislinn calmed now, thinking of that. A small smile touched her lips and a new confidence took root. Even if he did return with some trollop to fill his bed, would he forget her so easily? Did she haunt his memory as he did hers? He had enjoyed her well that last night together. Even in her inexperience, she knew this, so she must lay upon his visions of her as a woman to bring him back unfettered.

She turned down the lane that led to an empty cottage, made vacant by the deaths of a father and son who had fought with Erland against Ragnor and lost life in that battle. But Maida cringed away as Aislinn took her arm to lead her into the hut.

"Ghosts! I am afraid of ghosts!" she cried. "What will they do to me, alone and with no one to stand fast for me? They will take me away and harm me! I know it!"

"Nay." Aislinn soothed her mother's fears. "There were none but friends who lived here. They would not return to do Erland's widow ill."

"You think not?" Maida whined. With a sudden child-like trust she followed Aislinn nearer the cottage. The dismal dwelling stood separate from the rest of the town near a small scraggly copse of which in turn bordered on the marsh. Aislinn pushed the rickety door ajar and half choked on the dusty, fetid smell of the place.

"See, mother." She gestured within. " 'Tis of sturdy frame and needs only a clever hand to set it aright and make it a good home."

The interior was gloomy and Aislinn sought hard to quell her own doubts and keep her manner light and cheerful. The two small windows had thin oiled skins stretched over them which let in much less light than cold wintery wind and every footfall brought dust from the dry dirt floor thinly scattered with rushes. A crude hearth commanded one wall and a sturdy oaken bedframe covered with a limp rotting mattress was against the other. A single rough hewn chair stood beside a slab table near the fireplace and here Maida sank in dejected despair and began a low moaning song as she rocked back and forth on that simple seat.

Aislinn felt the same anxiety she knew her mother harbored. Wearily she moved to stand by the door and leaned her shoulder against the frame as she stared out into the dreary day. She knew what a battle it would be to confront Gwyneth and demand that her mother be reinstated in the chamber Wulfgar had allowed her. It was as if Gwyneth were possessed by some demon that spurred her on with sharp rowels of vanity and jealousy and would not let her rest or find pleasure in simple kindness.

Aislinn heaved a sigh and shaking her head, pushed back her long sleeves, seeing that she must do the work of making this filthy hovel a fit place to dwell. She found a flint and steel on a narrow shelf above the fireplace and soon had flickering flames to chase the gloom and chill from the room. She snatched filthy linens from wooden pegs where they had last been thrown by the unfortunate men and fed rotting shreds of old wool and leather gar-

191

ments to the greedily dancing fire where they were rapidly consumed along no doubt with a multitude of vermin. She wrinkled her nose in distaste at the foul odor of the mattress as she tore it from the wood framed cot. In the span of weeks food had dried to a rock hard consistency in the bottom of wooden bowls where it had been left when the warning of the Norman's approach was sounded from the tower. As Aislinn scraped the leavings she thought of Gerford and his son. When most families ate their meat from boats of stale bread, those two had been talented enough to fashion themselves utensils from hard wood. The absence of their handiwork would be sorely felt at Darkenwald, for they had lent their ingenuity to making tools, tableware and other useful objects. Now her mother would enjoy this small luxury, even if she didn't have the other comforts she was accustomed to.

All the while Aislinn labored Maida sat crooning her wordless song and rocking gently to and fro. She seemed oblivious to everything around her. Even when the door swung open, giving Aislinn a start, she did not move from her chair. Kerwick and Ham filled the portal, their arms burdened with blankets and furs.

"We thought she might find use for these," Kerwick said. "We took them from her chamber when Gwyneth bade us clean the place for her own use. If your mother is to be called thief, so must we."

Aislinn beckoned them in and closed the door. "Aye, we will all be called thieves, for I will not see her cold and hungry."

Kerwick glanced around at the humble interior. "Thomas makes tents and pallets for the Normans now. I'll see if he has some mats to spare."

"Would you ask him to come and put new hinges upon this door, too?" Aislinn asked. "I fear that panel would not keep out the humblest of beasts."

Kerwick peered at her. "Would you make your bed here with your mother?" Worry set upon his mind. " 'Twould not be wise, Aislinn. There is more to fear from lowly characters like Ragnor and those other Normans than any dumb beast. The men would do no harm to your mother, for they fear her mad, but you—"

Aislinn turned to watch Ham spread fresh rushes upon the dirt floor. "Doubtless you do not know Sweyn makes his pallet before my door at night. Like his lord he has little trust for women. He would not let me come here."

Kerwick sighed in relief. "'Tis well. I could not rest knowing you here, and Wulfgar would hang me from the highest tree as a warning to other men if I tried to give you protection, for he would surely think the worst."

"Yea," Aislinn murmured. "He expects betrayal from women."

Kerwick's blue eyes held her for a moment then he gave a wretched sigh. "I must go before word spreads to the Viking that I am here. I would not have Wulfgar unduly distressed at this simple meeting."

The two left again and Aislinn once more labored to create some homeliness in the hut that might dispell her mother's fears. It was midafternoon when Thomas came laughing into the cottage to deposit before her a neat mattress of heavy linen. She took it up to place it where the old one had lain and raised her eyebrows at the first scent of dried clover and meadow grass.

"Aye, milady," the former vassal chuckled. "I stopped by the barn for the filling and some Norman nag will go hungry tonight."

Aislinn giggled in delight and together they placed the pallet on the bed where she covered it with furs and blankets until a snug warm bed was made for her mother. Thomas stayed long enough to repair the door, replacing the large patches of oiled leather that served as hinges and taking care that it closed snugly on its frame and could be well barred from within.

Darkness was swiftly closing on the land when Aislinn gave her approval to the now comfortable appointments of the cottage. Her mother had eaten and was asleep on the bed when Aislinn left her and returned to the hall to seek food for herself. Her hunger was great, for her only nourishment that day had been the bread she had nibbled at morning.

Ham was cleaning partridges Sweyn had killed that afternoon and as she entered, the boy jumped up from his chore. Gwyneth sat leisurely before the hearth with her needlework and Bolsgar idly whittled on a short branch.

"Milady," the boy smiled. "I saved you food. I'll get it."

Gwyneth glanced up from her tapestry. "Latecomers must bide their hunger to the next meal." Her imperious voice rang clear as she set another stitch. "Promptness is a rewarding virtue, Aislinn. You would do well to learn it."

Aislinn turned her back and spoke directly to Ham, disregarding Gwyneth. "My hunger bites me deep, Ham, and I would dine. Bring the food."

With a nod and a smile Ham scurried to do her will, and Aislinn strode to her usual place at the lord's table and met Gwyneth's eyes with calm repose.

Gwyneth's mouth curled into a sneer. "You are not my brother's wife. Though you may have gained some confidence in being his whore, you are no more than slave here, so give yourself no airs that you are anything more."

Ham nudged Aislinn's arm before she could make a reply and she turned her attention to him. He placed before her food enough to satisfy two appetites. Aislinn did not question his loyalty to her, knowing his act might well bring Gwyneth's malicious attention upon him. She smiled her gratitude and accepted the food.

"Strange that so many Saxon women fell prey to the Normans while you did not, Gwyneth," Aislinn said as if half musing, and her eyes slowly swept the other's thin frame from top to toe and then back again. "But then again perhaps not so strange."

Aislinn turned her full attention to the food, dismissing offhandedly the now enraged woman. A chuckle rose from Bolsgar's chair, and Gwyneth flew to her feet. Seething with rage she spat the words at her father's back.

"Of course, you'd side with these Saxon swine against your own kin. The Duke William should throw you all in the gutters where you belong."

In frustrated fury she fled up the stairs and loudly slammed the door to her newly acquired quarters, the comfortable chamber that Maida had vacated that morning.

The nights grew long and what day remained dawned cold and wintery. Naked trees thrust aching branches into the cold air and sighed in painful agony when the north wind swept the moor. When the winds died fog climbed from the marsh to engulf the town while thin ice ringed the pools. Misty rains turned more and more to tiny wet flakes of snow, which settled on the ground and changed the village paths into ankle deep mires of freezing mud. Furs of bear, wolf, and fox covered the unchanging woolen garments of the people. The hall reeked of freshly slain game and the tannery cast its stench to the winds as more pelts were demanded. Aislinn assured herself that Maida was comfortable in the small hut. She had sent extra furs and Kerwick fetched wood daily for the hearth. It became part of the everyday ritual for Aislinn to visit her mother and see to her welfare, and on her return through the town tend the ills of her people. In spite of her daughter's attention, Maida became more withdrawn and remote and her appearance degenerated into that of a crone. Aislinn began to hear stories of how Maida's singsong voice could be heard late at night chanting to the spirits, sometimes talking as if long-dead companions of her youth answered her or even as if her husband were with her and shared the cottage. Gwyneth abetted every story she heard and when she saw Maida and thought Aislinn out of hearing dropped sly hints about the haunting of the place. She passed every tale to Maida but twisted the words to make it seem as if the townspeople were malicious and hated the old woman. Maida sank even deeper into depression and Aislinn found her mother less and less capable of coping with reality. The old woman turned her confused interests to making mysterious potions she declared would drive the Normans from English soil. Aislinn found it useless to argue with her or try to make her see the futility of her efforts.

It was a cold blustery day with churning gray clouds spitting alternate sheets of freezing rain and soggy snow into a fitful wind that set it rattling against the shutters or with stinging force against the face. Ham covered his reddened cheeks and turned his back to the blinding gusts, thankful for the good hunting season and the warm pelts it brought. These same were now wrapped snuggly about his arms and legs with pliant thongs of deerhide, and a large wolfskin sewn to a rough tunic held the meager warmth close to his body. Under the pelt Ham clutched the medicinal herb for which Aislinn had sent him to her mother's. Having made his way in haste, he paused now to catch his breath in the shelter of a cottage.

"Ho! You there! Ham!"

He turned at the sound of his name and saw Gwyneth wrapped in a long mantle, standing in the door of the hall.

"Come here! Quickly!" She gestured imperiously to him and immediately he made his way to her.

"Fetch me more wood for my chamber," she commanded when he stood at the foot of the steps before her.

"The fire grows low and this hellish rockpile has an unearthly chill about it."

"I beg pardon, my lady." Ham bobbed politely. "But I am set upon a task of some urgency by my mistress and must see it through. When it is done, I will fetch wood for the night for you."

Gwyneth's eyes grew cold, for she could see only insolence in his manner. "You surly clod," she sneered. "You prattle of some brainless errand while I am freezing! You will go now for it."

"But my lady Aislinn has bade me—"

"But your lady Aislinn," Gwyneth snapped in growing anger, "is nothing more than Lord Wulfgar's whore. As his sister I am mistress of this hall, and I command you fetch wood now!"

Ham's brow drew into a worried frown, but he still had no doubt as to where his duty lay. "My lady Aislinn waits," he returned stubbornly. "I will fetch you wood shortly."

"You sorry beggar." Gwyneth's voice came low and sneering with hate twisting each word. "I'll see your hide stripped from you inch by inch."

Two of Wulfgar's men had drawn near and Gwyneth sought to turn them to her purpose.

"Seize this whining oaf and strap him to the rack. I want him whipped till the bones show in his back."

Ham paled considerably at her words and the men seemed doubtful whether they should obey or not. They knew this woman as Wulfgar's sister, yet they were highly skeptical their lord would approve of such savage punishment for such a minor offense. They had served Wulfgar loyally, never denying his authority. They knew him a sensible and just man. Were they now expected to respect his sister's demands and do her bidding without question as they did his?

Their hesitation lent fury to Gwyneth's already soaring rage. Her thin arm and forefinger stabbed out to point at the distressed servant.

"In Wulfgar's name and as I am his only kin, you will obey me! Seize this one and fetch the heaviest whip."

The men were both well aware that Wulfgar usually reserved judgment for himself in matters involving the Saxons. He had no real title to the lands as yet and was in fact a caretaker, a war lord, thus the military route of accession would apply leaving Sweyn in authority in his absence, but as the Viking was not present neither of them could find the courage to gainsay Gwyneth or refuse her commands. Thus it was with great reluctance they came forward to obey her and took the lad in their grasp.

Aislinn lifted the small girl onto her lap and held the child upright against her own warmth. The tiny one's labored breath wheezed in and out in a deep rattling rail as she rested between fits of coughing. The camphor leaves Ham sought would brew into a thick pungent steam and placed beside the bed would ease the child's distress and bring her comfort. But where was Ham? Time had passed slowly and Aislinn could not help but wonder at his delay. She retraced the path in her mind and knew he had more than ample time to have gone the way and back. He had always been a good lad and quick to obey and now she grew worried at his continued absence. If he were dawdling needlessly somewhere when this babe struggled for every breath she took, Aislinn vowed silently she would personally drag him back by his ears.

The child's breathing eased somewhat, and Aislinn gave the frail form to the infant's mother and wrapped herself warmly for the journey without to see where Ham dallied. She closed the door behind her and braced herself against the chilling gusts, then raised her eyes to see the two Normans dragging a protesting Ham towards the whipping rack. It was only a moment later when the men found their way blocked by a small form with legs braced wide and arms akimbo. Long tresses were freed by the wind and flew like a fiery pennant from her head. Violet eyes blazed as the French words tumbled from her lips.

"What is the meaning of this?" Aislinn demanded. "What foolery have you Normans wrought that you must take this lad, bent upon my errand, and seek to scourge him upon yonder posts in the heart of this winter's gale?"

The foremost one made a weak answer. "The Lady Gwyneth gave the command as he would not do her bidding."

Aislinn's slim, booted foot stamped the freezing mud as she fought her rage. "Set him free, you nitwit!" she cried. "Set him free this moment or by Lord Wulfgar's steel I'll see you all in graves before this moon is out!"

"Hold!" Gwyneth's screech cut through the air. "You have no voice here, Aislinn."

The girl turned to face the approaching woman and waited until she halted before her. "So, Gwyneth." Aislinn's tone rang clear in the railing winds. "You have taken upon yourself the authority of Wulfgar. And do you seek to deprive him of one more useful serf?"

"Useful?" Gwyneth spat. "This sluggard deliberately disobeyed me."

"Strange," Aislinn returned, "I have no such problems with him. Mayhaps it be your manner that confuses him. He is unaccustomed to the chittering of a jackdaw."

Gwyneth choked in unrestrained fury. "Jackdaw! You bastard's whore! You flippant Saxon slut! How dare you question my manner? In Wulfgar's absence I am lady of this manor and no one shall question it."

"No one doubts what you would be, dear Gwyneth. Whether you are or not must be asked of Wulfgar."

"There is no need for asking!" The retort was ground out. "I am his sister and you are no kin of his."

Aislinn lifted her chin proudly. "Aye, no kin of his! Yet I know his reasonings beyond your ken. He brings justice swift and sure, not madness as you preach, for he knows the worth of treating his serfs kindly and with heart."

Gwyneth gave a derisive snort. "I find it indeed difficult to understand how in your rush to his bed you took time to know his very thoughts." Her eyes narrowed until they were but pale slits outlined with tawny lashes. "Or is it more that you feel you can bend his mind to your will?"

"If I could," Aislinn retorted, "then that man would deserve no better than to be so bent. But I doubt Wulfgar's mind so easily won."

"Bah! A harlot's sport to castrate a man to any but her own way and tie his gaze to her swinging hips that he should never know he is being led." Gwyneth fairly trembled with ire as her gaze swept Aislinn in rude appraisal. Her mind could not press down the memory of Wulfgar fondling this Saxon wench outside his bedchamber the morning he left or the tortured thought that Ragnor might have done the same. "Men! They will forever chase that plump harlot form that jiggles with each movement and ignore the trim and proper lady who feels it ill to display her sex so bluntly."

"Ho! What trim form do you boast?" Aislinn chuckled,

198

raising a winsome brow. "Why, a budding willow switch has that which you could envy."

"Harlot!" the other woman croaked. " 'Tis said that a woman's shape grows full and plump under a man's touch, and I see that you must have known many."

Aislinn shrugged. "If that were so, then you, dear Gwyneth, have known no other's touch since your mother's."

Gwyneth reddened profusely and could make no reply. "Enough! I grow tired of your endless bickering and I care not to dally in the cold." She turned to the two Normans who dared show no humor. "Take the serf hence and strip his back a while. We'll see if he doesn't mind a lady's words more meekly in the future."

"Nay!" Aislinn cried. She whirled to the Normans and in a cajoling manner pleaded. "A young child lies yonder seized in ague, and herbs are needed to ease her suffering." She turned a hand to Ham. "He bears no mark for sin, for he carries there the very leaves I bade him seek. Let the two of us see to this sick child first and when Wulfgar returns I shall place the matter before him and seek his justice whatever he will name."

Gwyneth saw the uncertainty in the men's faces and felt her issue failing. "Nay! 'Twould serve no end! Let his punishment be done now that he remembers and will serve the better for it."

Aislinn turned in frustration to the woman and flung her hands wide. "Would you place this matter above the life of a child? Will you see the child dead that this punishment be carried out."

"I care no whit for a Saxon brat," Gwyneth sneered. "Let the serf's insolent tongue be served its due and stay my will no further, slut. Yea, I bid you stay and watch his hiding that you would no more challenge my commands."

"You have no right to command here," Aislinn cried.

Gwyneth turned livid with unshackled fury. "You deny my rights, harlot, but as Wulfgar's only kin I am the one who must speak in his absence. And you are naught but serf here, his slave who has no choice but must bear his weight in bed at his whim. You say I have no say here? Well, 'tis you who are without rights and should taste the way of one who disobeys her betters." Her pale eyes glimmered with the thought of Aislinn's soft flesh stripped by scars from the whip. "Aye, you should also learn obedience." She thrust her arm toward the younger girl. "Seize her! Put her beside the stubborn chit!"

The French words were not lost upon the boy who had learned much of the Normans' ways since their coming. Ham struggled with the men violently.

"Nay! Leave her be!"

The men could only gape in mute astonishment at the infuriated woman. The whipping of a Saxon wench was nothing in itself, but when that wench belonged to Wulfgar, that made all the difference in the world. There would be severe repercussions over this deed and they themselves would not suffer lightly. Perhaps Wulfgar's sister was foolhardy, but they were of a different mood.

"Take her!" Gwyneth shrieked, unable to further tolerate their delay.

Ham broke from the men and fled as one Norman stepped forward, intending more to escort the girl from danger than to do her harm. The men laid a hand upon her shoulder, but Aislinn, mistaking his move, whirled from him in outrage, leaving her mantle in his grasp.

"Be careful of the garments, you dolt!" Gwyneth snapped, showing her greed. "And take the gunna from her. I have need of it."

"So, you have need of it?" Aislinn choked. With trembling fingers she snatched the gown from her body and before Gwyneth could stop her she flung it down in the mud at her feet and trampled upon it. She faced the woman, wearing nothing more than a thin kirtle in the biting wind yet she hardly noticed its icy chill with the furious storm raging within her. "Then, Gwyneth, you must take it as it is."

The woman's strident voice cut like a blade through the cold wind. "Begin the whipping and do not cease until fifty lashes have fallen upon her back." Then she sneered at Aislinn. "My brother will find precious little to entice him when he views your frame again."

But Gwyneth's bidding was not to be carried out by the men. The one dropped the whip and backed away, shaking his head, as his companion followed him.

"Nay, we will not do it. The Lady Aislinn has nursed our wounds and ills and we are not wont to repay that kindness in this manner."

"You spineless curs!" Gwyneth railed. She snatched up

the whip herself. "I'll show you how to mete out well earned discipline."

With all the fury bent of hatred burning deep within her, Gwyneth raised her arm, and the whip hissed like a serpent's tongue to bite through Aislinn's simple garment and taste the tender flesh of her hip. Aislinn writhed in silent agony and pulled away, tears of pain sparkling in her eyes.

"Cease!"

They turned abruptly and men and woman faced a raging Sweyn. Ham stood beside him and there was no doubt in any mind that he had fetched the huge Viking. But the heady knowledge of her power drove Gwyneth beyond caution and she whirled to Aislinn again, drawing the whip back for another blow, but as she brought it forward the butt was snatched from her hand. Gwyneth spun about in frustrated fury to find Sweyn's foot planted firmly upon the end of the whip and his brawny arms set akimbo to his large frame.

"I said cease!" he bellowed.

"Nay!" Gwyneth half sobbed, half shrieked. "The bitch needs be chastened here and now."

The Viking approached the thin woman until he stood tall above her and bent his head that he could meet her flashing pale eyes.

"Hear me well, Lady Gwyneth, for I fear your life may depend upon the care you give my words. My Lord Wulfgar gave this girl over to me to guard against harm in his absence, and that means from woman as well as man. She belongs to him by his word, and he will not tolerate your whipping of her. Unless he speaks otherwise the girl will have my protection, and thus far I have heard no order from him releasing me of my vow to keep her from danger. Wulfgar would not be above breaking you if he returned to find the wench maimed because of you. Therefore I am removing her to safety for your sake as well as hers. Peace be with you, Lady Gwyneth, but I must satisfy my lord's wishes before considering another's."

With that he brushed past her, giving her no further opportunity to speak, and went to Aislinn. Snatching her mantle from one of the Normans, he spread it about her shivering body. Aislinn's eyes were brimming with tears as she raised her gaze to his in mute gratitude. She put a

201

hand upon his arm and the great Viking made rumbling noises deep in his throat, embarrassed by this display of softness from a woman. Aislinn spoke no word but moved past him to take Ham's arm and steered the lad safely away from Gwyneth's glare back to the hut where the small girl still gasped for breath.

Aislinn huddled nearer the blazing fire on the hearth, drawing away from the chilled darkness of the hall. She thought upon the day as a hellish nightmare that she was at last waking from. She was thankful for the tiny girl's improvement. The fever had broken and in a few days the babe would be back to normal. But in those terrifying moments after the first cruel blow of the whip had struck, her mind had not lent itself to any thought other than that of Wulfgar meting out punishment on Kerwick's helpless form; then her mind had whirled in a vision and she had seen herself lashed to the beams waiting for Wulfgar to deal out his worst, his strong arm raised against her in hatred. A shiver passed through her now as she remembered that frightening apparition. She forced her attention to the task Ham and Kerwick were performing, braiding strips of hide into a bridle for one of the Normans. But she could not forget her own need, her own desire to be comforted and reassured in Wulfgar's strong arms. Never before in his absence had she longed so deeply to feel the touch of his hands or to have his lips upon hers and to know that she was something more than some wench he had toyed with for a time. If she closed her eyes now she could almost see him before her, his lips curved in a slow smile, his eyes soft and warm in the moments after their lovemaking.

Oh Lord, she was letting her feelings play havoc with her reason. There was no guarantee he would come back of the same mind as when he left. As Gwyneth had said, he might indeed return to Darkenwald with a wife and where would she be cast? To his men?

Aislinn shuddered as the icy tendrils of fear crept around her heart. He had declared his hatred of women in simple language. Would he seek to revenge himself upon her because she was of that same unpredictable gender? He might not care how much he hurt her. And what if she were with child? His hatred of her would only grow the more, for he could never know whether it was his own or Ragnor's.

Disparaging thoughts thrust upward to rob her of confidence, to steal away the deliciousness of that soft moment when they had clung together just before his departure and he had kissed her tenderly. She had been assured then that he cared, if only slightly. But had she been telling herself another lie? Were they all lies? His kisses? His fierce embraces? Lies to rob her of her sanity?

She rose from her needlework with a ragged, pensive sigh and stepped away, twisting her hands in mute frustration. What must she do? Should she go away that she might salvage what little pride she had left?

Kerwick glanced up from his labor and studied the slender figure now turned from him. Her fingers strummed across the strings of a crwth which had lain untouched since the Normans' coming. The strange chords of music broke the silence in the hall and echoed in the large room.

The scene seemed a re-enactment of another that he had been witness to many months ago when her father had announced his consent for their marriage. Kerwick had been overjoyed, more so than she, he knew, for when she grew troubled, her father had once told him, she always plucked idly upon the crwth as she had done that night long ago, making an odd melody that sounded eerie in the great hall. She had never learned to play the instrument, preferring instead to be played and sung to by some knight or troubadour. With a clear, lilting voice she could catch the gaiety of their song and enchant all those who listened. Yet it was a weird sound that came to his ears now, as if her soul was crying out for ease.

He rose to his feet and coming to stand at her side, reached his hand out to take hers in gentle understanding. Aislinn looked up through gathering tears into his compassionate gaze, her lips trembling slightly to show the uncertainty she felt and she heaved a sigh.

"Oh, Kerwick, I am so weary of this battle that rages between Gwyneth and me. What must I do? Relinquish my place as harlot to the lord and let Gwyneth have her way? If I were to leave, mayhap she would soften and show kindness toward the serfs."

"She would but do her worst having a free hand and with no one to call her game," he replied. "You are the only one in Wulfgar's absence who can lessen the tide of hate that flows from her. Her father sees little of her cruelty. Sweyn is too busy with the affairs of this hall and Wulfgar's men to notice the way she truly is. And I," he laughed. "I am but serf now."

"But what can I do to curb her?" Aislinn insisted. "I have no status. I am merely a plaything for a Norman."

Kerwick bent to her. "Wulfgar has given you his protection. She can do no harm to you. Wulfgar's men will know that after today. And Gwyneth knows it, too. You're safe from her hatred. Sweyn is proof of that. Would you leave the serfs to suffer from her whims when you are the only one who can help them?"

"You will not let me run from my obligations, will you, Kerwick?" she asked wryly.

"Nay, no more than you would me."

Aislinn laughed suddenly, her mood lightening. "Oh, Kerwick, how vengeful you are."

He smiled and spoke in sincerity though his tone was light. "Yea, to be a betrothed scorned does not make for a generous man."

Aislinn peered at him askance. "Your wounds have healed quickly, eh, Kerwick? I see no scars."

"What wounds you speak of, my lady? Those of my heart? Nay, I conceal them well, 'tis all, for they yet throb and pain me." He stared down into the violet depths of her eyes. "You are still beautiful, Aislinn, though you belong to another man."

Aislinn made to draw away, nervous at his words, but he tightened his grip on her hand.

"Nay, be not frightened, Aislinn. I meant no injury. 'Tis only that I seek to make amends."

"Amends?" she repeated.

"Aye. 'Twas well known I was bent upon my own selfish desires, for I wanted you badly and was not wont to give you up. For my outrageous demands upon you I can only beg in humble apology that you forgive me."

Aislinn rose up and pressed a kiss upon his cheek. "We are forever friends, dear Kerwick."

A short, satirical laugh broke them apart and they whirled to see Gwyneth leisurely descending the stairs, a smile playing about her lips. From her crouched position in a darkened corner, Maida rose and scurried out of the hall to brave the snowy winds, seeking the safety of her humble cottage well away from this half-Norman shrew.

Gwyneth paused at the foot of the stairs, her arms akimbo. A soft chuckle escaped her as she considered the two before her.

"My brother will be interested in hearing that his mistress amuses herself with other men in his absence." Her pale eyes brightened. "And he will surely hear of it, I swear."

Kerwick stood with clenched fists and for the first time in his life was greatly tempted to strike a woman. Aislinn smiled with a serenity she was far from feeling.

"I have no doubt you will tell him, Gwyneth, with your usual care for detail."

With that Aislinn passed the now silent Gwyneth and mounted the stairs to seek what comfort she could find in the bedchamber, knowing that she was not completely safe from Gwyneth's spiteful ways.

Wulfgar shifted in his saddle as his sharp eyes slowly scanned the countryside. Sharp, chill winds pressed the woolen mantle more closely against his sturdy frame and his cheeks tingled with its icy bite. Dreary skies lent no color to the wintery browns and grays of the forests and fields. Behind him the knights Gowain, Milbourne, and Beaufonte waited with the others under his command, sixteen men-at-arms ever ready with long bows, lances and short swords. In the protection of the trees the covered cart Gwyneth and Bolsgar had arrived with strained up the hill, loaded with food for his men and grain to supplement the forage obtained along the route. An old but sturdy Saxon, Bowein, who had returned from service to Harold to find his home burned and fields ravaged, had welcomed an offer of a new home for his allegiance and now swore at the horses in colorful language that was foreign but not totally unfamiliar to many of the Normans riding alongside.

Wulfgar's foresight provided a strong, yet mobile band. He had long studied the ways of an army and chose to mount all his men when it was the wont of most knights and noblemen to mount only themselves while the men-at-arms wielded bows and lighter swords and spears and acted as the footmen of the army. He had seen no future for his men to walk their feet raw on the stony soil of England. Those he took with him he set upon horses and they accompanied him so; they dismounted and acted as men-of-arms when battles raged.

In the span of weeks Wulfgar had been at Darkenwald, William had had to bide his time, waiting for the strength of his men to return. They had been unable to march for nearly a month due to a malady not unknown in armies, which in this case had spared not even William himself. It made them prone to stay in camp and near a deep trench. Since Wulfgar's band had not suffered this, he had been flung upon a wide patrol to see no Saxon armies gathered in the south or west. It had usually fallen his lot to ride far from the main body of the army to secure the smaller hamlets, villages, and towns that might gather against the Normans. He did this well and ranging far from the main body his men fared better; their food was of a higher quality and their horses foraged on sweeter turf.

His position now was well west of London in the heavily wooded hills near the turning point of his sweep. For the most part they had traveled unseen and made their presence as little felt as possible. All seemed quiet about them but as Wulfgar continued to scan the countryside a group of three knights appeared, riding across the hills. Turning, Wulfgar gestured to Milbourne and Gowain and bade the other men to wait yet keep their swords and longbows handy for he knew not what small force might lie and wait in the copse of trees. With these two knights he rode down from the hill toward the three in the vale. A shout brought their attention and as they turned and saw his group, the three couched their lances and displayed their shields, which named them English and thus foes of William. They ranged themselves wide to meet him. When Wulfgar was close enough that the others began to worry, he stopped and waited for a moment, giving them ample time to view his shields and arms.

"I am Wulfgar of William's men," he said in a commanding voice. "By your colors I see you are men of Rockwell. I must bid you yield, for we are set against him as he has not taken an oath for William."

The eldest knight of the three faced him squarely and met his challenge with words in kind. "I am Forsgell, and I do not abide this Norman Duke. I have sworn my lance and blade to a loyal Saxon lord and with God's help we will send invaders from our land. We will have no king but that which we abide."

"Then it is battle you have set us to," Wulfgar replied. He gestured toward his men waiting above. "They will take no part, for you are knights and sworn by the honor of the cross you wear."

With his words he whirled the Hun and rode back some paces. Now all gripped their lances tightly and with a shout spurred their horses forward, three against three. The Hun charged, his huge hooves thundering in the turf and his muscles pulsing with his effort. He knew the feel of battle as well as his master. Wulfgar grasped the heaving sides with his knees and leaned into the lance. The elder knight took him full on and the two met with a thundering crash. The first pass was harmless and the horses whirled and set toward each other again as if of one mind. This time the greater weight of Wulfgar made itself felt, for his lance took the shield of the knight and smashed it against his shoulder before his own could touch the Norman. The Saxon's lance was hurled aside and his shield was swept from him but he held his place in the saddle. His left arm was numb but the horse still answered to his knees. Wulfgar stood away and gave him pause. The man gallantly drew the heavy sword with his good right hand and spurred his horse forward again. Throwing his own lance and shield aside, Wulfgar drew the long, bright blade that had so often held his honor, and without touching the Hun the horse leapt forward. The blades met and rang and now the difference told for the steed upon which he sat held Wulfgar always face on to the other, never being turned, always thrusting forward, pressing his powerful chest against the lesser horse until it stumbled and clawed to keep its footing. Wulfgar's sword rang upon the other knight's armor and blade. A blow to the head and now blood trickled slowly from beneath the helm of the Saxon and his arm grew heavy and weary. He shook his head and tried to lift his other arm but it still hung numb against his side. Now it was all he could do to present his blade to Wulfgar and still the great steed pressed and the shining blade sang ever harder, ever heavier against his defense. Wulfgar seized his sword in both hands and with his war cry ringing loud, he brought it down from above in full force. It shattered the other's blade and sank into his shoulder. The man could no longer lift either arm and could only sit helplessly. Wulfgar drew the Hun back and the man said no word but simply nodded his head. He yielded the day and Wulfgar's battle was won. He turned to the other forays and they too were quickly solved. Now three knights were taken, stripped of their arms and shields, no longer bound of oath but prisoners to be sent back to William for whatever disposal he might seek of them.

Thus it was that William was able to march unhindered and without word of his advance proceeding him. Many castles and strongholds awoke on a morning to find that without warning they had been surrounded. The sight of this vast army covering the hills around them and waiting the signal to attack rapidly brought out bargainers to seek the most favorable terms.

Wulfgar continued to ride. The skies turned gray and heavy and soon the clouds were obscured by a drizzle that sent icy runnels down his neck and chausses. The saddles became wet and it took constant attention to remain well seated. Still, if it brought discomfort the rain also served them in their efforts, for it dampened the high spirits and did not urge his men to sing or shout or even speak. They rode in silence and were doubly alert, for they knew they could be easily surprised from the murk that surrounded them.

Wulfgar stopped and raised his hand. Ahead of them came the sound of angry cursing. At his signal the men-at-arms dismounted and giving their horses to the pages, quietly strung their bows with hardened willow shafts. The bows, strings, and arrows were well oiled and protected by quiver caps of oiled leather, for Wulfgar was well aware of the dampness that comes with winter on these islands.

His knights couched lances and moved slowly forward ahead of their supporting footmen. A small stream crossed the path at a low spot and would normally have given no more than a wetting of hooves to travelers, but now it made a mire several yards across and in its middle sat a four-wheeled wagon bearing four children and two women. Two men and a strapping youth strained at the muddy wheels while the elder of the women urged a pair of tired punches to greater effort. A man with his left arm gone, pulled back and cursed until his eyes fell on the four knights with their lances pointing at him. His sudden silence drew the attention of the others and gasps of surprise reached Wulfgar's ears. He urged the Hun forward and considered the situation for a moment before signaling

209

for his men to relax. There was no threat in these sodden serfs.

Wulfgar came forward until his lance almost touched the chest of the older man. "I bid you yield, for the day is miserable and not fit for dying."

He spoke casually but the tone of his voice carried more menace than his words. The one-armed man gaped and nodded, though his eyes never left the point of the lance. There was a scurry of sound from the wagon and the well-trained destrier turned of his own to meet this possible threat. A small boy struggled to lift a huge broadsword as long as he was tall.

"I'll fight you, Norman," the lad sobbed as he struggled. His dark eyes brimmed with tears. "I'll fight you."

"Miles!" gasped the younger woman as she jumped down from the cart. She caught the boy and sought to quiet him but he pulled away and stood bravely facing Wulfgar in the pouring rain.

"You killed my father," he boldly stated. "But I'm not afraid to fight you."

The tall knight looked into the boy's eyes, finding some of the fiery courage of his own youth there. Wulfgar swept his lance to the vertical, spreading its banner with his coat of arms upon it and smiled tolerantly.

"I have no doubt you would, lad. England and William will have good need of spirit such as yours, but at the moment I am heavily engaged on the Duke's business, so am not free to duel."

The woman who held the boy seemed to relax and her gaze bespoke gratitude as she stared up at the Norman knight.

Wulfgar turned to the men and demanded, "Who are you and where are you bound?"

The elder one stepped forward. "I am Gavin, the smith. I was an archer and went to fight with Harold in the North against the Norwegians and there lost my arm." He turned and gestured to the woman in the cart. "That one is my wife, Miderd, and this other is my widowed sister, Haylan." He dropped his hand upon the shoulder of the youth beside her. "This one who spoke to you is Haylan's son, Miles. The other children are mine and the man is my brother, Sanhurst. We are bound to find a new home for ourselves since the Normans have taken ours."

As the man spoke Wulfgar noticed the pallor of his face

and a reddish tinge where the empty sleeve was knotted. His gaze shifted to the younger man who was short of stature but brawny of frame.

"The town of Darkenwald—," Wulfgar said, considering the two. "Do you know of it?"

"The name is familiar, milord," the younger man replied cautiously.

"Yea, 'tis known," Gavin interrupted. "The old lord who lives there once passed through our burh. Contrary he was. He would have me shoe a horse he purchased for his daughter and would not brook delay since he wished to present it to her on the same day, to celebrate Michaelmas. He boasted that she could ride as well as any man, and she would have had to, milord, for the Barb he purchased was a spirited one."

Wulfgar's brow lowered at the memory of Gwyneth's accusations echoed the man's words. "Aye, the mare was spirited as is the wench, but 'tis no matter now. If you are of a mind, you may make your home at Darkenwald. There is need of a smith."

Gavin peered up at him as the misty rain fell against his face. "You send me to a Saxon shire?"

"The old man is no more," Wulfgar answered. "I hold the town for William until that time England is his, then the fief shall be mine." He gestured to Sanhurst. "He will go with me and his duty will be to guard my back. If he does that well, I will return to see your family settled."

The Saxons exchanged questioning glances among themselves before Gavin stepped forward. "Begging pardon, milord, but we are not looking to serve Normans. We would find a place yet where we can know our own."

Wulfgar shifted in his saddle and peered at them. "Do you think you will go far when Normans range the countryside?" He looked into the faces of each and saw the uncertainty in them. "I will give you my banner. None of William's men will harm you if they are shown this." He gestured to Gavin's arm. "There is also one at Darkenwald who will see to your wound. She is the old lord's daughter and wise in the ways of healing. It remains your choice, whether you go or try to find your way to some other town that is still English held, yet I warn you. Every town will be taken, for William is rightful heir to the throne and is determined to have it."

Gavin stepped back to Sanhurst and they spoke quietly

between them for several moments before the younger nodded and approached Wulfgar. He halted before the huge steed and squinted upward as the rain trickled down his face.

"They will go to Darkenwald, my lord, and I with you."

" 'Tis well," Wulfgar replied.

He wheeled the Hun about to where Bowein waited in the cart just behind the archers. With a quick word to the old Saxon, he received a rope from beneath the seat. This he carried back to the wagon where he looped the strand double about a ring set in front bringing the other end around to the high back of his saddle. Urging the Hun forward to the limit of the rope he gestured to the woman who sat holding the reins. She shouted and slapped them and the smaller horses strained once more against their harnesses. Wulfgar's stallion seemed to know what was required and casting a wary eye backward, took up the slack and leaned his bulk plus several hundred pounds of armor and rider against the cable. His monstrous hooves churned mud and appeared to sink low, but then surged forward in a series of short, powerful lunges. The wagon creaked and with a sucking sound the wheels began to turn, slowly at first, but picking up speed until the vehicle fairly raced up the farther bank. The men of the family slogged through the mud and gave Wulfgar their thanks while the rest of his force joined him. Bowein waited until all were clear, then charged into the muck full apace and with a large destrier pulling the lighter cart came through without a pause.

The delay brought evening upon them and Bowein spoke of a heavy woods nearby that lay in the bend of the river. Wulfgar led his men to that place, bringing his new charges with him, and camp was soon made. Darkness fell and the rain pattered ceaselessly on. Cold winds moaned through the tops of the trees, sending the last few stubborn leaves swirling down through the barren branches. Wulfgar saw misery in the shivering of the children huddled about the fire and hunger in their thin pinched faces as they gnawed the soggy crusts of bread the older woman carefully measured out. He remembered his own distress as a child on being sent from home and the confusion he felt, sitting across a campfire from Sweyn, realizing he could never again return to that place of happy memories where he had known the love of a father who was suddenly not his father at all.

Turning, he bade Bowein bring out a large leg of boar and slice it for the Saxon family and to give them bread more palatable than what they had. Wulfgar knew a warmth in his breast as he watched the bright eyes of the children when they dined on what must have been for them the richest meal in weeks. Thoughtfully he strolled away from them, crossing to the campfire and took a seat beneath a tree. He ignored the coldness of the damp earth and leaning his head back against the trunk, closed his eyes.

In his mind there slowly bloomed a face in the midst of curling red-gold tresses, the violet eyes dark in passion and half closed, the soft, warm lips parted and reaching for his own. His eyes flew open and he stared for a long time into the glowing embers of the fire, reluctant to close them again.

Wulfgar lifted his gaze from the flames and watched Haylan as she approached. Feeling his eyes on her, the woman smiled uncertainly in return and clutched her mantle more tightly about her shoulders against the chill of the evening. Casually Wulfgar wondered how it would be to lead this wench into the density of the forest and spread his cloak for her. She was comely, with dark, curling hair and eyes as black as soot. He might then be able to strike Aislinn from his mind. But much to his own surprise, he found the prospect only mildly interesting. He grew perturbed, for that copper-headed vixen he had left at Darkenwald roused him more in her absence than did this woman here before him or, for that matter, any other he had come across in his wanderings. If she were here, he thought he might be tempted to set her back upon her heels with the rage he felt at the moment. He wanted to make her cry, to suffer for the torment she caused him.

Aaah, women! They knew well how to torture a man, and she was no different, except she knew better than most how to make a man want her. That last night together was branded upon his memory with a sharpness and clarity that made him at times almost think he could feel her against him and smell the soft fragrance of her hair. She had yielded to him with a purpose and now when he was away from her he could see what end she had been about. He wanted to curse her, to call her the bitch she was, yet

213

at the same time he longed to have her beside him that he might reach out and touch her when he cared to. Oh Lord, he hated women, and her he thought most of all because she had cast a spell upon him and now shadowed his every thought.

"You know the English tongue well, milord," Haylan ventured softly at his continued silence. "Had I not seen your banner I would have thought you one of us."

Wulfgar grunted in reply and gazed into the fire. For a moment all was still around the camp. Wulfgar's men sought their rest upon soggy pallets and damp grass and now and then a mumbled curse was heard in the darkness. The children had settled on the rough floor of their wagon and among the pelts and threadbare blankets now rested peacefully.

Haylan cleared her throat and tried again to break into Wulfgar's moodish musing. "I wish to thank you for your kindness to my son. Miles is as headstrong as his father was."

"A brave lad," Wulfgar returned absently. "As your husband must have been."

"Warring was a game to my husband," Haylan murmured.

Wulfgar looked at her sharply and wondered if he had detected a note of bitterness in her tone. Haylan met his gaze.

"May I sit, milord?" she asked.

At his nod she took a place closer to the fire.

"I knew this time would come for me when I would be widowed," she said quietly. "I loved my husband even though he was the choice of my father and I had no say in our marriage. Yet he lived too fiercely and was careless with his life. If not the Normans, someone else would have dealt the blow. Now I am left to fare upon my own or upon my family." Her glance drew Wulfgar's. "I am not angry with his memory, milord, only reconciled to his passing."

Wulfgar sat silent in reply and she smiled, turning her head to the side that she could study him more closely.

"Strange, but you do not act like a Norman either, milord."

Wulfgar raised a brow at her. "And how do you visualize Normans, madam?"

"I certainly did not expect kindness from them," she explained.

He laughed shortly in response. "I assure you, madam, I have no forked tail, and horns have not yet grown upon my head. Indeed if you will look closely you will see that we resemble normal men although some tales about would have us more hellish than good reality abides."

Haylan blushed and stuttered in apologetic tones. "I meant no slander, milord. Indeed we owe you thanks for your assistance and the good provender was most welcomed. 'Tis many months since I last tasted good meat and knew a full belly. Even a fire we have been reluctant to set, afraid it would draw raiders."

She stretched her hands toward the heat, taking comfort in its warmth. Wulfgar watched this movement and thought of Aislinn's slender fingers against his chest and the excitement they stirred by their simple touch. Angry with himself for letting his thoughts revert to her, he wondered why his mind should dwell on that vixen when this comely wench here might not object too strenuously to warming his pallet. When he chose to be charming and persuasive, some of the haughtiest and most reluctant damsels had come into his arms sighing and submitting, and this Haylan did not seem overly arrogant. Indeed the way she kept watching him she might welcome his advances, being a young widow and, as she said, reconciled to her husband's passing. Her words had almost held an invitation for him to take her. Yet as he gazed at her ample bosom and generous hips, he realized his fancy was toward a trimmer figure. It rather amazed him that he should find Haylan lacking when several months ago he would have thought her worth his most zealous attention. Had Aislinn's uncommon beauty spoiled his desire for other women? At the thought he nearly cursed aloud. He'd be damned before he would play the game of some besotted bridegroom cleaving only to his wife. He'd lay any wench of his choosing.

With that he rose abruptly, startling Haylan, and caught her hand, dragging her to her feet. Her dark eyes were wide as they stared at him in stunned surprise but he inclined his head toward the woods, answering her silently. She resisted his pull with some doubt in her mind, knowing yet not knowing what he intended, but upon entering the darkness of the forest she threw aside her reservations and fled at his side with an abandon that matched his. They found a vine-shrouded oak where the hanging stems formed an arched haven and dry leaves beckoned. He spread his cloak and turning pulled her in his arms to kiss her once, twice, thrice. He held her tightly against him, his arms crushing her while his hands roamed her back. His fierce ardor warmed her and she began to respond with like passion, slipping her arms about his neck and rising on her toes to mold her body against his. They sank together until they rested side by side on the mantle. Haylan was no stranger to the thrusts of a man's body and knew his mood. Throwing aside her own cloak, she tightened her thighs against his and slid her fingers beneath his chainse to caress the hard-muscled chest. With eager fingers Wulfgar loosened the string that held her peasant blouse at the top, freeing her breasts. Haylan's breath caught in her throat as he buried his face between the soft mounds and she clasped him fiercely to her, arching her back against him. But in the heat of the moment Wulfgar forgot himself.

"Aislinn. Aislinn," he muttered hoarsely.

There was a sudden stiffening in the body beneath him and Haylan drew back.

"What did you say?"

Wulfgar stared down at her, realizing the words he had spoken, and against her thigh Haylan felt his desire ebb. His eagerness fled and he rolled off her groaning, with the heels of his hands pressed against his eyes.

"Oh, bitch," he moaned. "You haunt me even on another's loins."

"What say you?" Haylan snapped, sitting up. "Bitch? Bitch, am I? Well and good, then let your prithy Aislinn ease your manhood. Bitch is it! Ohhh!"

She rose in a fury and straightening her clothes left him to whatever thoughts stirred in his addled brain. Wulfgar heard her footsteps stamping back to the camp and in the darkness blushed at his own inadequacy. He felt like some untouched lad after failing with his first woman. He drew his knee up and rested an arm upon it staring unseeing into the night. For a long time he sat in his brideless bower and mused on the follies of love-smitten men. Yet he made no admissions even to himself and finally rationalized his reaction as being due to the easy, tranquil life of Darkenwald.

"I've grown soft," he muttered as he snatched up his cloak and brushed the leaves from it.

Still, as he slowly made his way back to the fire, reddish gold hair seemed to brush the back of his mind and the smell of it came from the forest around him. As he lay beneath the cart and pulled his mantle over him he curled his arm as if a head rested on his shoulder and lay half on his side as if a soft, warm body leaned against him. He closed his eyes and against his will his last waking thought was of violet eyes staring into his.

Beneath their wagon Haylan stirred fitfully upon the pallet she shared with Miderd, casting a glance toward the motionless black form under the other cart.

"What ails you, Haylan?" Miderd demanded. "Are there lumps beneath the pallet that you must toss upon it like that? Be still or you will waken the men."

"Aaah, men!" Haylan groaned. "They all sleep soundly, every last one."

"What are you talking about? Of course they do. Gavin and Sanhurst have been so for hours. Truly it must be the middle of the night. What plagues you?"

"Miderd?" Haylan began then could not find appropriate words to pose a question. She sighed in frustration and finally spoke after a long pause. "Why are men like they are? Are they never content with one woman?"

Miderd rolled on her back and stared up in the dim light of the campfire toward the bottom of their cart. "Some men are content when they can find the right woman. Others go on ever searching for the thrill of the moment."

"Which manner of man do you think Wulfgar?" Haylan asked softly.

Miderd shrugged her shoulders. "A Norman like any other, but one we must be loyal to lest we find ourselves at the mercy of some wayward rogue."

"Do you think him handsome?"

"Haylan, are you daft? We are but peasants and he our lord."

"Which is he, knave or good knight?"

Miderd sighed. "How can you expect me to know a man's mind?"

"You are wise, Miderd. Would he likely beat a peasant if that one angered him?"

"Why? Have you done so?"

The younger woman swallowed hard. "I hope not."

She turned on her side, dismissing Miderd's questioning gaze and after a long time she finally found the sleep she sought.

The first light of dawn touched upon teardrops of rain still clinging to bare branches, setting them asparkle like precious stones in the morning mist and reflected off the wetness of moss covered rocks. Wulfgar roused from sleep to the hearty aroma of boar's meat and brewis. Glancing about the camp he found the women already astir and in the process of preparing a meal for them. He rose from beneath the cart and stretched, taking pleasure in the quietness of the morning hour. Haylan had been eyeing him uncertainly as he slept, wondering how she might fare when he woke, but he seemed generally to have dismissed her from his mind as he stripped down to his chausses and began to wash. As she bent over the warming meat she eyed him obliquely. She could not help but admire his tall, broad-shouldered physique and remembered with clarity the firmness of his rugged body against her own.

Wulfgar had donned his garments and mail hauberk and coif when he came forward with Gowain and Milbourne to sample the food. As she served him, Haylan's fingers trembled and her cheeks reddened at the thought of their lusty embrace of the night before, but he spoke with Milbourne and chuckled at a jest of Sir Gowain's and seemed indeed to have forgotten their tryst in the woods.

It was a few moments later when the eldest knight came around to take another piece of meat and Haylan posed a question to him.

"Sir Norman, who is Aislinn?"

Milbourne started in surprise and glanced hurriedly toward Wulfgar then stuttered. "Why she—ahem—she is Lady of Darkenwald."

He quickly left her as Haylan stood silent, venturing no more inquiries. She was lost in contemplation when Sir Gowain interrupted her thoughts and smiled warmly at her.

"Madame, soldiers oft miss the many comforts of a woman. 'Tis a pleasure to break the fast on these delicious tidbits and gaze at you over them."

Haylan's brows drew together in painful thought. "Sir knight, who is Wulfgar? What is he to Darkenwald?"

Gowain's enthusiasm receded rapidly at her obvious dismissal of his words. "Wulfgar, madam, is Lord of Darkenwald."

"That's what I feared," she breathed in a strained whisper.

Gowain peered at her in some confusion but without further word he strode away, feeling sorely set aback by her interest in another man.

The third knight, Beaufonte, approached her, having just risen, and waited patiently before she finally noticed him and dished up some of the brewis. She looked at him and gingerly queried:

"Sir knight, we do go to Darkenwald, don't we?"

"Aye, madam, to Darkenwald."

Haylan swallowed hard and wondered how she could face Wulfgar's lady and what her chastisement would be if the Lady Aislinn caught wind of her and her husband's escapade in the woods.

For the rest of the time until they decamped Haylan stayed well away from Wulfgar, not knowing if she feared him or his lady more. If he were her own husband, she would be mightily angry if she learned he had rolled in the grass with some wench, no matter what the outcome.

Before they left, Wulfgar sought out Miderd and rather stolidly handed her a bundle carefully wrapped in a tanned skin.

"Give this to my lady——" He cleared his throat sharply. "Give this to Aislinn of Darkenwald when you find a private moment with her. Tell her—tell her it was honestly purchased."

"Aye, milord," Miderd replied. "I shall see that no harm comes to it."

He nodded yet made no move to leave. Instead he seemed quite at a loss.

"Is there something more you wish, milord?" she ventured, bemused at this tall Norman's hesitation.

"Aye," he sighed. "Say also——" He paused, finding the words difficult. "Say also that I bid her well and that I hope she is trusting Sweyn to see to her needs."

"I will guard the words well, milord," she said.

He whirled and with a quick command to his men, swung into the saddle and guided his horse from the glade trailing out his band behind him. Sitting on the seat of the cart, Haylan watched Miderd as she tucked the bundle away in the back.

"What have you there?" she asked. "Did he give you some reward?"

"Nay. I only carry this to Darkenwald for him."

"Did—did he say ought of me?"

Miderd shook her head slowly as she considered the younger woman. "Nay. Why should he?"

"I—I thought he might. He seemed ill-disposed when I left him."

"He was not so now." Miderd stared up at her sister-in-law and her brows drew together. "Why are you beset about him?"

"Beset?" Haylan laughed weakly. "There is no cause."

"What happened last eventide when all of us were abed and you were not? Did he make love to you?"

Haylan jumped and cried indignantly, "Indeed he did not. 'Tis truth. Nothing happened."

Miderd studied her flushed face suspiciously, then shrugged. " 'Tis your life. Lead it as you must. You have never heeded my advice, nor do I foresee you doing so. But I would guess by my lord's manner that his interest lies elsewhere."

"As you said, Miderd, 'tis my life," Haylan replied testily and turned to help the children into the cart.

The approach of Normans on horseback was heralded
from the uppermost perch of Darkenwald's tower as the
last cock's crow died. Aislinn hurried to dress, hoping that
a messenger had finally come from Wulfgar. Her hopes
vanished quickly when she descended the stairs and found
Ragnor de Marte warming himself before the hearth.
Vachel and two other Normans stood with him but at a
word from Ragnor made haste to remove themselves from
the hall. Ragnor had flung aside his red woolen mantle
and the heavy mail and stood now in a soft leather tunic
and woolen chausses, but he had strapped the broadsword
again to his side.

He turned to gaze at Aislinn and a slow smile widened
his lips, making her aware of her loose flowing hair, forgotten in the rush, and her bare feet, now shrinking from the
cold stone of the stair. She crossed to the hearth, driven
there by the aching chill that possessed the place. The
dogs strained at their leashes and whined and yelped to be
free. She came closer and before she glanced Ragnor's
way, released each one and let them out of the hall. Finally she took a seat before the fire and faced the Norman, more than alive to the fact that they were alone in
the hall. Sweyn and Bolsgar had gone hunting and
Gwyneth had not risen as yet. Even the serfs had found
duties more pressing elsewhere, remembering too well the

slaughter of their families and friends by this Norman's hand.

Aislinn spoke softly. "Are there no wars to fight, Sir Ragnor, or is that why you return? I suppose this place is a safer haven than William's camp. I assume the Duke is well recovered from the malady that beset him?"

Ragnor's dark eyes swept her boldly before coming to rest on the small, slender bare feet almost concealed by the edge of her gunna. He smiled and knelt before her, taking one icy foot in his hands and rubbed it briskly. In distress Aislinn sought to pull away from him, but he was most intent on performing this service for her.

"Your tongue grows sharp, my dove. Has Wulfgar made you hate all men?"

"Aaah, you shrinking knave," she retorted. "What do you know of men?"

His fingers encircled her ankle and tightened a small degree, and Aislinn remembered the pain she had suffered at his hands.

" 'Tis plain to see, my lady, that you know nothing of them. To choose the bastard over me; 'twas folly most rare for any damsel."

She kicked his hand away, unable to bear his touch for a moment longer and jumped to her feet.

"I have not seen the folly of it yet, Sir Ragnor. Nor do I trust I ever will. Wulfgar is lord of this hall and I am his. It seems that I chose rightly, for what do you have but the horse that bears you away from battle?"

He rose to his full height and reached out to run his fingers through her bright hair. "Would that I could stay and show you how you erred, Aislinn." He shrugged and stepped away. "But I stop only for a few hours to rest. I'm on my way to William's ship with letters bound for the home country."

"It must be urgent for you to dally so," Aislinn sniped.

" 'Tis urgent enough that I must hurry once ahorse, but I was wont to see this fair hall again." He grinned at her. "And you, my dove."

"And now you have. Do I delay you? Some food mayhap to eat along the way. What would hasten you upon your way?"

"Nothing, my dove." He laid his hand over his heart. "For I would court death itself to tarry at your side."

A door slammed and Ragnor moved away from Aislinn

as the sound of Gwyneth's footfalls came from above. It was as if he played a game and dared Aislinn to betray him, but as long as it took his attention away from herself she was more than happy to allow his infidelity.

Gwyneth came to the top of the stairs and Aislinn bit her bottom lip. The gown the other wore was the tawny gold one, Aislinn's favorite and the last of any worth that remained in her coffer. Gwyneth made free with her clothes and only returned them when they were singed, torn or stained. Then Aislinn would find them on her bed, discarded. But as the woman came down the stairs, Aislinn had to suppress a smile. Gwyneth's small bosom seemed almost childishly flat in the garment and the bones of her narrow hips stuck out unflatteringly beneath the soft fabric. She eyed them suspiciously before turning her gaze upon Ragnor.

"I had begun to despair of seeing you again, sir knight," she said.

"Ah, damoiselle, your slim grace is ever poised at the edge of my thoughts," Ragnor assured her. "I would have you know I cannot pass a day without some memory of your fairness marking it."

"Your words melt in my heart like snowflakes upon the hearth, but I fear you lead me on," Gwyneth answered. "Is it not the way with men?"

"Nay, nay, sweet Gwyneth. I would not do so, though to say truth, 'tis more the bend of a soldier to forget the beauty at home for the one in his arms."

"How fickle men are!" A shallow smile curved her lips as she rested her eyes upon the young girl. "They forget their mistresses with such ease as to leave the damsel breathless. 'Tis ever found that the loyal wait is fruitless and 'tis far better to fly and save the pain fo being cast aside for another."

Aislinn straightened. "Your measure of men is by the shortest rod, Gwyneth. I prefer to use a longer one that I may know their fullest worth. Thus I pay little heed to the braggart's boast and more to what the true knight lays in deed."

Without further word or backward glance, Aislinn strode from them and mounted the stairs. Gwyneth watched her go and sneered at her back.

"If she thinks my brother will mend his ways and come flying back to her arms, she is a fool. Why should he sample only the first fallen fruit when the whole tree of England lies at his feet?"

Ragnor hid a smile and shrugged. " 'Tis not my way to understand women, only to love them." He caught Gwyneth's arm and spun her about into his embrace. "Come, wench, and let me feel your softness against me."

Angrily she pummeled his chest with her fists. "Let me go!"

Immediately he did as she commanded and so abrupt was his release of her that she stumbled back in surprise and almost fell.

"You didn't tell me you bedded that Saxon whore!" she cried, nearly choking on the tears that threatened to come. "You laid with that trollop and played me false!"

Ragnor smiled confidently and took a seat before her. "I had no cause to think it any concern of yours."

Gwyneth flew to him and knelt before his chair, catching his brown hand between both of hers. She searched his eyes, her own showing despair.

"No concern of mine? You surely jest. We are lovers, thereby we must share each other and what we do." Her nails dug into his arm in her desperation. "I will not follow second to that slut."

Ragnor thrust her hand away unkindly. "Unfortunately, my dearest, you already have."

Fear cut like a sword through her heart and she clung to his knees as she felt her panic rise. "Oh, my love, you wound me deeply."

"I will not be dictated to," he stated coldly. "I will not be led about like an ox with a yoke upon my neck. If you love me you will not try to harness me in such a manner. I cannot breathe with you stifling me."

In her misery, Gwyneth began to weep. "I hate her," she moaned, rocking back and forth. "I hate her almost as much as I love you."

A smile twisted Ragnor's lips and he cupped her chin in his palm, lifting her face to his as he bent to kiss her. " 'Twas merely a thing born from the heat of battle," he murmured huskily against her lips. "It was not an act of love as ours was."

His mouth pressed upon hers, gently at first, then as he felt her response he became more demanding, pulling her up against him until she lay across his lap. His free hand moved to cup her breast and as he touched the smoothness of her gunna he remembered where he had first seen it. Aislinn had worn it the night before he left, when she had entertained Wulfgar with such zealous attention and he her.

"Come to my chamber," Gwyneth pleaded. "I will be waiting for you."

She slid from his lap and hastened across the hall to the stairs, glancing back at him with a beckoning smile. When she moved out of sight, Ragnor finally rose and leisurely poured himself a horn of ale. Thoughtfully he gazed upward toward the lord's chamber and began to mount the stairs slowly. For a long moment he stood before the heavy door to that room, the only barrier between him and the woman he truly desired. Without even testing it he knew it was barred against him. She was careful that way, careful that she would not lose her precarious perch as Wulfgar's favorite, and it was precarious because no one ever knew what Wulfgar thought or felt in his bastard heart. She was enticing and beguiling yet distant as the very moon. He remembered too well the sight of her in Wulfgar's bed, soft, warm, free in her manner with the bastard. But Wulfgar had Darkenwald or soon would have it, and she had told him herself that was all she wanted. Whatever man possessed this hall and town would possess her.

He bowed before the door. "Soon, my dove. Be patient."

His tread fell noiselessly against the floor as he made his way to Gwyneth's chamber. When he pushed open the door, he found her reclining on the bed, her pale body looking sleek and graceful without the hindrance of clothing. Her small bosom was pushed upward by her arms as she hugged herself tightly, making her breasts appear fuller and more tempting. Ragnor smiled and closed the door carefully behind him. He discarded his garments and crossed to her, taking her in his arms as he laid down beside her. Her hands upon him were insistent and low moans crept from her throat as he caressed her. Her mouth closed hungrily upon his as her passion mounted and her arms tightened with a quick urgency that drew him down to her.

The wind whistled through the barren trees and rattled the shutters, setting them astir. Gwyneth huddled deeper beneath the pelts, silently watching Ragnor as he once again donned his clothes. She raised on an arm as he reached to open the door.

"My love?"

He paused at the sound of her voice and turned to gaze at her.

"The hour is still early," she murmured. "Stay a while and take your rest with me."

"Rest?" he questioned in mockery and he laughed softly. "Another time, Gwyneth. Now I must be about the Duke's business."

Without another word he left her, pulling the door closed softly behind him. He glanced toward the lord's chamber door and found it open. When he drew closer he saw the room empty and going to the top of the stairs he found the hall likewise. Mild disappointment stirred that he would not have an opportunity to see Aislinn again before he left. He descended the stairs and crossed to the great door, swinging it wide. The day was bright and sunny with a cool, crisp breeze blowing. As he stepped from the portal into the sunlight he stretched, spreading his arms wide, basking in the warmth. A movement from the corner of his eye caught his attention and he turned to see a quick flash of reddish gold hair as a ray of light penetrated the forest. Vachel and his other men dozed beside the horses, so his departure could easily bear a slight delay. He smiled ruefully as he remembered another day before this portal and the night that followed. He had, of course, imbibed to no small degree and could easily understand that he had done nothing to impress Aislinn favorably. He had been rough with her. Yet shown tenderness, she might now come to him willingly.

He set out after her, but admitted to himself a moment of puzzlement why he should even make the effort. Although he had not matched Wulfgar's conquest here, he had never found the companionship of a woman difficult to obtain. Aislinn's loyalty to Wulfgar was difficult to understand. Surely she must know that he would soon leave her, as he had much higher ladies of the Norman court. All he need do himself was wait and Aislinn would be his. So why was he following her now when he had more pressing duties? But her face loomed upward in his imagination and he knew the reason and hastened his step. He entered the woods and found a narrow trail whereon could be distinguished the light print of a small foot and hence he had no difficulty in marking her passage.

Aislinn had fled the hall, feeling Ragnor's presence and not wishing to meet him again. Pain from Gwyneth's sharp tongue penetrated deep and Ragnor only abetted that one's wit. Her only memories of him were associated with loss and agony. She well remembered the night with the rope around her neck and his drunken pawing. Worse yet the memory of her father lying cold and still was torn afresh each time she faced Ragnor.

Pausing by the brook, Aislinn stared pensively into its dark, chuckling waters as she leaned against an ancient oak that grew on the bank. Lost in her thoughts, she bent and picked up a small stone, turning it over and over in her hand. She tossed it at a persistent spot of light then watched the ripples spread until they touched the bank at her feet.

"Would you frighten the fish from a meager winter's meal, my dove?"

The words brought Aislinn around with a shriek. Ragnor smiled and moved to stand a pace before her. To ease her trembling knees Aislinn leaned back against the tree and watched him cautiously.

"I was strolling in the woods enjoying the quiet and I saw you pass this way. 'Tis not wise to be alone and out of sight of the hall. There are those who would—" He paused and saw her uncertainty and leaned against the tree himself, grinning down at her. "Ah, but of course, my dove. I've frightened you. Forgive me, fair one. I was only bent to your welfare and meant you no harm."

Aislinn lifted her chin proudly and stilled the quivering that possessed her. "I fear no man, sir knight," she said and wondered if she lied.

Ragnor laughed. "Ah, dove. Wulfgar has not tamed you yet. I was afraid he might cool that hot blood."

He straightened and stepped past her to the edge of the bank, squatting down as if to ponder some great unspoken cause. He peered at her over his shoulder.

"I know that in your eyes I've played the knave and have done you pain and oft labored hardship to your door. But in the one, Aislinn, I was a soldier and laid my sword where duty called and in the other—" He sent a pebble to follow hers. "Call me a moonstruck lad. Say that I am caught up or enchanted with your beauty, the

227

better of which I've never seen." He rose and turned to face her. "Must I bare my very soul, Aislinn, to be the knight to win your favor? Have I not the smallest chance?"

Aislinn shook her head in confusion. "Ragnor, you bemuse me much. Have I ever given cause to you to seek my hand? And why should you desire it? Little have I to offer you, save that I am Wulfgar's. He is my lord and master and as his mistress, I have sworn to him my loyalty. Is this what you seek truly, that I should betray him?"

His hand reached out and lifted a coppery tress from her breast. "Can I not desire you for yourself, Aislinn? Are you so distrusting that you will not believe a simple truth? You are more beautiful than words allow and I want you. I wanted you when you were mine and now that you are not, I wish you back."

"I am Wulfgar's," she said low.

"You say nothing of your heart, Aislinn, where it lies. Honor is good and I applaud it, but your affection is what I seek." His dark eyes held hers. "Aislinn, would that I could draw back the sword that slew your father and let him rejoice in life again as we. I would give my family's fortune to bring it thus, for you." He shrugged his broad shoulders. "But alas, my fair Aislinn, 'tis done and naught can bring it back. Yet I appeal to your kindness to forgive me. Give me your love and ease the pain in my heart."

"I cannot," she breathed. She glanced down at his lean, brown hand near her breast and closed her eyes tightly. "Whenever I look at you, I remember the misery you brought, not only to myself but to others. No cleansing can wash the blood I see upon your hands."

" 'Tis a soldier's way and Wulfgar is no less guilty. Have you thought of the Saxons he has slain? Fate was unkind to let it be your father my sword felled."

His gaze tasted the beauty of her delicate features, the fragile eyelids lowered now and fringed thickly with black. Her fair skin shone of vibrant youth with the slight blush of pink at her cheeks and the full bloom of that hue upon her soft lips. His chest ached with the turmoil she awoke in him. If she could only realize how she tortured him, she'd allow him to ease his sufferings.

Aislinn raised her eyes to his and murmured low, "Who knows my heart in truth, save God, Sir Ragnor, yet I

228

would say it cannot soften here lest some great miracle transpired to win it anew. Wulfgar has claimed me and I am his. My affections would sooner fall to him—"

Ragnor's face darkened and he gritted his teeth. "You speak that whelp's name. What is he that I am not? A bastard, nameless, wandering about battlefields hither and yon, fighting another's war for a clutch of gold, nothing more. I am this while he is not. A knight of a well-born family often privy to the Duke. I could take you to court and lead you there upon my hand."

Ragnor raised his hand as if offering it to her, but Aislinn shook her head and stepped away, presenting her back to him.

"I cannot. If Wulfgar cared for me naught but a whit, I am his chattel and must do his bidding. He would never let me fly." Turning back, she relaxed against the tree again and smiled as she reached out a finger to gently touch his outstretched hand. "But take heart, Ragnor, the Lady Gwyneth finds you most handsome and would no doubt gladly do thy will should you but speak the word."

"You mock me," Ragnor groaned. "A scrawny hen beside the whitest dove! Surely you mock me." He seized her hand before she could withdraw and the mere touch of her sent the blood pounding in his head. "Aislinn, have mercy. Do not let me faint so for want of you. Do not torment me so." He remembered the soft, white swell of her breasts and his gaze grew warm as he yearned to view them again. "Give me one soft word, Aislinn. Let me know that I can hope."

"Nay, I cannot," she gasped, twisting her hand to draw it from his grasp and failing. Panic began to rise in her. She saw his eyes and where they wandered and needed no seer to guess his intent. He began to draw her closer to him and though she fought his strength she came ever nearer. "Nay, I beg of you. Do not!"

His hand grasped her elbow and he sought to place a kiss upon her neck as his free arm slid behind her narrow waist.

"My dove, don't fight me. I am mad for you," he murmured against her ear.

"Nay!" She twisted away. Her hand found the hilt of the small dagger and snatched it from its sheath and held it threateningly before her. "Nay, not again, Ragnor! Never!"

Ragnor laughed. "Ha, the wench has spirit yet."

His long fingers reached out quickly, seizing her hand and squeezed it cruelly until she cried out and the blade dropped. He caught his hand in her hair and twisting her arm behind her, drew her to him until he could feel her soft breasts against his chest and her thighs pressed hard to his.

"I'll sample this bird again," he chuckled and kissed her, bruising her lips in his fierce passion.

With a strength born of desperation Aislinn flung herself away, falling back against the oak. She faced him, her bosom heaving with her fear and anger, and he stepped toward her with an easy laugh. There was a whisper of sound and with a solid thunk a great war ax seemed to sprout from the trunk less than a hand's breadth from Ragnor's face. He turned with a jerk and a coldness gripped his belly as he saw Sweyn standing some ten paces from them. The Viking stood with bow unstrung and slung across his back and at his feet a quarry of doves and a brace of hare lay. Aislinn darted toward Sweyn and the safety he offered but for the first time Ragnor saw that the Viking now stood unarmed, his bow useless for the moment and the ax embedded in the tree. His sword flashed from its scabbard as he leapt to halt Aislinn's flight. She gave a shriek as he came at her and stepped away from his outstretched hand. She spun behind the huge Norseman and in the flash of a moment Sweyn had retrieved the ax by the leather thong tied about its handle and braced himself for attack. The great war ax was balanced and ready on his shoulder, its spike and finely honed edge gleaming dully as it caught the light of the sun. It seemed to be a mute harbinger of death.

Ragnor skidded to a halt several paces from Sweyn, his face contorted with rage at being so thwarted at his game. He meant to strike with his broadsword and hew the man down where he stood, so violent was his anger and frustration, but something in the Viking's pose brought a memory to mind of a day when the soldiers were in the thick of battle and an enemy threatened Wulfgar's back. The sickening sight of that ax burying itself deep in that foe's head remained ever with him as a warning. Anger fled from him and he knew full well the cold, close breath of death upon him. He calmed himself, and sheathing his sword, carefully spread his hands from his sides that the

230

Viking should not mistake his moves. They stood so, facing each other for a long moment. A rumble rose in the Norseman's chest and a slow smile twisted his lips and brightened his blue eyes.

"Take heed, Norman," he said softly. "My Lord Wulfgar bade me guard this woman and I guard well. Should I split a Frenchy pate or two in the course, 'twould not grieve me greatly."

Ragnor chose his words, but spoke with venom in each syllable. "Heed yourself, you white-haired heathen. This matter will be finished someday hence and fate willing, I will yet bloody my sword between your maiden-fair locks."

"Aye, Ragnor." The Viking's grin spread wider. "My back lies fair to thy will but this friend," he hefted the ax lightly, "sees quite well to my other sides and loves to kiss those who would test their steel upon my skull. Would you care to meet her?" he asked, presenting the edge of the huge blade. "Mademoiselle Death."

Aislinn stepped from behind Sweyn and laid her hand upon his mighty arm as she looked coldly at the Norman. "Seek your pleasures from some other source, Ragnor. Begone with you and let the matter rest."

"I go, but I'll be back," Ragnor warned.

With that he turned on his heels and left them. When Aislinn returned to the hall a few moments later, she found Gwyneth nervously pacing the hall. One look at the woman's face told her that something displeased her. She turned on Aislinn with a feral gleam in her pale eyes.

"What happened with you and Ragnor?" she demanded. "I would know now, you Saxon slut!"

Anger brightened Aislinn's violet eyes but she only shrugged and replied, "Nothing that would interest you, Gwyneth."

"He came from the woods where you were. Did you throw yourself upon him again?"

"Again?" Aislinn said, raising a brow at the woman. "You are surely daft if you think I would ever make the slightest advance toward that knave."

"He made love to you before!" Gwyneth choked, rage and jealousy cutting into her as if they were rough cords lashed about her. "You are not content to have my brother hanging to your skirt. You must have every man you meet panting after you."

231

Aislinn spoked slowly in barely controlled wrath. "Ragnor never made love to me in the way you seem to think he did. He raped me brutally and there is a difference. He murdered my father and reduced my mother to what she is now. In all of your imagination, Gwyneth, how can you think that I could ever desire him?"

"He has more to offer than my brother. He is gentle born and has a family of importance."

Aislinn laughed distainfully. "I care for neither. Your brother is more a man than Ragnor could ever hope to be. If it is in your heart to have him, however, seek him with my good blessings. You deserve each other."

With that Aislinn swept around, leaving Gwyneth raging furiously and mounted the stairs to her chamber.

Although he had spared his cousin, Ragnor had mercilessly booted the archers awake, and now the group thundered across the low rolling hills toward the coast road that led to Hastings. Ragnor took the lead as the pace slowed and even Vachel lagged back with the men to avoid his obviously sour temper. Questioning glances were exchanged and answered with empty shrugs as none could name the cause of his ire. As the miles were worn away his mood grew blacker and occasional curses drifted back to the men behind. Ragnor's lack of sleep did nothing to soften his failure to win over Aislinn and his thoughts raged on. Wulfgar must have rewarded her handsomely for her favor, for of a surety that baseborn knight had no social graces. He had never partaken of the refined banter that took place during lighter moments at the genteel court. If it was true what Vachel said of Wulfgar; he had found the most highborn ladies worth but a brief play, discarding them when they had filled his temporary need. Yet he must have chosen well, for Ragnor knew of none that sought to avenge her rejection.

Bah! What hold the bastard had upon his women! Ragnor snarled at the thought. If Wulfgar would only fail in a foray and Aislinn be brought to see her folly, he might still salvage an estate from this war. Schemes flew through his head and were rejected apace as he could foresee their failure.

Vachel heard sighs of relief when the fortifications of Hastings came into view and the masts of the ships could be seen in the harbor beyond. A good night's sleep was on the minds of all and once the letters were delivered a bellyful of meat and a good draught of ale would hasten it to hand.

Ragnor turned to face the man who hailed him from afar and recognized the awkward gait of his uncle, Cedric de Marte, as the man crossed the sandy beach toward him.

"Ho, Ragnor, finally I have caught you. What are you, in a daze? Did you not hear me calling before?"

Cedric's reddened face and his puffing breath bespoke his exertion.

"I have matters on my mind," Ragnor replied.

"So Vachel has said," Cedric said. "But he would not speak of what."

"They are of a private nature," Ragnor retorted.

"Private?" Cedric's dark eyes pierced his nephew's scowl. "What is so private that it keeps you from gaining lands from William?"

Ragnor sneered. "So Vachel told you that, too."

"He was reluctant to spill the news, but he managed finally to be truthful. He is too loyal to you, Ragnor. You will lead him astray."

Ragnor laughed but without humor. "He has wits of his own. He can leave my side whenever he desires."

"He chooses not, but it does not make it right the paths where you lead him. His welfare is mine since his father died."

"What plagues you, uncle? Is it the women he beds or the bastards he collects?"

Cedric raised a grayed brow. "Your father is hardly delighted with your scatterings of seed."

Ragnor grunted. "They grow more numerous in his head."

"You young lads have much to learn of honor," Cedric said. "In my youth if I dared touch a maiden's hand I was sorely chastened. Now you think nothing of crawling between their thighs. What is it, a woman that besets you?"

Ragnor turned away sharply. "When have I ever worried over a woman?"

"That time comes in every man's life."

"It has yet to come in mine," Ragnor gritted.

"What of this girl Vachel speaks of, this Aislinn?"

The younger man's eyes burned with wrath as he bent

233

his gaze upon the uncle. "She is nothing. A Saxon wench, that is all."

His temper soaring also, Cedric jabbed his finger against his nephew's chest. "Now let me warn you, you carefree swain, you are not here to add more wenches to your conquests but to gain lands and reward to extend the family's holdings. Forget the bitch and concentrate on what we outfitted you for."

Ragnor thrust his hand away. "Your similarity to my father increases with each day's passing, Cedric," he sneered. "But you needn't fear. I'll yet have all that is due me."

The sun was rising over France as the four urged their mounts up the steep roads away from Hastings. Ragnor rode again in the van, his mood little improved from the day before. His rancor made him kick his steed into a lope, and the animal, being well rested and fed, ground the miles beneath his drumming hooves. This time they took the inland road to avoid the chance that a band of raiders might lurk along the route, awaiting their return.

They passed the day in silence, riding hard, and set a meager camp to meet their needs throughout the night. The weather was mild and they rested well and were up again at dawn and on their way. The sun had mounted high above and thrust bright fingers through a thickening layer of clouds when they topped a rise and saw far out before them a goodly band of riders. They quickly took to shadow and waited for some hint of the arms this band displayed. They watched as the men before them drew together in conference then after a while divided in three. Now a shaft of sunlight crept across the group and there before them Ragnor saw the colors he knew were Wulfgar's. The other three beside him would have made themselves known but Ragnor halted them. A plan took form in his mind. He bade the two archers ride on to William with news of his coming and of the letters he bore, saying also that he and Vachel had paused to bring word of Wulfgar. When they had gone Ragnor turned to his cousin and spoke with a smile on his lips.

"Let us see if we cannot assure that yonder soldier has a busy afternoon."

Vachel returned a puzzled frown to Ragnor's words and to his relief the knight continued.

234

"There is a Saxon shire just ahead as yet unbowed and still leaning toward an English king." He laughed. "I know they will not cherish a Norman knight, for when last I passed the place they chased me far afield." He paused pointing toward the men below where two of the divisions rode off to either side and the third, headed by Wulfgar's banner, dallied along. "See there," he bade his cousin. "As I know Wulfgar he sends the others out in force to block the roads beyond the town then he will approach and demand its surrender. If the English flee they will be trapped in the open. If they attack Wulfgar they will be struck from behind by the others."

Now he grinned at Vachel like a great gray fox teaching his cub the hunt.

"But let us change the plan. If we approach the town within its sight and seem to dally along we may draw out some stout-hearted folk eager to gain themselves a bounty of two Norman knights. Then we would lead them into Wulfgar's band before he clears the glade."

Ragnor laughed in glee at the thought of Wulfgar's scheme gone awry, but Vachel seemed in doubt.

"My hatred of the English overrides the contempt I feel for the bastard," Vachel returned. "I would not see our own misused by these Saxons."

"It can do no harm." Ragnor shrugged. "Wulfgar will surely slay the fools. 'Twill only teach him what it means to be attacked by these Saxon swine and how easy it is to kill them. Let him meet the scythe and staff and set his blade to their stubborn skulls, then he may know that we did but defend ourselves at Darkenwald and acted in the best manner there."

Vachel finally ceded to the prank and the two made haste to ride around Wulfgar. As Ragnor planned, when they came close and seemed to watch upon the town, some score came out with spear and staff and bow and seeing the Normans' retreat, pursued them across the open fields. Ragnor and Vachel seemed to wander as if unsure of the way to flee, leading the townfolk on until they drew them along the road into the heavy forest beyond the fields. Once there they rode swiftly ahead, leaving a trail for the pursuit to follow. On rounding a bend, they left the path and posted to a nearby hill to watch what followed. They saw the townfolk round the bend and pause to listen. Hearing Wulfgar's approach, the English took to the brush and trees that grew close beside the way.

Ragnor gazed ponderingly toward the road and spoke as if he now doubted his own wisdom with this game.

"It seems this goes astray, Vachel. They set a trap for Wulfgar, but I am torn. I fear for the safety of our own two yeomen. Will you ride to them, Vachel, and guard them on their way while I go to Wulfgar and warn him of the trap?"

Vachel shrugged away his reluctance to see a few Normans slain by Saxon hand and leaned forward in his saddle peering toward the bend in the road.

"Will you, cousin? That would seem foolish to me." He turned to face Ragnor and they both chuckled in mutual glee. "Let me bide here until they have taken Wulfgar from his saddle, then I will leave to do your bidding."

Ragnor nodded and they moved to a deeper glade to watch the unfolding scene below.

Wulfgar's small force rode along the path that wound its way through the trees, drawing them nearer to Kevonshire. Gowain and Beaufonte had been sent on ahead to take their positions around the town, and Sir Milbourne rode at Wulfgar's flank with the three yeomen following. As usual, Sanhurst brought up the rear, keeping his distance from Wulfgar. He seemed to hold the Norman in fearsome awe and was reluctant to come within a staff's length of him, though he had been supplied with short sword and spear to guard the knight's back.

They crossed a small glade and re-entered the deep shade, watchful yet relaxed as they rode. A doe fled their path and quails leapt from the wayside with a flutter of wings. The Hun seemed to grow nervous and pranced and worried at his bit, yet Wulfgar thought the horse only sensed the excitement of the coming fray. Then, approaching a curve in the path, the beast snorted and skidded to a halt. Wulfgar knew the manner and stood in the saddle clawing for his sword as he shouted a warning to those behind him. In the next instant the road was filled with shouting Saxons swinging whatever weapon they could bring to bear. The Hun's hooves lashed out and Wulfgar struck with his sword before a blow from behind stretched him out across the neck of his steed. He knew he was falling. His sword slipped from his fingers. The world turned

236

gray and it seemed with a feather soft bump he hit the ground. The gray world darkened until only a single point of light was left, then it too went out.

It was some time later when Wulfgar peered upward and realized that the achingly bright ray that pierced his brain was only a patch of blue sky with black pine branches etched garishly across it. Painfully he raised himself on an elbow and gazed about. His head throbbed and he saw his helmet laying beside him and frowned at the dent across the back. As he raised a hand to cautiously feel the lump on his pate he saw a stout staff of English oak nearby with the heavier end shattered from its length and knew the cause of his acute discomfort. About the road lay scattered the bodies of several townspeople and he spied the leather jerkins of three of his men but of Milbourne he could see no sign.

"Have no fear, Wulfgar. I suspect you'll yet live this day out."

The voice came from behind him and though he recognized it in an instant, he rolled heavily over and rested on his elbows as he fought to steady his reeling head and focus his gaze upon Ragnor, who half-reclined on a fallen log with a bloodied sword thrust into the dirt beside him. He laughed in silent glee at Wulfgar's efforts and wondered at Aislinn's thoughts if she could but see the brave bastard now.

" 'Tis a poor place to take repose, Wulfgar," he grinned and swept his hand indicating the littered lane, "here in the midst of the road where many would do you ill. Indeed, within the last hour I have set to flight a band of hearty Saxons who'd have taken your ears to prove their fortune at finding a Norman resting so."

Wulfgar shook his head to clear his befuddled brain and half moaned. "Of all those I would have named to save my life, Ragnor, I doubted mightily it would be you."

Ragnor shrugged. "I but lent an extra arm. Milbourne was quite sorely pressed, yet when I came the Saxons took flight thinking I was no doubt one of many coming."

"And Milbourne?" Wulfgar questioned.

"He has gone to fetch your men with that peasant you set to guard you. It seemed the Saxon could not reach you in time, at least that is what he said."

Wulfgar rose to one knee and still smarting from the blow, rested there for the world to right itself. He squint-

237

ed painfully at the other man, considering this action he had not expected. "I have bought you shame yet you won the day and saved my life. Some poor bargain, I trow, Ragnor."

"Alas, Wulfgar." Ragnor waved a hand, brushing off the proffered apology. "In truth both Milbourne and myself thought you dead until we dragged the English away and perceived your breath still stirred the dust." He smiled slowly. "Can you rise?"

"Yea," Wulfgar muttered and stood belatedly wiping at the sweaty grime that covered his face.

Ragnor laughed again. "English oak has done for you what well-honed steel could not. Ho, to see you fallen to a peasant's staff. 'Twas worth the battle."

The dark knight also rose and taking up his blade wiped it clean on a peasant's cloak then pointed to the roadside. "Your horse stands yonder at the brook."

Ragnor watched the other go and his face grew dark as he looked at his blade. He had been too hasty to kill the Saxon swine. "Ah," he murmured to himself, "to ponder on opportunities lost to fate."

He slammed the sword into its scabbard and turned to mount his own steed. Wulfgar came again to the road leading the Hun and bent to see that he bore no lasting harm from the pitchfork's welts.

"I bear letters to William from Hastings and I soon must fly," Ragnor said, his voice emotionless and flat. "Pardon that I do not stay and see you well."

Wulfgar retrieved his helm and swung into the Hun's high saddle. He returned the dark knight's gaze and wondered if Ragnor also thought of another whose healing hands were much more agreeable.

"I, too, must ride on soon but for now yonder burh has earned its right to burn. As soon as it warms the evening air I shall move my men to the next crossroads and there make camp. I bid you thanks, Ragnor." He drew his sword and saluted him with it, then leaning over flipped his lance up to where he could seize it. He shook the dirt from his pennant. "My men come yonder and I would join them."

He saluted Ragnor again with the lance and under the lightest touch of spurs the Hun spun on his heels and charged away. Ragnor watched Wulfgar's back until it

238

disappeared, then reined his horse about in disgust and went his way.

Wulfgar rode to meet his men and saw that only part of them returned with Milbourne. The knight raised his hand and drew up as his captain neared.

"Are you well, Sir Wulfgar," he questioned and at his leader's nod he continued with his report. "When the townsmen quit our play, they carried back word of a great Norman force approaching and set the whole town to its heels. They gathered possessions and fled. But Sir Gowain and his men held the road some furlongs away and have turned them back. If we hasten we may halt them yet in the field beyond."

Wulfgar gave his curt assent and then turned to Sanhurst who lagged back in some shame. He frowned at the young man. "Since you are no benefit guarding my back, stay and bury the dead. When you are done, join us ahead and then you may serve as my lackey." He raised a brow. "Let us hope you meet more success with that."

Wulfgar raised his arm and his force set off to do their labors. He led the way with Milbourne keeping pace at his side. The dented helm would no longer fit comfortably upon his bruised head and as Wulfgar hoped to avoid a pitched battle, he rode with it set before him over the high pommel of his saddle and shrugged away Milbourne's worry. They rode apace through the village square and as they passed the last cottage saw before them some two score and more Saxons of an assorted age, sex and kin. The townfolk saw the force before them and knew of more behind. Then, with fatalistic courage, they formed a tightknit group straddling the road. Mothers pressed their children to the center giving them what protection their own bodies would offer while the men seized whatever weapon was at hand and set themselves in an outer circle for one last battle.

Wulfgar dropped his lance to the ready but halted short of the people while his men circled until they formed a ring all with points lowered and ready to charge. The cold wind blew and the doomed Saxons waited. A long moment passed in silence then Wulfgar raised his helm to full view and his voice rang out harshly as he noted a rustle of amazement at his English words.

"Who plied his staff so strongly against my brow?" He waited until the sheriff moved to face him.

239

"He fell beside you in the wood," the man replied. "And for all I know still abides there."

" 'Tis a pity," Wulfgar half sighed. "He was a stout soldier and worth more than a sudden death."

The sheriff shuffled his feet nervously in the dust but ventured no further comment. Wulfgar raised his lance and set the helm to its place before him but the other lances stayed down, ever threatening.

The Hun pranced, nervous with the tension and Wulfgar spoke a calming word to him and surveyed the huddled mass on the road with steel cold eyes. When his voice sounded again it crackled with authority and none listening could question it.

"You are wards of William, by right of arms, King of England, whether you admit it or not. You may waste your blood here in the dust if you like or you may spend your strength rebuilding your town."

At these words the sheriff raised his brow and cast an inquiring glance at the still-intact buildings of the shire.

"The choice is simple and will be quickly levied," Wulfgar continued. "Of that you have my word. But I must urge haste as my men grow anxious and would see their labor done."

He withdrew a pace and dipped his lance so the sheriff could almost see the point transfixing his own chest. Slowly the man let his sword fall to the ground and dropped his belted seax beside it, turning his hands palm upward and open to show his surrender. The other men followed his action and dropped pitchforks, axes, and scythes until they all stood disarmed.

Wulfgar nodded to his men and the lances rose as one. He spoke once more to the townspeople.

"You have chosen the possessions to take with you. I hope you have chosen well, for these are what I leave you with. Sir Gowain." He turned to that young knight. "Take your men and move these people to yonder field and hold them there." He raised his arm. "The rest of you, follow me."

Reining the Hun about, he set the great horse flying toward the town. There in the square he gave further orders to Milbourne.

"Search each house and bring out what gold and silver or other worth you may find there. Place them in the cart.

Bring also any ready foodstuffs and place them on the stoop of yonder church. As each house is done close the door and mark it. When the village is done, set a torch to every shelter, sparing naught but the church and the graineries."

Wulfgar then turned and rode to a knoll where he could watch both the people and the town. As the sun sank lower and the shadows lengthened it seemed as if the town with its black stark windows stared aghast as the soldiers ran like ants upon its face taking its wealth, gathering its food. A moment of stillness and the dark eyes reddened as a first flicker of flames began to grow; then a thick red tongue lapped hungrily up a gabled eave. The churning clouds above took on hues of red and orange from the flames and as he lifted his eyes Wulfgar felt the first cold chill of snow upon his cheeks.

The townspeople realized the fruit of the Norman labor and a low moan came to Wulfgar as their voices raised in anguished protest. Now his men withdrew from the town, hauling the creaking cart behind them and he descended from the hill in a rush of hooves, his mood blackened by what he had wrought. He came to a skidding halt before the Saxons and they cowered in fear before his towering rage.

"Watch!" he roared. "And know that justice is swift in William's land. But I bid you heed me. I will return again this way to see what you have done, thus I charge you build again and know as you labor that you build this time for William."

The snowflakes fell in earnest now and Wulfgar knew that he must hurry for there was still some way to go and a sheltered camp must be laid against the storm. He pointed his lance down the darkening road and the last of his men withdrew, falling in behind the heavily laden cart. Wulfgar bent his gaze a last time to the roaring flames eating at the village's walls and the growing column of smoke that flayed away as the wind whipped it in a great spiral. He shouted above the noise to the sheriff.

"You have shelter left and meager food and winter draws near." He laughed. "I vow you will have no time for battling other Normans."

He raised his lance in a last salute and kicked the Hun after his departing troops as the villagers watched them go. The people finally turned, their defeat written upon their faces, yet deep within each heart they knew what he had destroyed could be replaced. He had left them with life and with life they could build again.

The fresh coverlet of white crunched coldly beneath her feet as Aislinn made her way from her mother's cottage to the hall. Darkness had settled with an ear-nipping chill and errant flakes of snow swirled and danced through the few stray beams of light that crossed her path. She lifted her gaze to a featureless black sky that seemed to glower close above the rooftops and press her world to a narrow slice between it and the hard-frozen earth. Aislinn paused in her stride and let the stillness of the night ease her troubled spirit. After spending time with her mother she always felt drained of strength and somehow a little less capable of facing the plaguing doubts that seemed to belabor what confidence she could muster, until she swore another day would see her broken and begging for mercy. With each day's passing her mother slipped deeper into delusions that demanded revenge on the Normans. If Maida succeeded in her vengeance, William's justice would seek her swiftly. Aislinn knew of no potion that would help in drawing out the festering hatred that twisted her mother's reasoning. She felt deep frustration that she could be of benefit to others, curing their ailments and healing their wounds, yet could do nothing for her only kin.

An icy tingle of snowflakes upon Aislinn's face refreshed her, and with a quicker step she hurried to the hall. As she drew near, she noticed a cart drawn up before the doors. She casually mused on what poor soul was seeking shelter at Darkenwald this cold night and if he would find compassion in Gwyneth where others could not. That one's evil humor, crudely bent upon the hearty appetites of serf and soldier, was not warranted to stop there but quite often extended to the embarrassment of visitors and family alike. Gwyneth ridiculed her father and Sweyn behind their backs because they were prone to indulge themselves with meat and drink now and then, being of sturdy frame. Though in truth Bolsgar and Sweyn supplied the game that graced the tables and kept hunger well away from the manor's door. Even the kindly Friar Dunley found himself the recipient of malevolent thrusts of Gwyneth's aspish tongue when he came.

Thus conditioned to expect the worst from Gwyneth's irate disposition, Aislinn pushed open the door and set it closed again before glancing at the group before the hearth. With deliberate slowness she doffed her heavy woolen mantle and approached the warmth of the fire, looking first to Bolsgar to determine the temperament of his flaxen-haired daughter. When Gwyneth raged, Bolsgar frowned and grew tight-lipped. But for the moment he seemed relaxed and feeling some relief, Aislinn turned her attention to the three roughly dressed adults and the children who huddled near the blazing fire.

The youngest lad gaped in awe at the brilliant copper tresses that curled around her shoulders. His stare brought a smile to Aislinn's lips and his dark eyes twinkled back in immediate friendship. She was not met with amity when she faced the younger of the two women, however. Indeed the other seemed to regard her with great wariness and hung back from the group, eyeing her every move. Aislinn could not mistake the similarity she bore the boy and assumed that if not mother and son, they were surely closely related.

The man, Aislinn saw, was pale and trembling and wore his weariness in a tightly drawn face. His wife stood quietly at his side, watching all that transpired. Aislinn sensed here a deep wisdom and calm strength and returned the slow smile the woman gave.

The other youths were older than the dark-eyed boy. There was a large lad perhaps as old as Ham, a younger girl who barely showed the first bloom of womanhood, and a pair of boys that Aislinn could tell no difference between.

"We had almost given you up for lost, Aislinn."

She turned in wary alertness for Gwyneth had spoken with a hint of courtesy in her voice and that alone was enough to put Aislinn's defenses in high key. She did not know the game but waited, outwardly calm and poised as the woman drew the moment out.

"We have guests come from Wulfgar," Gwyneth continued and watched a new spark of interest light the violet eyes. Lifting a hand toward the group she called them by name and then added, seeming pleased, "He has sent them here to live."

"It is so, my lady," Gavin nodded. "My brother, Sanhurst, is with him even now."

"And my lord? Is he well?" Aislinn inquired, her voice warm and friendly.

"Yea, the Norman is fit," the man replied. "He pulled us from the mire and we made camp with him on that night. He gave us food and bade us journey here."

"Did he say his length of stay?" Aislinn questioned. "Will he be coming home to Darkenwald soon?"

Gwyneth sneered. "You betray your lust for him, Aislinn."

A rosy hue stained Aislinn's cheeks but Gavin replied kindly:

"No, my lady. He did not say."

Gwyneth's gaze passed from Aislinn to the young widow who studied the other intensely, her eyes measuring Aislinn's trim frame and the swirling copper hair that fell past her hips. Gwyneth's eyes sharpened and gleamed as she thought of her next words, a small lie but one that would serve her purpose well.

"Wulfgar has bade Haylan and her son in particular to abide here at Darkenwald."

Aislinn knew the sharp edge beneath Gwyneth's words as she glanced at the widow whose eyes had widened considerably. Haylan now managed a tremulous smile under her regard, but Aislinn could not find it in her to return the gesture.

"I see," she said. "And you have made them welcome, Gwyneth. Wulfgar will be pleased with your kindness."

Gwyneth's pale eyes grew cold. "Since I am his sister, should I not know that much better than you?" A sharp ear could have detected the bitter harshness in her tone.

"Wulfgar is a most gracious lord. He even treats slaves more kindly than they deserve and clothes them richly."

Aislinn feigned a moment of confusion, knowing well the woman made reference to her. "Truly? Forsooth, I had noticed none save you, dearest Gwyneth, more finely garbed than they were before."

A smothered chuckle shook Bolsgar's great shoulders and Gwyneth gave him a murderous look. It was well known that she had taken full possession of Aislinn's few remaining gowns and made no secret of the seizure. Gwyneth now sat in the younger woman's mauve gunna while Aislinn herself wore the somewhat frayed gown she had always donned when cleaning was to be done. Now it was her best and only one.

Gwyneth's voice rose cuttingly. "It has always struck me odd how a man can swear faithfulness to a woman and then when gone from her side immediately seek the more available warmth at hand. It must be doubly dear that Wulfgar would find a form so comely that he should send it to his home to await his return."

Haylan choked and coughed to catch her breath, drawing Aislinn's immediate attention. She frowned slightly at the widow, wondering what had transpired between her and Wulfgar to make her act in such a manner.

With quiet dignity Aislinn spoke. "Wulfgar is much of a stranger to all. Not one here can truthfully say they know him well enough to judge what his worth might be, if any. As for myself, I only pray that he is honorable and will not play the knave. Time alone will bring the answer to us, and I will rest my fate upon my trust in him."

Aislinn then turned abruptly, cutting off whatever Gwyneth had meant to reply and left her stuttering with open mouth as she bade Ham fetch her tray of medicines.

"I perceive this good fellow has need of my ministrations, unless of course one of you have offered to tend him."

She looked first to Haylan who shook her head and grimaced and then to Gwyneth who met her gaze in anger but shrugged and returned to her needlework.

Aislinn smiled wryly. "Very well, then I will do it since none of you seem willing."

She bent over Gavin's arm and busied herself as Miderd drew closer to help bending over her husband's arm with Aislinn as the stump was bared and cleansed.

Gwyneth's voice came sharp with malice. " 'Tis well known, of course, the ways of soldiers on the field. Does not the very mention of a battle bring kind memories to your heart, dear Aislinn? The Normans, so proud and great, sampling each wench that meets their fancy. I wonder how the vanquished woman finds that brave caress."

The words awoke a pain deep within Aislinn and she felt the anguish rise and seize her bosom until she fought to breathe. The cruelty it took to stir those memories was stunning to her mind. She inhaled deeply and found Miderd's eyes locked to her own. She saw compassion for her own distress mirrored there and knew a flow of kindness from the woman's kindred heart.

"I would to God that even you, good Gwyneth," she sighed slowly, "should never feel that moment."

Gwyneth sat back in her chair, not feeling particularly victorious and Haylan turned her back to warm her hands before the fire and reflect upon the words that had passed her ears.

Aislinn let the torment of Gwyneth's words ebb and finally rose, finished with her task, and moved to stand by Bolsgar's chair.

"My lord, you have just heard it said of men that they are fickle. How think you on this matter? Are you so, sire? And is Wulfgar, do you think?"

Bolsgar grunted. " 'Tis apparent my daughter knows little of men, never having had one herself." He took Aislinn's slim fingers into his grasp in consolation. "Even as a lad Wulfgar was true to the things he knew, his horse, his hawk—me." The old eyes grew moist before he averted his gaze. "Yea, he was steadfast."

"But you know nothing of his women," Gwyneth hastily pointed out.

Bolsgar shrugged. " 'Tis true he has sworn in the past he holds no great love for them, but Wulfgar is much like the iron wolf who haunts the fields of war and needs no softness of this world, but in his heart there burns a need for love so strong he can do naught else but deny it."

"Beasts of darkness!" Gwyneth snapped. "My own father who has of yesterday lost his home and land now approves of this match between my bastard brother and this Saxon—"

"Gwyneth!" Bolsgar bellowed. "Shut thy mouth or I will see it shut for you."

247

"Well, 'tis true!" Gwyneth cried angrily. "You would mate this Saxon whore to him with a solemn oath of marriage."

Haylan's mouth dropped open and she stared agog at Aislinn. "You are not his lady?" she asked before a frown from Miderd made her bite her tongue.

"Indeed she is not!" Gwyneth replied indignantly. "She has bedded one Norman and now seeks to bind my brother to her."

Bolsgar shot up from his chair and for the first time in her life Gwyneth cringed from him in fear. Aislinn stood with set jaw and clenched hands, not willing to ease her fury for fear that trembling would possess her. Bolsgar pushed his face close to his daughter's and sneered:

"You mindless nag! How many times must you cut with your blade of jealousy?"

Haylan cleared her throat and tried to set aside the wrath of the old man by turning his mind to some other matter. "My Lord Wulfgar wars much. Is he oft injured? The scar—"

Aislinn's head snapped up and she stared at Haylan with wide eyes, for her only thought was of Wulfgar's most recent wound that only she and Sweyn knew of and now perhaps this young widow.

"I have only been curious—," Haylan said weakly as she felt the heated faces turned to her. Even Gwyneth's jaw had slackened and Bolsgar's brow had darkened considerably as he turned away from his daughter to face her.

"Curious?" Gwyneth saw Aislinn's surprise and wondered what had drawn it. "What plagues your thoughts to such extent, Mistress Haylan?"

"The scar upon your brother's cheek, that is all," Haylan replied gingerly, shrugging her shoulders. "I desired only to know how it came there."

Gwyneth sat back in her chair, quickly glancing toward her father who had fallen back in his. A frown grew upon his brows like a gathering storm, and his hands tightened on the arms of his chair until the muscles of his forearms stood out like ropes beneath the flesh.

"And you were distressed by that unsightly scar?" Gwyneth ventured.

"Distressed? Oh nay!" Haylan replied. "He has a most handsome face."

She looked at Aislinn now as an equal, thinking that if

she had not been too hasty leaving Wulfgar that night she might have had him in her will. At least she would have had as much claim upon him as this vixen.

"It came by way of an accident when we were children," Gwyneth began somewhat cautiously.

"Accident?" Bolsgar bellowed again. "Do you lie, daughter? Nay, 'twas no accident. 'Twas done with malice."

"Father," Gwyneth cajoled, now striving to set aside his rage. " 'Tis past and best forgot."

"Forgot? Nay, never. I remember clearly."

Gwyneth tightened her lips in vexation. "Then tell them quickly how it came about if you must. Tell them how in a temper at learning he was bastard you struck the boy with a falconing glove, laying open his cheek."

With difficulty Bolsgar rose to his feet and stood trembling with wrath as he stared down at his daughter. His eyes swept Haylan briefly before returning to Gwyneth. Aislinn's own surprise had subsided. Bolsgar seemed so furious now that she had no doubt he was deeply ashamed yet in his own stubborn way could not cede his actions wrong.

"There is no need for me to speak, daughter," he bit out, "as you have told them enough yourself."

"Do sit and be a civil host, father," Gwyneth pleaded.

"Host!" Bolsgar sneered derisively. "I am no host here." He raised a horn of ale. " 'Tis Wulfgar's manor we abide in. I do not seek what is his and you presume too much." His morose mood did not lessen as he glanced about the hall. "Where is Sweyn?" he demanded. "I've a thirst for more ale and needs have a companion to ease my mind upon."

"He's with his horses, Father," Gwyneth replied, trying to hide her growing impatience with him.

"Then Kerwick?" he thundered. "Where is he? That lad is a worthy one to drink with."

"Not now, Father," Gwyneth hissed. Her annoyance grew at the thought of him tippling ale with a common serf. "I've sent him to ready cottages for these new families."

"At this late hour?" Bolsgar snapped. "Cannot the lad have some ease from toiling?"

Gwyneth gritted her teeth and spoke with measured care. She was reluctant to aggravate her father's sullen humor. "I thought only of these poor and weary people and what discomforts they might have suffered. This stone floor yields little ease and warmth to exhausted travelers and there is more privacy in the huts."

Bolsgar rose. "Then if there be no one to exchange a civil word with, I shall retire to my pallet and seek my rest. Good eventide, daughter."

Gwyneth nodded her head in return and the man showed his back to them as he faced Aislinn. He offered his hand to her.

"I am an old man, child, but still I favor escorting a beautiful damsel to her chamber. Would you honor me in such small manner?"

"Surely, sire," she murmured and smiled at him. While his daughter proved insensitive, Bolsgar was not, and often lessened the hurt by saying some kind word or doing some thoughtful deed. Laying her hand upon the brawny one he stretched out to her, she allowed him to draw her away from the group before the hearth and up to the chamber that was hers and Wulfgar's.

Bolsgar paused at the door of the bedchamber, seeming unsettled with his thoughts. Finally he sighed.

"I should speak to Wulfgar. He must deal with you more honorably. Yet I have no right to enter into matters that are his. I lost that when I sent him from my home. He is a man alone now."

Aislinn shook her head and smiled softly. "He must not feel trapped into showing me more kindness than he would give of his own accord. It must be freely rendered or it means naught."

Bolsgar pressed her hand gently. "You are wise beyond your years, child. Yet one more word of wisdom would I give you. Let the wolf howl at the moon. It will not come to him. Let him range the forests dark. He will not find what he seeks there. Only when that time comes when he admits to himself that he has need for love shall he find true happiness. Until then, be his in truth and kindness. If you hold any softness for him in your heart, Aislinn, give to him what his mother and I denied him. Cradle him in your love when he drops his aching heart at your feet. Place a tether of faithfulness about his neck and he will become tame and docile."

Aislinn felt the heartache the old man bore, for he had lost both wife and sons and spoke from experience.

"I am but one of his many women, gentle Bolsgar," she pointed out. "You see how fetching the young widow is. 'Tis the same with the others no doubt. How can I be assured of some place in his heart when there are so many who yearn for that spot?"

Bolsgar glanced down and away, finding no suitable answer. He could tell her she was beautiful and graced with charm, yet what Wulfgar thought no man knew. It was better not to build her hopes upon his own assumptions, for there was no guarantee he was right.

Gavin nodded toward the stairs, hearing the old man's feet trudge away from the door and the soft click of the latch as it was closed.

"She is the old lord's daughter?" he asked.

"Yea," Gwyneth sighed. "And a festering wound in the heart of this town."

Miderd and Gavin exchanged quick glances but remained silent. Haylan perked and her attention grew as Gwyneth continued.

"Yea, 'tis true, and she has weedled her way into my brother's bed and seeks to be lady of this hall." Gwyneth felt Haylan's attention and lifted her eyes to the young woman. "My brother only amuses himself for a time, but I fear she will cast some spell upon him."

Gwyneth clasped the arms of her chair as the torturing thought of Ragnor holding Aislinn close against his heart once again pricked her. Her eyelids lowered until they shielded the spark of malice that shone in their depths.

"That one called Kerwick is her lover in Wulfgar's absence," she said slowly. "She is a harlot, yet even my father thinks her fine and good. He is smitten by her beauty as is any man."

"Does my lord think her beautiful?" Haylan inquired, jealousy riding her hard. She could remember still Wulfgar muttering the name of that one.

Miderd frowned and warned. "Haylan, 'tis unwise to delve into Lord Wulfgar's affairs."

"Forsooth, I do not know what my brother thinks," Gwyneth interrupted, spreading her thin hands wide, palms upward. "She has the mark of evil in that red hair. Could any one of us doubt it? Who knows what soul she might steal with her potions and her ways. Beware of her.

251

Do not let the sweet words she mouths warm you to her. She practices them with great deception."

"Nay," Haylan murmured. "I will take care."

Miderd looked sharply toward her sister-in-law but the widow missed her frown. Gwyneth rose to her feet, putting aside her needlework.

"My eyes grow weary from the smoke in the hall and I must seek some ease from the irritation. Good eventide to you."

The Saxon family watched quietly until Gwyneth was out of sight and then Miderd faced Haylan in exasperation.

"You will respect your betters for the sake of all of us, Haylan, or we might find ourselves cast upon the road again."

Haylan shrugged and danced lightly away. "Betters? I have great respect for Lady Gwyneth. Whom do you mean? Lord Bolsgar was bad tempered but I was polite to him."

"I know when you set your mind to some matter you will not rest until it's to your liking," Miderd returned. "And I see you have set your eyes toward the Norman. Let him be, Haylan. He belongs to Lady Aislinn."

"Ha!" Haylan scoffed. "In a moment I could have him."

"You boast overmuch, Haylan. We were sent here to work, no more."

"No more?!" Haylan laughed shortly. "What do you know of it?"

Miderd glanced at her husband in silent appeal but he only shrugged and turned away.

"I will not argue with you, Haylan," Miderd said quietly. "Yet I would warn you that if the Lady Aislinn becomes mistress of this hall, she might be so disposed to send us on our way if you go after the Norman. And where would we go, with naught but famine and misery for our kind? Think of your son, pray."

"I do think of him," stormed Haylan. She glanced down at the nodding boy and stopped to smooth his hair. "Miles would be of benefit to any lord."

Miderd threw up her hands in disgust and shook her head, turning her back to the willful widow.

Upon Kerwick's return they woke the now sleeping Miles and wrapping him against the cold, led him out with the other children. After seeing to the needs of Miderd and Gavin and their family, Kerwick led Haylan and her son to a smaller hut. Here the hearth was warm and inviting with a blazing fire lighting the dreary cubicle of the interior. Haylan watched Kerwick closely as he laid more wood by the hearth, then ventured:

"Your Lady Gwyneth is a fine damsel. You must be pleased to serve her."

Kerwick rose and stared at the young woman without a flicker of emotion on his lean face. Haylan's dark eyes snapped with growing anger at his continued silence and she glared back at him.

"What do you know of your betters? You are but serf here. 'Tis easy to see you have cast your lot with that red-haired vixen."

Kerwick spoke with measured care, his lips curling in distaste as he spat out the words. "That red-haired vixen was once my betrothed before that warring Norman claimed her as his. I was once lord of my own hall and he took even that, but mostly I regret her loss. Do not speak with contempt when you say her name to me. If you have any wits about you, you will not listen to Gwyneth and the lies she spills."

"You may rest assured I have sense enough to see what's before me," Haylan retorted. "And that you are still smitten with Aislinn!"

"Aye," Kerwick admitted. "More than you can understand."

"Oh, indeed, I can well understand," Haylan replied heatedly. "Do you forget that I am just widowed and know what interests a man?"

Kerwick's brows raised. "What is this? Are you spreading false rumors about us already? You are a haughty wench for a serf."

"Serf?" Haylan laughed distainfully. "Mayhap and then mayhap not. Who knows until Lord Wulfgar returns." She raised her chin. "I can have him if I choose."

Kerwick chuckled in disbelief. "You? What claims do you have upon him? Are you saying he has made you his mistress also?"

Haylan's voice rose in unbridled fury. "I am not that kind of woman! But if I were, I could have had him. He desired me and who knows what will follow on his return."

Kerwick snorted his contempt. "Let me give you warning, fair widow," he said, bending his head until his nose almost met hers. "Wulfgar has striped my flesh when I dared defend Aislinn from him and his rage soared when I briefly touched her, yet he is quick to declare his hatred of women. Do not be fooled that he is a soft master without a will, for he is strong, and he would easily see through your simple motives to have him for your own. He might take you as he did my Aislinn, but I warrant he'd offer you far less than he has her."

"Are you telling me that I have no chance of being lady of this hall?" Haylan demanded. "Why, you bubbling cur, you are too addled by your lust for her to see why he has sent me here."

"To work like the rest of us, I vow. He needs more serfs," Kerwick replied easily.

Haylan squealed in irate temper. "Look at me! Do you find it so hard to believe that a man could fall in love with me?"

"You enlarge your importance, madam, and you are a pompous, conceited wench. You are comely, true, but there are many of the same value. Aislinn has no match. She is unsurpassed."

Haylan choked. "I will be the mistress of Darkenwald! You will see."

"Will you?" Kerwick raised a dubious brow. " 'Tis more likely you'll be a serf here, no more."

"Lady Gwyneth says that Wulfgar plays with Aislinn only for a time," Haylan bit out. "Mayhap I can hasten her descent."

"Bah! Lady Gwyneth!" Kerwick spat. "Do not listen to her. Listen to me instead. Wulfgar will not let the Lady Aislinn go nor would any man of good sense."

"Your opinion is not his and therefore of no value," Haylan flung, arrogantly tossing her head.

"You will be hurt," Kerwick warned. "For you see I forgot to mention another asset of Aislinn's." He smiled slowly. "She is wiser than most women."

"Ohhh, I loathe you with all my being!" Haylan cried.

Kerwick shrugged his shoulders, unperturbed. "Madam, I really don't give a blessed damn."

With that he spun on his heels and strode from the cottage, leaving Haylan standing in a flush of heated emotion.

In the loneliness of the chamber Aislinn felt her fears

254

well up anew. Doubts shredded her confidence as her imagination dwelled on the vision of Wulfgar clasped in the arms of the dark-haired Haylan. In roiling despair Aislinn drew the gunna and kirtle from her body, remembering in pain Wulfgar's warm caresses on their last night together and his gentleness with her. Had he found more pleasure in another's bed? Did he consider her after all but a passing fancy? Did he even now lie in some other wench's furs and play them all for fools?

The ache grew in Aislinn's chest until her breath came in ragged sobs and she flung herself upon the bed and muffled her cries of anguish in the pelts spread there. At last the tears were spent and she drew the wolfskins about her, huddling dejectedly beneath them, seeking to find some warmth to set the chill free from her heart. A light knock sounded on the door and pulling a fur about her shoulders she spoke for the late visitor to enter. To her surprise it was Miderd who had returned through the cold night to seek a word with her. In her hands Miderd bore a bundle.

"Milady, I bring tidings from Lord Wulfgar and he bade me give them to your ears alone."

Miderd knew Aislinn's anxiety from her reddened eyes and tear-stained face and spoke with a gentle concern.

"Milady, Haylan is a sorrowed soul and dreams of much beyond her ken and sets upon her fairness undue worth. 'Tis in my mind that your lord has not turned from you, for he set this gift within my hands and spoke with concern for your welfare, desiring that you go to Sweyn with your woes if there is need. 'Twould seem that you should not fear overmuch a young widow's dreams and dallyings."

She placed the package in Aislinn's hands and smiled kindly as it was opened with rare haste.

"He instructed me also to say, milady, that it was purchased with honest fare."

Tears came again but this time gently so as Aislinn drew the bolt of yellow cloth to her face and knew the touch of Wulfgar's hands had been of late upon the cloth. Happily she embraced Miderd, causing the woman to blush with her words of thankfulness.

"Oh, Miderd, do you not see?" she cried exuberantly. "Wulfgar said it was not his wont to buy women gifts, for his monies were hard earned and no wench was worthy of his labors."

Miderd smiled softly. She felt she had found a friend in Aislinn despite their brief acquaintance. She pressed the girl's hand tenderly. "'Twould seem you've won a battle, my lady. And let us hope on the morrow, the war."

Aislinn's violet eyes shone with a sparkling radiance as she replied gayly. "Oh, indeed, let us secure the morrow."

Happy for the girl, Miderd closed the door to the chamber, feeling a kinship with this young woman whom she barely knew and a confidence in the future she had not experienced for a long time. She sensed she would be at peace here at Darkenwald. Her husband would have a trade and her sons would give him aid. She and her daughter mayhap could help here in the lord's manor to further supply their needs. At last she felt that they would be secure.

Aislinn rose early in the morning before any in the household stirred. Taking the treasured yellow piece, she sat beside the coffer Wulfgar had claimed for his own and carefully removed each garment that belonged to him, smoothing the pieces absently as she unpacked and set them aside. When she had emptied the chest she then put the yellow neatly to the side where it would not be unduly crushed and returned Wulfgar's clothes to their place. Here Gwyneth would not dream of looking and the cloth would be safe. When she heard some word of Wulfgar's return she would take it and make a gown for herself and meet him more properly than in her old gunna and kirtle. Her heart grew light as she thought of him coming back and her head swam dizzily with excitement in the renewed confidence that he would be returning to her.

When she descended the stairs to the hall she found Haylan and Gwyneth before the hearth. The widow had been excused from any toiling by Gwyneth and now sat beside that woman trying to learn the more refined art of needlecraft. She did poorly with the tapestry given her and Gwyneth's patience was sorely tasked. Aislinn hid a smile of amusement as Haylan humbly begged Gwyneth's pardon for being so inept, not knowing that Aislinn had come into the hall and stood apart from them watching.

Gwyneth sighed in exasperation. "You must take smaller stitches as I have shown you."

"I pray for your forgiveness, milady, but I was never

talented at mending," Haylan returned apologetically. Then she added brightly, "But I can roast a boar and my breads are acclaimed by all."

"That is serf's work," Gwyneth replied shortly. "A lady is known by her stitchery. If you ever hope to become one, you must learn the value of a needle. Wulfgar will expect you to make and mend his garments."

Aislinn strode forward, surprising them with her presence and went to warm her hands before the fire.

"You are helpful, dear Gwyneth, but I need no assistance to mend my lord's clothes." She turned a smile to them, raising her skirts a trifle to let the heat rise beneath them. "Wulfgar seemed pleased enough with my talents."

Gwyneth snorted derisively. " 'Tis a wonder you found any leisure for needlework as much time as you spent in bed with him."

"Why, Gwyneth, how could you know when we were abed or when we were not?" Aislinn grinned. "Unless, of course, you make it as much of a habit snooping around doors as you seem to do in my coffer." She looked pointedly at the gowns the two women were wearing, for Haylan was donned in a third-hand gunna no doubt given to her by the generous Gwyneth.

"Your coffer?" Gwyneth repeated in mockery. "Slaves have no possessions."

A slow smile touched Aislinn's lips. "But, Gwyneth, if I am a slave, all that I have belongs to Wulfgar." She raised her brows in mock question. "Do you steal from your brother?"

Gwyneth's jaw grew tense and she spoke in heated fury. "My brother assured us that everything here was to be considered ours and that we were to abide as suited our tastes."

"Oh?" Aislinn chuckled. "Those words were spoken to Bolsgar, not to you, and that dear fellow is careful to take nothing more than his share. Indeed, he more than earns his keep with the game he brings in. You know Wulfgar needs many hands to prosper here. What do you, good Gwyneth, to aid his cause?"

The woman rose and snapped in irate temper, "I keep this house when he is gone and see that his larder is not robbed by those greedy drunkards who——"

She stopped abruptly, seeming to choke on her words, and Aislinn followed her gaze to find that Sweyn had entered and was approaching the hearth. He smiled at Gwyneth and with deliberate slowness tore a large chunk from the meat that roasted over the coals then washed it down with a hearty swig of ale. He smacked his lips and licked the grease from his fingers then wiped them on the shirt of his tunic. He turned to Aislinn and rumbled:

"Who doles the food that I and Bolsgar provide?"

Aislinn laughed. "No one, Sweyn. No one at all. We all eat well from your labors."

The Norseman stared at Gwyneth for a long moment, then mumbled, "Good. Good."

Belching loudly he left them.

Aislinn stepped back and spread her skirt in a half curtsey. "Your pardon, ladies. I must be about my work." She turned to leave and spoke over her shoulder. "Haylan, tend to the meat that it does not char."

She made her exit almost skipping in glee, and flinging open the doors, viewed the world and thought it marvelous.

At the crossroads near Kevonshire Wulfgar and his men camped for several days. The snows ceased and soon melted into the ground. They halted travelers and English messengers spreading word of William's march. These latter they simply held and released when they marched, as the information they carried had grown useless with the passage of time.

Now William's armies moved beyond them and no threat could come from this quarter. Breaking camp, they moved on to repeat their task time and again. They swung north and the Duke's hordes crossed the Thames west of London from the landward side. The city lay bare and alone, isolated, her would-be allies sealed from her. Hampshire, Berkshire, Wallingford, then at Berkhamstead Archbishop Aldred and an entourage including the Atheling Edgar, the pretender, met William and surrendered London. Hostages were left with William and oaths were pledged to him. He would be crowned on Christmas Day as King of England.

Wulfgar and his men were called into camp with the rest of the army. The cart was loaded heavily with gold and silver and precious items taken as tribute or plunder. This was sent to William who had his treasurers account it, remove a double tythe and return the rest to Wulfgar.

The monotony of camp life set in. Wulfgar paid his knights their shares and brought his other accounts up to date but he held his men close to their camp and did not release them to go a-wenching or a-wining as was the general trend.

Several days had passed yet nearly a week remained before Christmas when Wulfgar received a messenger from William informing him that as the army moved into London he was to occupy a manor near the abbey. There with his men he would await the day of the coronation.

As the day was but a youth, Wulfgar saddled the Hun and rode into London to find a place where he would lodge with his men. The city was tense and as he rode through the streets the English eyed him with open hatred. The houses and shops were stone walled and heavy timbered, crowded close or even overhanging the cobbled streets. The frequent open gutters ran with dark murky water afloat with the offal of the city. He neared Westminster and the press of bodies grew heavy as every free man journeyed to see where England would fall to the Norman Duke. Many times Wulfgar pushed his steed through throngs that filled the way. As he urged the Hun into the square his eyes were immediately drawn by a large stone house that stood a way off the square itself but whose roof opened on a commanding view of the place. With difficulty he made his way across to it and as it had not been claimed by another Norman commandeered its use in William's name. The somewhat overstuffed merchant who owned the place decried Wulfgar's manner and made loud complaint of this use of his property. His rantings turned to shrieks of rage when he was informed that no compensation would be made and trembled in anger when Wulfgar continued.

"Why, good merchant, 'tis naught but your just due to William and his crown." He spoke with heavy satire in his voice. "Be happy that your house still stands and is not reduced to rubble as I have left many others before this day."

It was a final blow and tears ran down the plump cheeks when the Norman knight further bade him take himself, his many in-laws and cousins to some other place of lodging for a fortnight—or two.

Wulfgar roamed the place for a while seeing to its appointments as the man scurried about informing his family of the move. Wulfgar listened for a moment and chuckled to himself as he heard a loud, strident feminine voice berating the merchant for not having resisted the Normans or at least demanded payment. Soon the man joined him again and now stayed close to him as if he found it safer there. There were stables for the horses and a fine kitchen on the street floor. In that room a stairway led to a cellar where a rich array of wines and sweetmeats lay. Wulfgar hastily eased the trembling merchant's worry by a promise that what was used of these would be paid for.

The second floor held small rooms and a large hall where his men could rest and game. From here Wulfgar climbed the narrow stairs to the loft. There the merchant's own apartments lay dressed in a rich comfort which would have graced the finest Norman castle. At one end of the entryway a small stair led to a cupola on the roof and from that height the view was unrestricted. Passing down, Wulfgar paused at the large bedchamber, its great bed draped with heavy velvet. As he reached out to test the down-filled mattress he could not suppress a vision of soft creamy skin and curving hips, laughing violet eyes and lips that moved in sweet caress upon his.

Wulfgar drew back sharply. Lord, what spells that vixen wove in his mind. He could almost see her standing, arms outstretched, wreathed in green and crimson smokes, chanting ancient runes as errant breezes lifted those tumbling brazen locks to send them curling around her brow and breasts.

As if willed by some greater force, Wulfgar returned his gaze to the bed and again saw the violet eyes twinkling with laughter. He grew angry with these imaginings and with a curse tore himself away. But as he descended to the street an ache grew in his belly and spread to his loins. He could not help but dream of Aislinn on that great velvet coverlet.

His return was lost in musings and he took no note of the city he passed. Pausing on a rise he stared at the sprawling encampment and knew a loneliness that touched his very soul. Though yet unvoiced, he knew also that a decision had been made, and with the thing settled in his mind, Wulfgar, in a gaiety of spirit he had not known for many days, kicked the Hun who snorted in surprise and charged down the hill to his tents.

It was two days hence and the move was made to London. The night had fallen and a welcome feast laid. His men were ensconced below and Wulfgar could hear their voices as they laughed and talked about the unfamiliar comfort of the place. He stood behind the balustrade and gazed upon the torchlit square beyond. Gowain had left and upon the morrow should find his way to Darkenwald. An unbidden eagerness filled Wulfgar's chest and he wondered at the quickening of his heart. Aislinn's face was vague in his memory but he could almost see those glowing eyes that changed their hue with every flickering light. He knew the brow he had so often traced and the impudent curve of her slender nose. He knew the delicate line of her lips, from the resistance he met on them to their eagerness when she warmed to his caress.

Wulfgar turned away from the night. These coltish musings did nothing for his peace, yea, rather stirred him to a lustful wakening. He disliked the feeling of bondage and strode irritably into the bedchamber where the great bed waited. Stripping, he fell upon it to take his rest but soon found it beckoned not with sleep but of gentle stirrings and mutterings as if one lay beside him.

In exasperation Wulfgar flung himself from its comfort and went to stand by the window, unmindful of the chill that crept into the room as he threw open the shutters and stared at the sleeping street below and the huge pale moon above. Strangely his mood grew gentle the longer he stood and there was naught else that plagued his mind but Aislinn of Darkenwald.

The tender bitch, he pondered, so fine and proud. Sorely used 'tis true, yet she dares stand before me like some Cleopatra of the heath. She pleads her plight so well my head grows soft. How can I refuse her when she bares her soul beguilingly and seeks to touch the very depth of my honor? She braves my temper for her people and bends me to her will when I might have it otherwise. He rubbed his brow as if it ached from thought, and he could draw no end from his meditation of her. Yet, somehow I find myself wishing that she—

"—he would pledge that loyalty to me," Aislinn sighed as she stared at the bright moon above the moor. If he would say a vow and express some love for me, I would be content. He is kind and just and tender even in his lust, and here I am bound to this maiden's shape that sets his blood afire. I did not ask that he should take me, yet I cannot damn him for the man he is. What must I do to gain his favor, when in his arms I cannot even hold myself from him? His kisses tear from me all resistance, and I am like the willow stems beneath a storm, swaying where he wills. He is content to have me at his beck and call, to use my body for his pleasure and never offer any promises in return. Yet I would have more. 'Tis true he was not the first to lay hand upon me, but his attentions have surely given me some small claim on him. I am not a woman of the streets to be used and left; he must be brought to that conclusion somehow. I am not without honor and pride. I cannot go on being his paramour forever, having only that small and minute part of him and no more.

She took her kirtle off and laid it aside, then crept into the pelts and drew the pillow to her where the last fragrance of his being clung. She hugged it to her and could almost feel the play of his muscles beneath her hands, the heat of his lips on hers.

I want him, she concluded. Whether I love him or not, I want him more than anything ever in my life. Yet I must seek him with wisdom. I shall resist him to the limits of my senses but try not to anger him. And if he will relent to me this much, I will give to him whatever love I have or can steal or can borrow. He will not regret doing so.

The day dawned bright and Darkenwald grew clamorous in its labors. Aislinn rose, and having broke the fast, set about her duties to the town, seeking out the sick and lame. She passed the hours avoiding Gwyneth and thus her aspish wit. Late afternoon the lookout shouted from the tower and soon Kerwick sought her out to bear the news that riders came with Wulfgar's colors.

Fleeing to her chamber, Aislinn quickly combed her hair and bound it with ribbons. She pressed a cool cloth upon her face to ease her blush. Her spirits fell when she went below and saw that it was only Gowain who strode into the room. He crossed the hall toward her smiling, but Gwyneth, sitting at her tapestry before the hearth, called to him and directed him to come near. Gowain looked hesitantly at Aislinn, wishing to speak with her first, but in good manner went to the other.

"What of William?" she inquired anxiously. "Is England his?"

"Aye," Gowain replied. "The Duke will be crowned Christmas Day if all goes well."

Gwyneth drew a sigh of relief. "Then Darkenwald belongs to us."

"Is my Lord Wulfgar well?" Aislinn asked, joining them. "Why did he not come himself? Has he been harmed in some way?" The fear betrayed itself in her voice and in her eyes as she searched Gowain's face for some obvious clue of his coming.

"Oh, nay," the knight quickly assured her. "He is well and hearty."

"Then why have you journeyed here?" Gwyneth interrupted. "It must surely be on some important errand."

Gowain smiled slowly. "Indeed, my lady. To Wulfgar it is a most urgent matter."

"Then what?" Gwyneth insisted. "Do not keep us waiting."

"I am here to fetch—someone." He finished lamely, recalling the strain between Wulfgar's sister and Aislinn.

"Fetch someone? Whom do you seek?" Gwyneth questioned. Her eyes lifted to the man's face and she tapped her cheek thoughtfully as she considered him. "What is it? The coronation? Does Wulfgar wish to present his family to the king? I will be happy to go, but I must insist upon a new gown from him to meet royalty in." She indicated the mauve gunna she wore. "These garments are not fit to feed the swine in."

Gowain reddened with his discomfort and cleared his throat, glancing uncertainly at Aislinn. He had made the matter worse in his delay to speak. Aislinn's gaze was fixed upon the seated one, and following her stare, Gowain suddenly recognized the gunna adorning Gwyneth as one Aislinn had worn several times prior to their leaving Darkenwald. He remembered well, because he had admired the maid's graceful form in its soft cloth and then had been caught gaping by Milbourne, who had made some hearty jest of his rutting after Wulfgar's woman. Gowain turned his regard to the gown Aislinn wore and was surprised at its poor condition. His chivalry was prompted to act in the lady's defense, for he immediately came to the conclusion that her clothes had been taken from her. But he swallowed the words tempting his tongue. It would be best to stay out of Wulfgar's affairs

263

and let him handle them. Besides, it was never wise to enter into a fray between two women.

The knight cleared his throat and ventured. "My Lady Gwyneth, I fear I have brought you to the wrong conclusion."

"Eh?" The woman looked at him sharply and saw his eyes go to Aislinn. Her own narrowed.

Gowain flushed deeper and he spoke with great care. "Lord Wulfgar has sent me to fetch the Lady Aislinn. The girl, Hlynn, is to accompany her to see to her needs."

"What?" Gwyneth nearly shrieked, coming angrily to her feet, nearly oversetting her tapestry frame. "You cannot mean Wulfgar is so careless with his position as knight to William that he must take this tart to bed beneath the king's nose."

She paced the floor before the hearth in a highly agitated state. Then her eyes fell on Haylan as she came into the room and approached them. She bestowed a calculating smile on the poor young man.

"You undoubtedly misunderstood him, Sir Gowain. Was it not some other maid he sent for?"

The Norman shook his head, most certain of his mission. "Nay, it was Aislinn of Darkenwald Wulfgar instructed me to bring to his side. He beckoned me to do so with all haste and we must ride on the morrow." He dismissed the raging Gwyneth and did not even notice the gaping Haylan and turned to the happily smiling Aislinn.

"Can you be ready, damoiselle?"

"Of a certainty, Sir Gowain," Aislinn returned, her eyes sparking with her delight. They dazzled him and he drew a quick breath as she pressed his hand warmly. "Indeed, there is little to prepare. 'Twill be no trouble."

"Then, damoiselle, I await your pleasure."

He bowed low and quickly left to see to his men, needful of the cold air that would cool his blood. He'd have to stay well away from the maid on the journey to London, for fear he might forget himself with her and do both Wulfgar and her dishonor.

The small group formed early and left Darkenwald with the first light of dawn. They wound their way first westward and then north to London passing the place where Atheling Edgar had made his abortive attack on William. Silence reigned as they rode through the ruined town of Southwark where tumbled houses still smoldered and homeless Saxons poked and dug in the rubble and snow for what lost treasures they might recover. They stared at the travelers in mute despair but as their eyes fell on the Norman knight the light of hatred glowed bright. They knew, however, the full weight of William's wrath and stood glowering their rage until the band was gone from sight.

Gowain led the small entourage across the Southwark Bridge into London proper early on Christmas Day and fought a path for hours through the milling throngs. There seemed to be a madness in the air as English men raised their cups on high to sneeringly toast William the Bastard and roamed about in confused frustration.

The party approached Westminster and the crowds grew even thicker. Gowain and his men were forced to use their spear points to clear a way. They entered the square and even the huge steeds were buffeted from side to side with the surging of the masses. Curses and threats did little to clear a path and progress was measured in feet. Gowain glanced back over his shoulder at Aislinn who rode a smaller mare. Her bright head was covered by the hood of her mantle but her face showed no panic. Her hands gripped the reins firmly and with a sure hand.

Then from ahead a roar of flames burst upon them, and as the people recoiled in fear, a force of Norman knights was thrust upon them. Aislinn fought to keep her seat as her mount stumbled and scrambled for footing beneath the onslaught of a huge steed that pressed upon them, crushing them against a wall. She felt the lesser beast going down under the greater weight and saw the threat of them both being trampled underfoot.

Wulfgar had risen early in the morn and donned his finest raiment for the coronation of William. With some reluctance he laid aside his great sword and hung a shorter, lighter blade at his side. He was garbed in black and red trimmed with gold and his tall broad-shouldered frame and weather-bronzed features were impressive indeed. His gray eyes and sunstreaked hair seemed pale against his dark skin.

On leaving the manor, he left orders with Milbourne and Beaufonte to hold the men in readiness and have the Hun saddled with his helm and long sword hung on the pommel. If the day turned amiss they would seek him out near the steps of Westminster, for as the moment neared William feared there might be a thrust of revolt and wished some of his force held ready.

Wulfgar placed himself just within the main portal of the cathedral and watched as William's tall and powerful frame bent before the Norman bishop. With slow ponderous pomp the English ceremony followed. The crown was lowered to his brow and shouts of "Hail William" from the English reverberated throughout the abbey. Wulfgar looked on with a feeling of relief in his chest. This is what they had sought to have. William, Duke of Normandy, had been proclaimed King of England.

Suddenly from without angry shouts rose up and Wulfgar stepped to the door to investigate this disturbance. Smoke curled from a rooftop and crowds of Saxons grappled with Norman men-at-arms as the latter carried torches to other structures. Wulfgar rushed from the church and fought his way to the nearest knight who struggled against the fray.

"What goes on here?" he demanded.

The man turned in amazement. "We heard the English shouting from the cathedral. They have attacked William."

Wulfgar groaned. " 'Twas not that, you fools! They only gave him a salute." He flung his arm toward the torch bearing soldiers. "Stop those men before they would fire all London."

Milbourne pressed the mounts forward through the crush to his lord's side, and Wulfgar snatched himself to saddle to lead his men crashing forward to halt the Normans in their mistaken purpose. He struck brands from their hands and shouting there was no threat, halted them. Yet others raced on unchecked. He urged the Hun on, then suddenly flames roared from a storefront and the people surged away from the heat in fear to crush him and his men against a wall, pinning them upon another mounted group. The Hun crashed against a smaller horse and Wulfgar fought to control him. The other steed's forelegs buckled beneath the crush and a feminine cry alerted Wulfgar. Leaning forward in his saddle he flung an arm out, wrapping it about the small mantle-enveloped form and snatching it from the saddle as the horse stumbled and went down. The cloth fell away from coppery hair as Wulfgar set the maid before him and the soft scent of lavender filled his nostrils.

"Aislinn," he breathed, thinking himself in the midst of another fantasy.

The face lifted to his with violet eyes wide in surprise. "Wulfgar?"

He felt the full impact of surprise as he stared down at her, realizing it was no illusion this time. He was tempted to kiss her, to crush her against him in an agony of longing but instead demanded:

"Are you all right?"

Aislinn nodded and was reassured as she felt his arm tighten about her, pulling her against his chest. Sweeping his gaze about, Wulfgar found Gowain struggling forward to reach her mount before it was trampled beneath the larger hooves. Doing so, the young man turned his eyes on Wulfgar and despite the dilemma of the moment the young knight grinned.

"My lord, you said deliver her swiftly and I did so, straight away to your lap."

A smile broke Wulfgar's stern face. "So you have, Gowain. Now let us see the lady safely away."

Before they could urge their horses forward a burly man, bearded and roughly dressed, shook his fist at them.

"Norman pigs!" came his cry and a cabbage barely missed Wulfgar's brow.

Wulfgar raised an arm to shield Aislinn as his men formed around them. She clung to his waist, glancing around at the angry English.

"Never fear, cherie," Wulfgar chuckled. "They will have to kill all of us before they can do you harm."

"I do not fear," Aislinn insisted. "Why should they do me hurt? I am English, too."

Wulfgar laughed softly. "Do you think they care as long as you're with us?"

Aislinn's assurance dissolved into uncertainty when a peasant chanted: "Norman slut, bed the swine! May your ears grow long like an ass's and your nose become as warty as a toad's!"

The man ended his curse by hurling a potato at her head but Wulfgar's arm deflected the missile.

"Are you satisfied now, my brave vixen?" Wulfgar inquired, raising a mocking brow.

Aislinn swallowed and nodded. Wulfgar spurred the Hun forward with Gowain, Hlynn and the returning party following. They worked along behind a wall of towering destriers until they reached the mouth of the narrow street leading to the merchant's manor and Wulfgar drew up, turning to Gowain.

"Take the lady to our quarters," he roared in command. "See her safe and guard that others do not kindle the place."

Before he passed her to the young knight, Wulfgar pulled Aislinn's face up to meet his and his hungering lips crushed upon hers in a fierce, passionate kiss that ended almost as quickly as it began, leaving Aislinn breathless and giddy. He lifted her across to the other knight and with a last look at her shining locks and soft smile, wheeled his horse about and returned from where they had come. Gowain led Aislinn into the manor, throwing the bar behind him and setting guards at it to halt the torch bearers from their zealous firing, while Wulfgar sought to restore some order and calm both Saxons and Normans. The noise finally receded to a low roar as the city relented to an endless bout of merrymaking and revelry for the Christmas Day, if not the coronation of a new king. Wulfgar's anxiety to return to Aislinn was unbounded, yet he found his duties drew him farther and farther afield. When late in the evening all rounds were complete and he, Beaufonte and Milbourne turned homeward, he drew a sigh of relief, but even then he found his time was not his own, for he and the knights were almost forcibly drawn into a celebration of a goodly party of noblemen. The men would endure none of his excuses but nodded in agreement as one of their group remarked:

"Indeed, my good knight, you must be honored as William's soldier."

Wulfgar looked painfully at Milbourne, who returned his gaze sympathetically and shrugged.

"'Twould seem, my lord, you are caught," he murmured, drawing close. "They might take it amiss you do not celebrate the Duke's coronation."

Wulfgar groaned in despair. "You are right of course, Milbourne, but it does not make it less painful."

Beaufonte grinned. "My lord, why do you not tell them that the fairest damoiselle in all of Christendom awaits your return? They might relent."

"Aye," Wulfgar grunted. "And they may follow me to the manor to see her for themselves." He laughed ruefully.

So, the three knights were feted, dined and wined, and while their hosts lavishly decorated and enlarged upon tales of their exploits, they squirmed uncomfortably. A troupe of entertainers was engaged and the festivities increased. Wulfgar's agitation heightened when a well-endowed Saxon wench leaped upon his lap and pulled his head to her breasts, holding it there until he almost choked on the sweet musky smell of her. His hosts guffawed as he tried to disengage himself and uproariously bade him take his chance with her.

"You'll not find another more worthy on this night," chortled a count. "And I vow your ride will be soft."

Milbourne and Beaufonte hid smiles as Wulfgar scowled and declined. When they finally freed themselves of the unwelcomed hosts and left, Wulfgar moaned to see the first red blush of dawn above the rooftops. But his spirit lightened and grew more gay as they neared the merchant's manor. There they stabled their mounts and climbed to the hall. While Beaufonte and Milbourne stumbled to their pallets, Wulfgar continued up the stairs. He took the steps three at a time, his finely made shoes ringing his eagerness on the treads. His heart pounded in his ears and he knew his breath came more quickly than could be accounted for by his rapid ascent. He expected to find Aislinn asleep or just stirring in the bed. It would not take him long to shed his clothes and join her there. But when he eased the oaken door open, he was both disappointed and surprised to find her already about and seated on a bench with a silken cloth draped about her. Hlynn arranged the coppery hair high atop her head with ribbons in preparation for a bath. A large wooden tub steamed in readiness near the hearth. Wulfgar entered and as he leaned his weight against the door, closing it, Aislinn turned to him while Hlynn backed away timidly.

"Good morningtide, monseigneur," Aislinn smiled. Her violet eyes measured him, glowing brightly. "I had begun to fear somewhat for your welfare."

In all of his imaginings Wulfgar realized he had not visualized Aislinn as beautiful as she truly was. He straightened and removed his mantle.

"My pardon, cherie," he grinned. "I would have been at your side earlier but the difficulties of the day occupied me until the evening had passed. I beg you not to think too harshly of me."

"No thoughts amiss," she replied, bending her head as Hlynn returned to tuck a last few curls into place. "I know you are bound by duties and would not think of amusing yourself otherwise when I am come." She cast him a glance awry. " 'Tis only widows you send to share my stoop."

Her voice was sweet but she watched him carefully as he bent at the tub to splash water over his face and hair then shook the tawny mane sending droplets flying. He drew a chair close beside her, sitting in it and propping his feet on the end of her bench while his eyes sought the curves where the cloth displayed them. His heated gaze seemed to devour her and Aislinn felt his nearness in every fiber of her body. His close scrutiny of her body set her own blood afire and drew her imaginings onward. The memory of his caresses and play of love served her well bringing a light blush to her cheeks. Without further hesitation she sought to turn their thoughts away from the matter which seemed uppermost in the minds of each, knowing she was most susceptible to him.

"I vow your Duke's coronation was met with some

dissatisfaction from the melee we entered into yesterday passed."

" 'Twas only a matter of misunderstanding."

"Then it seems the countryside is well at peace, for we had no trouble on the way here," she returned then added a bit more sharply, "The English have been duly quelled."

Wulfgar grunted a wordless reply and let the sight of her red hair coiled neatly above that flawless neck soothe his tired thoughts. He leaned forward intending to rise and place a kiss upon that tempting nape and take her in his arms, but Aislinn hastily drew herself up and went to the steaming tub, calling back over her shoulder.

"The weather was most pleasant also. We fared the way in good time. Gowain seemed most anxious to arrive."

Wulfgar settled back in his chair and smiled, anticipating the sight of her glowing body as she dropped the cloth to step into the bath. He frowned darkly, however, as Hlynn took the makeshift robe and held it high, shielding Aislinn from his gaze. When the cloth was at last lowered, Aislinn sat deep in the tub, her head the only part above its edge. Those fine features were most pleasant to look upon but Wulfgar was not satisfied at the simple viewing of her brows.

Aislinn turned to the choosing of soap and scents as Hlynn held the jars for her perusal, testing each until her favorite, a lavender was selected, a soft, beguiling scent that instilled itself with the gentle freshness of a spring-born breeze. It was well timed for here Wulfgar's feet struck the floor, heavy with his ire at this endless dallying over perfumes.

Both women started and stared at him as he rose, glowering at poor Hlynn. With a half smile leering from beneath his frowning brow, he caught the younger girl's eyes and held them in the steel of his own. Unclasping his belt he set it with his sword on the bench. He lifted the short gown from his shoulders and swept it over his head, laying it carefully upon the belt. His eyes never broke their hold and now he began to undo the fastenings of his chainse and as he folded that garment away, Hlynn's eyes widened at the sight of him in naught but chausses. When his hands went to his cross garters and began unwrapping them, Hlynn found his intent and fled the room.

Aislinn could not suppress a laugh as he came to sit

271

upon the stool beside the tub. "Oh, you rogue, Wulfgar. You frighten the lass."

He smiled leisurely. " 'Twas my intention, cherie."

She widened her eyes in feigned horror. "In my youth my mother warned me that crude and loathsome knaves might take advantage of my tender person, but I scarce believed they existed."

"And now?" Wulfgar grinned.

Aislinn flashed him an impishly wicked look. "Why, my lord, now I have no doubts."

Wulfgar chuckled and his eyes shone as he viewed her. She lathered her shoulders and arms lavishly with the scented soap, an item he had purchased especially for her though the rare bar had cost him a goodly sum. But watching her, he decided the coins were well spent. His gaze turned to where the water gently swirled about her rosy breasts, hiding them, yet ever promising to part and bring their ripeness to full view.

Reaching out, he drew a finger along the delicate line of her collarbone, setting her nerves atingle with the pleasure of his touch. He bent forward to press a kiss upon her lips, but Aislinn, feeling nervous and unduly excited at his attention, began to scrub her face.

"Aaah, wench, the fires in the hearth this winter have failed to warm your heart," Wulfgar breathed.

Aislinn smiled behind the cloth, feeling for the moment victorious. Her will, she had come to realize, was quite weak where he was concerned. When she lowered the cloth, her eyes widened and with a squeal she half rose to flee as Wulfgar stepped into the tub, unclad and unabashed. With a devilish laugh he sank into the water, pulling her down atop of him. His arms locked about her holding her close.

"My day and night have been wasted in endless trifles," he grinned. "And I would now set my teeth to more fleshy matters."

He moved upward slightly and his long-starved lips pressed hers with a fiery warmth that sent her senses reeling. Aislinn relaxed against him, feeling a mellow warmth within her as she slipped a hand behind his neck and yielded to his kiss. Then suddenly her whole manner changed. With an angry shriek she pulled away, her eyes flashing with her rage. Before Wulfgar could move, the soapy cloth smothered his face and with a vengeance

Aislinn pushed his head beneath the water. A splash and a foot against his chest and she was gone and free. Wulfgar sat up, spitting lather from his mouth and struggling to wipe the stinging soap from his eyes. When he could look at her again she was wrapped in her robe staring at him with brows arched and eyes blazing.

"Duties! Hah!" Her lips trembled in rage. "Why, the stench of the whore still clings to you. In truth, you smell more like a woman of the street than any Norman."

Wulfgar stared in surprise at her sudden fury, then a quick vision of heavy breasts crushed to his face and an odor of choking sweet musk flashed in his mind and he knew the cause.

With furious motions Aislinn began to dry herself, not realizing the dampened cloth clung to her and revealed more than it covered. Wulfgar leaned back, enjoying the view, and took the opportunity to scrub well lest any further offense remained. He rinsed himself and watched amused as she struggled to hold the cloth in place while trying to raise her kirtle over her head. When she would have succeeded his voice came soft but sternly.

"Nay, my love."

Aislinn turned in exasperation and he met her gaze calmly then inclined his head to the bed. She stamped her foot and groaned.

"But 'tis morn and I have had my sleep."

He laughed softly. " 'Tis naught of sleep I think."

In a single movement he rose and stepped from the tub, taking a linen towel to dry himself. Aislinn half shrieked, half moaned and bent to gather the cloth up that she might flee. With a gasp she found herself snatched up and held in those steel-thewed arms. Wulfgar's gaze plunged deep into hers, and for a long moment they were held motionless, caught in the mounting excitement that hurtled recklessly through them. He carried her to the waiting bed and tossed her upon it. Her cover fell away and Aislinn earnestly sought to drag the blankets close about her, but Wulfgar would have none of it. He swept her body in one long caress as he lay beside her, and he held her still while his hands roamed where they would and his kisses fell where he would place them. His fingers freed her hair from the ribbons and he pressed his face against the soft mass, breathing in the fresh scent that clung to it.

273

There was a light persistent rapping at the door and Hlynn's voice penetrated the moment.

"Milady? Are you well? I have brought food to break the fast."

Hlynn caught her breath as the door jerked open before her to present Wulfgar in all of his naked splendor. Her mouth formed a silent "oh" as the tray was snatched from her hands and the oaken door slammed in her face before she could move. Wulfgar stood with the tray in his hands, listening to the rapid beat of running feet fleeing down to the hall ending in the distant thud of a door and the rattle of a bar being hastily thrown. He sighed and turning, moved forward to place the tray on a table beside the bed. Aislinn had slid beneath the covers at the intrusion pulling them tightly beneath her chin. Now as Wulfgar leaned down to her, she smiled hesitantly and placed a hand on his chest, holding him off.

"Wulfgar, wait," she pleaded. "I beg a morsel. Let us eat."

He shook his head slowly and slipping in beside her enfolded her in his arms.

"In good time, cherie," he breathed against her ear. "In good time."

He smothered further protests in a manner which brooked no resistance and soon the thought of food had flown from Aislinn's mind. Her head spun dizzily with the fervor of his caresses and she felt herself weakening, yielding. She struggled against him, wanting to hold him off but her resolve waned more, then fled completely when he pulled her beneath him. His fierce ardor awoke yearnings she had little known existed. The cold nights, the lonely dreams, now added fuel to the fire in her brain. His kisses seared her and left her panting and breathless. She heard his voice in her ear, hoarse and indistinct yet with an urgency that betrayed his need and his longing. Her heart trembled under his demanding passion. It touched a quickness deep within her, a glowing spark that grew and grew until it seemed to shower her with burning embers. A thousand suns burst within her and spread their surging heat in ever flooding tides to the very limits of her senses. With a gasp she rose against him, her eyes widening and staring in amazement into the gray ones bent upon her. Then slowly she sank to the pillows as he lowered his mouth to hers and she dissolved in a flood of pleasure, knowing for the first time the full wide reach of love.

Aislinn slowly roused from ecstasy and flamed, aghast at her own abandon. Where did the difference lie between her and the women he had taken before? She was soft clay in his hands, unable to retain her dignity and pride, without the courage to withstand his merest advance. Wulfgar held her within his arms and stroked her hair, drawing his fingers through the soft, curling tresses that tumbled over and around them, but as she flung herself from him with a sob he stared at her in surprise.

"Aislinn?"

He sat up, reaching out a hand to bring her back but she shook her head vigorously. His hand dropped away, but he sat pondering her with a puzzled frown. She lay curled on her side with the covers clutched over her bosom and her slender body quaked with her tears.

"Did I hurt you?" he questioned softly.

" 'Tis naught of pain," she muttered miserably.

"You did not weep so before I left. What is it?" He bent over her, brushing the strands of hair from her cheek. "Tell me."

He was answered by another shaking of her head and no amount of inquiry would bring more than renewed sobbing. Wulfgar lay back and sighed, completely at odds with the ways of women. He knew she had experienced the full measure of her womanhood but now she wailed as if some vile thing had been done to her. After a time she quieted and with blissful mercy his night's revelry overtook him and wiped the troubles from his mind with sleep.

The sound of his breath fell heavy and regular when Aislinn carefully sat up on the bed, wiping the last traces of tears from her face. She hugged her knees close against her bare bosom as she stared down at him, letting her eyes roam his length as if she sought to memorize each small thing about him. Her failure to curb her own passion when he gave no hint of love or regard for her upset her greatly. Her body was more in his will than her own and it was only at times like these when he lay in exhausted slumber that she had some slight advantage. She laughed ruefully at the thought. Why, if she chose she could even press a kiss upon that handsome mouth without having the corners turn up in a mocking smile.

Her eyes traced his features in fascination. His tawny

275

hair was sorely in want of a trimming but she saw him no less than magnificent. There were men like Gowain whose features were so fine and fair that they could almost be called beautiful. Not so with Wulfgar. The strength and rugged character of his face added to its appeal and was far more intriguing than those which seemed to be without flaw.

In relief she noted that no new injuries marred his frame and that the wound she had tended had healed completely and only a reddened scar remained from the searing. Gently she drew the blanket over him against the light chill in the room then moving from his side, climbed from the bed. She donned her clothes, frowning in displeasure at the frayed gunna she must meet him in when he woke. She had hastily wrapped the yellow velvet he had sent her and brought it along but time had not permitted making it into a proper gown. But there was no help for it now and it did little good to curse Gwyneth for her thievery. She would have to make the best of what she had. With that conclusion drawn she began to groom her hair. It was one thing Gwyneth could not take from her, and many times at Darkenwald Wulfgar had sat silent and watched her comb the willful mass into shining beauty.

She remembered his warm, amorous gaze upon her and grew flushed, wakening to that strong memory as surely as if she were in his arms again. With a wistful sigh she went again to the bed and stood quietly at its edge as she gazed down at him. It seemed impossible for her to remain cool under his advances. If she could still the sweeping pleasure that possessed her then perhaps she could remain true to her own determination not to yield. But now, aware of what further heights she could reach, she feared it would be even more difficult to remain passive to him. Her mind would not slow but continued to grind with imaginings of what could be if only—

Annoyed with her ceaseless dreaming, Aislinn turned abruptly away and strolled about the room, admiring the rich trappings of the place. Then as she came upon his neatly folded garments she paused and smiled to herself. He had no great variety of clothes, yet what he had was carefully chosen for endurance and richness of cloth. Even the lowliest piece showed signs of constant attention. His apparel was never mussed nor strewn about but was either upon his frame or placed neatly aside. Even with himself he was neither indulgent nor extravagant. Perhaps raising himself up from naught had taught him frugality. Whatever the reason by his words he was not one to be overly generous and had yielded considerably to send the yellow velvet to her. Perhaps he felt some fondness for her after all. Ah, would she ever know the truth of his feeling for her?

Wulfgar slept for only a brief time and the morning was still young when he stirred and roused himself. He splashed cold water over his face to wash away drowsiness and as he donned his shirt and hose he gave Aislinn a long slow scrutiny that did not miss a detail. She blushed lightly and could not take a proper stitch in the chainse she repaired for him, finding her fingers too clumsy to deal with the shirt. When he was clothed she grew calm again and rising, directed him to a bench. There with a well-honed blade, warm water, and some of the precious soap, she scraped the whiskers from his cheeks and chin and put a neater edge to his cap of sun streaked hair. He sighed beneath her hands and opened his eyes to gaze into hers.

"Your talents have been sorely missed, Aislinn," he smiled. "Sanhurst replaces the beard with more scars than is my desire."

She laughed low and set his hand away as it was wont to wander. "Why, my lord, if nothing else you might keep me as your lackey."

He grunted. "I despair to see a lackey with so tempting a form." Then he sighed and smiled. "But indeed, it bears mark of a worthy notion."

"Ha!" she returned flippantly and rested the point of the knife against his chin. "I vow Sanhurst would protest at being so used as I and for the meager fare might well split your gullet." She lopped off an errant lock of his hair and threw it into the hearth.

Wulfgar cocked an eye to her. "Mind you well that blade, wench, ere I be like the barbarians of the south with but a knot of hair atop my pate to break its shining baldness."

" 'Twould serve you right if I shaved that fair mane," Aislinn retorted. She dipped a cloth in a steaming bowl then clapped it to his face and held it there against his struggles. "Mayhap I would have fewer widows bleating at my chamber door."

Wulfgar's reply was lost in the folds of the cloth but

277

when she withdrew it he turned a reddened face and jaundiced eye to her. "I think 'tis better I bear with Sanhurst."

Her laughter rang in the room as she stepped away from him to sweep her skirts in a low curtsey before him. "As you wish, sire. I am your slave and can do naught but obey you."

" 'Tis well," he replied with some humor.

Rising from the bench, he pulled on his gown and as he belted on his short sword he frowned slightly at her as his attention was brought back to her sadly worn garments.

"I would have seen the yellow piece on you, Aislinn. It seemed a bright and cheerful cloth and one well suited to your color."

She lowered her face and ran slim hands down the threadbare gunna. "There was little time to make it into a gown after Gowain came to fetch me, Wulfgar, and before he came I hid it to keep it safe."

"I fear you are becoming a miserly old crone, Aislinn," he sighed in disappointment. "But when we wend abroad, have you nothing better to wear?" He lifted a fold of her cloak from the peg where it hung and grimaced at the raveled hem. "I have seen your coffer and methinks you better garbed than this." He turned and raised a brow to her in question. "What do you seek, that I should feel some pity for your circumstance?"

Aislinn's cheeks flamed and she shook her head in quick denial yet his words stung her. "Nay, 'tis only that there were others at Darkenwald more in need than I. I bring no complaints to you, but my means are slim and I could not replace the loss, that is all."

Wulfgar frowned heavily but Aislinn hurriedly stepped to her small bundle and produced the yellow.

"But look, I have brought the cloth and will make of it a fine gown. 'Twill only take a few days, Wulfgar."

Perturbed with her shabby appearance, he grunted a sour reply then taking her arm escorted her to the hall below. As he handed Aislinn to a chair, Hlynn made haste to set a platter of meat before them, looking hesitantly at Wulfgar and blushing profusely. In a corner Sanhurst rose to briefly acknowledge their entry then returned to his chore of polishing Wulfgar's armor, sword and helm. From the latter he struggled to rub the last vestige of a dent but through it all kept a cautious eye bent to his lord.

Aislinn gazed inquiringly at the hearty-framed young man whose head and face showed signs of recent trimming.

Wulfgar smiled slowly as he saw her perusal. "Sanhurst," he replied to her unasked question.

Aislinn mused on the harried expression the man wore. "You seem to have him well trained."

Wulfgar grunted. "I gave him more credit than he was worth. He's found his just due."

She peered at Wulfgar. "Another Saxon taken under heel, my lord?"

Her words brought a spark of anger from the Norman knight. "Aislinn, would you defend this bumpkin to me? Be damned! You seek to shield all cloddish knaves and beggardly fools that sprout from English soil."

Her eyes widened in feigned innocence. "Why, Wulfgar, where is the need of my protection, when the lords are such fine and understanding Normans?"

Wulfgar gritted his teeth in hard-won restraint. "You would test the very saints, woman. But I must take into account that you are Saxon and thus partial to them."

Aislinn shrugged. "I seek only what is just, no more."

"And you immediately condemn me as being unjust," Wulfgar retorted. "Ask Sir Milbourne of my fairness when this beetle-headed dolt ran in the thick of battle rather than stand at my back. I have done naught save reduce his status from soldier to serf and that he well earned."

Aislinn's brows drew together in anxious worry. "Were you attacked, Wulfgar? You did not tell me. I saw no new scars—"

She stopped and her cheeks flushed as she realized that not only was Wulfgar looking at her with quizzical interest but the other occupants of the room including several of his yeomen had turned to stare at her.

"I mean"—she stammered in sudden confusion. "You made no mention—"

Wulfgar laughed heartily, his cheerfulness restored, then murmured in lower tones for her ears alone. "I do not mind your concern for me, cherie. It matches mine for you."

Aislinn bowed her head, unable to meet his mocking eyes or to endure the shame she felt. Reaching out, Wulfgar pressed a large hand over the slim ones folded tightly in her lap.

"No need for dismay, Aislinn," he grinned. "They are

aware of your skill in healing and will assume it is for that you see to me."

Raising her gaze, Aislinn found him smiling warmly at her.

"Only I know the truth for sure."

"Oh?" Aislinn raised a brow then smiled. "You would be the last to know."

Gowain joined them and seated himself beside Wulfgar. As the latter plied Aislinn with questions of Darkenwald and of Sweyn's welfare, the young knight listened with interest while he sipped a goblet of wine. In the midst of her replies Gowain raised his chalice and sniffed at it suspiciously, then frowned in puzzlement. As he glanced around his eyes settled on Wulfgar and widened. He turned away but soon his gaze returned to his lord once more. He glanced away again and again, each time bringing his gaze back as if drawn irresistibly until his odd behavior piqued Wulfgar to the core, causing him to gruffly inquire:

"What ails you, Gowain? Have I grown horns of a sudden or have you become faint from lack of wisdom?"

"My pardon, Wulfgar," Gowain said quickly. "I could not help but notice." The young man seemed to grow earnest and plucked his lip thoughtfully. "Yet—I do not think the scent of lavender becomes you overmuch, my lord."

Wulfgar's brows raised in surprise and Aislinn's squeal of laughter was quickly smothered beneath her hand. In a moment Wulfgar found the humor of it and chuckled at himself before turning a mock scowl to Gowain.

"When you come of age and must shave your face, lad, I will hold you accountable for those words."

As the mirth died Sir Gowain bent close to Wulfgar's ear.

"My lord," he whispered. "The one you sought is in the stables below. Will you see her now?"

A movement from the corner of his eye caught Gowain's attention and he glanced there to find Aislinn staring at them with a bemused frown troubling her fine brow. Her eyes questioned Wulfgar who hurried to allay her fears.

" 'Tis naught to concern yourself, Aislinn. 'Tis merely a bargain I've been seeking to settle. I shall return shortly."

He pressed her hand before he rose but Aislinn's worry was little abated as the two of them left the hall. The men entered the stables and there a merchant held a mare the color and stature of which Wulfgar admired greatly. He approached and ran his hand over the horse's flanks, feeling the strength and depth of her muscle, the straightness of her legs and the soundness of her hooves. She was a dapple-gray, almost blue where the coat was dark and a pale gray where it was light. Her brow was gray and blended smoothly into a dark muzzle on a finely tapered head. The eastern blood was well apparent yet she had the shortness of stature that marked the English mounts. She would add strength and wind to his line but better yet she would serve him other ways.

Wulfgar nodded to Gowain and then drew aside. The merchant watched greedily as he counted out the necessary coin, then exchanged it for a paper on which was painstakingly drawn the lineage of the fine creature. As the merchant went his way the two knights paused further to admire the steed.

"She is a worthy mount. The lady should be well pleased," Gowain said.

"Aye," Wulfgar returned. "But do not give word of this to her. I would save the news for a later time."

When they re-entered the hall Aislinn turned and seeing Wulfgar's pleased smile could not find it in her to make mention of the matter. Still she went and laying a hand upon his arm, looked into his gaze.

"I have never been to this fair London, Wulfgar, and I yearn to see the sights. May I stroll about this afternoon and"—here she hesitated and her cheeks reddened but to make a proper gown she had need of thread and trim and she had nothing to procure them with but what he might spare her— "and perhaps purchase a trinket or two."

A scowl deepened on Wulfgar's brow as he regarded her for a long moment and she blushed crimson when his eyes swept her tattered gown, but that was the least of her embarrassment. His words started a dull ache in her chest and brought a tightness to her throat.

"Nay," he returned somewhat gruffly. " 'Tis not a time for women to be wandering about unkept. I have no time myself and cannot send my men, for they are pressed with duties. You will do better to spend your day here behind stout doors and await my leisure."

She could only nod lamely in her disappointment, casting her eyes away as Gowain made to offer his services but was quickly frowned down. Soon Wulfgar swept his cloak about his shoulders and went to the stable, leaving Aislinn to watch after him dismally. She set Hlynn and Sanhurst to cleaning the hall and slowly made her way to the great bedchamber to set it to order. She was putting her meager belongings away when she heard the clatter of hooves on the cobblestones as Wulfgar left. She sat numbly on a bench before the window staring out over the rooftops wondering how he could use her so against her will and then dismiss her cruelly from his life.

The sun mounted the sky until it rode high overhead, but a heavy haze marked the city as the peat fires were stirred for the midday repast. Aislinn laid the bright yellow cloth carefully on the bed and stood working her shears as she planned a gown from it. Without trim it would be rather stark but a needle served her well and she was sure she could fashion a fetching gown if only some thread could be found.

The sound of voices came from the hall below and she guessed the men had returned to dine, then Hlynn's footsteps sounded outside the door and her rap rattled its hinges. Aislinn bade her enter and stood back in amazement as a whole troop of people pushed into the chamber behind her. Hlynn giggled and shrugged her innocence, spreading her hands wide to deny any knowledge of this invasion.

There were servants bearing cloth; velvets and silks, linen and wool; women with scissors, thread, trimmings and furs. Following the others came a lean tailor who swept low in a bow to her. He bade her mount a bench that he could measure. His cord was drawn and knots made and the tailor gave detailed instructions for the seamstresses to follow. Aislinn found she could halt the group only when it came to the yellow velvet she had spread on the bed. There she sat with the tailor and described while he drew, a special gown, one with full flowing sleeves and a tight bodice made low to show the best of a kirtle sewn from a pale yellow silk he had. She chose a gold braid for the trim and assured herself that more than usual care would be taken in the making.

The room began to buzz as the women snipped and stitched and the servants hurried to lay out the materials and gather up the scraps that fell from the scissors. Aislinn was hustled from hand to hand as progress was made and her approval sought. There were slippers half formed and sewn to fit her feet. There were strips of fur, fox, mink and sable, to warm the neck and cuffs. One garment in particular caught her eye, a rich cloak of fur-lined velvet. The tailor warmed to his task and smiled as the afternoon wore on. It was rare indeed that he plied his trade on a form so trim and fair or for a lord so generous.

The afternoon was half gone when Wulfgar found a small inn that was not crowded, where he could pass the time inconspicuously. He sat before a roaring fire and watched as the keeper set before him a jug of fine heady brew and a chalice for his pleasure. His duties were done and he would have returned to the townhouse but he knew the tailor would still be occupied there. He suppressed a shudder as he thought of the cost and poured another cup of the rich red wine. But damn, he would not have Aislinn seen in those rags she came in. He pondered the circumstance of her low estate and a mounting anger nettled him until he filled the cup again. Gwyneth, no doubt, he thought. She would take advantage of his absence and seek to better her own lot. But what of the coins he had left her? Spent on some trifling matter? Ah, women! Were they ever to be understood? Gwyneth, with a mother who had loved her and with a proper parentage, but endowed with the temperament of an asp. Why, when everything she had ever asked for had been handed her? What plagued her that she should be so vicious?

The more Wulfgar imbibed, the less his mind dwelt on his half sister and turned with eagerness toward Aislinn. What woman would not be pleased with such an elaborate gift of clothes? The coins spent might well be of immediate benefit to him. Surely, if anything, this would prompt her to end her resistance and come willingly into his arms and not act as if sorely set upon. Visualizing her before him, his mind lingered on the softness and grace of her supple body and flawless face. A more winsome lass none could name. But her beauty he had never questioned. She was one of many and the best of all. She made no demands upon him and yet seemed eager in all ways but this one to please him.

Damn, he thought and drained the cup. I've given her more than any other woman. He frowned at the empty chalice and cured the oversight. Why does she continue to be cool? What is her game? She seems to care and yet I touch her only through her passion and afterwards she cries as if I have cut her deeply. Others much more highly born have come to me eagerly. Yet she lies passive with indifference until I waken her and push beyond her guard. Then she finds a rapture of her own, but still she curls away and will not ask me more.

He slammed the empty cup down in disgust and filled it to the brim.

"But this will end the game," he sighed, his confidence boldly soaring. "What ere the cost I will find its worth and more in her compliance."

He sat silent for a long while imagining her in the raiment he had purchased. The thought warmed him and he drained the mug to its dregs. He found the jug but filled the shallow bottom of his cup and called for a full skin of that wondrous nectar. He felt light of heart and gay and was pleased with his own generosity, dreaming of its end and bringing to his mind a vision of red-gold locks spilled in splendid disarray across the silken pillows, of soft breasts pressed against him and of pale arms curved about him while her lips answered his.

Many hours had passed since he first entered the inn and as a shadow fell across the table, Wulfgar raised his eyes to find the keeper standing near him.

"My lord, the hour is late," the man reminded him. "And I would bar the door. Do you lodge here for the night?"

"Nay, nay, good fellow. This night of all will I seek my own bed."

Wulfgar rose unsteadily to his feet and tucked the wineskin beneath his arm. He counted out coins until the keeper was satisfied, then made his way with slow deliberation from the inn to where the Hun stood waiting. The horse snorted at the unusual gait of his master but held stone still while, after several tries, Wulfgar lay prone across the saddle and then eased himself upright and found the stirrups. Wulfgar urged his steed forward and bellowed loudly when the Hun made no move to obey. Finally the innkeeper opened his door again and untying the reins from the post handed them to the rider. The man returned to his inn, shaking his head and mumbling to himself as Wulfgar roared his thanks. Now the Hun moved off, and for the most part ignoring his master's signals, made a cautious way in the direction of the townhouse and its warm stable.

It had grown dark at the house and thick fogs crept in from the river. Alone now, Aislinn clasped her arms about her in happiness. The eight new gowns lay carefully arranged on the bed before her, finished and well sewn, a delight for any woman. But what spoke more to her was Wulfgar's generosity. She felt overwhelmed by it. Never in a thousand years had she expected anything like this from him. They were luxurious gowns, like any grand dame would wear. And he had bought them for her, with the coins he guarded so well.

She took the yellow gunna first and folded it gently away. The others followed but for one of a soft peach hue which she donned. Hlynn combed her hair long and tiringly, then twined ribbons through the lustrous braids she formed as a crown about her mistress' head. Aislinn descended to the hall to await Wulfgar's return and as she came into view the room fell silent. Her changed appearance was such that the men were struck dumb. It was Milbourne, the eldest of the knights, grizzled and scarred, who rose to give her his arm and guide her to a seat at the table. Aislinn smiled and nodded her thanks while Sir Gowain gulped and began to compose poems of praise in his ale. None seemed to be worthy of her, but his eyes glowed warmly whenever her smile turned his way.

The men were enchanted and Hlynn grinned with pleasure to see these Normans stumble over words to praise her mistress. Even Sanhurst in his corner ceased the rubbing of tallow into Wulfgar's boots to prop his chin in his hand and bend a wistful gaze upon Aislinn.

The meal was taken leisurely and was almost done when Beaufonte raised his hand for silence. Through the open shutters at the end of the hall drifted the sound of slow hooves accompanied by a loud voice bawling a song of love and devotion. The curse of an irate townsman was heard before the door slammed in the stable below. Raised brows ran about the hall and Aislinn giggled as Gowain rolled his eyes in mock anguish. The voice was muffled but grew louder as unsteady feet mounted the stairs. Without ceremony Wulfgar burst into the room with a half empty wineskin in his hand. He bellowed and swung his arm wide to greet them all, then his feet did a quaint step as he regained his balance.

"Ho, good fellows and most lovely damoiselle," he roared as his clever gait carried him into the room. His words were slurred in an odd mixture of English and French.

In Wulfgar's mind, he came forward and made a graceful bow before Aislinn as she rose to greet him and taking her hand, kissed it gently. In reality his feet tangled as he stepped before her and many caught their breaths, fearful he would crash upon her. His hand seized hers as he swayed and his kiss found a place half way to her elbow. He straightened and his eyes wandered independently about the room until they focused upon her. Aislinn had never seen Wulfgar in this state. Indeed she had always known him to be abstemious.

"My lord," she murmured softly. "Are you ill?"

"Nay, cherie. I am drunk upon this beauty that bursts upon my eyes and leaves me gasping in its tumbled wake. Forsooth I raise a salute to you." He gestured to the room at large. "To the Lady Aislinn," he shouted. "The fairest wench in any man's bed."

He raised the skin high and managed skillfully to collect some of the brew in his mouth as Aislinn glared at his crudity. Wulfgar set the wineskin aside and took her hand in both of his, pressing it to his lips and murmured in his most romantic fashion:

"Come, cherie, let us retire for the night. To bed!"

He smiled a drunken leer of goodnight to his men and, turning, put his foot in a woven basket. It was several moments before he could shake the vicious beast from him, but only Sanhurst had the gall to laugh aloud though there were choking coughs aplenty.

Wulfgar straightened, casting a glare to the guffawing Saxon and rearranged his gown. With the majestic dignity of his kind he missed the second step of the stairs and measured his length back into the hall. With a sigh Aislinn grasped his arm and beckoned to Gowain who struggling with laughter took the other. Between them, and after many false starts, they guided him up the stairs and into the chamber where he was set upon the edge of the bed. Dismissing the young knight and closing the door behind him, Aislinn turned to Wulfgar. He lurched forward as if he would sweep her into his arms, but the cloaks hung behind the door filled them instead as she easily sidestepped his lunge. One fell over his head as he flailed about to free himself and Aislinn seized his hands.

"Hold, Wulfgar." Her voice took on an edge of command. "Hold still, I say."

She disentangled him and seated him again on the bed before returning the garments. That accomplished, she stood before him, arms akimbo, shaking her head. She began to remove his gown and lifted it over his head, but with delicate timing Wulfgar rose to fling his arms about her. Aislinn squealed in exasperation, pushing against his chest and Wulfgar found himself sitting again. This time he waited as the wench was obviously eager to lay with him.

Avoiding his persistent hand, Aislinn slipped off his shoes and his chausses, pressed him back and laid the covers over him. His eyes followed her with avid warmth as she went to stand by the glowing hearth and remove her gunna, carefully folding it and placing it with the others. She loosened her hair, shaking the long length free then slipped the kirtle off placing it too, neatly aside. She kicked the slippers off as she crept beneath the covers and waited for his hand to come searching, but heard only a soft, gentle snore. She giggled and curled safely against his warm side and resting her head against his shoulder, drifted contentedly off to sleep.

Aislinn's eyes opened at the bright sunlight streaming in through the windows. They had slept unusually late she surmised but even then something had awakened her, a strange moaning sound, oddly muffled and coming from the corner where the chamber pot stood. She chuckled to herself and snuggled deeper in the covers. There was a splashing of water and then the bed creaked as Wulfgar's weight settled upon it. She turned toward him with a cheerful morning greeting upon her tongue, but it died unspoken as she found herself staring at the broad expanse of back. She rose to an elbow and pulled at his shoulder until he rolled face up. His eyes and lips were tightly clenched and a rather greenish pallor extended well down his chest. Drawing a blanket over his nakedness, she tucked it in about him then raised her eyes and found his steel gray ones regarding her from pools of livid red beneath swollen bluish lids.

287

"The shutters, Aislinn," he sighed, gesturing toward them lamely. "Close them. That light pierces me with a thousand blades."

She scampered up, dragging a heavy blanket with her to wrap about her shoulders and darkened the room, easing his pain. She paused to throw more fuel on the fire then coquettishly leapt back into the bed and snuggled against him for warmth. Wulfgar gritted his teeth as her movements bounced his head.

"Gently, my sweet, gently," he groaned. "My head feels the size of a wineskin and I swear the fur still clings to my tongue."

"Poor Wulfgar," she murmured consolingly. "The wine makes you ill when taken in such great amounts and its joys of the night are well bought with the morning's misery."

Wulfgar heaved a sigh and rolled his head. "And I am couched with a philosopher," he muttered softly as if to himself. "Perhaps your talents include some remedy for an aching pate."

Aislinn chewed on the tip of her finger as she thought for a moment. "Aye, but the cure is near bad as the ailment."

He took her hand and laid it on his fevered brow. "If I live to survive the day," he promised. "I will reward you handsomely."

She nodded and rose from the bed, snatching the blanket about her. She thrust a fireplace iron deep in the glowing coals. While it heated she mixed herbs and potion in a cup, then filled it from a jug of wine. When the iron glowed red, she plunged the heated tool into the brew until the liquid steamed. Bringing it to Wulfgar she met him with a hesitant smile.

"You must drink it all and quickly," she directed.

Wulfgar struggled upright to accept her offering. The noisome mixture wrinkled his nose when he would draw it near and his greenish color seemed to heighten. He raised his eyes in mute appeal but she placed a finger beneath the cup and pushed it firmly toward his lips.

"All and quickly," she repeated.

He drew a deep breath and held it as he tipped the chalice and drained it in a single gulp. He lowered his hand and sat hanging his head, shuddering as the bitter draught tore its way into his belly. Aislinn drew back, clearing a path. There was a small rumble which drew him upright and then another as his eyes widened. He flew from the bed, not caring of the chill and made straight way for the chamber pot.

Aislinn climbed into the bed and settled deep beneath the blankets while he was held racked with spasms over the receiving bowl. She clasped her hands and turned an innocent gaze to him when some time later he returned to her side. He dragged himself beneath the covers and flopped back too weak to move.

"You are evil, wench, beyond your years. If I live to see this out, I will have you exorcised by the monks."

Aislinn sat up and smiled down at him. "What is your proposal, Wulfgar?" she inquired gayly. "As you know only a husband truly wed can exorcise his spouse."

"Aaargh." Wulfgar writhed as if in pain. "You even bait me in my hour of need when I am stretched up the rack of your spell."

He opened his eyes and peered at her and even now some of the red had left them and a more healthy color returned to his cheeks.

" 'Tis but a cleansing balm," she sighed in feigned disappointment. "With the poisons gone you'll soon feel much better."

Wulfgar probed with his fingers about his head. "It does feel almost normal and I vow I could devour the Hun."

He drew another pillow beneath his shoulders and regarded her more warmly.

"Are you pleased with the garments the tailor made for you?"

Aislinn nodded happily, setting her coppery locks tumbling over the blanket she clutched about her. "I have never known such finery before, Wulfgar. Thank you for the gift." She bent and pressed a light kiss to his cheek. "The gowns are worthy enough for any queen." She lifted her eyes to his. "The price must have lightened your purse sorely."

He shrugged, noncommittal, as his gaze dipped to where the blanket gaped away from her breast, but Aislinn sat back upon her heels, his lustful regard unnoticed, and frowned slightly.

"But I fear the garments might meet the fate of my own. They are far too lovely to be let alone."

Wulfgar half grunted his reply. "I'll attend to that."

Aislinn plopped down beside him again and snuggled close against his side. "Then they are truly mine? To wear as I will?"

"Of course. Would I give you gifts then take them back?" he questioned, peering at her from the corner of his eye.

She brushed a cheek against his shoulder. "What can a slave claim without the will of the lord?" She sighed then laughed lightly. "I vow I must be the first slave ever to be robed so richly. I will no doubt be the envy of many at Darkenwald. What will you tell them when they ask you about dressing a slave so?"

Wulfgar snorted. "Only Gwyneth is rash enough to dare such an inquiry. But what I do with my wealth, whether meager or large, is my own affair since it was my labors which accumulated it. If I chose I could give it all away and she could say naught to me. I owe her nothing nor any other woman."

Aislinn traced a finger across his hardened chest, following the path of the scar there. "Then I must feel doubly grateful for your generosity since I am, after all, only a woman."

Wulfgar turned on his side to face her and lifted a curl from her breast. "You are more worthy than most. That you are here with me is proof."

Aislinn shrugged her lovely shoulders. "But I am still your whore and that title bears no proof of your fondness. What am I to you that other women have not been? I am the same, no more."

He laughed derisively. "Do you think I would open my purse so freely for another woman even to see her nakedness covered? I have told you in the past my thoughts for the fairer sex. Be honored that I place you above the rest."

"But, Wulfgar," she murmured softly. "Wherein does the difference lie? In this gift you give? In others' eyes I am that and no more."

He bent to her lips. "I care naught of wagging tongues or what others think," he said then kissed her, silencing further words from her. He could not resist running a hand down that finely curved back and over a full hip, but Aislinn bit her lip and drew away as his fingers touched the tender spot that remained from Gwyneth's stroke of the whip. Wulfgar frowned and held her still as he lifted

290

the blanket to view the ugly welt that curved across her hip and buttock. Aislinn could almost feel his anger build.

"What is this?" he demanded.

"A bruise, nothing more, Wulfgar," she returned lamely. "I but fell—"

He snarled and raised to his knees. drawing her up to hold her by the shoulders. "Aislinn, you play me for a fool." He spoke softly but spit the words out as if they soured his mouth. "I know the mark of a lash when I see it."

Tears welled in her eyes as their soft violet met his. "You hurt me, Wulfgar." As his grip relaxed she raised a hand to his chest. " 'Tis nothing." She shook her head vigorously. "A pretty squabble now set aright." She rubbed her hand on his chest and murmured softly, " 'Twill heal and in time be gone, but spiteful words are never so. Speak no more of it I pray. 'Tis done."

She drew away from him and stepped from the bed and set about clothing herself while he watched with a puzzled frown. In her he never ceased to find new cause for amazement. A strength, a beauty, a wisdom, her understanding when he himself could scarcely name his mood. A softness grew in him, a yen to hold her close and see that the world would never prick her more. He squelched the feeling quickly.

Bah! Women, he thought. Ever playing the tender heart. I have no need of weakness nor of prattling mouths to ever bind me down.

He rose and stretched and wondered at his recovery.

"Truly, cherie, your cures mend me well. But come, let us be about and see this day out. There is a Yuletide fair and you may view the city as is your wont."

He reached out and pulled her to him, gathering her close within his arms. He kissed her brow and then her lips and smiled down at her.

"Or better yet," he murmured huskily. "We will let London view you."

The morning sun had burned the early mists from the streets when four knights and a lovely maid left the merchant's manor and strolled leisurely through the streets of the awakening city. They soon came to a broad thoroughfare where the city folk had set their stalls and bid for the attention of wandering lords and ladies with their hawking voices. There were mimes and mummers, some with carved masks who strove to gain an audience and prattled lines of crude jokes. There were groups of acrobats who sailed high in the air from boards. There were venders of sweetmeats and wines and every sort of fare. There were also thieves and cutpurses and tricksters who would hide a pea beneath one of many shells and sought to confuse the eye.

Aislinn's gay laugh rang as the four Norman knights escorted her through the throng that grew in ever surging numbers. Young smitten lads trailed behind to catch another glimpse of that winsome face and if they pressed too close were met with a darkening scowl from the one who towered full head above them all. They strolled and stopped whenever a trinket or show caught the lady's eye. Aislinn soon found that she had but to admire a bauble and it would be purchased for her by one of her four guardians. It was Beaufonte who saw her lift a silvered mirror and rushed to her side to lay coin for it and press it into her hand. She had never seen the like of the thing

292

and thanked him for the gift most sincerely. Still she grew cautious at openly displaying interest in such wares.

Sir Gowain's subtle witticisms were met with giggles of delight from her and Wulfgar's dry humor added to the revelry. Beaufonte, himself a quiet man, stood back and laughed at their play as Milbourne chortled and repaid twice over Gowain's playful jibes.

The day was late when Aislinn tugged at Wulfgar's sleeve and pleaded succor from the crushing mob. They sought a side lane and soon found their haven where Hlynn awaited with a savory repast. A messenger from William had come in their absence with a command for all lords and knights to be present at a Yuletide mass hosted by the King, followed by the presentation of the court and then a feast. Aislinn felt her hopes dashed, for she had anticipated spending another day with Wulfgar before his duties interfered.

When the food was removed they sat awhile around the warming hearth before seeking their beds in preparation of the long day to come. Aislinn found herself again the object of attention from Wulfgar as he brusquely dismissed Hlynn and then with eager fingers sought the fastenings of her clothes himself. She was lifted up in his arms and placed gently in the great bed, but that Norman knight was sorely pressed to find that he had not yet met the price of her willingness, for though she knew again the ultimate in pleasure, afterwards he stared at the ceiling while she sobbed into her pillow.

Aislinn sat on the bed with her knees drawn up beneath her chin watching Wulfgar as he laid out his raiment for the day. Again he chose the black and red of his colors. He called Sanhurst to prepare him a bath and in deference to Gowain carefully added a touch of sandalwood to cover the hint of lavender that still clung to him.

Aislinn laughed at this last precaution. "If you would share my bath again, my lord," she said through her mirth, "I will leave the choice of scents to you."

He grunted and lowered himself in the steaming tub and began to wash.

"Will you be late this eventide, Wulfgar?" Aislinn asked somewhat hesitantly. "Or shall I wait the evening meal for your return?"

He lowered the cloth from his face and peered at her.

"My men will dine as is their wont, but knowing these affairs I vow we shall probably be out till a late hour indeed."

Aislinn sighed in disappointment. "The day will be long without you, Wulfgar."

He chuckled. "The day will be long for sure, my sweet, but you will spend it at my side."

Aislinn gasped at his words and rose from the bed, her red hair swirling about her naked form in resplendent disarray. Seeing Wulfgar's appreciative gaze lower she snatched up a blanket to cover herself and came to stand beside the tub.

"But, Wulfgar, I am Saxon. My place is not there."

He scrubbed his chest undismayed. "Your place is where I choose to take you. There will be Saxons." He smiled slowly as he lifted his gaze to hers. "Though to be sure, their loyalty is not as yours. I trust you to use some discretion. You are not a simple maid and can hold your tongue when warranted. As for you being enemy"—he raised a mocking brow—"I would swear I have never found such pleasure with a foe before."

Aislinn's cheeks brightened with color. "You are vile," she returned impatiently.

Wulfgar threw his head back and guffawed his mirth, but Aislinn whirled and strode from him.

"I have never been to court," she argued. "I could embarrass you."

He grinned as his eyes consumed her. "The English court is overfilled with stout Saxon dames and it seems that I have met every last one of them—from the giggling lass to the pinch-faced spinster—and had them pressed upon me because I chose to come without a wench upon my arm. Embarrass me? Nay. 'Twill do them good to witness my standards."

"But Wulfgar," she sighed in exasperation. "All the nobility and William himself will be there to see—I have no proper escort. They will know I'm your mistress."

He snorted. "Because you have no fat dame eyeing your every move?" His eyes smiled at her. "I could say you are my sister." He lathered the soap up in his hands and shook his head. "Nay, that would not do. They would think something amiss when I look at you and we would only be accused of a greater sin. Nay, 'tis best we bear with their questioning stares and say naught of what we are."

Aislinn groaned and tried again. "Wulfgar, I can bear the wait here—"

"But I cannot. I'll hear no more of it," he returned sternly. "Prepare yourself."

By his tone Aislinn knew he would not yield in this matter and in sudden panic realized she wasted valuable time in trying to dissuade him. Flying to the door, she pulled it open and called for Hlynn. Wulfgar sank lower into the tub as the girl quickly answered the summons. He watched in wry amusement as the two of them rushed about the room sorting out what Aislinn would wear and planning the most becoming style for her hair. Finally he caught Aislinn's eye.

"Cherie, I would not frighten young Hlynn, but should I rise I fear she would tear the door asunder in her haste to leave. The water cools and I have wrinkles to my knees. Could you spare me a moment to end this bath?"

Aislinn sent the young girl out on an errand, and with considerable relief Wulfgar climbed from the tub and resumed his dressing while Aislinn began to comb out her hair.

"I would have you wear the yellow gunna today, Aislinn," Wulfgar said over his shoulder. "The gown will do you justice."

"I beg to decline, monseigneur," she returned and waited as his questioning gaze turned her way. She smiled. "I would save it for another affair."

Wulfgar seemed somewhat bemused. "What affair is more important then meeting a king?"

Her smile widened into a beguiling grin and she shrugged her shoulders innocently. "I dare not say for what, Wulfgar, but did you not give me leave to choose as I may?"

He nodded. "I would but have you at your best and the color is becoming."

She rose and came to him, setting her hands upon his bronze chest as she lifted her gaze to his. "There is another gunna I would wear and it is a rich gown."

Her violet eyes plumbed the depth of his in silent plea. Wulfgar was dazzled by their beauty and found it hard to remember the cause for argument. Aislinn caressed his chest lightly as she waited for his reply and he could only sigh in submission.

"'Tis your choice."

Aislinn threw her arms about his neck and managed to place a kiss upon his cheek while thanking him profusely. Wulfgar scowled and turned away. But some time later when she stood before him adorned in her finery he had cause to silently vow he would not interfere again with her choice of gowns.

The gunna was of a rich creamy hue trimmed about the neck and long flowing sleeves with a silken braid sewn with tiny pearls. The girdle of delicate gold links rode her trim hips with her own jeweled dagger occupying its sheath. Her hair had been woven upon her head into an intricate fashion and twined about with narrow ribbons with a sprinkling of dainty, silk flowers of the off-white color. Her fair face glowed with its own radiance and her eyes against the black of her lashes were clear and sparkling violet.

In all of his rovings Wulfgar could not remember seeing a maid so fetchingly beautiful. For a moment he grew concerned, knowing Ragnor would be there, and he wondered what the day held for them. Perhaps the wisest thing would be to leave her behind, but he did not fancy the thought of long hours apart from her. He admitted to himself he had come to enjoy her companionship and did not grow bored with her as with other women when they were not abed. It was purely a selfish reason he had for taking her with him. He never felt entirely at ease at court. The whining complaints of fat spouses, the treachery of ambitious lords, the roving eyes of cuckolding ladies gave him reason to be ever on his guard. He was more at home on a battlefield, where he knew his enemy and could meet him face to face. With Aislinn's presence beside him he could find comfort with the day and ease the monotony of the long mass.

At Wulfgar's continued silence Aislinn turned about in a circle before him, holding her arms wide.

"Do I please you, monseigneur?" she asked.

She missed the glow in his eyes and raised her gaze to his sardonic stare when she again faced him. He folded his arms across his broad chest as he grinned.

"Do you try to weedle praise from me, cherie?"

Aislinn made a face at him. "You are stingy with your words," she accused, then laughed gayly as she swept around, tossing over her shoulder a roguish look that drew the length of him. "But I am more generous, my lord.

You are indeed a fine sight. I do not wonder that you are beset with widows and giggling lasses."

The mass was indeed long and tiring. They knelt and rose only to kneel again as the archbishop began another prayer. Wulfgar's gaze repeatedly went to Aislinn and he took pleasure in moments when others did not. The serenity of her slender hands clasped in prayer was soothing to his thoughts. She was quiet and uncomplaining beside him, only raising her head when a prayer ended and dutifully bowing it when another began. Her gaze, when he lent a hand to assist her to her feet, radiated warmth and softness. He marveled at her long-enduring graciousness when later in the throne room of the castle they were pressed into a corner by high ranking nobility seeking an introduction. His companions of two nights prior pushed others aside in their haste and with a great display of amiability clapped him on the back while their eyes dwelt mostly on Aislinn. With long suffering patience Wulfgar presented each to her and wore a stoical countenance as they casually let drop their closeness to William, as if to distinguish themselves above the ill-born knight who stood at her side. Aislinn gently withdrew her hand if they were wont to linger over it and answered their inquiries courteously, but with such skillful evasion that only Wulfgar knew she had not told all. He smiled to himself and knew she would be able to hold her own in any court, even William's.

Her elusive dignity seemed only to arouse further interest from the zealous Normans and many by their regal airs thought to win her favor. It was with considerable relief that Wulfgar heard a command for attention as the King entered and knew that knights and nobility would shortly be presented to him. In their corner Wulfgar felt Aislinn's slim hand slip into his and he glanced down to find her glowing eyes upon him. For a moment he stared down at her, wanting to say some gentle word of praise for her wisdom with his fellow Normans, but he found that his reserve with women did not lend easily to glibness here. He smiled lamely instead and pressed her hand. Aislinn's gaze searched his somewhat worriedly.

"My lord, does the day distress you or is it me you find disfavor with?"

He chuckled. "Nay, cherie, I can find fault with neither."

Aislinn smiled in relief. "You should not scowl so when you are thoughtful, Wulfgar. If I were a maid of lesser heart you would frighten me."

"Ah, lady," he sighed. "If you were of a softer mold, mayhap you would come to my bed more willingly."

Aislinn's cheeks grew flushed and she glanced quickly about to see what ears might be near to catch their words. Finding none attentive to their exchange, she smiled at Wulfgar sweetly.

"Why, my lord, it takes all my perseverance to accept your casual rape of me with meekness. 'Tis not farfetched that you may know the full flood of my wrath at being so misused by your hand."

His hand squeezed hers again. "You are not so misused," he replied and his eyes laughed at her. "What English maid has been so cosseted by her Norman lord? You must admit this is better than being chained to the foot of my bed."

Aislinn shrugged and her fingers straightened his short velvet mantle. "At least you did not dishonor me then."

Wulfgar smiled, undismayed. "I do not dishonor you now. In truth, I honor you above all other women. Do you see any other upon my arm or wearing clothes my money has purchased? For those coins I sweated and could have given my life if the foe had been the better one. I treat you kindly. You do not toil nor break the sod. You occupy a place beside me as if you were my lady. There is only a small difference in that I have no vows to forever confine me."

Aislinn opened her mouth to reply but the call to present for another knight she knew made her start and glance about. She saw him immediately and as her gaze fell on him, Ragnor de Marte smiled and saluted her and she knew he had been watching them all along. He seemed confident of himself as his eyes roamed her form, and Aislinn's cheeks reddened as she felt stripped of her clothing. Abruptly she turned back to Wulfgar who regarded the other calmly.

"You did not tell me Ragnor would be here," she said.

Wulfgar glanced down at her flushed face. "You must learn, cherie, it is better to face Ragnor whatever he's about than let him come upon you unawares. That small precaution eliminates a dagger piercing the back."

"And leaves my breast bare for his blade," Aislinn returned with sarcasm.

Wulfgar smiled. "Never fear, my lovely. I doubt if you'll ever feel that sharp instrument against your fair bosom. He is not a complete fool."

" 'Twould be a lesser evil than anything he could deal me," she said snidely.

Wulfgar peered at her dubiously but she turned to watch the brief ceremony which seemed stiff and formal and without warmth. William was of a commanding frame, as tall as Wulfgar yet a great deal broader through his body. The robes of state gave him a massive appearance and as Ragnor knelt before him the King seemed to dwarf the younger man. William's eagle eyes watched him solemnly until the knight rose; then he nodded to Ragnor's salute, calmly accepting his due. As with many of the nobles before Ragnor, William sat sternfaced, giving little hint of comraderie or friendship. Yet Aislinn noticed something subtly different when Wulfgar approached several moments later. William seemed to relax in his chair and his austere countenance softened a bit. If William felt some slight favor for this knight he was to let it go undiscerned, for his sake as well as Wulfgar's. A warm glow filled Aislinn as she watched Wulfgar bow before his king and her eyes were no longer for William.

Aislinn noticed the interest stirred among the Saxon women over his tall Norman knight and the heads coming together and the whispers that followed. When he returned to her side Wulfgar appeared unaware of the attention he aroused and took her hand once more, unconcerned with the stares directed toward them, now from the women as well as the men.

"Ah, my lord, you seem to have captured a few more roving hearts," Aislinn commented. "Is that how you've collected so many mistresses?"

Wulfgar laughed lightly as if at some jest she had made. "You are the first I've had, my love. A night or two passed with the others, no more." He kissed her hand and for the benefit of the onlookers kept a tender smile on his face. "But I've grown so enchanted with the custom that I wonder why I didn't try it before."

Aislinn smiled sweetly but gritted out her words. "No doubt in the Norman court there were so many you had difficulty choosing." Well aware of the many eyes that watched them, she fluttered her lashes downward like a coy maid. "You would have been so busy there my plain face would not have attracted your slightest attention. Oh, that such would have been the case at Darkenwald."

Wulfgar lifted her hand to his lips but whispered above it. "Have care, cherie, the chain is still at the foot of the bed."

Aislinn laughed lightly then murmured softly, "I have no fear, Wulfgar. You could not bear that cold iron bruising your shins at night."

"'Tis truth of course," he chuckled and yielded the exchange to her. "I would much prefer you willing than a beaten slave."

Growing more serious, Aislinn gazed into his eyes as she gave him answer. "Willing? You have not yet named the price. But yet neither a beaten slave, I think."

Wulfgar met her gaze and knew a strong desire to take her in his arms and kiss her despite the looks directed toward them, but a loud voice gave him pause as the feast was announced.

As Wulfgar seated her in the hall, Aislinn glanced up and across the way saw Ragnor standing beside his own chair. He smiled leisurely and when she had taken her place, seated himself as if he only waited for her. The food was placed before them and as the odor of the rich roast meat struck her nostrils, Aislinn knew the full length of a ravening hunger and realized it had been many hours since she had eaten. She gave the meal all of her attention for some moments then her eyes rose and with a start met Ragnor's. He nodded and smiled and in haste she turned away. She was careful not to look at him again, for almost in fear she knew he watched her closely. She replied lightly to the inquiries made by the other knights at the table while Wulfgar seemed undisturbed and spoke with her quietly, pointing out to her the more important nobility and those that had accomplished some heroic act. At the conclusion of the meal Wulfgar was approached on an important matter by an earl and drawn away from her side to discuss the affair openly and at length. Aislinn sat alone, amazed by the press of royalty which seemed to fill every corner of the elaborate room. Then she realized someone was taking Wulfgar's chair and glancing up, found Ragnor smiling down at her.

"Your pardon, my dove. May I sit for a moment?"

Aislinn frowned at him but could think of no good reason to deny his request.

"Wulfgar—," she began but was quickly interrupted.

"Is well occupied and I would have words with you." He took the seat and pulled the chair close beside hers. "Can you not see that Wulfgar is only using you for a time?" He saw her anger begin to rise and sought to allay it. "Has he asked you to wed him? Has he spoken any word of it? Has he given you any title or place other than as his slave? I have even heard that he has sent another damsel to abide at Darkenwald. You play him fair but should you ever lose his favor it will be the other who warms his bed and fills his nights."

Aislinn glanced about seeking some escape from his heated yet tormenting words. With a start she felt Ragnor's hand upon her thigh beneath the table.

"I would make you lady of Darkenwald and Cregan, too," he murmured, leaning toward her.

"How can you?" she snapped, pushing his hand away. "The towns belong to Wulfgar."

She would have pulled back but his arm around the back of her chair held it still and little abashed he again laid his hand upon her thigh. She struck it away and again it returned more bold than before.

"Ragnor!" she gasped and rose, moving away from him. He stood with her and taking her arm drew her close. As eyes turned to them he whispered feverishly in her ear, but she did not hear his words as she sought to pull away from him.

"Take your hands from her." Wulfgar's voice sounded low but startingly near. His open hand clamped down on Ragnor's shoulder and spun him about. "Did you forget my warning of long ago? What is mine I hold."

Ragnor sneered. "I have some claim to Darkenwald. You denied me the merest share of its worth yet 'twas I who fought the battle."

Wulfgar met his glaring stare with cool dignity. "You earned nothing there, for it was you who caused the battle."

Ragnor's dark eyes narrowed and grew dark. "You are a knave, Wulfgar," he snarled. "I have even saved your life yet you give me no quarter."

"You saved my life?" Wulfgar raised a questioning brow and did not pause for answer. " 'Twas learned by some of my men that two Norman knights rode close to Kevonshire and drew the townsmen out, leading them to a bend where they could sit in ambush for me. The arms of one knight plainly seen were Vachel's and I can well guess who the other was. Saved my life? Nay, you nearly cost it."

Aislinn's eyes widened and she gasped at Wulfgar's words. Ragnor could say nothing, but snarled in his fury. Without thought he snatched his heavy gauntlets and threw them in Wulfgar's face. They struck and fell to the floor. Wulfgar slowly drew his sword and pierced the gloves where they lay, picking them up on its point. With a sweep of his blade he returned them full force to Ragnor's face.

"What ho! Have I a battle between my own knights?" A voice demanded behind them and William joined them.

Wulfgar held his peace and returned his sword to its sheath, bowing before the King.

William turned to consider Aislinn who met his stare unshrinkingly. His eyes passed from her to Ragnor and then back to Wulfgar.

"A quarrel over a woman, Wulfgar? 'Tis not like you."

Wulfgar's face darkened. "Sire, I beg to present Aislinn of Darkenwald."

Aislinn sank into a low curtsy before the King as he further studied her. When she rose she stood before him proudly, her chin lifted and her gaze meeting his.

"You are not afraid of me, damoiselle?" William asked.

Aislinn's glance went quickly to Wulfgar then returned. "Your grace, I once answered that same question to your knight and if I am permitted to reply in kind. 'Tis God I fear."

William nodded, impressed by her frankness. "And these knights of mine fight over you. I can well see their cause." He turned to Ragnor. "What do you have to say on this matter?"

Ragnor stood stiff in his ire. "Your pardon, sire. This bastard has no right to Darkenwald nor to the Lady Aislinn, for she is part and parcel of it all, the daughter of the lord whom I did slay with my own good sword."

"Do you, Sir Ragnor de Marte, then claim these lands by right of arms?" William inquired.

"Yea, sire," Ragnor affirmed and for the first time bowed to his king.

William faced Wulfgar. "And these lands are the same you claim, Sir Wulfgar?"

"Yea, my liege. As you bid me secure them against your crown."

William considered the men then turned to Aislinn. "Have you ought to say of this, damoiselle?" he asked gently.

"Aye, your grace," she answered him proudly. "My father died as a warrior should and he is buried with his shield and sword, but he went out to meet a flag of truce. 'Twas in his mind to yield if we could but stay in peace, but he was needlessly insulted until he was forced to wield his arms to his honor. There were naught but serfs to aid him and they were slain with him." She gave a rueful smile. "He had sent all to Harold. He kept not even a horse to die upon."

William again faced the two knights. "The gauntlet has been cast I see and well returned. Sir Ragnor, will you agree to a contest of arms and abide by its end?"

Ragnor bowed his assent.

"And you, Sir Wulfgar, will you agree?"

"Yea, sire," Wulfgar replied.

"And Lady Aislinn?" William turned to her. "Will you bend yourself to the victor?"

Aislinn met Wulfgar's gray, brooding eyes for the briefest moment but knew she could give no other answer.

"Yea, sire," she murmured and dipped low before William.

The king then addressed them all. "The turn of the year approaches and on the first day of the new, we will have a joust, a contest of arms to the fall but not to death, for I have need of my knights. In this manner we will determine the lord of Darkenwald. The field and weapons will be set under my eye and let no one say after that it was less than true and just." He turned again to Aislinn and presented his arm. "Until that day is out, my lady, you will be my guest. I shall send for your possessions and attendant, and we shall see a room prepared here for you. You are under my protection from both these knaves till then and I hereby declare you a member of the royal court."

Aislinn glanced hesitantly toward Wulfgar and saw his scowl. She wanted to protest at being taken away but knew she could not. Before he led her away William smiled.

"Have patience, Wulfgar. If the day is well met we will yet see this turn to the best."

Ragnor grinned his momentary triumph but Wulfgar frowned after them feeling a loss he could not put to words.

It was late that night when Wulfgar returned to the huge bedchamber. The fire was low on the hearth and all signs of Aislinn's presence were removed. What had been a place for him to seek after a wearisome day was now a torture chamber. He saw Aislinn everywhere, standing before the window, kneeling beside the hearth, sitting on the bench, laying on the bed. He idly smoothed the cover with his hand then turned and stared about the empty room, and it was barren, an empty husk of anything it had ever been, its luxury faded, its comfort rough and cruel. Then his eyes held. Folded neatly beside the tub was a small scrap of yellow velvet. He picked it up and the scent of lavender clung to it. Closing his eyes, he passed it beneath his nose and almost could feel her beside him. He sighed in mute frustration, wanting to call the day back, wanting her here with him, her softness filling his arms. He tucked the piece carefully within his chainse and smoothed the bulge until no one would guess its presence. Taking his heavy mantle, he went below to make his bed on an empty pallet in the hall. Here the loneliness was less apparent and he again felt the soldier. Still he lay for a long time, yearning for her warmth beside him.

He rose early the next day and found his knights unduly quiet, but their eyes followed his every movement. It was Milbourne who finally broke the silence as he sprang from his chair with an oath and proceeded to curse Ragnor for a wretched knave. Gowain only raised saddened eyes and appeared much like a love-sick swain. Beaufonte stared moodily into the fire as he quaffed a warming brew.

"You are a sorry lot," Wulfgar chided and sighed. "Ready the mounts. We might as well put this day to some use."

Wulfgar lost himself in hard, rigorous labor that gave him little time to dwell upon his own low thoughts. When he returned to the manor he found a note awaited him asking him to take his evening meal with the king. His spirits lightened considerably and he dressed carefully and was soon led into the hall where William and his retinue were wont to dine. It was with some anger that he found Ragnor was also present and his mood grew almost surly as he was the one seated next to Aislinn. His irritation did not ease when the page led him to a chair of equal rank but on the other wing of the table opposite them. Aislinn could only glance his way briefly before her attention was drawn by a count seated beside her. Wulfgar conceded her beauty gave a lift to the court and saw that more than William obviously enjoyed her presence. She seemed light of heart and answered gayly when spoken to, even quipped and told stories of ancient Saxon feuds, yet she kept well clear of Ragnor's hands. That fellow, in the company of the king, donned his best manner and made light fun with his quick wit and ready tongue. His eyes remained on Aislinn, however, and if his hands were properly tame his eyes devoured her greedily beneath the guise of innocent glances. While forcing a smile Aislinn snapped at him beneath her breath:

"Will you allow me to remain clothed in the presence of the King?"

Ragnor's laughter rang out and Wulfgar's brow darkened. The evening dragged for him. He was continuously aware of Aislinn and chafed when her laughter tinkled brightly in the hall. He felt out of sorts. He could not chatter endlessly of nothing as seemed the wont of others. Yet often during the meal he felt William's eyes upon him and knew that he was watched. He respected William's wisdom in allowing the duel, for if he won the day there could never be any question of his title. Yet the absence of Aislinn marked him. He hid himself in the guise of a soldier and responded to the wit of the lords with a forced grin, mumbles and a nod. He sipped a chalice of wine that grew warm in his hand and gave him no ease. He could find no moment alone with Aislinn and aware of William's scrutiny he would not press the point.

The whim of the king was difficult to plumb and Wulfgar knew he was fiercely loyal to his own Matilda. With so much at stake Wulfgar could not risk a scene that would leave it all amiss or give Ragnor cause to say he had acted less than fairly. Finally he gave up trying to speak with her and, making his adieus, left the hall and dismally made his way to his own lonely pallet.

Aislinn found a moment of peace and glancing about the hall realized Wulfgar was gone. Her gay mood fled and left her with an ache that would not be eased. She made a poor excuse and sought her own chambers, finding Hlynn awaiting her there. She fought back tears until she could with cause dismiss the girl for the night. When she was safe abed and could smother them in a pillow the sobs came long and hard. The court was a fascinating place and the Normans treated her with a deference that was easy to accept. When she had learned Wulfgar was to be present, she had been elated and had waited eagerly for the first sight of him. None could have named her a bumbling country lass, not even Gwyneth if she had been present. Even Ragnor had been charming, when his eyes were not seeking out her pleasing assets. But whenever she looked to Wulfgar his eyes were elsewhere and from his frowns she knew his mood was far from good. He had worn a soft brown gown that on his tall, lean frame had rivaled William's richer garb. In the whole of the evening no word had passed between them, no note of tenderness or care had come from him, and she sobbed anew at his neglect.

I am shameless, she thought. A heated vixen, for even though I have no vows to bind us I lie here and crave his arms about me. Oh, Wulfgar, make me more than a harlot. I cannot abide these things I feel.

She longed for his hard-muscled warmth beside her in the bed. The silken pillow had no firm ribs for her to caress nor gently rising chest for her to lay her head upon nor arms to even in sleep draw her near. She remembered each scar, each bulging of his arm and even the chafing of his beard along her neck. She tossed and turned, taking small peace from her enforced chastity and more than once shook her thoughts away from waking dreams of him gently caressing her in the night.

Once more a note came from William and though Wulfgar had little cause to enjoy the night before, this time he had no choice, for the King demanded his attendance. Now the day drew out with painful slowness and Wulfgar chafed, for his duties did little to occupy his time and he was not looking forward to another evening of watching Aislinn from afar. Thus he entered the palace with dragging feet and to his amazement was led immediately to Aislinn. The radiance of her smile nearly intoxicated him, and her eyes seemed to caress him with their tender touch.

"Wulfgar, you would dally so long the evening is well spent. Come, sit."

She reached up and tugged at his sleeve, pulling him down in the chair beside her. The glow of her beauty and the warmth of her greeting struck the wit from his tongue and he could only mumble a simple reply.

"Good eveningtide, Aislinn." Then he ventured further in clever repartee. "Is all well with you? You look fit."

"Do I?" She laughed low and smoothed her hands down the ice blue silk of her gunna. "You were kind to give the gown to me, Wulfgar. I hope you are not distressed at them taking the garments without your permission."

Wulfgar cleared his throat. "Nay, why should I be? I gave them to you, therefore I have no further claim on them."

Aislinn laid her hand casually upon the one he had resting on his thigh and her violet eyes held him softly. "You appear well too, my lord."

Wulfgar sat in awkward silence, struggling with himself to keep from crushing her to him. Her hand upon his gave him difficulty, for its softness led to imaginings of other parts of her body which he knew were softer yet and more pliable beneath his caress. Feeling the hot blood stir in his loins, Wulfgar withdrew his hand only to heighten his torture, for her hand remained on his thigh. He paled somewhat and glanced around in discomfort. He saw Ragnor across the way occupying his seat of the night before and that knight's eyes centered upon Aislinn.

"He watches you like a hawk," Wulfgar complained, "as if he were already tasting the sweetness of your flesh."

Aislinn laughed softly and ran a finger down Wulfgar's sleeve. "It has taken you long enough to see his aims but now you see his threat overmuch. Others have leered at me with more open intent." As his scowl turned upon her, her eyes twinkled into his. "Never fear, Wulfgar. I have turned them away, assuring them my hand is already spoken for." She raised the mentioned member and he took it in his own. "See, Wulfgar," she smiled. " 'Tis not so hard

307

to claim my hand in public. You have taken all else, why not my hand?"

"Your hand?" he sighed. He brushed her fingertips against his lips. " 'Tis more than that I crave. I called you here to warm my bed and now to find companionship must seek out my men."

"Poor Milbourne," she chuckled. " 'Tis hard to see him meeting your tastes in entertainment. And Gowain harder still. His poetry and prose must ill dispose your ear. Or do you sit like four ancient lords before the fire and exchange memories of feats long past?"

"Nay," he replied and in dour truthfulness continued. "It seems the three of them have grown dotty in your absence. Gowain moons about the place as if 'twere his love lost while Milbourne rages at this abuse and Beaufonte sits before the fire ever deeper in his cups." He laughed at his own words. "I have seen more cheer in the dungeon than in that house."

Aislinn dropped a consoling hand upon his arm. "But what of you, Wulfgar? Does not Sanhurst see to your needs?"

"Ha!" Wulfgar sneered. "Do not mention that Saxon's name in my presence. The fool would put a saddle backwards if left alone."

Aislinn laughed and caressed his arm as if to soothe him. "Be easy with him, Wulfgar," she lightly admonished. "He is but a lad and does not know the ways of lords and knights. He will learn if given time to know your whims and will serve you well."

Wulfgar sighed. "I must be ever counciled on the treatment of my serfs and as if I were blind, led to believe that hulking bear is some tender-faced lad."

So the evening wore until the meal was done. But every time Aislinn touched him, Wulfgar fought an urge to take her from the room to the nearest bed and there make her kindle to his caress until the flame consumed him. Beneath the table he felt the innocent brush of her thigh against his and where it touched he burned. He clamped an iron-hard self-control on his passion, answering others easily when they questioned or commented but with Aislinn it seemed he was ever given to stilted words. As she laughed with some lord he hardly knew over that one's clever tale, she leaned against his arm and he felt the softness of her breast. Wulfgar silently groaned and nearly turned away in his agony. William's approach gave him a diversion and excuse to rise. He started up but William waved him back in his chair.

"So, Wulfgar," the conqueror said, "on the morrow we will see this matter done. But tell me true, what plagues you? You do not seem the amiable companion I've known of yore. Let us lift the horn and taste the ale and be of lightened heart as we have done on many nights long passed."

"Your pardon, sire, but all that I have strived to accrue in this world will rest upon the field of honor. I do not fear my cause but I grow weary with the wait."

William chuckled. "Indeed, you have little changed. But I fear I have erred. You seem a poor companion for a lady so fair and lively. You may desire her but your manner speaks little of it. Were I the maid I would prick you sorely."

Wulfgar flushed and glanced away. "The lady has been within my care of so long I find her absence much unsettling."

William peered at Wulfgar closely, pausing a moment. "Indeed, Sir Wulfgar? And have you seen to the lady's honor? It has been our lot to cast her from her home. 'Twould be a sorry thing were we to abuse her name as well."

Wulfgar raised a doubtful brow to the king, wondering at the meaning of his words, and as William met his eye he continued in a lighter almost flippant manner.

"Be at ease, Wulfgar. I know you well and have every faith in you that you would do anything but see so fine a jewel cast in less than a perfect setting."

William rose, dropping a hand upon the warrior's shoulder and then left him. As Wulfgar turned back to Aislinn she gazed hesitantly into his brooding face.

"Is there anything amiss, Wulfgar?" she inquired softly. "Has the king brought distressing news?"

"Nay," he said shortly. "Would that the morrow be done and I could take you from here. Ragnor is a fool if he thinks I will give you up to him. You are mine and I will not abide encroachment."

"But, Wulfgar," Aislinn murmured. "What will you do? The king has spoken."

Wulfgar raised a brow at her. "Do? Why, cherie, I will win of course."

16

The first day of January 1067 came slowly in the murky skies of London. The low mists lightened first and then the blackness overhead faded to a dull, smoke-laden gray. The air was cold and as a rare breath stirred it was damp and moist against the skin. Before Wulfgar broke the fast he donned full armor and rode the Hun to an open field near the townhouse. There he worked the war horse upon the frozen turf renewing an old acquaintance with the heavy weight on his back. The sun was high and mists of morn long fled when Wulfgar was satisfied and returned the steed to the stables. He fed the horse and rubbed him, still the mount felt the coming fray and stomped and chafed in eagerness to be about the day's labor. Wulfgar climbed the stairs and made a late breakfast for himself from the kettle of brewis that simmered over the fire. Finishing the meal he went to the hearth and settled himself before it, propping his feet on a low stool. He sat musing upon the battle to come until he realized the light had grown strangely dim around him. He looked up to find Gowain, Milbourne and Beaufonte had approached him and were awaiting his attention.

Gowain was first to speak as he perched on the raised hearth near Wulfgar's feet. "My lord, take heed. I have watched Ragnor often in battle. It seems that on the charge he has a tendency to lean—"

Wulfgar held up a hand to stop him.

311

Milbourne leaned forward. "Wulfgar, hear me out. 'Tis more important that you know he carries his shield high and a bit across his body, thus weakening his defense. If a blow was struck so, it would push aside and bid you enter."

"Nay, nay, good fellows," Wulfgar laughed. "I hear your words and in another case would heed them, but there is only one thing I need to know, that he has more a coward in him than knight and I will have no one on the field to guard my back. I thank you for your care, but here is in any other battle what I do on the moment will be of more import than what I plan here. The day is set and well away. See you there to cheer me on and lend a hand if I fall. Sir Gowain, will you be my second?"

With the young knight's eager nod, Wulfgar rose and made his way up the narrow stairs to the huge, empty bedchamber. In closing the door, he paused, thinking of the glow that seemed to fill the room when Aislinn was present. He swore an oath as again he recognized the signs of the dismal mood which held him of late. The coming battle would demand the use of all his mental faculties to see it done rightly and to his gain. He could not be forever dwelling on thoughts of that saucy wench as Gowain was wont to do. His determination of the night before must hold firm. He told himself it was not Aislinn he fought for so much as Darkenwald, but he knew deep within him there were other lands to be got but there was only one Aislinn, and he had not grown tired of her yet.

He disrobed, and washing, donned garments that would see him to his tent at the field. He laid out his mail and shield upon the bed. Sanhurst had labored long to polish and shine them yet Wulfgar frowned at the helm as he put it with his armor. He could still trace the outline of a dent across the back. He wondered at his opponent and what lengths he would go to have Aislinn. The ambush at Kevonshire had near cost him his life and if that was the end Ragnor sought, today's tournament would not appease him if he lost. He had always been wary of the knight, never fully trusting him. Now he had good reason to distrust him as long as he had life.

Before leaving the chamber he stood in front of the hearth where the coals glowed red, yet there was no fire to warm him. Sanhurst had been lax again and failed to put kindling beside the hearth, but it did not matter now.

He would be gone in a few moments and Aislinn was not here. With a sigh he picked up the small scrap of yellow velvet from the table beside him and stared at it for a long time before tossing it on the coals where it scorched, then ignited, and was gone in a small burst of flame.

Whirling abruptly, Wulfgar flung a heavy mantle about his shoulders and strode to the bed where he gathered his equipment into a bundle, then strapped on his sword and tucked within his belt an ax which Sweyn had given him as a companion upon his journey. With his gear he descended again to the hall where the three knights awaited him. Sanhurst glanced up from the task of clearing away the remains of his lord's meal and Wulfgar scowled at the young man, noticing his lateness at doing so, but bit off the sharp words that baited his tongue. For once since having the Saxon in his service he was determined to be patient, nettled by Aislinn's pleading words.

Gowain came to him and taking the bundle from him left the hall. Wulfgar followed with Milbourne and Beaufonte and chuckled as the older knight with much humor pleaded with him not to damage the goodly Sir Ragnor overmuch.

"After all, my lord," Milbourne grinned. "If he were gone, who would you have about to exercise your anger upon except us three?"

It was a heady sight, though rare. Every favored lord in London came to view the coming combat. Small pavilions were draped with cloth that pulled aside. Other seats were simple and crude affairs and intended only to form a perch for their bearers. The edges of the entire field were draped high with multicolored banners to shield the fray from the preying eyes of serfs and peasants, for this was an affair of honor and not meant for common folk.

Wulfgar and his party entered the field. As he and Gowain made their way to the tent that bore his colors, Wulfgar surveyed the grounds. William's pavilion was still closed against the chill breeze that swept the field and no sign of Aislinn was to be seen. There was great activity around Ragnor's tent and Wulfgar surmised he had arrived early and was as anxious as he himself to get the deed done.

Wulfgar dismounted at his own tent, and as Gowain entered he paused to caress the Hun and hang a bag of grain over his nose. Sweeping into the shelter, Wulfgar found

313

Gowain inspecting the links of his mail and the enarmes of his shield. In silence Wulfgar donned the leather garments he wore beneath the armor and with Gowain's help shrugged into the heavy hauberk.

A plate of meat and wine was brought to them. Wulfgar declined the brew but Gowain took a second draught that equaled the generous amount of the first. Seeing this, Wulfgar raised a dubious brow.

"'Tis not meet that we should lose the maid with this small skirmish, Gowain. 'Twould take a heartier one to see that done."

The young knight saluted him. "My liege, I have all faith in you."

"Good," Wulfgar replied, belting on his sword. "Now lay aside that cup and hand me my gauntlets before I must give assist to you."

With a grin Gowain postured a bow and then accommodated him.

Time dragged out and Wulfgar gave no thought to William's intent, but only that he must win. In the past he had been noted for his jousting and he must be at his best today, for he knew Ragnor was both strong and cunning. They had never met before in a tourney of arms, yet he was not fool enough to believe that Ragnor could be easily beaten. It would take great strength and wit to win this day.

Trumpets blared, and he knew they announced the arrival of the king and his party. Aislinn would be with William, the only woman in the King's group. If it had been another king, Wulfgar knew he would have had cause to worry, but William was not wont to take mistresses nor be anything less than a loyal husband to Matilda.

Wulfgar swept the flap aside and strode from the tent to where the Hun stood waiting. He removed the bag from the steed's nose and caressed its velvet softness, speaking to him in a low voice as one would talk to a close friend. The horse snorted and nodded as if in reply. Wulfgar mounted and Gowain handed him up his helm and shield. The front of the tent was hidden from the king's pavilion and though he desired to he could not see Aislinn nor she him.

Across the way, Ragnor strode from his tent with Vachel, the former nodding his head while the latter spoke to him. As he swung up onto his horse Ragnor caught sight of his opponent already mounted and waiting for the signal. He settled into his saddle, bending his body forward in a mock bow, and his laughter rang with exaggerated confidence.

"At last, Wulfgar, we are met," he called. "Come see me at Darkenwald with the fair Aislinn as my own when this day is done. I will not begrude you a glimpse of her, since you gave as much to me."

Gowain stepped forward with fists clenched.

"Hold, lad," Wulfgar counseled him. " 'Tis my affair. Let me have the honor."

Ragnor's mirth rose as he rocked back in his saddle with glee. "What, Wulfgar? Another swain smitten by the tender wench? You should be hard pressed by now keeping them from her. I vow even your favored Sweyn has had the urge to tussle her. Where is that good heart by the way?" Ragnor laughed, knowing full well the answer. "Guarding my lands?"

Wulfgar knew the game and gave no word or gesture but sat mute in reply. Vachel murmured a word to Ragnor that caused him further peals of laughter and only the blare of trumpets sobered him. The two knights rode as if to meet each other—then swerved and galloped toward the king's tent. Now Wulfgar caught sight of a yellow snood covering Aislinn's head and as he neared could see she wore the yellow velvet gown beneath her fox-lined cloak. He felt pleased with her choice. Without spoken words she gave him her favor by choosing to wear that garment.

William stood as they neared the pavilion and acknowledged their salutes. He then read the order of the day, which commanded all to honor the outcome of the meet. Aislinn sat next to William, tense and pale, obviously distraught at the thought of what would come. Though Wulfgar's gaze remained on the king her eyes held him. Aislinn wanted to cry out her preference and let the world know whom she would have, but as part of the prize of combat she was not asked to declare herself.

The trumpets sounded again, seeming strident against her ears, and as the horses whirled Aislinn thought she saw Wulfgar glance her way but she could not be sure, for if he had, his look had been brief. The knights went to their places, each marked with a banner bearing their

315

crest and colors. As they turned and faced each other they drew on their helms. Both were handed a lance by their seconds and again both saluted the king. Now the trumpets began to play and when they ended it would be time for the first charge. Aislinn was tense and fearful yet outwardly sat proud and aloof. Her heart would not cease its rapid pace and thudded hard against her breast. As she clenched her hands together beneath the mantle she silently renewed the prayer she had murmured within the chapel that morning.

She held her breath as the last note of the trumpets fell. The great horses bunched their muscles and charged forward, the rapid tattoo of their hooves echoing the beat of Aislinn's heart. The knights came together with a crash of arms that made Aislinn start. Wulfgar's lance glanced off his opponent's shield and Ragnor's splintered against Wulfgar's arms. Aislinn released a grateful sigh as she saw that Wulfgar was unharmed and still astride and for a moment her heart warmed. The two men wheeled and returned to their boxes, each taking new lances and she again knew fear. The second charge was made with no warning. This time Wulfgar struck fair but his lance shattered into a thousand splinters. Ragnor took the blow and was rocked back, his own lance rising and missed Wulfgar completely. They returned to their places and took new lances. The great Hun was warming to this fine play, and Wulfgar could feel his muscles tremble as he waited. Now Ragnor whirled and the sound of the charge was like thunder. Wulfgar leaned into his lance and took the edge of Ragnor's shield. The Hun slammed into Ragnor's horse and he was thrown to the ground. Aislinn bit her lip as Wulfgar's Hun stumbled over Ragnor's destrier but he kept his feet. Wulfgar withdrew slightly and seeing Ragnor struggle to rise, cast aside his own lance and dismounted to meet his opponent on foot. With an angry snarl twisting his lips, Ragnor snatched the spikeless mace but quickly flung it down. With spikes it would have been a deadly weapon indeed, but William sought to save his knights. It did little to appease Ragnor's blood lust.

Where he stood Wulfgar drew the ax from his belt and hefted it but cast this weapon aside also. Both knights now drew their heavy broadswords and began to walk toward each other as Aislinn watched in pained silence. The first blows rang smartly in the cold winter air. It was difficult

316

to follow the blows for the blades flashed in the sunlight and seemed to continuously ring on one another. Aislinn sat rigid, willing her body from any outward display of her emotions. The tall, heavy shields provided a wall from behind which each knight fought. The blades glistened in the sun and again and again thudded into the shields. Sweat began to run from the faces of the two men and trickled unheeded beneath the leather coats that padded the hauberks. Ragnor was fast and deft, Wulfgar while a bit slower wielded his strokes with more sureness. This was no mere duel of rapiers but a test of sheer strength and will. Whoever could last out the other would win the day. Ragnor began to feel the weight of his sword on his arm and sensing this, Wulfgar drew vigor from some unknown source and pressed his attack the harder. But of a sudden there was a weight about his leg and his foot tangled in the chain of the fallen mace. Ragnor seized upon his advantage and rained his blows stout and heavy. Wulfgar fell to a knee as the weight about his ankle held him fast. Aislinn half came to her feet and smothered a gasp with her hand. Still, William heard the sound and took full note of whom the maiden favored.

Wulfgar shook the fetter from his leg and managed to rise beneath Ragnor's stunning blows. He stumbled back and gained respite and met the other's renewed attack with both feet now solidly on the ground. The battle raged and it seemed that neither could gain the upper hand until again by sheer strength Wulfgar began to tell on the other. Suddenly his great long sword reached out, not with a swinging blow but with a thrusting motion. It caught Ragnor's helm and knocked it askew. Before he could recover the blade had swung high in the air and now crashed down, biting into the edge of the shield and striking the helm again. Ragnor stumbled and Wulfgar fought to draw his sword free from the other's shield. Ragnor discarded the piece as Wulfgar freed his blade. He now wove an ever pressing net of steel about the dark knight. Ragnor was forced to retreat, having to provide with his weapon both defense and attack. He found more and more that his sword was held to meet the other's or turned aside. A stunning blow caught his shoulder and sapped the arm below its strength. His ribs smarted as the ever threatening blade rang against the mail that covered them. Ragnor stumbled again and his sword fell for the barest instant.

The helmet flew from his head as Wulfgar's sword smote heavily. Ragnor dropped and rolled upon the frosted grass, trampling it beneath his flailing limbs. Wulfgar stood back and rested, panting heavily as he watched the other try to rise. Again and again Ragnor strained to gain his feet but always fell back upon the sod. Aislinn held her breath as she waited, praying with every ounce of her being that the contest was at an end. Ragnor finally lay motionless and Wulfgar slowly turned to William, saluting him with the hilt of his sword against his forehead. It was Aislinn's wide eyes and look of fear upon her face that warned Wulfgar of the movement behind him. He spun in time to turn aside Ragnor's blow and laid the knight flat with the broadside of his sword hard against the ribs. Ragnor let out a yelp of pain as he was flung to the ground by the impact. This time he made no move but moaned in agony against the earth.

Now Wulfgar approached the king's pavilion. He caught a glimpse of Aislinn's joyful face out of the corner of his eye before directing a question to William.

"Is the contest met, sire?"

William smiled and acknowledged him. "I never doubted the outcome, Wulfgar. You have done this day a worthy battle and have upheld the field of honor." He peered askance at Aislinn and remarked with dry humor to Wulfgar, "Poor maid, she thinks to thrive upon your meager ardor. Should I warn her to take less heart in your winning?"

Wulfgar stabbed his sword into the ground and tossing his gauntlets upon the earth beside it, cuffed his helmet and coif from his head and perched them upon the hilt. With bold strides he mounted the steps of the pavilion and came to stand before Aislinn, startling a gasp from her as he snatched her from her seat. He kissed her with deliberate slowness, holding her crushed against him as if he would draw her within his own body. His lips parted and moved upon hers with a searing hunger she had known only in the privacy of the bedchamber.

Ragnor was helped to his feet by his cousin and the two stood alone on the empty field, watching the embrace. Ragnor's body ached and his face twisted in a grimace of pain that hid his inner rage. As he leaned against Vachel, the other heard him speak with vengeance heavy in his voice.

"Someday I will kill that bastard," he muttered, then he turned and limped toward his tent.

When Wulfgar released Aislinn, she sank slowly back into her chair, no strength left in her knees, and struggled until she could draw an even breath. Wulfgar turned to William and made a brief bow.

"Does that meet your pleasure, Sire?" he asked.

William laughed heartily and winked at Aislinn. "Aah, the truth will out. The lad is more eager for you than the lands."

Aislinn blushed but found pleasure in his words. The king became more serious as he turned back to Wulfgar.

"There are contracts to be drawn as the result of this and the time will be well taken. I bid you come tonight to my table and sup with myself and your charming lady, for I would extend her presence to the limits. The court has been dull without the benefit of feminine companionship. We shall see you then. Good day, Wulfgar."

William turned and left, gesturing for Aislinn to accompany him. She did as bade, drawing the hood of her cloak over her brilliant hair, but before she descended the steps she cast a glance back over her shoulder at Wulfgar and bestowed a farewell smile upon him.

Now with the hardship of the day behind him, Wulfgar could relax, yet as he returned to the townhouse and waited for evening to approach he found himself champing at the bit. Each time he thought of Aislinn he felt the excitement stir within him and he grew more anxious for the night. He chafed at the delay as Sanhurst labored up the stairs with buckets of steaming water, impatient for the bath that would soak the aches and pains from his bruised body. He sorted through his garments with a critical eye, finally settling again on the brown, a sober hue and one he would not feel conspicuous in.

A gay abandon overcame him as he rode through the streets that evening to the castle and he hummed an ancient air, his spirits considerably lightened. He was greeted differently now at the court. The Hun was taken and openly admired by the men. He was guided by a page to the hall, where he was met by a large group of lords immediately upon passing the door. They paid him compliments and congratulated him on the battle. As they parted he saw Aislinn across the room standing quietly with another woman. Yet her eyes were upon him. Their gaze met and held as they exchanged smiles. She was a poised beauty, seeming unattainable, yet of all the high lords present Wulfgar marveled that it should be him to have claim upon her.

Begging leave of the men, he strode toward her and she moved to meet him.

"Again, my lord," she murmured. "You have won me."

The expression on his face did not change as he presented his arm and she laid her hand upon his.

"Come," he bade her and esco..ted her toward their chairs at the table. His manner was that befitting a victorious knight claiming his prize and none present guessed the truth. Within his chest there was an ache to take her in his arms and smother her protests with his kisses. It sapped the strength of his will to walk beside her, feeling her touch light as down on his arm and not turn and astound the court with what he felt.

The meal was passed in light repartee and amid many toasts to Normandy, the Crown, England, William, and finally to Wulfgar's victory of the day. The food had been devoured, the wine drunk, and Wulfgar's courage and skill at arms well noted when the guests began to melt quickly away. A page came and bent to Aislinn and whispered in her ear. She turned to Wulfgar.

"The King wants a private word with you, and I must go make ready. Farewell for now, monseigneur."

Wulfgar rose and waited as the table was moved away by servants then knelt before his king. He heard the doors close behind the servants as the chamber was emptied, and Bishop Geoffrey moved to stand behind William's chair.

"Sire, I am at your call," Wulfgar said, bowing his head.

"Rise, sir knight, and hear my words," William returned firmly. "You have fought this battle and the day is won. The lands of Darkenwald and Cregan with all between and around are yours as is the Lady Aislinn. Let no one from this day forward question your possession of them. It is known to me that the lands are small and thus I would not give you lordship over them. Instead I give you full title. They lay in command of the roads east and west and the shortest route to the coast from London. It is my wish that you build at Darkenwald a fine stone castle able to quarter a thousand men or so, should the need arise. Though Cregan sits at the crossroads, it is also in the lowlands and poorly protected. A castle there would bear witness to all of our hand upon the land. Darkenwald will serve the same purpose and nestles in the hills beyond. There the castle should be built. You will pick the site and build it strong and well. The Norwegians still lend an eye to England and the kings of Scotland would also bend them to their heel. So we must plan."

He paused and raised a hand to the bishop who moved forward taking from his voluminous robes a scroll which he spread and slowly read. When it was done the King affixed his seal upon it and the bishop handed it to Wulfgar and withdrew from the room. William sat back and clapped his hand to the arms of the heavy chair.

"It has been a day to remember but again I say to you, Wulfgar, I had no doubt."

"My liege is overkind, I fear," Wulfgar murmured, somewhat abashed at this rich praise.

"Yea, Wulfgar, I am overkind," William sighed. "I am overkind but I do naught without cause. I know that you are loyal to me and will see to my affairs, for soon I must return to Normandy. Even in that fair land there are those who would see me set aside for their own purpose, and I have few enough truly loyal men to do my business here. Build the castle strong, I bid thee, and hold the lands for your own sons. I know well a bastard's plight and 'tis the least of fair that I should share my fortunes with another of my kind."

Wulfgar had no words to answer him and the King rose and stepped forward, holding out his hand. Wulfgar clasped it and they stood for a moment as two soldiers looking eye to eye.

"We have shared many a cup, good friend," William said softly. "Go your way and make the best of it and do not in a foolish moment cast away the Lady Aislinn. It comes to mind that she is a rare woman and would do any man honor as his wife."

Wulfgar dropped to his knee again and paid homage to his king.

"The lady will be sent to you in all good time, Wulfgar," William continued. "I shall see you again before you leave London and before I leave for Normandy. Good tidings, Wulfgar. Good fortune, friend."

With that, William left the room and Wulfgar made his way to the yard where the Hun awaited him. He mounted and left the castle courtyard yet had little cause to hurry home. He could not help but wonder when William would release Aislinn to his custody once more, and chafed at his failure to plead for his cause. He wandered aimlessly, gazing at the buildings he passed. He found a small tavern and went within, calling for a jug of ale from the keeper. It was in his mind that perhaps this brew could ease his loneliness. Enough of it, he sneered to himself, might even make the night more bearable. He raised the cup and the stuff was bitter in his mouth. It gave no ease and he soon rose, leaving the cup half full. He rode again and wandered afield, stopping at another inn and this time ordering a thick red wine. But it, too, could ease his pain no smallest amount. Again he was on his way and he found himself standing once more before the townhouse. He gazed at it with saddened heart, reluctant to enter. It was late when he made his way into the hall, and all others had long since sought their pallet. A low fire burned in the hearth and he paused to bank it for the night. He climbed the stairs with lagging step, but as he passed the small chamber Hlynn had occupied he heard a sound.

What's this? He paused. Can it be? Hlynn? 'Tis Hlynn. If she is here then Aislinn must be—

Now his feet carried him on with urgent haste to the main chamber's door and he threw it open to reveal her standing beside the window combing her hair. She turned at his entry and smiled. He closed the door behind him and leaned against it, his eyes going about the room. All was in its place, her gowns where they should be, her combs on the small table. It was as if the room gained new life from her presence. She was dressed in a soft, clinging white kirtle. She seemed to glow with a radiance of her own, and her smile shone warmly in the soft light of the candle burning beside her. Aislinn could not see him well in the darkness beyond the candle, but suddenly he was there taking her in his arms, pulling her face up until his lips pressed against hers, smothering all words, all greetings, in a greeting more ageless than all. He gave her no time to breathe but lifted her in his arms and carried her gently to the bed. She gasped for air and would have spoken but his lips covered hers again and he was on top of her, crushing her into the soft coverlet. His hand slipped down the open neck of the kirtle, and his burning lips traced a path across her throat down to where his hand trapped tender game. He pushed the garment up to take it from her but he drew back confused. Aislinn's lips trembled and her eyes were tightly closed, yet tears slid from between the lids and ran across her cheeks. He frowned.

"Aislinn, do you fear, my love?" he ventured.

"Oh, Wulfgar," she breathed. "I fear only that you will cast me aside. Will you ever know my plight?" She opened her eyes and looked at him. "A goblet may be often filled with wine and tasted with full pleasure, but when it's bent and turns the lip then it is cast away, no longer used. 'Tis a thing. Purchased. Owned. Used. I am a woman. My purpose was made in Heaven and I fear the day when I am bent and cast away and another fills your need."

He laughed away her fear. "There is no goblet that also tastes the wine nor finds the brew more heady once it's filled. Yea, poor cup, my hand has grown accustomed to the grip and you provide much more than I would ever raise up to my lip. Bent or not, I find your brew more filling than what the vine could bear." Then he chided her lightly. "And you have your pleasures too, I know."

She rose, tucking her feet beneath her and straightened her gown around her. "Monseigneur." She met his gaze. "I spent these days in William's court. I made myself a gentle maid and he looked at me a gentle maid and all the lords treated me as such, yet the falseness of it all was bitter in my mouth, for I know what I am."

"You belittle yourself, cherie, for this day I've laid my life on the field for you. What greater price would you demand?"

She laughed in mockery, waving a hand. "What price did you pay for your women in Normandy? The cost of one gown or two? A copper or a handful? What difference one coin or a thousand? But the woman is still a whore. For tonight the cost was some hour of your life today. The price is dear, I grant you." She laid a hand upon his arm. "Even unto me, for I value your life perhaps more highly than you. What price did William pay for your life, for your loyalty sworn by oath? Could I purchase it from him? Would you then make your oath to me? But whatever cost you lay to me I am still a woman, gentle reared. If I come willingly for your price, I will still be a whore."

Wulfgar rose and stared down at her in anger. "You are mine, twice pledged from your own lips."

Aislinn shrugged and smiled at him gently. "A choice of

evils, once to ease the burden of a loathsome sort, once to see your honor held. Wulfgar, can I make you see?" She held out a hand to the door. "I can go yonder out upon the streets and would you say me not that I could bring to my bed this night an even dozen lords of high repute?"

Wulfgar shook his head and would have denied it but she spoke earnestly as if she could force the thoughts into his mind.

"Wulfgar, hear me out. What matter one or a dozen? What matter the cost? If I come willingly, then I am whore."

Now he almost sneered at her, having lost his amorous bend. "Then what matter your handful of coppers or words spoken in some hallowed hall? What makes the difference but that you bind a man for his lifetime?"

She turned her face away from him and the tears welled again as she knew he little understood what made her the very woman he desired. Her words were spoken so softly he had to strain to hear them.

"I am here when you would have me. I may cry out and yield to you again, but again I shall resist you to the limit of my will."

She hung her head in dejected defeat and tears dripped slowly on the back of her hands folded in her lap. Unable to bear the sight of her crying and equally unable to ease her mood, Wulfgar finally turned and angrily strode from the room.

He stood before the fireplace in the hall, staring broodingly into the flames. He gritted his teeth. "Must I ever rape the wench?" he murmured to himself. "When will she come to me as I would have her?"

"You spoke, my lord?" A nasal voice sounded behind him and he whirled to find Sanhurst staring at him.

"Saxon swine!" he roared. "Get from my sight."

The young lad made haste to do his master's bidding and in the chamber upstairs Aislinn heard Wulfgar's voice and knew why his anger showered on others. She rose from the bed and went to the door, almost yielding from her own resolve. She sighed and shook her head and going to the window, leaned her head against the panes and stared out over the dark, murky city.

The fire had died on the hearth when Wulfgar came again to the chamber. In the bed Aislinn closed her eyes and feigned sleep, listening to him move about the darkened chamber, then the bed dipped as his weight came upon it. She felt him press close and she only sighed and stirred sleepily. Still Wulfgar could not resist her nearness. His hands moved and soon caressed her boldly. He pulled her beneath him until his weight held her on her back. His lips joined the attack and played upon hers, softly at first then fiercely until she was breathless and weak, pliant to his will.

"No, no, please," she whispered, but he gave her words no heed, and she knew her battle was lost again. He took her and she sobbed as her body answered of its own. Again beneath him, the torrent grew until it obscured all else, then seemed to lift her up on its rising waves and sweep her swiftly to her doom.

As the passion ebbed, she lay exhausted in his arms and oddly felt no sobs or tears. She wondered at the strange contentment that seemed to fill her now and of his tender manner with her. He gave her gifts when he had vowed it was not his way. He had said he did not fight over women, yet he still did battle over her. Thus it was evident he could change his mind and he might change it again.

The next few days passed quickly as Wulfgar attended to his duties and was called often to the castle to see to the details of his estate. When they were in public together, Wulfgar and Aislinn seemed much as lovers; there was a lingering in their touch and when their eyes met it was with a gentle warmth. But when they were alone in their chambers, Aislinn became cool and aloof and seemed to fear Wulfgar's merest touch. Her resistance began to wear on him. Each time he must start anew and attack her fortress with vigor and with patience, yet when their play was done, where before she had drawn away, now she lay close to him and enjoyed the comfort of his arms about her.

It was three days hence that a letter came from William releasing Wulfgar from his duties at court and bidding him to return to Darkenwald and attend to his duties there. He was drawn away by a number of matters that day and was late returning. Aislinn made her meal alone and later in her chambers waited for him with a platter of meat warming by the hearth and a mug of ale cooling on the window sill. Their last night in London they stood at the window, looking at the city until the moon rose high overhead, and between them there was a quietness, a serenity and contentment never felt before. Aislinn leaned against Wulfgar as he stood behind her with his arms folded about her, and she gloried in those tender moments as none before.

There was a rush the next morning. The last items were packed into bundles and carried down. Aislinn dressed and wrapped herself in the warm fur-lined cloak that she cherished and made her way to the hall where she had a quick breakfast before going to the stables. Her small roan punch was tied to the back of the cart without saddle or trappings as if to be led. With a puzzled frown she turned in bemusement and found Gowain standing near.

"Sir knight, am I to ride the cart?"

"Nay, my lady. Your mount is yonder."

He raised a hand and pointed. There was an odd smile on his lips but he would say no more and turning, walked away. Aislinn frowned after him and went to see for herself, following his gesture. There in the stable was the fine dapple-gray mare. Upon its back sat her sidesaddle and before it, a warm robe to cover her legs on the journey. She ran a hand down the mare's flank to admire the depth of muscle there. She caressed the mare's muzzle and shook her head at its soft bluish gray. Suddenly feeling a presence behind her, she turned to find Wulfgar watching her with an amused smile. She opened her mouth and he spoke instead.

" 'Tis yours," he said brusquely and shrugged. "I owe you one."

He turned and led the Hun outside where he mounted. Aislinn again knew a warming in her breast and again was reminded of his words that he never spent much on his women. Happily she led the mare outside and cast her gaze about as there were none to help her mount. Seeing her predicament, Sir Gowain made a great show of leaping from his own horse and giving her a hand, settling her carefully in the saddle and tucking the robe snugly about her. Then he swung up on his own horse and the party was off. Aislinn had no word or gesture from Wulfgar and so sought a place in the caravan some few paces behind him. They made their way carefully through the streets of London with the cart creaking along behind the knights and the bowmen bringing up the rear. They crossed the bridge and traversed the road through Southwark and out into the open country. Here Wulfgar looked over his shoulder again and again as if to assure himself that all was well behind him. At last he lifted the Hun's reins and slowed until Aislinn was at his side. The pace picked up again and she smiled, for she now occupied a wifely place beside her lord.

The day grew cold and a camp was made that night with tents, one for Wulfgar and Aislinn, one for the knights and one for the rest of the men. Hlynn was left to what space she could find in the cart which rested close beside Wulfgar's tent. A great fire was built and after a warm supper they retired to the tents against the cold night air. All was quiet and Aislinn could see the flickering of the dying fire through the walls of the tent. Great robes covered them and soon she felt Wulfgar move close beside her, and then his hand began to explore. A rattle came from the wagon where Hlynn made her pallet, and Wulfgar's mood was broken. But a few moments passed and again Aislinn felt his touch and again as if by design a noise came from the cart. He withdrew. She heard a mumbled curse and then his voice came in an aggravated whisper.

"That one beats about out there like a bull in a breeding pen."

He came close and tried again, and again Hlynn settled herself in the cart. With a disgruntled curse, Wulfgar rolled over and drew the pelt close about his neck. Aislinn giggled at his chafing and knowing herself well safe for the evening, snuggled close against his back to share his warmth.

The next day dawned bright and cold, and the horses breathed great clouds of steam which misted on their bridles and frosted the bits. They set out again and Aislinn's heart lifted, for she knew that night she would spend in her home at Darkenwald.

327

The day was cold and clear as January days are wont to be. There was no fanfare of trumpets to greet them, but it was the only thing missing as the gay procession entered the courtyard of Darkenwald, for it seemed as if every person from miles around had turned out to welcome the lord back to his manor. Aislinn was warmly wrapped in the voluminous folds of the fox-lined cape as she sat lightly on the mare. The animal was long legged and spirited and pranced with excitement, but she checked her to stay carefully behind Wulfgar. He guided the Hun through the mass of people and dismounted before the hall. As a lackey took the bridle of Aislinn's horse, Wulfgar swept her from the saddle to stand her beside him. He bent forward as Aislinn lifted her head to ask him a question, and Gwyneth's brow furrowed as she watched the couple from the doorway, noting that when they touched it was almost a caress. As they came toward the hall, a cluster of people jammed close about them—the knights who had accompanied Wulfgar and the Normans who had stayed; a rabble of children daring each other to touch the knights, particularly Wulfgar; and a press of townspeople seeking news from afar. Gwyneth moved back into the hall and when the door was thrown open, the sounds from within mingled with those from without. Dogs barked at the strangers and shouts of greeting rang loud. The sweet smell of a roasting boar drifted from the hearth where two young lads were set turning it. It blended with the stench of sweat and leather and the tangy spice of newly tapped ale.

Here Aislinn knew each voice and each odor. The bedlam assailed the senses, but she seemed to grow more alive and alert in this cacaphony of sound, sight and smell. Her heart thumped wildly as she was welcomed by familiar faces. She was home, away from the stilted posturing of the court. Women shouted to hasten the feast and the knights and warriors found horns of ale to quench their thirst. Many were lifted and toasts were shouted back and forth across the hall. The crushing noise dulled to a low roar, and Aislinn found herself among the circle of men as they bantered back and forth with Wulfgar. Feeling out of place, she tried to draw away from his side to join the women, but though he did not cease his conversation, his hand on her shoulder held her and drew her back to his side. Content to stay, Aislinn relaxed against him where he stood, enjoying the deep sound of his voice and his ready laughter.

The hall grew still as the ring of Gwyneth's words overrode the gaiety. "Well, Wulfgar, have you had your fill of slaying Saxons?"

She came toward him with a deliberate pace and others made way for her.

"Have you won this fair place and all with it or must we soon pack our belongings and move elsewhere?"

Wulfgar smiled tolerantly. " 'Tis mine, Gwyneth. Even Ragnor found it impossible to take it from me."

Her brows raised questioning. "What do you mean?"

His gaze was mocking. "Why, Gwyneth, we did joust for this fair land and the Lady Aislinn."

The woman's eyes narrowed as she looked at Aislinn accusingly. "What has the whore been about now? What deception brought you and that worthy knight to arms? 'Twould be like her to further fill your head with vicious slander of me. I can well imagine her simpering lies as she rolls her eyes in innocence."

Wulfgar felt Aislinn stiffen against him, though she gave no outward sign of her anger.

Gwyneth held out her hands to him and spoke pleadingly as Wulfgar met her eye in calm regard.

"Oh, don't you see her game, brother? She seeks to rule Darkenwald through you and turn your head from us.

You must fight down these basic urgings of a bastard and thrust her aside before you are undone. You would do well to watch the finer bloods at court. Your habits and your frolics with this whore do not become a lord, and she will be the end of you."

Gwyneth considered Aislinn with haughty distain as she continued with her tirade.

"She set the serfs against me. In truth, she even barred my way when I would have punished that insolent Ham for disobeying my command. Yea, even Sweyn was drawn into her treachery and no doubt will side with her."

She raised a brow to Wulfgar and smiled.

"Has she told you of her fondness for her former swain and their games while you were gone? 'Twas convenient for them that you brought that slave here so they could dally together in your absence."

She did not miss his darkening brow and saw success in her game.

"Why, good Haylan whom you sent to share the hall"—she turned and smiled toward the object of her words who stood somewhat uneasy but beautiful and arrayed in another of Aislinn's former gowns. "Aislinn set upon her and would not share the merest rag to clothe her body until I made the matter right. I could not see the harm in making her share her garments when we were in need. Above all that she has done, this slave demanded a free woman roast meat and prepare food like any serf."

Wulfgar glanced about him at the silent faces gathered around them. In some he saw doubt and in others rage. Gowain stood stiff and angry beside him, ready to defend Aislinn if his lord did not. Wulfgar turned back to his sister.

"I heard no slander until you appeared, Gwyneth," he remarked quietly and watched Gwyneth's eyes widen in surprise. "Indeed, Aislinn spoke nothing of you nor Haylan."

Gwyneth stuttered in confusion and Wulfgar smiled sardonically.

"It seems, dear sister, no lips but yours have betrayed you. But now that you have aired your complaints, I beg you to take this close to your heart." He spoke tersely. "I am lord here, Gwyneth, and now so titled. I am also judge and if I choose, executioner. Understand, no punishment is given here but in my name and you have no privy claim to my authority. 'Tis mine alone and cannot be usurped by any other. You must as anyone here abide under my laws, and I will tell you true, I would not be against giving you the same as you would another, so tread carefully, sister.

"As for those I sent." He, too, marked Haylan with his eyes much to that one's dismay. "I sent them here to serve these lands with every talent they possess and none of them was meant to take a place within this hall."

His attention moved to Aislinn for a moment before meeting Gwyneth's eyes again.

"You refuse to see that Aislinn serves me well and faithfully in all things and mends what you would set atroubled. I enjoy her company and she abides within my house, thus within my guard as you have. I must tell you again that she is the lady of my choosing. What is hers I gladly cede her for her labors, if not for my own desire. Kerwick knows this well and also knows the weight of my hand, so I have little doubt that he would lay the lightest touch on any of my possessions."

He gestured to the clothes both Haylan and Gwyneth wore.

"I see you have shared those meager rags well, but what is hers she owns and henceforth, if taken will be considered stolen. I do not fancy you wandering in my chambers as you will. Do not enter there again without my leave or Aislinn's."

Gwyneth stood in embarrassed silence and could find no retort to hurl in his face.

"In deference to your father and our mother, I say this gently," he continued. "But venture you with the most of care that you do not press my mercies again."

"I had not expected you to see my sorry plight, Wulfgar," Gwyneth sighed. "What am I to you but sister?"

She turned and made her exit carefully with a quiet dignity that deceived the hearts of some. Haylan watched her in bewilderment until she disappeared, then went to the hearth where a boar and other game roasted. She found Kerwick regarding her with mockery in his clear blue eyes.

"Your garments are too fine for this labor, my lady."

"Cease your prattling, lout," Haylan hissed. "Or I will see you bereft of the simple wits you boast. My brother, Sanhurst, is here now and will come to my defense."

Kerwick cast an eye to the one mentioned who at that

331

moment was laboring up the stairs with Wulfgar's chest. His laugh rang with an edge of spite.

"It seems Sanhurst is too busy with his own to care much of your woes. A good lad, he does not seek to share his master's table but is content to be about his duties."

Haylan bristled at his jibe and with a glare at him turned to test the meat.

The feast was done and the hour was late when Aislinn followed Wulfgar up the stairs to their chamber. Wulfgar closed the door behind them and watched as Aislinn pirouetted about the room, entranced with being once more at home.

"Oh, Wulfgar," she cried. "This happiness is too much to bear."

He frowned at her inanity and glanced about the chamber, half feeling the welcome here. His mood had been disrupted by Gwyneth's words. They could not be dismissed lightly, and now his mind sought an answer.

Aislinn stopped and swayed giddily as a dizziness caught her then with a giggle threw herself full length upon the bed. Wulfgar moved to the side of it and stood gazing down at her as she rolled about and in joysome frolic scattered the pelts, flinging some to the floor.

He bent the full frown of his countenance upon her. Aislinn saw his scowl but knew no reason for it. She gazed up at him, sitting back upon her heels.

"Are you ill, Wulfgar?" she asked, somewhat worried at his manner. "Does some wound perchance hurt?" She patted the bed beside her. "Come, lay here. I'll knead the pain away."

His brows knitted in a dark storm. "Aislinn, have you played me false?"

Her eyes widened in stunned dismay.

"Before you speak," he counseled slowly, "be it known I must find the truth. Did you bed your Kerwick while I was gone?"

She rose slowly until kneeling on the bed, her eyes level with his. The gray ones were clouded with indecision, but the violet eyes grew darker until they snapped with anger. Aislinn trembled with rage at the thought of his affront. To take her pride and then question her faith. Her fury broke. Her fist, clenched tight and backed with every ounce of strength she could muster, struck squarely the center of that broad chest. Pain numbed her hand and brought tears to her eyes but he stood unmoved. Her temper flared the higher.

"How dare you! You made me your slave and took what virtue I could call my own, then you dare ask such a thing of me! Ohhh, you betraying ass—"

Angrily she snatched up a pelt and flung herself from the bed. She flew to the door where she whirled to face him, yet she still could find no words to vent her wrath. In outraged ire, she stamped her foot and spinning on her heels, fled down the stairs and across the hall, unmindful of Bolsgar who turned from the hearth to stare at her in some surprise. She marched across the courtyard, then having no better destination in mind, turned along the narrow path that led to Maida's cottage. She startled her mother no end when she flung open the door and slammed it closed behind her, dropping the heavy bar in place and nodding her head once in definite satisfaction of this deed. Without a word of explanation Aislinn threw herself into the single chair and gathering the pelt around her, pouted her petulance at the fire. The old woman read the signs and saw in her daughter's rejection of Wulfgar a high revenge indeed. A cackle burst from her lips and she pranced from her bed in glee, dancing about her daughter who scowled at her from beneath her brow. But Maida silenced suddenly as heavy footsteps sounded without and the door was tried and then rattled under a heavy pounding.

"Aislinn." Wulfgar's voice rang.

Aislinn threw an angry glance over her shoulder at the offending portal and returned a stony gaze to the flames.

"Aislinn!"

The rafters shook but Aislinn gave no response. Then with a crash the bar splintered from its brackets and the door was torn from its leather hinges and fell to the floor. Maida shrieked and scurried into a dark corner. Aislinn came to her feet and whirled to him in rage. Wulfgar stepped over the broken panels and faced the exercised Aislinn.

"You Saxon wench!" his voice rumbled. "No locked doors will ever keep me from what is mine."

"Am I yours, my lord?" she jeered.

"You are," he roared in reply.

She spoke slowly, biting out each word as if it hurt. "Am I yours, my lord, by right of conquest? Or perhaps,

333

my lord, am I yours by the words of a priest? Or am I yours but by your own simple tongue?"

"Did you bed the cur?" Wulfgar shouted.

"Nay!" Aislinn stormed, then continued more softly and slowly as if to make each word crystal clear. "Could I have bedded the cur with Hlynn, Ham and my mother present and Sweyn guarding my door? Would I have played the game for their enjoyment?" Her eyes brightened with turbulent tears. "Would I say you nay on every turn of hand and bid you spare me some dignity if I had none? Believe what Gwyneth says if you must, but do not expect me to bow and scrape before you in amends for that which is naught. 'Tis your choice whether you hold my words dear or Gwyneth's. I will not answer you again of those accusations, and I will not plead for you to see my way."

Wulfgar stared at her for a long time then reached out and gently wiped a tear from her cheek.

"You have found a place within me, Saxon wench, where only you can do me hurt."

He snatched her to him and gazed down into her eyes, his own aflame with passion and desire. Without a word he lifted her in his arms then stepping over the shattered door, bore her through the night to the dimly lighted hall. As he crossed the hall with her, Bolsgar chuckled softly in his ale.

"Ah, these young swains, they will have their way."

It was early in the second month of the year and the
snows of winter had gone, but the cold wet rains still
came with regularity and clouds hung low on the hills. Often heavy fogs rolled in from the marsh and laid over the
small town all day. The damp cold bit to the bone and
made the warmth of a roaring fire welcome to drive the
chills away.

Maida's hut grew cold as Aislinn carefully banked the
remaining embers in the corner of the fireplace that she
might sweep away the accumulated ashes and clean the
hearth. Aislinn knew Wulfgar would be in the barn with
his horses, tending them himself as was his habit on his leisure days. Aislinn had taken this opportunity to see to her
mother's comfort and bring food so that Maida would not
have to venture out in the cold rain after it. The old
woman sat on her crude bed with a half-mad smile twisting her lips and her eyes gleaming in the endless twilight
of the cottage as she watched her daughter work.

An ache grew in the small of Aislinn's back and she
stood erect to ease it. The sudden movement made the
room swim briefly and she put a hand upon the stone
chimney to steady herself. As she brushed a droplet of
moisture from her brow, her mother's words echoed in the
stillness of the room.

"Has the child moved yet?"

Aislinn started and turned to face the other, her brows

arched in surprise and her lips parted in a quick denial. She stepped down from the hearthstone and sat down. Her hands tightly gripped the small twig broom in her lap and she raised her eyes in mute appeal.

"Did you think you could hide it from me forever, child?" Maida asked, the old eyes glowing with protracted glee.

"Nay," Aislinn murmured, feeling half smothered in the close air of the cottage. "I've hidden it too long from myself."

She realized she had known for some time that she bore a child. There was a thickening in her breasts and her time had not come since that night with Ragnor. A sadness grew with a dull pain in her chest and the weight of her mother's words seemed to settle in a cold lump in her belly as she acknowledged to herself for the first time the growing seed that formed there.

"Aye." Her mother's words crackled in her ears. "I know you are with babe, but, my little Aislinn, whose?"

A wild laugh rang in the room as Maida rocked back, throwing up her hands to slap them on her knees. She leaned forward and held up a crooked finger in a beckoning gesture. Wheezing laughter broke her words as she whispered hoarsely:

"Behold, my daughter, be not sad. Behold." She rocked back in her mirth. "What sweet revenge we've brought from these prancing Norman lords. A bastard for the bastard."

Aislinn raised her gaze half in horror at the thought that she would bear a bastard child. She could take no solace in her mother's chortling glee and suddenly felt a need to be alone. She sought out her cloak and retreated hastily from the stifling odor of the place.

The coolness of the mist on her face refreshed her and she strolled slowly, taking the long way back toward the hall, down among the willows that marked the edge of the marsh. She stood for a while on the bank of a chuckling rivulet and thought she sensed it laughing at her. Once proud Aislinn brought down so low. Whose bastard do you bear? Whose? Whose?

She wanted to cry out her anguish, her torment, yet she only stared dumbly at the dark swirling waters and the gray hulking shapes of trees half hidden in the fog, wondering how she would broach this matter to Wulfgar. He

336

would not be happy, for he took much pleasure from his evening frolic and would be sorely afflicted by this state of affairs. A thought came to her, but she quickly shook it from her mind; she would not consider that he would turn both her and the babe away. Her task was clear. She must approach him the first time they were in private.

That occasion presented itself more quickly than Aislinn had dared to hope, for she realized as she stood outside the stable in the gathering darkness and looked in that Wulfgar was quite alone. She had thought to wait until evening when they retired, but she knew this would be better, when he had some other chore to occupy his hands and mind.

A tallow lantern hung from a rafter and Wulfgar worked in its smoky light. He stood with one of the Hun's hooves clamped between his knees. With a small, short knife he was paring the edge of it to shape. Aislinn grew fearful as she imagined him flying into a rage when she told him of her condition. Indecision flooded her, but the great horse turned his head in her direction and snorted, warning Wulfgar of another's presence. Taking a deep breath, Aislinn entered as Wulfgar looked up. He straightened as he saw her, letting go of the hoof, and moved to wipe his hands. She came near and Wulfgar noted the hesitancy in her manner. As he waited for her to speak, he began to groom the chestnut flanks of the animal.

"Monsiegneur," she murmured softly. "I fear that what I have to say will anger you."

He laughed lightheartedly. "Let me be the judge of that, Aislinn. You'll find me more willing to hear the truth than to deal in lies."

She looked up into the gray eyes smiling at her and blurted out, "Even if I told you I am with child?"

He stared at her for a moment, ceasing his labor, then shrugged. " 'Twas to be expected. 'Tis known to happen on occasion." He chuckled as his gaze drew the length of her. " 'Twill be a few months yet before your size impairs our pleasure."

Aislinn gave a snarl that made the pigeons stir in the loft. The Hun threw a wide eye over his shoulder and pranced away from her, but Wulfgar displayed less wisdom than the beast and stood his ground, grinning at her anger.

"I suppose I can stand the drought, cherie."

337

He turned, chuckling at his own humor, and before he could take a step, Aislinn was at his back, pommeling its broad expanse with her fists. Wulfgar turned in stunned surprise and without a pause she continued thumping his chest until she glanced up into his face, saw his amazement and realized that she had not dented him in the least. Aislinn's lips drew back from gnashing teeth as she stepped back slightly and chose a second line of attack, swinging a hard-soled shoe against his shin. Wulfgar stumbled back under her assault and stepped behind the Hun, rubbing the injured member while he berated her.

"What madness has seized you, wench?" he groaned. "What have I done to warrant this abuse?"

"You blackhearted boor!" she railed. "You have the meager wit of a squawking chicken."

"What would you have me do?" he questioned. "Act as if it were a great disaster or miracle when I've been expecting it all along? You were bound to get caught."

"Ohhh!" Aislinn shrieked in undying wrath. "You insufferable, pig-headed, addled-pated Norman!"

She whirled on her heels, sending her mantle billowing wide and stalked passed the Hun, kicking angrily at a bundle of straw near him. The loose stuff filled the air with chaff and the horse shied away again. Wulfgar's breath left him in a loud "whoof" as he was caught between the animal and the wall.

As Aislinn stamped out, it lightened her mood to hear Wulfgar's muffled curse.

"You stumbling nag! Move!"

Aislinn pushed open the heavy door to the hall and flung it closed behind her as she strode angrily into the room. The group of men standing near the hearth turned to stare at this interruption. Through their midst Aislinn could see Bolsgar and Sir Milbourne seated at a game of chess, musing over the board and so engrossed with it that they did not glance up. The others turned back to watch seeing that there was no matter for alarm, and Aislinn hurried across the room and ascended the stairs in restrained fury. Meeting Kerwick on his way to Gwyneth's chamber with an armload of firewood, she remembered that she had not made a fire on Maida's hearth. She paused beside her former betrothed.

"Kerwick, would you mind fetching wood for my

mother if you are not sorely pressed? I fear I left her poorly fit for the night."

He peered at her closely, noticing the flushed cheeks and the set of jaw that often bespoke of agitation in her. "Is there some matter troubling you, Aislinn?"

She returned his stare with aloofness. "There is no matter worthwhile."

"You storm in here like a wind from the sea," he returned. "Do you tell me 'tis naught that makes you fly with such temper."

"Do not pry, Kerwick," she retorted.

He laughed and nodding with his head indicated the men downstairs. "They leave but one who could have caused your wrath. A lover's quarrel?"

" 'Tis none of your concern, Kerwick," Aislinn said brittlely.

He set aside the wood. "Did you tell him of the child?" he asked slowly.

Aislinn started and stared at him aghast, but he smiled kindly.

"Did he take the news poorly? Does he not enjoy facing the rewards of pleasure?"

" 'Tis like the lot of you to determine my circumstance on your own," Aislinn muttered peevishly, recovering from the blow of his question.

"So, the great Norman did not know," Kerwick surmised. "He wars too much to know aught of women."

Aislinn's head snapped up. "I did not say he knew nothing of it," she protested, then pouted, folding her arms before her. "Indeed, he was expecting it."

"Will he claim the deed or let Ragnor have the credit?" he asked derisively.

A feral gleam shone in Aislinn's violet eyes at his inquiry. " 'Tis Wulfgar's babe, of course."

"Oh?" Kerwick raised a questioning brow. "Your mother said—"

"My mother!" Aislinn snarled, stepping close to him. "So, that is how you knew!"

Kerwick took a step backwards at her outburst.

"She babbles overmuch, I fear," Aislinn gritted. "No matter what she spills from her tongue the babe is Wulfgar's."

"If you wish it so, Aislinn," Kerwick said carefully.

"It is what I wish because 'tis truth!" she bit out.

Kerwick shrugged. "At least he is more honorable than that knave."

"Indeed he is!" Aislinn said huffily. "And pray, good fellow, do not forget!"

She strode into the bedchamber, slamming the door behind her and leaving Kerwick quite bemused by her loyalty to Wulfgar when to all his knowledge the Norman had crudely rejected marriage to her.

Aislinn crossed the chamber in irate strides, fuming at Kerwick's impertinence. How dare he even insinuate that it might be Ragnor's seed growing within her when she loathed the very thought of him.

She scuffed her foot across the floor. Even if Ragnor were in truth the sire, Wulfgar would be the father, and she was determined toward that end, whatever came.

Kerwick crossed the courtyard on his way toward Maida's hut when he paused outside the stable and watched his lord at work, though by Wulfgar's movements and his tone of voice one could tell he was greatly vexed.

"You surly beast, afraid of a little twit like that. I've a mind to see you gelded."

The Hun snorted and nudged his master's arm.

"Leave off," Wulfgar flung. "Or I'll set her on you again. That might indeed be worse punishment."

"Trouble, my lord?" Kerwick asked, entering the stables. He was determined to know where the Norman stood with Aislinn and if he would do the right thing by her.

Wulfgar's head snapped up sharply. "Can I find no peace in toiling?" he growled.

"Beg pardon, my lord," Kerwick returned. "I thought something amiss. I heard you speaking—"

"There is naught amiss," Wulfgar replied sourly. "At least nothing I cannot set aright with my own hand."

"I saw Aislinn in the hall," Kerwick said carefully, fighting down the prickling fear that tugged at his throat. He remembered too well the stripes on his back not to be a little anxious for himself when he even mentioned her name to this man.

Wulfgar straightened and looked at the younger man, raising a brow. "Oh?"

Kerwick swallowed hard. "She seemed greatly disturbed, sir."

"She seemed greatly disturbed!" Wulfgar snorted, then muttered, "Not half as much as I."

"Does the child displease you, my lord?"

Wulfgar started as Aislinn had and his eyes narrowed as he stared at the Saxon. "So, she told you, did she?"

Kerwick paled considerably. "Her mother did some time ago."

Wulfgar threw the rag he was holding against a small, rough hewn table nearby. "That fool Maida has a loose tongue."

"What are your intentions, my lord?" Kerwick choked out before apprehension could make him swallow the words.

Wulfgar's gray eyes pierced the man. "Do you forget your place, Saxon? Have you taken leave of your wits? Have you forgotten that I am lord here?"

"Nay, sire," Kerwick replied hurriedly.

"Then remember also I will not be questioned by a slave." Wulfgar stated clearly, emphasizing each word.

"My lord," Kerwick returned slowly. "Aislinn is gently born and raised. She could not endure the humiliation of bearing her child outside the bonds of wedlock."

Wulfgar snorted, turning away. "I believe, Saxon, you sorely underestimate the maid."

"If you claim it as Ragnor's, then—"

"Ragnor's?" Wulfgar whirled on Kerwick and his eyes held him like cold steel. "You go too far, Saxon, to raise the question of the sire. 'Tis naught of your affair."

Kerwick sighed. "It seems that Aislinn is of like mind. In fact, her words were much the same."

Wulfgar relaxed. "Then you should have heeded her, Saxon."

"She has no other to defend her honor, my lord, and I would but see the best for her. I have known her since she first came into the world, some ten and eight winters ago. I cannot bear to see her shamed."

"I would do her no harm," Wulfgar replied. "The child can be sent to Normandy and none will know the circumstance. There are friends of mine who will see the babe properly tended and raised. The child will have far more advantages than I."

Kerwick gazed at him. "Do you mean to send Aislinn away, too?"

"Of course not," Wulfgar answered in some surprise. "We will go on as before."

Now Kerwick snorted in derision. "Nay, lord, you may know women of the court, but I fear you have much to learn of Aislinn. She will not let her child go."

Wulfgar scowled. "She will see the wisdom of it in time."

Kerwick gave a short laugh. "Then take heed, my lord, until the act is met, say naught of it."

Wulfgar raised a brow. "Do you threaten me, Saxon?"

Kerwick shook his head. "Nay, my lord, but if you wish to keep the Lady Aislinn at your side, speak nothing of this to her or to others who would warn her."

Wulfgar peered at Kerwick and suspicion was heavy in his tone when he spoke. "Then you would keep the child here to mark my sins and keep alive some hatred for the Norman kin?"

Kerwick signed in frustration and lowered his head in a mock bow. "Again nay, my lord." He raised his eyes to the other's and spoke earnestly. "But, sire, do you think Aislinn to be a mild maid that you could snatch her child from her breast and send him across the seas? Would she then fly to your arms? Nay, could you long avoid her dagger's point? Or could you heft yon blade and smite her before she fled or struck." He held up a hand to halt Wulfgar's reply. "Think well, my lord," he cautioned. "You can have them naught or both." He shook his head. "But never only one."

Wulfgar stared at him for a moment, then returned in anger to his work. "Begone with you, Saxon. You task my temper. She will do as she is told."

"Yea, my lord."

The smirk in Kerwick's voice made Wulfgar turn again and stare intently at the man. He read both contempt and disbelief in the young man's face and opened his mouth to berate him, but Kerwick turned on his heel and left him gaping. He stood for a long moment with his mouth open then closed it and returned thoughtfully to his grooming of the Hun.

Aislinn was seated before the hearth in the bedchamber with only a blanket wrapped about her when she heard Wulfgar's footsteps in the hall. They seemed slower than usual as if he were hesitant at entering the room. She bent

342

over the soft linen chainse she was making for him, paying close attention to the small, neat stitches she was taking, and when he entered there was nothing about her to indicate her prior rage. He had seen her many times at this same task and in this same manner. Lifting her head, she smiled a greeting though he scowled and looked at her somewhat mistrustingly. Aislinn saw that he had washed in the stables for his hair was moistened around his face and the sleeves of his chainse were folded back.

"Are you feeling better?" he inquired.

"I feel fine, my lord. What of you?" she replied sweetly.

Wulfgar grunted a noncommittal response and began to disrobe, setting his clothes, as always, neatly aside and in their place.

Aislinn put away her sewing and rose from the blanket, drawing Wulfgar's eyes as she crossed naked to the bed. She shivered as a cold draft caressed her and hurriedly climbed into the bed, drawing the pelts up high under her chin. She lifted her eyes to Wulfgar as he continued to gaze at her, but he turned away abruptly. She watched his movements as he banked the fire, and it was a long time before he finally moved to the bed. He unsheathed his sword to place on the floor. Though he no longer barred the door each night, this simple act he had not relaxed.

He stood for a moment staring down at her, his hands low on his hips and an ominous frown upon his brow. Aislinn rolled on her side, presenting her back to him, not giving him a chance to say whatever he had on his mind. After a time he blew out the candle and Aislinn felt his weight on the bed. He slid beneath the pelts but made no move to draw closer. Indeed, he seemed to lay tense and unyielding beside her. Aislinn shivered again, huddling beneath the covers. Usually he shared his warmth with her, but by his manner she knew he was of a different mood. Time passed slowly. When finally she turned she was startled to find his eyes fastened upon her in the glow of the fire, staring at her intently as if he would read her mind.

"Are you troubled, monseigneur?" she asked.

"Only by you, my love," he replied. "What else there is would not delay an ant."

Aislinn rolled back to her former position and lay quietly, feeling his unrelenting gaze upon her. The moments

343

slipped by, seeming to lag on each new borning of time, and still he made no move to draw closer.

"I'm cold," she complained softly.

He came a small measure closer yet not enough to share the heat of his body. Aislinn could not hold back another shivery spasm and after a long pause he finally came near enough to do some good, but he lay with only his chest against her and his whole body rigid.

A thousand thoughts in Wulfgar's mind fell away under the onslaught of just one. The soft press of Aislinn's skin against his chest drove his imaginings to other parts of her body, the full ripe breasts, pink and creamy ivory, velvet smooth beneath his hands; the long legs, slim and lovely, straight and perfect; those narrow hips—

Aislinn almost started as she suddenly felt Wulfgar's body full against her own. His arm settled tight about her and her eyes opened wide as his hands went on with things that had nothing to do with warming. He turned her and she stared for a moment into the gray eyes, hard and shining with his desire.

"You know what I want," he murmured huskily before his mouth lowered and moved over hers.

Wulfgar first tasted the coolness of her mood while his hand enjoyed full freedom of her body. But he persisted. His lips stayed and nibbled and played, parting hers in fierce, hungry kisses that left her breathless. Aislinn felt the chill no longer. Indeed, the coals of her ardor were fanned aflame until they all but consumed her. A soft, rather forlorn moan escaped her as she slid her arms about his neck and her lips yielded to the intensity of his. Wulfgar knew once more he had broken through the ice that encased her. Her mouth now clung to his and she answered his deep thrusts with all the vigor in her trembling body. In this moment they took and gave until they were fused as one in the heat of their passion. Wulfgar's lips brushed against her brow, her ear, and the soft scent of lavender rose to fill his head. He pressed his face against her throat and his lips seered her with their warmth. Aislinn quivered beneath him, turning her face to meet his and as his name escaped her with a quick, sighing urgency his mouth took hers again and they were caught in a whirlwind that swept them on its twisting currents to unfathomable heights, thrusting them ever upward until it released them and they seemed to float, entwined in their mutual bliss.

Wulfgar rose and gazed down at Aislinn, now still and sleeping soundly. A light frown troubled her brow and her lips were parted as she breathed. The red gold hair was spread among the furs and her shoulders were white and soft. He shook his head, befuddled with her moods, and his thoughts drove away sleep. He slipped on his chausses and tunic and made his way quietly from the room down into the hall. Bolsgar was there relaxed in his chair before the hearth, sipping from a chalice of choice vintage. Wulfgar dragged another chair beside the older man's and after pouring himself a cup from the same skin settled himself into it. The two of them watched the hissing logs for many moments in silence before the old man spoke.

"What troubles you, Wulfgar?"

Another long moment passed before the younger man answered with the question that tormented him.

"Where lies the bend of a woman's mind, Bolsgar?" he sighed. He turned his face to the other's and the gray eyes frowned in painful thought. "Does she torment me thus, caring naught for me or seeking vengeance?"

"Poor fool," Bolsgar chuckled. "A woman is the softest yet the sharpest steel this earth can bear. She must be coddled and tended ceaselessly. She is a weapon to be hurled into the fiercest fray but to serve you well must be whetted and honed and protected and above all kept close beside you." He smiled. "And 'tis even said that the best of blades must be bound by an oath of loyalty."

"Bah!" Wulfgar snarled. "I have always purchased my blades with a handful of coin and then carefully set down how they would be shaped."

"Yea," Bolsgar answered. "But with my words remember this: the blade is tempered well to pare life from a simple husk. Woman's lot is to start life anew within her, to bring it to its borning and nurture it from that day forth."

Wulfgar raised his brows and stared at the old man again before he rejoined. In his mind he discarded Bolsgar's statement. He turned to the fire in anger.

"I know naught of these wiles and have little need for further oaths and bonds. I am sworn to William and his crown and to Sweyn as a good companion. I have no urge to venture further. I see it that I must live this life as well I may." His voice grew harsh and sneering. "Women are but softlings which I use. They pleasure me and if I give them pleasure in return, what more? Should this be bound about with fancy trappings and entered into a moldy tome in some dark abbey?" He paused in his tirade then continued more gently. "Or better set in a moment's splendor and then called fair and just and remembered with tenderness."

Bolsgar leaned forward in some ire. "We speak not of women, Wufgar, but of one. There comes a time in each man's life when he must face the full image of all that he has done and know how well he's gone or if he's failed." He shrugged his shoulders and settled back in his chair. "I failed." He stared into the fire. "I take no pleasure from what I see. All that I have done has led to pain or naught. I have no lands. I have no arms. I have no sons. The very best I claim is a daughter soured with this world. In anger I rejected that which I would have held." He turned to Wulfgar with an earnest plea. "You have a chance, a beautiful woman, wise, worthy to walk at your side to Heaven's gate itself. Why do you blunder about and play the fool? Do you detest her? Do you seek vengeance for some imagined wrong?"

He seized Wulfgar's shoulder and turned him so they faced each other.

"Do you torture her because she has injured you? Would you see her kneeling on the floor to beg for mercy? You've used her, first with force and now with candor. You take her openly each night and make her whore on the lips of all and give no promise for tomorrow. If you seek revenge, cast me out. I did you wrong. Or Gwyneth. She cuts you every moment with her tongue. But this one, what has she done that is not your bidding? You are a fool indeed if you cast her from you, or if you stumble on your pride and turn her thus away. If this be your way, you are the same in my eyes as a dim-witted warrior who roars in his cups of what a hero he might have been—if only."

Had this been another man he would have long been seeking in the rushes for his teeth, yet Wulfgar looked into the furrowed face and could raise no hand. He shrugged the restraint away and rose.

"I can stand no more," he said between clenched teeth.

"First her, then Kerwick, now you. I vow that simple Hlynn will set upon me in a rage before this night is out." He squared his shoulders and glared at Bolsgar. "She will bear the child where she will, and mine or nay, I will send it where I will."

He stopped at the surprise in the old man's face.

"Do you say that Aislinn is already with child?" Bolsgar asked.

"You did not know?" It was Wulfgar's turn at surprise. "It seemed that everyone knew but me."

Bolsgar's manner became insistent. "What will you do now? Will you wed the maid as well you should?"

Wulfgar's anger returned and he gritted his teeth again as he half shouted, "I will do what I will!"

With a final glare he turned away and strode angrily up the stairs to his chamber. As he entered the room Aislinn was sitting up in bed with a frightened look about her, but when she saw him returning she smiled her relief and laid down again, curling on her side. His anger could not last and soon he lay curled around her and they went to sleep.

Wulfgar strode down the stairs the next morning somewhat later than usual. Sweyn and Bolsgar were already into their meal as were the other men in the hall. At his appearance the two men ceased their conversation. While Bolsgar bent to his food, Sweyn leaned back in his chair and boldly stared at his lord with amusement sparkling in his pale blue eyes. A chuckle shook his broad shoulders as he continued to gaze at him and there was no need for Wulfgar to be told that the news that Aislinn was with child had spread a bit further. As Wulfgar took a seat the Viking passed him meat and boiled eggs. His voice fairly boomed in the hall as he spoke, making the serfs and those Normans who understood the tongue of England turn and listen with acute interest.

"So the wench is with child, eh?" He chuckled again. "What does she have to say on the matter? Is she effectively chastened and ready to call you master now?"

Wulfgar glanced up toward his men and knew by their gaping faces that they had heard Sweyn clearly. Miderd and Haylan had stopped in their serving and Hylnn straightened from over the kettle to turn and stare at him with mouth slack in surprise as Kerwick continued to pay close attention to his chore.

347

"Sweyn," Wulfgar muttered. "There are times when your mouth far outpaces your mind."

The Norseman threw back his head and guffawed his delight then choking down his amusement, clapped Wulfgar heartily on the back.

" 'Tis a secret that's bound to be known sooner or later, my lord. It would be different if the maid were stout, but being lean she has no chance of holding the matter hushed for long."

His voice gentled somewhat as he leaned near, yet everyone now was most attentive to his conversation and sat eagerly awaiting his next words. There was no strain placed upon their ears, for Sweyn's voice seemed to echo in the hall.

" 'Tis the best way to keep that shrewish vixen at your beck and call, keep a babe in her belly and the clothes off her back."

Wulfgar looked at him in pained silence wondering if there was a fox hole nearby that he could stuff the Viking in. In sour humor he cracked an egg and began to peel it as the Norseman continued.

"You're right to keep these Saxons at heel. Show them who is master. Keep their women abed and little bastards running at their heels."

Bolsgar's brows raised questioningly as he turned to stare at Sweyn. Wulfgar choked on the yoke of the egg he had just bitten into and Bolsgar gave him assist by pounding him heavily on the back. The younger man turned a silent scowl upon his friend when he had regained his breath and took an ample draught of milk to wash the egg down.

Sweyn nodded agreeably. "Aye, there should be some celebration for the wench's comeuppance. Ah, she was a haughty one, but no matter. When she's gone, there will be more to conquer. Never fear."

Fnding the last straw that broke his calm, Wulfgar slammed his palms down on the table in silent rage. Without a word he strode past Sweyn and crossed to the door, snatching it open, and making his escape from the stares of all.

Sweyn leaned back in her chair, and tipping his head back, loudly vented his amusement. Bolsgar had shifted his gaze from Wulfgar's back to stare at the Norseman.

Slowly the dawning came and he could see the lay of the Viking's words and he, too, joined in Sweyn's high humor.

Aislinn descended the stairs shortly after Gwyneth. Haylan had wasted little time informing Wulfgar's sister of the expected addition to the family. Gwyneth turned a mocking gaze upon Aislinn as she spoke on the side to Haylan yet loud enough that Aislinn might hear too.

" 'Tis best that an unwed slave take advantage of her master's tenderness while she can, for the lord will soon grow tired of her ripening shape and pack her off to some hovel or some distant country to have the babe in shame."

Aislinn's brows drew together at the woman's words but she replied with dignity. "At least I'm capable of bearing children," she sighed. "There are those who are unable though they would try hard. 'Tis sad, isn't it?"

She turned away from their gaping faces with small sense of victory. Gwyneth's words had destroyed her slight spirit and she could not bear the sight of the food-laden table. She wondered what fate her child would suffer if Wulfgar could not be convinced to marry her. She could not nag him on the matter, for he would surely turn from her in disgust and find some other wench to amuse himself with. She must deal with her state with all the honor and honesty heaven allowed her. In that way she might win him and nothing else would satisfy her.

It was toward dusk when Wulfgar returned from Cregan and mounted the stairs to his chamber, removing his helm and coif and tucking them beneath his arm. Aislinn was bent over her needlework before the hearth when he flung open the door, but seeing that his mood was morose and untalkative, she quietly rose and assisted him in removing the hauberk.

"I've heated water for your bath," she murmured and took his leather tunic as he handed it to her to fold it in the manner she had seen him so often do.

Wulfgar grunted in reply but when she went to lift the heavy kettle of water from the hearth, he paused in taking off his chainse and asked sharply:

"What are you about, woman?"

Aislinn stopped and stared at him in surprise. "Why, I'm readying your bath as I have done these many months past."

"Sit down, wench," he commanded then strode to the door and throwing it open, bellowed: "Miderd!"

It was but a moment before the woman showed a worried face in the portal. She looked hesitantly at Wulfgar, a rather awesome sight garbed only in chausses. She swallowed convulsively as she measured the broad expanse of his chest with her eyes, wondering what she had done to rouse his wrath.

"My lord?" she said weakly.

"You will keep these chambers clean and prepare baths as the Lady Aislinn desires. You may have Hlynn to help you," he directed. He pointed to Aislinn and startled both women as he shouted, "And you will see that she lifts nothing heavier than a chalice."

Miderd almost breathed a sigh of relief, but his scowl did not allow for ease of spirit. She hurried to ready the bath, glancing at Aislinn as the girl stared somewhat amazed at her lord. Miderd withdrew, closing the door behind her, as Wulfgar began to take off his chausses. He stepped into the steaming water and relaxed back against the rim of the wooden tub, letting the heat soften the ache that a hard ride drew forth. He had driven the Hun almost to the limits as he tried to sort out in his own mind the thoughts that plagued him.

Aislinn took up her sewing again, settling back in her chair, and glanced up at Wulfgar between the stitches she set.

"My lord," she murmured, after a while. "If I am a slave, why do you command others serve me?"

Wulfgar scowled. "Because you are slave only to me, for my enjoyment, none other's."

Aislinn drew her needle through the linen. " 'Twas not my intention to let my state be known to any other than yourself, my lord, but I fear there is no help for it now. It seems my position of child-bearing slave has spread to all corners of Darkenwald."

"I know," Wulfgar replied brusquely. "There are many here at Darkenwald cursed with loose tongues."

"And will you send the babe and me off to Normandy or some other place distant from here?" She would not bite her tongue to keep the question unsaid. She must know, for it tortured her every moment.

Wulfgar looked at her sharply, remembering his words to Kerwick. "Why do you ask?"

"I would know, monseigneur. I do not wish to be away from my own kind."

Wulfgar frowned heavily. "What is there different between a Norman and a Saxon that you must say this is your kind and yonder is mine? We are all flesh and blood. The child you carry is between, half Norman, half Saxon. Where will he place his loyalty?"

Aislinn laid her sewing in her lap and stared at him as he continued speaking in anger, realizing he had not answered her. Had he avoided the question deliberately because he did intend to send her away?

"Can you not place your trust in someone other than a Saxon?" Wulfgar demanded. "Must you forever spur me for their cause? I am no different from any Englishman."

"Indeed, my lord," she said softly. "You remind me much of one."

Wulfgar scowled at her but he was silenced and could find no further words with which to berate her. He rose from the tub and, toweling off, donned his clothes and escorted her down the stairs where they took their meal in silence under the stares of serf and Norman.

Aislinn sat alone in the bedchamber, carefully sewing small gowns and other garments for the child to come. It had been a month since she had told Wulfgar of her state, and her mood was near the depths of despair. Wulfgar had been gone from the hall since early morning and in his absence, Gwyneth's sharp tongue came into play. Aislinn recalled the snide remarks that had driven her almost in tears from the noon meal to seek the privacy of her chamber. Wulfgar's sister had casually asked if Aislinn had her things packed and was ready to leave Darkenwald then had viciously carried the subject further to imply that Wulfgar would soon be sending her away, probably to Normandy as soon as Aislinn's belly began to hinder his lovemaking or when it could no longer be hidden. Aislinn sniffed loudly and shook her head as the tears threatened to spill again. At least here was a place Gwyneth dared not roam and where Aislinn could find a moment of peace.

Even Maida had unwittingly done her part to ruin Aislinn's day. It was not too long after she had sought the shelter of the room that her mother had come scratching at the door. Her plea was that she came to see to her daughter's welfare, but in reality she did little to enhance it. She had begged Aislinn to leave with her, hinting that

351

the time was short and it was far better to flee to a haven of their own choosing than to wait Wulfgar's pleasure. The visit had ended in an argument, as this subject always did, and only when Maida faced Aislinn's flaring temper had she wisely retreated.

So it was that Aislinn worked on the tiny clothes and arranged them on the bed, smoothing them pensively as she thought of the wee form that would fill them. Still she found no solace, for even as she dreamed of her child her thoughts came full circle and she remembered her mother. She felt the pain of seeing Maida's fragile grasp on sanity weaken and slip and knew she could do nothing to save her.

" 'Tis naught to be done now," she sighed. "Best I put away the past and look to the future." She straightened a tiny robe. "Poor wee child. I wonder if you are lad or lass." Aislinn felt a movement as if the babe would have answered her. She chuckled lightly to herself. " 'Tis the least of my worries. I would be satisfied if you were born of a marriage true and not a bastard."

She lifted a small blanket and tucked it tenderly into the crook of her arm, feeling its softness. A lullaby came to her lips and she rose and strolling idly to the window, hummed the refrain and dreamed of how it would be to hold her own baby and know its helpless trust as it slept against her breast. She might well be the only one who would love it and give the warmth and kindness that would nourish it more than milk.

A light rain pattered on the sill before her and an early southern breeze played in her hair, bringing a smell of wet sod from the outdoors, of growing things, of spring not too far off. A shout came from the stable, followed by a rush of voices and she knew that Wulfgar and Sweyn had returned. Thinking he would come and seek her out as was his custom, Aislinn rushed to put away all the clothes in a chest and set the room to order. She ran her hands over her gunna to chase the wrinkles and sat down before the hearth to wait.

Time passed and no one came.

Aislinn could hear Wulfgar's voice in the hall, laughing and making jokes with the men who gathered there.

He cannot come to bid me the time of day, she mused petulantly. Already he finds his ease with his men and that hussy, Haylan. He readies himself for the day he will send me away to bear his brat in some far off hovel where his tender eyes will never see the truth. Her eyes narrowed. 'Twill not be so.

Tears were near flowing again, but with an angry shake of her head, she sought a cool cloth to press upon her face and drive the redness away. There was no need for weeping. Wulfgar was gentle with her and of late more than considerate, especially after learning she was with child. He did not press her to play his game as often.

Indeed, she thought sadly, one might even call his manner cool. 'Tis sure he sees my ripening shape and finds that hefty widow more to his liking.

There was a light rap at the door and Miderd's voice came.

"My lady, the table is set and my lord bade me come and ask if you will sup with him or take a platter here?"

No solace there, Aislinn mused derisively. He sends others to fetch me instead of troubling himself.

"Give me a short time, Miderd," she replied, "and I will take my meal in the hall. My thanks."

Wulfgar and the others were in their seats at the table when Aislinn entered and joined them. He rose to greet her with a smile, but she would neither meet his eyes nor answer him and brushed past him to take her chair. He frowned slightly, wondering what had set her to brooding, and finding no answer for his thoughts, took his place beside her.

The meal was good but not unusual as winter had considerably narrowed the available fare. There was fresh venison and mutton and what vegetables that could be stored, all cooked in a rich stew that lined the belly well. The talk was scant and forced, and the knights were wont to fill their cups more often, Wulfgar not the least of them. He sipped his wine and considered Aislinn as she daintily nibbled at her food. Her aloofness was unmistakable, but more than not these days she was somber and serious, her manner cool and withdrawn, as if she had lost all gaiety in life. He could find no cause but the babe and wondered after the child was born if she would detest it as his mother had him. It would be better that the child was sent away where he could find the love and attention he would need. Wulfgar knew well by experience the heartbreak a boy could suffer if left with an unloving mother. No matter what Kerwick's words, he must consider the advantage for the babe. There was a kindly couple he knew of, who had long hoped for a child of their own but had been unable to have one. They would make good and doting parents.

With Aislinn's moods, Wulfgar admitted to being at a loss. It took only some small, misplaced gesture to anger her and he would feel the bite of sharp words from her tongue. Still, in bed she was as she had always been, reluctant at first, then yielding, then passionate. And he thought he knew women—he smiled to himself.

Gwyneth had taken note of Aislinn's manner and once the meal was well joined, leaned toward her brother and ventured:

"You seem to be gone overmuch of late, Wulfgar. Has something here lost its flavor? Or perhaps this hall displeases you?"

Aislinn glanced up to meet Gwyneth's smug smile and knew the last was meant for her. She realized immediately that it had been a mistake to join the meal, but there was nothing to do now except face it out or admit defeat. Bolsgar snorted and sought to change the subject.

"The game comes out of the deep forest, Wulfgar," he tried in a conversational tone. " 'Tis a sure sign of spring as are these light mists we've been having."

Gwyneth sneered at her father. "Light mists! Indeed! 'Tis the sorry whim of the south of England to see us cold and wet. It seems either that snow is blowing in my face or the fog is heavy and wets my hair. And who cares if spring comes or naught. This dastardly weather is foul all year long."

"You should care, Gwyneth," berated her father, "for 'tis on this year and its success or failure, we'll see the truth of Wulfgar's ways or even William's. The land is much wasted as are the poor English lads, and if this summer's harvest is slim, then so will your belly be come the next cold."

There was silence all around the table and the cups were quickly emptied to be refilled by Hlynn and Kerwick as they made their rounds. Aislinn saw that Wulfgar's eyes wandered to where Haylan labored, and her temper flared no small bit as she took note that in the warmth felt near the hearth, the widow had opened the simple dress she wore until her bosom swelled well into view.

The meal was done but still the men lingered on. Their

manners grew lively and Gowain brought out his cithern to pluck loud chords from it as bawdy songs were roared by Sweyn and Milbourne. The knights called for more wine and ale and Kerwick set out skins of the red stuff and tankards of the amber brew before them.

Haylan had finished her duties and stood watching as the men warmed to the spirit of revelry, making contests of the drinking. It was Beaufonte who offered her a horn of ale. Without hesitation she took it in a hearty manner and raising it high, held it for a moment before bending a smile to the men who waited for her to taste it. She set the cup to her lips and, amid cheers, drained it. She slammed the empty horn on the table and her eyes challenged them all. Gowain filled his own and matched the feat, then Milbourne did the same. Beaufonte would have passed the sport, having imbibed too much as it was, but Sweyn seized a skin of wine and poured until his cup ran over and the poor knight begged him to stop. Beaufonte took a deep breath and began to drink. Gowain strummed a beat on his strings and a low chant rose to mark time with the swallows. He finished and a cheer rose as with a gesture of triumph he licked a last drop that threatened to fall from the edge of the mug. Lowering the cup to the table, he took his own seat, then, bearing a contented smile on his lips, he slid slowly beneath the planks.

Sweyn roared in mirth and Bolsgar laughed as he filled a tankard with cold water from a pail and dashed it into the knight's face.

"Ho, Beaufonte!" he chortled. "The night is yet young and you will miss a good round of drinking if you nap like this."

His victim struggled to his feet and tried to stand and as he lurched to and fro, Gowain began to pick out a rhythm that matched his steps. Haylan laughed and taking the drunken knight's hands, led him in a slow dance. The men cheered them on and even Wulfgar began to chuckle at the inane play. Aislinn watched the foolery and as her mood was not light, saw them as grown men playing at childish games. They were all knights of William and seasoned warriors, yet they pranced and leered at Haylan's opened bodice like untried lads.

Beaufonte warmed to the game but was bent toward a more romantic frame of mind and tried to take her in his arms and dance in that manner. With a laugh Haylan pushed him from her and he staggered back to come up against a bench where he sat abruptly and could not rise again. The widow whirled away and halted before Gowain, there stamping her foot until he picked up the rhythm on his instrument and began to play a tune that made her feet beat a quick tattoo on the stone floor. The others shouted their acclaim and began to clap their hands to urge her on. She paused with arms akimbo and her right foot took up the beat then her left joined and soon she was twisting and swirling in a dance that was marked with a tempting sway of her body. Wulfgar sat back in his chair to watch and turning away from the table, stretched out his long legs before him.

Haylan saw his movement and her chance. Under his full attention she moved toward him, ignoring the heated glare from Aislinn and swirling her skirts as Gowain's fingers quickened the pace. Then she was dancing over Wulfgar's feet, weaving an intricate pattern about them, stepping lightly between his legs and then quickly away as if to tease him. Her sultry eyes held him and her skin, wet with sweat, gleamed in the dim light of the hall. She lifted her skirts above her knees and her feet seemed to dazzle the eye as they kept the rapid rhythm, then she moved back and with a last twirl, came to her knee bowing before Wulfgar. Her bodice opened as she bent, leaving little to the imagination of the men and showing the full ripeness of her body to Wulfgar.

Aislinn stiffened and eyed Wulfgar who seemed not in the least upset by this wanton display but clapped his hands and roared his approval with his men. Aislinn's violet eyes burned and she could find no relief, for Gowain started another song which prompted Haylan to start another dance. Aislinn turned in her chair in disgust and refused to watch this new taunt. Drawing in his feet, Wulfgar moved around to raise his horn and take a leisurely draught. His eyes roamed slowly over the full curve of Aislinn's breasts as his fingers lightly drummed on the table in time to the music. None could guess his thoughts, but Gwyneth found cause to smile as she watched Aislinn's unsmiling face and listened to the beat of Wulfgar's fingers. The lord and his mistress did not appear the loving couple at all this night and at the thought Gwyneth laughed aloud, a rare sound that drew the attention of everyone. Wulfgar peered questioningly at his sister while Aislinn withdrew further into her morose mood, knowing well the spur to Gwyneth's gaiety. As Haylan continued her prancing, Aislinn sat quietly in her chair, her doubts marching like devastating tides across her resolve. Wulfgar would have little use for her when she grew round with child, she mused in dismal dejection. He was already casting about for game more lively. And the most lively game about seemed to be Haylan.

When Wulfgar bent toward Sweyn and laughed over some exchange of wit about the well-endowed widow, Aislinn silently rose from her seat and made her way from the hall, unnoticed by all but Gwyneth. She stepped into the courtyard and took a ragged breath, shivering under the impact of the cold night. She felt her way down the dark path to Maida's cottage. It was in her mind to spend the night there and make her home with her mother, freeing Wulfgar for a more compatible arrangement if he found someone else to sate his desire. She was tired of seeing her hopes dashed by a negative word from him. Where did her dreams lead but to more heartache and misery? She felt beaten, unable to go on. Her fear was that he would send her away and it rode paramount in her mind. He had never denied it and had of late begun to speak more and more of Normandy in her presence as if preparing her for the change, assuring her that it was a fair country where a lad could grow and flourish. Oh, yes! It was his intent to be rid of them.

She hastened through the dark along the narrow path much as she had the night they returned from London when Wulfgar had questioned her about Kerwick. She smiled ruefully at the thought that he could so easily question her faithfulness and she could not his. A slave! Nothing more to him. A slave to do his bidding and to bear his weight in bed without the right to say him yea or nay.

She eased open the cottage door and found her mother sitting before the hearth near the remains of her supper. The old woman looked up with some semblance of sanity in her eyes. She beckoned Aislinn in.

"Come, my pretty. The fire is warm enough for two."

Aislinn moved slowly forward and it was Maida who hurried to fetch a pelt and wrap it around her daughter's shivering shoulders.

"Ah, love, why come ye in the cold? Do you have no care for yourself or the babe? What ill bodes in the lord's chamber that you must seek my poor hut at this late hour?"

"Mother, I fear 'twill be the way of things henceforth," Aislinn sighed and choked on her tears.

"What? Has the bastard cast you out? That rutting Norman ass sets you aside?" Maida's eyes gleamed as she considered this for a moment, then smiled. "A bastard for the bastard you shall give him true. 'Twill bite him sorely to see the babe with his own pale locks."

Aislinn sniffed and shook her head. " 'Tis his plan I fear to send me away where he will not be pricked by the sight of his bastard kin."

"Away?" Maida gasped and stared hard at her daughter. "You will not let him send you away from me." It was half a fearful question.

Aislinn shrugged and smothered a deep pain.

"He is lord here and I am but his slave. There is naught else I can say."

"Then flee, daughter. Before he can do the deed," Maida pleaded. "For once think of yourself. What good will you do those here if you are in Normandy or another far off country? Fly with me to the North where we may seek out our kin and bid them give us shelter. We can stay there until the babe is sprung."

Aislinn sat quietly before the hearth, thoughtfully gazing into the flickering tongues of flame that curled about the logs and licked at the hard wood until it grew black and charred. Her mind would not ease and turned ever on the road that would lead her to escape. Would he care? Or would he feel relief and be glad to be rid of them? She did not relish leaving the place of her birth and this hall that had been the only home she had ever known. Still, Wulfgar's manner of late left her little choice, for she could not imagine herself faring well in Normandy. She rested her forehead in her hand and knew that the decision was already forced upon her.

"Aye," she breathed softly, and her mother had to strain to hear the words. " 'Twould be the best. If he cannot find me, then surely he cannot send me from England."

Maida clapped her hands in glee and danced a jig about the small, littered room. "Bastard! Bastard! Norman foe! We will be gone before you know."

Her mirth was not shared by Aislinn who numbly rose and went to the door.

"Gather your belongings at the morning's break, Mother mine. He rides to Cregan on the morrow and we will part for the northern climes soon after. Make ready. I must return to his bed this one last time or we mayhap will find our plans gone awry."

Aislinn left without another word and returned to the hall, leaving Maida to cackle long and hard before the hearth. Aislinn paused at the great oaken panel, gently closing the door behind her. Wulfgar stood leaning against the stone wall of the fireplace as Gowain plucked a softer tune, and Haylan swayed before them as if she were some temptress of the Nile. Her dress fell loose over her shoulder and her bosom swelled wantonly but the cloth held at the peaks of her breasts. Aislinn wondered if it was held there by a spell that eluded the men who seemed to await its fall with fascinated attention.

Aislinn saw Wulfgar's gaze wander about the room, then settle and hold upon her. She crossed the room under his regard, but before she reached the stairs Haylan whirled, seeing Wulfgar's interest elsewhere, and came to dance before Aislinn as if flaunting her talents before her. Aislinn looked at her coolly; then suddenly the music stopped and Gowain laid aside his instrument in some embarrassment. Haylan turned on him in a huff, allowing Aislinn to mount the stairs in quiet dignity. Wulfgar swept past the irate widow in his haste to follow after Aislinn and slowed when he caught up with her at the head of the stairs.

"Where did you go?" he inquired softly. "You left so suddenly I thought you might be ill."

"I am quite well, my lord," she replied. "I'm sorry to have distressed you. I only went to see to my mother's needs."

He pushed open the chamber door for her and allowed her to precede him then closed it quietly behind them. Leaning back against it, he watched her move away into a darkened corner of the room and there disrobe with her back to him. His eyes slowly drank their fill, moving along her long, slender legs over her hips to the waist that was still fairly narrow. When she turned, her bosom came into view before she hastily slipped into bed pulling the pelts up high under her chin. Wulfgar crossed to the bed and

359

laying across it, pulled her in his arms and began to kiss her. Pressing his lips against her fragrant hair, he muttered against it.

"Ah, wench, you are the gentlest delight. What would I do to fill my leisure if you were taken from me?"

Aislinn turned her face away and sighed. "My lord, I do not know. Pray tell me."

He chuckled as he nuzzled her shoulder. "I would find some wench as beautiful and as lusty, and then mayhap I would be content," he teased.

Aislinn did not take kindly to his humor, but replied in measured tones. " 'Twould be to your advantage to find one as talented as Haylan also. You never know when there is cause to be entertained."

Wulfgar laughed at her sarcasm and rolled from the bed to shun his clothes, returning a moment later when he had laid them away. Her back was now presented to him, but Wulfgar was little daunted since many of their most pleasurable evenings began in this manner. Moving close against her, he brushed the curling tresses from the nape of her neck, for his lips were hungry for the taste of her.

Aislinn could not find the will to deny him even with her mind set and the plans for escape formed. Only by leaving would she regain some portion of her self-respect. Still, he would plague her mind and the memory of his bold caresses that could send the full depth of her being reeling in giddy delight, would forever bring a longing to her breast. She sighed again as she surrendered to his arms and gave him kiss for kiss, parting her lips beneath his and clutching him to her as if she could not hold him close enough. Their ardor drove them on and the roaring furnace of their passions consumed them. Aislinn trembled in his arms and as they lay in the aftermath of the storm, she wept softly in her pillow.

Aislinn woke at the bright twinklings of light escaping through the shutters and drowsily searched the bed with her hand. The pillow beside hers was empty and glancing about the room, she found that Wulfgar had gone. She sat up sleepily and in deep dejection dropped her chin wearily in her hands, thinking of the day's chore. It all seemed like some horrible nightmare, but Maida's scratching at the door a moment later reminded her it was not. The woman entered and began in haste to pack her daughter's gowns into a bundle until Aislinn stopped her.

"Nay. I take only the rag Gwyneth left me with. The others are his—" And she added with a choked sob, "For Haylan if he so chooses."

It did not matter that he had given them to her. She'd have little peace taking them with her, for every time she wore one she'd be reminded of all that had passed between them, and she wanted no more unwelcome memories than she had already.

She called Miderd and swearing her to silence, enlisted her aid in the hurried leavetaking. The woman gave her argument until she saw Aislinn's determination, then could do nothing other than assist her. Sanhurst was instructed to saddle an ancient nag, little knowing it was for Aislinn he did so. At the sight of the ragged mount, Maida quelled, then ranted furiously at Aislinn's choice.

361

"Take the gray. We'll need her strength to see us through."

Aislinn shook her head and murmured firmly, "Nay. 'Tis this or naught. No fine steed will mark my passage through these climes."

"The Norman gave her to you and the clothes you set aside. They are yours and 'twould do him good to see them gone."

"I will not go bearing his gifts," Aislinn said stubbornly.

The choice of food yielded Maida no more assurance of her daughter's good sense, but gave her cause to wail.

"We shall starve. You beggar us upon this stumbling nag, then expect us to survive on that meager fare."

"We will find more," Aislinn assured her and turned away further argument. As they rode from view, Miderd slowly turned and made her way into the hall, wiping a tear that traced down her cheek.

Darkness had approached and Miderd could not shake away the sadness that burdened her heart. She watched Haylan as the young woman tested a side of vension roasting for the evening meal. She knew Haylan would accept the news with gladness and wondered at her continued flirtation, for she herself saw Wulfgar as a man of honor and could read the signs of his true concern for Aislinn.

Miderd turned away in disgust as she remembered the night before. "Why do you seek to tempt the Lord Wulfgar?" she asked, more than a trifle piqued with her sister-in-law. "Will you still play the strumpet if Lady Aislinn is the mistress of the hall?"

"There is slim chance of Aislinn becoming mistress here," Haylan snapped. "Wulfgar admits he hates women."

Miderd swung round. "Does a man hate a woman who bears his child in her belly?"

Haylan shrugged. "That is not love, but lust."

"And you would have him lust after you until you're as round as she?" Miderd questioned increduously. "Last night you danced before him like Salome before that king. Would you ask for Aislinn's head to satisfy you?"

Haylan smiled. "Were she gone," she sighed, "Wulfgar would be mine."

"And she goes," Miderd said bitterly. "Are you so happy?"

Haylan's dark eyes widened in surprise and at her stunned silence Miderd nodded.

"Yea, even now she hastens from him. She takes nothing but herself, her mother and his child and the old nag she leads her mother on."

"Does he know?" Haylan questioned slowly.

"Upon his return from Cregan he will know, for I will tell him. She bade me hold silent but I fear for her safety. The wolves range wide in the forests where she goes. I cannot keep my tongue and let her fall prey to those savage beasts nor the human ones who would take her with no regard for her soft condition."

"Who is to say whether Wulfgar will go after her or not?" Haylan shrugged. "She grows fat with child and he will tire of her soon anyway."

"Your heart is sheathed in ice, Haylan. I would not have thought you so pitiless nor so bent upon your own desires."

Haylan let out an enraged howl. "I am wearied with your fault-finding, and your sympathy for that wench grows tedious. She has done naught for me. I feel no obligation toward her."

"If you ever have need of her," Miderd returned softly, "I hope before Heaven that she has more compassion for you."

" 'Tis not likely I'll ever require her help," Haylan retorted and then she shrugged her shoulders flippantly. "Besides, she is already gone."

"The townspeople will miss her. They can turn to no other for what milady gave them."

"Milady! Milady!" Haylan mimicked sourly. "She is not my lady nor will she ever be. I will be more crafty than she. I will make Wulfgar love me and want me as his own."

"*Lord* Wulfgar," Miderd corrected testily.

Haylan smiled and licked her lips as if anticipating some great feast. "Soon he will be only Wulfgar to me."

The sound of heavy hooves thundered near and passed in the direction of the stables. Miderd rose and faced Haylan.

"He returns and I go to tell him. If he does not go after her, be assured I will blame you for the death of Lady Aislinn, for it is very likely she will die in the wilds."

363

"Me?!" Haylan cried. "I did naught but wish her gone. She left of her own free will."

"Yea," Miderd agreed. "But it was as if you placed your hands upon her back and pushed her out."

Haylan flounced back to the hearth in a fit of temper. "I care naught. Away with you. I'm glad she's gone."

Without further reply, Miderd sighed and left the hall and made her way to the stables where Wulfgar and his men unsaddled their horses. Hesitantly she approached the big Hun and glanced at Wulfgar a bit nervously. He was speaking with Sweyn and failed to notice her until she stretched out a hand and pulled at his sleeve. With a hand resting on the Hun's backside, he turned to her, still smiling at some jest, and raised a questioning brow.

"Milord," Miderd said softly. "I fear your lady is gone."

The grin faded from Wulfgar's face and his eyes grew cold.

"What is this?" he demanded.

Miderd swallowed hard, fear almost washing her resolve away. She held on grimly and repeated her statement.

"The Lady Aislinn has gone, milord," she said. No longer sure of herself, she wrung her hands. "Shortly after you left this morn, milord."

In a single motion Wulfgar snatched his saddle from the ground and flung it to the back of the Hun, startling a snort from the steed with his unexpected action and drawing the immediate attention of his men. He braced his knee against the horse, pulling the girth tight as he spoke aside to Miderd.

"She went north, of course. To London?" He turned a questioning to her.

"North, yea, but not to London. I think more westerly to ride around the city and seek some haven with the northern clans," she replied and then added softly, bowing her head, "where no Normans abide, my lord."

Wulfgar swore a hearty oath and swung into the saddle. He saw Sweyn readying a mount to accompany him and halted him.

"Nay, Sweyn. I go alone. Again I bid you stay and see the lands secure until I return."

He turned and his eyes swept the stables seeing everything in its place and her mare in its stall.

"She took no horse nor wagon? How does she fly? Afoot?" Again his glowering gaze turned toward Miderd.

She shook her head. "Milady took no mount save the old nag and for some provender a few blankets and other meager trappings. They will seem like homeless Saxons fleeing the wars." She remembered sadly her own long journey then continued in worried haste. "I fear for her, milord. The times are bad and scavengers range wide. Wolves—" She stopped, unable to go on, and raised her eyes half in fear.

"Allay your thoughts, Miderd," Wulfgar said, leaning forward in his saddle. "Be assured you have earned a place this night for ten score years to come."

Wulfgar's hand moved the reins and the Hun whirled away and was soon on the north road, swinging easily into a mile-eating gait that took them rapidly on their hunt.

Miderd stood long and listened to the sounds of hooves dying in the night. She shook her head and smiled to herself. In spite of this man's fierce manner and his liking for battle, he had a heart which she knew had borne much pain. So he spoke gruffly and blasphemed his own feelings for others and bragged that he needed no one else. So he lent himself to war, perhaps half hoping that his gnawing ache might end on another's blade. Yet here he rode the night to halt a fleeing love as if it were a hunting bird once tamed and brought to hand, but having thrown the jess, now refused to come to glove.

Wulfgar rode easily in the saddle, still fully garbed in mail with his mantle billowing out behind him. He snatched the helmet off and let the cold March wind drive sleep from his head. He felt the thrust of the Hun beneath him and knew the pace would cover in a matter of hours what had taken Aislinn most of the day.

A bright three-quarter moon rose high in a cold, black sky and seemed to draw low mists from the fens and bogs. He measured its passing for the time he would slow and search for the starved glow of a waning fire. He frowned and looked northward, his mind trying to sort out the reasons that had brought her to this action. He couldn't remember anything different that had happened in the past few days to cause her to be dissatisfied with their life. But what did he know of women, except that they were not to be trusted.

Aislinn rechecked the reins tied about a small tree and ran a comforting hand along the trembling sides of the ancient mare.

"Sorry lot, we," she thought. "Feast for wolves and naught else."

Aislinn put her hand to the small of her back where a dull ache was beginning to bloom and crossed to the fire near where her mother slept peacefully upon the damp earth, wrapped in a shoddy blanket against the chill. Aislinn shivered as a cold breeze rattled the winter-cleaned branches above them and trembled even more as a far-off howl warned of wolves roaming the countryside. Sitting beside the small fire, she poked at it aimlessly, thinking of the warm bed she could be sharing with Wulfgar now. She had not wanted to stop here in the woods, hoping instead to reach the town some two hours away before fatigue grew too apparent in her mother. But it was the mare who had held them back, going lame in one of her forelegs.

Aislinn wrapped her arms about her knees, gazing thoughtfully into the flickering flames. At her continued stillness, the child within her belly stirred and moved with faint featherlike motions. The baby was content, lulled to sleep in the warm, safe haven of his mother's womb. Aislinn smiled softly as tears came to her eyes, blinking them away when they threatened to overflow.

A babe, she thought in wonder. A treasure, a miracle, a sweet joy when two beings came together in love and made a child.

Lord, if she were only able to reassure herself and Wulfgar that it was truly his, but always that doubt hung above them, setting Ragnor's face between them as if he were more than their imagination. But even if the babe were Ragnor's, she could not abandon it and send it away from her sight nor could she bear the thought of being isolated from her home. Now at least with her leaving, Wulfgar would not have to look at her anymore and wonder.

The tears began again and flowed unchecked down her cheeks.

"Oh, Wulfgar," she sighed miserably. "Had I been properly betrothed to you and unspoiled by Ragnor's hand, perhaps I could have won your heart, but I see that your eyes wander already from this melon shape of mine to the trimmer one of the widow Haylan. I could not bear the way you looked at her—or was it my imagination that placed the lust within your eyes?"

Aislinn dropped her cheek against her knees in despair and gazed thoughtfully into the darkness of the woods, her vision blurred by the tears that came much more freely now. Everything was still about her. It was as if time had ceased and she was forever caught in the limbo of the present. Even the stars appeared to have strayed from the blackened sky overhead, for two bright lights glistened from the darkness beyond.

Something prickled along Aislinn's spine and set her nerves on edge. Slowly she raised her head, blinking away the moisture in her eyes, and fixed her gaze on those shining points. Fear etched deep in the shadows of her mind, for she knew now it was not stars at all but two eyes that stared back at her. They were joined by others and more until the dark across the fire seemed scattered with glowing coals. One by one the wolves crept nearer, jaws opened, tongues lolling as if they laughed at her helplessness. The poor old mare snorted and trembled but could muster strength for nothing more. Aislinn added another log to the fire then seized a small stick in one hand and drew the slim dagger in her other. She could count some dozen furry bodies now as the wolves drew closer, snapping and snarling, seeming to bargain among themselves for the best position. Suddenly a stronger voice rent the night with a snarl and the wolves tucked their tails and drew aside as a beast easily twice as large as any of the others trotted forward into the light. As he came he glanced casually about, appraising the scene, then placing himself in front of the pack, turned his back on Aislinn and raised again a threatening snarl until they withdrew to the edge of the glade. He turned to face her and the slanting yellow eyes met hers with an intelligence that was amazing. Her lips moved and formed the word before she knew their intent.

"Wulfgar!" The hoarse whisper escaped her.

The black beast lay down, seeming so perfectly at ease that he could have been some trained hound to do her bidding.

Aislinn lowered the stick and returned her knife to its sheath. The wolf's jaws opened as if he smiled and confirmed the truce. He dropped his head to his outstretched paws but the eyes remained alert and never left her. Aislinn leaned back against the tree and the feeling came over her that she was secure in this wild wood, as much as she had ever been in Darkenwald.

A wolf snarled from the dark and Aislinn came fully awake, realizing she had dozed for some time. The great wolf raised his head and fastened his eyes on the darkness behind her but made no other move. Aislinn waited, her hackles rising as the tension grew. Then a stone rolled and she slowly turned.

"Wulfgar!" she gasped.

His eyes went to her as he came forward leading the Hun and then went to the huge beast beyond the fire. It was both surprise and relief that she felt as he came to stand fully in the light, for she had almost convinced herself that he was were-beast as the rumors held and had somehow become that great, black wolf who had guarded her so well.

The animal now rose and shook himself, his golden eyes gleaming as he and Wulfgar stared at each other across the dying flames. The black wolf finally turned and with a yelp to his pack led them away into the night. The forest was silent for a long moment and Aislinn waited as Wulfgar stared at her. Finally he sighed and spoke with some humor in his voice.

"You, madam, are a fool."

Aislinn raised her chin a notch and returned quite tartly: "And you, sir, are a knave."

"Agreed." He gave her a brief smile. "But let us share the comfort of this glade until the morning breaks."

He tied the Hun beside the tired mare and from a pouch behind his saddle gave them both several handfuls of grain. Aislinn resigned herself and in spite of her failure to escape, felt great comfort at his presence and thus made no resistance when after doffing his mail and laying it across his grounded saddle, he stretched out beside her, drew her near and wrapped them both in his heavy cloak.

Maida sat up suddenly with a snort and rose mumbling to herself to lay more sticks on the fire. She stopped short as she saw the great Hun beside the mare and her quicksilver eyes searched about until she spied Wulfgar beside Aislinn.

"Ha!" she grunted. "You sly Normans can find a warm bed in any thicket, can't you?" She stamped back to her bed but cast a last glare at Wulfgar. "Turn my back for just one moment! Huh!" She flopped down and pulled the blanket high over her shoulders.

Aislinn smiled contentedly to herself and snuggled more comfortably against Wulfgar. Maida was not happy to see this stalwart Norman in their camp, but her own heart swelled jubilantly within her breast to be once again within his embrace and to have his large hands upon her, holding her close.

"Are you cold?" he murmured against her hair.

She shook her head and her eyes shone with more warmth than the fire offered, yet her gaze was cast downward where he could not see and he had no way of knowing she was deliriously happy. Her slim body was pressed full length to his side, and with her head upon his shoulder she knew the full comfort and security of their bed at Darkenwald.

"The babe stirs," Wulfgar said huskily. " 'Tis a sign of strength."

Aislinn bit her lip, suddenly uncertain. He rarely spoke of the child and when he did, she had the feeling it was only to make conversation with her as if to ease her mind some small whit. Yet she grew more troubled each time she caught him gazing toward her belly in mute consideration of it as if by staring at that slight roundness he could find some assurance that it was his babe who grew there.

"It moves often now," Aislinn replied, her voice so low he had to strain to hear.

" 'Tis good," he said and pulled his mantle more tightly around them, ending the stilted conversation as he leaned his head back and closed his eyes.

In the early morning hours Aislinn came slowly awake as Wulfgar eased from her side. Through half-closed eyes she watched him rise and go into the woods, then she sat up, pulling his mantle close against the chill and cast a glance around at their camp. Her mother still slumbered heavily on, curled in a tight ball as if she would forbid the world and reality to disturb her.

Running her fingers through her long hair to loosen the soft tangles, Aislinn stretched and grew warm within herself at the beauty of the morning. Dew glistened off leaves of grass and bedecked a spider's airy web. Birds flittered about through the budding limbs above her head and a soft scurrying in the grass proved to be a small furry rabbit. There was a scent of newness in the air and she filled her lungs on its heady fragrance. She sighed, content with the world and its marvels. Her face shone radiantly as she lifted it to the sparkling rays of sunlight invading the glade. How sweet the bird's song. How sweet the morning dew. She mused briefly on her feelings and the happiness she knew. Why? When in fact she should be disconsolate at having been intercepted. She might see Normandy after all. Yet her heart sang with the fullness of spring.

The sound of Wulfgar's footsteps came behind her, and she turned to greet him with a smile. He paused, seeming for the moment confused by her manner, and then crossed to where she sat and dropped down beside her. He took up the small bundle she had hastily prepared upon leaving Darkenwald and sorted through it. Raising a questioning brow, he held up their meager fare.

"A joint of mutton? A loaf of bread?" There was a derisive note in his voice. "You must have planned well for this long journey north."

"Gwyneth guards your larder well. She counts the very grains for meal and surely would have sent out an alarm had I taken more."

Waking at the first sound of their voices, Maida now rose and rubbed a hip grown stiff in the night. She sneered through a crooked grin.

"You must forgive the child, my lord. Her mind is weak in these matters. She thought we would have seemed the thieves if we took too much of *our* food."

Aislinn pouted at her mother. "We would have found more generous provender on leaving William's lands."

Wulfgar snorted. "From your kindly Saxon kin no doubt? Those heroes of the north?"

"Those loyal friends would have welcomed us and seen to our needs as victims of the bastard duke," Maida scolded, chafing at his scorn.

Wulfgar sneered. "William is the king by all acclaim, save you. Your loyal friends, bedamned. The northern clans exact a heavy duty for passage on their roads and many a far richer band than you has arrived quite penniless."

"Ha!" Maida waved her hand at him in disgust. "You prattle like a raven with the croup. Time will tell who knows the Saxon breed the best, a Norman rogue or one of true English blood."

She dismissed further argument and made her way into the brush.

Wulfgar tore a piece from the loaf and laying upon it a slice of meat, handed it to Aislinn. He prepared the same in greater proportion for himself and munched thoughtfully on the cold fare, watching her as he did so. His eyes passed briefly over her frayed gown.

"You took no coin nor gold to pay your way?" Knowing the answer to his question before he spoke, he continued with a sour humor in his voice. "I can see some northern laird welcoming you in his chambers, but your mother might have found more toilsome labor to meet the cost." He laughed low as his gaze raked her again. "Yet had you paid the full toll, cherie, I vow you would have found it difficult to move from pallet to bench."

Aislinn tossed her head, dismissing his crudities, and daintily licked her fingers. Wulfgar ignored her distain and moved to sit close beside her.

"In truth, my love, why did you flee?"

Aislinn's eyes opened wide and she turned to him in surprise, but saw the earnest question in his gaze.

"You had everything a maid could desire," he said, running a finger along her forearm. "A warm bed. A strong protector. A gentle arm to lean upon. Food aplenty and love to keep you busy on a long, cold night."

"Everything?" Aislinn gasped, finding her tongue in amazed protest. "Oh, I beg you consider what I have. The bed was my father's who now lies slain in a grave. My protectors I have seen meet the sword or the lash. Indeed, I must protect more than I am protected. A strong arm to lean upon I have not yet found. The ample food is doled out from that which once was mine." Her voice broke and tears pushed close to the surface. "And love? Love? I am raped by a drunken fool. Was that my love? I am made the slave of a Norman lord. Is this my love? I am chained to the bed and threatened." She caught his hand and pulled it to her waist. "Feel my belly. Put your hand here and feel the child move. Conceived in love? I cannot say. In truth I do not know."

Wulfgar opened his mouth as if to speak but Aislinn raged on, shrugging off his hand.

"Nay, hear me out this once and tell me what I have. I am abused in the same hall where I played as a child, my clothes and every treasure taken from me one by one. I cannot call the simplest gown my own, for on the morrow I may see another wearing it. My only pet, a beast of burden, is broken and all be it in mercy, slain. Tell me, my lord Wulfgar, what I have."

He scowled at her. "You have only to ask and if it be in my power I will bring it to your feet."

Aislinn looked into his eyes and spoke slowly. "Will you marry me, Wulfgar, and give this child a name?"

He frowned more deeply and turned away to roll a half burned log into the fire.

"The ever-present trap," he growled, "to snare the unwary foot."

"Aaah," Aislinn sighed. "You enjoyed me well enough when I was slim, but now you evade the issue. You need not tell me of your passion for Haylan. Your eyes bespoke the lust as she danced before you."

Wulfgar jerked his head around to stare at her in surprise. "Lust? I but enjoyed the entertainment."

"Entertainment, ha!" Aislinn jeered. " 'Twas more like an invitation to her bed."

"Upon my word, my lady, I have not noticed you trying to please me half so well."

"What?" she cried in amazement. "With this round shape of mine? Would you have me dance and play the fool?"

"You give excuses where there are none," he retorted sourly. "You are as slim as she and there is naught to stay you. I would enjoy your coddling for once instead of fighting you in bed and being pricked by your tongue."

Aislinn stiffened and her violet eyes flashed with anger. "Whose tongue does prick, my lord? 'Twould serve me better to wear your mail than be ever wounded by your jibes."

Wulfgar snorted. " 'Tis not my nature to be a cocky swain like Ragnor. I find it hard to cosset a maid, but with you I have been generous."

"Do you love me perhaps some small bit?" Aislinn asked softly.

He caressed her arm. "Of course, Aislinn," he murmured. "I will love you every night until you cry out for me to cease."

Aislinn closed her eyes and from between her grinding teeth an anguished moan escaped.

"Do you deny that my caress awakes in you an answer?" Wulfgar inquired.

Aislinn sighed and murmured simply, "I am your slave, milord. What would you have a slave say to her master?"

Frustrated anger showed in his eyes. "You are not my slave! When I caress you, you come to me in warmth."

His words brought a deep scarlet flush to her cheeks as she glanced warily toward where her mother had disappeared into the woods, fearful that Maida would return and hear. He laughed in mockery.

"Are you afraid she might learn you relish a Norman's bed?" He drew up a knee and rested an arm upon it while he leaned a bit nearer to her, bending his head as she bent hers. "You may be able to fool your mother, but I am the one to know. 'Twas not my lovemaking that made you flee."

With a cry of rage, Aislinn drew back her hand to strike but found it seized in his. With a quick movement he pushed her back upon the ground and held her there with his weight.

"So, your honor has been abused. Is that why you suddenly flew after these many months?"

Aislinn struggled in vain. His knee was thrust between her own and his arm easily held her immobile. She felt the hard muscles of his body, now tense against her own frame and his large hand pressed against her back. Realizing that resistance was useless, Aislinn yielded and relaxed beneath him. Tears crept from her tightly closed eyes and ran down her cheeks.

"You are cruel, Wulfgar," she sobbed. "You play with me and decry that which I cannot suppress. I wish I could be cold and uncaring then perhaps your touch would not torment me so."

He bent low and lightly kissed her nose, her eyelids salty with tears, and then his mouth moved over her lips and even now Aislinn could not withhold the surge within her and answered his caress with passion of her own.

Maida's voice crackled in the morning air. "What ho! A Norman rolling in the dew? M'lord, should not we mount the steeds instead and be upon our way?"

She cackled in glee at her own words. As Wulfgar sat up and ran his fingers through his hair, he gave the old woman a glare that would have fair split her skull. Aislinn turned her face away from them both and brushed the grass from her skirt.

Wulfgar rose and saddled the horses and brought them forward. His hauberk he folded and lashed in front of the saddle on the Hun, preferring to ride unfettered this bright spring day. Maida groaned as she tried to lift her foot into the high stirrup then found herself seized by the waist and placed astride the ancient mare. Wulfgar stepped around Aislinn, swinging into his own saddle then sat looking down at her. He met her questioning gaze with an amused chuckle.

"The mare is lame and cannot bear you both."

Aislinn set her gaze coolly upon him. "Am I then to walk, milord?" she inquired haughtily.

He leaned an elbow on the high pommel of his saddle. "Is that not what you deserve?"

Her glare grew hotter but without speaking again she spun on her heels and began the long trek to Darkenwald. Wulfgar smiled and lifted the reins, following her. Maida brought up the rear on the limping nag.

The sun was high and the morning well along when Aislinn halted and flounced down on a log, taking off her slipper to shake a pebble from it.

Wulfgar halted and waited until she looked up, then asked her solicitously, "Does milady weary of this stroll?"

" 'Twas you who set me upon it, milord," she replied with much feeling.

"Nay, my love, not I," he denied innocently. "I but asked if it was what you deserved."

Aislinn rose and stared at him, then she flushed.

"Oh, you beast!" She stamped her foot but winced as the tender heel struck the ground.

Wulfgar gestured to her and slid back to sit on the skirt of his saddle.

"Come, my love," he admonished her. "The day will be tiresome as it is and I would soon be home."

He reached down and Aislinn reluctantly placed her hands in his and with an easy movement Wulfgar swung her up into the saddle before him, guiding her knee around the large pommel.

Maida had drawn up beside them and now sneered at Wulfgar's attentions. " 'Tis better to walk than to warm a Norman's lap, daughter."

Wulfgar flung a sideward glance at the woman and

spoke not gently. "Would you like to escape, old hag? I would gladly turn my back if you will."

There was a strange sound from Aislinn, but when both turned to her she stared serenely into the distance, yet the corners of her mouth quivered with suppressed merriment.

Wulfgar urged the Hun forward while Maida sulked and grumbled to herself, giving him a snarl behind his back, but otherwise for the next few miles she held her silence.

As the Hun finally slowed and plodded along, Aislinn began to feel a great drowsiness creep over her. The saddle was worn smooth and far too roomy, thus she found it difficult to hold her place upon it. She felt the close warmth of the man who rode behind her and looking down could gaze musingly at his hands holding the reins. They were strong and capable of wielding a mighty sword, yet his long fingers were lean and supple and even gentle when the moment warranted. A sly smile spread her lips as she thought of their strength. With eyes aglow she leaned back full against him and pulled his mantle about her shoulders, laying her head against his neck with her face hidden beneath his chin. The smile stayed as she relaxed and left it up to his strong arms to keep her there. Wulfgar found the chore not unrewarding. Her softness and fragrant scent teased him, yet he wondered again at her sudden change.

It seemed like only a short time had passed when Maida rent the silence with a whining screech. Aislinn came upright, startled out of her dozing, and glanced around at her mother.

" 'Tis naught but dust I've swallowed these many miles," the woman wailed. "Would you have me die of thirst, you hedge lord, so that you can have my daughter when is thy wont without my bridlings to keep you in check?"

At Maida's complaints, Wulfgar turned his steed off the road beside a swift flowing stream and pulled him to a halt. Swinging down from the stallion's back, he reached his hands up to catch Aislinn around the waist and drew her down beside him, lingering a moment to wrap his mantle about her shoulders. He gave Maida a look askance before he went to her side and reluctantly helped her down.

"Huh," she snapped. "You have much to learn of

gentleness, Norman. 'Tis no doubt that rape got my daughter with child, 'twas naught else from your hand."

"Mother!" Aislinn scolded, but Wulfgar looked at Maida pointedly.

"How came you by the assurance, old grouse, 'twas me who sired the babe and no other?"

Maida peered into his face and cackled gleefully. "Aaah, if the wee one comes with the black of a crow's wing in his hair, then 'tis Ragnor who played the maid rightly, and if the summer's wheat falls upon the babe's pate and disappears into the tuff, then 'tis bastard's brat for sure. But——," she paused, seeming to sample each word with delight. "If the child's crown springs forth with the red of the morning sun"—she shrugged and hugged herself joyfully—"then his sire is not known, of course."

Wulfgar's brows drew together before he turned abruptly away, brushing past Aislinn, and led the horses to water. Aislinn frowned at her mother who giggled her delight and scampered off into the woods by herself. Aislinn glanced uncertainly at Wulfgar's broad back. It seemed now so cold and forbidding that she knew he wanted no company save his horses which he stroked distractedly. With a sigh Aislinn turned and slowly entered the thicket herself, knowing he must settle the problem himself within his own mind.

He was waiting for her when she returned and had sliced bread and meat for them. Her inquiring look found him still broodingly silent and no further words were exchanged between the three as they dined. Maida had noted his temperament and for once carefully held her tongue, desiring no bruises from this Norman knight.

The ride home continued in the same manner, though Aislinn dozed in Wulfgar's arms and drew some comfort from his gentleness with her. His deep voice speaking low against her ear woke her as they reached the hall of Darkenwald. With an effort Aislinn straightened, blinking away sleep and found that darkness had fallen. Wulfgar swung from the saddle and Aislinn dropped her hands to his wide shoulders as he reached up to help her from the Hun. He set her carefully down beside him and turning to her mother, saw that Maida's small frame sagged wearily upon the mare. The torches burned beside the great door and by the light Aislinn noted her mother's face was drawn and bespoke of her fatigue. Aislinn took Maida's thin arm and spoke softly in her hear.

"Come, I'll take you to your hut."

Wulfgar stretched out a hand, stopping her. "I will take her. Make your way to our chamber and await me. I will be there soon."

Maida looked at him suspiciously before moving slowly ahead of him into the dark. Aislinn paused, listening to the sound of Wulfgar's footsteps following behind her mother, then fading slowly. After several long moments a dim light was seen in the distance from Maida's cottage window, and Aislinn finally turned and with lagging steps, trudged into the hall and up the stairs to their bedchamber.

The room was lit by a cheery fire prepared no doubt by some thoughtful soul who never doubted Wulfgar's success in anything he did—undoubtedly Sweyn, ever loyal and ever seeing to his lord's comfort.

With a sigh Aislinn dropped her soiled gunna onto the coffer as she stood near the warmth of the hearth. Drawing off her kirtle, she reached for a pelt to wrap around her naked body but as the door creaked open behind her she clutched her kirtle to her breast again and faced the intruder.

"So, you're back," Gwyneth murmured, leaning against the frame.

Aislinn swept her hand before her. "As you see, still alive and breathing."

" 'Tis a shame," Gwyneth sighed. "I was in hopes you'd meet some hungry wolf."

"I did, if you are anxious to know. He should be along any moment now."

"Ah, the brave bastard," Gwyneth returned derisively. "Ever flaunting his valor."

Aislinn shook her head. "You know so little of your brother, Gwyneth."

The woman straightened and strode forward brazenly, raking Aislinn's slim body contemptuously with her gaze. "I admit I do not understand him nor why he should go flying off in the night to search for you when he will in time send you to Normandy or some other land far from here. Foolishness to be sure and naught of wisdom."

"Why do you hate him so?" Aislinn inquired earnestly. "Has he ever sought to hurt you? You bear such venom for him I find it hard to understand your reason."

Gwyneth sneered. "Nor would you, you Saxon slut. You are content to spread yourself upon his bed and play his games. What will you get from him but more bastards?"

Aislinn's chin raised a notch as she choked back angry words. Then a movement out of the corner of her eye caught her attention and looking there, she found Wulfgar standing in the doorway, listening with quiet interest to their words. His arms were folded across his chest and his hauberk rested casually across his shoulder. At Aislinn's silence Gwyneth turned to follow her stare and met her brother's gaze.

"Do you come to welcome us back, Gwyneth?" he inquired somewhat roughly.

He closed the door behind him and crossed the room, laying his mail across the coffer beside Aislinn's gown and regarded Gwyneth who eyed him coldly.

"You make your contempt for us well known, Gwyneth. Are you not happy here?" he asked, placing his arms akimbo.

"What? Here in this beggardly hall?" She snapped.

"You are free to go," Wulfgar said slowly. "There is no one who would stop you."

Gwyneth's pale eyes stared at him coldly. "Are you casting me out, brother?"

Wulfgar shrugged his shoulders. "I but wish to assure you I will not hold you here if you choose to go."

"If it weren't for my father, you'd find a way to be rid of me," Gwyneth accused.

"True," Wulfgar admitted, a slow, sardonic grin spreading his lips.

"What? The roving knight has found that being a lord of lands has its disadvantages?" Gwyneth sneered sarcastically. "You must find it tiresome indeed to deal with the burdens of your many serfs and your household as well, when all you had to bother about before was yourself. Why do you not admit you are a failure here?"

"It does prove tiresome on occasion." Wulfgar looked pointedly at his sister. "But I believe myself capable of bearing the weight."

Gwyneth snorted derisively. "A bastard trying to prove himself worthy of his betters. 'Twould make a wooden image laugh."

"Do you find it so amusing, Gwyneth?" He smiled and moved to stand close beside Aislinn. Admiringly he lifted

378

a shiny coppery tress as she raised her eyes and he placed a gentle kiss upon it, his gaze caressing her with more than passing warmth. "You must find us all worthy of your scorn, we being human and imperfect."

Gwyneth watched his attentions to Aislinn and lifted her lip jeeringly. "Some must be tolerated with more patience than others."

"Oh?" Wulfgar faced her, raising a brow. "I was under the impression you held us all in the same contempt. Whom do you not?" His countenance seemed thoughtful for a moment then he smiled slowly, turning again to Aislinn who grew warm and weak with his nearness. "Ragnor, perhaps? That knave?"

Gwyneth straightened her spine. "What do you know of the gentle born, being a bastard yourself?" she snapped.

"A great deal," Wulfgar replied. "I had to take the abuse of those like Ragnor and you since I was a young lad. I know much of their high born ways and 'tis not worth a pauper's purse to me. If you really want to choose a man, Gwyneth, and I give you this advice freely, look to his heart and you will see the true measure of a man, not by what his ancestors before him have done or not done. Beware of Ragnor, sister. His kind is treacherous and should never be trusted overmuch."

"You speak from envy, Wulfgar," she charged.

He chuckled and ran a finger around Aislinn's ear, making a delightful shiver run through her body. "If you must believe so, Gwyneth, but be it known I warned you."

Gwyneth walked proudly to the door where she paused for a moment, glowering at them coldly, then left without another word, slamming it behind her.

Wulfgar laughed softly, dismissing her, then pulled Aislinn into his arms, slipping a hand to the small of her back while the other hand raised her chin. She did not resist but neither was there the response to him he desired. As his lips pressed lightly against hers, Aislinn willed her mind to think of other matters that greatly disturbed her and thus met his kiss with a coolness he was not accustomed to in her. After a moment he raised his head to gaze down into violet eyes lifted innocently to his.

"What plagues you?" he demanded in low voice.

"Do I displease you, milord? What is thy desire? Tell me and I will obey. I am your slave."

379

Wulfgar scowled heavily. "You are not my slave. I have told you once this day."

"But, milord, I am here to please you. What is a slave but one who must do her master's bidding? Do you wish my arms about your neck?" Stiltedly she turned, raising a silky limb while still holding her kirtle with the other and slipped her hand behind his neck. "Do you wish my kiss?" Rising on tiptoes, she lightly brushed her lips against his, then dropping her arm again to her side, she resumed her former position. "There, I have pleased you, have I not?"

With a disgusted movement, Wulfgar tore his tunic over his head and folded it angrily away. With long strides he crossed to the bed and sat down on its edge, pulling off his chainse. When he stood up to remove the chausses, Aislinn went to the end of the bed where the chain still lay and sat down upon the stone floor, catching her breath at the coldness of it against her bare buttocks. As he stared at her in some amazement she slipped her slender ankle in the circlet of iron and snapped it closed.

"What the devil?" he cried and stepped to her. He yanked her to her feet, making Aislinn lose her grip on the kirtle. She stood naked as he stared down at her, his face black with ire. "What do you think you're doing?"

Her eyes widened in feigned innocence. "Are slaves not chained, milord? You see I am not aware of their treatment because I've only been a slave these past few months. Since the Normans' coming, milord."

Wulfgar swore and bending, impatiently removed the iron from her ankle. He lifted her in his arms and tossed her onto the bed.

"You are no slave," he bellowed, glaring at her.

"Aye, milord," she replied, barely able to keep her mouth in sober lines. "As you wish, milord."

"For mercy's sake! What do you want of me, woman?" he demanded, throwing his arms up in frustration. "I have said you are no slave. What more do you want?"

She batted her eyelids coyly. "I wish only to please you, milord. Why do you show such anger? I am here to do thy will."

"What will make you listen?" he raged. "Must I cry it to the world?"

"Aye, milord," she said simply and smiled as he looked at her more closely.

For a short moment Wulfgar stared at her as if trying

to find her meaning, then as it dawned on him he straightened and began snatching up his clothes again. He strode to the door and there paused as her voice halted him.

"Where do you go, milord? Am I not pleasing?"

"I go to join Sweyn," he growled in return. "He does not badger me so much."

With that he left the room, slamming the door behind him in a fit of temper. Smiling to herself Aislinn drew the pelts up around her and, wrapping her arms about his pillow, breathed in his scent that lingered upon it and presently went to sleep.

"What saucy wench, that?" Wulfgar swore as he strode angrily across the courtyard to the stables. "She would have me wed to her, declaring to the world she was my lady proper. I am not the one to be led about by a ring in my nose. She'll have to be content."

He found some fresh hay beside the Hun and thumped about until he had prepared an adequate bed for himself. The noise he made stirred the animals and then drew aggravated grumbles from his men. At a sharp word from a lowly archer, he flung himself down on the straw at the Hun's head, drawing his mantle about him and tried in vain to get the rest he sorely needed.

He rode hard and fast the next day, tiring his mind and body in hopes he might drift into a well deserved sleep that night, yet as dawn painted the horizon with soft magenta hues he still lay fitfully tossing and turning upon his bed of straw. He had avoided the hall since leaving it that other night but now and again he caught a glimpse of Aislinn as she crossed to her mother's hut or went upon some other chore. At these times he would stop and watch her go, admiring the gentle swing of her skirts and the brilliance of her coppery tresses as her hair shone in the sunlight. She cast furtive glances his way but generally stayed out of his reach. His men looked at them questioningly, glancing from one to the other, and scratched their heads at his bed in the straw. They were careful to remain silent if some sudden oath or snarl woke them in the night, recognizing his voice, and huddled upon their own pallets, hoping greatly that he would soon find sleep.

The third morning he rose and took his breakfast in the hall, casting glances toward the stairway until Aislinn finally descended. For a moment she seemed surprised to see him but then quickly recovered her composure and went to help Ham serve the meal. She brought a platter around to the men and finally came to him with it, offering the quail to him without a word. He selected a plump bird and then peered at her.

"Fill my cup," he commanded. Complying Aislinn reached across him, her breast brushing his shoulder, and took up the mug. She returned a moment later with it filled with milk and set it before him.

Wulfgar frowned. "Did you find it thusly? Move it to where it was, slave."

"As you wish, milord," she murmured.

Again she reached across him, her breast brushing his shoulder and placed the horn as it had been.

"Does that please you, milord?" she questioned.

"Aye," he replied and bent his attention to his meal.

Gwyneth seemed delighted with this arrangement and took her meal beside Wulfgar that evening sitting in Aislinn's chair. She bestowed a bit more kindness upon her brother and tried to draw him into conversation but was met with noncommittal grunts and silent stares. His attention seemed mainly centered upon Aislinn as she labored with Ham and Kerwick to set the food before him and his men. She struggled with the large platters, and Kerwick often came to her aid when it seemed she was about to drop the heavy load. His solicitude aggravated Wulfgar sorely and brooding stares followed them about the hall. Wulfgar's hand tightened upon his cup as he watched Aislinn at one point laughing with the young Saxon.

"You see how she plays with him?" Gwyneth murmured near her brother's ear. "Is she worth your concern? Look to Haylan instead." Her thin hand swept the hall toward the young widow who eyed Wulfgar longingly. " 'Twould seem she has more love to offer. Have you tried her in bed yet? She might prove a healing potion."

Yet with all Gwyneth's efforts, Wulfgar's gaze returned to Aislinn. Bolsgar watched him silently for a while, then leaned near.

"The wolf roams the countryside but always returns to his one mate. Have you found that one yet?"

Wulfgar turned to him sharply. "What price have you taken to make this match?"

" 'Twould seem it was low, whatever." Bolsgar laughed softly, then grew serious. "Make your choice, Wulfgar. Free the maid Aislinn or take her for your own."

Wulfgar gritted his teeth. "You conspire with Maida!" he accused.

"Why do you keep such a mean and vengeful maid in your household?" Bolsgar inquired, gesturing to Aislinn. "I see how she tortures you with her presence. She knows you are watching and plays with other men. Kerwick is no fool. He will take the girl to wife and be father to her babe. Why not give her to him? He would be happy. But you, milord fool—," the old knight chuckled. "What of you? Can you bear the thought of her sharing his bed?"

Wulfgar's fist banged down on the table. "Cease!" he roared.

"If you do not take her, Wulfgar," Bolsgar continued imperturbed. "Then in good faith you cannot keep the young Saxon from marrying her to give a name to her babe."

"What difference would it make to the child? My mother was married to you and I still am called bastard," Wulfgar returned bitterly.

Bolsgar's face paled. "I disclaimed you," he said slowly, struggling with his words. "Say that I was then the fool, for many times I've regreted my action and yearned to have you back. You were a truer son to me than fair Falsworth. My mind is ever tortured with the agony I caused you, but it cannot be undone. Will you be so foolish?"

Wulfgar turned away, disturbed by the old man's words. Finally he rose and strode from the hall, not noticing that Aislinn's eyes followed him with worry drawing her brows together.

The next morning Aislinn was startled rudely out of sleep when Wulfgar tore the pelts from her and gave her a hearty whack upon her bottom.

"Rise, you wench. We will have important guests this day and I would present them with your best appearance."

Aislinn sulked, rubbing her abused posterior and finally

rose under his all too careful regard. As she reached for her kirtle, he clapped both his hands together loudly and the door immediately opened to admit Hlynn and Miderd who carried in water for a bath. Clutching her kirtle over her nakedness Aislinn glanced from the women to Wulfgar in confusion.

He raised a brow. "For you, milady. A scented bath will liven your spirit." He whirled on his heels and strode to the door, there to turn again to her. "Wear the yellow gunna I bought for you. I like the color on you."

Aislinn flounced down angrily upon the edge of the bed.

"Tsk! Tsk!" he scolded. "You seek to please, do you not? Or have you forgotten a slave's duty?" He smiled. "I will be back shortly."

With a laugh he stepped through the portal, quickly closing the door behind him before some missile could find his head, and strode down the stairs.

Reluctantly Aislinn let the two women assist her with the bath and finally relaxed under their massaging hands as they smoothed a scented oil upon her body. Then they combed her hair long and painstakingly until Aislinn thought they would never cease. They pulled it from her face and caught the mass high on her head, intricately coiling it with yellow ribbons. They helped her don the silk kirtle and the rich velvet gunna, then placed her gold fila-gree girdle about her hips, completing her toilet.

Miderd stepped back to admire her and smiled through happy tears. "Oh, milady, you are too lovely for words. 'Tis glad we are that he brought you back."

Aislinn embraced her fondly. "To state the truth, Miderd, so am I, yet I wonder at his moods, if he will have me now or seek some other."

Timid Hlynn slipped a comforting arm about her mistress' waist and patted her back consolingly, failing to find the right words to comfort her. Aislinn hugged her close, tears brightening her eyes, and then Miderd and Hlynn hurried to tidy the room before Wulfgar returned. At his entrance several moments later they quickly scurried out, closing the door softly behind them.

Wulfgar came across the room to stand before Aislinn, clasping his hands behind his back and setting his feet apart. His eyes slowly traveled her length and then re-turned as leisurely to her face. Bristling slightly under his close scrutiny, Aislinn returned his gaze coldly. He came closer and his knuckles beneath her chin raised her head. Very lightly he pressed a kiss upon her soft lips, and his look was warm and devouring.

"You are beautiful," he murmured huskily against her mouth, and it took all of Aislinn's willpower not to relax against him and slip her hands around his waist. He laughed softly as he stepped away. "But a slave must not be made vain. Come down to the hall; the others wait," he called over his shoulder as he left.

Still feeling the brush of his lips, Aislinn scuffed a small foot disconcertedly against the stone floor.

"A slave to do his bidding, nothing more. 'Twould take all Heaven to convince him I would be a just mate."

Gwyneth had donned her finest also and stood rankling at the mystery and the delay. Wulfgar leisurely quaffed ale as he watched her pace the floor giving him a glare now and then as she passed him.

"You drag me out of bed and do not tell me the reason, except that someone comes. Who would venture to this Godforsaken place other than the slow witted?"

"You came, dear Gwyneth," he said with humor and watched the flash of anger he aroused. "Do you make yourself the exception or are we all slow witted?"

"You jest, brother, but I do not see your precious William come to view your holdings."

Wulfgar shrugged. "Would you have the King visit a commonplace lord with small lands? His duties as king are far greater than mine as lord. I can well understand that his time is well met, especially if his subjects continually grumble as mine are wont to do."

Gwyneth made a sneering reply with a toss of her head and then went to where Ham and Kerwick were turning a boar, venison, and an abundance of smaller game and fowl on spits above the fire. She gestured derisively toward the meats.

"This would feed us all for a month. You are careless with food, Wulfgar."

"The grains in the meal," Wulfgar sighed under his breath and turned to meet Bolsgar as he came down the stairs, a handsome man still when in fine garments. Wulfgar had shared with him from his own coffer, presenting to the older man some of his best. Though the belt had proven too narrow for Bolsgar's waist the shoulders and length of his robe fit well enough. The elder man chuckled as he turned before them.

"I've regained my youth, I swear."

Gwyneth scoffed. "In borrowed clothes yet."

The old eyes measured Gwyneth, taking in Aislinn's tawny gold gown that she wore.

"What ho! The pot calls the kettle black. It seems to me you have borrowed some yourself," he said.

Gwyneth spun around, turning her back to him, and Bolsgar dismissed her as Wulfgar handed him a horn of ale. They sat enjoying the mellow taste of the drink until the great door swung open admitting one of Wulfgar's men who hurried to his lord carrying a rather large bundle wrapped in skins. The man bent over Wulfgar's ear as he set the package before him and spoke softly of some matter. Wulfgar nodded and as the man turned to go Wulfgar began to cut the cords binding the bundle. He drew it apart and pulled several men's garments from it and threw them over his arm. He crossed to Kerwick who paid no heed to his approach so intent was he with the task he had been set to.

"Kerwick."

Wulfgar spoke and the younger man immediately rose to his feet, turning. His eyes flew to the garments and widened slightly in surprise before he quickly straightened.

"My lord?"

Wulfgar held the clothes up. "Am I right to name these garments yours?" he questioned a bit gruffly so that he added confusion to the Saxon's countenance.

"Aye, milord," Kerwick returned uncertainly. "But I have no idea how they came here. 'Twas not I who carried them from Cregan."

"If you had noticed, Kerwick, they have only just arrived. I sent a man for them."

"Sir?" Kerwick looked doubtfully at Wulfgar's taller frame and knew no alteration could make the garments fit the Norman.

"They are not for me, Kerwick, but for you," Wulfgar returned, reading his eyes. "Take them and rise from this chore and dress yourself as one who is gently born."

Kerwick stretched his hands out to take the clothes then drew them back hurriedly to wipe them upon his rough tunic. With care he accepted the apparel yet still wore much bemusement on his face.

Gwyneth whirled sharply in disgust at her brother and strode to the other end of the hall to sulk in silence by herself.

Wulfgar turned and spoke to the hall in general. "My man tells me our guest is on his way and will arrive anon."

Aislinn's descent of the stairs caused a stir and many admiring stares fell upon her, for by the time she joined the group in the hall many of Wulfgar's men had also entered, dressed in their best garments. Sir Milbourne and Sir Gowain stood near the bottom of the stairs, and the younger man gaped so hard at her, the older reached up to wave a hand before his face drawing chuckles from those near. Gowain offered up his hand to her and smiled happily as she let him assist her.

"My lady, your radiance bedazzles me overmuch. I find my tongue grown lame and I cannot think of words to express the full measure of your beauty."

Casting a glance awry to Wulfgar in time to see Bolsgar nudge him, Aislinn smiled beguilingly up at the young knight.

"Your tongue is smooth, sir knight, and no doubt many a young maiden has fallen to its charm."

Pleased at her compliment, the knight glanced around at the other faces near him then swallowed convulsively as Wulfgar joined them. He stuttered and grew deeply flushed as Wulfgar raised a questioningly brow at him.

"What is this, Sir Gowain? Have you so much leisure upon your hands that you must dally with my slave?"

Gowain nearly choked on his tongue and was thoroughly confused by what had transpired in the days prior to this one, when Wulfgar had ignored the Saxon beauty, giving him to wonder if there was some hope.

"Nay, my liege. Nay," he denied profusely. "I was but attesting to her exquisite beauty, that is all. I meant no harm."

Wulfgar took Aislinn's slender hand in his, pulling her slightly to him and bestowed a grin upon the flustered knight.

"You are forgiven. Only give good heed to this matter hence and venture but with care. I have not been one to split hairs over a wench or two, but this one, Sir Gowain, I might fairly split your skull over."

With that warning to the young knight and all those that heard, Wulfgar drew Aislinn away from the men and returned to Bolsgar's side. The old man's eyes twinkled merrily as he viewed her.

"Ah, what a comely maid you are, Aislinn. You do these ancient eyes of mine good to behold you. Nearly three score years have I lived and in that time I cannot remember viewing such perfect beauty before."

"You are kind, my lord." She curtsied to him and glanced up at Wulfgar, feeling his eyes upon her. "And do I please you also, milord? 'Tis my duty whatever you command, but 'twould seem difficult to change my appearance if it were not worth enough to draw your approval."

He smiled into her eyes, his own burning and intense, yet his lips spoke without committal.

"As I've said, a slave should not be made vain."

He squeezed her hand as he held it down against her side. His mouth widened into a grin as she looked at him icily, but her fingers trembled in his hand, giving the lie to her gaze.

"You are lovely," he murmured. "Now what else would you have me admit?" She opened her mouth to retort, but he put up a hand before she could speak. "Cease your demands. I am wearied of being hounded. Give me rest."

Miffed at his words, Aislinn whirled, snatching her hand free and crossed to the hearth where Ham labored.

"A feast?" she surmised, gazing at the roasting meats. "His guests must indeed be important."

"Yea, milady," the lad agreed. "He has not spared a thing to make this day to be remembered. Even now they labor in the cooking chamber to please him."

Aislinn turned and considered Wulfgar from a distance. He made a splendid figure in a tunic of deep green velvet, edged with gold braid. A short mantle of deep crimson was clasped at his neck and flowed over one shoulder down to his knees. Beneath his gown he wore a soft linen chainse and Aislinn thought of the care with which she had sewn that simple garment for him. It fit his broad shoulders well and she admitted only to herself the garment never looked so fine as now that he wore it. His long, lean legs showed straight and well muscled beneath the tawny chausses and cross garters, and his appearance was such that a deep painful pride began to grow in Aislinn's chest as she stared at him.

"Aislinn?"

Her name came from a familiar voice behind her and she whirled and stared in surprise at Kerwick now dressed in rich attire. Her eyes went over him in astonishment, then a radiant smile broke upon her lips.

"Why, Kerwick, you are beautiful," she cried in pleasure.

"Beautiful?" He shook his head. "Nay, 'tis a word describing you."

"Oh, but you are," she insisted.

Kerwick smiled. "It feels good to wear fine clothes again. He sent for them—especially for me," he said in amazement.

"Who?" Aislinn questioned and her eyes followed Kerwick's to where Wulfgar stood. "You mean Wulfgar sent to Cregan for them? For you?" she asked in astonishment.

Kerwick nodded, bringing a warm, jubilant smile to her face. With a happy catch in her throat, Aislinn begged the pardon of her former betrothed and made her way to Wulfgar's side again, though she did so slowly, eyeing him as she went and puzzling at his motive. He turned as she touched his hand and welcomed her with a smile.

"Cherie," he murmured warmly, gently squeezing her fingers. "Have you decided you can stand my humor?"

"On occasion, milord, but not overmuch," she returned and the corners of her lips turned upward winsomely. Wulfgar found himself mesmerized by her eyes shining into his. For a long moment they stood thus, enjoying the nearness of one another and experiencing once again the exciting attraction that always seemed to draw them together. Gwyneth's voice broke them rudely apart.

"A bastard and his trollop," she hissed. "I see you've found each other again. What more can one expect from the common born."

Bolsgar snapped at Gwyneth sharply, commanding her to silence, but the insolent daughter ignored him and slid her eyes down Aislinn.

"Fit enough for royalty I suppose, but your belly spoils the costume."

Before she could think to hide her reaction, Aislinn lifted her hand to that slight roundness and looked a bit worried.

Wulfgar scowled heavily at his sister and bit back a sharper reply. "Do not be cruel, Gwyneth. Today I will have none of it. Either show respect to Aislinn or you will be dismissed to your chamber."

"I am no child," Gwyneth gasped. "And I will not show respect to a slut."

"Nay, you are no child," Wulfgar agreed. "But I am lord of this hall and you will not challenge me. Will you obey?"

Gwyneth's lips drew tightly together and her pale eyes narrowed but no words spilled from her mouth. Instead as she saw Haylan approach, her gaze grew cunning and she smiled up at Wulfgar.

"Here is dear Haylan. You will of course notice I've taken the liberty of sharing my meager garments with her."

They turned their gazes upon the young widow, and Aislinn recognized her own mauve gunna adorning her frame. Haylan was a bit shorter and plumper than Aislinn but nevertheless the clothes accentuated her dark beauty. Encouraged by the events of the days past, Haylan came to stand beside Wulfgar, managing deftly to slip between him and Aislinn and smiled boldly into his eyes. With a finger she traced a path down his chest where the edge of his mantle lay.

"You look fit, milord," she breathed.

Aislinn stiffened and beneath lowered lids she glared at the woman's back. She was possessed of a great urge to tear the long black curling hair from the woman's head and give her round buttocks a firm kick. Absently she toyed with the hilt of her dagger while her eyes fixed in distant concentration on the back of Haylan's dark head.

Haylan leaned against Wulfgar, her round bosom pressing lightly against his chest, and rubbed the soft velvet of his tunic with her hand while her eyes raised coyly to his.

"Is it your will that I leave, milord?" Aislinn's voice cut in with knife's edge sharpness. " 'Tis not my intent to interrupt thy—pleasure." The last word dripped with sweetness but her voice rose slightly as if in question.

Wulfgar hastened to disengage himself from Haylan and led his mistress away, leaving both Gwyneth and Haylan frowning at his back.

"And they call me wanton," Aislinn muttered to herself.

Wulfgar laughed low. "The widow sees more than there is, no doubt. Yet truly, I feared for her welfare when I saw the blood lust in your eyes."

Aislinn snatched her arm free. "Do not turn your day with worry, master." She bowed in humbleness though her eyes belied the gesture. "I am but a slave and would bear the cruel whim of others calmly and if attacked in rage would only seek to defend myself unless you spake it other."

Wulfgar grinned and rubbed his chest where he still bore the marks of her temper. "Aye, I've tasted your tender, helpless manner and know well that should the widow test you, she would goodly fare to rise with but one small lock of hair still attached."

Aislinn opened her mouth to retort, but her expression changed to one of surprise as the door of the great hall slammed open and a strong gust of cold March air swirled in. When the dust settled Sweyn stood in the portal arrayed in all his Nordic finery. His arms were akimbo and as he saw the faces before him, he laughed heartily, setting the hall atremble with his mirth.

"The man approaches, Wulfgar," he thundered. "He will arrive forthwith."

Wulfgar took Aislinn's hand without a word and led her to Bolsgar, there placing that hand carefully upon the old man's arm and bade the old man to keep her there. Ignoring her sudden pout, Wulfgar left her to stand beside Sweyn to greet the arriving guest.

Soon there was a clatter of small hooves accompanied by much huffing and puffing, then a slip-slap of sandals and Friar Dunley hove into view smiling broadly in obvious joy. Wide eyes and puzzlement marked the faces of all present and a low murmur of confusion filled the hall. The holy man joined Wulfgar and Sweyn and for a time the three of them talked with heads close together and in low tones. A moment passed and the bemusement of the others grew deeper, then Wulfgar led the friar to the table where he poured a chalice of wine for the monk.

The priest took the offering and with a quick genuflection, drained the cup to the last drop and nodded his thanks. Clearing his throat and assuming a serious manner, the man turned and mounted to the fourth step of the stairs where he faced them all, holding a small, golden cross before him and waited expectantly. The hall grew hushed as the people breathlessly waited for what the moment would bring. Bewilderment still dwelled on the gaping faces.

Wulfgar went to stand before the priest and, turning, raised a brow to Bolsgar who now grasped the meaning of it all. He raised Aislinn's hand high before him on his arm and led the stunned maid forward until she stood beside Wulfgar. Friar Dunley nodded his head, and taking Aislinn's hand, the Lord of Darkenwald knelt in the rushes on the floor, pulling her gently down beside him.

Maida sat down suddenly on a bench near her and stared in numb surprise. Kerwick for a moment felt a choking in his chest, but this eased and he grew strangely happy for Aislinn, seeing what she wanted most take place. Gwyneth gaped in sinking despair as her hopes to gain power and a place of honor at Darkenwald faded with the friar's words. Finally grasping the meaning of the ceremony, Haylan sniffled and began to sob as her aspirations dwindled rapidly with the soft drone of the priest's voice laying the blessing of the faith on the union.

Wulfgar's voice came strong and clear as he repeated his vows, and strangely it was Aislinn who stumbled and faltered as she repeated the words in a daze. Wulfgar drew her to her feet and she stood dumbly as the monk spoke the final binding statement. She realized that he had repeated a question for the third time to her.

"What?" she murmured, still dazed. "I didn't—"

The friar leaned forward and spoke earnestly. "Will you kiss the man and seal the vows?"

She turned to Wulfgar, hardly able to believe what had passed and half thinking herself dreaming, stared at him in wonder. A loud thump broke the silence as Sweyn slammed a tankard of ale on the table, sending foam flying and raised it high.

"Hail Wulfgar, Lord of Darkenwald!" he roared.

A fair thunder of cheers came from his men and even the townfolk present joined in. Again the heavy tankard slammed down on the table.

"Hail Aislinn, Lady of Darkenwald!"

And if the shouts had been loud before, this time the rafters shook and threatened to fall.

Aislinn finally accepted the truth and with a shriek threw her arms around Wulfgar's neck and between shouts of laughter and tears of joy, covered his face with kisses. Wulfgar finally held her at arm's length to calm her and laughed at the throbbing gaiety that filled her. She was snatched from his hands by Sweyn who crushed her in his arms for a moment then planted a resounding kiss upon her cheek and spun her away to Gowain thence to Milbourne, Bolsgar, Kerwick and on to the whole host of them. Finally she was once more placed before Wulfgar, rosy with excitement and breathless with laughter. He took her in his arms and kissed her long and hard, and she held nothing from him but answered him in the fullness of the joy she knew in her heart. They turned slowly full circle locked in their embrace amid the hearty shouts and cries of encouragement from the folk.

The hall dissolved in a heavy crush of merriment, but unnoticed were the grim faces of three of the women. Maida broke from her stupor and with a low moan of despair, fled from the hall clawing at her hair. Gwyneth slowly mounted the stairs to her chamber where she sat in lonely silence before the hearth, and Haylan fled sobbing on Maida's heels.

Around Aislinn there were good wishes from all and thumps on the back that left her gasping. She danced through it all with a single thought branding itself into her mind.

Wulfgar! My Wulfgar! My Wulfgar! The words rang in her deepest being and obscured all else.

More barrels of ale were broken and skins of wine emptied. The meats were cut, bread broken and words grew slurred as toast after toast followed. Wulfgar leaned back in his chair enjoying the festivities and entertainment. Jugglers, acrobats and musicians had been hurriedly summoned and performed for the amusement of the revelers. But it was Gowain who spoke the words, Aislinn remembered above all else as he postured in front of the newly wedded couple.

> "No fairer rose has my heart seen
> Nor knight errant ever won.
> Her beauty reigns on the highest peak
> Where no other maid can touch or seek.
> No blacker night nor darker day
> Than when this rose was snatched away,
> And bound in wedlock, how forlorn!"

He raised his ale high and ended:

> "To my one last pleasure, the drinking horn."

Aislinn laughed in obvious glee and the merrymaking continued until Wulfgar rose, clearing his throat for attention. He gazed around him at the joyful faces, serf and warrior, archer and vintner. They turned to him expectantly, and as he began to speak in French for the benefit of his men, the serfs gathered around Kerwick that he could put the words to English for them.

"In our towns, this day is to be remembered as the joining of Norman and Saxon," Wulfgar began carefully. "Henceforth this will be a place of peace and it will be a shire that profits. Soon we will begin building a castle as the king has bade, to protect the towns of Cregan and Darkenwald together. Around it there will be a moat and it will have walls as strong as we can make them. In times of danger both Norman and English will take shelter there. Those of my men who wish, may take up professions and raise shops of trade or skill that will support them. We shall make these towns safe and comfortable that visitors will seek them out. Masons will be needed and carpenters, tailors, venders of all types. Sir Gowain, Sir Beaufonte and Sir Milbourne have consented to stay on as my vassals and we shall continue to give our protection to all the people."

Wulfgar paused and there was a rush of speculations on his words. Then he continued.

"I have need of a money changer or sheriff of sorts that will be honest to Saxon and Norman alike. He will act in my stead on minor matters and keep records of all that transpires. No act of barter, sale, marriage, birth or ownership will be complete until he has entered it in the books. My marriage to the Lady Aislinn will be his first entry."

Again Wulfgar halted, looking at the faces around him then pressed on.

" 'Tis to this end I bring you. My attention is drawn to the fact that among the Saxons there is one who speaks both tongues well, a man of much learning whose skill with figures is unequaled and who can be depended upon for his honesty. 'Tis to Kerwick of Cregan I entrust these duties and I name him Sheriff of Darkenwald."

Gasps of surprise filled the hall, but from Aislinn there was only stunned silence. An astonished Kerwick was pushed forward as cheers roared forth and the hall was shaken again with merriment. As he came to stand before them, Kerwick glanced from Aislinn, whose elation now shone brightly in her eyes, to Wulfgar, who returned the stare with an earnest frown.

"Kerwick, do you think yourself capable of this task?"

The young Saxon raised his head proudly and replied, "Yea, my lord."

"So be it. Henceforth you are no slave but the Sheriff of Darkenwald. You have authority to speak in my name on those matters I leave to you. You will be my hand as much as Sweyn is my arm, and I shall put my faith in you to be just and fair to all."

"My lord," Kerwick said humbly, "I am honored."

A smile curved Wulfgar's lips as he added softly for Kerwick's ears alone.

"Let us be at peace, Kerwick, for my lady's sake." He extended his hand and Kerwick took it with a nod of agreement.

"For the sake of your lady and England."

They clasped hands as brothers and Kerwick turned away to receive the congratulations of both Norman and Saxon. Wulfgar resumed his seat and feeling Aislinn's gaze, he turned his eyes upon her.

"Husband!" she breathed as if marveling at the word, and her eyes gleamed.

Wulfgar chuckled softly and brought her fingers to his lips. "Wife!" he murmured in return.

Leaning toward him she drew a line upon his chest with a finger and smiled invitingly. "My lord, do you not think the hour is getting late?"

His hand gripped hers tightly and his grin deepened. "Indeed, my lady, the hour is growing very late."

"What must we do to cease its rapid fleeing?" she asked, her voice low and rich with warmth. Her free hand dropped against his knee and rested there. To the casual eye it was a small gesture yet between them flowed a surging excitement that could not long be denied. A devilish twinkle sparkled in Wulfgar's eyes.

"My lady, I would not know of your need for rest, but I am wont to find our bed soon."

Aislinn concurred with a smile. "Aaah, my lord, you read my mind. I was also thinking of the comfort to be had there after so long a day."

Their eyes met warmly and held promises each was anxious to collect, but suddenly they were startled apart as Wulfgar's men swarmed upon them, snatching their lord up and lifting him high over their heads, passing him on to the uplifted hands that waited. Aislinn looked on in amusement, dissolving into a fit of laughter. But she soon gasped in surprise as Kerwick lifted her in his arms and passed her to Milbourne and thereon to Sweyn and Gowain. In the middle of the hall they set the newly wedded on their feet and Aislinn collapsed into Wulfgar's arms, thankful for her safe arrival yet unable to cease her laughter. Wulfgar chuckled and held her close, but he was torn from her again. A cloth was tied over his eyes and Sweyn whirled him about, then they bade him find his bride if he had any intention of bedding her that night.

Wulfgar threw back his head and laughed heartily. "Oh wench, where are you? Come, let yourself be caught."

Aislinn found herself surrounded by Hlynn and Miderd and a host of women who motioned her to silence. Aislinn smothered her giggles and watched fondly with eyes aglow as her husband spread his hands toward the maze of women and began his search.

He stepped lightly at a rustle of a skirt and caught Hlynn. The young maid giggled in glee and Wulfgar, shaking his head, moved on without pausing. They thrust Miderd at him and one touch of her sturdy arms told him those were not the slender ones of his wife. He moved on, passing a lusty wench who smelled of hay and sweat. He walked easily through the women, lightly touching one then pausing beside another. Then suddenly he stopped, the slightest fragrance catching his nostrils and he whirled abruptly. His hand reached out, closing over a slender wrist. He was met with silence from his captive though as he pulled her close there was much snickering and smothered giggling from the onlookers. His fingers touched a woolen garment over her shoulders, much different from the softness of Aislinn's velvet gunna, but his questing hand moved with deliberate slowness downward over a well-rounded breast to the mirth and merriment of all.

"Your lady is watching," someone called.

Wulfgar was not daunted. His hands slipped around the slender waist, pulling the maid in his embrace and his head lowered to find the soft lips waiting his. His grin deepened before his mouth moved over hers hungrily and he felt the fiery response to his kiss. His limbs were pressed tightly to hers and he felt every soft curve against him stirring his blood.

"My lord, you have the wrong wench!" another cried.

Wulfgar reached up and snatched the cloth from his eyes without interrupting his kiss and opened his eyes to peer into the violet ones which stared back. Aislinn melted into laughter, giggling against his lips and as they broke apart, shrugged out of the woolen mantle someone had thrust upon her. Her hand slipped again into Wulfgar's as Sir Gowain pressed a horn of ale onto him.

"What is your secret, my lord?" the young knight grinned. "That you knew her before you touched her was certain yet you were hampered by a blind. The truth now, pray, that we might play the game as well."

Wulfgar smiled slowly. " 'Tis the truth now I speak, sir knight. A wench has a fragrance of her own. There are scents to be purchased at fairs, but 'neath it all is the sweetest smell of woman and in each it is different."

Sir Gowain threw his head back and guffawed his delight. "You are a crafty one, milord."

Wulfgar grinned. "Agreed, but you made a desperate man of me. I was not wont to spend this night warming the Hun's straw."

The knight raised a finely arched brow at Aislinn. "Indeed, my liege, I see your reasoning."

Coloring lightly at the compliment, Aislinn slipped from Wulfgar's side, breaking free from the merrymakers and made her way to the stairs. Halfway up she paused and sought out Wulfgar once more with her eyes. He watched her over Gowain's shoulder and though he nodded at the man's questions, his gaze was only for her and it was warm. Aislinn smiled softly in return and felt his gaze follow her until she closed the chamber door.

Miderd and Hlynn had arrived early and were there awaiting her. They embraced her fondly before drawing her to the warmth of the fire. There they helped her doff the yellow gunna and kirtle and wrapped her in a soft, sheer cloth of silk. Aislinn sat dreamily before the fire while Miderd combed out her hair. Hlynn tidied the room, carefully folding her clothes in the coffer, and laid the furs back invitingly on the bed.

The night was black outside and the shutters were set ajar to let a breath of cool air set the hangings of the room astir. With last good wishes, Miderd and Hlynn left her and Aislinn waited now alone yet with breathless anticipation. She could hear the laughter and gaiety in the hall, and she felt like dancing about the room. She laughed, remembering everyone's bemusement when the little friar hurried in. It was Wulfgar's way to keep her guessing till

398

the last. Her heart now swelled with pride as she thought of his plans and his benevolence to Kerwick. A man for men was Wulfgar, no better lord.

Lost in her happy musings she started when a small sound came from the door, and she glanced up to see it swing slowly open. Maida scurried into the room, carefully closing the door behind her.

"Those two have left," she whined. "They turn the sweetest milk to curds with their simple chattering."

"Mother, speak not so of Hlynn and Miderd. They are friends and have given me good solace in times of need."

Aislinn's eyes dropped to Maida's ragged garments and she frowned.

"Mother, Wulfgar will not be pleased with your attire. Would you háve others think he abuses you? 'Tis not so, for he has treated you kindly despite your pricks and jibes."

Maida screwed up her face and spoke as if she had not heard her daughter. "Married! Married! Blackest day of days!" She threw her hands over her head. " 'Twas the best of my revenge that you should bear the brat a bastard. To a bastard give a bastard," she sneered then snickered at the thought.

"What say you?" Aislinn drew up in surprise. "This is the happiest of days for me. I would that you too rejoice that I am wed."

"Nay! Nay!" the old woman cried. "You've stolen from me the last inch of vengeance. All I had was to see the slayer of my poor Erland twist in agony."

"But Wulfgar did not the deed. 'Twas Ragnor who swung the blade."

"Bah!" Her mother dismissed the words with a fling of her hand. "They are Normans everyone and everyone the same. It makes no matter who swung the blade. They must all bear the guilt."

Maida continued ranting and raving and screeching in rage. She wrung her hands and turned away from all of Aislinn's efforts to calm her.

In frustration Aislinn cried, "But Ragnor is gone and 'tis Wulfgar here and he is a fair lord and my husband!"

A change came over Maida at her words. Her lips twisted in a set sneer and her eyes flickered to every corner of the room. She crouched and stared into the fire for some time unspeaking, unmoving.

"Mother?" Aislinn asked after watching her for a while. "Are you all right?"

She saw Maida's lips move and leaning close barely heard the words so softly whispered.

"Yea, this Norman lies at hand—even yonder in my bed." The woman's eyes gleamed and she turned suddenly as if Aislinn had surprised her. Her eyes flew wide and then narrowed and she chuckled to herself.

She stopped and stared at Aislinn with no recognition in her gaze, then gathering her ragged garments close to her, swept a vacant gaze about the chamber and hurried from it.

There was a scuffle of feet in the hallway and laughing voices and crude jests followed before the door burst open and Wulfgar was thrust inside, having been carried ceremoniously to its threshold. Where she sat before the fire, Aislinn saw Sweyn and Kerwick bar the way that others would not enter and Wulfgar hastened to close the door against the press. He turned, panting heavily, and his eyes went to her. The firelight etched her body through the veil of gossamer, stirring his blood, yet he paused, unsure of her reception, for her manner was quiet now and no words from her encouraged him to act the husband. The moment was at hand and he became no lord and master but a fumbling newly wedded groom. He gestured lamely toward the door.

"They seemed to think that we should meet and fill the night together."

Still no answer came from her and he drew his mantle off his shoulders, folding it neatly, and removed his belt, setting both to place. Aislinn's gaze followed him, but the firelight was behind her and Wulfgar could not see the tenderness that filled her eyes. He sat on the foot of the bed and rose again to hang his tunic from a peg. At her continued muteness he tried to peer into her face yet the shadows were deep and he could discern nothing.

"If you feel awry, Aislinn," he murmured and disappointment drew each word. "I will not press you on this night."

He fumbled inanely at the top tie of his chainse, for the first time in his life feeling completely at a loss with a woman. Did marriage lessen the pleasure, he wondered dismally.

Aislinn finally rose and went to stand before him and, taking the loops from his stumbling fingers, with a quick pull untied them. She lifted the shirt from his ribs and placed her hands upon them.

"My Lord Wulfgar," she breathed in softest whisper. "You play the sotted groom so well, must I lead you where you have so often gamed?"

Her hands slid upward pushing the shirt over his shoulders and from his head then went further to clasp behind his head and pull him slowly down until he met her parted lips. She lay full against him and her hand caressed his back while her kisses gave him cause to sigh. Wulfgar's mind spun like a boulder crashing down a hill and exploded into a flurry of emotions: confusion, surprise, and, not least of all, pleasure. He had thought it impossible for her to respond more fully than she had in the past yet now she aroused him purposefully, pressing feverish kisses against his throat, his mouth, his chest, and doing little tempting things with her fingers that made him catch his breath. He had thought foolishly at one time that he knew well a woman's mind. Now this one was teaching him that women were different and should not be taken lightly.

Aislinn dropped the silken garment from her shoulders, letting it fall to her feet and slid her arms around him once more, pressing warmly against him. For a moment Wulfgar's own limbs seemed weighted down. Her soft breasts against his chest seemed to burn into his flesh, and he dismissed his earlier thoughts of marriage as he bent and swept her up into his arms and bore her to their bed. He laid her there and hastily discarded the rest of his garments, flinging them heedlessly aside. For the first time in Aislinn's memory he made no effort to place them away. He lay beside her and she responded fully to his touch, improvising on her own as her hands boldly stroked his body. His eagerness overrode all else and he pressed her down into the bed. His lips trembled at her ear and caressed her neck then moved downward where he could feel the rapid thud of her heart. She arched in ecstasy, opening her eyes for a moment, and the breath suddenly locked in her throat.

A dark shadow stood over them and there was a glint of metal over his back. Aislinn screamed in terror and tried to thrust him away. Wulfgar half turned in surprise at her cry and the blade struck a glancing blow on his

401

shoulder. Pure rage clouded Wulfgar's mind. With an oath he swung a fist then clasped the throat of the unlucky assailant, wrenching a strangled cry from it. With a surging roar he bore the intruder from the bed to the hearth. There the fire lit the attacker's face and Aislinn screamed again, seeing her mother's face twisted in soundless agony. Flinging herself from the bed, she flew to pull at her husband's arm.

"Nay! Nay! Do not slay her, Wulfgar!"

Frantically she tugged at the arm again, but it was like iron, and she was unable to break the hold. Maida's eyes bulged and her face seemed blackened. With a sob, Aislinn reached up to turn Wulfgar's face to hers.

"She is mad, Wulfgar. Let her be."

Her words broke his fury and he released his hold, letting Maida slip to the floor. The woman lay writhing and twisting upon the hearth, struggling for breath through her bruised throat. Wulfgar bent and picked up the seax from the floor beside her and turned it over in his hand examining it closely. Some memory pricked the depth of his conscious mind then surfaced with full realization. This weapon had been Kerwick's, the one used once before in an effort to slay him. A slow dawning lit his face as he looked down at the crone. He whirled to stare at Aislinn and she read his thoughts and gasped.

"Nay! Not so, Wulfgar!" Her voice grew strident. "I had no part in this. She is my mother true, but I swear I was not forewarned of this."

She caught his hand with the blade and turned the dagger against her own heart.

"If you would doubt me, Wulfgar, end your doubts here and now. 'Tis a simple matter to end a life." She pulled his hand closer until the point pressed against her breast. Tears blurred her vision and trickled down her cheeks, falling softly on her trembling bosom as she gazed up at him. She whispered low, "So simple."

Maida found her breath and her feet and fled unseen by the two who stared into each other's eyes, trying to read what truth was to be found. The slamming of the door marked her going but still they did not move.

Seeing Wulfgar's uncertainty, Aislinn urged his hand once more, but he resisted her and she could not bring the blade nearer. She leaned against it until it pricked her skin and a tiny drop of her blood mingled with his upon the point.

"My lord," she murmured softly. "Today I spoke my vows before God and as He is my witness I hold them sacred. As our blood joins on this blade so are we one. A child grows in me and I pray earnestly that he is thine and we be one in him, for he will need a father such as you."

Her lips trembled as he stared down into her eyes. Wulfgar felt the heavy weight of her words upon him and he could deny her no longer. With an oath he flung the seax at the offending portal where it clattered on the wood and then on the floor. He bent and, snatching Aislinn up in his arms, whirled her about in complete abandon until she begged him to cease. Impatient once more, he turned to the bed, but she touched the wound on his shoulder and silently shook her head. Expertly she applied salve and bindings as he sat on the edge of the bed. When at last she tied the knot and set her healing notions aside, she turned to him, leaning forward until her breasts lightly pressed against his chest and she met his mouth eagerly with her own. His arms went around her trying to urge her down beneath him, but she placed both hands against his chest and pushed him firmly back upon the pillows. He stared up into her eyes in the firelight, wondering at her game, then she gave an answering smile and laid full length upon him. The hot blood surged through Wulfgar's body, and the wound hindered him not then—nor later—nor later.

Wulfgar woke in the morning at first light and lay still
lest he wake his wife who slumbered peacefully against
him with her head resting on his shoulder. His thoughts
were clear and keen this early morning hour, and he knew
that never before had he experienced pleasure so rich and
fulfilling. He was still filled with amazement at her abandon. He had known ladies of the court who responded as
if offering him a high favor, passively waiting to be
aroused. He had known the common women of the street
who pantomimed their passion by predictable rote and were
eager only when it meant an extra coin. But here was one
who met him—nay, more than halfway, who met his advances and aided them with an eagerness to match his
own and who built their passion to a blinding, consuming,
overwhelming height that in a brilliant flash of ecstasy collapsed upon itself and left the smoldering foundation
ready for a new experience.

She lay warm against him now, her leg casually across
his, her breath softly caressing his chest. It was difficult to
believe this soft and tender fluff beside him was the bold
and brazen hussy of the night just past.

Another happening of the night before crossed his mind
and his brow furrowed in thought. Maida was an element
he could not deal with, but if Aislinn had spoken truth, he
could leave the matter to her. Well aware of her strength
of purpose, he could be sure she would deal with her

mother. And if she lied—he made a mental note to be more wary in the future.

Aislinn stirred and he pulled the pelts more snuggly about her shoulder. He smiled to himself as his thoughts came to rest once more on her. He pondered at the words spoken yesterday and upon their effect on her. In simple terms he had vowed complete responsibility for her welfare and safety, and she, it seemed, had promised herself as his wife to honor and obey. He almost chuckled at the thought, and in his own innocence he did not begin to realize what being the master of this woman would mean.

Aislinn sighed and snuggled against him, opening her eyes to glance across the broad expanse of his chest toward the cold hearth. She lifted her gaze and found him watching her quietly then lay across his chest to press a soft kiss on his lips.

"We let the fire go out," she sighed.

Wulfgar smiled with a twinkle in his eye. "Shall we kindle it?"

Aislinn laughed gaily and bounced naked from the bed.

" 'Twas the fire on the hearth I spoke of, my love."

Wulfgar bounded out of bed and caught her as she was rounding the end. Pulling her to him, he sat on the pelts and nuzzled her throat as he slipped his arms about her waist.

"Ah, wench, what enchantment have you cast on me. I scarce can mind my duties when you are near."

Aislinn's eyes sparkled as she looped her hands behind his neck. "Do I please you, milord?"

"Oh-ho," he sighed. "You leave me atremble with the merest touch of your fingers."

With a little laugh, she nibbled at the lobe of his ear. "Then I admit it is thus with me."

Their lips met and it was some time later that they descended the stairs to break the fast. Though the hour was late when they finally appeared, only Miderd and Hlynn were about. The hall had been carefully cleaned and new rushes scattered with a sprinkling of dampened herbs to clear the stench that was wont to linger after a night of heavy celebration. A tasty porridge garnished with pork and eggs simmered on the hearth and as they seated themselves, Miderd came bringing bowls of the stuff to place before them while Hlynn fetched tankards of fresh cool milk.

The meal was begun in silence. The entire village seemed to lay strangely quiet outside the open doors. There was no sign of the gaiety expressed the day before until a few moments later when Kerwick entered. He walked with studied care and his hair still dripped with water from the stream. Hesitantly he sat at the table with them and gave Aislinn a weak smile, his pallor accentuating the redness of his eyes. The smile faded as he caught the scent of the porridge and stared into the steaming bowls bobbing with chunks of pork and coddled eggs. He clasped his hands over his stomach and with a strangely muffled apology fled again in the direction of the brook.

Aislinn smiled in wonder as Miderd sent a peal of laughter after the distressed young man.

"The poor lad took the best of a keg of ale," the woman chuckled. "And got the worst of it, I fear."

Wulfgar nodded and swallowed, smiling. "I shall be more gentle with my gifts to him hereafter," he murmured. "He seems to take them too much to heart."

The repeated rattle of a door from the chambers above punctuated his words, and they raised their eyes to see Bolsgar at the head of the stairs, one arm braced against the wall while the other hand raked his tousled hair. He cleared his throat and steadying himself, hitched up his braccos and began a slow descent, carefully watching his feet as they seemed to wander a bit from where he would place them. As he neared they could see the blood-shot eyes and the stubble of a beard that gritted as he rubbed his hand across his chin. He, too, gave Aislinn a smile of greeting that came through as a lopsided leer. He seemed in high spirits that spoke of some lingering essence of ale or wine. He approached the table until he caught the odor of the porridge then sobering, swerved and half fell into his chair near the fireplace.

"I don't think I'll eat just yet," he rumbled, and covered his mouth with his hand for a moment while his eyes clenched tight. He shuddered and then settled back in his chair with a trembling sigh.

Miderd brought a sympathy offering of a horn of ale, and he took it nodding and sipped it gratefully. Wulfgar spoke and at the sound of his voice, Bolsgar flinched.

"Sir, have you seen aught of Sweyn this morn? I wished to talk to him of some matters dealing with the castle."

Bolsgar cleared his throat and weakly replied. "Not since we split that last keg of ale."

"Ho!" Miderd guffawed. "No doubt that fair swain is groaning with pain and trying to bury his head in the straw of his pallet." She chuckled and gestured with a large ladle toward Hlynn. "The poor lass will do good never to come within an arm's reach of him again."

Aislinn looked up in surprise, wondering at the woman's words. As far as she knew Sweyn had always handled himself quite properly with the women of the village.

"Hlynn still bears the bruise of his embrace," Miderd continued jovially. "But no doubt his cheek will smart for days to come."

Hlynn blushed and turned to her task, hiding her face in embarrassed silence.

"Aye," Wulfgar chuckled. "Sweyn looses a winter from his years with each empty horn, then fancies himself a prancing buck again to rut after any free bosom."

Aislinn smothered a giggle as another shadow darkened the door. Sir Gowain entered, shading his ravaged brow from an overly bright sun. The cool shade of the hall drew a sigh of relief from him, and he almost walked a straight path to the table. He paused for a moment then sat as far as possible from the porridge and braced his arms on the table as if to hold it steady. He nodded a greeting to Aislinn but could not venture a smile and fought to keep his eyes from the steaming bowl.

"Your pardon, my lord," he said with strain in his voice. "Sir Milbourne is ailing and has not risen as yet."

Wulfgar suppressed his mirth and frowned a bit as Aislinn fought with hers.

"No matter, Sir Gowain," Wulfgar replied. He sat back and took a bite of meat as the one addressed hastily averted his eyes. " 'Twill be a day of rest as I find my loyal folk are good for little else this morn. Can you bear it, have a cup of ale to clear your head and see to your own welfare." He leaned forward and spoke with mock concern. "You seem a bit at odds with the day yourself."

Gowain took the proffered cup from Hlynn's hand and raising his eyes but once, gulped the cool draught and left.

A gale of laughter set Aislinn back in her chair and Wulfgar heartily joined the gaiety while Bolsgar cringed at the unwarranted attack on his ears, until Gwyneth's voice crackled with anger from the top of the stairs.

"Well, I see the sun is high enough for my lord and my lady to rise."

Bolsgar took the bait and hurling his cup across the room, half rose. "Ye gods," he roared. "It must be noon. My fairest daughter rises to break the fast."

Gwyneth descended the steps and in a whining voice answered his jibe. "I could not sleep until the early dawn broke. There were strange noises in the chambers all night." She frowned pointedly at Aislinn. "As if a cat were tangled in the briar." She raised her brow sardonically. "My Lord Wulfgar, did you hear the sounds?"

Aislinn's cheeks flushed with color, but Wulfgar laughed aloud, unabashed.

"Nay, my sister, but whatever they were, I vow you would not know their like or kin."

Gwyneth sniffed and dabbled in the pot. "What would you know of gentle folk?" she sneered and plopped a morsel of meat in her mouth.

Both Miderd and Hlynn found themselves busy with urgent chores so Gwyneth dipped herself a cup of milk and sipping it went to stand before her father. Her voice rang sharp within the hall.

"So, I see the sham of youth has fled as quickly as it came."

"My lines have come of life well lived. What excuse of yours, daughter?"

Gwyneth whirled in fury and stared hard at Miderd as she coughed loudly.

"What few there are," she sniped, "are there from bearing the cruel barbs of my father and my bastard kin."

Wulfgar rose, taking Aislinn's hand and drew her up with him. "Before the day is rent beyond repair, will you take a space and ride with me?" he asked.

Glad for this reprieve from Gwyneth's tongue, Aislinn murmured softly, "With happiness, my lord."

Wulfgar led her from the hall as Gwyneth's voice rose in new attack on the sore-beleaguered Bolsgar. As they leisurely crossed the paddock, Aislinn without reason laughed in gay abandonment and pleasure. She grasped Wulfgar's hand and danced around him like a child around a Maypole. Shaking his head at her, he caught her in the crook of his arm to stop her and leaned against the stable wall.

"What a tempting vixen you are, wench," he murmured

408

huskily against her hair and finding her arms about his neck, was inspired to kiss her. As, the night before, he found himself amazed by her willingness. He wondered at her mood and at the ardor of her answer; at this vibrant being in his arms that touched him and set his every nerve alive with pleasure.

A rattle of hooves broke the moment and they pulled apart to see the friar's donkey trot from the stable, his master hunched upon his back, grasping the small beast's mane as if he fought to stay astride. The monk's hood was pulled low over an ashen face as he rushed by them and on to Cregan.

Aislinn giggled and snuggled once more against Wulfgar's chest, slipping her arms behind him and holding tightly. Playfully she nipped his neck with her teeth. With a quick movement Wulfgar swung her into his arms but he almost dropped her in surprise as she struggled frantically against him.

"You beastly Norman, would you rape me here?" she demanded in feigned anger and then chortled at his bemusement.

Wulfgar grinned. "To pick you up was the best way I knew of getting you to move. If you are determined to gambol all day, a strong hand must be taken to you to curb you."

She shook her fist beneath his nose in mock threat, and as he set her to her feet, she kissed him, murmuring against his lips, "Fetch the horses, my lord. England waits."

The Hun felt an urge to stretch his flanks and run and show off a bit before the gray mare, but Wulfgar, in deference to Aislinn's gentle state, plied a firm hand on the reins and held him back. The stallion gave a jump or two and raised his feet to rear, but at a warning bark from his master he set them down again and, letting out a disgusted snort, settled into an easy trot.

Aislinn laughed and in the sunny day her heart flew with the swallows above the trees. They passed a portion of the road where ancient carved stones lay edge to edge to form the surface. The hooves of their mounts made a clicking rhythm and Wulfgar began a song in French. The song became risqué and he turned, smiling at Aislinn, to whistle the last refrain while he ogled her with lusty attention and much rolling of the eyes. Aislinn giggled in glee at his mimicry then lowering her voice to a gruff tone, sang an old Saxon ditty until he bade her stop.

"Such words were not made for a lady's tongue," he sternly reproved, then grinned. "Or for Saxon harlots either."

"Pray tell me, milord," she smiled sweetly. "Have you grown old womanish in your dottiness?"

She reined her mare quickly to avoid his sweeping arm and spurred her steed to a faster pace. Waving a hand, she raised her nose in the air and spoke in mincing tones.

"Norman dog, keep your distance. I am a lady of my master's court and will not brook this ceaseless fondling."

This time she turned her mare hard away to avoid the charge of the Hun and seeing Wulfgar's determined gaze, she kicked the mare across a low hedge and sent her fleeing across the greensward. Wulfgar and his mount came crashing after.

"Aislinn, stop!" Wulfgar bellowed. As this had no effect, he urged the Hun to a faster pace and roared again, "You witless vixen, you'll kill yourself."

He finally caught her reins and drew the trembling mare to a halt. Leaping from the Hun, he reached up to snatch his wife from the saddle, angry at her foolery and the fear she caused him.

With a laugh, Aislinn threw her arms about his sturdy neck and as he would have set her to the ground, she slid full against him, her face flushed with excitement. It seemed more natural to kiss her than to speak and as he swept her into his embrace she did not protest but tightened her arms about his neck.

Some time later they rested in the warm sun at the top of a small knoll. Aislinn half sat, half lay, and plucked early spring flowers, weaving them in a garland. Much pacified, the Norman knight rested his head upon her lap while he considered the fairness of his mate and leisurely traced a finger across her bosom. Aislinn giggled and pressed a light kiss upon his lips.

"My lord, it seems you are never sated."

"Ah, wench, how can I be when you are ever tempting me?"

She feigned sympathy as she sighed. " 'Tis true. You are sorely beset by women. I must speak with Haylan——"

Wulfgar sprang up and snatching her to her feet, enfolded her within his arms. "What is this of Haylan?" he queried with a grin. " 'Tis you I lay the blame to, you jealous vixen, none other."

Pushing from him, she danced away with a flippant manner and setting the garland upon her head, bowed before him. "Do you say that you were not tempted by the lusty Haylan when she danced for you and showed her bosom? You must have been blind not to see."

Wulfgar slowly advanced as she retreated, backing away from him with a delighted giggle. She held out a hand warily.

"Now, my lord, I've given you no cause to beat me."

He swooped upon her and she shrieked in playful glee as he caught her up in his arms and whirled about with her.

"Oh Wulfgar. Wulfgar." Her voice rang with a joyful note. "You are mine at last."

He raised a dubious brow but smiled into her eyes. "I vow you planned this marriage from the first moment of our meeting."

She nuzzled her face against his throat and sighed. "Oh nay, Wulfgar, 'twas our first kiss that set my mind on the matter."

They dallied through the day, giving no thought to others. The sun was low and had lost much of its warmth when they guided their mounts into the huge barn. As Wulfgar tended the horses, Aislinn watched him with glowing eyes, then they walked in blissful silence hand in hand like young lovers barely met. Just before they passed into the hall, Wulfgar laughed and swept the garland from her head then placed a kiss upon it before he sent it sailing through the door. Wrapping his arm about her, they entered to the cheers of his men and warm greetings from the others.

Sweyn sat at the foot of the table and seemed still more inclined to slip under it than meet their gaze. From him Aislinn's eyes went to Hlynn. The Viking's followed, then he buried his face in a mug of ale and strangely seemed to choke upon its tartness. At a whispered comment from Aislinn, Wulfgar threw back his head and roared heartily while Sweyn squirmed and flushed a deeper shade.

"I vow you're right, Aislinn," Wulfgar grinned. "For his waning years he must find a gentler maid to fondle."

Still chuckling at her wit, Wulfgar swept Aislinn along

411

with him to their table and met Gwyneth's cold stare as he handed his wife into her chair.

"The way you coddle these Saxons, Wulfgar, I would believe you are one," she said derisively, then gestured toward Kerwick, who now ate with Gowain and the other knights. "You'll have cause to regret trusting him with your affairs. Mark my word."

Wulfgar smiled, undisturbed. "I do not trust him, Gwyneth. 'Tis only that he knows what reward I hold in store if he should fail me."

Gwyneth sneered in contempt. "Next you will be giving Sanhurst some title of importance."

"Why not?" Wulfgar shrugged and mocked. "He has come to know his duties well."

Gwyneth looked at him in distaste then continued with her meal in silence as Wulfgar turned to Aislinn, dismissing his sister as he would any burdensome matter.

Haylan brought trenchers for them to fill though she kept her reddened eyes and glum face downcast. The meal was passed in good grace with jovial banter tossed back and forth. After a few more draughts of ale, Sweyn joined in and mirthfully raised his horn to Wulfgar.

"Ho, lord, if I am wont to choose a gentle maid like Hlynn to fondle and I know of none more tame, 'tis cause you've shown me the folly of rutting after a more determined wench." The hall filled with roars of laughter at his quip. The Viking lifted his horn of ale and saluted his lord with a grin. "Good marriage, Wulfgar. Long life."

Wulfgar chuckled his approval and lifting his own chalice, drained it without pause. The evening's merriment continued but on a quieter note as Milbourne challenged Bolsgar to a game of chess. The men rose with followers and as they also stood, Aislinn leaned to Wulfgar, slipping a hand into his.

"I would see to my mother if you will permit. I fear somewhat for her health."

"Of course, Aislinn," he murmured, then added with more concern, "Take care."

She rose on tiptoes to press a kiss to his cheek. His eyes followed her warmly as she retrieved her cloak and left the hall, then he turned to join the men. Haylan bit her lip and watched him as he crossed the room, then as Kerwick passed her, he grinned tauntingly.

"Lady of Darkenwald, eh? It seems you misjudged your abilities."

Haylan glared at him then whirled with a most unladylike word and began to help Miderd clear away the meal.

Aislinn strolled the path to Maida's hut in the dark as she had many times before, but this time it was with a different purpose in mind. Without a knock or call, she pushed open the door. Maida was seated on her bed, staring morosely into the weak fire on the hearth, but when she recognized her late guest, she sprang to her feet and began to berate her daughter.

"Aislinn! Why did you betray me? At last we had a chance to revenge—"

"Cease your prattle!" Aislinn interrupted angrily. "And listen to my words well. Even your addled mind should make sense of them, though I fear your madness is much of your own making."

Maida cast her eyes about as if looking for some escape and she would have denied her daughter's words. Aislinn threw the hood back from her head in a fury.

"Listen to me!" Her voice rang firm and commanding. "Hold your tongue and listen to me." She continued more gently yet spoke distinctly. "Should you succeed and slay a Norman knight to avenge my father, and especially Wulfgar, for he is William's friend, you would only bring the Norman heel hard upon us all. What do you think the Norman's justice is for those who slay his knights while they sleep?

"Had your blade struck home last eve you would have seen me stripped and nailed to the door of Darkenwald. As for yourself, you would have danced on a rope for all of London to see. You gave this no thought and only dwelt on your own revenge."

Maida shook her head and wrung her hands and would have spoken, but Aislinn stepped forward and seized her mother's shoulders, shaking her until fear widened her eyes.

"Heed me, for I'll beat it in until my words reach whatever sanity you have left." Tears came to Aislinn's eyes and a desperate plea twisted her fair lips. "You will cease harassing the Normans here and now. William is King, and all of England is his. For anything you do in the future against the Normans every Saxon is honorbound to hunt you down."

Aislinn released her grip and Maida sank upon the bed, staring up into her daughter's wrathful face. Aislinn bent close to her and each word came from her hard and earnest.

"If you would lend no thought to that, then give full care to this. Wulfgar is my husband, vowed and sworn before a man of God. If you would do him further injury, I will do the like to you. If you slay him, you have slain my chosen one and I will see my own mother flayed and hung upon the castle wall. I shall fill my hair with ashes and evermore lay naught but rags upon my body, that all who see would know my sorrow. I love him."

Aislinn's eyes widened at her own words and she straightened in wonder at them, then repeated them again more tenderly.

"Yea! I love him. I know that in some ways he loves me. Not fully yet, but that will come." She bent again to her mother and her voice hardened once more. "You have a grandson aborning in my belly. I will not let you make him part orphan. When it is meet that you find your mind again, then I will greet you with open arms, but till then make no threat to Wulfgar's safety or I will see you banished to the farthest corner of this earth. Do you mark my words and know them for the truth?"

She stared down angrily and Maida's face sagged and she hung her head then slowly nodded.

Aislinn softened. "Good."

She paused, wanting to ease her mother's burden but well knew the harshness of her warning would bear more fruit.

"I will continue to see to your comfort. Fare thee well for now."

With a heavy sigh she turned and left the hut, wondering what Maida's tortured mind would make of this. She entered the hall and went to Wulfgar's side where he stood near the hearth watching the game of chess. He welcomed her back with a smile and, slipping his arm about her, returned his attention to the match.

Spring burst upon the land and of its myriad blossoms the most beautiful was Aislinn. She bloomed in a glorious color of spirit that stunned even Wulfgar. She reveled in her new position as Wulfgar's wife and lady of the hall and did not shirk her responsibilities in either, nor did she hesitate to exercise her authority when needed, especially when Gwyneth was wont to charge someone unjustly. She had a strength of mind that made even the men of the village seek her out and come to her for advice. Bolsgar marveled at her wisdom and when he told of it, Kerwick simply nodded and smiled, knowing well of what the other spoke. She continually interceded for her people and that fierce Norman knight whose stern visage they yet feared. Yet when Wulfgar's justice was demanded she stood back and let it have its way. She tended the aches and pains of Darkenwald's people and rode many times with Wulfgar to Cregan when her skill was needed there. She was a welcome sight at his side and the people, seeing her trust and fondness for her Norman husband, began to lose their fear of him. They ceased to tremble when they saw him coming and a few brave ones even ventured into conversation with him and were surprised to learn that he understood the peasant well and had compassion for their needs. They stopped thinking of him as the conquering foe and began to regard him as a reasonable lord.

Wulfgar was the first to realize the assets of making Aislinn his wife and not only in dealing with her people. He was amazed at the difference in her, a few spoken vows had made, for now at the softest touch of his hand she would turn to him warm and willing, giving herself without reservation. He dallied less and less in the hall after the evening meal but sought their chamber early. He enjoyed the quiet moments with her as well as their lusty passion. Often in those times he was content just to watch her. The sight of her sitting across from him with her fingers nimbly stitching some garment for him or the babe was strangely comforting.

The end of March had approached and it was a time of plowing, planting, and shearing; a time for building. Kerwick was sorely pressed to meet the demands of his new profession and set into his books, as Wulfgar had bade him, the birth of each kid, lamb, and child, as well as the circumstance of every soul who dwelt in the town and the time each man spent for the castle and credit him the amount on his taxes.

Wulfgar passed an order that two days of every man's were his and lads were drafted from the fields to assist the newly arrived masons. A deep foss was dug about the base of the high hill and a single drawbridge would cross it, to be guarded by a stone tower. The brow of the hill was scooped level and a stone wall began to form a crown about the flat field thus created. In the middle a tall keep began to rise.

It was during this time that word came from William that he would be returning to Normandy for Easter. Wulfgar knew that Edgar Atheling and many of the English nobles rode with him as hostages of war, but he held the news from Aislinn, realizing she would be little pleased with the information. On his journey William would be passing close to Darkenwald so that he might come and view the progress of the castle. For the next few days there was a busy rush about the hall and its grounds as every corner there was tidied and readied for the visit of the King. Nearly a week passed before a watchman shouted from the tower that the standard of the King approached and Wulfgar rode out to meet him.

William came with some fifty men-at-arms and much to Wulfgar's surprise Ragnor rode with him. Wulfgar frowned at sight of the other knight but kept his silence, taking some ease in the fact Ragnor would be returning to Normandy with the King. William greeted Wulfgar with the warmth of friendship and as the procession continued Wulfgar pointed out the terrain and spoke of plans for its defense as William listened and nodded his approval. Along the side of the road peasants paused from their work in the fields to gape in awe as the King and his cortege rode by. Finally the procession came up before the hall of Darkenwald and William bade his men to alight and relax, for he would be some while here.

As William and Wulfgar entered the hall, Gwyneth and Aislinn sank into deep curtsies as Bolsgar and Sweyn and those present paid homage to the King. William's eyes scrutinized Aislinn as she rose and seeing she was with child, he lifted a questioning brow to Wulfgar and looked at him without a word until the younger man replied.

" 'Twill be no bastard, sire. She is my lady now."

William chuckled and nodded. "Good. There are too many of us in the world."

Gwyneth watched coldly as the King greeted Aislinn with familiarity, laughing with her over the jest he made of her growing a little since he last saw her. Gwyneth bristled with jealousy yet held her waspish tongue in William's presence. When he and Wulfgar left the hall to ride to the site of the castle, she whirled in a temper and fled to her room, little knowing Ragnor was just outside the hall.

Seeking to share the hospitality of Darkenwald, Aislinn bade Ham, Miderd, Hlynn and Haylan to help her serve the waiting men some ale that had been cooled in the depth of the well. It was a pleasant day, for the warm winds of the south swept away the chill and Aislinn stepped from the hall without fetching a mantle, having little need of it in this fair weather. The men gratefully accepted the brew and as they remarked in French of the beauty of this Saxon maid, Aislinn smiled and accepted the compliment quietly, not letting on that she now spoke the tongue fluently. She paused beside a man in noble dress who sat with others similarly arrayed. Here there were no smiles to greet her but from some sneers that drew up the corner of their lips. Feeling much bemused by their manner, Aislinn frowned and was about to draw away when the one jumped to his feet and made his apology in a voice which held no hint of a foreign accent.

"Do you know who we are?" the man inquired.

"Nay," Aislinn replied and shrugged. "How can I when I've never seen you before?"

"We are English captives of the King. We are being taken to Normandy."

Aislinn's mouth formed a silent "oh" as her eyes moved to the others.

"I am sorry," she murmured.

"Sorry," one of the elder men snorted. He looked derisively to her belly. "You did not waste precious moments bedding the enemy it seems."

Aislinn drew herself up with dignity. "You judge me without hearing the circumstance. But 'tis of little matter to me. I do not beg for an ear. My husband is Norman and I give him my loyalty, yet my father was Saxon and died upon the Norman sword. If I have accepted William as my king it is because I can see no use in a hopeless struggle that would only mean more death and defeat for the English. Perhaps it is because I'm a woman that I see no future in further efforts to place an Englishman on the throne. I say let us bide our time and give William his due. Mayhap he will bring some good to England. I vow you can do naught else with only dead men to raise their bones behind you. Would you have us all dead before you

417

realize the truth? I would say William does right to keep you under his thumb to ensure peace for England."

She turned without further word and strode across the greensward past her father's grave to where she saw a lone Norman knight sitting beneath a tree with his back to them. He had removed his helm and had propped an arm upon a knee as he gazed toward the forest in quiet repose. Aislinn was upon him before she recognized him and drew back in surprise. Ragnor turned at her gasp and stared up into wide violet eyes as a slow grin grew upon his lips.

"Ah, dove, I missed you," he murmured and rose to his feet, sweeping a bow before her. As he straightened his gaze took her in and his amazement showed clearly upon his face. He smiled down at her and chided, "You did not tell me, Aislinn."

She raised her chin and met his warm gaze with coolness, "I saw no need," she replied haughtily. "The child is Wulfgar's."

He leaned a shoulder against the tree and his dark eyes danced. "Indeed?"

Aislinn could almost see him mentally counting the months, and her temper flared. "I bear no child of yours, Ragnor."

He laughed with ease, dismissing her words. " 'Twould be a just reward were it mine. Yea, I could not have planned as well myself. 'Tis not likely the bastard will claim my cub, but then he may never know who the sire is." He stepped before her and gazed down into her snapping eyes, growing serious. "He will not marry you, Aislinn," he murmured. "He never was one to dally long with a woman. Mayhap you've already seen his interest wane a bit. I'm willing to take you from here! Come away with me now to Normandy, Aislinn. You'll not regret it."

"On the contrary, I would," she returned. "I have all that I want here."

"I can give you more. Much, much more. Come away with me. Vachel shares my tent but he will gladly find some other resting place. I have only to ask and he will obey. Say you'll come." His voice took on a gay note as he was encouraged by her silence. "We must hide you from the king, but I know of ways to disguise your fair looks and he will be none the wiser. He will think I've come across a small lad to be my lackey."

She laughed distainfully and played the game a moment longer. "Wulfgar would come after you."

He reached up and took her face between his hands, sliding his fingers through her hair. "Nay, dove. He'll find someone else. Why should he come when you carry a bastard?"

He bent to press his lips against hers, but she murmured quietly:

"Because I am his wife."

Ragnor jerked back from her in surprise and her pleased laughter filled his ears.

"You bitch," he said through gritted teeth.

"Do you not love me, Ragnor?" she mocked him. "Poor maid I, discarded from fellow to foe." Then she ceased her laughter as she sneered. "You murdered my father and robbed my mother of her wits! Do you think I will ever forgive you? Heaven help me if I do! I'll see you in hell first."

Ragnor glared back at her. "I'll have you, bitch, and I'll take you at my leisure. Wulfgar or no, you will be mine. The marriage means naught to me. Wulfgar's life even less. Bide the time well, dove."

He scooped up his helmet and whirling from her, strode angrily down the path to the hall, there to fling the door wide and enter with bold strides. Trembling, Aislinn leaned against the tree for support and silently wept, knowing the fear that often nagged at her that her child would show the dark skin and hair of Ragnor.

The hall was empty and Ragnor mounted the stairs unchallenged. Without a knock he flung open the door to Gwyneth's small chamber and slammed it closed behind him, meeting her startled gaze as she sat up in bed with reddened eyes.

"Ragnor!"

She stared agape at the sight of him then made to run to him, but he crossed to the bed, removing his hauberk and throwing it aside. She gasped as he fell upon her and his savage kisses bruised her mouth, but she clutched him to her, delighting in his fierce ardor. It mattered little that he hurt her; she even gained pleasure from the pain. Her spirits soared that he should desire her enough to cast caution to the wind and seek her out when there was so much risk of being discovered. The thrill of danger added to the excitement of their violent passion and she crooned in his ear her love for him. Ragnor took her with no such tenderness in his heart. His lust and rage combined without compassion for his prey. But in his mind he could not cease comparing this lean and eager form to Aislinn's more pleasingly apportioned, though much less willing, frame and with thoughts of her perfection riding his mind he found ease with this one.

With his desires sated Ragnor could once more feign some fondness for Gwyneth and pretend some gentle care for her. She lay in his arms, stroking the hard, lean muscles of his chest and he bent and pressed a soft kiss upon her lips.

"Take me with you to Normandy, Ragnor," she whispered against his mouth. "Please, love, do not leave me here."

"I cannot," he breathed. "I travel with the king and have no tent of my own. But do not fear. There is time enough and I shall return to you perhaps in ways more to your liking. Wait for me and be ever wary of lies told of me. Listen to naught but from my lips alone."

Again they kissed, long and passionately, but with his hunger appeased Ragnor was eager to be away and made his excuse as he rose from her side reaching for his clothes. He left her chamber with more care than he entered, and seeing no soul about, he hastened down the stairs and out the hall.

Wulfgar reined in the Hun behind the King's mighty charger and dismounted, glancing around at the men who lounged beneath the trees. Seeing Ragnor taking his rest in the shade of a spreading oak, he relaxed somewhat yet his gaze swept on until he found Aislinn refilling a cup a young archer held out to her. So doing, she crossed to them with a warm greeting and from where he sat, Ragnor watched the couple from beneath lowered lids, feigning sleep. Vachel had rode in their party to view the castle and now made his way to his cousin, but Ragnor gave him little heed as he considered Wulfgar's casual embrace of Aislinn.

"The dove has tamed the wolf it seems," Ragnor muttered to the younger man. "Wulfgar has married the lass."

Vachel dropped down beside him. "He may have wed the wench, but he is no less the Norman. He builds that castle as if he expects to hold off all of England behind its walls."

Ragnor sneered. "The bastard thinks to keep the lady for sure, but there will come a time."

"Do not judge his ability too lightly as with the tourney," Vachel warned. "He is clever and has great strength to support his ventures."

Ragnor smiled. "I will take care."

Summer waxed and the child grew in Aislinn's belly
apace with the castle. The people watched both, her glowing warmth that seemed to set the air around her alive
with her energy, and the castle with the sense of security
that upheld Wulfgar's promise to protect them. Yet a new
threat dawned. Even the serfs and peasants found a
wealth they had never known before under Wulfgar's
guidance and it was not long before a murdering band of
miscreants and thieves found the richness of his flourishing
lands. He set patrols to ride the roads and warn of
strangers but even this proved fruitless as time and again
families were forced to flee to the hall as their homes
were looted and sacked.

It was by some chance Wulfgar came about a quicker
method of warning. Aislinn had retired to the cool shelter
of her chamber after the midday meal to rest a time from
the sluggish warmth of the late June day. She removed her
gunna, leaving on the light linen kirtle beneath. Feeling a
bit bedraggled by the sultry heat, she began to tidy her
appearance. She splashed water on her face and the
coolness of it did much to refresh her. Taking out the silver mirror Beaufonte had purchased for her at the fair in
London, she began to comb her hair, but hearing
Wulfgar's voice in the courtyard below, she went to the
window and leaned out.

The three knights and Sweyn were with him and the

five were dressed in battle gear, not wanting to be caught unawares if another alarm was sounded. They had returned from Cregan shortly before midday and were relaxing now in the shade of a tree before riding off again to make a wide sweep of the countryside. Aislinn called to him several times but the men's voices overrode hers and he could not hear her. Finally frustrated, she drew back, but the sun's rays caught the face of the mirror she held and the burst of light from it was reflected on the men below. Wulfgar sat up immediately and glancing toward the source of the brightness, raised a hand to shield the glare from his eyes and saw her at the window. As she lowered the mirror, Aislinn laughed, pleased she had finally caught his attention, and waved to him, having nothing important to say. With a smile he waved back and was relaxing once more against the tree when suddenly he sat up again, then leapt to his feet. Aislinn watched him in puzzlement as he ran toward the hall and soon she heard his feet on the stairs then in a moment he was beside her, taking the mirror from her. He went to the window where she had stood and experimented with it, soon drawing the attention of the group below. Wulfgar laughed in amazement as he turned the thing in his hands, then coming to stand beside his wife bent and placed a hearty kiss on her mouth. At her surprise he chuckled.

"Madam, I think you have saved the day. No more riding long patrols that wear men and horse alike." He raised the mirror as if it were a treasure. "Only a few lads on hilltops with these and we'll have the thieves." He laughed and kissed her again fiercely before striding out the door, leaving her bemused but happy.

It was nearly a week later that a shout from the top of the castle tower brought the knights out in full battle dress and the village was nearly emptied as the men stood to arms. A mirror signal from one of the watchmen had marked the approach of a group of raiders. Wulfgar rode out with his small army, many doubled or even tripled on whatever mount was to be found. They took the path that led south to Cregan, which was an hour's leisured ride or a half hour's gallop from Darkenwald. The trap was set on a blind curve where Wulfgar's charge would be downhill and thus the weightier. Men were carefully hidden in the brush or hillside to harass the raiders with stones and arrows, and Wulfgar's well-trained band of archers and spearmen set to seal the retreat. Thus the ambush was met. Wulfgar, Sweyn and the knights held their horses quiet, well back from the curve. Soon laughter and shouts could be heard as the raiders neared, little suspecting that their progress was known and the way well guarded. The leaders came, talking loudly and wearing the loot of their last attack. Suddenly they halted as they saw the four knights and the hulking Norseman before them. Their laughter froze in their throats, and behind them the others pressed close to see what was amiss. Wulfgar lowered his lance and leaned forward in the saddle. The road trembled beneath the hooves of the five chargers. The thieves shouted and sought to flee and the lane became a mad tangle of bodies.

One raider, braver than the rest, dug the butt of his spear into the ground and held its point to meet the charge, but Sweyn's great ax whistled to shear the man's arm and the shaft before it could do harm. The thief screamed and grasped the stump in his other hand and died as the short, Viking spear took him full in the chest. Wulfgar's lance spitted another and pinned him to the ground. Then the long sword rang free and left a trail of gore where the Hun's flailing hooves passed. It was over in a moment. Some had sought to flee and now lay in the dust studded with arrows. A dying man told where their camp was located deep in the marsh and there Wulfgar took his men when the bodies had been stripped of loot and arms and pushed from the road.

Wulfgar found the wretched place in the midst of the peat bogs. The inhabitants of the camp had been warned and fled deeper into the marsh, leaving their possessions behind. Four naked slaves, chained in the open, had been abused for the entertainment of the thieves. Their ribs stood out from hunger. When struck free and given food, they knelt and humbly wept their thanks. One of the freed slaves was a young girl who had not fled fast enough from the raiders. Another was a Norman knight who had fallen wounded far afield, the other two were serfs and had been seized from a small village west of London.

Wulfgar and his men dallied only long enough to search the hovels, bringing out what little of value they could find. They mounted the four on captured steeds then set the torch to the entire place, setting a warning to other thieves who would tarry here.

The girl was returned to her family amid cries of joy and the others remained at the hall until they regained their strength before going their own ways, and Darkenwald returned to peace and its labors. Yet there were those who seemed out of pace with the life there. Gwyneth was sorely chafed by the awareness she was little more than a guest and had to abide within the charity of the lord and lady of the manor. Even Haylan had ceased to heed her and began to draw away. Finding no more charity from Gwyneth, the young widow had her own and her son's welfare to look after and found little time to converse and conspire with the other woman. Gwyneth knew a loneliness deep within her, but soon found that without facing Aislinn directly, she could extract some vengeance from carrying to Maida greatly embroidered tales of Wulfgar's cruelty to his wife and at every opportunity weakened the woman's already strained sanity. To see Maida scampering hastily out of Wulfgar's path amused his sister and her pale eyes glowed as she baited the poor woman time and again to stir her fears for her only child. A good lie was worth a year's wear and tear upon the woman's confidence and to this end Gwyneth would go well out of her way to seek the woman out.

Maida watched her daughter closely when Aislinn came to the cottage to tend her or when she saw her about, looking for the telltale signs that would mark her abuse. Instead, Aislinn's glowing happiness further confused her and she sank lower in dejection.

The hot days of July simmered by with grinding slowness and Aislinn lost the last hint of grace. Her passage was slow and made with studied care, for quick movements were well beyond her capabilities. At night she curled close against Wulfgar's back and many times they were abruptly wakened by the strong stirrings of the babe. She could never see her husband's face in the darkness of the room. In the warmth of July there was no need for a fire in the hearth, therefore she was unable to determine his moods and worried that she disturbed him overmuch, but his kisses silenced her fears and apologies. He was gentle with her and many times his helping arm assisted her on her way.

In the few days past, her burden had lowered and now even sitting became a chore. When taking meals, she continually shifted her weight to ease the ache in the small of

425

her back, and only nibbled at her food while listening with half an ear to the conversations that floated around her, not taking any verbal part, only nodding or smiling when a question or statement was directed to her.

Now as she sat beside Wulfgar, she suddenly gasped and pressed a hand to her taut and rounded belly, amazed at the vigor with which the child moved. Wulfgar's hand took her arm and she met his worried frown with a reassuring smile.

" 'Tis nothing, my love," she murmured comfortingly. " 'Tis only the stirring of the child." She laughed. "He moves with all the strength of his father."

She had begun more and more to think of Wulfgar as the child's sire, unable to bear the thought of Ragnor fathering it, but she knew that she had used the wrong words as Gwyneth sneered.

"Unless you know something we do not, Aislinn, it seems the blood of your offspring is well in doubt. In truth it could be fully Saxon."

She turned a derisive eye to Kerwick who stared at her in surprise, then reddened as he realized her meaning and in his haste to reassure Wulfgar, stammered a poor denial.

"Nay, my lord, 'twas not the way. I mean—," he looked at Aislinn in his helplessness then turned again to Gwyneth, his anger flaring. "A lie you say! A lie!"

Wulfgar smiled though his tone betrayed little humor as he answered his sister. "You have with your usual charm brought another tasty conjecture forth for our entertainment, Gwyneth. I seem to remember Ragnor the villain instead of this poor lad."

Gwyneth's anger showed itself as she snarled. "I bid you consider well, Wulfgar. We have only your wife's word and the ramblings of some drunken fools to back her say that Ragnor ever laid a hand on her. Indeed, I doubt that Sir Ragnor ever touched her or could act in the manner she lays to him."

While Aislinn gasped at the twisted reasoning, Kerwick choked and flung himself to his feet.

"Maida herself saw her daughter carried up those stairs. Would you say he done her naught?"

Wulfgar's face had hardened and as Gwyneth snorted he scowled blackly at her.

"Maida, ha!" Gwyneth jeered, and flung up a hand in disgust. "That addled fool cannot be trusted."

426

Aislinn forced herself to remain calm and murmured softly, "In all good time, Gwyneth, the truth will out. As for Kerwick, either he was chained or I was chained well beyond the time that he could be the sire. That leaves two and I deny the first along with the gentle manner some lay upon him."

Gwyneth turned in rage and glared at her, but Aislinn continued on gently.

"And I pray, God willing, that time will prove I give life to Wulfgar's seed. As to your bid that a gracious Ragnor could not have used a lady so, I pray you recall, good Gwyneth." She leaned forward and spoke each word carefully. "Ragnor himself gave truth to the fact that he was the first."

Gwyneth's rage knew no relief at this defeat. Without thought, she seized a bowl and raised it as if to hurl it at Aislinn, but Wulfgar came to his feet with a loud roar and clapped both hands down upon the table. His angry glare held his sister.

"Take heed, Gwyneth," he rumbled. "This is my table you set your feet beneath, and I will not have you question the father of the babe again. 'Tis mine because I make it so. I bid you go with care that you may continue to abide here."

Gwyneth's anger fled and left a bitter frustration. Tears came to her eyes and she shook with sobs but she lowered the bowl again.

"You will rue the day, Wulfgar, that you placed this Saxon slut above me and denied me what little honor I have left."

With a last look of loathing contempt flung at Aislinn, she turned and made her way up the stairs to her chamber. Her reserve fled as she closed the door behind her and she flung herself upon the bed to sob out her misery there. Her mind was a confusion of tumbling thoughts but it settled on one burning theme. It was cruel fate that her brother, bastard Norman that he was, should be the one to cast her from her rightful place and take a weak-faced Saxon bitch to wife. But Ragnor—she trembled at the memory of his touch. Ragnor had promised her much more. Yet was he in truth the father of Aislinn's babe? The thought seared her brain that Aislinn would bear first fruit of that gentle-born knight and that her child might grow thin and dark with the look of a hawk in his brows or have the black and moody eyes of her lover. She silently vowed that when Ragnor returned, as he must to raise her from this sty, she would see that Wulfgar knew the full weight of her displeasure.

In the hall the meal was ended with strained silence and as Haylan cleared away the food before them, Aislinn struggled to her feet, reddening slightly under the woman's amused stare that seemed centered on her oversized belly. Self-consciously she turned and begged Wulfgar's leave to go to their chamber.

"It seems I tire easily of late," she murmured.

He rose and took her arm. "I'll help you, cherie."

He guided her slow progress up the stairs and to their chamber where she began to undress for bed. As she unfastened her kirtle, he paused behind her and reached up to stroke her bright hair. With a sigh, Aislinn leaned back against him and he bent to press a kiss beneath her ear where the flesh was soft and white and fragrant.

"What are you thinking?" he breathed.

Aislinn shrugged and pulled his arm across her bosom, hugging it close. "Oh, just that you have cause to hate women."

He laughed softly and nibbled at her ear. "Some women I cannot abide and then there are others"—he folded his arms about her above the rounded belly—"I cannot do without."

Her parted kirtle stood away from her bosom and her full, rounded breasts were pressed together until the plunging valley between them seemed to beg for his exploration. His hand slipped within her garment and he knew a hunger in his loins as he roamed those soft, warm slopes. He was sorely strained to pull away and leave her be and now an ache grew in him as he yearned for the day he could satisfy his longings.

Bolsgar had taken his usual chair before the hearth and Sweyn joined him there as the old man gazed thoughtfully into the low fire. Kerwick and the others made their way from the hall, ill at ease at what had passed and eager to be away. There were no words between the Viking and his old lord, nor were they needed. As Sweyn knew Wulfgar, he also knew the elder and could guess his moods. Gwyneth's irascible disposition sorely nettled her father and he was at a loss as to how to deal with her.

From above came the sound of a chamber door opening and closing. Bolsgar raised his gaze and meeting it, the Norseman laughed aloud as they exchanged a wordless thought. Wulfgar had spread his bed with a bachelor's eager lust and now well-fed, found the same pallet lumpy and hard and not at all to his liking. They held their amusement and glanced up as Wulfgar appeared at the head of the stairs, a scowl blackening his brow and his manner short and coltish. With little concern Wulfgar made his way to the barrel and drew a full cup of ale, emptied it and drew another. He came to sit beside Bolsgar and the three of them stared at the fire for a long time before Wulfgar mumbled in his cup and Sweyn turned a quizzical glance to him.

"Did you speak, Wulfgar?"

Wulfgar lowered the cup and slammed it on the arm of the chair. "Yea, I said this marriage is a hellish affair. Would that I had married some narrow-flanked primp like Gwyneth, then I would have no worries or other urgings when I could not see them out."

Bolsgar grinned over his shoulder. "What say you, Sweyn? Think the buck will fly to seek another doe?"

"Mayhaps, my lord," the Norseman chuckled. "The hunting lure is ever louder than true love's call."

"I am no rutting stag," Wulfgar snapped. "I made my vows with my own mouth and of my own will. Yet I feel the trap of wedlock sorely and with a comely maid 'tis more the rub. My loins ache with the sight of her and yet I find no ease. I would seek another but my vows bid otherwise and I am left to lie beside her yearning yet cursing the very thought."

Bolsgar grew serious and sought to ease the young man's chafing. "Have patience, Wulfgar," he gently chided. " 'Tis the way of life, and you will find the prize well worth the wait."

"You prattle of things that stir me not," Wulfgar sneered. " 'Tis in my mind that one so fair brings naught but pain. I must ever bare my sword to see her honor cleared. Every mewling lad with fuzz upon his cheeks grows addled at her smile. Why, even Gowain grins like a dolt at her merest favor and still I wonder about Kerwick and what fond memories he might bear."

Bolsgar was pricked that Wulfgar should question Aislinn's honor and lay the blame at her feet. "Why say you, Wulfgar," he scolded. "You do the lady wrong I fear.

429

She bade no Norman knight come pounding on her door or take her upon her mother's bed nor asked a simple lord to chain her there." He smiled ruefully. "I did hear her say you chained her, did I not?"

Wulfgar stared in amazement at the other's rising anger and even Sweyn felt disappointment that he had failed to teach the young man an easier acceptance of responsibilities.

"Do not berate me so," Wulfgar flared. "At least she has the ease of knowing who the mother is, while I will never be assured and may well raise a brat that's not my own."

"Then do not set your mind against the Lady Aislinn," Bolsgar returned sharply.

"Yea," Sweyn muttered, nodding his head in agreement. "My lady had no say in all of this and has come through more true than any. Would this be done again, I would hold you from her till my death."

Wulfgar laughed derisively. "Look to yourselves," he scoffed. "The two of you come so late to her colors. Even old fools are not free of her wiles. She can charm the—"

Wulfgar found the front of his tunic seized tightly by the ham-sized fist of Bolsgar and he was lifted from his chair with a speed few other men could muster. He saw the other fist draw back and there it held. Slowly Bolsgar's rage left him. His face sagged and he dropped his arm from Wulfgar's front.

"I struck you once in anger," the old man sighed. "And I will never again."

Wulfgar threw back his head to laugh at the pathos of Bolsgar's remark but suddenly the entire hall seemed to burst inside his skull. Dust settled slowly around his long form as it stretched out on the rushes of the floor. Sweyn rubbed the knuckles of his hand then lifted his gaze to find Bolsgar staring in surprise.

"I felt no such restraint," Sweyn explained then nodded his head to the slumbering one. " 'Twill do him good."

Bolsgar bent and grasped Wulfgar's ankles while Sweyn lifted his shoulders and together they carried him to his chamber. Bolsgar rapped lightly on the door and at Aislinn's sleepy answer, pushed the door wide. As they entered she sat up in surprise, rubbing her eyes.

"What happened?" she stammered, her eyes wide and staring.

"He drank too much," Sweyn grunted as they dumped Wulfgar unceremoniously on the bed.

Aislinn looked at the Norseman with a puzzled frown. "Wine? Ale? Why, it would take a full skin and half the night to—"

"Not when lapped by a foolish tongue," Bolsgar interrupted.

She bent over her husband and as her hand touched his face, her quick fingers felt the growing lump on the side of his chin. Her brows knitted in confusion.

"Who struck him?" she demanded, her hackles rising.

Sweyn rubbed his knuckles again and smiled. " 'Twas me," he said smugly.

Aislinn's frown turned to one of bemusement but before she could question more, Bolsgar leaned forward and gently spoke.

"He was acting like a babe and we couldn't find a switch."

With that the old man beckoned to the Viking and they left Aislinn staring at Wulfgar in bewildered consternation. Finally she rose and pulled his clothes from his limp form, leaving him undraped upon the bed with the warmth of the summer's night.

A peal of thunder seemed to fill the chamber and Wulfgar sat up with a start half ready to do battle as he stared wildly about. Then he realized it was but a summer squall rolling off the sea and marching inland. He lay back and closed his eyes, listening to the gentler sounds that followed, the first splash of huge droplets on the stone outside, the quicker rattle of rain as it beat upon the shutters and the sudden gust of wind that set them jerking. The cool breath of the summer's breeze that stirred against his naked form was a welcome respite from the hot and muggy days which had passed before.

He felt a weight settle upon the bed and he opened his eyes again to find Aislinn's concerned face close above his. Her hair fell in a giddy torrent from her head and seemed to frame that milky visage. Deep violet pools caught him in their depths and gently wrung a smile from his aching skull. Reaching up a hand, he slipped it beneath the shining tresses to draw her down and quietly taste the wild freshness of her lips as her hair made a coppery curtain about their embrace.

431

Aislinn sat up smiling. "I was fearful of your health, but I see that you are well."

Wulfgar reached his arms above his head and stretched like a great, lean beast, arching his back against the bed, then drawing back he winced as his fingers brushed his jaw and tenderly felt the longer line of it. He frowned and sat up, propping an arm against a knee.

"Sweyn must be getting old," he mumbled and at her puzzled frown, hastened to explain. "The last face he so caressed was more than a little broken."

She laughed softly for a moment, returning with a platter of meats, warm bread and fresh honey in the comb. Resting her burdened body against his, she drew a morsel from the trencher and laid it to his lips, and Wulfgar knew the tenderness of her care. Her eyes were warm and liquid as she gazed at him and he could not resist their plea. Once more his mouth moved upon hers, this time with the softness of a bee resting upon the petals of a blossom to taste the nectar deep within. She lay in the shelter of his arm against his upraised knee and felt the tendons of his strength surround her. Yet there was a tautness in her womb that robbed her of serenity and made her wonder if her time was at hand.

Wulfgar saw the dimming of her eyes and the thoughtful bend of her mood. "Does Satan prick you with some unkind memory, Aislinn?" he inquired softly. He laid his hand upon her belly. "It has worn me ill that even if the babe be mine, he was made not of love but of my brutish taking of you in my own lust. I would have you know that in my thoughts I am prepared to take him as my own whoever be his maker. He shall bear my name and arms and shall never be cast from my house. 'Twould be unkind if having that he finds a fault in mother's love."

She lifted her gaze to his and smiled gently, thinking of the cruelty of his own rejection. "Have no fear, Wulfgar. He of all of us is innocent of his making and I would love him the same. I will hold him within my arms and bring him to manhood with all my finest care." She sighed deeply. " 'Tis only a woman's doubt as the time grows near. So many things beyond my ken will shape his life. But, you know, if may be a daughter and not a son!" She stretched an arm to rest upon his shoulder and toyed with a lock of his tawny hair.

Wulfgar smiled. "Whatever God wills it, my love. We

shall seed a dynasty to hold these lands and if a girl, I would that she wore your witch's locks to tempt all men as you have me." He turned his head and kissed the inner bend of her arm. "You have torn my life's ways and habits asunder. When I would say no vows to bind me, you made me sing them in my fairest voice lest I should lose you. When I admitted to a miser's thrift, you never asked a thing, but I would spend my life to shoe your feet and love the last moment of it." He chuckled ruefully. "I give up laying boundaries to build my life within and now lend my cause to faith that you will tenderly lead my errant feet and deal with my helpless soul in honor."

"Wulfgar," she scoffed. "What great Norman knight kneels and lets a simple-minded Saxon slave take him by the locks and swing him to and fro? You jest and mock my haggish face."

In spite of her words she leaned her swelling breasts upon his chest and kissed him softly, her lips clinging warmly to his, then she lingered close and searched his eyes as if to find her answers there.

"Is something born of love within me?" she murmured low. "I want your arms about me and yearn for every touch of you. What is this madness that sends me ever to your beck and call? I am more slave than wife and yet would have no other way. What hold have you taken on my will that even when I fought you I prayed you would ever press upon me again and never leave me lonely?"

Wulfgar raised his head and his gray eyes seemed almost blue as he held her with them. "No matter, cherie. As long as you and I are bent upon one purpose, let us revel in the pleasure of it." He scowled at her. "Now let me rise, err you be forced again against your will."

Aislinn giggled happily and withdrew. "Against my will? Nay, nevermore. But should you pass a babe on the way, treat him gently lest he should take offense."

Wulfgar rose with a hearty laugh and donning his clothes, left the chamber with the sound of her gay, lilting voice drifting after him in a merry tune. He smiled to himself, looking forward to the day when she would croon to the babe, for she had a pleasant voice and one that gave him ease. He left the hall and crossed the puddle-laden courtyard and looking to the sky, saw that it was clearing already.

The sun rode high overhead, marking the noon hour, as

433

Wulfgar returned to the hall. Bolsgar and Sweyn were seated at the table and as he joined them they sat back and regarded him, a bit uncertain of his mood. Seating himself at his usual place, he returned their gazes as he fingered his jaw and then waggled it as if testing its working.

"Methinks a young lass kissed me overhard last night," he remarked dryly. "Or perhaps an old man or child smote me."

Bolsgar chuckled. "Some gentle kiss indeed. You would not rouse to bid a fair good night. Forsooth! You took repose so suddenly poor Sanhurst labored out the morn to fill the hole in the floor."

He and Sweyn guffawed at the jest, but Wulfgar gave little to their mirth but sighed pensively.

" 'Tis much burdened I find myself with two aging knights who in their long-fled youth do dwell and smite me sharply if my words should turn naught but their tempers. Not only do their heads grow soft, I fear the strength has also fled their arms."

Wulfgar looked squarely at Sweyn who slapped his thigh at the slur.

"Would you brace an elbow with me I could yet in my dottering age break your arm," the Viking returned. " 'Twas only that I thought to spare the beauty of your face, you stripling lad."

Wulfgar laughed at having piqued the Norseman. " 'Tis more your tongue I fear than strength. The blow was well struck and I had no cause to so decry my lady." He grew serious and murmured, "As in my youth I would that words in anger loosed could be taken back to silence, but 'tis never such. I beg the pardon of you both and would forget the folly done."

He looked at them, waiting for some sign. Bolsgar exchanged glances with Sweyn then they nodded and, sliding him a mug of ale, lifted their own and the three drank an unspoken toast.

A moment later Wulfgar turned his gaze to find Aislinn making her way cautiously down the stairs. He rose quickly and rushed to assist her, drawing smiles from his men as they watched and remembered Wulfgar's earlier days at Darkenwald when it seemed naught could pass between the couple but with a quarrel.

Wulfgar led Aislinn to a chair beside his and at his anxious question assured him all was well. Yet before long the dull pressure in her belly became a wrenching surge that caught her by surprise and left her gasping for breath. This time when Wulfgar's concerned face turned to her, she nodded and held out her hand to him.

"Will you help me upstairs? I fear I cannot make it alone."

He came to his feet and brushing aside her hand, lifted her in his arms. As he bore her to the stairs he threw a brusque command over his shoulder that stirred some action among the staring men.

"Fetch Miderd to my chamber. The lady's time has come."

There was a mad scramble among the knights and Kerwick, and seeing their confusion, Bolsgar rose from his chair and went immediately to the task. Wulfgar took the stairs two at a time, unhampered by the burden he carefully held in his arms. Kicking open the door, he carried Aislinn to the bed that had seen her brought to life. His arms were slow to draw away and Aislinn wondered at the strain she saw in his face, if it was concern of her or some deeper thought of the child and its sire. She took his hand comfortingly, drawing it to her cheek, and Wulfgar carefully eased his weight onto the bed beside her to sit and gaze down at her, worry etching his brow. Here was a thing his training and experience had not prepared him for, and he knew the full weight of his helplessness.

The painful pang returned and Aislinn clutched his hand tightly. Wulfgar was well acquainted with the sufferings of war, having many scars to prove his stamina and his casual acceptance of pain. But this slim girl gave him an almost fearful dread of the agony she suffered.

"Gently, my lady," Miderd advised from the door and came to Aislinn's side. "Save your strength for later. You'll have need of it then. From the signs you will labor long with this one. The child will have his way, so rest and save yourself."

The woman smiled as Aislinn breathed easier, but Wulfgar's face seemed suddenly drawn and haggard. Miderd spoke to him gently, seeing his distress.

"My lord, will you see that Hlynn is summoned? There is much to be done and I would stay with my lady." She glanced to the hearth and seeing it cold, called after him as he left. "And tell Ham and Sanhurst to bring wood and water here. The kettle should be filled."

Thus Wulfgar was moved away from Aislinn's side and he found no chance to venture near again. He stood quietly at the door, watching the women attend his wife. Cool damp cloths were ever at hand to cleanse Aislinn's face as the heat of July built in the room with the added warmth of the fire. He watched and waited and caught an occasional smile from Aislinn as she rested. When the pains came he dripped with sweat as she labored and as the hours fled he began to wonder if all was right. His questions often went unanswered as Miderd and Hlynn made preparations. Then a line of worry snared him and he began to fear the babe would be dark-skinned and ebon-haired. The vision haunted him until he could not bear it. That the fair and lovely Aislinn should give birth to a child obviously of Ragnor's kin made his mind ache. And then a new thought dawned, He remembered hearing often of women dying in their labors. It would be Ragnor's triumph if the child were his and took Aislinn from this world forever. But what if it were his own that took her life? Was that any kinder? He tried to imagine his life without her after these many months of contentment by her side and his mind grew blank. Dark clouds seemed to shut all reason from him and the room became stifling. In roiling fear, he fled.

The Hun was startled as Wulfgar threw the saddle onto his back. The beast snorted and drew back as the bit was forced into his mouth and Wulfgar vaulted onto his back. Astride the great charger Wulfgar rode long and hard across the countryside, never easing his pace until the winds blew the shreds of confusion from his head. At last man and beast paused on a lower hilltop beneath the mound bearing the castle. As the Hun panted for breath Wulfgar gazed at the framework which rose taller with each day's passing. Even now in the late evening, men strove to set a few more stones before darkness overtook them. He was amazed at the people's ambition to see it finished. They worked without grumbling and often upon finishing other chores they would bring some stone to be hewn and set. But it was for their defense as well as for his, and he could well understand their reasoning after the slaughter Ragnor had brought. They were as determined as he that it should not happen again. He looked to the keep where he and Aislinn would some day reside. Its construction progressed slower than the wall but when finished would be an unscalable fortress where no foe could enter. Except death—

He turned away, knowing it would not be so fine without Aislinn to share it with him. Black thoughts invaded his skull and he was no longer content to sit and muse. Whirling the Hun away, he shook out the reins and rode the boundaries of his lands.

His lands!

The words rang solid in his head. If the other portion of his life should turn awry at least he would have these. He remembered the gray old knight that Aislinn had buried the first time he met her. Perhaps the old man would have known his feelings now. Here was his land. Here he would die and lay beside that other grave upon the hill. Perhaps some greater lord would come and slay him, but here he would remain. No more wandering. Let Aislinn give him what she would, bastard or his own son or daughter. He would claim it as his, or if things came to worse, join them beneath the oak upon the hill. A strange peace settled over him and he could now meet his fate in whatever form it came.

The Hun slowed and his master became aware that Darkenwald lay before him. He had covered his lands and returned as the sun sank beyond the western moors. He paused beside the grave of Erland and dismounted, squatting beside it and watching the village below. As darkness spread its raven wings about him he still remained, conscious of the slackening activity of the people.

"All of them," he sighed "will look to me in trouble. I must not fail them." Thoughtfully he gazed down at the grave beside him. "I know your mind, old man. I know what gathered in your head when you went out to meet Ragnor. I would have done the same."

He reached out and plucked a wild flower that grew nearby and placed it beside the ones Aislinn had left the day before.

"Rest well, old man. I will do my best for them and Aislinn, too. God willing, you will feel the feet of many grandsons cross this turf and when I come to rest up here I will take your hand as ever any friend's."

He waited under the shelter of the tree, not willing to descend and face the questioning stares of those below.

The stars passed overhead as he watched the lighted hall below. People came and went and so he knew the event had not yet occurred. The early hours of a new morn saw him still there, then he was brought upright by a scream.

The hairs bristled on the back of his neck and a cold sweat dampened his brow. He stood immobilized by fear. Had it been Aislinn's cry? Oh God, he had come so late to know the tenderness of a woman. Was it meet that he should lose it now? Long moments dragged by until he heard the loud and lusty cry of a babe.

He waited still longer as the word was passed from hall to cottages. He saw Maida creep through the shadows to her hut. Others left and at last the hall was darkened. Finally he rose and led the tired horse to the barn. Passing silently through the empty hall, he climbed the stairs to his chamber. He pushed the door open slowly and saw Miderd sitting before the glowing hearth holding the babe in her arms. Peering through the darkness toward the bed, he could make out Aislinn's form. She lay still and silent but he could see the gentle rise and fall of her breasts. Asleep, he mused and smiled, thankful for the day.

Softly he strode to Miderd's side and she uncovered the child that he could see. It was a boy, wizened, more like an old man than a babe and upon his pate a blazing thatch of red hair grew.

No help there. Wulfgar smiled to himself. But at least it was not black.

Turning, he went to the bed and stood quietly by its side trying to see Aislinn's face. When he bent nearer, he realized her eyes were open and watched him carefully. He eased his weight down beside her and as she raised her hand took it in both of his. He sat thus for a moment thinking that he had never seen her eyes so warm and tender. Her hair spread over the pillow and curled in splendid disarray upon her shoulders. A smile played around the corners of her mouth though her face was drawn and pale. The cost of her struggle to bring the child forth had etched its passing on the gentle features, yet there shone behind them a calm strength that made pride rise in him. She was indeed a wife to stand beside a man and meet whatever life could offer.

He bent low and kissed her tenderly and it was in his mind to beg her forgiveness. He drew back bracing himself on his arms that he might watch her as he spoke, but

438

as he raised she sighed and closed her eyes, a slow peaceful smile spreading over her face. He held his silence and Aislinn found sleep as he stared down at her. She had waited to see him and this done, exhaustion took over to bring to her the needed rest. Leaning close again he laid another light kiss upon her lips and left the room.

Wulfgar made his way to the stables and as he shaped a bed in the sweet-smelling hay, the Hun snorted his displeasure at this intrusion. The Norman warrior looked over his shoulder at the mighty steed and commanded him to silence.

" 'Twill only be for the night," he assured him and went to sleep.

The babe was named Bryce and Aislinn knew joy, for he was bright and cheerful. One loud cry when hunger stirred his belly and that quickly turned to gurgles of delight as he nuzzled at her breast. Wulfgar in his doubt could find no solace in the locks that faded fast to a reddish gold or in the baby's eyes, deep and blue. Maida had seen the birth and for the first weeks had not come near, but now whenever the babe was about Aislinn knew her mother would be somewhere in sight. She would not enter the hall unless so bade by Wulfgar or Aislinn, but if the day was warm she squatted beside the door and watched him as he lay on a pelt before the hearth. At these times Maida was in a distant mood and seemed to ponder on older memories. She knew the child of her blood and could not say him other than kin. Years before she had watched her own fiery haired young daughter playing on her blankets in this same hall. Now she remembered the gay times, the love, and the happy moments and with the passage of time Aislinn hoped the evil things her mother's eyes had viewed would dim and fade.

The long warm days of summer shortened and September brought the first chill of winter to the night air. The townfolk watched as the fields ripened. Under Wulfgar's guidance the crops had been tended regularly and young boys set with slings to scare away the birds and beasts. The harvest promised to be rich as never before. Kerwick, in his rounds, kept a full account in his book, and the sight of the young man coming on horseback with his ledgers lashed behind him became a common sight. The people even sought him out to measure their wealth before putting it in the larders or graineries.

Oxen plodded in a circle turning the millstones of Darkenwald. Here to this town the people came and bartered and bought from Gavin's smithy the tools that would see them through the winter's cold or set the fields ready for next spring's seed. The end of the first harvest neared and the late crops still ripened in the sun. Already the graineries bulged with stores and the larders grew crowded as slabs of various dried and smoked meats and great loops of sausage hung from the rafters. Wulfgar claimed a lord's share of all and the great bins beneath the hall began to fill and the cellars hung with plenty. Young maids gathered grapes and other fruits for wines and sweetmeats which likewise were added to the rest. Huge combs of honey were melted in earthern jars and as the wax rose it was skimmed and made into candles. When a jar was full the last thin layer of the stuff was left to harden and seal it and the container was placed deep in the cool cellar. The hall was a constant rush of activity and as the herds were culled with only the best stock kept for the next year's breeding, the reeking odors of slaughter and tanning hides added to the smell of the place. The smoking shed was always full and salt was laborously carted across the marsh and meat preserved in the brine made with the stuff.

Haylan's hand was ever present and her skills in flavoring and curing were much in demand and so she was content that her son, Miles, had found a friend in Sweyn. This good fellow could teach many of the things a boy needed to know. In the days they spent together, Sweyn taught the lad the habits of geese and other fowl and where to loose an arrow to bag them; of stags and does and where they wandered through the woods; of fox and of wolves and how to set a snare, skin the animals and turn the bloody stiff pelt into a soft warm fur. They became the two most seen together and where the Norseman went, the lad was wont to follow.

The trees were beginning to show red when a hard and early freeze gripped the south of England. This day the youth had missed his friend, for the big Viking had gone to Cregan on an errand. Thus young Miles ventured on his own to empty the traps they set and reset them. Sir Gowain saw him go and watched him out of sight into the swamp. Haylan did not miss him until the midday meal was set. She went to the stables and there was told Sweyn was gone. She went to the hall and Gowain, dining there, heard her questions and spoke of seeing the lad go into the swamp. Kerwick ceased his labors and with the Norman knight set out to follow the trail of footsteps in the heavy frost. They found him where a heavy log was set to snatch the unwary fox or wolf and drag him into a nearby brook and hold him there. The lad lay up to his armpits in the stream and was shivering and blue about the lips. For several hours he had lain and held a bush against the current and dragging log. He had shouted till his throat was raw and was not heard. When they dragged him from the freezing water he hoarsely croaked:

"I'm sorry, Gowain. I slipped."

They wrapped him well and hurried to his mother's cottage, but even swaddled in heavy pelts and placed before a roaring fire, he shivered and would not stop. Kerwick would have sent for Aislinn but Haylan grasped his arm and bade him nay.

"That one is a witch," she shrieked. "She'll cast a spell on him. Nay, I'll care for him myself."

The day wore on and the young boy's brow grew hot and his breath became a rattle in his chest and he fought to draw each one anew. Still Haylan would not see the lady of the hall and snarled her defiance in their faces.

The hour was dark when Sweyn returned and hearing the news, ran his horse to Haylan's cottage, throwing himself from the saddle to slam open the rough-hewn door and crouch beside the lad. He took the boy's hand in both of his and felt the heat it bore. He paused but a moment before he turned to Gowain who had followed him there.

"Fetch Aislinn," he commanded.

"Nay, I will not have it!" cried Haylan, distraught and torn but with a vengeance heavy on her breast. "She is a witch!" More earnestly she continued. "She cast a spell upon your own Wulfgar to bind him to her, to see that no other could find his eye. She is a witch, I say. I will not have her here."

Sweyn turned half crouched and his voice came low with a growl in it. "Haylan, you decry a saint for your

442

own lost end, but I forgive you that. I know this lad and I have seen the likes before and he will die unless well tended. There is one who has the skill and I will have her here. So be it that I care little for you, but this lad I would save and cannot stand to see him waste away while you condemn another. If you would stop me, I will see you mounted on my ax to ride it into hell. Now step aside."

He rose and looking into his eyes, Haylan let him pass.

Aislinn played with Bryce on the hearth of their bedchamber while Wulfgar watched from his chair as the boy was bounced astride his mother's slim waist. Her hair spilled to the fur pelt beneath them in brilliant display and with an ache in him Wulfgar longed to touch it.

A thundering at the door drew wide eyes from Bryce and a trembling lip. His mother cuddled him and at Wulfgar's answering call, the door was thrown aside and Sweyn charged in.

"Lady Aislinn, your pardon," he thundered. "The boy, Miles, fell in the water and is taken with a fever and chills. His breath comes hard and I fear for his life. Will you help?"

"Of course, Sweyn."

She turned about and stopped in confusion, Bryce still in her arms. She spun to Wulfgar, who had risen from his chair, and thrust her son into his arms.

"Wulfgar, take him, please. I cannot with me. Tend him well and if he cries, call Miderd."

She gave no choice and her voice held a stronger command than William's. She threw her mantle over her shoulders, caught up her tray of potions and a sachel of herbs and in a twinkling had gone with Sweyn.

Wulfgar stood staring after them, holding the son he could neither accept nor fully reject. He gazed down at the child who returned his perusal with a seriousness and intensity that brought a smile to Wulfgar's lips. He tried bouncing him on his chest as Aislinn had done but the wideness of his chest and his hard, flat stomach were not as comfortable and drew nothing but a whimper from the lad. With a sigh Wulfgar sat in his chair and propped the chubby cherub on his lap. There the boy seemed happy. He pulled at the sleeves of the chainse and soon was sprawled upon Wulfgar's chest, showing little fear of the savage Norman knight as he tugged in glee at the ribbons that tied the chainse at the throat.

Aislinn threw aside the door of the cottage and found her way barred by Haylan, who was waving a sprig of mistletoe as if she would drive away a witch. Without a pause Aislinn brushed her aside and hurried to the boy. Haylan had just gathered her balance and stepped forward to protest when Sweyn entered the room and pushed her aside once more. This time she sat where she fell to stare dumbly as Aislinn began to rush about the room. Snatching a shallow kettle, Aislinn scooped it through the hearth, half filling it with glowing coals then placed it near the bed with a smaller kettle inside full of water. As the first steam rose she took several herbs from her pocket, crushing them between her hands before scattering them in the bowl and then from a large vial she poured a thick, white substance into the water. Immediately the room was filled with a heavy tangy odor that made one's eyes and nose smart. She stirred a mixture of honey and several good pinches of a yellow powder with a bit of the brew from the simmering pot then lifting the boy's head against her arm, Aislinn poured it into his mouth and rubbed his throat until he swallowed. She laid him gently back and dipping the rag in cool water, wiped his fevered brow.

This way the night wore on. When Miles's brow grew hot, Aislinn cooled it with a damp cloth. When his breathing grew troubled and rough, she took the milky stuff and rubbed it on his chest and throat. From time to time she would take a spoon and dribble some of the simmering brew down his throat. She dozed at times but with each movement or gasp she came awake.

The dawn was breaking when Miles began to shake and tremble. Aislinn threw every pelt and blanket in the house upon him and bade Sweyn build the fire higher until they all glistened with sweat. The boy grew red and flushed but still shook so hard he could barely breathe.

Haylan had not stirred from her place and from time to time she mumbled a prayer. Aislinn's own voice whispered for assistance from a greater force than her own. An hour passed. The dawn was bright now. Each kept their own vigil in their own way.

Then Aislinn stopped and stared. There was a trace of moisture on Miles's upper lip and a bead of sweat on his brow. Beneath her hand his chest grew damp and soon he was dripping wet with sweat. The trembling ceased. His breathing was still ragged but grew steadier by the moment. His color faded to a normal hue and for the first time since Aislinn had entered the cottage, the boy slept peacefully.

Aislinn rose with a sigh, rubbing her aching back. She gathered her potions and herbs and stood before Haylan, who stared up at her with red rimmed eyes and sobs trembling on her lips.

"You have your Miles back now," Aislinn murmured. "I will go back to my own, for it is long past his feeding time."

Aislinn went to the door and wearily shaded her eyes and squinted against the glare of the bright sun. Sweyn took her arm and walked her back to the hall. He did not speak nor did she, but in this great hulking Norseman she was assured of a friend. She entered the bedchamber to find Wulfgar and Bryce sprawled on the bed still asleep. The baby's hand was tangled in Wulfgar's hair and his tiny legs were propped across his sturdy arm. Aislinn stepped out of her clothes and left them where they lay. Then, dragging herself across Wulfgar, she drew her son against her. She smiled at her waking husband and before he could speak, closed her eyes and was soon asleep.

It was nearly a week later when Haylan approached Aislinn in the hall as she sat quietly nursing the babe. It was a peaceful moment, for the men were about their affairs, leaving the hall to the women.

"My lady," Haylan ventured timidly.

Aislinn lifted her gaze from her son.

"My lady," Haylan began again. She paused and took a deep breath to rush on. "It has come to me that I have greatly wronged you. I believed the vicious words that another spoke to such an extent that I thought you were a witch and sought to take your lord from you." She paused, wringing her hands as tears trembled in the corners of her eyes. "Can I beg your pardon? Will you see my folly and forgive my trespass? I owe you much that I cannot repay."

Aislinn reached out a hand and pulled the young widow into a chair beside her own, smiling gently. "Nay, Haylan, there is naught to forgive," she consoled. "You did nothing to me nor harmed my cause." She shrugged and laughed softly. "So take heart and never fear. I can well understand your plight and I know 'twas little of your making. So let us be friends and never rue what yesterday has laid away."

The widow smiled in agreement, admiring the chubby babe who greedily nuzzled his mother's breast. She would have spoken of her own boy in his wee age, but Wulfgar strode through the open door, breathless from a vigorous ride. Haylan rose and took her leave. Wulfgar crossed to his wife, casting a doubtful eye after the widow then peered questioningly at Aislinn.

"Is all well with you, my love?"

Aislinn looked into his face and saw his concern. She laughed lightly. "Of course, Wulfgar. What think you amiss? All is quite well."

He took the chair beside her, stretching out his long legs before him and setting them on a low bench. "There are often hard words in this hall it seems," he said musingly, stroking his cheek. "Gwyneth ever shuns what kindness we would show her and seeks to prick our tempers. 'Tis a mystery to me why she casts herself from our companionship and sulks endlessly in her chambers. Why does she act so, when if she would soften her ways, we would be gentle, too?"

Aislinn smiled and gazed at him with loving eyes. "You are in a thoughtful mood today, my lord. You do not often ponder a woman's mind."

He turned to her, his gaze warming at the soft beauty of her. "Of late I find there is more to a wench than rosy breasts and thrusting hips." He grinned slowly, his eyes sweeping her with passion's fire and leaned close to her, resting a bold hand alongside her thigh. "But of the two, mind and body, I vow there's more pleasure for a man in the latter."

Aislinn giggled her delight then caught her breath as his mouth pressed warmly against her throat, sending quickening fires shooting through every nerve.

"The babe—," she whispered breathlessly, but his lips found hers silencing them, and she found herself too weak to resist. A noise outside the door made them bolt apart, and with cheeks glowing, Aislinn rose to put her sleeping son in the cradle beside the hearth, while Wulfgar came to his feet and faced the fire as if to warm his hands. Bolsgar entered, carrying over his shoulder a bag of quail for the feast that was planned on the morrow. He gave them a hearty greeting and as he went to give the birds to Haylan, Wulfgar watched the old man, chafed a bit with the interruption. It seemed of late there was always someone or some matter demanding his or Aislinn's attention. He had bided his time after the baby's birth, not wanting to press the issue too hurriedly, but now it seemed that every moment worked against him. If the babe was not squalling to be fed, some serf came seeking her care or wanting to consult the lord. Then when the moment seemed finally at hand and they were alone together in their chambers, he would see the tired droop of her shoulders and know he must bide his time a bit longer.

Over his shoulder he watched her move about, following the gentle sway of her hips with his gaze, and his eyes took on a hungry look. She has grown slimmer than before, he mused, yet there is a fullness about her that speaks of woman and no longer a girl.

Was this to be his lot? To find her ever close at hand yet never know again the privacy with her that had been before. Was this marriage? To have a babe more oft between them than finding a moment to share long suffering passions? He sighed and turned his stare to the fire. Winter comes, he thought. And the nights are long. He would have more leisure to seek her out. She can not sport the babe forever. He had taken her first in a quick, lusty moment. He would not quell at doing the same again.

Aislinn raised her gaze and saw Maida standing at the door peering timidly in. She noted that her mother was well washed and had combed her hair and wore clean garments. She found pleasure in the thought that Maida might love her grandchild and would abandon her mad dreams of vengeance. She could name no better balm than a wee babe.

Lifting a hand, Aislinn beckoned her mother in and with a quick nervous glance at Wulfgar's back, the woman scurried in and went to crouch beside the cradle, drawing herself into a small knot as if to escape the Norman's eye. Wulfgar gave her little heed. Instead, his stare followed her daughter across the hall as she went to seek out Haylan on the matter of the morrow's fare.

A day of feasting and rejoicing was planned to celebrate the harvest and its good yield. A boar hunt would see the knights and their ladies mounted at the noon hour to either slay or drive the beasts from the fields. It would be a gay event and one they all looked forward to.

As Wulfgar stood before the hearth, the knights and Sweyn entered to pour themselves a horn of ale and toast the morrow. Having little else to occupy him at the moment, Wulfgar joined them, and when Bolsgar returned, it was a merry group. The afternoon dwindled into evening and the evening into morning and their voices could still be heard in the hall as Aislinn tossed upon the bed in the chamber above, fretting at Wulfgar's delay at coming. She could not know that whenever he sought to leave the men, a hand would draw him back and another would replenish his cup.

The gurgling sounds of Bryce rooting for his breakfast awakened Aislinn and she opened her eyes to find that Wulfgar was already up and donning his clothes against the day. She lay still a moment, admiring his long, muscular frame and his tawny good looks, but the baby's cries became insistent and there was no help for it. She rose, slipping on a loose kirtle, and went to sit before the hearth to nurse the babe. Bryce quieted at her breast, and she lifted her eyes to meet her husband's and smiled a bit devilishly.

"My lord, is it that you find the sport of drinking more to your liking than of old? I vow the cock crowed before you saw our bed."

He grinned. "Forsooth, cherie, it did crow twice before that pillow felt my weary head, but 'twas not to my liking. My knights ever feted me with tales of yore and I could do naught but stand and bear the pain."

The sight of her made Wulfgar's blood run searing through his veins, but there were loud sounds coming from the hall below and he knew that his men would soon be coming to fetch him if he did not shortly present himself. With a sigh he brushed a kiss upon Aislinn's brow and, shrugging into his leather jerkin, left the room to join the group below.

When Aislinn came downstairs it seemed that she had entered a madhouse. Laughter and shouting came from every corner. The uproar stunned her ears at first and she could make no sense of it all. Bryce clung to her, somewhat afraid of all the noise. She spread a pelt in a corner of the hearth where he could be warm and yet could view the rushings of those about him. She was careful to place him near where Wulfgar stood with his knights and merchants of the towns so that they could watch him and keep him safe from the hounds that were given to wandering about the hall. The dogs barked as they ran underfoot, and the odors of cooking filled the room. Bets were made on horses, first boar, largest boar and who would be the first to drop his spear. Gowain, the youngest of the knights, suffered much ribbing over his fair face, especially as Hylnn was caught with fits of giggles whenever she came near him. Crude jests were tossed across the room and bandied back and forth. Men laughed and women shrieked as their nether parts were fondled in passing. Aislinn might have suffered the same had she been wife to any other besides Wulfgar. Though there were many tempted, the men kept a respectful distance, not wanting to test the point of his blade.

Near the hearth loud curses rose from the group of men as a great hound fled from beneath their feet with yelps of pain from well-laid boots. Wulfgar's voice came loud and clear.

"Who sees to these hounds? They roam the hall unfettered and would nip the ankles of our guests. Who sees to these hounds?"

No one answered and then his voice came louder.

"Kerwick? Where is Kerwick, sheriff of the hall? Come here, sir."

Kerwick blushed and made his way to where Wulfgar stood. "Yea, my lord?"

Wulfgar took him by the shoulder and lifting a horn to the group of men who stood beside him, spoke with humor heavy in his voice. "Good Kerwick, your friendship with the hounds is known by all, and knowing them so well, you must be made master of the hounds. Think you able for this job?"

"Aye, milord," Kerwick readily replied. "Indeed, I have a score to settle. Where is the whip?"

A great lash was handed to him and he hefted it to crack its end loudly.

"Methinks that reddish mongrel was the one who set his teeth upon my thigh." He rubbed the place, remembering the nips on a cold night. "I vow, my lord, he will hunt well today or bear the bite of this good weapon."

Wulfgar chortled. " 'Tis settled then, good master of the hounds." He clapped the younger man heartily on the back.

"Get them from underfoot. Put them to their leashes and see that they hunger for the hunt. We'll have no fat-bellied hounds crawling in among the trees."

The men laughed and a toast was drunk. Indeed, it was amazing to see how much ale was needed to keep these voices rich and full.

Bryce whimpered near the hearth and Aislinn pushed aside great shoulders and heavy chests to make a way to him. Wulfgar stepped out of her path with a stiff, decorous bow, sweeping his arm before him, but as she bent to lift the mewling babe and comfort him, his hand descended upon her behind with a lusty familiarity that made Aislinn straighten much faster than she had planned.

"My lord!" she gasped and whirled, clutching the babe to her.

Wulfgar drew back and flung up a hand in feigned fear, adding to the guffaws of his companions. Though chafed at his public caress, she could not hold back her laughter at his manner.

"My lord," she chided gently, the corners of her mouth lifting in a winsome smile. "Haylan is across the hall. Did you perhaps mistake my gangling frame for her fairer form?"

At the mention of the widow's name, Wulfgar lost some of his cheerfulness and raised a brow at his wife. It was only at the sparkle in her eyes that he eased and grew again more careless in his cups.

They lifted mugs and drank again until Bolsgar paused and held his jaw agape. They turned, following his stare and found Gwyneth mincing down the stairs in full regalia for the forthcoming hunt. She joined the group near the hearth. Casting a disparaging eye at Aislinn holding the babe, she turned to Kerwick.

"Is it overmuch to presume that you would make a horse ready for me today?"

He bobbed his head and looking to Wulfgar for excuse he left the group, then Bolsgar came forward and dipped a sweeping bow before his daughter.

"Does my lady mean to join the peasants today?" he mocked.

"Indeed, dear father, I would not miss this gay party for all the treasures in England. I've been too much the maiden here of late and would be out and seek some genteel exercise. 'Tis the first I've noticed in this place."

And thus having chastened them all for their crudity, she turned and made her way to the table and sampled the foods being prepared there.

The rest of the morning was mostly lost in the mad hustle to make preparations for both the hunt and the feast. Before the noon hour Aislinn took the babe and went to her chamber where she filled his belly and laid him down to sleep, leaving Hlynn to watch over him. When she again joined the group, she was dressed in a long full skirted gown of yellow and brown, sturdily made for the sport of the hunt. The diners mostly took their meat and bread standing, for there was little room to sit. A band of wandering minstrels entered the yard, there to entertain the folk with gay music. The horses were led out and Gwyneth found little cause for joy, for the one that Kerwick had chosen for her was the small roan that had borne Aislinn to London. It was a sturdy horse and one quite well-mannered but it lacked the long-legged grace of Aislinn's dapple-gray.

The hunting party rode off. Kerwick held as many leashes in his hands as there were hounds following him, and the young man had much to do to keep them straight. The dogs sensed the excitement of the chase and bayed and snarled at one another as they were led along behind the hunting party.

The day was gay and all but Gwyneth made merry and joked. Aislinn rode beside Wulfgar and laughed at his ready wit, covering her ears at his ribald songs. Gwyneth's hand was heavy on the reins, and the poor punch bridled and pranced and worried at the bit. The hunters left the road and soon topped a hill and there before them in the glade at the edge of the forest could be seen a herd of swine with several large boars present. Kerwirk leapt from his horse and made haste to set the dogs free. The hounds were off with baying voices marking their progress. It was their duty to see the boars brought to bay, those great shaggy beasts of the woods, bold, black, and vicious with long tusks sprouting from their jaws. Once at a stand, the hounds would hold them until the riders came. This was mean duty and it took courage to face a charging hog. The spears were short, for much of the hunting was done in heavy brush and some arm's length behind the point a crossbar was heavily bound, this to keep the swine, so hard to kill, from charging up the spear and tearing at the hands that held it.

As they entered the woods, Aislinn and Gwyneth were left far behind, Aislinn holding back, well aware she was unused to this harsh activity. She reined her mare in and found herself apace with Gwyneth, who had found a stout switch and was beating her horse mercilessly trying to make it heed her signals on the reins. As the small mare sensed Aislinn beside her she quieted and Gwyneth held her hand, realizing she betrayed a vicious mood. They rode along apace and Aislinn shrugged away Gwyneth's abuse of the horse and finally sought to make some light comment. There was a crispness of autumn in the air and the smell of leaves heavy on the ground beneath the bright-colored trees.

" 'Tis a marvelous day," she sighed.

Gwyneth's reply was short. " 'Twould be if I had a proper mount."

Aislinn laughed. "I would offer you mine, but I've come to treasure her."

Gwyneth sneered at the gentle chiding. "You always manage to better yourself, especially where men are concerned. Yea, you gain twofold what you lose."

Aislinn smiled. "Nay, ten or a hundred fold, you can say, since I lost Ragnor, too."

It was too much. Gwyneth, already sorely pricked, flew into a rage. "Saxon slut," she snarled. "Have care whose name you degrade."

She raised the switch and would have struck Aislinn with it but she reined aside and the blow fell instead against the dappled mare's flanks. Unused to this crude use, the gray started and hurtled into the heavier brush beneath the trees. She had gone but a few yards when she struck a small thorn tree and twisted away from the sudden pain of the barbs, causing the reins to jerk from Aislinn's hands. The steed slipped, half fell, and then reared, throwing her rider from her back. Aislinn struck the ground and lay stunned, trying to shake the fog from her head. A dark shape, outlined by the sun, came to stand above her and vaguely she recognized Gwyneth on her horse. The woman laughed and then spurred her horse away. Long moments passed before Aislinn struggled upright, but she winced at the pain in her thigh. She rubbed it and decided that she had only bruised herself in the fall. She steadied herself and dragged free of the heavy brush.

Her mare stood some distance away, the reins hanging beneath her head. She made to approach the horse, but it shied, frightened by the pain where the cruel thorns had raked her chest. Aislinn crooned and tried to quiet her. Just as she would have succeeded there was a crashing in the brush behind her. The mare snorted and fled as if the very devil dogged her heels.

Aislinn turned and saw a great boar thrusting its way through the shrubs toward her, snorting and squealing as it found the scent of those who had of late forced it to run. And here it smelled the helplessness and fear of one afoot. He seemed to sense her pain and turned its beady eyes to stare at her, its white tusks gleaming. Aislinn backed away and flung her gaze about for some haven from the beast. She saw an oak with a branch that she could reach and made her way to it. The boar followed her with a vengeful gleam in its eyes. But Aislinn found that she could not raise on her injured leg high enough to grasp the limb. She tried to jump but her fingers would not hold and she fell against the huge trunk and there lay still as the beast halted, no longer seeing a movement before him. He snorted and tore the ground with his tusks, hurling great chunks of moss and grass into the air. Suddenly, on shaking his head from side to side, he saw the bright color of her cloak. He squealed in anger and began to move forward, thrusting his tusks against the branches that brushed near him, tearing the leaves asunder.

Aislinn felt her panic rise. She had no weapon, no way to defend herself. She had seen before long gashes in dogs and in the legs of men made by those ravening tusks. She drew back against the tree, seeking what shelter it could offer and as the boar came forth in the glade she could not suppress a scream. Her voice rang in the trees and seemed to anger the swine more. She pressed her hands against her lips to still another that would follow.

There was a sound in the forest behind her and the boar swung its head to see what new thing menaced it. Wulfgar's voice came low and soft.

"Aislinn, do not move. As you value your life, do not move. Hold still."

He swung down from the Hun, bringing the spear with him. He crouched low and eased forward, his every movement closely watched by the boar that now stood silent, waiting. He eased forward until he was beside Aislinn but several yards away. She made a movement and the boar swung his head toward her.

"Be still, Aislinn," Wulfgar's voice warned her again. "Make no move."

He crept forward until the spear was some two lengths away from the boar. Then he braced the butt against the sod and put a knee upon it, keeping the point carefully aimed. The boar squealed in anger and thrust back upon its hind legs. It tore again at the turf with his tusks and it began throwing up clumps of dirt with its forelegs, then lunged back upon its haunches and charged. Wulfgar, with his great shout ringing in the forest, held the point of the spear full against the snout. The beast screamed in pain as the long, slim iron head pierced its chest and it was impaled on the lance. It nearly broke the barb and almost jerked the haft of the weapon from Wulfgar's hands, but he held on, bearing his weight upon it and the two fought, thrashing across the glade until the life blood of the great pig had run out. He quieted, gave one last jerk and died. On his hands and knees, Wulfgar dropped the spear and knelt there for a moment, panting with the strain of the fight. Finally he turned his head toward Aislinn and she, with a tearful gasp, struggled to stand but fell full length upon the ground. He rose and hurried to her.

"Did he strike you? Where?" He bent to her anxiously.

"Nay, Wulfgar," she assured him and smiled. "But I fell from my horse. It ran into some brush and was frightened and I fell. I bruised my leg."

His hands lifted her skirt away from the injured thigh and his fingers gently traced the growing bruise. His eyes raised slowly to meet the deep violet ones holding him softly, and her parted lips gave breath short and fast. She stretched her arm to him and slid her hand behind his head, drawing him close until their lips could meet. Her arms went around him and his around her and they lost themselves in the fierceness of their embrace.

He drew her up, the bruise forgotten, and bore her to a leafy copse where he spread her mantle and lay beside her.

It was much later when the sun had lowered in the sky that there were voices from afar and much crashing in the woods, then into the glade thrust Sweyn and Gowain.

They glanced about and found Wulfgar and Aislinn lying together beneath the great oak tree, resting as if the day was meant for lovers. Wulfgar raised on an elbow.

"Where go you? Sweyn? Gowain? What hies you through the wood in such a rush?"

"My liege, your pardon," Gowain swallowed. "We thought the Lady Aislinn had come to harm. We found her mare—"

Another thud of hooves and Gwyneth came on the scene. She took one look and fought with a frown then tightened her lips and whirled away.

"Naught is amiss," Aislinn smiled. "I but fell from my steed. Wulfgar found me and we—rested for a bit."

24

The last harvests were under way and October's frosty
nights had sapped the brilliant hues of autumn and drawn
a darker cloak of brown upon the forest. Since the boar
hunt Gwyneth had given up her constant baiting of Aislinn
and to the amazement of all, carefully held her tongue
and at times was almost charming. She made it her habit
to come to the hall for her meals and would sit sewing at
her tapestry while listening to the light flow of conversation
about her.

Kerwick and Haylan were familiar figures in the village,
but whenever they came together harsh words were exchanged. It seemed as if neither could pass the other without making some biting comment. They bickered endlessly
over trifles and their battle became so renowned the children came running whenever their angry voices sounded
to dance about them and mime their rage. With her skill
in cookery, Haylan was given authority over the food and
its preparation. She gathered wool and flax in her private
moments and labored hard to learn the finer points of
weaving and sewing. She even sought to learn French and
did very well in the language.

It was of considerable happiness to Aislinn that Maida
now bathed regularly and garbed herself in neat, well-
cleaned gunnas. When she thought others were not about,
she would venture forth from her cottage to play with
Bryce and always brought him toys she fashioned from

discarded remnants of cloth or wood. Once she even came to Aislinn's side and sat quietly watching the babe as he nursed at his mother's breast. She would not speak but kept her silence, yet every day she became more the old Maida of Darkenwald.

The boy had Aislinn's fairness of skin and his hair faded to a light reddish gold. The only mark upon the days was that Wulfgar held himself aloof from the child and seemed to regard the lad as a necessary demand on Aislinn's company. Still the babe thrived on his mother's love, and Miderd, Hlynn, even Bolsgar saw that he was little wanting for attention.

The days wore on, the nights grew colder, the bounty of the land swelled the graineries, and the castle wall neared its last stone. Only the central keep was not complete and here the work was slow. The huge blocks of granite were hauled from the quarry and careful measurements laid upon them. They were shaped on the ground and hoisted into place by teams of horses straining at heavy cables.

Then late one morning in early November, a messenger came with news that brought a frown to Wulfgar's face. Rebellious lords of Flanders had made a pact with the deposed English lords of Dover and Kent. They had landed troops between the great white cliffs and marched to take the town of Dover from William's men, but the castle the King had ordered built on the heights had held them at bay. William led a force from Normandy north to Flanders to set the rebellion aside at its source, but the Atheling Edgar had escaped and joined the Scottish kings in the North to stir up trouble there.

The worst of the news was that broken bands of men from the invading Flemish force were fleeing inland and might soon come to lay waste to the country in anger at their defeat. William could send no help now but bade Wulfgar to stand ready to defend himself and if possible to close the roads to retreat.

Wulfgar surveyed his resources and with little delay set all hands to work. The castle would serve as it was for the time being, for there were other matters to be tended now. The land was to be stripped so that any band would find no provender here. Herds of goats, swine, sheep and oxen must be brought near the fortress. Graineries and storehouses must be emptied and all brought to the castle to fill the huge bins and cellars that lined the inner wall and lay beneath the keep. Cregan first would yield its larders, for it was more distant and thus hardest to defend, then Darkenwald if time permitted. While Wulfgar with his knights and men patroled the reaches against attack until all was done, the men of the village had to form the castle's garrison. Beaufonte and Bolsgar were given the task of seeing to these preparations in Wulfgar's absence. When all of Cregan was withdrawn to the castle, two bridges near the town would be felled to block the roads.

Thus set, the labors began. Every cart, wagon, mule and horse was bent to the task and Cregan gave of its stores until there was an endless stream of coming and going between the town and the castle. Items of value were brought and entered in Kerwick's books then placed in a vault in the keep. The outlying farms were shuttered and the families came to the castle. They formed the first compliment within the walls. The women went to the marsh and cut straight willow and yew branches, bringing them to the yards while the men made bows, spears, and arrows from them. Large barrels of the black, odorous fluid that oozed from pits in the swamp were carried within the walls and lifted to the battlements. It was easily fired and once alight could be poured down upon the heads of attackers. Gavin's smithy rang day and night as he and his sons hammered out the heads for spears and arrows and made crude but effective swords. Everyone worked. Everyone served.

Aislinn gathered blankets and linens in the keep and assured the looms of Darkenwald worked throughout the day on more. The cellars and stalls of the castle took all of Cregan's stuffs and still seemed almost empty, but they had been built to carry several years' bounty and what lay within them now would see the people of both towns through the winter and more.

Finally trouble came. A tall plume of smoke rose near Cregan, and Wulfgar roused his men from their breakfast and rode out to meet the foe. Not far from Darkenwald, he came upon a column of people who had refused to leave their town. Now they choked the road and were shocked at having been driven from their homes by this new enemy. Wulfgar learned that a small band of knights and bowmen had set upon the village at first light and though the townsmen had tried to defend it, they were soon put to rout. The raiders had fired the houses as they came and seemed more bent on destroying the town than gaining plunder. They had brutally cut down all who had come in their path.

Friar Dunley brought up the rear of the procession, pulling a small cart which held his beloved crucifix and other relics from the church. He paused as Wulfgar approached him and wiped his brow.

"They have fired my church," he gasped. "They had no mercy even for the things of God. They are worse than the Vikings. Those thieves were after loot, but these brigands seem more bent on simple destruction."

Wulfgar shaded his eyes toward Cregan as he spoke. "If your church is gone and we survive, sir priest, you shall have the old hall of Darkenwald for your worshipping. 'Twill be a fitting place to wait the Lord's day out."

The monk murmured his humble thanks and bent again to his cart as Wulfgar gave orders for Milbourne to take a few of the men and form a guard for the people to see them safely to Darkenwald.

When Wulfgar came to Cregan, the town still smoldered but was little more than a pile of rubble. There were a few bodies scattered about, those who had sought to defend their homes or had not fled fast enough. As Wulfgar gazed about him he was reminded of another day he had viewed another scene of slaughter and another village littered with dead. His scowl darkened and his heart grew hard. Who had laid this town to waste would surely suffer for the deed if he must pursue the ones at fault to the ends of England.

With a heavy heart he motioned for his men to follow and they returned to Darkenwald. He entered the hall and met both Aislinn and Bolsgar awaiting his return. Quietly he answered the unspoken question in their eyes.

"We found the rebels gone, but I think we have not seen the last of them. They got little from Cregan and one of them was killed with his mount and both were lean and well starved. The raiders will not go far until they gain some food for themselves and fodder for their horses."

Bolsgar nodded in agreement. "Aye, they will lay up and let their steeds graze on our rich lands and then hunt game for themselves until they are fed and able to move on. We must be wary lest they find our flocks the easier picking."

Aislinn called for food to be brought as Wulfgar took

his place at the table, and Bolsgar seated himself nearby to continue their discussion. Haylan came with a huge platter of meat and bread then returned to fetch pitchers of foaming ale. A cold draft swept them as Sweyn entered the hall and made his way to the table. He made no comment but seized a whole rib of mutton and filled his mouth. He sighed at the taste of food and seated himself while he chewed happily and washed the whole down with a horn of ale. The breeze of Sweyn's entry had not died when the door was again flung wide and the three knights came into the hall. They attacked the remaining food and set about devouring it with gusto and washing down their meal with large amounts of ale. Wulfgar was left staring at the empty dish before him in some bemusement.

"Would I be the king, my hearties, I fear I would yet starve with you as companions."

The men roared in loud glee and Aislinn laughed and called for more food. The sound of their mirth brought Gwyneth down to join them although she had dined earlier. She sat quietly at her tapestry as was her manner of late and seemed to enjoy the company. Kerwick soon joined them also, looking somewhat haggard and harried. He complained of the mess this affair had made of his books, and held up his hand with the fingers stiff and twisted as though deformed.

"Why look!" he exclaimed. "I've taken a cramp from clutching my pen all day and making changes and corrections in the book."

There was a round of laughter at his play and when it stilled, he turned to Wulfgar more soberly.

" 'Twas with some pain that I entered the deaths of eight from Cregan," he said sadly.

The hall grew quiet as the horror of the day was brought home to all who sat at the table.

"I knew them all," he continued. "They were friends. I would put aside my books for a space and join you as you hunt the vandals down."

"Rest easy, Kerwick," Wulfgar bade him. "We will see them brought to justice. Your value lies much more in staying here to make some sense of this confusion."

He turned to the others and spoke more firmly, giving them his plans.

"The watchers will be set as before." He turned and directed his words to Bolsgar. "Choose the men who know the signals and see them well hidden in the woods and hills. They should go out tonight that they will be ready at the morrow's first light."

He faced the knights.

"We will stand to ride if the rebels show again. When we go, we will signal the castle of our path and will be informed of the raiders and their whereabouts. Beaufonte, you will stay and continue to prepare the castle for possible attack. Did all go well there today."

Beaufonte nodded but frowned as he gave his report. "The castle is being armed and the men are directed in the defense of the walls. But there is one matter I would bring to you." He paused, unsure, then continued. "The people of Cregan find themselves much crowded in the bailey and many have built huts close against the outer wall. 'Twould bode ill for us if there should be an attack."

"Aye," Wulfgar agreed. "On the morrow see them moved beyond the lower moat. With the watchers out we will have warning aplenty for them to get within the walls."

He looked questioningly about the table and met no other problems.

" 'Tis done then." He raised his cup high. "To the morrow. May we send them all to their maker."

All joined the toast but Gwyneth and as she sat somewhat aside; no one even offered her a cup.

Unnoticed but by one, Haylan entered and brought wine to fill the cups and a fresh platter of steaming meats, bread and a large bowl of hot gravy to dip them in. Kerwick boldly seized a piece of meat and as he tasted it he wrinkled his nose.

"Ugh! There is too much salt on this meat."

His voice was louder than those at the table needed and all watched him as he took another piece and tasted it also. He threw it down in feigned disgust.

"And not enough salt on this one. For shame, Wulfgar. At least you could find someone who knew how to flavor meat."

He laughed at his own prank and turned to speak to Aislinn, at the same time reaching for a piece of bread. Haylan leaned over the table and turned the platter so that the steaming gravy was beneath his unwary hand. He squalled in pain as his fingers sank into the hot stuff and

461

jerked them quickly back to plunge them into his mouth to ease the hurt.

"Is that meat flavored more to your liking?" Haylan asked innocently. "Mayhap it needs more salt."

She lifted the small salt cellar up invitingly and laughter rang about the table. Even Gwyneth smiled.

The next morning a young serf who had gone out to gather the last of his crop wakened the manor as he loudly beat on the door. When Wulfgar threw open the door, the peasant gasped out his story as his lord rapidly dressed.

Late on the evening past a group of knights had approached his farm. He was wary of strangers and had fled to hide in the woods nearby. After burning his house and scattering the grain he had labored so hard to gather, they had withdrawn but a small way and made camp near a brook.

When the lad had completed his tale, he was given a hearty meal while Wulfgar and his men mounted and rode out to seek the raiders. They approached the camp from a sheltered gulley but found only blackened scars where the campfires had been laid. The remains of a young oxen, a stray from one of the herds, lay near the camp. The rebels had taken only the choicest parts and left the rest to rot. Wulfgar shook his head as he stared down at the carcass. Gowain neared him and was bemused at Wulfgar's concern for the slain animal.

"What bothers you, my lord?" he asked. "They slew a beast to feed themselves. 'Tis simple."

"Not so," Wulfgar replied. "They took no part to smoke or cure but just enough to fill their bellies for the moment. They must have other plans to gain provender for their journey and I fear that we are part of those plans."

He gazed around toward the barren hilltops that surrounded them and the small hairs crawled on the back of his neck. Gowain saw his frown.

"Aye, Wulfgar." The young knight also gazed about. "I also feel there is something amiss here. These men sneak in the night not like soldiers but like sulking beasts."

Again they returned to Darkenwald with no word of victory and were met with news that as he rode to the south a farm was burned to the north and a small herd of goats slain. No meat had been taken from them. They had been left as they fell for the scavengers. It seemed senseless, as if the band would simply destroy as much as they could.

Wulfgar chafed cruelly at his folly. He paced the hall and raged that he had let himself be led astray while the enemy raided and laid waste to his holdings. Aislinn wondered at his mood, for she knew he chastised himself more harshly than any other would, but she held her tongue. He calmed after a bit and at her urging ate a light supper after which he seemed at ease again. He cast off the heavy hauberk, leaving on the leather tunic he wore beneath and sat before the hearth, discussing the day with Bolsgar and Sweyn.

"The thieves have been to Cregan and then north and today south. Tomorrow we shall set out at the first light of dawn and ride to the west. Mayhap we can intercept them in their thievery."

The others could name no better plan. They would rely upon the signals to mark the band of raiders and hope they could catch them before more damage was done.

Gwyneth's rasping temper had worn them all through the evening as she ranted on their failure to find the rebels. Now as she began again, Aislinn looked away to where Bryce played on a pelt before the warm hearth, letting the sight of him ease her vexation.

" 'Tis in fear I cower here amid these moldering ruins that could hardly slow a well cast spear," Gwyneth said, glancing around at the ancient timbers that roofed the hall. "What have you done to see to our safety, Wulfgar?"

He lowered his brow and stared into the fire without reply.

"Aye, you wear the hooves of your horses low and plow the roadways well, but have you set a sword to a single one of those thieves? Nay. They still roam as free as the wind. Indeed, on the morrow I may have to take a blade and defend myself against them while you wander the countryside."

Wulfgar turned to stare at her as if he half wished her words would come true.

Bolsgar grunted and his voice fell sour from his mouth. "Leave the sword, my daughter. Take your tongue to them instead. It has far the sharper edge and since it smites your protectors so, it should lay low the worst of our enemies. Who could stand before it? 'Twould surely pierce the stoutest shield and split the holder in twain."

Aislinn choked and coughed at Bolsgar's comment, trying not to laugh, and in the process won a glare from Gwyneth. She busied herself at twirling her distaff, drawing a long yarn from the ball of wool that capped its smaller end.

"My good father jests while thieves burn and pillage and make us hide behind our walls," Gwyneth snarled. "I cannot even take a ride to ease my spirit."

Sweyn chortled. "My thanks for little favors. At least we need not fear for the horses."

Bolsgar joined his mirth. "If we could but teach her to turn them about. She is ever riding out but always walking back."

Gwyneth placed her sewing on the hearth and turned to glare at them, standing with her arms akimbo.

"Laugh, you croaking ravens," she railed at the two men. "I do not prop my leg in the tower and look for silly flashes from the hills nor do I slobber on my food or swill ale like a boar."

"Aye, but what do you do?" Bolsgar interrupted and was rewarded with another flare of her temper.

"As any lady should I keep to myself." She cast her eyes askance to Aislinn. "I mind my stitchery and naught else as my lord Wulfgar bade me. I am careful not to injure the gentle pride of others."

She paused and a whimper came from behind her. She turned and saw that Bryce had found her sewing where she had laid it and pulled it to him. He did much damage to it now as he struggled to free himself from the snarled yarns. Gwyneth shrieked and bending, snatched the stuff from him, jerking it free of his tiny arms.

"Brat!" she cried and slapped him on the arm, leaving a reddening welt. He puckered his lips and drew a long breath to cry.

"Brat!" she spat again. "I'll teach you to—"

There was a sudden thud as she sat firmly on the dusty floor. Aislinn's ankle had swept her feet from beneath her. Gwyneth's eyes flamed with her fury then widened in startled fear as she looked up to find Aislinn standing above her with feet braced, coppery hair ablaze in the light of the fire and violet eyes striking sparks of rage. In her hands she clutched the distaff like a spear about to be thrust. The lips parted and the words came breathless but hard.

"What you lay to me, Gwyneth, I can bear. I am a woman full grown." She leaned forward and the distaff moved threateningly. "But Norman or English, light, dark, red or green, that baby is *mine*—and if you would lay hand to him again, you would best seek a sword, for I will tear you end from end." Aislinn paused but a moment before demanding, "Do you hear me?"

With gaping jaw Gwyneth nodded slowly. Aislinn stood away from her and lifted the awestruck Bryce to her, cooing into his ear as she soothed the sting of his arm. Gwyneth gathered herself and her sewing and dusted her skirts. Unable to face the grinning men, she made her way to her room.

Later in their chambers Wulfgar stood watching as Aislinn laid the babe before the hearth. He marveled that she could be at one time the wild tempered vixen when her offspring was threatened and then another this graceful nymph who did the slow, mesmerizing dance of a wife before him as she went about her duties in the room. Her every movement was a study in rhythm and grace. The white kirtle she wore flowed about her as she moved, showing a thrusting breast now and curved hip or a narrow waist then. He could feel the urge grow in him and as she came near he caught her in the crook of his arm, bringing her to meet his questioning kiss, but a cry from Bryce soon proved a distraction.

"Wait till the child is asleep," she whispered against his lips. "Then we will see your rutting ways well met."

"Rutting?" He grunted, disappointed. "And who is the maid who swings her coltish hips and fondles me in public until I would fair burst my seams?"

He kissed her again softly before stretching out in his chair, and from beneath lowered lids watched her closely. She bent low to pick up her wool cards from the hearth and presented him with a view of her swelling breasts pressed almost free of the open front of the kirtle.

"Have a care, my love," he murmured softly. "Or I may yet startle the babe."

She rose quickly, blushing at his boldness, but knew full well it was no idle threat.

"Watch the child for a while," Aislinn bade him sweetly. "I must see Miderd about some things and set tomorrow's fare."

Gathering a shawl about her shoulders, she left him to

Bryce's care. Wulfgar closed his eyes for a moment and relaxed, feeling the sense of peacefulness that seemed to flood him with the warmth of the fire. He opened his eyes again at a tug on his ankle and saw that Bryce had rolled to him and now struggled to sit up with the help of his leg. The lad succeeded and sat unsteadily while he looked up at Wulfgar with those wide, quizzical blue eyes. He showed no fear of the huge Norman lord but wrinkled his eyes in a smile. He waved his chubby arms in glee, chuckling heartily and toppled abruptly. Eyes, suddenly sad, raised as his chin quivered and great tears began to stream down his face. Ever at a fault before tears, Wulfgar reached down and lifted the babe to his lap.

The eyes instantly dried and the child chortled, happy at his new position in the world and plucked with wondering fingers at the collar of Wulfgar's chainse. He stretched upward along the broad, hard chest and explored the smiling mouth of the face that loomed above him. Wulfgar reached down beside his chair and lifted a wood and cloth doll to place it in the boy's hands. After a few moments the babe yawned, tiring of the toy, and dropped it. He moved about until he was comfortable on this unyielding bed then sighed and went to sleep.

Wulfgar sat for a long time without moving, afraid of disturbing the boy. There was an odd warmth that grew in him as he realized this tiny, helpless being trusted him beyond all reason. The small chest rose and fell with the soft, quick breath of a child's sleep. Could this one have sprung from his loins and the lust he had eased on a young, beautiful captive?

This lad lies lovingly and in full trust upon my breast, Wulfgar mused. Still I shun his love. What is his motive that he comes hither though I gave no word to him?

Wulfgar's mind was in a turmoil, yet he slowly became aware that he was bound by more than vows. There were other ties that sank tender hooks within the heart of a man and would never set him free without deep scars that marred the soul. The vows of wedlock were a promise just the fulfillment of which chained him more firmly than the words.

He gazed down at the innocent slumbering face and knew the sire made no difference. This would be his child from this day forth.

The fierce Norman knight bent low and gently kissed

the head that rested on his chest. He felt a presence beside him and raised his gaze to meet Aislinn's shining eyes. She looked down upon the man holding her child and felt an overwhelming love for them both.

The new day dawned and Wulfgar set out with his men, riding to the west as planned. It was not long before a flash from a hill warned of an attack to the east of Darkenwald. Wulfgar swore and swinging about, pressed his men to a hard pace as one stayed long enough to give word of his direction. They had passed the castle when one of the bowmen called and pointed to the tower where another watchman signaled. The band had split and was now burning cottages to the north and south. Wulfgar's rage and frustration mounted. At his order his man flashed back that they would divide and go after them. He had barely made the parting from Gowain and Milbourne and headed northward when word came that the band had reformed and set a torch to a field in the west of his holdings. Wulfgar's face blackened. He and his men had rested there only a few hours ago. How could the Flemish know his whereabouts that they could elude him so well? He growled a command and a message was sent for Gowain and Milbourne to meet him near Darkenwald.

Thus the troubled day wore on. He saw nothing of the invaders, everywhere he went they were pillaging elsewhere. Before the sun had set, word had ceased to come of the raiders and Wulfgar could only surmise that they had gone to ground somewhere in the myriad places of forests and swamps where they could not be found. He cursed the day and with his men slumping wearily in their saddles, they returned to Darkenwald.

Wulfgar strode into the hall in great agitation, flinging the portal wide with a loud crash, frightening Bryce who lay on a pelt before the hearth. The lad's lips trembled and soon his face was a caricature of youthful distress. Aislinn set aside her distaff and lifted him, cuddling him close to soothe his fears. Her gaze followed Wulfgar as he paced in front of the hearth, slapping his gauntlets against his thigh.

" 'Twould be no different if they knew my every move before I made it," he raged. "If I told them of my thoughts, they could not escape me better."

He paused suddenly and stared at his wife.

"How could they know unless——" He shook his head as if confused by the thought. "Who would tell them?" He strode away then turned back to Aislinn. "Who here left the town?"

She shrugged. "I did not watch closely, but the people held close to the castle and most of them went about on foot."

Wulfgar pressed the question. "Kerwick, mayhap? Or Maida?"

Aislinn shook her head vehemently. "Nay. Kerwick was with Beaufonte at the castle the entire day and Maida stayed here with Bryce."

"'Twas but a thought," Wulfgar sighed, yet Aislinn knew he still worried on the matter.

He called Sanhurst to bid him fetch Bolsgar and Sweyn. When they came, he climbed with them to the top of the tower where no prying ears could overhear. Wulfgar looked out upon his lands spread wide below him.

"I own this small estate, yet I find I cannot protect it from a few straggling soldiers. Even the lookouts do not give us the advantage."

Bolsgar watched him as he spoke and knew his concern. "They report only bands of men," he said slowly. "If the Flemish raiders divide singly or in pairs and wear Norman cloaks, they would pass unnoted and when they rejoined 'twould be too late for us to forestay them."

"True," Wulfgar ceded. "Then let the lookouts report all riders and their direction. 'Twill take a few new signals, but you can see to it, Bolsgar."

"Wulfgar." Sweyn now spoke his piece. "There is a thing that gnaws at me. You ever tell this place of our intentions and we find no enemies where we go. It bodes of a traitor in our midst. Let us inform no one and ride where we will."

"You are right, Sweyn, and it eats at me that I can put no name to the Judas." Wulfgar beat the railing with his fist. "Or perhaps someone reads our signals as well as we. Though if that were true, it would be as simple to slay or drive the watchers in. We will do as you say on the morrow. Say no word of this to anyone." He turned to Bolsgar. "Let no watcher pass a signal as to where we ride from here, then we shall see."

Bolsgar went to see his task performed, and when all was done to make the morrow safe, they met in the hall and did justice to Haylan's cookery. The meal was concluded and Wulfgar took Bryce from his mother's arms and mounted the stairs to the chamber with Aislinn at his side. Bolsgar and Sweyn exchanged glances over this unusual happening and then silently toasted the day.

Bryce gurgled with glee as Wulfgar gently tusseled with him on a pelt spread in front of the hearth. When the babe grew tired of the games and yawned, Aislinn put him in the cradle. On her return across the chamber, she drew a cup of wine for her husband and handing it to him, sat crosslegged beside him as he sipped it. His eyes warmed to her and setting the goblet aside, he reached out an arm to pull her down against him. He pressed a soft and tender kiss upon her lips, and she sighed as she traced a finger along his cheek.

"You are tired, my lord."

"There is an elixir of youth you add to my cup," he whispered as his lips caressed her cheek. "It makes me feel as if the day has yet to begin." He loosed the strings of her kirtle until her bosom lay open to his gaze.

Her arms slipped around his neck and they came together as lips melted to lips, and in his bed Bryce slept on through the sound and fury of their play.

Wulfgar and his men rode out the next morning shortly after sunrise and waited in a wooded copse until the first sign of the band had been seen by the watchers and signaled, then they rode hard. The first cottage was barely set afire when they arrived. The haystacks were scattered as if waiting to be torched and the signs were that the raiders had left in haste. They doused the flames, salvaging most of the structure.

A hill twinkled with reflected sunlight and Wulfgar called his men to horse and they rode again. This time the hut was not kindled, but a small fire to light the brands was still smoking in the yard. Again the thieves scattered into the forest, but in their haste to flee they left a trail. Now the heat of the chase and near success seized the Norman pursuers and the pace quickened. A new signal beckoned and they swung south, this time to see the colors of Flanders as the band of raiders gathered and then had to fly. The quarry scattered again and Wulfgar's men spread out to search the runs and warrens.

A new beacon flickered and at Wulfgar's call his men

came together to ride north. They mounted the top of a hill just as the raiders regrouped and the chase was rejoined. The thieves fled into the edge of the swamp and scattered once more. Wulfgar's men followed, flushing two Flemish from cover and as they raised their swords the two were slain as many arrows studded their leather tunics. Wulfgar confirmed they were Flemish, but they bore no coat of arms to name their leader.

The others had eluded the chase, and as Wulfgar waited for his lookouts to come to life with further news, he and his men rested their mounts and took a light repast. The hunt bore ever closer on the invaders, and thus the day was filled until, with the dark, no further sign was visible. A return was made to the hall and Wulfgar felt secure. The pillaging marauders had found no rest or food and would be hard pressed to meet their own needs, at least till dawn. He vowed he would wear the raiders down until they fled his lands or surrendered. And to that other thought, his mind had already formed a plan, yet who it was who worked against him in his own hall or town he could not name though he considered and rejected several possibilities.

Much later that night he drew Aislinn and Bolsgar out for a stroll in the frosty evening brightly lit by a full moon.

"There is one who betrays us here and we must find him out," he told them. " 'Tis my plan that my men will leave by twos before first light and wait beyond the hill. I will go with Sweyn and Gowain as if to seek signs of the raiders."

Aislinn decried his scheme, clinging to his arm. "But, Wulfgar, there is danger in you riding with so few. There are still a score or more of them. 'Tis folly."

"Nay, my love, hear me out," he bade. "I will join my men and ride slowly east beyond Cregan where we left the raiders. They should have camped nearby. You and Bolsgar will watch the hall and town. If someone leaves to betray us, you will see him and can send a rider to me. Once we know them warned we will ride hard to scatter them again before damage is done. Mayhap we may slay a few and with their informer found out, we will surely win the day."

Bolsgar agreed and when assured no danger would

come to Wulfgar, Aislinn finally nodded her assent. Wulfgar dropped an arm about her shoulders.

"Good lass, we'll have the best of them yet."

Wulfgar roused from bed long before daylight and watched from the chamber window as the men left by twos and threes, carefully keeping to the shadows and being quiet in their passage. When they had all gone and the first light of dawn drove the stars from the eastern sky, he donned his clothes and with his hauberk over his arm left the room with Aislinn to break the fast. Bolsgar and Sweyn joined them at the table and soon Beaufonte. Gwyneth came down sleepily rubbing her eyes and yawning as if the noise of the men's stirrings had awakened her. When Wulfgar was assured all was there within hearing he rose.

"Come, Sweyn. The thieves will not wait upon our table. Let us fetch Gowain and see if we can search out the rebels."

Sweyn rose mumbling through a mouthful of rich brewis as Wulfgar threw on his hauberk and coif and set his helm to his head. The Norseman hefted his sword and battle-ax, testing the edge of the latter with a gleam in his fair blue eyes.

"She seems eager to bite today," he laughed. "Mayhap we will find a skull or two to split."

Gwyneth sneered. "Let us hope you fare better than you have in the days passed. Forsooth, I'll have to bolt the doors of Darkenwald against those scavenging few to save my maiden's virtue."

Wulfgar peered at her with a mocking grin. "Prithee, sister, do not fret. That danger seems far-fetched and I would guess you have naught to worry you."

Gwyneth threw him an ugly scowl that drew a guffaw from Sweyn who rumbled:

"Nay, Wulfgar, she does not fret. She only counts the moments till they come."

With that Sweyn left the hall with Wulfgar following. Gowain joined them and as they took the road to the west, every eye watched.

Bolsgar stood in the tower of the hall with the signal man and held his gaze to the village spread out beneath them. Beaufonte rode near the castle and Aislinn sat in the bedchamber at the window with the shutters barely ajar where she could see the lower end of the village and the path to the swamp and forest. She could not see Maida's hut where it crouched by the willows, yet worried that her mother might have found a way to spend her vengeance upon Wulfgar without her daughter's knowledge. Aislinn toyed with the sewing in her lap, unable to set her mind to it. She fretted that something might go amiss and Wulfgar would fall into a trap set for him. She could not bear the thought of losing him and grew more anxious with each passing moment.

Suddenly her heart leapt, for she saw a movement in the thick brush by the edge of the marsh. She watched closely and saw it was a woman's figure that crept along in the shadows. A cold dread began to build in her breast as she thought of Maida again and her eyes strained to catch some familiar mannerism that would bare the identity of the person. A dark mantle shrouded the figure from head to toe, giving her little aid. Her mind would not still. Perhaps it was some other. Haylan perhaps? Had she found a lord of Flanders for her own?

The figure passed an open spot and she saw that it was not her mother, for it moved with a agility and speed the old woman would be hard pressed to match. Now the figure stopped and turned to glance behind her. Aislinn smothered a gasp. Even from this distance and in the shadow she knew the slim, bony face as Gwyneth's.

Aislinn watched as the woman made her way deeper into the willows and straining she could see the shape of a man dressed as a peasant who met her in the shadows there. Words were exchanged between them before the man disappeared again into the denseness of the forest. Gwyneth waited in the shade for some time before picking her way back to the hall.

Glancing back over her shoulder to see that Bryce still slept, Aislinn hurried to call Bolsgar from the tower. As she waited for him to join her she paced before the hearth, wondering how she might tell him gently of his daughter.

"What be it, girl?" he asked when he faced her. " 'Tis important that I watch for the traitor and I do not fully trust the watchman."

Aislinn took a deep breath. "I know the traitor, good Bolsgar. I saw—" Then she blurted it out. " 'Twas Gwyneth. I saw her meet a man by the swamp."

He stopped and stared at her, the agony showing in his eyes. He searched her face for some hint of a lie and glimpsed only her own pain and sympathy for him.

"Gwyneth," he breathed low. "Of course. She would be the one."

"She will be here soon," Aislinn warned him.

The father nodded, his mind grown distant. He went to stand before the fire with his broad shoulders sagging and stared into its depths.

Gwyneth swung open the door and strode in, humming to herself as if light of mood. She was almost striking with a rosy bloom upon her cheeks and her flaxen hair tumbling over her small bosom. Bolsgar swung to glower at his daughter from beneath beetled brows.

"What ails you, father?" Gwyneth chirped gayly. "Does your breakfast sit ill on your gut?"

"Nay, daughter," he growled. "Another matter eats at my heart. One of a traitor who betrays her own kin."

Gwyneth's eyes widened and she swung to Aislinn. "What lies have you set in his head now, bitch?" she snarled.

"No lies!" Bolsgar roared, then he continued in a calmer voice. "I know you best of all and never in your life have you given care to ought but your own ends. Yea! Traitor I believe. But why?" He turned his back upon her, for his eyes found little ease in beholding her. "Why do you aid a cause that will only bleed the life from our land? What friends you choose! First that Moorish boor Ragnor and now the Flemish!"

At the mention of Ragnor's name Aislinn saw the other woman's chin rise and a proud look come over her. At once everything seemed to settle in place and all of Aislinn's questions were answered and she knew the cause of Gwyneth's actions. She came out of her chair with a cry.

" 'Tis Ragnor! He leads the raiders! Who else would know the land so well and where each cottage lay? 'Tis Ragnor she betrays us to."

Bolsgar swung around and with a dark scowl on his face bore down on Gwyneth. "By God, I swear," he ground out, "you have made this day the blackest of my life."

"Blacker still than the day you found your precious son a bastard?" she sneered in his face and righteous pride rang in her voice. "You, he and that Saxon slut tore from me my last trace of pride. What was I here but a nothing in a hall where I should have been the lady? I was forbidden the right to answer the lies and slurs that were set to me by others. My own father chortled like a foolish babe when I was stripped of every—"

Bolsgar's hand caught her full across the mouth and the force of the blow spun Gwyneth about until she staggered back against the table.

"Do not name me again your father," he snarled. "I give lie to the fact and deny your kinship."

Gwyneth braced her arms behind her on the table and glared at him with hatred burning in her eyes. "You love Wulfgar so much even though the world calls him bastard?" She rubbed the bruised cheek. "Then draw this day as long as you can, for the night will see him dead."

Aislinn gasped at her words. "They set a trap for him. Oh, Bolsgar, they will draw him out and kill him!"

She crossed to Gwyneth, her eyes narrowing and her hand resting on the small dagger in her belt.

"Where, bitch?" she demanded, all trace of the gentle Aislinn flown. "Where or I will carve your neck until the breezes draw a tune from it."

Gwyneth's eyes flickered with uncertainty as she faced the other, remembering well Aislinn's rage at things past. "'Tis too late to aid my bastard kin, so I will name the place. He may even now lay in the forest just outside of Cregan."

She lowered her gaze from the two who glared at her and slid into a chair, folding her hands in her lap. Aislinn questioned her further while Bolsgar stared in disbelief at his daughter. When Gwyneth would yield no more Aislinn turned to him.

"Go to him, Bolsgar," she begged in her distress, tears coming to her eyes. "Ride hard and warn him. There is yet time as he ventures slowly awaiting word."

Without another glance to his daughter, Bolsgar snatched up his mantle and helm and hastened from the hall.

Wulfgar had left the hall and ridden out of sight to the west then swept around and joined his men. There was no haste and he flung riders wide to guard the flanks and search out any ambush. He dallied on the way, pausing often to scan the hills and the road behind.

The first hint of a rider was a small cloud of dust that rose to the rear and they halted to wait. Wulfgar's brows lifted in surprise when he saw that it was Bolsgar who approached them. The old man reined to a skidding halt beside him.

"Ragnor leads the vandals," he panted. "And it was Gwyneth who betrayed us. The Flemish set a trap for you at Cregan. Let us ride and I will give you the news as we go."

Wulfgar set spurs to his horse as Bolsgar began to relate the events at Darkenwald. The younger man's brow had clouded and now as Bolsgar ended his tale, he rode in silence, musing on Gwyneth's treachery. A column of smoke began to rise from beyond the forest and gave more weight to Bolsgar's warning. When they came to the edge of the forest, Wulfgar halted the men. His commands rapped out in quick succession.

"Bolsgar! Sweyn! Stay with me. See to your arms. Gowain! Milbourne! Take half the men and ride deep in the forest. Place yourselves behind the spot and when you hear my call, charge with lance and sword. We will drive them to the open and see the game met there."

The forest was quiet and eerie. It seemed the slightest noise echoed from every tree. Great oaks with moss festooned trunks stood on every side. Fallen trees blocked the way again and again, but above all the game had fled. There were no hares bounding to cover or birds singing or startled deer fleeing with graceful leaps. There was only silence and the men.

Wulfgar's force rode away from the path and deep into the brooding darkness where only spots of sunlight dappled the shadows and lightened the gloom. Now they turned and paralleled the path until the light of the farther side could be seen and the ruins of Cregan were glimpsed through breaks in the brush. They turned again and went stealthily forward until they could hear the hushed murmurs of men ahead. The first charge would be with all men mounted and once the foe was flushed and in the open, the archers would dismount and hurl their barbs into the fray.

They waited. Nerves grew taught. Wulfgar decided the others had had time enough to take position and his wavering war call shrilled through the forest. As one the men leaned forward and urged their mounts into the charge.

475

The mad chaos of battle was joined and in the tangle of the wood it seemed a thousand men charged. The mottled shadows lent to the confusion as men on horseback appeared everywhere and on every side. The Flemish, seeing the hopelessness of a stand here, fled further to the open fields before the ruined town.

The one knight who led them bade them stand and hold their shields up into a wall. He brought a few within the circle to bend their bows and give some protection. Their horses had been left in the forest and now the raiders stood boldly exposed.

Wulfgar dismounted his archers at the edge of the woods where cover was plenty and full. He brought his five knights into view, Bolsgar on his left, Sweyn on the right and Gowain and Milbourne at either end. He raised his pike with its standard and called out.

"Yield yourselves," he offered. "The day is lost."

The single knight shouted back. "Nay. We've heard of William's justice to raiders. Better we die here than under his ax." The knight raised his shield and sword and shook them. "Come to the killing, Norman."

At the last words, Wulfgar glanced to his left then to his right. He couched his lance and a shower of arrows fell among the enemy. He set spur to the Hun and charged. His long lance reached past the shorter spear of the man before him and bore him to the ground, opening the wall of shields. They crashed through the defenders and whirled to charge again. The lone knight labored to form the men again, but Wulfgar and his knights were on them. This time he struck not the center but the corner of the square. He peeled the foe back and opened the way for the others. Dropping the lance he swung his long sword out and hacked a path about him as the Hun thrashed forward. Half of the Norman archers drew swords and with spear and blade joined the battle. The others held back and let slip an arrow when an opening was presented or a foe sought to flee.

The field lay silent but for a moan here or there and only the single knight still stood. As Wulfgar drew his men back, the knight rested his arms on the hilt of his sword with its point upon the ground. Without a word Wulfgar dismounted and with shield and sword met him fairly. It was no match but the knight died with honor.

Sweyn and Bolsgar searched the fallen for Ragnor or

Vachel and found neither. Three of the Normans were slain and six were wounded but able to ride. The Flemish were stripped of arms and armor and laid together to await a grave. Wulfgar scanned the horizon and sat the Hun uneasily, wondering where Ragnor and Vachel were.

Aislinn paced the hall, her mind in a turmoil. Wulfgar was in danger and all because of a woman's folly. She whirled on Gwyneth in a temper, intending to berate her sorely, but she found the woman's eyes fastened intently upon the door. Aislinn followed her gaze but could see nothing. She returned her gaze to Gwyneth who now sat looking at her hands folded in her lap. Aislinn frowned in puzzlement and went to sit at her sewing, setting a stitch now and then as she watched the other. Gwyneth sat quietly, but her eyes continually went to the door as if she waited.

"We knew a traitor was in the hall, Gwyneth," Aislinn said with deliberate care. "Wulfgar rides slow and waits for word from us. 'Tis far more likely your Ragnor will be the one to meet his end today."

Gwyneth only stirred slightly and returned, "Ragnor will not die."

"The men rode out early but only to wait upon Wulfgar beyond the hill," Aislinn further needled and watched Gwyneth carefully. There was no reaction, only the words calmly spoken.

"Ragnor will not die."

Aislinn clapped her hands to the arms of her chair and came to her feet abruptly, bringing Gwyneth's eyes sharply to her.

"Ragnor will not die," Aislinn repeated, "because he comes here!"

By the triumphant look on Gwyneth's face Aislinn knew she had struck the truth. She wasted no time but called up the tower for the sentry there to fetch Beaufonte and any men with him. The man went off to do her bidding as she returned to watch Gwyneth, her hand on her small dagger. There was a rattle of hooves outside and Aislinn drew her blade, ready to do battle with the slim weapon if Ragnor burst into the room. To her relief Beaufonte entered with one man running at his heels. The knight glanced about the hall and seeing nothing amiss, turned questioning eyes to her.

"My lady?"

They turned as Kerwick came running into the hall, gasping in his haste with the watchman close behind. Now the men all stared at her.

"Ragnor is on his way here while his men seek to ambush Wulfgar," she informed them. "We must secure the hall against him."

They all ran to close shutters and bolt them, then Beaufonte threw the heavy bar across the door. Aislinn remembered well the night Ragnor came and could almost hear the crashing of another bolt being splintered beneath the pounding of a heavy, ramming log. It was well her mother was safe in her hut. Her mind could not bear a repeat of that horrible night. Aislinn chafed further, wondering at what more could be done to see them safe, then thought of the obvious.

"Beaufonte, the watchers! Send a signal to Wulfgar to return to Darkenwald and let us pray he sees the message!"

The knight called up the tower well and the lookout climbed down to him. They were discussing the message when there was a heavy pounding on the door and Ragnor's voice called for entry. Before anyone could stop her, Gwyneth leaped to the portal and threw the bar to the floor. The sturdy oaken panel was flung aside and two strange men surged through followed by Ragnor, Vachel and two more. They were all dressed in Norman trappings, yet Beaufonte drew his sword and confronted them. One of the men behind Ragnor threw a spear and the watchman died with the shaft in his chest. Beaufonte's man joined him and the two battled valiantly, but Vachel took that man on his blade and laid him low. Beaufonte stood alone and engaged Ragnor and the others while Kerwick pushed Aislinn up the stairs to her chamber. Vachel drew aside and worked behind Beaufonte. Taking his sword in both hands, he swung it upon the brave knight's back, hewing through the links of mail and biting deeply into his neck. Beaufonte fell with a cry of warning then sank to his back and stared at the huge timbers of the ceiling as his eyes dimmed and his breath stilled.

Kerwirk thrust Aislinn into the chamber, closing the door behind her then snatched an old shield and sword from the wall beside the door. He stood ready to meet the foe and delay them as long as possible. Two of the raiders came forward with Ragnor close behind.

"Saxon dog, give up this play," Ragnor beckoned with a confident grin. "What have you to gain in defense of the lady? She will be taken anyway when you are dead."

Kerwick held his stand. "If my life is all I have to give for her, then so be it. Come, Ragnor, I've longed for this since you first took my betrothed."

"You too, Saxon?" Ragnor chided. "Is everyone smitten with the wench?"

Kerwick brushed aside a spear thrust and plunged his blade into one of the men's stomach. He fell but Ragnor's sword struck the one Kerwick held and snapped it near the hilt. The next blow fell upon the shield but the other raider's spear caught the Saxon's arm. Ragnor swung again and passed Kerwick's guard to strike him down. Blood streamed from his head and he rolled beneath their feet as Ragnor rushed by to throw open the door to the chamber.

Aislinn whirled with a gasp and Ragnor grinned, advancing into the room.

"I said I would have you, dove," he laughed. "And the time has come."

Aislinn's eyes flashed but she gave no outward sign of her fear. A stirring from the cradle made Ragnor pause and he stepped to it, raising his sword. With a cry Aislinn threw herself upon his arm, but Ragnor struck her free of him with the back of his hand, flinging her to a heap against the foot of the bed. She came to her feet in an instant, blood trickling from the corner of her mouth.

"You would slay your own son?" she taunted him.

"There is that possibility, but also some doubt," he calmly returned. "He is better dead than Wulfgar's."

He turned and raised his sword again.

"Nay!" Aislinn screamed.

There was something in her voice that gave him pause and he looked to her. She held the blade of her dagger against her own breast and in her eyes he saw the threat.

"Touch the babe and I will kill myself. You know Wulfgar and you know there will be no corner of hell for you to hide in if I am dead."

He laughed cruelly. "That bastard is of no worry to me. Even now my men push the dirt upon his grave."

"Have care, my love," Gwyneth's voice came from the

doorway. She had sought him out, unwilling to leave him alone with Aislinn for long. "Wulfgar is warned. They found me out and my father rode to him. They knew of someone here and have set their own trap."

Ragnor sheathed his sword and for a moment was lost in thought. "Now that bodes ill for us, my pet," he mused aloud. "If I know the bastard's luck, he will survive the day and while I had thought to hold the rest at bay with his wife as hostage until we ruined his lands, now I am afraid we must flee. I spent what few men I had to buy his death."

He looked at Aislinn now holding Bryce in her arms and knew he could not easily separate them now and the moments had become precious. He turned to Gwyneth.

"Fetch foods from the cellars. We will seek out Edgar with the Northern Scots and pledge to him. Hurry, pet. Time grows short." He whirled to face Aislinn. "Bring the lad! He will be as much a hostage as you, though I doubt Wulfgar finds him more than a hindrance." Then he spoke sharply. "But I warn you, my dove, if you would see the babe live, do nothing to delay or mark the trail."

She sneered an answer to his threat. "You will mark your own trail wherever you go. My babe will be no hindrance. Still, I could leave him here. There will be those who come." She tried to speak casually. "Wulfgar thinks the babe is yours and does not value him highly though he will see him cared for."

Ragnor looked at her narrowly. "Dear Gwyneth says otherwise, that he named the child his and dotes upon him of late. I think we will take him, too."

"That bitch has seen to you well," Aislinn hissed.

"Speak not harshly of her, my love. She has served me faithfully," replied Ragnor.

"Yea," Aislinn choked in rage. "But she has served no one else and I think not even herself."

"She would have the world at her feet," he laughed. "And who could deny that tender blossom anything?" The tone of his voice belied his words and now he straightened and became harsh. "Enough of this dawdling. Bring what you will, but quickly. I grow weary of chatter."

Aislinn threw clothes in a bundle for Bryce and snatched up her fur-lined cloak to keep them warm.

"That's all," he commanded. "This will see you through."

He followed her out of the chamber, pushing her past Kerwick as she would have knelt to him and led her out of the hall, giving her little time to pause beside Beaufonte.

Gwyneth was already mounted on Aislinn's dapple-gray mare. She wore a fine gown, one she had finally purchased with the money Wulfgar had left for her and her father when he went with William. The small punch was led up for Aislinn, and Ragnor placed her upon it as she clutched the baby to her. Gwyneth eyed them suspiciously as Ragnor set her foot to the stirrup. His eyes raised to Aislinn's.

"Remember well, dove, I'll kill the babe if you give me cause."

Aislinn swallowed and nodded then he swung up on his own steed. Gwyneth delayed the party for one more petty gambit. She seized the woolen cloak from her own shoulders and made Aislinn trade her fur-lined one for it. Ragnor casually sat the back of his horse and waited, amused at the exchange. Gwyneth took a place beside him and smiled.

"Am I not a fine figure now, my love?" she questioned coyly.

As they set off Ragnor laughed but bent his eye above Gwyneth's head toward Aislinn.

481

Wulfgar scanned the hills again and it was as if he heard voices in the back of his mind. He canted his head to listen better and the words came clear. Ragnor! Aislinn! Bryce! Darkenwald! The names came together and of a sudden he knew where Ragnor was.

The Hun snorted in surprise as he jerked the reins, wheeling the steed about and he bellowed to Bolsgar.

"Stay here and see these men into the ground. They fought bravely. Milbourne, stay with him and hold ten here to dig. The rest who can ride, come with me."

Sweyn, Gowain and fifteen or more mounted, some of them wounded, but all eager. They rode apace, giving their mounts no rest until they thundered into the courtyard and brought their horses to a halt before the hall. Wulfgar noted briefly that no shout rang from the tower to mark their approach and that Aislinn was not out to meet him. He dismissed the worst of his thoughts as he swung from the saddle and threw the reins to Sweyn. He ran into the hall and the scene that greeted him was far from his expectations.

Wulfgar's blood ran cold as he surveyed the damage. The main hall was a shambles and the watchman lay slain at the door to the tower. Beaufonte was sprawled in a pool of blood, staring with sightless eyes at the ceiling. Propped on the stairs, where Haylan carefully tended a gash that ran down the side of his head from hairline to chin, was Kerwick. He still grasped in his hand the shattered butt of an ancient sword. A stranger lay near the head of the stairs with the other part of the blade buried in his gut. Miderd wrung her hands and Maida cowered in a dark corner.

" 'Twas Gwyneth!" Haylan half screamed. "That bitch, Gwyneth, opened the door for them. And she has gone with them." A sob of anger shook her. "They have taken the Lady Aislinn and Bryce."

Wulfgar was calm, indeed quiet. But his skin grew pale and his eyes took on the hue of polished steel. Even Maida, where she crouched by the empty cradle, read death in them.

Haylan blubbered on, crying and sobbing. "They took the babe and I heard him say he would kill him if she gave them any trouble."

Wulfgar's voice was soft and almost gentle as he spoke. "Who, Haylan? Who was it who spoke?"

She stared at him for a moment in surprise, then answered. " 'Twas the one who came with the king—Ragnor. He was with another knight and four men. Beaufonte killed a man before he was slain and the other stayed Kerwick's sword. The rest took Aislinn and the boy and fled."

Haylan turned away and bent to carefully fold a fresh cloth against Kerwick's wound. All the while Maida rocked on her heels by the crib and made a low moaning sound as she rent her hair. Wulfgar came to stand beside Haylan and gazed down at his battered sheriff.

"Kerwick?"

The young man's eyes opened and he grinned weakly. "I tried, my lord, but there were too many of them. I tried—"

"Rest easy, Kerwick," Wulfgar murmured and dropped a hand upon his shoulder. "You have been twice flayed for my lady's sake."

Sweyn slammed through the door, his ax in his hand and a snarl on his face. "They killed the stable boy. A young lad and unarmed. They slit his throat."

His eyes widened as he saw Beaufonte and he muttered a low curse that rolled from the depth of rage. Wulfgar's jaw tightened as he gazed again at his slain knight, but he gave Sweyn no pause and rasped out orders in a growl.

"Feed and rub the Hun and your own." And he added

as an afterthought, "For the ride, no armor, no packs. We travel light."

The Viking nodded and spun on his heels, departing as Wulfgar turned to Miderd.

"Go to the larder," he bade her, "Cut long strips from the dried venison. Bring two small bags of meal and two skins of water."

Before she could move he had gone up the stairs to his chamber. When a few moments later he returned, he wore no mail or helm but a soft cap of doeskin and a shirt of the same, overlaid with a rough jerkin of wolf fur held in place by a belt from which hung his broadsword and a well-honed dagger. Over his doeskin boots he wore leggings of wolf fur bound in place in the Viking manner. He passed Haylan and Kerwick, who now managed to sit and as he paused, his voice came low and harsh.

"This is a thing I have delayed too long and now it has struck me sore. Until I return, Kerwick, mind this hall. Bolsgar and my knights will give you aid."

Miderd approached with the required items and he took them from her and with no other word hastened out. At the stables he divided the provisions with Sweyn and nodded his approval when he saw that the Norseman was dressed much as he and had included a goodly bag of grain for each horse. Then the two of them mounted and in a moment were out of sight.

Bolsgar had finished his labor and set the battlefield at peace. The graves were well marked and he left some twenty horses laden with plunder in the stables then hastened to the hall where he found Kerwick seated at the table, still pale and drawn. Haylan tied the last strips of a bandage about his head then sat beside him and held his hand.

The old Saxon listened to the tale Kerwick spun and his face grew dark with rage and shame.

"Gwyneth sprang from my loins and I must see this done," he murmured, half to himself. "Wulfgar may give his sister pardon, but not I. I will follow and if he hesitates I shall lend assurance that her traitor's days are done."

He went sadly to his chamber and returned in a short moment. He chose only a bag of salt and a strong bow to add to his sword. In a moment he too had left Darkenwald.

Ragnor rode as if Satan dogged his heels and raged at each delay. Aislinn struggled with Bryce. To keep him still in her arms, yet guide the mare proved a test of her abilities. She complained bitterly when Ragnor whipped her horse into a brief gallop, but knew that in his rankling mood he would not spare her the blade if she gave him reason.

They pressed on, swinging wide of London and any Norman patrols, resting only a brief few hours at night to rise with the first light of dawn, choke down cold gruel and meat and ride on again. Though it gave her little respite, Aislinn was glad for the brevity of the rests. Ragnor's eyes turned to her more and more and she knew his thoughts would have quickly found some ease if there had been time to spare. She could not escape his gaze at night though Gwyneth pressed close to him, and at dawn when she nursed the babe, he always found reason to be near.

Bryce slept in her arms for the most part, giving her some rest as they rode, but when he woke he squalled with renewed vigor at his enforced inactivity. Ragnor grew more savage with each passing hour and even Gwyneth, who had ridden silently these many miles, began to feel the bite of his tongue. Aislinn wondered at the man. He might succeed in reaching the northern hills and live out a hard life in the bleak barren lands, stealing from others for livelihood or join Atheling Edgar and his cause, but there would still be Wulfgar.

With his name in her mind, tears came to her eyes. She could only hope that he could somehow contrive to rescue or ransom them. Indeed, she could only hope that Bolsgar had reached him in time to warn him of the trap that lay in wait and that he still lived. She could not bear Ragnor's boasting of the snares he had set for Wulfgar and knew a deep fear that he might have fallen.

The sun rose high and the road became dusty. Bryce woke and fed fitfully, then whined and mewled when his mother would not put him down for a romp.

Ragnor turned in his saddle and snarled, "Cease that bastard's whining!"

Aislinn crooned and sang softly to her son, rocking him in her arms and he finally quieted and settled himself for another nap. They had left the lowlands of the rivers and entered the rolling, heath-strewn, midland hills. They passed the ruins of a small village, the cottages tumbled and roofless. As they trotted slowly through what had been the square, a withered crone sidled forth from the shadows. She had lost an eye and her right arm hung stunted and useless while in the left she held a crude wooden bowl which she thrust toward Ragnor.

"A copper, your lordship?" she said with a twisted smile. "A copper for a poor old—"

Ragnor kicked at her and with amazing agility for her ravaged frame she avoided him. Aislinn paused and the hag renewed her plea.

"A copper, a bauble, a morsel, your ladyship."

In pity Aislinn tossed her the remains of a dried loaf of bread, realizing as she did so she might be giving away her own meal. Ragnor sneered at her charity and urged them onward. He halted suddenly at the edge of the square, drawing his sword and facing Aislinn.

"That brat delays us and I have no use for two hostages."

Aislinn drew Bryce to her and spoke with the determination of a mother. "You gave your word, Ragnor. To kill him you must take me first and then you would have no hostage when Wulfgar comes."

Her hand came from beneath the woolen cloak with the small dagger clutched desperately in it. The other men drew away agog and Ragnor cursed at his folly of not having taken the weapon from her sooner. Vachel rested his arms on the horn of his saddle and grinned.

"What say you, cousin? Will you let the proud vixen kill herself?"

Gwyneth of all knew Aislinn and seeing a chance, kicked her own steed forward to crash into Aislinn's and snatched the dagger while the other grasped for support and clung fearfully to her son. Regaining control of the punch, Aislinn turned anger bright eyes toward Wulfgar's sister.

"Traitor!" she hissed. "Always the traitor. Poor Gwyneth."

Ragnor laughed and sheathed his sword. "Aah, my dove, will you never yield? I would slay whom I will and you can change it naught. But I have given my word and unless you force me to, I have no intention of harming the lad. I would but leave him with yonder hag and give her ample food and a few pence for her trouble."

"Nay!" Aislinn gasped. "You cannot!"

"There are goats in yonder glade," he argued. "And the old woman would have no shortage of milk. And if as you say Wulfgar, Sweyn, or others do follow, they will surely find the child and fetch him home."

Aislinn found hope in the last statement and realized she bore a better chance to escape unburdened. Finally with a heavy sob and tears flowing down her face she yielded her son to Gwyneth who took the babe and carried him back to where the crone squatted in the dust clutching her crust of bread. Bryce raised a howl in a lusty voice for one so young and even from a distance Gwyneth seemed glad to lay him in the arm of the old crone. She could be seen to haggle and then she counted out coins, gave over a small skin of wine and a portion from their supplies. Mounting the dappled mare she returned in haste as the old woman raised wondering eyes after them.

Now the journey began in earnest. Ragnor pushed the band as he could not before. Soon their steeds began to wheeze and gasp for breath. They halted in a shaded spot and the saddles were drawn off the exhausted beasts and placed on fresh mounts that Ragnor had taken from Wulfgar's stable.

As they rested, Ragnor and Gwyneth drew off to one side and could be seen laughing and talking as if they exchanged some jest. When the new steeds were finally readied and watered, Aislinn dragged herself again into the saddle and watched with saddened heart as her own dapple-gray was turned loose and trotted slowly away. Ragnor closed up beside her on his mount and with a strange smile on his lips, took the reins from her hands, shaking them over the destry's head.

"I'll lead a while, my dove, in case you would like to return."

He led off slowly, letting Gwyneth and Vachel and the other men move a distance ahead. After some moments he laughed aloud and slowed until they rode side by side.

"It seems Gwyneth has done us both one better," he chuckled. To Aislinn's raised brow he explained, "She convinced the hag she would soon need someone to beg for her and that a young lad well trained would be worthy aid."

Aislinn gasped, fear making a cold hollow in her stomach, but Ragnor continued.

"And before Gwyneth left she warned the hag of an

evil Norman knight who might possibly come searching for the boy."

He laughed aloud and before Aislinn could recover, spurred his horse to a gallop dragging hers with it. She clutched for support and as they neared the others he shouted back over his shoulder:

"Don't think of jumping, Aislinn. You'd surely break a bone, and even not, I'd tie you across the saddle and that, my dove, might somewhat bruise your dignity."

Aislinn held on in dejection and fear and with lowered eyes watched the flashing hooves beneath her churn mile after mile between her and Bryce.

That night she choked down a meal barely warmed before the fire was doused. She was lashed by her wrists to a tree, and drained by hopelessness, she soon sank into the full stupor of utter fatigue.

Wulfgar and Sweyn rode side by side. The two great destriers lightened of heavy chain and armor loped easily along. No word was spoken but in absolute necessity and then brief questions at village and farm, thus the trail was drawn and the pace never slackened. The close observer might have seen that the great ax never left the Norseman's grip and that the hilt of the long broadsword was fondled constantly by the Norman knight.

There was a deadliness about the two and a sense of purpose that would not be denied. When a halt was called, a double handful of grain was carefully fed to the huge horses and then they drank and briefly grazed while the men chewed on leathery strips of meat and caught quick naps in the sun.

Well past midnight a restless peasant wondered at the steady drum of hooves thundering by his cottage. Wulfgar knew no exhaustion. He was well trained to the hardship required by the martial calling. He rode relaxed in the saddle yet his thoughts ranged far ahead. Perhaps Aislinn and the babe had both been slain by now. His mind recoiled at the idea, trying to imagine life without Aislinn's happy laughter ringing in his ears and here his musings found only a black, gaping dread. It came to him as bright sunlight in the night that he loved Aislinn beyond all reason, beyond his own life. He accepted the fact and found he relished the taste of it.

He smiled to himself in the blackness and spoke to the

Viking who rode at his side. Though his voice was soft, there was a note of death in it that made Sweyn try to see his face in the gloom.

"Ragnor is mine! Come what may, Ragnor is mine."

Soon there was a trail to follow, the cold coals of a campfire, the flattened grass where a maid might have rested. The eagerness of the two men became intent and they rode steadily past other wayfarers who paused to stare after them.

Then in the broken highlands of the north shore near Scotland, they topped a hill and on a distant knoll caught a glimpse of six riders, one whose mount was led. The great warhorses seemed to catch the fever of their masters and, though tired, stretched their mighty sinews a bit more.

Three slowed slightly in the group ahead, dropping back while one knight and two women fled on. The distance narrowed and the three saw a favor in that only two pursued. At a shout from Vachel they halted, drew swords and braced themselves against those two.

As the hunters saw their game to earth, a long, undulating war cry from Wulfgar's throat ended on a note that raised the hackles of a nearby fox and sent it scurrying to its den. The great sword flashed on high and hummed in the wind and the war ax swung in a tight circle above the Viking's crown. At the wailing sound from the far off hill, Ragnor pulled his steed to a halt and cursed the fates for he knew Wulfgar's cry and worse, he knew Wulfgar.

The two warriors raced, never pausing, at the three who confronted them. Both stood in their saddles and leaned far forward. Wulfgar clasped the Hun's heaving flanks hard with his knees and a short lance length away he jerked the reins and the Hun raised up and crashed not into the other steed but crushed the hapless rider beneath his shield. His sword hued through the other's shield and half the arm that held it before the man could strike. Another blow and it was finished.

With a surge the Hun thrust himself free of the tangle and whirled about, but there was no need. Vachel had fallen with his leg shattered and knelt in the dust glaring up at Sweyn.

"For Beaufonte!" Sweyn roared and the ax hurtled downward. Vachel sank slowly into the dust and paid full score for his loyalty to Ragnor.

Sweyn jerked his ax free from Vachel's helm and shouted thanks to Wodin but too soon. His great destrier slowly slid to its knees with the hilt of Vachel's sword protruding from its ribs. Sweyn stepped free and as the horse writhed in agony, the Norseman's broad face mirrored the pain he saw. His ax rose and fell and the loyal charger collapsed in the dust.

Wulfgar dismounted and cleaned his sword on the cloak of one that had fallen. With his foot he turned Vachel face up with eyes wide and unseeing and with trickles of blood marking uneven paths from his brow to his jaw. Wulfgar's gaze lifted to the now dwindling figures that rode beyond.

"I must go on," he said. He met Sweyn's eye. "See to these and return to Darkenwald. God willing I will meet you there with Aislinn and the babe."

Sweyn nodded and gave a last bit of warning. "See to your back."

They grasped each other's hands for a moment, then Wulfgar swung back into the saddle and was off at a merciless pace that spared neither man nor beast.

Ragnor had wasted little time. As Wulfgar's battle cry ended he led the women off again as fast as the winded steeds could race across the steepening hills. Aislinn rode behind him, strangely calm. Assured now that Wulfgar lived, she knew a warmth in her breast and a smile half parted her lips. Glancing over his shoulder at her, Ragnor found little ease in the serenity he saw in her face.

The afternoon drew out and still they raced on, the horses stumbling and wheezing, froth covering their sides but whipped ever onward. The three riders paced along a cliff above a wide, still loch that glistened silvery in the lengthening shadows. They came to a break in the sheer wall and began a slow, careful descent. Their breath frosted and swirled out before them. Aislinn's hands, gripping the horse's mane, grew numb with the cold yet she dared not loosen her hold for fear of tumbling down the rocky ravine. Before them stretched a thin bar of sand leading to a low island where there was the tumbled remains of some ancient Pictish stronghold. Ragnor led them down the break in the cliff along the sandy bar into the ruins. They halted in a large courtyard, bordered on three sides by a low stone wall and on the seaward side by the higher remaining wall of a temple. Within the ancient courtyard rose a block of stone with crude loops at its corners, possibly where the living sacrifices of pagan rites were offered up.

Ragnor snatched Aislinn from the saddle and bore her to the stone, leaving Gwyneth to dismount herself and tie her mare secure with the other two horses. Ragnor bound Aislinn's wrists together to a loop with the use of leather strips and as she shivered with the cold, removed his own mantle and drew it close about her. He lingered a moment beside her, gazing upon her fine features with an odd mixture of lust and respect, and he wondered how it might have been with this woman had their meeting been different. Perhaps the world would have been an easy apple for him to pluck with her at his side. His thoughts took him to that sorry night he first laid eyes upon her. How could he have known then that in his efforts to have her he would be led to ruin? Now Wulfgar, if he had managed to escape Vachel and the other two, was on his trail like a wolf scenting blood.

Wulfgar pushed the Hun to his limit and as the beast stood wheezing, knew that he had given his last. He dismounted and gave the horse the rest of the grain and rubbed him well with the empty bag. Turning the steed back towards Sweyn, he slapped him on the rump and sent him off in a flurry of hooves. Wulfgar started walking and as he went he chewed a mouthful of dried meat and grain, adding water until he could swallow, then washed it down with a healthy draught. He took off the belt and broadsword and slung it over his shoulder so the blade lay along his spine with the hilt easily reached just behind his neck. Now he broke into a trot, loping along, his head down following the faint trail of hoofprints on the hard ground. He was in the gloaming when he came to the brow of a cliff and saw an island and the glimmer of firelight on it. The tide was rising and the sand bar was slim. By the time he reached it, dusk had deepened and a good foot of water covered the strip of sand. Ragnor had planned well, he thought. Now a silent approach was impossible.

Withdrawing to a rock in the shadows Wulfgar waited the rising of the moon, chewing another mouthful of dry food as he watched the mists rise from the water in the frosty night. The black hills about the loch seemed to gather their shoulders and hunch their backs against the

491

darkening night. He climbed the cliff a ways that he might look down into the square and from there he could see three figures in the firelight; Gwyneth moving about near the fire, Ragnor standing where he could watch the shallow strand and Aislinn huddled in the folds of a mantle by a great block of stone. And the babe—where was he?

Slowly the night lightened and a great orange half moon rose to perch on a moor. Wulfgar knew the hour had arrived and he smiled. Tipping back his head he gave vent to his battle cry, a low pealing moan that rose on the night winds and echoed from the cliffs, ending in a wail of rage.

In the tumbled ruins below, Ragnor started and flung up his head. The howling cry that resounded across the loch held him motionless as if he could hear naught but the ring of death in it. Beside the stone Aislinn lifted her gaze to peer into the blackness beyond the fire. She knew Wulfgar's battle cry, yet the raising moan sent a shiver up her spine. It brought to mind a great black wolf who had stared at her across another fire with the wisdom not of his kind.

With a gasp Gwyneth whirled to Ragnor with a fearful look, her pallor appearing ghostly white in the glow of the meager light, but as the last echo of Wulfgar's war cry ended Ragnor's face twisted in a snarl. With long, angry strides he crossed to Aislinn, slipping a short knife from his belt. Aislinn's breath caught in her throat then she glared at him in open defiance, expecting to feel that sharp blade plunging into her breast, but with a quick motion Ragnor cut through the thong binding one wrist, setting it free. She stared up at him, wondering what next would follow, but he gave a cruel smile, sheathing the blade, and pulled her to her feet. He crushed her against his mail clad chest and his dark eyes pierced hers to their very depth. She gave him no resistance but hung limp in his arms. His hand moved slowly, caressingly down her cheek as if he were held for a moment in a trance by her beauty. His lean brown fingers took her chin in their iron grip. With no regard for Gwyneth who gaped at them in stunned surprise, he kissed Aislinn, bruising her soft lips as he forced them apart beneath his. Her hand came up against his side, straining to push him away, but he gave her no respite. His lips lingered above hers with his breath falling hot and heavy against them.

"He'll not take you, dove, I swear," he muttered huskily. "He'll not have you."

Gwyneth approached behind him and her tired face struggled to shape itself into an alluring smile. "Ragnor, love, what is it that makes you bestow your favors on her? Do you seek to raise my brother's ire? Take care, dear one. He is angered enough without you fondling his bitch before his eyes."

Ragnor threw his head back in mirth, his laughter echoing from the cliffs. Slowly the sound died, leaving only silence to hold the land. He stepped behind Aislinn and pulled her back against him as his eyes swept the darkness beyond the sand bar.

"Wulfgar, come and see your mate," he called. He snatched the mantles from Aislinn's shoulders, letting the garments fall in a heap at their feet. The fire cast its flickering light against her slim form clothed in velvet gunna and with a slow deliberateness that made Aislinn gasp his hands moved over her breasts, fondling them leisurely as if to torture the man who might be watching somewhere in the ebony shadows of the cliff.

"See, Wulfgar, bastard of Darkenwald," Ragnor shouted to that blackness. "She is mine now as she was before. "Come and take her if you can."

Again silence answered him and Aislinn could hear only the sound of Ragnor's heavy breathing against her ear. With a choked and angry sob she struggled, but in vain, for he held her firm in his savage grip. Ragnor chuckled evilly and his hands moved again, this time to the narrow waist then more boldly down along her hips.

"Ragnor!" The protest came from Gwyneth who saw his intent, and her brows drew together in her agony. "Would you torture me also?"

"Be still," he flung. "Leave me be!"

His caressing ventured further as his hand slid downward over Aislinn's belly and she bolted against him in outrage.

"Must I take her before your eyes, bastard?" he yelled with a laugh.

There was no reply from Wulfgar, only the pressing quiet. For a moment Ragnor continued with his lustful strokes until he finally realized nothing would come of it. Wulfgar would not let rage goad him into a foolish act.

"I'll finish with this later," he sneered in Aislinn's ear. "But first there is the matter of your husband's death."

He stepped from behind her, pulling her wrist to the other corner of the stone where another loop was carved and tied it there so she again faced the fire but now stood with arms spread.

With a half crooning sound Gwyneth sought to cling to Ragnor, but he snatched away with a growl.

"Begone, she dog," he spat, venom crackling in his voice and his dark eyes sneering. "I have tasted the honey of Heaven itself. Do you think I fancy the favors of a skinny bitch over hers? Take your quivering flanks into the streets if you find them lacking."

Gwyneth's features sagged in despair and she gazed at him unable to believe his words.

"Ragnor, you must relent. Soon you will meet Wulfgar and 'tis evil omen to take the kiss of an unwilling maid into battle. Let me give you a token to carry into the fray."

She half spread her arms in her anxious plea, but Ragnor retorted in rage.

"Silence!" he commanded.

He strode to the fire and threw more wood on the blaze as he peered at the hills, but Gwyneth sobbed and ran to him, trying to throw her arms about him.

"Nay, my love," she wept. "You have found me in passion willing. Do you yet strive upon that purloined piece? Take my love with you."

Ragnor flung his arm up and pushed her from him in distaste, but she returned to him again. With a curse he lashed out with the branch he held in his hand, striking her head. Gwyneth stumbled back, half falling against the wall where her head struck with a sickening thud. A dark stain was smeared down the stone as she slid down it then fell to her hands and knees with her head hanging between her arms. A dark glistening stain spread through her flaxen hair as blood flowed and matted her pale tresses. She groaned softly and Ragnor threw the stick which careened off the wall and struck her in the back.

"Get thee gone, bony one," he sneered. "I have no further use for you."

Gwyneth dragged herself to the stone portal and into the darkness beyond. Ragnor watched her go, hurling a last sneer of contempt in her direction before he turned to scan the shoreline opposite the island for some sign of Wulfgar. As before there was nothing. No sound, no sight of him. Ragnor paced the grounds, now and then to stop and stare off into the distance as if he sensed Wulfgar's nearness. With a curse he swung into his saddle and began to make a wide sweep outside the ruins, bending low over his steed so he could see any trail that might have been left. He reined his steed to a sudden halt on the upland end of the island when he came across a log pushed against the shore and a wet trail leading from it to a jumble of fallen blocks. He paused for a brief moment before he charged the horse to the far end of the spit and urged him into the shadows there.

Silence reigned once more. It was broken only by the nervous stamping of the other two horses that stood tethered in the square. Aislinn held her breath as she strained to hear some sound of Wulfgar's presence, then from the darkness behind her she heard her husband's voice rise tauntingly.

"Ragnor, thief of Darkenwald. Come and taste my blade! Will your black heart forever war on women and children? Come out now and fight a man."

Aislinn's heart pounded in her ears.

"Wulfgar!" Ragnor's call echoed in the night. "Show yourself and I will do likewise, bastard. Let me know that you are not at my back."

Aislinn heard a gasp of surprise from Ragnor as Wulfgar seemed to raise from the ground at the upland of the square like a spectre, shaggy and menacing in the blackness of the night. He drew the long blade from the scabbard and shook it over his head.

"Come out, thief!" His voice rang clear and he began to trot forward. "Come and meet my steel, or must I turn the very rocks in search of you?"

In answer Ragnor's destrier thundered out of the dark beyond the fire. Aislinn screamed in terror for in the small space it seemed he came at her. She fought her bonds until her wrists bled but swallowed any other outcry, fearing more that it would distract Wulfgar.

Ragnor swung a chained mace with long deadly spikes as he charged at his enemy. He must do the slaying while weight of arms made the difference. Wulfgar waited until the mace swung high for the stroke then dived to the right, across the path of the horse. The spiked ball whistled through the air where he had been. Wulfgar struck on his shoulder on the ground and rolled, then as the destrier swept past him he swung his sword at its heels. The edge took the tendons just above the rear fetlock and the beast screamed in pain as he stumbled and crashed to the ground, unable to stand.

Ragnor threw himself clear and turned with the mace in his hand. It was not a weapon to be used against a skilled swordsman and he hurled it at his adversary, Wulfgar easily avoided it but it gave Ragnor a chance to draw his sword and set himself for battle. His eyes flashed in hatred as he faced the other and he gained confidence in seeing that Wulfgar was unarmored and bore only the long broadsword. Any touch of his blade would scar and maim. A warrior once lamed was worthless and Ragnor held a brief vision of the great Wulfgar begging in the streets. He laughed and braced his shield against his shoulder as he closed to combat. Ragnor swung but Wulfgar moved swiftly away and left a wide gash ringing on the edge of the dark knight's shield.

Ragnor could only stand feet planted and take the brunt of the two-handed blows on his shield and strike when Wulfgar closed with him. Wulfgar kept up a constant rain of steel, more to harass than damage. The weight of the armor and shield began to tell on his opponent. As on the tourney field Ragnor could find no opening in the front his antagonist presented him. He felt the same sickness in his gut and knew this was no joust but a battle to the death. He slowed, sweltering in the sweat beneath the mail and leather. Wulfgar reached the shield and took his sword in both hands. Now they met toe to toe and still Ragnor's blade was ever met to Wulfgar's and went no further.

Ragnor saw that Wulfgar was suffering under the strain as well as he. Wulfgar wore no armor and thus must meet every blow with a parry and still seek to punish his enemy. He stepped back before Ragnor's renewed attack which struck at the momentarily exposed leg. The blow was partly blocked but still laid open the legging and the boot beneath, drawing blood. Ragnor roared his success and raised his sword high as Wulfgar fell to one knee. Aislinn cringed in terror for her husband, but Wulfgar saw Ragnor's intent. Still crouching, he laid his sword flatside along his shoulder to turn the chopping stroke away and send it into the ground, half numbing the other's arm.

Wulfgar's vest and tunic were cut through by the force upon his own blade and blood streamed from his shoulder, yet he struck in return and Ragnor staggered back, his arm severed to the bone.

Ragnor shrieked, clutching his arm and leapt across the fire. He snarled in frustration then paled as he saw Wulfgar approach him with the long blade ready. He looked death in the eye and fled.

He ran to the doorway in the standing wall and there stopped short, seeming to pause. A rattling gasp came from his throat and he grasped the doorway to brace himself. Aislinn looked questioningly to Wulfgar who waited, prepared to do further battle. He stepped to her quickly and cut her free, keeping an eye on that one by the stone portal.

Ragnor leaned against the wall and slowly turned to face them, his mouth gaping in surprise. Their gazes followed his as he stared down to where the jeweled hilt of Aislinn's dagger stood out from his left breast. The long, narrow blade had slid neatly between the links of his mail and plunged deep. Grasping it with his good hand, he pulled it from him and a gush of blood followed to run down his chest. He lifted his eyes to them in stunned disbelief.

"She's slain me, the bitch."

His knees crumpled slowly and he pitched forward onto his face and lay still. A movement in the darkness behind him drew their attention and Gwyneth staggered from the shadows. An ugly bruise swelled on her temple and stood stark against her pale ashen face as she gazed down at Ragnor's form. It was a macabre mask she turned to them. A slim trickle of blood ran from her ear and another from her nose. Her eyes were blank and the sad pathos of her seemed to plead their forgiveness.

"He said he loved me and took all I could give, then he cast me aside like some dirty—"

She sobbed and took a step toward them but stumbled and fell to lay still weeping in wretched misery. Aislinn flew to her and cradled the flaxen head upon her lap.

"Oh, Aislinn, I've been a fool," Gwyneth sighed as her eyes found the other's. "I listened to naught but my own vanity and desires. Forgive me, for I baited you cruelly in my lust to have some worthy post and honors. 'Twas never mine to possess. What is a bastard's lot?"

Wulfgar came to stand near her feet and gaze upon his sister. She lifted her eyes to him and smiled lamely as if at some wry jest.

"I could not bear the thought of walking in your stead and taking the world's abuse, though you tutored them well on the merits of honoring a bastard." She coughed and a red spittle came to her lips. "Our mother spoke to hurt your father and began an endless lie, Wulfgar." She closed her eyes and took a deep breath. "On her deathbed she pleaded that I should bear you the news and set all aright, but I could not. I was a coward. So now you will finally learn." She opened her eyes and gazed at him once more. " 'Tis no bastard you be, Wulfgar, but true son of Bolsgar." She smiled at his lifted brows. "Aye, 'twas I and our brother, long dead, who should have borne your title. Falsworth and I were sired by her lover when Bolsgar roamed the lands to do battle for the king. Forgive me, Wulfgar."

She coughed again.

"Oh Lord, forgive my sins. Forgive my—" With a long sigh she relaxed and gave up her life.

Wulfgar knelt and watched in thoughtful silence as Aislinn carefully wiped the blood and grime from Gwyneth's at last serene face. When he spoke, his voice was soft and husky.

"I hope she has found her peace. Be it known that I forgive her. Most of the sin belonged to our mother and in her twisted vengeance she tortured us all."

Aislinn's voice came sharper. "I will forgive her only if we can set this one thing aright. She gave our son to some haggard crone, one who begged among the ruins of a town."

Wulfgar rose, his face twisting in anger. He went to where the two remaining horses stood and seized a saddle from the ground, but suddenly calmed, remembering the scavaging gulls which would come with the dawn. He could not bear the thought of his sister's bones lying bleached and naked on the sand. Replacing the saddle, he turned to Aislinn and sighed.

"One more night will make no difference."

He spread pelts upon the ground away from the two who lay near the portal and drawing Aislinn down with him, pulled the mantles tightly about them against the chill winds that sighed among the tumbled stones. Aislinn lay with her head upon his shoulder and took comfort in his strong arms that encircled her and held her secure against him. In their exhaustion they found sleep.

The first hint of dawn broke the eastern haze to find them awake and while Aislinn prepared food Wulfgar scraped two shallow graves in the hard packed sand. He buried Ragnor with his saddle, shield and sword and Gwyneth with her hands clasping the small dagger that formed a cross upon her breast and the fur lined cloak shrouding her thin frame. The graves were filled and Wulfgar labored hard to place slabs of heavy stone above each one to keep them safe from wolves. He stood for a long time searching for words but found none. At last he turned away and now hurrying saddled the horses. They eased their hunger, and lifting Aislinn onto her steed and swinging into the saddle of the other, Wulfgar led the way, splashing across the shallowing bar.

They rode with no thought for themselves, urging their mounts along the road at their fastest pace until they reached the tumbled ruins. They beat among them well, finding a crude hut of leaning planks and boards yet the ashes were cold and the pallet stripped. There was no trace of the path the old woman took leaving the town. They swung wider, stopping at every village and though some knew of the hag, none had seen her on the roads.

The second day wore out and darkness threatened and they stood, having come full circle once again, amid the ruins of the hamlet. Aislinn groaned her despair and sank slowly to the ground sobbing in abject defeat. Wulfgar bent and tenderly raised her to her feet, wrapping her in the shelter of his sturdy arms. Her cries were muffled against his pelts as he gently brushed her hair away from her ear and kissed her there. Of all the trials Aislinn had known this was the one that broke her. She had no more spirit, no will or drive. She was robbed of strength and simply hung in his arms, sobbing her sorrow against his chest. It was a long while until the tears would come no more. Her chest ached with the weeping and her throat was raw. Wulfgar lifted her gently in his arms and bore her to the shallow shelter of a broken wall where he sat her down. He labored until he had a small fire to drive away the chill of the lowering night. The sky to the west was stained red as blood but faded and arched above their heads with a deep blue, and as he gazed up Wulfgar saw cold bright stars appear one by one. It seemed he could almost touch them. He glanced down at Aislinn where she sat dumbly staring into the fire. Kneeling, he took her hands in his and would have given her of his own strength if he could. She turned violet eyes to him and there was nothing in them but the empty agony of her loss.

"My son, Wulfgar," she moaned. "I want my son."

A racking dry sob shook her shoulders and he sat beside her, drawing her across his lap until she lay cradled in his arms. He stared into the fire for a long time and his voice was low and tender as he spoke.

"I know little of love, Aislinn, but much of things lost. A mother's tenderness I could never win. A father's love was torn from my aching arms. I have hoarded my love with a miser's zeal and now it all burns within me here."

He looked into the eyes that watched him carefully now. His gray ones were light with the open innocence of a youth. He smoothed a coppery curl from her cheek.

"First love," he whispered softly. "Heart's love, do not betray me. Take what I would give and make it part of you as it is all of me. Bear my love within you full time as you did with the child then with a glad cry bring it forth and we shall share it ever more. I offer you my life, my love, my arm, my sword, my eye, my heart. Take them all. Spare not the least portion. If you cast it away then I am dead and shall wander the moors howling like a mindless beast."

Aislinn smiled now and he kissed her lips with tenderness.

"There will be other sons, perhaps a daughter, and none shall doubt the sire."

Aislinn threw her arms about his neck and with a low sob, murmured, "I love you, Wulfgar. Hold me tight. Hold me for all time."

He whispered softly in her ear, "I love you, Aislinn. Drink of my love. Let it be your strength."

She drew back and lay against his arm, caressing his cheek.

"Let us go," she said, half pleading. "I cannot stay here another night. Let us go home to Darkenwald. I have a need to feel my own things around me."

"Aye," he agreed and with the word he rose and began to scatter the fire.

As she neared the horses, Aislinn grinned ruefully and

rubbed her bruised posterior. "I shall never again enjoy a ride as much as of old," she mused.

Wulfgar stopped and considered her thoughtfully. "There is a craft I spied while quenching my thirst. Aye, 'twould ease your plight considerably. Come, 'tis but a short way."

Taking her hand and leading the horses, he led her to a nearby copse of willows. Parting the hanging branches he showed her where beneath them lay a boat, a long and narrow craft hewn from a single trunk. He bowed graciously.

"Your royal barge, milady." At her puzzled frown, he grinned. "This stream joins the one that sweeps the marsh near Darkenwald."

Her relief at not having to take to the saddle again was complete as she lifted her gaze to him. He nodded and turned the horses loose to wander where they would, placing the trappings and gear in the prow of the boat. He seated Aislinn in the middle where she could lay back comfortably against the saddle and tucked her mantle around her. Pushing the craft into the water, he stepped in and seated himself near the stern, then lifting the short paddle, steered it into the swift current.

Time ceased to be. Aislinn slept for a while then woke briefly, feeling the even thrusts that drove the boat onward. She stared upward at willows that waved against the sky as if sobbing their anguish to the world. She watched stars drift through the gaunt, barren branches of an oak and the moon rise blood red, then golden, paling as it tore itself free from the breast of the moor. She drifted again into restless slumber. Thus through the night it was. For her a snatch of sleep, a moment of waking and Wulfgar ever driving the boat along the winding stream.

Wulfgar's mind was blank. The son he had just begun to love was lost from him now and he might never again see that bright tousled hair or hear that cheery gurgle. His thoughts began to churn and against that labor he lifted his arms, dipping the paddle again and again until the ache drove some of the pain from his brain.

The first gray light of dawn outlined a friendly oak on a well known hill, a sleepy town then the great hall looming black in the midst of it and on a further rise the near completed castle of Darkenwald. The boat grated on the sand and Wulfgar stepped into the water to drag it ashore.

He returned and taking Aislinn in his arms, carried her to where her feet could touch the dry leafy bed of the shore. He led through the trees, holding her hand behind him on the narrow way. The path was familiar to him now. It had been another November morn, a little warmer perhaps, that had seen him on the back of the Hun, searching out the unknown trail leading through the woods and copse and finally to a fair maid bathing in a cold stream. So time did fly, with joy mending the wounds, or the hurt wrenching the gaiety from their hearts.

Aislinn sighed and lifted a sad and weary gaze to the growing light of dawn, holding an empty ache within her. They neared the manor and Wulfgar held the portal open as she entered then stepped in behind her.

They stopped and stared about them for a moment in confusion, stunned by the light and noise of the place. No one it seemed was missing. Bolsgar and Sweyn were loudly debating with Gowain and Milbourne; and Kerwick, sitting in a chair by the hearth, was carefully tended by Haylan. His leg and head bore bandages but his spirits seemed high. When his eyes met Haylan's there was a mutual softening. And in a dark corner with her back to the rest, sat Maida, giving no recognition of the arrivals.

The entire scene was completely out of place for a hall that should have been hushed and in mourning, especially at this early hour. Both Aislinn and Wulfgar were unwilling to break the easy mood of the place with the dark news they bore yet approached closer to the hearth until Bolsgar spied them and with a jovial greeting came up from his chair.

"So, you are finally here," he chortled. "Good! Good! The watchers saw you coming from the tower." He turned his gaze to Aislinn and with a quick perusal, formed his own conclusions. "Well, daughter, I see that smitten knave did you no harm." He peered at Wulfgar as he lifted a questioning brow. "Did you kill him, I hope? I've grown to favor this lass's company and would take it much amiss if that dandy would threaten her again."

Wulfgar shook his head negatively and before he could explain Sweyn jumped to his feet.

"What is this?" the Viking roared. "Can I not leave you foundling youths to perform a simple deed?" His laughter rumbled in his throat and he gave Bolsgar a hearty clap on the back that left him at a loss for breath. " 'Twould

502

seem we two must take up the chase and see this matter finished. Mayhap this time you'll not find an excuse to delay you."

Wulfgar glanced from one to the other, unable to correct the two as Sweyn's comment roused another question in his mind.

"Aye," Bolsgar returned with jovial sarcasm. "And I would not trust you to lend a hand in the slaying as you seem to have a penchant against sparing me any labors."

Sweyn hooted. "Why, you old Saxon warhorse. Could you not see my hands were full already keeping that rutting stud from those flimsy mares Ragnor let loose? When I passed you on the road, I could do naught but wave a hand."

The Norseman turned to Wulfgar and explained.

"I camped at night and the Hun awoke me in the cold morn with his nose in my face." He chuckled, glancing briefly at Hlynn who stirred a brewis at the hearth, and continued loudly. "Why, I dreamt at first 'twas some fair young lass who nuzzled me, then that stinking stallion snorted down my neck and it seemed the only thing to do was ride him back behind those other steeds I found along the way." Sweyn guffawed. "They all turned out to be mares and that braying mule of yours, Wulfgar, nearly killed me in his zeal, especially when I came across that dapple-gray of Lady Aislinn's." He gestured toward Bolsgar. "Now this ornery Saxon claims I deserted him when he was in dire need."

"A lame excuse," Bolsgar grunted. "You could see 'twas I the more burdened."

Wulfgar gazed questioningly at his father. "What pressed you so sorely?"

The old man shrugged. " 'Twas a bit of baggage you left behind."

Sweyn interrupted, giving no regard for Wulfgar's puzzlement. "But what happened to that knave, Ragnor? Did he escape to the northern climes with Gwyneth?"

Wulfgar shook his head again. "Nay," he murmured. "They did each other in."

Bolsgar shook his head sadly and his voice grew husky as he spoke. "Aaah, Gwyneth, poor lass. Perhaps she's at peace now." He sniffed and wiped his sleeve across his face.

A brief mourning silence held the room and Aislinn

leaned wearily against Wulfgar who drew her close with an arm about her shoulders. She felt the warmth of home yet it fell lacking. There was an emptiness in her that did not fit with the gaiety and laughter that had greeted them. Her eyes roamed about, noting Haylan and Kerwick in close companionship, Miderd and Hlynn laboring at the kettles to prepare the morning meal and Maida, still huddled in her corner.

Sweyn coughed, breaking the quiet. "We buried good Beaufonte."

Gowain rose from his chair, nodding. "Aye, we did. But the three of us and the Friar were poorly met to keep the Viking from laying him in a boat and setting a torch to it."

"Forsooth," Milbourne chuckled. "We did see our friend laid to rest, but Sweyn's manner of mourning has put us all to rout."

"Yea," Bolsgar agreed. "In truth, it has lowered by no small amount the supply of ale and wine for the winter's chill."

" 'Twas to honor a valued friend," Wulfgar murmured. He looked to Sweyn. "Rest the day, for tomorrow we must be upon the roads again with Gowain and Milbourne to search out an old woman with a withered arm."

"Why need you that old crone?" Bolsgar inquired. "She'll rob ye blind."

Wulfgar gazed at the elder in some surprise. "Do you know of her?" he demanded in anxious tones and he became aware that Aislinn's attention had perked up with his father's words. Was it too much to hope Bolsgar could lead them to the old hag and mayhaps to the babe also?

"I had dealings with her," Bolsgar replied. "She sold me a bit of baggage upon my urging and it took some haggling, for she was set on the piece and would not easily come around. But with a handful of silver and a show of my blade, I managed to best the bargain."

Wulfgar peered at him suspiciously. "Of what baggage do you speak?"

Bolsgar called over his shoulder. "Maida!"

"Yea!" That one answered as if piqued at being so rudely summoned.

"Fetch the baggage here! We must teach these two not to cast aside their baggage so carelessly. Yea, fetch me my grandson!"

Aislinn's head snapped up and Wulfgar turned a surprised gaze on his father. Maida rose and faced them, holding a bundled form in her arms. At sight of the tiny head adorned with coppery curls, Aislinn gave a happy shriek, tears flooding her eyes, and ran to her mother to snatch the babe from her arms. Cuddling him close against her, she whirled around in an ecstatic circle as everyone looked on with broad smiles. Wulfgar laughed as Bryce let out a squall of protest at being so heartily squeezed.

"My love, take care. He cannot bear so much loving."

"Oh, Wulfgar! Wulfgar!" she cried gayly, coming to him, and she found no better words to speak.

Wulfgar smiled down at her tenderly and then feeling as if a great burden had been lifted from his chest, he took the lad from his mother's arms, swinging him up in the air to Bryce's delight. He squealed in glee and chuckled but Maida clucked as if she were a mother hen.

"That youngling will rue the day at having a sire such as you. Go gently with my grandchild."

Wulfgar looked at her, doubting her sanity, and held Bryce more carefully, yet he saw in Maida a new found firmness of mind and body and glimpsed a beauty he had never noted before. The scars on her face had faded and a healthy glow replaced them. He knew that in her youth she would have rivaled Aislinn to behold.

"What is it that assures you that I'm his sire?" he asked.

"Of course he's your son," Bolsgar broke in. "Just as you are my son."

Wulfgar raised a questioning brow to him, but the old man reached out a finger and pulled Bryce's swaddling down to reveal a reddish mark upon his buttock. " 'Tis a birthmark of mine—if you will accept my word since I will not display it for your eyes. As I brought the babe back home there came a need to change his britches. As soon as I saw the mark I knew you were my son and he your son."

Wulfgar seemed bewildered. "But I have no such mark."

Bolsgar shrugged. "Neither did my father, but his father bore it, as well as the grandsons of each so marked."

"Gwyneth gave the news to me that I am your true son," Wulfgar murmured. "And our mother gave Gwyneth

505

the tidings on her deathbed that she and Falsworth were sired by another."

Bolsgar sighed deeply. "Perhaps if I had left your mother less in my venturing after war, she might have been content. Now it seems I failed you all sadly."

Wulfgar clasped his shoulder and smiled. "I have gained a father but lost William's sympathy. Still, the trade is one of wealth unknown."

In Wulfgar's arms Bryce gazed wonderingly about, chewing on a small fist, his eyes wide with curiosity. Maida crooned as she reached out to pet him then looked askance to his father.

"There was never any doubt he came by your seed, Wulfgar. Can you not tell a virgin when you've laid one?"

"What is this?" Wulfgar demanded. "Have you gone daft again, woman? Ragnor—"

Maida cackled and turned to peer at her daughter. "This one wielded well what Ragnor could not raise, eh, daughter? And that crowing Norman cock claimed what he never had."

"Mother," Aislinn pleaded.

Maida lifted a small packet hanging from her girdle and waggled it before her daughter's eyes. "Know you this?"

Aislinn gazed for a moment at the small bag, feeling a bit perplexed, then suddenly she giggled.

"Oh, mother, how could you have dared?"

Her laughter drew a confused frown from Wulfgar.

"Aislinn, what is it she bears there?" he asked.

"A sleeping herb, my love," Aislinn smiled, with adoring eyes turned to him.

"Aye, 'tis true!" Maida agreed. "The night she and Ragnor would have bedded I slipped a potion in the wine. For him! Just for him! But he made Aislinn drink of it too. I was in the room and he did not know. He sought to take her. He tore her clothes and cast the shreds aside." She gestured up the stairs. "He fell upon her—on the bed," Maida cackled gleefully. "But before his body met his will they both did fall into sound sleep and there they rested thus entwined until I roused her with the morning's light and we did fly." She shrugged. "I would have killed him, had I not feared his men would then fall upon my daughter and kill her."

Wulfgar continued to scowl at the woman. "There would have been other signs."

506

"I took the proof away," Maida laughed, her eyes asparkle. "Her torn kirtle of your night on her with the virgin's stains still on it."

"Mother!" Aislinn interrupted, her voice of a sudden angry and questioning. "Why did you let me go these many months adoubting?"

Maida turned to her and raised her chin proudly, showing a shadow of the beauty she once bore and had passed to Aislinn. "Because he was a Norman and you would have flown to him to tell the news." She shrugged her thin shoulders again. "Now he is only half Norman and the other part Saxon."

Wulfgar threw back his head and relented to the hearty laughter that swelled within him. After a while he managed to calm a bit and muttered:

"Poor Ragnor, he never knew."

Aislinn came into his beckoning arm and as Maida took the babe from him, Wulfgar drew his wife in the circle of his embrace. His eyes swept the hall and he felt the warmth and friendliness of the place which Aislinn had always known. His gaze took in the knights, Milbourne and Gowain, who had fought by his side in the thickest of battles; Sweyn, who had brought him up from his youth; Bolsgar, a father restored; Maida; Miderd; Hlynn; Ham; his man Sanhurst; Haylan and Kerwick, friends all. He smiled as he stared at the latter two then chuckled.

"You have my leave to marry the widow, Kerwick. The castle will be completed in a few days and we shall have a feast and festivities. 'Twould be a joyous time to wed."

Kerwick threw a glance at Haylan and grinned. "Aye, lord, if I can rise and be about by then."

Haylan dipped to Wulfgar and Aislinn. "He will be about," she assured them, her dark eyes twinkling. "Or he will have a deeper wound than now."

With an easy laugh, Wulfgar pulled Aislinn along with him to the portal and drew her outside into the crisp morning air. She shivered slightly as a cool breeze stirred beneath her cloak and he hugged her close against his side to share his warmth. They strolled together across the courtyard in the direction of the castle. As he pulled her beneath the branches of an ancient oak, he grinned and enfolded her within his embrace, leaning back against the trunk of the mighty tree. He pressed a kiss upon her cheek and another further down against her throat.

"I never thought I would love a woman as much as I love you," he sighed. "You hold my world in the palm of your hand."

Aislinn laughed as she rubbed her face in the wolf fur of his vest. " 'Tis time you came around."

She turned in his arms, lying back against him and gazed toward the castle which rose like a great towering sentry to guard the land.

" 'Twill be a safe place for our sons," Wulfgar murmured against her hair.

"Yea, our many sons," she breathed, then she pointed to where a wind vane had been mounted on the highest tower of the castle. "Look!"

A huge iron wolf had been fashioned by Gavin's hammer and swung with the morning breeze as if seeking some scent of prey. Wulfgar watched it for a time.

"Let that beast search out the winds of war," he said softly. "I have found my peace here in you. I go no more to wander in the wood and seek battle. I am Wulfgar of Darkenwald."

He turned her in his arms and their two shadows were joined as one in the new sun's light.

Darkenwald had found a place for all.

America Loves Lindsey!

The Timeless Romances of #1 Bestselling Author

Johanna Lindsey

America Loves Lindsey!

The Timeless Romances
of #1 Bestselling Author

GENTLE ROGUE	75302-2/$6.99 US/$8.99 Can
DEFY NOT THE HEART	75299-9/$6.99 US/$8.99 Can
SILVER ANGEL	75294-8/$6.99 US/$8.99 Can
TENDER REBEL	75086-4/$6.99 US/$8.99 Can
SECRET FIRE	75087-2/$6.99 US/$8.99 Can
HEARTS AFLAME	89982-5/$6.99 US/$8.99 Can
A HEART SO WILD	75084-8/$6.99 US/$8.99 Can
WHEN LOVE AWAITS	89739-3/$6.99 US/$8.99 Can
LOVE ONLY ONCE	89953-1/$6.99 US/$8.99 Can
BRAVE THE WILD WIND	89284-7/$6.50 US/$8.50 Can
A GENTLE FEUDING	87155-6/$6.99 US/$8.99 Can
HEART OF THUNDER	85118-0/$6.99 US/$8.99 Can
SO SPEAKS THE HEART	81471-4/$6.99 US/$8.99 Can
GLORIOUS ANGEL	84947-X/$6.99 US/$8.99 Can
PARADISE WILD	77651-0/$6.99 US/$8.99 Can
FIRES OF WINTER	75747-8/$6.99 US/$8.99 Can
A PIRATE'S LOVE	40048-0/$6.99 US/$8.99 Can
CAPTIVE BRIDE	01697-4/$6.99 US/$8.99 Can
TENDER IS THE STORM	89693-1/$6.50 US/$8.50 Can
SAVAGE THUNDER	75300-6/$6.99 US/$8.99 Can